Winning Rylie

Winning Rylie

A multicultural, age gap, forced proximity, friends to lovers, drunk vegas marriage, sports romance.

Galactic Wrestling Association
Book 4

Leah Mae Wright

Copyright

Contents

Dedication

To the 1982-1983 fifth grade class at Park Elementary School. While my memories of our class Christmas party inspired Rylie's memories in this book, I am admitting to absolutely nothing by writing her recounting of the red food coloring incident. But even if I were, I'd like to point out that my mother is the one who added the food coloring to the chocolate Santa candies, not me.

Introduction

After getting married while drunk in Las Vegas back in the summer, Liam Connery and Rylie Long spent months fighting their mutual attraction to one another. Until fate and their matchmaking friends intervened to push them together. Unfortunately, their combustible chemistry wasn't enough to keep them burning up the sheets past the fall, and a winter cold front seemed to be hitting their marriage.

As Liam filled in for their boss and took the GWA plane to New York City for upgrades over the end of the year holiday break, Rylie accompanied him, presumably so they could both sign off on the paperwork to dissolve their marriage. But neither one of them were prepared for the mischief and magic of Christmas with the Connerys.

Would spending their break with his big Irish family bring them back together for their happily ever after? Or would they start the new year as newly single people?

DISCLAIMER: This multicultural, age gap, forced proximity, friends-to-lovers, drunk Vegas marriage, sports romance contains profanity, graphic sex scenes, struggles with infertility issues, and reconciling their lives with their religious beliefs. It is intended for adult readers (18+) who are not easily offended.

Author's Note

While this book can be read as a stand-alone story, it is highly recommended that you read **Mistakenly Married?** before reading **Winning Rylie**, so you have a better understanding of Liam and Rylie's backstory.

As you're reading this book, you will notice some words that appear to be misspelled or used improperly. For some of those, specifically the misspellings, that is my artistic license for spelling things phonetically for how they sound when Liam is speaking in Irish or putting on an Irish accent for his wrestling persona, or when his Irish grandparents are speaking. If you have problems reading them, please try to "hear" them in an Irish accent so they'll make more sense. You will also notice that the Irish terms of endearment Liam uses with Rylie are spelled phonetically when she hears them and spelled correctly in Irish when the scene is from Liam's point of view.

My apologies to my Irish ancestors and the entire Irish population of the world if I've totally butchered the language. You can blame it on my Wright ancestors, who came to the US from Ireland about two-hundred years before I was born, for not passing the language down through the years, so I had to rely on what I could learn online.

There are also several terms in this book that have different meanings in the professional wrestling industry, which people outside the industry might not know. For those who might need it, you can refer to the _Glossary of Professional Wrestling Terms_ while reading this book if you come across a term that doesn't make sense as the GWA characters are speaking.

Finally, my apologies to anyone who might be confused by this "sports romance" primarily taking place while the GWA is on a holiday break. But even though there is no off season in professional wrestling, the wrestlers need time off too. I promise, there will be some behind the scenes wrestling action later in the book.

Prologue

Liam Connery's phone rang just as he got out of the shower. "Feck," he groaned, knowing he'd miss the call by the time he finished drying off, so he wouldn't drip all over the hotel carpet between the bathroom and bedside table, where his phone was currently sitting on the charger. Still, just in case it was his attorney's office calling to confirm his appointment on Monday, he rushed through toweling off, wrapping the towel around his waist, and running out of the bathroom. Unfortunately, he'd only made it halfway across the room when his phone stopped ringing.

"Hopefully, they'll leave a message with the direct line I need to call back to confirm." Liam didn't bother going to check the caller ID, turning around and grabbing a pair of boxer briefs from the suitcase he'd left on top of the dresser to start getting dressed for the day. Once he dried his dick and balls a little better than he had in the bathroom, he discarded the towel and put on the boxer briefs before reaching into his suitcase once more for a pair of black dress socks, knowing they'd match no matter which of his black or gray suits he chose to put on that day.

As he walked over to the closet to pick a suit, tie, and shirt for the day, his phone rang once more. This time, he was able to grab it, seeing Da flash on the screen just before he answered it on the second ring. "Good morning, Da."

"Oh good, you answered this time. I wasn't sure if you didn't the first time because you were already on the plane headed home, or if I called early enough to catch you still in bed." Brian Connery wasn't big on greetings and pleasantries, always seeming to be two or three sentences ahead of Liam whenever they started a telephone conversation, almost like his da had said his greetings while the phone was still ringing.

"I was actually in the shower," Liam clarified as he finally made it to the closet to settle on a medium gray suit, black dress shirt, and black and gray houndstooth-patterned tie.

"Good, good, then it's not too late for me to tell you to bring your wife home for the holidays with the family."

FECK! Does he know about the wedding in Vegas? Or is he just fishing to find out if there's any chance of making our wrestling angle real in the new year? Liam was torn about how to reply, knowing if he tried to lie and say the marriage was just a work for the GWA, then his da would be upset if he already knew the truth. But he also couldn't agree to bring Rylie home for the holidays and pretend they were a happy couple, when she was only speaking to him when they had to interact for their jobs. Even their car rides between the airports, hotels, and arenas they'd shared since *Christmas Chaos* had been quiet and somewhat awkward. *Guess I'll just have to go with honesty, then, since her discomfort with being around me would be obvious to him and everyone else in the family, if I miraculously convinced her to come home with me.*

"Da, we're not really a couple," Liam started, planning to explain that they were annulling the marriage, so he couldn't make plans like that for Rylie, when Brian interrupted.

"Quit being an eejit. I already know you married her in Las Vegas," Brian informed his son, sounding exasperated, even as he surprised Liam by not calling him out as a liar. "Rick called to see why you hadn't asked for our normal passes for the show you had here last week and told me all about it."

"Then why didn't you come to *Christmas Chaos*, so you could have personally invited Rylie for the holidays?" Liam didn't mean to vocalize the question, but he was so gobsmacked by finding out his da knew he'd gotten married that his mouth didn't get the message to keep his thoughts in his head.

"Oh, I thought about it," Da chuckled. "But after talking it over with the rest of the family, we decided to give you the time you needed to man up and come clean."

"So, this call is to let me know my time is up?" Liam shook his head, as he put his phone on speaker and sat it on the bedside table, so he could continue getting dressed. Once he put on his slacks, he donned his shirt next.

"Only because Rick called back to let me know you were planning to come home alone and file the paperwork for an annulment."

Fecking Rick! I guess D was right when he said he thought our boss was playing matchmaker after seeing him deconstruct the wedding favor bags we had to put back together last month.

"I think you both need to talk to the rest of the family, and maybe Father O'Malley, before you make such a final decision about your marriage," Brian advised, not seeming to comprehend that Liam didn't really want to talk about how he'd screwed things up with Rylie, especially if his da intended to include his brothers in that discussion.

But maybe I can talk to him about some of our issues now, so he'll understand why bringing Rylie home to talk with the rest of the family isn't an option.

"I think it's too late for that, Da," Liam confided with a sigh as he tucked in his shirt and put on his belt, not really wanting to mention how he'd screwed up by kissing Jen after he'd married Rylie.

"Do you love her? 'Cause it's not too late if you love each other."

"We're just friends, Da." As he looped his tie around his neck and shirt collar, Liam tried deflecting the question, not wanting to confess his love to anyone else when he couldn't say those three little words to Rylie.

"Ha," Da scoffed. "Friends don't have the chemistry the two of you show the world every week on TV. So if I were a betting man, I'd bet you're in love with her and just haven't told her yet. But that's okay, you don't have to say the L-word to anyone but her. Just answer with a simple yes or no. Do you love her?"

"Yes," Liam reluctantly admitted, bungling the knot in his tie and having to start over. "But sometimes love isn't enough. Not when we've got so many obstacles to overcome."

"Ah, that's where you're wrong, Son. There's no such thing as an obstacle that love can't overcome."

"She's ten years younger than me, Da," Liam started, hoping to convince his father that he and Rylie couldn't work, even though he really wished they could. "And she's only been with the GWA for nine months, so she's got at least another ten years before she'll be ready to retire, while I'm planning on leaving the business in the next two to five years. We can't exactly have a relationship and raise a family if I'm in Belle Harbor while she's still touring. And even if she were to decide she loves me enough to cut her career short and retire when I do, I don't want to risk her getting hurt by not feeling welcomed in our neighborhood because she's Black and not Irish, or having to put up with snide comments because we didn't have a Church wedding."

"I hope you're not implying we'd discriminate against anyone just because our family and community are proud of our Irish heritage," Brian barked defensively. "I know I raised you better than that. I don't care what color her skin is or where her family is from, she's a Connery now, so she's family. And family will never be made to feel unwelcome here."

Liam felt like an arse for even bringing up that possibility, knowing his family would never discriminate or make her feel unwelcome, even though the same couldn't be said for all of their neighbors.

"Is that why you're planning to spend the holidays apart? Because her family wouldn't accept you?"

"No, Da," Liam sighed, sitting down on the bed to put on his socks and shoes. "The reason we're not planning to spend the holidays together is because we only got married because we were drunk and some of our friends were getting married, so in our inebriated state we wanted to join in, but we're not really a couple. We've never even gone on a date, only hung out as friends. The fact that she doesn't have any family left has absolutely nothing to do with it."

Fucking a few times doesn't count as dates, right? And neither does going to our friends' wedding stuff together, since we were mostly pretending to be happily married and married people don't date, no matter what Josh and Crockett call their lunches and sightseeing with their wives.

"She doesn't have any family left?"

Liam could hear the mix of concern and compassion in his father's voice and knew he'd said the wrong thing to convince him that Rylie wouldn't be coming to Belle Harbor for the holidays. "No, she's an only child, whose parents died a few years ago when their car was hit by a drunk driver. From what she's told me, her parents cut off contact with their extended families when they didn't approve of them getting married almost thirty years ago. So she's planning on spending the holidays with her friends, whom she doesn't get to see often since she joined the GWA."

"If they're not off visiting family out of town."

Liam remembered Rylie's words from a few weeks earlier and hoped withholding the possibility that she wouldn't be able to catch up to any of her friends from his da wasn't considered lying by omission. *If so, then I guess I have something else to add to my confession while I'm home.*

"While friends like that are important and can feel like family sometimes, seeing them for the holidays isn't as important as getting to know her new family. So, you need to convince her to come here at least through Saint Stephen's Day, even if she wants to go be with her friends for New Year's," Da insisted, making Liam feel like he had no choice but to agree to ask her.

Feck! I know she's going to decline, but the only way he's going to let me off the phone, so I can meet Rylie in the lobby and get to the plane on time, is if I agree with him.

"Okay, Da, I'll ask her as soon as I see her this morning," Liam finally caved, making sure he had everything packed to leave the hotel before putting on his jacket. "But she's a grown woman with a mind of her own, so don't be surprised if she refuses."

"Tell her you love her, Son, and she won't refuse you. And maybe say it in Irish, because de ladies lahve de accent," Brian advised, putting on a stronger than normal Irish brogue before disconnecting the call.

"If only it were that easy." Liam chuckled self-deprecatingly as he finished gathering his things, preparing to meet Rylie in the lobby so they could ride together to the airport, since they had to keep up the pretense of being happily married in public after he "won" her managerial services at ***Christmas Chaos***. "But as bad as I hurt her by stupidly kissing Jen, I know she'll only agree to come home with me if her presence in my lawyer's office on Monday will expedite our annulment."

~~~

Friday, December 20, 2019, Flying from Memphis, Tennessee to San Antonio, Texas

As Rylie Long took a seat in the same quad with her fellow members of Protection Detail on the GWA plane for the first of multiple flights she had scheduled that day, she pushed aside her guilt for not waiting around in the hotel lobby for Liam and riding with her teammates. Instead, she started to question if the savings from booking a round-trip ticket between San Antonio and Atlantic City, instead of two one-way tickets from Memphis to Atlantic City at the beginning of their holiday break and then Atlantic City to San Antonio when it was time to go back on tour, was worth all the extra travel time. Granted, she didn't have to deal with the holiday crowd at the private airports the GWA used, but she still wasn't looking forward to having to deal with cranky passengers and potential airline delays for her commercial trip home and then again for the commercial trip back to meet up with the rest of the GWA crew.

Maybe I should consider spending my holidays wherever the GWA plane is from now on, she contemplated while tuning out the conversation between Harrison Thorne, who used the ring name Magnum, and Cameron Wentworth, who used the ring name Trojan. *If I book my stays in extended-stay hotels, instead of the nicer places like we use with the GWA, I bet the cost would be about the same as all the round-trip flights. And it's not like there's anyone back in Atlantic City that I'll be spending my breaks with, so it doesn't really matter if I don't go back there all the time. For that matter, I could probably have all my mail forwarded to the GWA headquarters and get a storage unit for what little stuff I have in my apartment, and save quite a bit more of my salary by not having to pay rent and utilities every month.*

Considering her first year GWA salary was more than four times the highest combined yearly income she'd seen on her parents' tax records after they passed, she knew it probably seemed silly for her to be so frugal. But knowing she'd most likely end up having to go through multiple rounds of costly fertility treatments to have a family
~~~

one day, and would need to have enough money saved to live on while going through all the medical procedures and for at least the first few months of her babies' lives, she knew she had to save as much as she could while working in the highest paid job she'd likely ever have. And if she was really lucky, her salary would increase every year as her coworkers had implied theirs had, so she could save up enough to not have to go back to a crappy secretarial job, like the ones she'd had to pay the bills while waiting for her big break in sports entertainment, until after her children were old enough to go to school.

Or maybe one of the investments the Hunters recommended will pay off big enough that I can be a stay-at-home mom, like I've always dreamed of.

While she'd always assumed that fantasy life would only be possible if she met her soulmate and they combined their lives, and incomes, to make it happen, she was now resigned to doing it all on her own, since her marriage with Liam had imploded. After meeting and falling in love with him, she couldn't imagine making a family with any other man.

If I can stay on with the GWA long enough to start earning those multimillion-dollar contracts I've heard about, so I can invest more and really make my money grow, then my dream just might be within reach, even if I can't get past the pain of breaking things off with Liam and have to use a sperm donor to have my babies.

Almost three weeks earlier, when she'd told him she needed space and time to deal with her feelings before they could even hang out as friends again, she'd really thought she'd be able to convince herself to forgive him, since they technically didn't know they were married when he kissed Jen. But every time she tried to get her brain to listen to her heart and pussy, so she could forgive him and try to have a real relationship with him beyond the brief friends-with-benefits thing they'd tried, her brain kept getting stuck on what he'd said about wanting to sleep with someone else to get over her. And her pain and anger at him for his utter rejection just made her resent the time she had to spend with him. Which she now realized was probably why she was in such a pissy mood when he was late meeting her in the hotel lobby earlier, triggering her to act out by riding with Protection Detail instead of him. Unfortunately, she didn't know how to get past her anger, making her wonder if they'd ever get to the point where they might have a second chance.

Regardless of the fact that he was as attracted to her as she was to him, that statement made it clear that he didn't love her. Or at the very least, that he didn't want any deeper feelings to develop between them, so he wanted to decrease the risk of one of them falling in love by getting his physical needs met with anyone but her. It made her feel like he was saying, "I think you're hot enough to bang, but you're not hot enough for me to only want to bang you for the rest of my life." Only without actually being man enough to say the words.

Since Jen Burleson was only a couple of years older than Rylie and was so ensconced in her family business in Texas that she'd never move to New York to be with Liam, Rylie had at least convinced herself that he hadn't been lying when he said he didn't want to be more than friends with Jen. Considering their age difference and career paths keeping them apart were the two things he blamed for why their marriage couldn't work, she had to assume the same would be true for him and Jen. Combined with how epically bad Liam had described their two attempts at kissing, Rylie felt like an idiot for ever being jealous of the other woman.

But regardless of no longer believing those two kisses in September were grounds for breaking things off, she still couldn't bring herself to forgive him and ask to start over with their friendship, or possibly try for more, because the reason behind the attempt at being with another woman was the actual issue she had a problem with.

Is that because I'm afraid friendship is all we'll ever have? Or am I just trying to protect myself from a bigger broken heart later, if he rejects me again when I tell him I'm ready to move past friendship to something more?

Rylie was so lost in her thoughts that she didn't realize the plane had taken off until Liam appeared beside her seat, wearing a gray suit and black shirt, which almost perfectly matched her outfit.

"Can we go talk privately for a few minutes?"

Shit! I bet he's pissed that I didn't wait in the lobby for him this morning like I was supposed to and rode to the airport with Cameron and Harrison instead of him.

"In a plane full of people?" Rylie arched an eyebrow curiously at him, unsure how they could have a private talk unless they both went into one of the lavatories. *Gross, no, not happening.* "I don't think that's possible 'til after we land."

"Actually, we can go upstairs or to the back galley and not be overheard," Liam pointed out.

Rylie had only realized the plane had an upstairs a couple of weeks earlier, after seeing the staircase when Rick opened the door in the middle of the plane, which she'd always thought was a closet, before he and Liam disappeared up those stairs. Since she'd been in the back galley before to get bungee cords for securing her largest suitcase, she opted to go upstairs, wanting to see the previously unknown space. When she got to the top of the stairs and saw the top level was set up as a bedroom, however, she started to question if she'd made the right choice.

No, he just wants to talk, probably about how I broke kayfabe this morning by riding with Protection Detail. He didn't bring me up here so we can join the mile-high club. While intellectually, she knew Liam wasn't trying to get back in her panties, her hard nipples and wet pussy clearly hadn't gotten the memo. *Damn, I knew I should have worn pants today, instead of this gray skirt. Now I have to keep my legs crossed in case my thong can't contain the moisture, so he doesn't notice any drippage.*

Hoping he also wouldn't notice the prominent pebbling of her nipples under her black lace bra and thin stretch turtleneck, she squeaked out, "What did you want to talk about?"

"Rick asked me to take this plane back to New York and pick out the pods that are going to be replacing all this stuff up here, and filling up the second plane he just bought for the ring crew whenever we travel someplace they can't drive the trucks they usually take to beat us to the arena each day," Liam stated, not really getting into why she needed to know any of that information. But also surprising her by not berating her for not riding with him that morning, either.

So, this is our last chance to break in the bed and join the mile-high club?

"And I thought you might want to cancel your flight home to come to New York with me, so we can both meet with my lawyers Monday to find out what we need to do about the annulment."

Of course, he still thinks we can get his entertainment lawyer to convince the judge to give us an annulment instead of a divorce.

"Can't you just file everything and send the paperwork to my lawyer's office for me to sign? Or maybe just bring it back with you when we go back on tour, so I can sign it without having to hire a lawyer?"

"Yeah, I can if that's what you want," Liam sighed, shaking his head, which she took to indicate neither of those options were what he wanted to do. "But I thought it might be faster if we're both there on Monday, so maybe we can file and sign off on everything without having to take time off later to appear in front of the judge."

Don't cry, Rylie Ann. You knew he wanted to end the marriage as quickly and quietly as possible since the moment he found out, even when we were having sex and trying to see if we could eventually be more than friends with benefits. So this is not a surprise. There's no reason to cry over dissolving our marriage, no matter how much I wish we wouldn't.

Damn it! Damn it! Damn it! Why am I getting upset about ending our legal connection when I was just lamenting why I can't forgive him to be able to try to make our marriage real?

"Okay, I'll have to see if I can find a hotel that's not already booked up with the hordes of people from all over the world about to descend on the city for the holidays." Honestly, while she assumed she'd be able to find a place for the next few days and probably even through Christmas, she wasn't sure what her chances were of finding a hotel that would still have a room available through New Year's Day because of the ball drop in Times Square.

"You don't have to find a hotel," Liam disagreed, reaching out and stopping her from pulling her phone from her wristlet and doing a search on the plane's Wi-Fi. "I have a big empty house, where you can have your choice of guest rooms."

"And how are you going to explain my presence there to your family, when they're dragging you off to all the parties and stuff you mentioned a few weeks ago?" *Surely, he's not suggesting introducing me to his family, just in time to tell them we're ending our marriage.*

"Actually, my family already knows about you," Liam admitted sheepishly. "Da called me this morning and insisted I bring you home for the holidays. That's why I was late getting down to the lobby and missed meeting up with you to drive to the airport."

Rylie's jaw dropped in shock at hearing the news that his family knew they were married, totally missing the fact that he thought her riding with Protection Detail that morning was his fault. *Is that because you finally told them we really got married in Vegas? Or because the matchmakers in your family are hoping to push us into making our gimmick marriage legal?*

"I didn't tell them," Liam blurted, holding his hands up in surrender, and making her wonder if he'd just read her mind, or if she'd actually voiced the questions she'd thought were only in her head. "Apparently, Rick called Da when I didn't request passes for the family to **Christmas Chaos** and he told them about us."

Rylie had to wonder if Rick calling Liam's father was part of the matchmaking Fiona had talked him into while they were in Heart's Destiny for Allissa and Dean's wedding. But she wasn't about to mention that to Liam at the moment, knowing he'd be as irritated by that as he was about them having to share a room and reconstruct the wedding favors.

When she didn't immediately respond to his revelation, Liam continued telling her all about his conversation with his father that morning. "Apparently, the whole family is eager to meet you, so I wouldn't be surprised if Ma and Granny have a welcome-to-the-family party planned already. I'm just not sure if they'll try to spring it on us before or after the intervention Da mentioned to try to help us work through our issues, so we'll call off the annulment."

"He actually mentioned an intervention?" *Are they really trying to keep us together? Or hoping an ambush by the whole family will scare me off?*

"He didn't call it an intervention, exactly," Liam back peddled, shaking his head. "But he suggested we wait to decide on an annulment until after sitting down with the family, and possibly Father O'Malley, to discuss everything. At first, I thought he meant the whole family, and was absolutely against it because there's no way I want to hear my brothers' opinions on our marriage. But now that I think about it, I'm pretty sure he only means for us to sit down with him, Ma, Granda, and Granny, so they won't take a chance on my single brothers bringing any anti-marriage views to the table."

"And you want us to sit down with your parents and grandparents to discuss our marriage?" Rylie found that hard to believe, considering how adamant he'd always been about getting the annulment.

But if there's a possibility that they can help us work through our issues, shouldn't we try it? Even if their intervention isn't enough to change his mind about the annulment, maybe the women in his family can help me figure out why I'm having such a hard time forgiving him when I'm still madly in love with him.

I mean, I know it won't be the same as if I could still talk to my mom about everything, but a mother-in-law seems like the closest I'll ever have to getting Mom back. Not that I imagine Liam's mom is anything like mine was. Or that she'll want a close relationship with me like I had with Mom. But it's possible she'll be as open to mothering me a little when I need it as Mandi and the other women of Heart's Destiny were last month. And if not, then I'll just make another stop for a motherly hug from Mandi when we fly back to San Antonio on the first.

"Honestly, I don't know what I want," Liam huffed, running his hand through the longer strands of hair on the top of his head and making it stick up in all directions, instead of sweeping forward and off to the side as it normally laid. "That's not exactly true. I know I want us both to be happy. I just don't know how to make it happen without disappointing anyone else I care about. If my family or Father O'Malley can share the wisdom of their experiences to give me the insight to make us all happy with whatever happens next, then I'm willing to listen. But I'm also afraid that sitting down to discuss everything with them will just lead to more disagreements and none of us being happy with whatever we decide to do going forward."

Rylie's heart broke from the anguish in Liam's voice. She wanted to do or say something to comfort him, but she had no idea what might be effective without muddying the waters between them even more than they already were.

Joining the mile-high club will make us both happy, her pussy suggested.

No, sex is why everything is so muddy now, her brain argued.

Just hug him and tell him we'll go meet his family, her heart pleaded. *And maybe his family matchmakers will have better luck than the ones in Heart's Destiny, so we can get our happily ever after for Christmas.*

I don't agree with the hug yet, but going to New York is our best option, her brain chimed in once more. *If his family can't convince me to forgive him, then we'll at least be able to get a clean break by taking care of the annulment paperwork all at one time.*

"Okay, I guess I'm cancelling my ticket to Atlantic City, then," Rylie finally conceded, wondering if she could do it online from the plane, or if she'd need to wait until they landed to actually call the airline. "Will I have enough time on the ground in San Antonio to take care of that before we take off again?"

"Yeah, plenty," Liam assured her with a smile. "We're not flying to New York until tomorrow morning."

Thankfully, she knew Rick kept a block of hotel rooms booked for the first night of any of their breaks, so any of the talent who couldn't get an immediate flight out to their hometowns would have a place to stay. *At least, I don't have to room with Liam tonight. And hopefully, I'll be able to stay in his guest room without losing the fight with my libido to sneak into his bed, if we decide to go ahead with the annulment.*

No, hopefully, we'll work things out and spend every night in his bed for the rest of our lives, her pussy and heart chorused in unison as Liam led the way back down the stairs for them to take their seats for the rest of the flight.

Does thinking of my subconscious inner voice having three distinct personalities as various parts of my body mean I'm having some kind of psychotic break? If so, then I think I now understand why so many romance authors have their main characters tell their love interests, "You drive me crazy." 'Cause if I'm going crazy, Liam has definitely been the man to drive me there.

Chapter One

Rylie wasn't sure what she was expecting to find when they arrived at Liam's house after flying to New York and picking out the new seats for the GWA planes, but it certainly wasn't the modern design of the four-story building that he directed their driver to at the end of the street, which dead-ended at the beach. The boxy white marble and glass construction stood out among all the more traditional homes in the area, reminding Rylie more of an office space than a house. Though she supposed the wood garage doors, which matched the excessively tall privacy fencing and decorative accents on the building, were designed to make it obvious it was indeed a home and not a commercial space. *As much as he talks about the history and tradition of his family in the community, I'm surprised he lives someplace so obviously new. I wonder if that's because the house that was originally here was destroyed during Hurricane Sandy?*

Not wanting to think about her own experience with Hurricane Sandy, Rylie refocused on her current surroundings as Liam got their bags out of the cab. Apparently, instead of leaving his car at the airport in long-term parking, he always used a cab or Uber if he went home, where he would have access to his personal vehicles. Or if he stayed at the hotel with the rest of the GWA when they were all in New York for shows, he just shared a rental car with the other guys as if they weren't in his hometown. Considering his driveway was packed with cars, she assumed the cab was a necessity because he wouldn't have been able to park if they had gotten a rental or he'd left his personal vehicle at the airport.

Why are there so many cars here? Do random people just park in his driveway because it's the closest to the beach access and he's normally not home to stop them? Or are there actually people in his house? Surely, his family would wait to hear from him that we've arrived before coming over, right?

She took her luggage and followed Liam, who was mumbling something incoherent under his breath, through the maze of vehicles and the hidden gate in the fence to get to the bright yellow door, which was surrounded by horizontal wood-slatted accent walls, where they entered his home. As soon as they walked inside, they immediately went up a set of stairs with a banister made of wood-topped glass panels that turned to the left at the halfway point between floors. Once they reached the second floor, they entered the main living space, which was filled with an oversized, plush, tan, sectional sofa and modern-style tables. The white walls were accented by ocean blue columns, which she assumed were support posts due to their positioning in the corners and along the center of the structure.

Rylie didn't have time to notice the decorative pieces on the walls or tables around the room before several people, whom she assumed were all members of Liam's family, even though only half of them shared his reddish-brown hair and fair complexion, filed out of the dining room, which she could see was open to the living room between two of the blue columns.

"Hey, they're finally here," a slightly shorter, thinner version of Liam shouted back over his shoulder, presumably to the rest of the family who were still in the kitchen, which she assumed was behind the wall alongside the second set of stairs going up to the next floor. "That means we can eat now, right?"

"You have to ignore my baby brother, Finn. He thinks with his stomach ninety percent of the time," Liam chuckled, tilting his head down toward her momentarily before redirecting the rest of his comments toward the crowd. "What are you guys doing here, anyway? I thought we were meeting at Granda and Granny's for dinner later."

"Granny and Ma decided to move your wedding feast here instead, where they knew you'd show up," another one of the men, who looked like he could be one of Liam's brothers, only his hair was browner and his skin tone wasn't quite as pale, explained. "So there's plenty of room for them to invite all the aunts, uncles, and cousins from both sides of the family."

Wedding feast? Is that like a wedding reception, only for people who eloped since it's not right after the ceremony? And if so, why is his family ambushing us with it now, when he's told them we're planning to get an annulment? Is this the intervention he told me to expect? Or just the welcome-to-the-family party he mentioned his mom and granny planning, since it's obviously more than just his parents and grandparents here?

"Feck," Liam groaned, dropping his chin to his chest for a second before lifting it and shaking his head. "Please, tell me they didn't call this our *'wedding feast'* like it's some kind of official celebration."

"Hey, don't shoot the messenger." The brown-haired man held up his hands. "But I thought I should warn you before you see the three-tiered fruitcake Granny made that's currently sitting on your kitchen counter." He then redirected his words to Rylie, extending his hand to her as he introduced himself. "I'm Quinn, by the way. I'd call you by name as I welcome you to the family, but big brother here seems to have forgotten his manners and hasn't told us what it is. So I didn't want to offend you by assuming it's Chastity, just because that's what they call you on TV."

"My real name is Rylie, but I'll answer to either," she chuckled nervously, smiling and releasing the handle on her rolling suitcase to shake Quinn's hand. "Nice to meet you."

"Welcome to the family, Rylie," Quinn smiled back. "Now if you'll hand me your luggage and coat, I'll carry it all upstairs, so you can stay down here and meet everyone else."

"Oh, um, thank you," Rylie sputtered before relinquishing her luggage and removing her long black trench coat, wondering if he knew to take her bags to a guest room, or if she'd have to hunt her stuff down in Liam's bedroom later.

"Sorry, everyone, I should have started with introductions." Liam raised his voice so everyone who'd come out of the other part of the house could hear him. "This is Rylie. She uses the ring name Chastity, so you can call her either one." Liam redirected his next words to her. "You've already met Quinn, the brother closest to me in age. The next youngest is Rory, who's hiding in the back of the room." He pointed to a man with bright red hair, who waved at her across the crowd. "Then we have Aiden, who is going to be a wonderful brother and carry my stuff upstairs."

"Welcome to the family, Rylie," Aiden chuckled, holding his hand out for a fist bump from her before he took Liam's bags and overcoat and followed Quinn up the stairs to their right.

"And the youngest is Finn, who apparently snuck back into the kitchen for the food since everyone else has come in here." Liam looked around the room as if verifying his youngest brother wasn't just hiding somewhere in the huge crowd.

Geez, he told me about his four brothers, but he never mentioned the other fifty or so people that appear to be part of his family. Unless, maybe, his family invited a bunch of his friends and their families to this party?

"Ah, dat dosser," an elderly blonde woman scoffed before heading back into the other room, presumably to run Finn off from the food.

"That was Granny Breena," Liam chortled before pointing at the elderly man with matching blond hair, who was standing near the empty space left by Granny Breena. "And that handsome gentleman who was standing beside her is Granda Neilan."

"Welcomb ta de family, Rylie," Granda Neilan greeted her with a wide smile, making it clear where Liam learned his Irish accent, just as a middle-aged woman with bright red hair only sporting the faintest blonde highlights at her temples pushed through the crowd to get to them.

"And this beautiful woman is my ma," Liam barely got the introduction started before his mother threw her arms around Rylie, "Cathleen Connery."

"Oh, my first daughter!" Cathleen gushed as she embraced Rylie, rocking them both from side to side in her excitement. "I can't wait to get to know everything about you."

Rylie returned the hug, unsure how else to respond to such an exuberant welcome.

"Don't smother the girl before the rest of us get to meet her, Cathleen," a middle-aged gentleman, whom Rylie assumed was Liam's dad now that she could see the family resemblance between Liam, his brothers, grandparents, and parents, advised as he gripped Cathleen's shoulders and lightly tugged her back while giving Rylie a warm smile.

Leah Mae Wright

"And the man rescuing you from my octopus ma is my da, Brian Connery," Liam chuckled, stepping closer to her and putting his arm around her shoulders. "Da, Ma, this is my wife, Rylie."

What the hell, Liam? Did you decide to get out of the intervention by pretending we're happily married in front of your family the same way we did back in Heart's Destiny last month? Rylie was so shocked by him claiming her as his wife, when she thought he'd made it clear that their marriage was a drunk mistake while they were in Vegas and would be dissolved while they were in New York, that she almost missed Brian's words.

"We're very pleased to meet you, Rylie. Welcome to the family."

"It's nice to meet you, too, Mr. Connery," she sputtered out in response, trying to be polite without letting on that she had no idea what kind of game Liam was playing at the moment.

"Please, there are too many Mr. Connerys in the room for such formalities, especially since we're family now. Call me Brian or Da," he instructed, smiling warmly.

"Yes, thank you, Brian." Rylie returned his smile, realizing that Liam had been correct in thinking his dad wanted them to work things out. *Maybe Li's just acting like a happy hubby right now because he's biding his time until it's just us and his parents and grandparents?*

"Alright, we'd better hurry to make the rounds and introduce you to everyone else before Finn eats all the food," Liam chuckled before guiding her through the room to introduce her to several aunts, uncles, cousins, cousins-in-law, and several of his cousins' children. Along with all the Connerys, there were several Sullivans and McCarthys as well, but he introduced them all as relatives, not the friends she'd expected earlier.

Considering there had to be close to fifty of Liam's relatives in attendance, Rylie was so overwhelmed by the sheer number of people that she knew she'd never remember all their names, much less how they were all related to Liam. They were all exceptionally welcoming though, making her question Liam's honesty when he'd told her his family knew they were planning to annul the marriage as soon as they could meet with the lawyers on Monday.

I should probably wait until everyone leaves before asking him what's going on, she thought as he guided her past the large marble table in the dining room, which was almost completely covered with various platters and bowls of food, to meet back up with Granny Breena in the kitchen. *But if I wait that long, then I won't know what to say about our relationship if I end up in a conversation with someone while he's otherwise occupied this afternoon. But I don't want to ask him why nobody seems to be acting like we're only temporarily married when his entire family can hear me. Especially since I know he wasn't even sure he wanted to sit down and talk about our issues with his parents and grandparents, and was adamantly against including his brothers in that discussion, so I'm pretty sure he wouldn't want to include the whole extended family either. Come to think of it, that's probably why he just introduced me as his wife that one time and hasn't mentioned anything about our marriage being temporary.*

"Granny, was this all your idea?" Liam removed his arm from around Rylie as he bent down to hug his petite grandmother, whom Rylie could now tell had the faintest hint of red undertones in her blonde hair.

Does red hair turn blonde with age instead of gray? Rylie wondered as she realized that none of the older adults in their midst had any silver in their hair like she was used to seeing as people with darker hair aged. Even Brian's hair, which was more of a medium brown like a couple of his sons' hair, seemed to have platinum blond highlights, instead of the silver that had started to appear in her dad's dark brown hair just before he died.

"Naht entirely, Cathleen 'elped," Granny Breena replied, her Irish accent as strong as her husband's, as she returned Liam's hug.

"But whose idea was it to call this get-together our wedding feast?" Liam pointed to the tiered cake on the island separating the kitchen and dining room. "And who made a wedding cake?"

"Ah, it's naht a weddin' feast. It's a welcomb ta de family party fahr Rylie." Granny Breena smiled mischievously before winking at Rylie, even as she continued stirring whatever was in the pot in front of her on the stove. "And dat's joehst a fruit cake, naht necessarily a weddin' cake, oehnless ye want ta save de tahp layer fahr yooehr first baby's chrestenin'. Boeht if ye're already wahrkin' ahn makin' me a great granny, den yooehr bride prahbably shooehldn't eat any o' it."

"Why shouldn't I eat any of it?" Rylie questioned, assuming she accurately understood Breena's strongly accented words, and looking back and forth between Liam and his grandmother.

"Because she's soaked the whole thing in Irish whiskey," Liam chuckled. "But considering how much of a lightweight you are when it comes to holding your alcohol, I'd suggest only taking a couple of bites to prove to everyone you're not pregnant, but don't eat a whole piece unless you want a repeat of the memory loss from our wedding night."

Considering the only clear memory she had from that night was the burn down her throat of that first shot of Irish whiskey, Rylie wasn't sure she even wanted to try taking a couple of bites of the booze-laden cake. *But if I don't, are they all really going to think I'm pregnant?* "Can I skip the cake and just have a glass of wine instead?"

"I got you covered, Rylie," one of Liam's cousins, whose name she couldn't remember, shouted as she opened what looked like an extra-large cabinet door, revealing a hidden refrigerator and pulling out two wine bottles. "Do you prefer red or white?"

"Red," Rylie decided, thinking white wine was too similar to champagne and might still send the signal that they were celebrating their marriage. While she wished they were all gathered there to celebrate her union with Liam, she knew better than to even let herself pretend for the afternoon when she knew Liam was still planning to end their marriage in just a couple of days.

"No wonder you married her, Boyo," Finn grinned between bites of what appeared to be some kind of stew, which he was eating with a plastic spoon from a paper bowl. "How long did it take you to brainwash her into choosing all things red in homage to your wrestling persona?" After taking his next bite, he waved his spoon up and down while pointing it at Rylie.

She looked down at her red, long-sleeved, blazer dress, which the GWA wardrobe department had recently added to her gimmick clothing trunk, along with quite a few other red dresses, and had to laugh. "No, I didn't pick this dress. I mean, yeah, I picked it out of my wardrobe trunk, but only because it has long sleeves, and coming here meant I wasn't going home to Atlantic City, where all my winter clothes are, so I had to improvise with the new stuff from the wardrobe department. They're the ones who basically chose an all red wardrobe for me, so I can match Liam while I'm booked as his manager."

"Is Atlantic City where you grew up?" Cathleen asked as she held a gravy boat up for Breena to fill it with a hearty brown gravy from the pot on the stove she'd been stirring.

"Yes," Rylie smiled as she took the plastic cup of wine Liam's cousin handed her.

"That must have been a fun place to spend your childhood," Cathleen gushed as she carried the now full gravy boat to the table. "I really enjoyed the Boardwalk there when we took the boys on vacation years ago. That's where I'd spend every weekend if I lived there."

Maybe at first, you would, but eventually it'd get old like it did for Mom and Dad. Although, now that I look back on our few visits to the Boardwalk as an adult, maybe it was more that most of the activities I wanted to do were too expensive to do more than once in a while on their teacher salaries.

Before Rylie could think of a response that didn't sound rude, Breena called everyone to gather around the table, or at least as close as they could get while filling up the kitchen and dining room and spilling into the living room. Then Neilan offered the blessing, saying an extra thanks for the addition of Rylie to their family. Rylie was touched by the warm welcome, but she still felt a little uncomfortable because she knew she most likely wouldn't be part of their family for long.

Once Neilan finished the prayer, the scene seemed to turn into a feeding frenzy as all the men and children in attendance grabbed paper plates and bowls to dish up their food. Unlike how the GWA crew lined up in an organized manner for the nightly buffet in catering, the Connerys, Sullivans, and McCarthys, all seemed to surround the table and reach over and around each other to get to the various dishes in a chaotic manner. Well, the men and children did anyway. The women all seemed to back away from the table, moving behind the safety of the island in the kitchen to pour drinks in more plastic cups for their husbands and children to take once they had their plates filled.

Rylie found herself huddled in the kitchen with the rest of the women, while Liam joined his male relatives and their children. She turned to the woman who'd handed her the cup of wine and asked, "Is it always this crazy when your family gathers for a meal?"

"Only when there's not enough room for everyone to sit at the same table," the woman replied before taking a sip from her own cup of wine. "But anytime more than one part of the family gets together, it's pretty much like this. Don't worry, though, the guys will all clear out in a few minutes and go sit out at the tables by the pool, and we'll be able to take our time politely walking around the table to fill up our plates."

"Wit de way dahse boyos act, you'd dink we never feed dem," Breena chuckled as she slid into the space to Rylie's right. "Since I 'ad ta chase down Finn earlier, I'm sure I missed bein' intrahduced ta ye, Rylie. I'm Breena Connery, boeht everyahne in de family calls me Granny."

"Even those of us who are only related by marriage," Liam's cousin chuckled. "Right, Granny?"

"Right, Caitlyn," Granny agreed, unknowingly helping Rylie remember the woman's name.

"Wait, I'm confused," Rylie shook her head, looking back and forth between Caitlyn and Breena. "Liam introduced you as his cousin, but you actually married into the family?"

"No, I'm not married," Caitlyn clarified, shaking her head. "Aunt Cathleen, my dad's sister, married into the Connery family, so I'm Liam's cousin on his mom's side, but I'm not biologically related to Granny and Granda because they're Uncle Brian's parents."

"Yeah, I'm going to need all of you to find some really big name tags, so you can draw little family trees under your names to help me learn who's who," Rylie quipped before taking a big gulp of her wine. "And I should probably switch to water, so I can remember who's who for the rest of our break from work."

Several of the women around her laughed. But as the men all made their way out of the dining room through the glass doors to the tables set up under the overhang of the building and around several large heaters surrounding the pool, which she assumed were necessary since none of them put on coats before going out in the thirty-something degree weather, the women all took turns reintroducing themselves and explaining how they were all related to Liam.

Rylie joined them in filling a plate with the meats and vegetables she recognized, only opting to take a small serving of the dishes she didn't recognize after Cathleen told her what each was, and only then if it sounded appetizing. Thankfully, her lack of knowledge of traditional Irish foods steered their conversation toward her telling them how, as the only child of Peter and Tammy Long, she'd grown up eating what her mom called soul food and her dad called good southern cookin', so she didn't have to worry about any questions about her relationship with Liam. Well, other than when Caitlyn discreetly pointed out she was wearing her rings on the wrong hand.

"Yeah, we opted to use my parents' rings for our wedding," Rylie quickly explained as she moved the rings from her right hand to her left after looking out the windows to see that Liam had the band he'd bought in Heart's Destiny on his left ring finger. "And I'm so used to wearing them on my right hand since they passed that I keep forgetting to put them on my left since we got married."

"Brian mentioned that you'd lost your parents," Cathleen informed her, thankfully not asking anything about why she didn't leave her rings on all the time to bring the faux pas to the attention of the rest of the women. "We're so sorry for your loss. We know we could never truly fill their shoes, but we hope one day you'll see us as your backup parents and feel comfortable calling us Ma and Da."

Rylie was touched by the heartfelt sentiment, but knowing she most likely wouldn't be their daughter-in-law for long, she couldn't in good conscience call them Ma and Da as if she was a permanent part of the family. Instead, she planned to avoid addressing them by name or title if at all possible for her short stay in Liam's home. "Thank you."

"How long have you been on your own?"

"Seven years," Rylie calculated, blinking back tears as she continued. "Well, it'll be seven years on New Year's. They were hit by a drunk driver on their way home from a party to ring in the new year."

She went on to tell them about being between her first and second semesters of college when she lost them, but didn't mention how she'd had to juggle studying with making sure the Hurricane Sandy repairs were completed, so she could sell their house and other belongings to pay for the surgeries that failed to save their lives. She was extremely grateful when Liam's Aunt Keira asked what she'd studied in college, effectively changing the subject when Rylie told them about softball and changing majors several times without getting into why she hadn't stuck with getting a degree in education like her parents.

Eventually, the guys got too cold outside, even with the heaters set up a few feet away from the tables, so everyone ended up back inside. At that point, Granny Breena finally cut into the cake, informing them that she'd only soaked the top layer in whiskey, so the majority of it was safe for the kids, pregnant women, and anyone who still had to drive home to be able to have a slice.

I guess since Liam and I weren't the ones to cut the cake and they clearly didn't save the top layer for us to eat later, his brothers were only teasing him about this being our "wedding feast" earlier.

While she was pretty sure Liam's family all really hoped they'd work things out to stay married, unfortunately, Rylie still wasn't sure what the day meant for how Liam felt about their marriage, or their plans to annul it. And it was rather disconcerting to realize her future relied so much on him, when she had no idea what he was thinking or feeling.

Even when she'd thought they'd really connected the previous month while making love as part of their friends-with-benefits arrangement, she now realized she'd projected her feelings onto him. *I just thought every time we made love was as meaningful for him as it was for me because I naïvely wanted him to love me as much as I love him. But clearly he didn't, since even us having sex didn't change his opinion about ending our marriage. Which means he probably hasn't changed his mind now, just because his family seems to want us to stay married. So, I can't let his current happy-hubby act give me false hope that we won't go through with the annulment when we meet with his lawyers on Monday.*

~~~

After several hours of catching up with everyone, and a second round of food for dinner, his family finally left Liam and Rylie alone. Now that it was just the two of them, Liam could no longer put off showing Rylie around the upper levels of his home and letting her pick which of his guest rooms she wanted to stay in while they were there for the holidays. As much as he wished she'd opt to stay in the master bedroom with him, where he knew his brothers put all their luggage earlier, he knew it was most likely that she'd pick the third-floor
~~~

bedroom on the opposite side of the house from his fourth-floor master, if only because it was the farthest from where he'd be sleeping. *Considering how bad my nightmares have gotten recently, that's probably for the best, so I don't wake her up if my screams for her are louder than the decibel rating of the soundproofing insulation I had installed in the walls when this house was built.*

"Okay, I'm confused," Rylie confided as they walked back up to the main living space on the second floor after seeing everyone off. "Other than everyone welcoming me to the family when we first got here, no one really said anything about us being married, or asked about our wedding, much less mentioned our plans to go to the lawyer's office on Monday. Are you sure they all know we're planning to get an annulment?"

They might not have asked you, but they certainly had plenty of questions for me about our wedding. But now that I think about it, none of them were about the annulment.

"Honestly, I'm only positive Da knows about our plans because of our talk yesterday," Liam admitted as he directed her up the stairs to the third floor, not wanting to tell her about how he hadn't mentioned the annulment to anyone when they'd questioned him earlier. "He made it sound like the rest of the family knew we really got married, but I'm not even certain that's the case, since some of my cousins were surprised to find out it wasn't just an angle for the GWA."

"I wonder if that's what Caitlyn was trying to figure out without actually asking," Rylie pondered as they reached the third floor, "when she commented on me wearing my mom's rings on the wrong hand. Since I didn't know how we were handling telling everyone about the annulment, I just played it off as habit from wearing them on my right hand since Mom and Dad died and switched them so nobody else would notice and start asking questions I didn't know how you'd want me to answer."

"Sorry, I guess we should have planned a little better for what we're telling everyone." Liam winced, spinning the Claddagh wedding band on his left ring finger in his pocket before temporarily changing the subject. He knew they'd have to finish their discussion before going to Mass the next morning, but he hoped to have some time to himself to figure out what he wanted them to tell his family before he made his suggestion and discussed their options with her further. "So, there are two guest rooms on this floor. The first one is the smaller of the two, but it has a balcony where the larger one doesn't."

He directed her to the doorway of the smaller room first before showing her to the second guest room on that level for a quick peek. "They're basically identical to the guest rooms on the next floor, so again, you'll have your choice of a smaller room with a balcony or a larger room without." He redirected her back to the stairs for the climb up to the fourth floor, where the other two guest rooms and the master bedroom were all located. "They all have their own bathrooms, with the bathrooms attached to the smaller rooms having bathtubs while the larger bedrooms only have showers."

"Do any of them have views of the beach?" Rylie questioned as they continued up the stairs to the fourth floor.

"They all do," Liam grinned, not mentioning that he'd specifically picked this house design because all the bedrooms would have a view of the Atlantic Ocean. "Just in the smaller rooms and the master, you have to go out on the balcony to get the best view, while the two larger guest rooms just have windows overlooking the beach."

"Then I'll probably take one of the two smaller rooms, so I can soak in the tub," Rylie decided as he directed her to the left at the top of the stairs on the fourth floor, toward his bedroom.

"Well, whichever one you choose, we'll have to move your luggage, 'cause I'm almost positive Quinn put your bags in my room." Liam was proven correct when he opened the door and saw all their bags and both their coats piled up on his bed.

"Then let's just go across to the smaller room on this floor, so we don't have to carry everything downstairs until it's time for us to rejoin the GWA tour." Rylie surprised him by not picking the absolute farthest room from his, even though the one she chose was the farthest from his room on the same floor.

Hopefully, the hallways and stairs between us will add to the soundproofing in all the walls, so she'll be less likely to hear me if I wake up with a nightmare than if she'd picked the room that shares part of a wall with mine.

He assisted her in carrying her things to her room and was just about to wish her goodnight and go back to his room when she beckoned him to wait a moment. *Feck, Rylie, couldn't we have talked while we were still downstairs and nowhere near a bed?*

"So, um, what exactly do you want me to say if anyone asks about us while we're here this week?"

Liam was torn about how to reply. On the one hand, he wished he could ask her to pretend to be happily married the way they had while they were in Heart's Destiny, so he could avoid any lectures from his family about how marriage was a lifelong commitment and that they shouldn't get an annulment. He wanted everyone to be nice and welcoming to Rylie, like they were all day, so she could enjoy the holidays without feeling like an outsider. And he could enjoy another week and a half of living out his fantasy life of being her husband, even if it didn't include having her in his bed.

But on the other hand, he kind of wanted to tell everyone the truth about their relationship, so more than just his parents and grandparents would be able to advise him on how they should move forward. Yeah, he'd be setting himself up for lots of lectures, but knowing his family, Rylie would be getting quite a few of those lectures, too. And maybe in the mix of all those lectures, someone would have the right combination of words to guide them through dealing with all the obstacles they faced to be able to stay married and have a long happy future together.

With Rylie looking up at him expectantly, though, Liam didn't have time to run through all the pros and cons of each option to make a decision. So, he suggested the only thing he could without feeling like he was manipulating the situation.

"The truth, just like I've been doing since Da called me yesterday," Liam advised, running a hand through his hair as he fought the urge to step closer to her and try kissing her until she agreed to give him another chance, even if it was only for a fling while they were staying together over their holiday break.

"Did anyone ask you about us today?" Rylie questioned, nervously fiddling with the strap of one of her bags. "Like when you were outside with the guys and I didn't hear it to know how you responded?"

"Yeah, a couple of my cousins asked if we're really married or if it was just a work," Liam shrugged. "That's why I mentioned earlier about not being sure Da told everyone."

"And what exactly did you tell them? Just that we got married? Or did you tell them we're planning to go to the lawyer's office Monday to find out if we can get an annulment or have to get divorced?"

"Just that we got married while blackout drunk in Vegas," Liam admitted. "And then they were too busy ragging on me for not being Irish enough to hold my whiskey for me to get a chance to mention any of our plans."

"So, you don't want me to mention looking into our legal options either?" Rylie's expression was impossible for Liam to read, clearly a mask because she didn't want him to know anything about her emotions.

"Maybe not with anyone but Ma, Da, Granny, and Granda," Liam shrugged, taking a page out of her book and schooling his features to cover his true feelings on the matter. "We're going to have a hard enough time convincing the four of them not to interfere in our plans to meet with the attorneys on Monday, so it's probably best not to get the rest of the family riled up about how marriage is supposed to be sacred and forever, when we've still gotta spend the next ten days seeing them at church and various parties and get-togethers."

"Okay, then I'll just keep acting like your blissfully happy wife," Rylie agreed with a sigh, not seeming pleased with the advice he'd given her, which he knew was the only way to keep her from having to suffer through lectures from everyone in his family.

But feck, I can't take the chance that having everyone in my family gang up on her will guilt her into forgiving me, so we can make our marriage work, and coerce her into giving up her wrestling dreams to retire when I do, so we can start a family. I love her too much to use them to manipulate her into doing what I want. And because I love her, I have to set her free, so she can decide for herself what she wants for her future. I just pray that we can at least maintain our friendship, so she'll know I'll still be here waiting on the off chance that she'll eventually forgive me and love me enough to want us to get back together after her wrestling career is over.

"You don't have to pretend to be my blissfully happy wife," he finally offered with a sad smile. "Just be yourself. My friend Rylie, who apparently can't hold her Irish whiskey any better than I can." *And I'll sell the dopey, lovestruck hubby routine enough that nobody will pressure you about calling off the annulment.*

Rylie at least chuckled at his lame attempt to lighten the mood. "Goodnight, Liam."

"Goodnight, Rylie." Liam knew when he was being dismissed, so he closed her bedroom door on his way out, heading back to his room to unpack.

Feck, the next ten days are gonna suck! Not that making all my extended family think I'm madly in love with my wife, so they won't say anything to her about the annulment, will be that hard, since I won't have to pretend any of the attraction I feel toward her. But it's gonna be hard as feck to keep from following through and acting on my desire for her when we're alone. Not that she'd let me get too far outta line, since it's clear my gobshite confession about Jen killed any attraction she had to me.

As he unpacked his stuff to settle in for a week and a half at home, Liam pulled her vibrator from his bag along with the Claddagh wedding band he'd purchased for her in San Antonio a month earlier. While he'd continued wearing his matching wedding band anytime he was in public and needed to maintain kayfabe, he still hadn't mentioned buying her a matching ring to anyone, assuming she wouldn't want it after they annulled their marriage anyway. But seeing the ring box side by side with her vibrator box, Liam felt really guilty for not giving her back her toy after they left Heart's Destiny last month.

But feck, I couldn't give it back to her after everything that happened that week. Since we didn't end up using it together then, I couldn't figure out when and how to hand it over without embarrassing one or both of us. Besides, if I'd have given it back to her after we ended our friends-with-benefits arrangement, then I'd have just driven myself crazy for the last month, imagining her using it every night. And I can't even give it back now, even if I could somehow sneak it into the bedroom she's using while she's otherwise occupied this week, 'cause I'll be right back to torturing myself with fantasies of how she's using it every time we go to our separate rooms.

As he put both her vibrator and the ring box in his bedside table to deal with later, Liam berated himself once again for screwing up the friends-with-benefits arrangement he'd reached with Rylie in Heart's Destiny after only a few days of getting to make love to her. While he still didn't think they could have made it work past the couple of years he had left of being a decent in ring performer before he retired, he knew he'd regret not getting to spend the last couple years of his career making love to her every night.

But no, I had to be a gobshite and admit to the one thing that was a deal breaker for her. So, now I'm gonna hafta make the memories of the five wonderful nights I got to be inside her last for the rest of my life.

Unless, maybe Da was right when he suggested we talk to him, Ma, Granda, and Granny before following through on the annulment plans? Could they possibly have the perfect advice for how I can make up to her for being stupid and kissing Jen, so we might have a chance at making a go of our marriage? Feck, even if we can't make it work forever, maybe talking things out will help us find a way to keep trying, at least until I retire from wrestling? I know the long-distance thing after that is a long shot. But maybe if she can somehow forgive me and give me a second chance now, then by the time I'm ready to retire, maybe I'll have earned her love enough that she'd consider retiring at the same time to start our family?

No, I can't ask her to quit wrestling early. But maybe Rick will have another opening for a booker, so I can travel with her for a few more years? And if not, then I'll just make sure she knows that I love her so much that I'm willing to wait however long it takes for her to be ready for us to get back together after her time in the ring is over.

Deciding he needed an outside opinion on the possibility of her being able to forgive him, even if it meant they weren't able to be together for another decade or more, Liam decided to call his best friend. He rushed through his nightly routine to get ready for bed, so he could pick up his phone from the bedside table as soon as he sat down propped against the headboard. Then, he quickly dialed the number, wanting to know how Dion was doing as much as he wanted his advice about Rylie.

"Hey, Li," Dion greeted him when he answered the call. "Freezing your balls off in New York yet?"

"No, the high today was thirty-four, so not quite freezing," Liam chuckled, glad to hear his friend in good spirits.

"Yeah, traveling up north in the winter is definitely one thing I'm *not* gonna miss about being on tour with the GWA," Dion chuckled.

"We were only about ten degrees shy of double your high here today, and that's plenty cold enough for me."

"You're still in Heart's Destiny, right?" Liam knew Dion was planning to stay there through the end of the year, but he wasn't sure if he had to make a short trip back home to get his records from the hospital and doctors he'd seen after the injury to take them to the new doctors he planned to see in Texas. He also didn't know if Dion planned to make the move permanent now that he was going to be a father, or if he planned to travel back and forth between there and his hometown of New Orleans, or if those trips would be with or without Julie and their babies. And if he was making it a permanent move, he wasn't sure if D had already gone back to New Orleans to pack up his condo before going back to Heart's Destiny for good. "How long are you planning to stay there? Just 'til New Year's like you said before? Or are you moving there now and need to run back to NOLA to pack?"

"Yeah, Dare and Mama Marcel are still planning to head home in the new year, but I have no plans of leaving here anytime soon, even to pack my stuff. At least, not until I can convince Jewel to go on a family vacation with me. And if that takes longer than I hope, then I'll just have Dare and Mama Marcel bring me anything I might need while I'm living at the B and B that I don't already have with me."

Liam still couldn't believe his first guess of Julie Burleson had been correct when Dion had asked about the woman he'd dreamed about while in the hospital, whom he'd only called Jewel. Especially since Dion was so adamant that her name was Jewel and not Julie for the first month after losing his memory. All it took was Dion actually seeing her again before his friend finally figured out Jewel was in fact Julie, but now they had other issues facing them that were still keeping them apart.

"Any luck getting back together with her since the last time we talked?" The last Liam had heard, Julie Burleson had only agreed to co-parent their twins with Dion, but he knew D was still holding out hope that she'd forgive him for his brother being an arse when he answered D's phone while Dion was still unconscious in the hospital back in October, so they could get their happily ever after as a family of four.

"No, she's still insisting I focus on my recovery and not our relationship," Dion sighed. "But we're talking or texting daily and went baby shopping together earlier this week, so it's just a matter of time before I convince her to give me another chance."

"And you've been following up with the doctor she referred you to there?"

"Yeah, Doc Hayes is coordinating with a bunch of specialists and doing all kinds of tests, trying to find the best treatment plan so maybe I can get a little closer to normal," Dion informed him. "Or at least, maybe I can quit having the pass out spells that scare me for possibly dropping one of the babies. In fact, I spent last night and this morning at the sleep specialist's clinic doing a couple of sleep studies to see if maybe the brain injuries made me narcoleptic."

"Yeah? Did they give you the results while you were there? Or do you have to wait to go back to the doctor to find out?"

"I have to go back to the doctor to find out. But I also did some tests with a neuropsych and found out I have A.D.D., and the medicine they started me on for that is one of the meds they'd recommend for narcolepsy, so I'm hoping those spells will go away before I go back to the doctor next month. And they also started me on some dementia medicine to help me retain my new memories, even though it probably won't do much to help me get the old ones back."

"Well, that's good. You'll have to let me know if any of those things work, or if I need to start looking into bubble wrap onesies for your babies," Liam quipped, glad to hear that his friend was closer to having the diagnoses he needed to properly treat his residual issues after his injuries.

"If Mama Marcel is right and they're both girls, I'm probably gonna wanna look into a full line of bubble wrap clothing to keep them safe from any bumps and bruises," Dion chuckled. "And maybe with the outer layer being made of Kevlar so nothing can pop the protective bubble around them."

Liam could only laugh at the mental picture Dion's plans for baby armor conjured in his mind.

"Well, at least if you have girls, you'll have Anthony and all the Burlesons to back you up with keeping the boys away from them." Thinking about his best friend becoming a dad in a few months made Liam wish for his own family. *If only I knew how to make my dreams of me and Rylie making things work to stay married and have kids together come true.*

"True," Dion chuckled before changing the subject, as if reading Liam's mind to know his wife had just popped into his head. "How are things going with you and Rylie?"

"Feck if I know," Liam grumbled, picking at a loose string on the edge of the right leg of his dark purple boxer briefs. *I hope I can find more in this color, since Rylie seemed to like the irony of me wearing eggplant-colored underwear.* "We've been back in the awkward friend phase since we had to start riding together after **Christmas Chaos**. But then Da called me yesterday to make sure I brought my bride home for Christmas to meet the family, so today's been more like when we first got to Heart's Destiny for Dean and Allissa's wedding and were pretending to be happily married."

"How'd your dad find out? I thought you were telling them the marriage was just part of your current angle?"

"Rick called and filled him in," Liam scoffed, still unsure how he felt about his boss interfering in his personal life. "Considering how many times Rick seemed to have his head together with the Matchmaking Mommas last month when we were all in Heart's Destiny, it wouldn't surprise me if bringing Rylie here to meet the family was all his idea."

"Yeah? Ya think he's trying to help ya'll figure out you should stay together?"

"Maybe," Liam sighed, wishing he could go along with all the matchmakers' plans for him and Rylie. "Even knowing I'm planning to file for an annulment while I'm here this week, he's got plans to continue the marriage angle after the feud with Protection Detail is over."

"Really? He's gonna permanently separate them from their manager?"

"As permanently as anything is in professional wrestling," Liam chuckled. "So, he could basically have a whole new plan by the time we get back from break, but as of now, we're planning for Protection Detail to go over at the **Massacre** show, but pin my temporary partner, so I can claim that he could lose us the titles, but not my wife, and keep her as my manager going forward."

"And once they have the tag titles, you'll go back to singles matches?"

"Yeah, no point in putting me in another tag team, only to have to find my replacement in a couple of years to keep the team going after I retire." Liam was glad to hear that Dion's brain injury issues since being shot hadn't impacted his mind to the point that, along with his memories, he also lost his ability to be an outstanding wrestling strategist. "And since Cooper is planning to retire from the ring to start booking in the next few months, Rick wants me and Vaughn to feud for the heavyweight title while our wives feud for the women's title."

"So, is he playing matchmaker to keep you from screwing up his booking again? Or has him being happily married this time changed him to the point that he wants everyone else to get their happily ever after so bad that he's changing his booking as part of his matchmaking plans?"

"I think that's as hard to determine as whether the chicken or the egg came first," Liam chortled, finally pulling the entire thread out of the hem of his boxer briefs, leaving the edge unrolled where it could fray. *Definitely have to go look for more in this color sometime this week now.*

"The chicken came first," Dion stated confidently. "'Cause I'm sure our creator is gentlemanly enough to make sure the chick always comes first."

"Feck, man, I miss your sense of humor," Liam laughed, knowing he'd have to share that one liner with the rest of the guys in the locker room once the GWA's break was over. *And maybe with my brothers and cousins while I'm home, but only if I can get them alone so Da or Granda don't hear it.*

Once their jovial moment passed, Liam brought the conversation back around to why he'd originally called. "So, one of the things Da mentioned when he called me yesterday was possibly having me and Rylie sit down with him, Ma, Granda, and Granny, and maybe Father O'Malley, to try and talk things out for us to stay together instead of going through with the annulment. But before I agree to that, I'd kinda like an outside opinion about the odds of them being able to help me make things right so she can forgive me, or if we'll just be rubbing salt in the wound and making her uncomfortable with being here. Which is why I called you, 'cause you're the best at helping everyone whenever we have issues with each other backstage."

"I think that'll depend on what she has to forgive you for," Dion advised, his voice softening with compassion. "I know we talked about it some that last day you were here, but I honestly don't remember what you said you did to make her mad enough to break things off."

I guess that new memory medicine isn't working for him yet.

"I confessed to going into the back room at Tully's with Jen at Charlotte and Ian's joint bachelorette and bachelor party," Liam admitted, feeling like a gobshite all over again. "I told her it was only two really bad attempts at kissing, but I don't know if she believes me or not. Feck, even if she does believe me that I never had sex with Jen, and haven't had sex with anyone but her since she first started with the GWA, I think the fact that I kissed Jen after we were married, and technically it was in the wee hours of the morning on Rylie's birthday, both contributed to making it seem like a worse offense than it really was."

"Why the fuck would you kiss another woman after you married Rylie? And especially on Rylie's birthday? Granted, I don't remember the last couple of years to know how you've changed recently, but the decade of memories I do have of you don't fit with a cheating asshole."

"First of all, I didn't know I'd married Rylie when we went to Heart's Destiny for our Labor Day break," Liam defended his reprehensible actions to his friend, whom he knew didn't remember the night in question at all. "Second, I didn't know it was Rylie's birthday until after we got back from the break and celebrated her birthday backstage a week and a half later. Third, you were my designated driver that night, so I drank way more than I should have, so I don't know what the feck I was thinking when Jen suggested hooking up in the storeroom and I stupidly tried to agree. Fourth, I probably had a mild concussion from banging our heads together the first time we tried to kiss, so I wasn't thinking straight when we attempted it the second time and realized it felt like we were kissing our cousins. And finally, even after all that, my dick knew she wasn't Rylie, so he tried to turn himself inside out to get away from Jen. So, there was no way I could have followed through with more, even if I'd wanted to in my delusional state."

"Did you tell her all that? Or did you just confess to kissing Jen without explaining all the extenuating circumstances?"

"I definitely didn't mention that it was on her birthday. Although, I'm sure she's smart enough to figure out that the party was the night before her birthday to realize that the kisses probably happened after midnight." Liam banged his head back against the headboard, unsure if he was glad it was padded or not, since at least if it wasn't, it might knock some sense into him.

"Okay, good. Don't mention that unless she does," Dion advised. "And then only to apologize and let her know you didn't know it was her birthday at the time. What else did you tell her when you confessed the first time?"

"I didn't mention how much I had to drink in my misguided attempt to get her out of my head that night," Liam remembered, shaking his head when he realized what he had said he'd done to try to stop thinking about her instead. "Feck! But I did say I thought fucking someone else would help me get over my attraction to her."

"Were you drunk the night you told her all this?" Dion's voice sounded incredulous at Liam's sheer stupidity.

"Not drunk, just lightly buzzed from the champagne at Dean and Allissa's wedding reception." Liam shrugged, unable to really claim he was all that impaired, considering how much he'd had to eat along with the three or four glasses of champagne he'd had at the reception. "But I did tell her about us butting heads the first time we tried kissing and how my dick didn't want anything to do with Jen."

"Well, that's good," Dion laughed. "At least you don't have to repeat how it tried to turn inside out in front of your parents and grandparents. Fuck, man, how am I supposed to keep a straight face the next time I see Jen after hearing that?"

"Don't take your dementia medicine for a few days so you forget this conversation by the time you see her again?" Liam jokingly suggested, unable to keep from laughing along as he pictured D fighting not to laugh while trying to talk to Julie with her twin sister right beside her.

"Yeah, sorry, I already took it tonight and I'm sure I'll see her at church tomorrow since Justin and Amy's wedding shower is right after. Does she know she gives you an innie? Or am I gonna embarrass her if I comment on it?"

"Feck if I know," Liam shuddered, not wanting to picture his dick as an innie, like it was a second belly button, even though he'd been the one to initially mention it wanting to turn inside out. "With Jen, I imagine she could take it one of two ways. One, she'd remember she was the one who first mentioned feeling like she was kissing her cousin and think it was funny. Or two, she'd be hurt by thinking the kiss was bad because I don't find her attractive, which isn't true. She's a beautiful woman. She's just not the woman for me."

"Considering how easy it seems for women to misunderstand things, especially from me right now, I'll keep that info to myself."

"Yeah, no need to piss off your girl by coming across as saying her twin sister isn't attractive," Liam agreed.

"Exactly," Dion chuckled momentarily before turning more contemplative. "But seriously, just apologize to her and promise she'll never have to worry about you doing anything like that again. Tell her you were too drunk to think clearly, or you'd have realized what a stupid idea it was to think being with anyone else would help you get over her without having to try it to find out what your body already knew was the truth, which is that Rylie's the only woman for you. And then regardless of what she decides about forgiving you in the moment, just keep being her friend. Even if she needs a little time to get there, that's the only way you stand any chance of her eventually forgiving you and wanting more than just your friendship."

"Thanks, man," Liam sighed. "That's exactly what I needed to hear."

They talked a little while longer about the various activities Dion had recently done with Julie, including how even her dad seemed to be in favor of them getting back together and wanting Dion to move onto the Burleson Ranch to live with her and their twins. Dion also told Liam all about the house Julie moved into, which was over a hundred years old and originally built by Julie's second-great-grandfather. It was also apparently where Julie's father, Jon, wanted Dion to move and remodel the attic to provide bedrooms for more than just the two babies he and Julie were expecting in May.

While they didn't get back around to discussing Liam and Rylie's relationship or how Liam should proceed after apologizing, specifically with regard to trying to win her heart while staying married, or going through with ending the marriage and hoping she'd come back to him after he set her free, hearing Dion's plans for him and Julie and their future family made Liam's hopes for his own future clear. He wanted a family with Rylie and he knew his only shot at that would be if he followed his da's advice to have them sit down with Father O'Malley for some marriage counseling before deciding whether to follow through with the annulment or not. While he knew his da really meant for him and Rylie to sit down with the elders in their family first, being accustomed to confessing his sins to a priest made him think meeting with Father O'Malley might be easier, or at least a little less uncomfortable, than talking things out with the older generations of Connerys.

I wonder if he has any openings for after Mass tomorrow? If not, I guess we'll go ahead with the legal appointment on Monday, but maybe not sign anything until after we have time to talk to him first. And maybe talk to my family if Father O'Malley can't get us in this week because of the holidays, or if his advice isn't helpful since he's not married.

Chapter Two

Sunday, December 22, 2019, New York City, New York

Rylie was surprised to hear music playing as she walked downstairs, already dressed for Mass since Liam's granny had made it clear that they were expected to attend as his family left the night before. Yeah, Liam had popped his earbuds in and listened to something whenever they had downtime in their hotel room in Heart's Destiny the month before, when they were pulling off the charade of being happily married. But she'd assumed that was only because he was trying to avoid talking to her at the beginning of that week, since he didn't keep it up the whole time they were there and didn't normally listen to anything on their plane rides or downtime backstage. He was always more focused on carrying on conversations with everyone else and didn't seem into the passive activity of listening to music.

   When the music changed from a classic rock anthem, like her dad used to enjoy, to an old-school hip hop song by The Notorious B.I.G., like her mom had loved, she was even more surprised, not identifying Liam as a fan of either genre. Since he didn't seem to really pay attention to the music playing whenever they went out, and he'd danced to everything, from the current dance hits that played at most of the clubs they went to after GWA shows to the country music that was most popular at the bar in Heart's Destiny, she assumed he didn't have a preference when it came to music. That lack of a favorite genre of music was something she thought they had in common, since she'd always been happy to listen to whatever her parents or friends played, but usually picked audiobooks to listen to in her spare time over a music app.

"What are you listening to?" Rylie questioned as she walked into the kitchen, where she found Liam standing beside one of the two stovetops stirring something in a fry pan. He was only wearing a pair of gray sweats that set low on his hips, allowing her a mouthwatering view of his muscular back and trim waist.

"*Rock Hits Radio* on Pandora," Liam informed her as he turned away from the stovetop to look at her.

Holy abs, Batman! Rylie was so enamored with his chiseled physique that she had to stop and sit down on one of the barstools on the opposite side of the island from where he was standing to keep herself from giving in to the urge to lick her way from his eight-pack and the sexy V-cut of his obliques up to the light brown disks surrounding his nipples on those perfect pecs. "And they classify Biggie as rock and not hip hop?"

"Yeah, I think D screwed with the algorithm for my Pandora feeds by favoriting a bunch of hip hop and old-school rap. So now it doesn't seem to matter which station I pick, I get a mix of everything from the Rolling Stones to Nirvana mixed with Biggie, Snoop, and even some Sir Mix-A-Lot." Liam walked over to the island and swiped his phone screen until the music playing on built-in speakers in the kitchen, dining room, and living room turned down so they could talk without having to shout over it, and unknowingly tempting her even more with each step closer to her he took.

"That sounds like a prank Dion would pull," Rylie chuckled, finally dragging her gaze up to Liam's face, so hopefully he wouldn't catch her drooling over him. "Speaking of Dion, have you heard anything new about him and Julie?"

"Yeah, they're talking daily and looking forward to co-parenting, but he still hasn't convinced her to go out with him again." Liam smiled sadly. "She's making him focus on healing before revisiting their relationship."

"And is he healing?" Rylie wanted to know how their friend was doing but felt like a nosy Nellie for asking anything regarding Dion's medical information. "Have those zone out spells he was having last month gotten any better?"

"Not yet, but when I talked to him last night, he mentioned some new meds the doctors are trying and some tests he just had done to see if there's anything else they can do to stop them, so he'll feel safer holding their babies once they're born." Liam leaned against the island and picked up his coffee cup to take a drink.

How on earth does he make taking a drink of coffee look so freaking sexy?

Once he set the cup back down, he continued. "Oh, and apparently Mama Marcel thinks the twins are both going to be girls, so now he's on the hunt for baby clothes with a bubble wrap layer covered in Kevlar to keep them safe."

"I think he was pulling your leg on that," Rylie laughed, grateful for the mention of Dion's fortune-teller adoptive mom to help her redirect her thoughts. Though to be honest, even trying to think of Dion, Julie, and Mama Marcel trying to dress the twins in Kevlar once they were born didn't divert her attention for long. She knew Liam at least had to go put a shirt on before anything else might steal her attention away from how hot he was.

"Maybe, but I'm still tempted to ask the ladies in the GWA wardrobe department if they know anyone who can make up a couple prototype baby bodysuits I can send him as a baby shower gift."

"Yeah, I can't imagine those would be comfortable for the babies to wear," Rylie laughed, trying to conjure the image in her mind to keep from looking back down at Liam's tempting torso.

"Probably not," Liam chuckled with her. "But I'm sure Julie is more than capable of keeping him from actually putting them on their kids."

Their laughter soon died down as they started to smell smoke, which actually worked to redirect Rylie's attention from Liam's bangin' bod.

"Oh, feck, the eggs!" Liam turned back around and jogged the three steps from the island to the counter with the second stovetop where he'd been working when she first walked in. He quickly removed the pan from the burner before turning it off. "Guess I'm not making breakfast for us this morning after all."

"I'm sorry, I didn't mean to distract you from cooking," Rylie apologized, feeling guilty for sitting down at the island, instead of walking all the way into the kitchen, so he could talk to her while also watching the food in the pan. *But if I'd have gone around the island, I probably still would have distracted him from cooking, just with licking the ridges of his abs and that sexy V, instead of waiting for breakfast.*

"No worries," Liam said, shaking his head as he turned away from the stove once more. "Since we always go to the late Mass, we still have time to stop for breakfast on the way to Saint Stephen's. I just have to go throw some clothes on first, since I showered after my run earlier. I just didn't want to take a chance on messing up my suit with my notoriously disastrous cooking."

Before Rylie could volunteer to take over cooking duties, Liam scooped up his phone, turned off the music, and practically ran out of the kitchen. *Yeah, I probably would have been just as distracted as I made him anyway,* Rylie decided as she sat there waiting for Liam to come back downstairs. *So we'd have just wasted even more time and still would've had a burnt breakfast. And hopefully, now I have time to get my libido back in check before we go sit in church with his family.*

Unfortunately, she didn't take into consideration how his bergamot and sandalwood scent would envelop her in the confines of his sports car as they rode to breakfast and then to the church.

An hour later, as Rylie walked into Saint Stephen's Cathedral alongside Liam and his family, the smell of incense not only helped cover Liam's enticing scent, it also helped banish her lustful thoughts by instantly bringing a wave of memories to the forefront of her mind. Memories of attending Mass with her mom and dad regularly throughout her childhood and teenage years, and especially how her parents always seemed to be a half-beat behind everyone else whenever kneeling or crossing themselves. Rylie smiled as she remembered how her parents had explained that neither of them had grown up Catholic, so all the rituals weren't ingrained in them, causing them to always feel like they were following along with what they saw, no matter how many years it'd been since they converted. Being lost in her thoughts, and having not stepped foot in a Catholic Church in almost seven years, Rylie felt like she was following in her parents footsteps with being that half-beat behind Liam and his family as they crossed themselves with holy water and bowed to the altar as they took their seats.

She thought back to the various times she'd attended the services at the Heart's Destiny Community Church when she was there for weddings in the last several months, trying to remember if Liam had adhered to the Catholic rituals while entering, or if he'd conformed to the behaviors of the members of the non-denominational church, as she had. *I know he didn't cross himself or bow toward the altar any of the times we were there over our Thanksgiving break, and I don't think he did at any of the services over our Memorial Day or Independence Day breaks either. But I can't help but wonder if he did on one of his first visits when I wasn't there. And if he did, did he stop because Jen pointed out that they don't do those things there?*

Not wanting to rehash any of her jealous feelings over Liam's friendship with Jen, Rylie tried to refocus on the service as the music started and the priest entered and greeted them with an opening prayer. As the service went on, crossing herself and replying along with the rest of the congregation at the appropriate times soon came back to her as the ingrained habits they'd once been, making her feel guilty for being so angry at God that she'd turned her back on the Church after losing her parents. So much so that during the Penitential Rite, the way she'd misbehaved and lashed out in the angry phase of her grief were the only sins she could think of to pray about and ask for forgiveness.

Mom and Dad would be mortified if they knew all the stupid stuff I did back then. Especially how my grades slipped to the point that I almost lost my scholarship and flunked out of school because I was just too angry at them for leaving me that I skipped going to the classes they were most excited about me taking that first semester after they were gone.

She'd planned to follow in her parents' footsteps and become a teacher after getting her degree in elementary education, but she'd only taken core general education classes in her first semester of college, having to wait until the second semester before taking her first degree track classes. With them being killed between her first and second semesters of college, she just couldn't handle the emotions of being in classes similar to the ones her parents had told her about taking for their elementary education degrees.

Yes, she knew they'd also had to take the core classes everyone had to take in college. But since neither her mom nor her dad had specifically mentioned anything about the math, composition, science, history, or other core classes they'd taken, those classes hadn't been difficult for her to attend. Which was how she managed to cobble together enough credits in the next few years to graduate with a bachelor's degree in general studies. Not that her degree actually qualified her for any kind of career.

It was precisely due to her degree not being in a specific career field that she ended up working for a temporary service, filling receptionist and secretarial jobs at a variety of businesses around Atlantic City after she graduated. Luckily for her, one of those temporary positions was in the office of the local arena, where she saw the GWA live for the first time. And as the receptionist, she answered the phone when Patrice Jacobs, Rick's executive assistant, who worked exclusively from the corporate office in New York City, called to confirm the next date the GWA was scheduled to have a show there.

While she'd watched wrestling on television with her dad as a kid, she'd never considered it a viable option for her future career. But after seeing the matches live for the first time in January 2017, she knew she had to find out if her athleticism from participating in sports in high school and college would be enough for her to get out of the temporary office rut for a more lucrative career in the wrestling ring. So, when she had the opportunity to speak with someone who worked with the GWA, she took it to ask a few questions about the training requirements and how to get an opportunity to eventually interview for a job as a wrestler.

Patrice cautioned her about the long arduous training period and the crazy schedule of GWA performers, but she also gave her the contact information for an independent wrestling promotion in Atlantic City, where she could train and get some in-ring experience. She also instructed Rylie to call her directly to schedule her try-out match whenever she felt she was finally ready. It took two years of training and working indie shows on the weekends while continuing to work her temp office jobs during the week, but with perseverance, she finally made it.

While we're in Manhattan tomorrow, I'll have to pick up a gift card for the coffee shop closest to the GWA headquarters for Patrice to thank her for all her help over the years and drop it off at the office. While Rylie knew the GWA corporate office was closed for the holiday break, she assumed the security guard for the building would be able to hold a Christmas card for her at the desk and pass it along when Patrice returned to work on the second of January.

"Just cross your arms over your chest like this to show you just want a blessing and aren't taking communion." Liam's whispered words brought her out of her head, just as it was time for their row to line up to walk to the front of the church.

Oh, wow, I guess we haven't really discussed our religious backgrounds for him to know I didn't need him to tell me that. But I guess only seeing me attend services when they were associated with wedding events in Heart's Destiny hasn't exactly given him any insight into my Catholic upbringing. And the fact that I opted to have him drop me off at the mall when he mentioned needing to go to confession last month, when we escaped Heart's Destiny for a few hours, certainly didn't make it clear that I'm just a lapsed Catholic and not a total non-believer or member of another religious congregation. So I suppose it's to be expected that he doesn't know my religion.

As she followed Liam back to their pew after receiving her blessing and him receiving communion, she had to wonder if thinking she wasn't Catholic was another reason why Liam believed they were incompatible and should annul their marriage. *Surely, there's more to him still pushing for us to end our marriage than just our age difference, especially after I told him my plans to cut my wrestling career short to have children. I know it's certainly not due to a lack of attraction, even if he doesn't want to be attracted to me for some other reason. But if it was only because of our ages and possibly not quitting wrestling at the same time, then that doubt should have been laid to rest last month when we agreed to do the friends-with-benefits thing.*

Or I suppose it could be that I told him about probably having to do in vitro fertilization to have kids because of my risk of P.C.O.S., and he firmly agrees with the Catholic Church's views on IVF? I guess I can see why he might feel like I'm not wife material because I'm probably not going to be able to fulfill my wifely duty of bearing his children the old-fashioned way and he doesn't want to have to decide between sinning with IVF or not having children.

I mean, I didn't really think about it being a big deal when I first started researching it, but I also haven't been practicing my Catholic faith for the last several years, at least, not the way Liam and his family obviously do. Now that I'm here in a Catholic Church for the first time in years, and am feeling compelled to start practicing my faith again, I'll have to rethink that plan to one day have children.

Of course, that's still a few years off and not necessarily a foregone conclusion for what it'll take for me to carry a baby. And when the time comes, it'll also require me to decide with my husband and not just on my own. Well, if I'm married then, anyway. Not that I can see myself falling in love with anyone else if Liam gets his way and we're able to annul our marriage. And I guess not being able to easily give him children is legal grounds for an annulment for a valid reason. But dang, it still hurts to think he can't love me enough to want to be with me anyway.

Geez, I'm so stupid for thinking that he called me "Moh Graw" because he loved me. It might mean "my love," but it's just a generic term of endearment, kind of like the way Jax calls all the women in the company "Doll," or how so many southern ladies call everyone "Hun" or "Sugar." It doesn't mean anything. It's just his go-to phrase in the heat of the moment.

Maybe he thought he could love me when he first started using it. But since he hasn't called me "Moh Graw" at all since we were in Heart's Destiny, even though he'd used it out in public when we weren't having sex before that, obviously he's decided not to keep giving me false hope that he could love me. I just wish I knew what happened to make him decide he can't love me, 'cause I swear it felt like he did when we made love.

Unless, maybe he thought he loved me then, but my overreaction to hearing about him kissing Jen after we were married changed his perception of me to the point that he thinks I'm too immature for him now? Or too petty and jealous?

I thought pressing pause on the benefits would help clear my head, so I could look at our relationship more rationally. But maybe that was wrong? Maybe I should have followed my heart and used our physical relationship to strengthen our emotional connection? At the very least, I should have continued trying to talk to him about everything, instead of shutting him out and only interacting with him for work and our very brief conversations about coming here on break to meet with the lawyers.

As the rest of the congregation finished receiving communion, and then the priest led them in prayer, blessing everyone in attendance, Rylie stole a glance at her husband, trying to figure out how she really felt about Liam. While she thought she was in love with him, she was still so hurt by the way he'd tried to get over his attraction to her by sleeping with another woman that she wasn't sure if it mattered how she really felt.

Hearing him admit that he'd tried to get her out of his system with another woman made her feel like his feelings for her were just a passing lust and not the true love she longed for with her significant other. She couldn't believe his claims that his failed attempt at hooking up with Jen had proven he would only ever want to be with Rylie.

In her opinion, all that had proven was that his plan was flawed because he'd chosen someone he already knew he could only think of as a friend. And she couldn't help but wonder if one day he'd meet someone he could actually love and not just lust after, and would break her heart by kicking her to the curb. It was that doubt about his feelings that made her want to go to the meeting with the lawyers to annul their marriage if possible.

She still wasn't sure he was right about an annulment being possible. But now that she was sitting in a Catholic Church again, she also didn't think she could go through with the divorce the attorney she'd spoken with in New Jersey recommended. Catholic guilt was a very real thing, at least for Rylie. And that guilt over not honoring her marriage vows as the sacred commitment they were meant to be made her question whether or not she'd be able to go through with any legal process to end her marriage to Liam, especially when combined with her strong feelings for him.

Even if Liam's lawyers could convince the judge that their GWA characters didn't reflect anything about their real lives, so they didn't consider Red and Chastity's marriage announcement as proof that Liam and Rylie had lived as a married couple, she wasn't sure she'd be able to stand up in court and say she didn't want to be married to him. Doing so would feel too much like telling a big fat whopper of a lie, which she really couldn't do if she'd sworn on the Bible to tell the truth.

Leah Mae Wright

Oh, Mom, I really wish you were still here to give me some advice.
While her mother obviously couldn't be there, Liam's mom and
granny stepped up to take her around and introduce her to what
seemed like everyone in the congregation once the service was
dismissed, much like Rylie remembered her mom doing whenever she
convinced a friend to go somewhere new with her. *Is that just the
basic nature of moms? Or are their exuberant introductions of me as
the newest member of their family a sign from above that I'm supposed
to try harder to work things out with Liam, so we can skip the legal
stuff and stay married?*

Knowing her and Liam's families shared the same beliefs in the
sanctity of marriage, she had to wonder if she was subconsciously
seeing the way the older Connery women were pushing for the same
thing her mom would have, if she were still alive and able to give her
opinion, as a sign that she should push for what she really wanted to
happen between her and Liam. *Am I just not strong enough to fight for
what I want on my own? Or am I just so uncertain of what I want that
I'm following along with his family's desire for us to stay married, so I
don't have to make a decision about any of it myself? Considering
until we came here, I was just following along while Liam made the
decisions about us going to talk to his lawyers and file for the
annulment, I think it might be the latter.*

*So, instead of just blindly going along with Liam's plan to go to his
attorney's office tomorrow, or agreeing with Breena and Cathleen that
we need to make our union work, I need to take some time to figure out
what I want for my future. Do I want to forgive Liam for having
doubts about us and wanting to block out his feelings for me before
they took root, so we can have a chance for a future together? Or do I
want to hang onto my anger and jealousy and end our marriage?*

She was so lost in her thoughts that she missed the majority of the
conversations going on around her. But when she looked up at Liam,
as if seeing his handsome, clean-shaven face would give her the
answers to her inner questions, his words quickly brought her back to
the moment.

"Father O'Malley, you'll have to excuse Ma and Granny for getting
ahead of themselves. Rylie and I have a lot to discuss before deciding
how we plan to proceed. So, I think you can hold off on putting

together an online conversion course until after she has some time to decide whether or not she wants to convert to Catholicism."

"Um, actually, I'm already Catholic," Rylie interjected, surprising everyone around her. "I haven't attended Mass since my parents' funeral. But until they passed, we were at Our Lady of Hope in Atlantic City every Sunday, so I'm sure they still have the records of my baptism, confirmation, and first Communion."

"Ah, well, den we can go ahead and schedule de cahnvalidation ceremahny." Granny Breena was the first among them to recover from Rylie's declaration, but Liam wasn't far behind her.

"No, Granny, we can't," Liam sighed, shaking his head. "Again, Rylie and I have to talk a lot of things out before we decide what we want for our future." Liam's clipped tone and stiff posture made it clear that he was uncomfortable, but Rylie couldn't tell if that was because he didn't want to discuss the annulment with the priest while half the congregation could hear them, or if he was irritated by his family pushing for them to not only stay married, but also to complete a convalidation ceremony, which was basically the Catholic Church's version of a vow renewal to make their marriage valid under canon law.

Wanting to smooth things over with everyone so they didn't get into a debate about her and Liam's marriage in the middle of the vestibule, Rylie spoke up, directing her words to the priest. "Actually, regardless of what we decide as a couple, I really need to know the confession schedule here, so I can repent before Christmas Mass."

"Confession is on Saturdays at eleven or by appointment," Father O'Malley informed her with a gracious smile. "But I'd be happy to take your confession now, if you'd like."

"Thank you, Father," Rylie smiled and nodded before following the priest back into the nave and over to the confessional.

"Please take a few minutes to pray and examine your conscience before stepping in to begin," Father O'Malley instructed her before entering his side of the confessional booth.

Rylie followed his directive, walking over to the nearest pew and bowing toward the altar before kneeling to pray. Since reflecting back on the last seven years of her life would take a lot longer than the few minutes Father O'Malley had given her, she cut herself off after only thinking about her major sins from the first year after her parents died, knowing a lot of those were repeated over the other six years. Then she looked back over the last few months, specifically since she joined the GWA roster and met Liam, adding a few more transgressions to the list of sins she needed to confess. Finally, she quietly prayed once more, this time for the ability to speak intelligibly as she gave her confession through the tears that had already started streaming down her face.

When she entered the confessional, the first thing she did was pull a couple of tissues from the box on the shelf below the screen separating her from the priest, even before exchanging greetings with Father O'Malley. She wiped her tears as best she could while exchanging pleasantries, trying to compose herself before beginning.

"Bless me Father, for I have sinned. My last confession was seven years ago, right before my parents died. After losing them, I was extremely angry. Angry at Mom and Dad for leaving me. Angry at the doctors who couldn't save their lives. Angry at God for not answering my prayers to keep them here on Earth with me. And pretty much angry at everyone around me for happily going on with their lives as if the catastrophic loss of the two most important people in my life hadn't happened. I expressed my anger by acting out in a sinful manner by turning my back on the Church and our beliefs. I drank excessively on occasion, but only after I turned twenty-one and when I knew I wouldn't have to drive afterwards. I disrespected my parents and professors by skipping the classes that Mom and Dad had been most excited about me taking the first semester after they passed, and continued disrespecting their wishes by dropping my elementary education major and barely squeaking by with good enough grades to get a general studies degree instead of something that could lead to a career."

She paused long enough to wipe her tears once more before continuing. "I also acted out in my anger by temporarily getting back together with my high school boyfriend, a boy they didn't like, and having sex for the first time. I also started dressing more provocatively and flaunted my body in a way I wouldn't have before. Since breaking up with that boyfriend again a few days later, I've had sex a few more times over the last seven years, sometimes with boyfriends and sometimes just one-night stands, but never with anyone I was married to until Liam. I used condoms every single time, even with Liam, the few times we had sex, but that was only once in October and for a few days in November. The only time I haven't used a condom was when I masturbated using my vibrator, but I haven't used it since Liam hid it in his suitcase last month and didn't give it back when we went back to separate rooms."

Ugh! How embarrassing to have to admit all this to Liam's priest. But I guess at least being embarrassed helped dry up my tears after thinking about Mom and Dad.

Rylie tried to shake off her mortification at having to admit all that before continuing, specifically asking a question that she knew would probably make Father O'Malley as uncomfortable as she was at the moment. *Hopefully, embarrassing a priest isn't a sin, since I kinda need his opinion on whether or not these next couple of things are sins or not.* "I've also been on birth control pills since I was a teenager to regulate my periods and hopefully prevent the P.C.O.S. symptoms my mom suffered from. I know back then, I was told that wasn't a sin because I was still a virgin. But now that I'm married, is it a sin? Or is it okay, since Liam and I aren't having sex anymore? And was having sex with him a few times a sin, since we're planning to annul the marriage? Also, is it really okay to annul the marriage, but a sin to divorce? 'Cause I'm not sure we'll be able to get an annulment."

"Um, technically, the Church finds it acceptable for a woman to take contraceptive medication for other medical reasons as long as she is not explicitly taking them to prevent conception," Father O'Malley explained with only the slightest stutter over his initial words. "However, married couples are expected to have sexual relations, not only to procreate, but also to build intimacy in the relationship. So, your sins would be using contraceptives when you have sexual relations with your husband if preventing pregnancy is the primary reason for taking them, instead of for the treatment of a legitimate medical issue, and possibly withholding intercourse. In First Corinthians seven, verses three through five, the Bible states, 'The husband should fulfill his duty toward his wife, and likewise the wife toward her husband. A wife does not have authority over her own body, but rather her husband, and similarly a husband does not have authority over his own body, but rather his wife. Do not deprive each other, except perhaps by mutual consent for a time, to be free for prayer, but then return to one another, so that Satan may not tempt you through your lack of self-control.' So, unless you and Liam have mutually agreed to abstain while you pray for your marriage, you should be having relations that could lead to procreation and building the intimate bond every marriage needs."

"Even when he's still adamant that we need to go talk to his lawyers about getting an annulment because we were too drunk to remember when we got married? And I'm still struggling with forgiving him for wanting to be with another woman a couple weeks after we got married? And really, do I have a right to be upset about him kissing Jen then, when neither one of us knew we were married at that time because we were so out of it that night that we totally forgot the wedding?"

"If you've mutually agreed not to have intimate relations because you're ending your marriage, then no it isn't a sin to abstain," the priest clarified, making Rylie feel a little better about having ended the friends-with-benefits arrangement they'd shared for a few days in Heart's Destiny. "Going back to your question about divorce and annulment, neither are sins, but they also don't nullify your marriage in the eyes of God or the Church. In addition to your civil divorce or annulment, you'd have to request a Church Tribunal to annul or dissolve your civil marriage before you can remarry in the Church, otherwise you're still considered married, just living apart from your spouse, and sexual relationships with anyone other than your spouse would still be considered adultery. As for your other questions, you're going to have to explain in more detail before I can answer. When exactly did you get married? And how long was it before you found out you were married?"

That was when Rylie realized the Connerys hadn't shared the circumstances surrounding their Vegas wedding with the priest, other than to indicate they got married while touring with the GWA. "That goes back to my bad coping skills after my parents died leading me to over imbibe on occasion. And back in August at the after-party for the GWA's big summer pay-per-view in Las Vegas, I wasn't the only one who drank way too much. The mother of one of our coworkers made the suggestion that we go take pictures at one of the wedding chapels to create a buzz on social media, and several of us ended up hitched while we were too drunk to remember it. Since Windy paid for all our licenses and ceremonies, none of us knew we'd tied the knot until almost two months later, when I found mine and Liam's marriage license in my mail while we were in Atlantic City for a show. That's when Liam first started talking about annulling the marriage because we were just friends and not actually dating."

She went on to tell Father O'Malley how the other two couples had decided to date and give their marriages a chance, but Liam hadn't wanted to do the same. She explained how she'd always had a crush on him, and had used flirting as part of their GWA angle to try to get his attention and maybe change his mind about them trying to be a real couple, confessing to how she'd flaunted her body in some of their earliest promos for the marriage angle, much like she had when she first started working in the wrestling business. She went on to tell the priest about the incident that occurred at the *Halloween Horror* fan expo, including how she'd tried to be there for Liam as he dealt with the trauma of seeing his best friend being shot, which led to the first time they had sex. She continued with how the very next day, they'd reverted to only interacting for their jobs and staying in separate hotel rooms until the trip to Heart's Destiny.

Of course, once she got to that point, she had to go back and tell him all about the matchmaking that happened every time they were in town for one of their friends' weddings to explain why they'd had to share a room. Then she explained how the close proximity of sharing a bed led to them doing the friends-with-benefits thing for a few days, confessing again to overindulging in alcohol and masturbating. Finally, she told him about how jealous she felt every time Liam's previous fix-ups with Jen were mentioned, and how his confession to her about kissing Jen only a couple weeks after they'd gotten married had hurt her so bad that she'd called off the benefits part of their friendship and went back to only interacting with him for work, until he'd suggested she come with him for the break to speak with his attorneys about the annulment. When she was done, she was crying again, having felt the ups and downs of reliving their entire relationship in the span of a few minutes.

"And honestly, I'm still not sure what to do, but I'm leaning toward getting the annulment, even though I think it'll feel like lying to stand up in court and say I don't want to be married to him, 'cause I really do want to be his wife. But still, it might be best if we start over as two single people to see if we can fall in love and decide to get married again when we're sober. 'Cause getting married in Vegas was a drunk mistake, not because we were madly in love, which should be the only reason for getting married. Yeah, I'm pretty sure I'm in love with him, but his actions have made it clear that he doesn't feel the same way. I honestly think he's just a typical guy, who was horny enough that he wanted to have sex with me, but he's already realized he's not in love with me. And even if we skip the annulment and stay together now, he'll eventually dump me when he meets the woman he can actually fall in love with."

"Since you were married while inebriated, which rendered you unable to give consent, and the officiant wasn't a Catholic priest, with you both being Catholic, I'm sure you'll be able to qualify for an annulment through the Church," Father O'Malley assured her. "But that won't be the case if we go through with the ceremony in the Church that Mrs. Connery suggested. So, my best advice is for you and Liam to spend some time in prayer before having an honest discussion about your feelings for one another. And regardless of what you both decide for the future of your marriage, you need to forgive him for anything that happened when he didn't know he'd committed to you. You also need to pray and meditate on the act of forgiveness and finding peace, so you can forgive yourself for everything we've discussed today, as well as your parents for dying, the doctors for not being able to save them, and God for calling them home, so you can truly banish that anger from your heart."

Father O'Malley went on to quote several passages from the Bible about marriage and forgiving others as she expected God to forgive her, advising her to study them, meditate on them, and pray for the ability to enact them in her life. She agreed and apologized for all her sins before he assigned her penance. She continued wiping her eyes of the tears that just kept falling, as she recited her act of contrition and the priest absolved her of her sins and concluded with a blessing.

Once she left the confessional, Rylie returned to the closest pew to kneel and pray, wanting to immediately complete her prayers of penance before rejoining Liam and his family. *Hopefully, all these prayers and the meditation Father O'Malley recommended will help me figure out if I'm meant to be a part of their family, or if we should follow through with annulling our union.*

~~~

The black streaks smeared down Rylie's face as she exited the confessional surprised Liam. Not because she was emotional and cried during her confession, but because he hadn't ever realized she wore any makeup, other than maybe a little eyeshadow and lip gloss to add a little color to her face when she appeared on camera for GWA promos. He'd always believed she was naturally beautiful enough that she didn't need makeup otherwise and wouldn't want to wear it to wrestle when she'd just sweat it off.

From where he stood by the door between the nave and narthex, he didn't think she saw him before she knelt in the last pew to pray. Father O'Malley clearly did, however, heading straight for Liam as soon as he exited the confessional booth.

Liam had known Father Declan O'Malley for as long as he could remember, since the priest, who was twenty years older than Liam, had grown up in the same neighborhood and attended Saint Stephen's long before he was ordained. While Liam only had the vaguest memories of him before he was a priest, he'd attended enough of Father O'Malley's sermons, as well as seen him at various community gatherings over the years, to recognize the fleeting look of disappointment on his face as he walked up.

Feck, what did Rylie say in confession? And why do I have a feeling that whatever she said made him think I should have been in there right behind her?

While Liam always tried to honor his Catholic upbringing, as he got older, he'd started seeing a few areas where he disagreed with the Church's view on some sins. For example, things like masturbation and condom usage shouldn't be classified as sins in his opinion. And since there weren't actual references to either in the Bible, he felt he was justified in lumping those acts together when he confessed his sins instead of listing out each and every infraction individually.

But if Rylie mentioned me using a condom every time we had sex or catching me masturbating in the shower when we were in Heart's Destiny, then I suppose he could think I need to confess those things too, even though he doesn't know when I last went to confession or what all I confessed when I wasn't confessing to him.
~~~

Leah Mae Wright

"Liam, do you need to give your confession now too?" Father O'Malley questioned, arching an eyebrow curiously. "Since it's been over a year since you've been here?"

Yep, read that one right.

"It's been over a year since I've been in Saint Stephen's, but I've still physically attended Mass and gone to confession at least once a month while touring, and I always watch the live stream of Mass on Sundays, even if I have to do it while on the plane, if we don't have a pay-per-view that week so I can go in person." Liam assured the priest with a smile, unsure if he was grateful his family had already left or if he wished they were still there to overhear this conversation, so he wouldn't have to repeat it later, when they all asked if his not attending services regularly was why he hadn't known Rylie was Catholic. "Thanks again for telling me about the Mass Finder app. It's helped tremendously in figuring out where the nearest Church is, so I'm not late for work or getting to the plane for our morning flights, like I was a few times back when I had to look up Catholic Churches online, call to find out the Mass and confession times, and then got lost or stuck in traffic whenever they weren't as close to our hotels as I thought."

While Liam wasn't as stringent in his beliefs as the rest of his family, he did try to adhere to the teachings of his Catholic upbringing for the most part. And he always confessed the things he did that the Church considered sins, even when his personal view was that the Church hadn't caught up with the times in determining if something was a sin or not. Which was why most of his confessions over the years had been about listing out each specific time he'd had sex before being married, with masturbating and always using condoms so he only engaged in safe sex only being briefly mentioned once, lumping together a month's worth of incidences. Though now he had to wonder if he was really following the intent of the Sunday Mass obligation when he counted online Mass and going to the non-denominational church in Heart's Destiny as meeting his obligation.

"I'm glad it's worked well for you. When was the last time you used it?"

"Thursday in Memphis, for both a midday Mass and confession."

"Has Rylie not gone with you any of the times you've gone to Mass or confession since you got married?"

"No, she hasn't." Liam sighed, feeling guilty for having to admit to the priest that he and his wife weren't living as a married couple. "Our marriage is only a legal technicality at this point. She's staying at my house while we're here on break, but in a guest room. When we're on tour with the GWA, we only act married when we're in character for the shows. But we stay in separate hotel rooms and only hang out together in our free time when it's with a group of our other coworkers."

"I see," Father O'Malley nodded solemnly. "I know we all have a lot going on this week, but if possible I'd like to schedule a counseling session for you and Rylie on either Friday or Saturday. That should give you the time you need to talk as a couple first. And then I'll be able to either counsel you on your duties to one another as husband and wife, or advise you on the process to have the Church nullify your marriage."

Guess Da didn't just talk to me about trying marriage counseling with Father O'Malley before deciding whether or not to go through with the annulment. Which is probably good, since I hadn't figured out how to ask him about it without making it appear to Rylie that I'm trying to manipulate the situation for us to stay together and her to give up her career before she's ready.

"I thought we just had to file for an annulment through the court, which is why we have an appointment with my attorneys tomorrow." Liam nervously ran a hand through the longer strands of hair on the top of his head, probably spiking it up in a bit of a faux-hawk instead of leaving it combed flat to the front and right side of his head the way he typically wore it to look professional.

"As I told Rylie a few minutes ago, that only dissolves your marriage in the civil system, but not in the eyes of God or the Church. If you'd have planned your wedding in the Church instead of getting married at the spur of the moment, you'd have had to go through the Pre-Cana Rite as a couple beforehand to learn these things. But it's no big deal. We can just schedule a counseling session now to give you the information you need, even if we don't end up going through all the Pre-Cana sessions to prepare the both of you before a convalidation ceremony."

"Yes, of course," Liam agreed, trying to remember what his family had planned for the days between Christmas and New Year's, so he could schedule a time with Father O'Malley. "What time Friday or Saturday?"

"Two?"

Before Liam could agree and set a specific date, Rylie walked up, clutching a handful of wadded up tissues streaked with what he assumed was the mascara she'd already wiped away with her tears. The sight of her momentarily distracted him from the conversation he was having because, even with puffy eyes from crying, she was the most beautiful woman he'd ever seen. But still, seeing her upset gutted him, even though he knew her tears were probably cathartic after her confession and not because she was truly hurting, leaving him unable to stop himself from acting on his desire to take care of her.

She arched an eyebrow curiously when he pointed to the tissues in her hand, trying to indicate he wanted to take one.

"You missed a spot." He smiled as he rubbed his own face with the tip of his pointer finger to indicate where she still had a black smudge on her cheek. "But since there's not a mirror nearby, I figured you'd want me to help you with it before anyone else notices."

"Thanks," she agreed, opening her hands for him to see what was left of the tissues she'd been using to wipe her tears.

He took the cleanest looking one from her hand and gently rubbed the small spot she'd missed under her right eye when she'd wiped her tears away after finishing her prayers. Once it was removed so only her natural glowing complexion was visible once again, he took the rest of the tissues and stuffed them in his pocket, so she didn't have to keep carrying them around until they could get out of the church and find the nearest wastebasket.

"I think we need to plan for two o'clock on both Friday and Saturday for now," Father O'Malley stated, smiling knowingly after quietly observing the exchange between Liam and Rylie. "So we can possibly do a couple of the Pre-Cana sessions in person before you have to go back to work and do the rest over the internet."

Is he implying that he thinks we'll need to do the Pre-Cana Rite because he thinks we'll decide to stay married and will want to do a convalidation ceremony to make our marriage officially recognized and blessed by the Church? I mean, I hope he's right, but how did he come to that conclusion without me having to tell him that's what I'm hoping to get from doing counseling sessions with him?

And what all do we have to do for these Pre-Cana sessions? Just talk to him? Or are they like marriage classes with homework and stuff?

He didn't have time to ask all his questions then because he'd promised his family that he and Rylie would meet them at Granda and Granny's house for Sunday dinner. So, instead of bringing them up, Liam just agreed to the two o'clock meeting times for both Friday and Saturday before double checking that he had Father O'Malley's contact information in his phone, just in case he'd forgotten something his family had planned at those times and would need to reschedule one or both of the sessions. Then they parted ways with the priest, knowing they all had plans for lunch with their families.

When they got out to his car, a red 2018 Porsche 911 Carrera 4 GTS Cabriolet that he hadn't gotten to drive nearly as much as he'd have liked since spending all his holiday breaks in Texas after he bought it, Rylie finally asked the question he'd expected her to ask Father O'Malley while they were standing there setting the appointments a few moments earlier.

"What are Pre-Cana sessions? And why do you have to do them?"

"I'm not exactly sure, but I think it's like pre-marriage counseling," Liam admitted as he unlocked the car and opened the passenger door for her. "And meant to be done by couples who wish to get married in the Church. But I think he wants us both to be there for the counseling he's talking about this week, 'cause it's most likely just going to be to give us the information we need to annul our marriage through the Church."

Why the feck did I say that? If I wanna postpone the annulment, I should probably start laying the groundwork to get her to agree by telling her that I want to go through this counseling first before signing anything with the lawyers. I know she'll fight me if I tell her I want to try staying married before she forgives me for kissing Jen. But I should at least make it clear that I'm open to the possibility, instead of seeming to be militantly clinging to the annulment plans.

"Oh, okay." Rylie tried to hide how her smile fell as she got in the car, but Liam could clearly see her disappointment in his answer, confusing him even more than he already was about how he should have replied a moment earlier.

Leah Mae Wright

Why is she disappointed? Since she's the one who ended our friends-with-benefits arrangement, I thought she'd be happy to know what we have to do to end our marriage in the Church as well as the courts. Liam dropped his gaze to the ground, noticing her long, red skirt still hanging out and dragging on the pavement just in time to keep from shutting it in the car door. He bent down and lifted the hem, tucking it into the car before closing her door. *Unless maybe she's not irritated by my answer, but more concerned about getting her skirt dirty because I insisted on driving the Porsche instead of the Navigator today since the weather is supposed to be clear and sunny all day? But feck, I thought she'd enjoy riding around in my fun car, instead of having to climb up in the SUV while wearing a skirt, even though it's still too cold outside to put the top down. Of course, I also expected her to wear one of the knee length pencil skirts she usually wears, not one that goes all the way to her ankles with so much material that it's hard to contain in a car.*

Remembering how the red material hugged her hips before flaring out from her thighs to her ankles, Liam's cock responded in a manner that was definitely not appropriate for being in the parking lot of Saint Stephen's Cathedral. *Feck, not now,* he mentally groaned, feeling like a perv for not being able to control his erections any better than he had as a young teenager.

As he walked around to the driver's side to get in the sporty, fire engine red vehicle, Liam tried to push away all thoughts of how attractive Rylie looked, regardless of her choice of skirt length. But as much as he loved seeing her sexy legs in the shorter skirts she wore most often, he couldn't help but appreciate how the longer skirt kept all other men from seeing what temporarily belonged to him. *Feck, I wish I hadn't screwed up so bad that she can't forgive me, so we could go back to enjoying the benefits of being married for a little while longer.*

"So, where are we going now?" Rylie asked, bringing him out of his thoughts as he buckled in and started the car.

"We're supposed to be going to Granda and Granny's for lunch," Liam informed her. "But we can take a few minutes to stop by the house and change first, if you want to wash your face or reapply your makeup."

"Is this *lunch* going to be an all-day event like yesterday, where we end up staying and also having dinner? Or will we have time this evening when we can be alone at your house to talk before we go to your lawyer's office tomorrow?"

"Um, it'll probably be a repeat of yesterday, only with just the Connerys and with everyone going downstairs to watch football between meals," Liam sheepishly admitted as he pulled out of the church parking lot to drive home. "But we can eat whenever we get there, so if there's something you think we need to take the time to talk about before tomorrow, then we can discuss it at home before heading over to Granda and Granny's."

Surely they won't be too upset if I text and let them know that Rylie and I are talking about our issues to see if we can stay together instead of getting the annulment, right? They won't have to know that it's probably just a formality that won't actually lead to us staying together. As much as Liam wanted to spend the rest of his life married to Rylie, he knew her forgiving him and falling in love with him was a long shot.

"I don't know if we have to talk about it before tomorrow or not," Rylie sighed, her shoulders slumping as she shook her head. "If we're just getting the information on what the steps are, and not actually filing anything tomorrow, then it can probably wait. But Father O'Malley suggested we take some time to pray, meditate, and discuss everything before deciding whether or not to file anything legally."

"Okay." Liam felt relieved that she seemed to want to follow Father O'Malley's advice, instead of going along with his original plan to file everything on Monday, so they could have everything resolved before they went back on tour. But even though he'd already wished to be able to put it off, he hadn't been holding his breath in the hope that she'd agree not to go ahead and file while they were meeting with the lawyers. *Did she say something in confession to make Father O'Malley think we might not go through with the annulment? And if so, is that because she's having second thoughts about the annulment, too? Like maybe she's already closer to forgiving me than I thought?*
"He said something similar to me, but I thought he only meant that we needed to talk to each other before our meeting with him on Friday, so I could fill you in on why we're meeting with him. I didn't realize he meant we have more to discuss than just what I already told you about

the counseling stuff, or that we need to talk before meeting with the lawyers, too."

"Yeah, I think he wants us to really examine our hearts and share our thoughts and feelings with one another before deciding something so important."

Liam knew the priest was probably just trying to get them to stop and think before doing something else rash, like they had back in August when they got married on a drunken whim. But he still held out a sliver of hope that Rylie had said something in her confession that made Father O'Malley think they might be able to reconcile, so they wouldn't have to annul their marriage.

"Okay, so this is definitely going to take longer than our drive home, which means I should probably text and let everyone know that we'll be over later, so they don't hold lunch waiting on us."

"Unless you think it would be easier to leave early so we can talk this evening," Rylie offered.

"No, once we get there, we won't be able to leave until all the food's gone and the football games are over," Liam chortled, knowing how his family got during football season.

"They aren't going to get upset if I cheer for the Atlanta Thrashers instead of the New York Emperors, are they?" Rylie questioned, smiling mischievously.

"You're an Atlanta Thrashers fan? Seriously, not the New England Yankees? I thought that's the team most people from Jersey pick?"

"No, my dad was originally from Atlanta, so moving to Jersey when he met my mom didn't change his team affiliation. And I pretty much had to follow in his footsteps with picking a favorite team."

"Well, they'll probably razz you a little, but you won't be kicked out of the family or anything," Liam chuckled. "At least, that's what they did when I started rooting for the New Orleans Gators after Dion introduced me to his childhood friend, Jamal Fontenot, who just so happens to be their starting tight end."

They spent the rest of the drive back to his house discussing their experiences meeting other athletes and celebrities, as well as their shared loves of watching sports and superhero movies. When they got there, they went to their separate rooms to change into jeans and sweaters, assuming they would eventually go to his grandparents' house after they finished talking. Liam sent a quick text to his da to let everyone know not to hold lunch for them. Then they met back up in the living room, where they sat facing each other on the sectional.

"So, um, I guess this should be ladies first, since Father O'Malley seems to have given you more information about what we're supposed to discuss," Liam suggested after an awkward silence had settled around them.

"Unfortunately, I don't really know what to say," Rylie sighed, fidgeting until she was turned sideways and could rest her arm on the back of the sofa and lean her head on the crook of her elbow.

"How about you tell me what you said in confession to lead Father O'Malley to think we need to talk before meeting with the lawyers tomorrow?" Liam suggested, assuming something she'd confessed had led to the priest recommending they talked.

"Since this was my first confession since my parents died, I had to go back seven years to start with how angry I was and how I rebelled and lashed out. Looking back now, I feel stupid for the way I behaved, but at eighteen, I wasn't emotionally mature enough to handle feeling like they'd abandoned me. And not just them, I was mad at God too, because He didn't answer my prayers to save them."

Feck! I knew it had been a few years, but I didn't realize she was only eighteen when she lost both her parents. And the way I've been acting like a gobshite with immediately insisting on an annulment and avoiding her instead of continuing to hang out with her as friends since finding out we got married probably hasn't helped her deal with the abandonment issues she most likely developed from losing them so young.

Liam had learned early on in his acquaintance with Rylie that she'd lost her parents in a drunk driving accident, which was why she'd always been adamant about everyone she knew having a designated driver or planning to use some kind of car service or taxi to get back to their hotels whenever the GWA crew went out to a club or party after one of their shows, or even at the various wedding functions they'd attended in Heart's Destiny. But he thought it'd only been two or three years ago, not seven. *Feck! Was she even out of high school then?*

Yes, she was. 'Cause she said something about it being when she was in college when she explained why she was so adamant about everyone having a designated driver at the first bachelor and bachelorette party she attended after joining the GWA roster, which is why I thought it was only two or three years ago. He remembered back to James and Randi's bachelor and bachelorette party and how cute she'd been when grilling Bobby Burleson about his standards for assessing sobriety before letting everyone leave at the end of the night. That was the first night he'd seen her get drunk. Before then, she'd always stopped with one or two drinks to make sure she wasn't too impaired, so she didn't risk her safety by passing out while taking an Uber or cab back to the hotel.

Since then, she'd only really gotten drunk a handful of times, most of which had been at the bachelor and bachelorette parties in Heart's Destiny, when she knew the police chief would make sure whoever drove her back to the B and B was sober first. The other two times she'd really let go like that were at the *Sin City Showdown* after-party and again on Halloween. Considering he now remembered her saying something about it being safe to drink a little more at the *Sin City Showdown* after-party because the club they were partying at was in their hotel, so none of them had to drive anywhere, he now understood how she'd gotten so drunk that she couldn't remember their wedding. It was probably the same reason he'd let loose a little more that night, too.

But we weren't at our hotel on Halloween. Did she ask someone else to help her get back there safely if she got too drunk? Or was she just so upset by me being surrounded by ring rats that she didn't think of the risk before she started drinking? Either way, thank God, I noticed and was able to keep her from drinking too much more and shared an Uber with her back to the hotel, so I could keep her safe.

Liam was so lost in his thoughts that he only half heard what she said about skipping classes and almost losing her softball scholarship because of her grades slipping so low the first year after her parents died. But he quickly tuned back in when she mentioned getting back together with her high school boyfriend, only to lose her virginity and then break up with him again less than a week later.

While none of the things she'd mentioned so far that she'd revealed to Father O'Malley in confession seemed to be the reason why the priest might have formed the impression that they could work things out and stay married, Liam was definitely interested in the insight he could glean from learning more about her sexual history. He just hoped his jealousy from hearing about her time with other men wouldn't be too evident in his expression.

"I didn't get too detailed other than to confess that I'd had sex several times since then, sometimes with boyfriends, and sometimes just one-night stands, and that I always used condoms, even with you."

"You told Father O'Malley we had sex?" *Feck! No wonder he seems to think we'll work things out and stay married, since there's no way the Church will agree to annul our marriage when the priest knows we consummated it. Feck! Is her telling Father O'Malley that we consummated our marriage the sign I've been hoping for that indicates she doesn't really want to end our relationship, since everyone knows not having sex is one of the major conditions to qualify for an annulment?*

"Yes, but I explained the circumstances, with Dion being shot and how we were both trying to deal with our emotional trauma that day, and with the sexual tension being high in Heart's Destiny because of my drinking too much and masturbating when we had to share a bed that week, as well as my jealousy over Jen, and how our benefits ended, so he knows each time was just a casual thing and not the intimate bonding experience of married couples in love." Rylie sat up straight once more, almost like she was bracing herself for him to get angry and scold her. Not that he would reprimand her in any way, even though her words just made it clear that her confession of sleeping with him wasn't the sign that she still wanted to be married to him that he'd hoped it was. At least, not consciously, anyway. "So, I don't think it'll matter in whether or not we can annul our marriage with the Church Tribunal."

Feck! If she told him all that, it's no wonder he thought I needed to spend some extra time in the confessional today. Who knows? Maybe he's right. Lord knows the penance I was assigned each of the times I've confessed to kissing Jen hasn't been enough to make me feel absolved of all the guilt. But feck, I doubt anything I do as penance will lift that burden from my heart if Rylie can't forgive me for it.

He didn't want to think about how hearing her say they'd only casually had sex in Heart's Destiny felt like a knife to his heart. She might think it was just a casual thing, but each time he'd made love to her had been exceptionally meaningful for him.

"If you don't think us having sex is the reason Father O'Malley seems to think we need to postpone the annulment until after we talk some more, then what do you think his reason is?" Liam wasn't sure what else she could have said in confession to make it seem like they should stay married, so he was still leaning toward believing it was because they'd consummated the marriage. But he had to give her the opportunity to share more, though he wasn't sure exactly why.

Probably because you're secretly wishing she told Father O'Malley that she's in love with you, and you want to hear her say the words to you at least once.

Before Rylie gathered her thoughts to answer his question, or Liam could argue with his inner voice, his phone dinged in the pocket of his Gators hoodie. When he pulled it out, he found a text from his granda.

Granda: Food's getting cold, Garmhac. And your granny won't let any of us eat until you get here. So hurry your arse up before we miss the first kickoff.

"Everything okay?" Rylie questioned, looking nervously down at the phone in Liam's hand.

"Yeah, but apparently, hearing we're gonna be late isn't going over well with Granny," Liam scoffed, shaking his head and turning his phone around so she could see his screen. "And she won't let anyone eat until we get there, so Granda is telling me to hurry my arse up before we miss the first kickoff."

"Wow, they really do take their football seriously," Rylie chuckled, as she pointed to the word she didn't understand. "And what does Garmhac mean?"

"Yeah, both kinds, football and American football, and Garmhac just means grandson," Liam laughed along with her as they both stood to leave and he tucked his phone back into his pocket. "If you think this is bad, just wait until soccer season starts. But don't call it soccer in front of anyone in the family. While they've learned to enjoy American football too, they'll still tell you all about how there's only one *real* football and one sport that should be called handball."

They didn't get the chance to discuss their marriage any further that afternoon or evening. But as he watched Rylie fitting in perfectly with his family, especially when she did a victory dance every time the

Atlanta Thrashers scored against the New York Emperors, Liam knew their appointment with the lawyers of the Kelly Legal Group the next day would just be to gather information and not to file anything. He might not know exactly what she said in confession to give Father O'Malley the impression that they might be able to work things out and stay married, but the glimpse of their possible future he got from having her spend time with his family certainly made him hopeful for the possibility.

Feck, even if we just end up postponing the annulment for a little while and don't actually get back to the point in our relationship where we can make love again, maybe the praying, meditating, and talking Father O'Malley suggested will be enough to get her to forgive me for being stupid right after we got married, so we can be better friends going forward.

Chapter Three

Monday, December 23, 2019, New York City, New York

At eight o'clock on the dot Monday morning, Liam stood in his kitchen waiting on his coffee to brew as he called his attorney's office, trying to find out the specific time of his appointment that afternoon. Unfortunately, as had been the case several months earlier, all he got was Boyle's voice mail. The eerie similarity between the way he felt right then and the way he'd felt when he couldn't reach his attorney right after he'd first found out he'd gotten married made Liam wonder if his family had known about his marriage long before Rick called his da. *Boyle never did explain why it took him almost a month to return my calls when I first mentioned getting married in my messages at the beginning of October. But it wouldn't surprise me one bit if he was dodging my calls then because he'd talked to someone in the family when the certificate of marriage first appeared on his desk. And he's probably dodging my calls again now because my family put him up to avoiding me to try to stop the annulment.*

"Hey, Boyle, it's Liam Connery," he stated, leaving a message while planning to look up the main office number to call next. "I haven't heard back from you since you said you'd schedule me an appointment with the family law division for today, so I wanted to find out what time I'm supposed to be there. I'm assuming you scheduled it for this afternoon, since we normally meet after lunch, but I don't want to miss it if you could only get a morning appointment for me. Give me a call back ASAP, so I know when to head into Manhattan."

Liam hit the icon on his phone screen to disconnect the call before swiping the icon to access the internet to look up the main phone line for the Kelly Legal Group. Once he found the number, he retrieved his now full coffee mug from his Keurig, taking a sip as he walked over to sit down at the dining room table to place the call.

I should have gone to the bakery earlier to pick up some donuts or muffins or something for breakfast, so we'd be prepared to go straight to Boyle's office this morning if he set up a morning appointment. After the disaster of burning the eggs in his attempt to make breakfast the day before, he knew he'd need to plan for other options for the rest of their time in town, but he hadn't thought about it while he was on his morning run or he would have jogged around the neighborhood instead of down the beach.

As the phone started to ring, Liam got distracted by Rylie walking into the room. She was wearing a red turtleneck, which he knew she'd cover with a blazer before they left like she often wore while traveling with the GWA, a pair of figure-hugging, black slacks, and a pair of black, stiletto ankle boots with little, shiny, silver dots covering them from the pointed toe to the top of the ankle, only not covering the pointy heel.

Feck! Liam mentally groaned, fighting to keep from popping a boner at the sight of his sexy-as-fuck wife, who smiled at him as she walked over to fix her own cup of coffee. *What I wouldn't give to be able to bend her over this table and fuck her from behind while she's still wearing nothing but those shoes.*

"Happy holidays from the Kelly Legal Group," a way too cheerful voice chimed from his phone, thankfully helping to redirect his blood flow back to his brain. "Our offices are closed for the holidays between Saturday, December twenty-first, twenty-nineteen, and Sunday, January fifth, twenty-twenty. We will reopen at eight a.m. on Monday, January sixth, twenty-twenty, to serve all your business and civil legal needs. If you are in need of immediate legal representation in a criminal matter, please press one to be transferred to our criminal law department and leave a detailed message for how our on-call attorney can reach you. Otherwise, enjoy your holidays and we look forward to serving your legal needs in the new year."

"Feck," Liam grumbled as he hung up the phone. While he really didn't want to file the annulment papers anytime soon, he knew he needed to find out the process while he was home for the holidays, just in case the counseling with Father O'Malley didn't work and they needed to do it later. "Why the feck did Boyle say he'd make me an appointment for today, when he knew the office would be closed?"

"It's barely past eight, so maybe they just haven't unforwarded the phones from their weekend answering service," Rylie suggested, having not heard the message that the office was closed for the holidays since his phone wasn't on speaker. "When I was calling around to find a lawyer in Atlantic City, I found that a lot of them didn't open until nine, so maybe you should wait until then to call again?"

"Yeah, that won't help," Liam chuckled, shaking his head. *I guess I'm getting my wish about not filing for the annulment yet. But Rylie's still gonna be pissed that I made her come here with me for a meeting that wasn't actually scheduled. Hopefully, she won't think I did it on purpose to try to coerce her into forgiving me and giving me another chance.* "The outgoing message said the office is closed for the holidays until the sixth of January."

"But your lawyer told you that you had an appointment today?" Rylie arched an eyebrow curiously at him as she stirred cream and sugar into her coffee before taking a sip.

"Yeah," Liam confirmed, nodding his head. "The last time I talked to him, he promised to schedule it for today and get back to me with the time after he coordinated his schedule with one of the lawyers in the family law department, so they could both be there. But I guess now I know why I never got a confirmation call on Friday like I expected."

"So, what are we supposed to do now?" Rylie questioned as she joined him at the table. "Wait until our Memorial Day break to meet with them? Or can we possibly schedule a video conference with them, the way I did with the lawyer I consulted with in Atlantic City?"

Or we could call around and find another family law attorney that's not closed for the next two weeks. Not that Liam was going to suggest that, since he really didn't want to meet with anyone who might actually be able to file the annulment papers before he tried talking things out with Rylie to see if they had any kind of a chance at a relationship going forward.

"I guess," Liam shrugged before pulling up the GWA schedule on his phone to see when they'd be able to coordinate with the attorneys, and secretly hoping it wouldn't be anytime soon. "But even if I can get Boyle and his colleague to schedule a video conference, it'll be the end of February or beginning of March before we'll be in the Eastern time zone to match up our schedule with theirs to book the appointment. And we still won't be able to sign anything until April, when we have a few hours free while in New York before our next European tour."

"I guess that gives us plenty of time to talk with each other, and with Father O'Malley too, so I guess it's not a big deal that we can't meet with them today."

Thank feck, she's not pissed about this.

"True," Liam agreed, taking another drink of his coffee while trying to decide how best to get back to the talk they'd started but hadn't finished the day before.

"I'm so excited about all the new places we're going with the GWA this year," Rylie gushed, smiling as she changed the subject before he had the chance. "I was so bummed to find out I'd just missed the European tour last year."

"This year's will be even better and almost twice as long, since Rick added stops in Switzerland, Germany, Denmark, Sweden, Norway, and Iceland, as well as a few new places in Canada before we get back to the US."

Liam was exceptionally looking forward to the European tour this year because they were kicking it off with the *No Remorse* weekend in Dublin, Ireland. As soon as he'd heard about it, he'd immediately started setting everything up for his grandparents, parents, and brothers to fly over to reconnect with the Connerys still in Ireland and attend the show. He'd been a bit wary of inviting everyone to the show, just as he'd been before the *Christmas Chaos* show, but ultimately decided that they'd probably have the marriage annulled by then, so it would be safe to have his family mingling with the GWA crew and meeting Rylie. *Guess I didn't have to worry about that after all, since Rick told them all about our marriage.*

When he'd called the charter company Rick recommended, however, he found out he could technically charter a plane big enough to take the whole extended family over for not much more than a smaller plane that would only hold his immediate family. Now he couldn't wait until Christmas morning, when he planned to present the trip as a family Christmas present, and find out how many of his uncles, aunts, cousins, cousins-in-law, and their kids could make the trip with them. Of course, that meant he had to stop himself from giving his Sullivan and McCarthy relatives their passes when they all met up at his parents' house for dinner on Christmas Eve, so they wouldn't ruin the surprise for the rest of the Connery side of his family.

I should have just told everyone about the trip on Saturday when they were all here, instead of thinking I needed to wait until I pick up the **No Remorse** *passes at the GWA office today to have something tangible to give them as a Christmas gift. Now I probably need to spend this afternoon shopping for another gift for everyone, since we can't meet with the lawyers like we'd planned.*

"Hey, um, I just realized that I need to go Christmas shopping today, in case any of my family members can't make the trip to Dublin I planned for them over the ***No Remorse*** weekend," Liam informed Rylie, grinning as he hoped to coax her into giving him more ideas for what to get her for Christmas without her actually realizing it. "What do you think about going to see the tree at Rockefeller Center and helping me shop? I'll even let you pick out my ugly Christmas sweater for the party we're going to tonight."

Rylie's eyes widened as she looked over at him. "Oh. Em. Gee. It's been so long since I've really celebrated the holidays that I totally forgot to ask you what your family usually does for presents so I can go shopping. So, yes, I will definitely go shopping with you and we can help each other pick out gifts and ugly Christmas sweaters."

"We used to each bring a single gag gift and play one of those gift swapping games," Liam explained, wondering if this would be the first time she'd celebrated Christmas since her parents passed away. "But since some of my cousins have gotten married and had children, we've gone back to buying something for everyone like we did when we were all kids. Only now, the married cousins team up with their spouses to share credit for giving gifts, so I was planning on saying all my gifts for them are from both of us."

"Okay, then you're definitely going to have to help me out with keeping track of who's who and how they're related to you, so I can make sure we don't miss anyone while we're shopping today." Rylie pulled her phone out of her wristlet and opened her notes app. "I know Granda Neilan and Granny Breena had four sons, but other than your dad, I can't remember which of your six uncles I've met are their other three sons. And yes, I know I saw them all yesterday without your Sullivan and McCarthy uncles there, so I should be able to figure it out, but since we weren't reintroduced, I only remember their faces, not their names."

"Okay, my Connery uncles are Callen, Flynn, and Owen. Uncle Callen is married to Aunt Kiera, and they have four sons: Callen Junior, who we all call CJ; Cian; Conner; and Cory." Liam paused in listing out his family tree to let her type all their names in her notes app, along with their relation to him, giving her correct spellings when she was unsure before going on with the list. "Uncle Flynn is married to Aunt Nora, and they have five sons: Donovan, Fallon, Grady, Rogan, and Sloan. Uncle Owen is married to Aunt Rihanna, and they have four sons: Ronan, Kegan, Lennon, and Devin."

"So every woman with the last name Connery married into the family? How many generations has it been since there was a girl born in the Connery family?" Rylie didn't bother to look up as she continued typing on her phone, but he could still clearly see her sarcastic smirk.

"At least three that I know of, since Granda only had brothers, too." Liam shrugged, fighting not to joke with her about how they'd probably only have sons too, since he wasn't sure yet that they might eventually have kids together. "You ready to move to the Sullivan side of the family, since they at least have a few girls mixed in?"

"Yes, go ahead," Rylie directed, moving down a couple of lines on her app to start the other half of his family tree.

"My mom's parents, Liam and Saoirse Sullivan have both passed on, but they had four children, too, my mom being the youngest. Uncle Quinlan is married to Aunt Shannon, and they have three sons and a daughter: Murphy, Gannon, Keenan, and Kelsea. Murphy is the only one of their kids who's married. Uncle Brogan is married to Aunt Tara, and they have two sons and two daughters, alternated in birth order: Kiernan, Kerry, Shay, and Caitlyn. Kiernan is the only one of them who's married. And finally, Aunt Chevonne married Ryan McCarthy, which is why the Sullivans and McCarthys are lumped together on my family tree. They have four sons: Sully, which is short for Sullivan; Riordan; Kevin; and Brendon. And all four of my McCarthy cousins are married."

Liam waited for her to get all those names down with the proper spellings before going on. "Starting with the McCarthys since they've been married the longest, Sully is married to Kelly and they have two kids, a boy and a girl: ten-year-old Sully Junior and eight-year-old Casey. Riordan is married to Aisling and they also have two kids, also a boy and a girl: nine-year-old Brady and seven-year-old Cassidy. Kevin is married to Lynn and they have a son, Ronan, who's six years old. And Brendon is married to Sheridan and they also have a son, Brendon Junior, who we all call BJ. He just turned one."

He waited to make sure she had all their names and ages down before going on to his Sullivan cousins who were married with kids, knowing they'd need those ages to pick out the right toys as gifts. Thankfully, he'd remembered to ask all the kids' ages when they were all at his house on Saturday.

"Kiernan is married to Cianna and their daughter, Taryn, is four. And finally, Murphy is married to Finola and their son, Declan, just turned three."

Once she had all their names and the kids' ages in her notes app, she went back to the top of the list to start trying to put gift ideas beside each name. "Okay, so what are you thinking of getting for your grandparents?" Rylie questioned, finally turning her gorgeous topaz eyes on him once more.

"Granny's easy to shop for," Liam smiled. "I'm sure you noticed her doll collection yesterday. So we should be able to find one she doesn't have yet at FAO Schwarz. Actually, now that I think about it, we can probably find something for most of my cousins and their kids at FAO Schwarz, too. And maybe even my da and uncles, but I'm at a loss for what to get Ma and all the aunts, female cousins, and cousins-in-law."

"There are other stores there besides FAO Schwarz, though, right?" Rylie looked skeptical of his plan to buy all his family Christmas presents at the toy store.

"Oh, yeah, lots of high-end designers and stuff that I'm sure will have great gifts, and Saks isn't far from the tree and ice rink, so we can check out the Christmas window displays, too. But I really need a woman's opinion to decide what to get for each of the women in my family." Liam did his best impression of puppy-dog eyes, hoping to get back to the playful friendship they'd had before they found out they were married. *And hopefully, while we're shopping today, I'll be able to figure out what to get you for Christmas, Mo Ghrá, besides the Claddagh wedding band I bought in San Antonio last month. 'Cause I know you're not ready for me to give you the ring I'd love for you to wear on your left hand for the rest of our lives.*

~~~

After Liam helped Rylie remember the names of all his family members that she'd met two days earlier, they planned their schedule for the day. In addition to the shopping they both needed to do, she needed to go buy the gift for Patrice she planned to leave with the security guard at the GWA offices before they stopped by there for Liam to pick up all the **No Remorse** tickets and backstage passes, which Rick had made up early so Liam could give them to his family for Christmas. They got breakfast on the go and took care of those errands first before going to Rockefeller Center to see the tree and shop for Liam's enormous family and pick out ugly Christmas sweaters for the party they were attending that evening.

They found their ugly Christmas sweaters while checking out the window displays at a few of the local department stores before going to see the tree and ice rink. While she appreciated him trying to show her the tourist attractions of the tree and window displays, they kind of fell flat for her, since the lights were her favorite part of Christmas decorations and they went during the day when the lights weren't very visible. Still, it was nice of him to think about making sure she saw the iconic sights of the city at Christmas, so she wasn't about to mention any disappointment she felt. Instead, she enjoyed getting in a mid-morning workout on the ice rink, when they could goof around like the friends they'd been before getting married, feeling thankful for the much smaller crowd at the rink than what she'd expect it to be in the evening.

Once their hour on the ice was up, they grabbed a quick lunch before planning how to hit the various shops to find all the presents before they had to leave to be on time for the party that evening. Liam obliged her by focusing on the women's gifts first, other than the doll for Granny Breena, since it seemed they'd be harder to find than what
~~~

he had planned for the men and kids. Surprisingly, it didn't take them long to pick out enough different scarfs and gloves at all the women's wear stores that none of the women in Liam's family would have to worry about matching each other if they all wore them to the same event after Christmas. They also picked up a variety of candy gift boxes at Sugarfina for everyone in the family, plus a few extras for the various service providers who took care of Liam's house while he was on tour. Then they picked out gifts for his dad, Granda Neilan, brothers, and uncles at Nintendo NY and Saturdays Football before splitting up for an hour to shop for each other. She was able to find him a New Orleans Gators jersey and an Irish knot tie clip, since they'd be exchanging gifts twice with the different parts of his family, before meeting back up to stash their wrapped presents in Liam's SUV, and finally finishing their shopping at FAO Schwarz.

While they didn't talk about their relationship or what they each wanted to do about their marriage, Rylie enjoyed spending the day shopping with Liam, as if they really were the happily married couple they portrayed on every GWA show for the last few weeks. She especially relished the way it felt like she was legitimately a part of his big, welcoming family, wishing she knew how to make that feeling into reality instead of only her temporary fantasy.

She'd been relieved to find out they couldn't meet with the attorneys after all. Yeah, that meeting had been the only reason she'd agreed to spend the holidays in New York with him. But after meeting his family, and especially after her confession with Father O'Malley the day before, she was even more torn about whether or not she'd be able to go through with the legal process to end their marriage. While she knew it was probably best for them to start over with a clean slate and let their relationship develop more naturally, she couldn't help but worry that, if they went through with legally ending their union, then they might not ever develop into more than friends.

Unfortunately, she knew she wasn't the only one who got a say in their future plans as a couple, and she didn't think Liam had the same reservations about ending things between them that she had. Well, ending the romantic parts of their relationship, anyway. She knew he was fine with them staying friends and coworkers, just not lovers, and especially not husband and wife.

If only him insisting on signing both our names to the gift tags for all these presents meant he wanted us to stay married, she thought whimsically as they ventured from the collectables section of FAO Schwarz, where they'd picked out various Funko Pop figurines for several of his cousins, over to the doll section, where she knew he thought they'd find the perfect gift for Granny Breena, who was the last person they had to pick a gift for before heading back to Belle Harbor for an ugly Christmas sweater party at the home of one of Liam's family friends. *But I know he's only insisting on that because he doesn't want me to spend a bunch of money on gifts for people I'm only temporarily related to by marriage.*

Seeing Liam act like a big kid while they were shopping in the world famous toy store only strengthened her love for him, even though she was pretty sure he was only trying to get them back to their easy friendship with his playfulness. When he had to take the time to try out every floor model before deciding which toys to buy for his cousins' children, she could easily picture him playing with those same toys with their children one day.

Geez, I really need to stop with the fantasies about a future I'm not likely to ever have. Rylie tried to push the image of Liam with their children out of her mind, but it was really hard when an adorable little girl approached him just as he picked up a doll from the shelf. *But, man, I'd love to be the first woman in almost a century to deliver a little girl in the Connery family.*

"No, mister, you don't want that doll. You want Ken 'cause you're a boy," the cute little blonde girl told Liam as she tugged on his sleeve with one hand while trying to hand him a Ken doll with her other hand.

"Well, yeah, I would want Ken if I was buying a doll for me," Liam agreed as he placed the Madam Alexander collectable doll he was looking at for his grandmother back on the shelf and knelt down to be on eye level with the child, who couldn't be more than five years old. "But I'm trying to pick out a doll for my granny and I don't think she wants Ken. But since you're obviously an expert on dolls, maybe you can tell me which one to get for my granny for Christmas, if your mommy or daddy don't mind. Where is your mommy or daddy, so we can ask them?"

Rylie looked around then, noticing for the first time that this child didn't appear to be with an adult, as she and Liam were the only adults in that part of the store at the time.

"Mommy is looking at the train sets with my brother," the little girl pouted, making it clear she was going to be an eye roller when she got a little older. She momentarily turned away from Liam to put the Ken doll back on the shelf behind her before turning all her attention back to Liam and his search for the perfect doll. "But I can help you find a dolly for your grandma. Does she like Barbie? Or the bigger dolls that are like real babies?"

"The ones she has are bigger than Barbie, but they aren't like babies. They're dressed up like they're going to a fancy party." Liam pointed to the display of dolls he'd just been looking at to show the little girl what he meant.

"Like princesses going to a ball?" The little girl twirled around like she was dancing with her imaginary prince, taking ahold of Liam's fingers to get him to dance with her.

"Yeah, something like that," Liam chuckled as he stood and swayed while holding the little girl's hand in the perfect position for her to twirl in place without bumping into any of the shelves of dolls around them. "What's your name, Princess?"

"Princess Ashley," the little girl declared, curtsying just before the music playing throughout the store changed from a slower waltzy type song to something a little more rock and roll. Ashley apparently knew the different songs required different types of dancing as she released Liam's hand to start dancing on her own.

"It's nice to meet you, Princess Ashley," Liam bowed to the little princess before joining her in a more freestyle dance. "I'm Prince Liam, and this is my wife, Princess Rylie. Do you know your mommy's name, so we can go find her to ask permission for you to help us pick out a doll for my granny, Queen Breena?"

Seeing Liam interacting with Ashley, Rylie would have sworn she felt her ovaries release all her eggs in hopes of spontaneously conceiving his babies.

"Mommy's name is Maggie Maguire. I'm Ashley Maguire. And my brother is Robby Maguire."

As soon as Ashley listed their names, Liam looked right at Rylie and signaled for her to help him flag down a store employee, presumably to have them page Maggie Maguire to reunite mother and child. At least, that's what Rylie thought he meant with the way he used dancing with Ashley to cover his hand signals of pointing to his eyes, twirling a finger, and holding a hand up to his ear like it was a phone. She barely managed to turn around to go find the store associate who'd just helped them a few minutes earlier with taking the things they'd already picked out to be gift wrapped, before she was almost run over by a frantic woman, whom she assumed was Ashley's mom.

"Ashley! There you are!" Maggie screamed, running over to scoop her daughter up in her arms as a boy, who looked to be about eight or nine years old, slowly followed behind her, looking down at the toy train set in his hands. "You scared me half to death, disappearing like that. You have to stay right with me when we're shopping, not wander off with strangers."

Liam stopped dancing when his dance partner was lifted off the ground and securely in her mother's arms, stepping back from the family reunion just as Rylie moved back by his side.

"But they're not strangers," Ashley protested, arching her back as she tried to escape her mother's bear hug. "They're your favorite wrestlers. The ones Daddy said you need a hall pass to meet. Is that why I'm in trouble? 'Cause I met them without getting a hall pass from Miss Christy?"

"Miss Christy doesn't give out that kind of hall pass," Maggie stated, blushing profusely as she obviously came up with a cover story that was appropriate for her children. "And Daddy was talking about needing additional tickets to the meet and greet the day before *Christmas Chaos*. He just called those tickets a hall pass because he thought you having to get a hall pass from your kindergarten teacher to go to the bathroom during class would make more sense to you than us not having the right kind of tickets to go to both the meet and greet and the wrestling show the next day. So you're not in trouble for meeting them now because you don't need a ticket to randomly run into someone while we're out shopping."

Rylie had to chuckle as Liam blushed in response to Ashley's announcement about them being "hall passes" and her mother's awkward attempt at trying to explain the term, which all the adults there knew meant the couple agreed that their spouses were free to cheat if they met their celebrity crushes. She stopped laughing, however, when Liam put his arm around her shoulders. She wasn't sure if he was staking his claim on her as off limits to Maggie's husband, or trying to make it clear he wasn't available to be anyone's hall pass. Regardless of which way he meant it though, her jealousy spiked enough that she looped her arm around Liam's waist to claim him back.

"Oh, wow, it is Red!" The little boy, whom she assumed was Ashley's brother, Robby, exclaimed as he looked up from the toy in his hands for the first time. His eyes practically bugged out when he recognized Liam. "You are Red. Man, I hate that Dark Chocolate got hurt and can't wrestle anymore. Red Velvet is my favorite tag team, and also my favorite kind of cake." The little boy turned to look at Rylie then, his jaw dropping when he also recognized her. "And you're Chastity. Too bad Dad's not here, 'cause you're his favorite wrestler."

I guess it was partially to claim me, Rylie thought as Liam tightened his hold on her in response to the little boy's last statement.

"No, she's Princess Rylie and he's Prince Liam," Ashley corrected her brother, finally wiggling enough that her mother let her down.

"Shuhh!" Liam held his finger up to his lips as he shushed the little girl. "Don't say that too loud, Princess Ashley. Those are our secret identities that we don't share with everybody. Kind of like Superman doesn't let everyone know his real name is Clark Kent."

"Oh, sorry." Ashley looked a lot more contrite about blurting out their names than she did for sneaking away from her mom a few minutes earlier.

"It's okay, Princess Ashley," Rylie offered to keep the little girl from feeling chastised. "Red only told you our real identities because you're also a princess. And since you're a princess, then obviously, your mom and brother are also royalty, so it's okay that you told them who we are. We just don't want to announce it so loud that the non-royals in the store overhear us."

"Wow, Rob is never going to believe we met the two of you," Maggie gushed, finally seeming to regain her composure as she got her phone out of her purse. "Can I get a picture of you with the kids to show my husband later?"

"Of course," Rylie agreed, smiling at the still somewhat harried mom and feeling a little bad about being jealous of her when she was only asking to take pictures of them with the kids and not selfies of Maggie with Liam.

"Your husband's name is Rob Maguire?" Liam inquired at the same time. When Maggie nodded, he continued questioning her. "Did he go to Saint Stephen's Catholic School?"

"Yes," Maggie said cautiously, lowering her phone as she eyed Liam dubiously. "How'd you know that?"

"He was a year behind me, so we didn't have any classes together, but we were both on the same wrestling team for a couple of years. Such a small world," Liam chuckled.

Liam pointing out that he was a year older than the father of the two children they'd just met gave Rylie a little unwanted perspective about their age difference. *Geez, if he'd have started his family a decade ago like Rob and Maggie, or some of his cousins, then he could have had a child before I was even able to get a driving permit.*

Looking at Liam right then, she suddenly realized she'd watched him wrestle long before she ever considered becoming a wrestler herself. *Yeah, I don't want to think about all the times I watched wrestling with Dad, and he made fun of Liam the Red being confused about whether he was Irish or a Viking and obviously had no idea how to play the Irish bagpipes he carried to the ring.*

"Yes, it is," Maggie agreed as she motioned for her kids to stand in front of Liam and Rylie, so she could start snapping pictures. As she continued speaking, she reached over and took the train set from her son, presumably so a Christmas present wouldn't be visible in the photos. "I can't believe he knew you and didn't tell me. But I guess now it makes sense why he didn't want to look in his old neighborhood when we were house hunting a few years ago. I knew it had to be more than just the long commute to work."

Because he was afraid she'd use her hall pass if she met Liam? Rylie's inner jealous bitch reared her ugly head again.

"We need to do some wrestling moves in these pictures," Robby insisted, turning to look up at Rylie and grinning mischievously, unwittingly helping her stifle the green-eyed monster living inside her. "Can you put me in a side headlock for the next one?"

"She won't, but I will," Liam grumbled, mumbling something under his breath about the boy being too young to try to cop a feel like that and making Rylie laugh at his outrageousness, even though she agreed that she wouldn't be comfortable having the kid's head pressed into the side of her boob. "Or better yet, I'll bend down and let you put me in a side headlock, and as your mom is taking the pics, I'll pick you up like I'm gonna drop you in a side suplex."

"Cool!" Robby was apparently excited to wrestle with either of them, and not actually mature enough to realize the move he'd requested from her could be sexualized inappropriately by anyone viewing the photographs later.

"Yeah, I don't think there's really enough room here to wrestle around like you do at home with Dad," Maggie corrected her son, vetoing Liam's recommendation. "So, we'll just stick to the pictures I've already taken of you standing beside Red and Chastity."

"Okay," Robby sighed, his shoulders slumping in defeat.

"We can still make our best mean, growly wrestler faces for some of the pics, though," Rylie offered, trying to console him some. She dropped her arm from around Liam and crouched down in the ready position from her softball days, since it sort of resembled the neutral position of amateur wrestling, which a lot of wrestlers used as their basic pose for gimmick photos. Then she bared her teeth and squinted her eyes, trying to look fierce in the most comical way she could think of at the time.

Robby mirrored her position, making his own ferocious face as Maggie snapped a few more pictures. Liam and Ashley soon joined them, only cycling through random silly faces and not just the mean ones. Their antics caused lots of laughter, drawing more than one strange look in their direction from the other patrons of the toy store.

"Alright, guys, we should probably stop, so we don't get kicked out of the store before we finish our Christmas shopping," Liam pointed out when they started drawing a crowd to the previously empty section of the store.

"But we still need to get pictures of Mom with Red and Chastity," Robby asserted, holding out his hand to have Maggie give him her phone.

"Just a couple with normal smiles," Maggie agreed, handing her phone to her son and stepping between Liam and Rylie. "No silly faces."

Rylie plastered on a fake smile as Robby held up the phone to take the pictures, not wanting to let on to the kids that she was uncomfortable with the way Maggie put her arms around Liam's waist and snuggled into his side, while basically turning her back to Rylie. *Seriously? Does she think our marriage is just a work for the GWA? Or is she really angling to use that hall pass while her kids and Liam's wife are watching?*

I mean, really, resting her head on his chest like that in public? I haven't even gotten that close to him today and he was actually just hugging me into his side a few minutes ago. Hell, the only time I've been that close to him was when we were sleeping together and when we had to tape the vignettes where I was sitting on his lap. So someone who's married to another man really shouldn't be pressing her tits into his side like that when we're in the middle of a freaking toy store.

Rylie was so caught up in her jealous thoughts and fantasies of how she could extract her husband from Maggie's clutches that she missed the rest of the conversation between Liam, Maggie, Ashely, and Robby. But luckily, she snapped out of it when Liam picked up the doll Ashley recommended for Granny Breena, so she was able to say their goodbyes to keep from being rude to the kids before they parted ways to continue their shopping.

After meeting back up with the sales associate to pay for all their purchases and have the doll gift wrapped, they finally carried the last of their purchases out to Liam's 2018 Lincoln Navigator Black Label. While riding in his Porsche the day before was a lot less nerve-racking because it was easily able to maneuver through the narrow streets and small parking spaces, the large luxury SUV was necessary for the cargo space to carry all the presents they had to bring back out to Belle Harbor. She just had to close her eyes a few times while Liam was driving through heavy traffic to keep from freaking out about how close the larger vehicle always seemed to be to the vehicles around them.

You'd think I'd be less scared of getting in an accident in this giant tank of a vehicle, assuming it would provide more protection from being injured if anyone crosses the lane lines and runs into us. But I think my fear of accidents is worse because we're so close to the lane lines on both sides that he can't swerve to avoid a collision if somebody else crosses the line near us.

And seriously, what is up with me suddenly having my fear of car accidents come back now? I thought I dealt with this years ago when I talked to the counselor in student health after Mom and Dad died, she thought as she felt her heart racing to the point that she almost felt like her chest was vibrating. *I haven't had a panic attack like this in years, even when I've ridden in some cabs and Ubers with crazy drivers. So, why am I freaking out now?*

Is it because of the third row of seats in here like in the minivan Mom and Dad were killed in? No, that can't be it 'cause Dion's SUV had three rows of seats too, and I was able to drive it without freaking out when we were in New Orleans. Of course, at that point I was so focused on trying to be there for Liam when he was having a breakdown because of Dion being shot that I didn't have the wherewithal to worry about myself at the time. So, maybe my concern for Liam, Dion, and everyone else in the GWA was able to override my fear to the point that I didn't notice the extra seats until we got out after parking it in D's garage?

"Hey, are you okay?" Liam reached over and pried her hand off the padded armrest on the center console, lightly massaging her hand to relax her enough that he could lace their fingers together before resting their joined hands on top of the console once more. "You've been really quiet since we finished taking pictures with Ashley, Robby, and Maggie. Did I miss something happening then that made you uncomfortable? Or is it just the rush-hour traffic that has you gripping the armrests like you're bracing for impact?"

"I, I don't know," Rylie stuttered out, unconsciously squeezing Liam's hand as she tried to focus on her breathing to calm her heart rate. Not wanting to admit to the jealous urge she'd had to yank Maggie off of Liam by her hair while they were taking the last of the photos, she didn't comment on why she'd been quieter for the last part of their shopping trip than she'd been earlier in the day. Instead, she latched onto the excuse he'd inadvertently given her and blamed her behavior on the increased traffic and the fear she'd developed after losing her parents in a car accident. "I haven't had a panic attack like this in about five years. So I don't know what exactly triggered it now. Maybe it's the increased traffic and being so close to the other lanes in such a big vehicle? Or maybe it's being in an SUV with a third row of seats like the minivan my parents drove that night? Or maybe it's just because I've been thinking about them so much lately and it's getting close to the anniversary of when they died?"

Or maybe it's because I was already on edge and getting angry because of my jealousy over the way Maggie was hitting on you pushed me over the top of what I could handle. And that spike of adrenaline hadn't dissipated enough when we got in here to drive back to your house, so my anxiety seems ten times worse now than it did on the drive into Manhattan this morning.

"Probably a combination of all those," Liam proclaimed, squeezing her hand reassuringly. "What can I do to help you feel better? Other than pulling over somewhere you can get out of the car, which isn't gonna be possible for at least an hour now that we're on the parkway."

"Yeah, I guess they don't really want me to get out in the middle of traffic when you stop to pay the tolls," Rylie choked out, wishing her lame attempt at joking around would help her calm down.

Inhale. Exhale. Inhale. Exhale. She kept repeating the words in her head as slowly as possible, trying to match her breathing with the mental chant. Unfortunately, instead of getting a whiff of Liam's bergamot and sandalwood scent, which had blissfully filled her nostrils on the trip into the city, she smelled the cloying scent of Maggie's perfume, which smelled like she'd sprayed herself down with every tester bottle in Perfumania without worrying about whether they went together well or not.

"Definitely not," Liam agreed, his voice lightening with mirth.

"The counselor I saw in student health back in college when I had these episodes before taught me some breathing exercises to do to calm my heart rate and ease the anxiety, but it's been so long I can't remember the different patterns she suggested," Rylie confided when she felt like she'd mostly gotten her breathing under control. "I just know it wasn't that hee-hee-hoo breathing that Kay practiced for months before having Sam."

"No," Liam chuckled. "I imagine it was slow, deep breathing, more like the inhale for a certain count, hold for a certain count, and exhale for a certain count that they do in yoga classes."

"Yeah," Rylie agreed, placing her right hand on her belly to make sure she was at least breathing diaphragmatically like she remembered from the yoga classes she'd taken. "But the counts were never the same from one yoga class to the next, so I don't know which one I should try."

"Well, maybe just keep breathing slow and steady and count to see how high you can comfortably go on each part of the breath," Liam suggested. "And maybe lay your seat back, so you can relax in a half seated, half laying down version of corpse pose."

"How do you know corpse pose?" Rylie asked as she followed his suggestion to recline her seat.

Inhale, two, three, four, five. Exhale, two, three, four, five.

"I tried a yoga class once," Liam shrugged. "And I thought it was ironic that corpse pose was the only pose in the whole class that didn't feel like the instructor was trying to kill me. I mean, seriously, even the ones she said were supposed to be easy rest poses were torture, like cow face. How did it get that name? While I haven't been out on the Burleson Ranch to check to be sure, I highly doubt any of their cows sit down and cross their legs like that. That pose needs to be renamed the nutcracker pose. And then she combined it with what she called eagle arms, which was even more ridiculously named. Eagle arms to me, sounds like you should extend your arms like an eagle flapping its wings. But no, not to the sadist teaching that class. She wanted us to twist our arms around each other and practically break our forearms to be able to put our palms together in a prayer position. It was insane."

Rylie couldn't help but laugh at the mental image of Liam trying and failing to contort into some advanced yoga poses, as he described in great detail how uncomfortable each of the positions he remembered from that class were, surprising her with how many pose names he remembered. Her laughter didn't help her with her breathing at all, but it did help ease her anxiety, so she considered it a win. She still left her seat reclined, though, so she could look up at Liam as he drove and didn't see the other cars around them to think about how close they were to getting into an accident for the rest of the ride back to his house.

While his comedy routine helped her tremendously with her anxiety, she felt a little regret that they hadn't been able to use that time to talk about their marriage, how they felt about one another, or what they each wanted for the future. She had at least looked up the scriptures she'd noted in her phone after talking to Father O'Malley the day before. But since her Bible and rosary were both in her apartment in Atlantic City, she hadn't felt comfortable trying to meditate on the passages she'd only been able to read on her phone screen. Which meant she also hadn't yet prayed for the ability to apply them to her life and her relationship with Liam.

I guess I should at least do that before I talk to him, so I have a better idea of what to say to Liam about what I want. Maybe we'll have time after this party tonight when I can ask Liam to borrow his Bible? And maybe showing him the scriptures Father O'Malley suggested I study will help him with figuring out what he wants too, so we'll both be better equipped for the talk we need to have with one another.

~~~

Liam wasn't sure how he and Rylie got roped into attending the O'Donnells' annual Christmas party, since it had been one of the events that his grandparents, parents, aunts, and uncles usually attended without the rest of the family. Of course, most of his memories of the event were from his teenage years, when it was a black-tie affair that he and his brothers and cousins had no interest in attending. Since the O'Donnells' children were several years younger than him, he hadn't hung out with any of them to keep up with when the party changed to the much less formal ugly Christmas sweater party. But apparently, in the fifteen years when he was off traveling with the GWA, the younger generation of the O'Donnell family had taken over planning and hosting the annual event. And his brothers and cousins had all attended at least once in the last few years, depending on their work schedules. When he asked why he'd never been asked to join them when he was home for the holidays before then, he was told that the party was usually held earlier in the month of December but had been put off this year until after the due date of one of the O'Donnell granddaughters, so she'd be more likely to be able to attend. Still, he found it hard to believe that all four of his brothers and all thirteen of his Connery cousins either had to work or already
~~~

Leah Mae Wright

had other plans this year, leaving only him and Rylie to represent the younger generation of Connerys at the party.

I bet half those guys are lying about their plans to get out of having to be here tonight. But I guess, at least, having to go to this party is another good excuse to put off talking to Rylie about our relationship and whether or not we should go through with the annulment. And having to wear this hideous sweater in public seems like an appropriate punishment for me not being able to figure out how to tell her I don't want to end our marriage, but I also don't want to pressure her to cut her career short to move home with me. Feck, maybe I should have had a sweater custom made to say exactly that, so I don't have to look her in the eye and tell her I'm breaking my own heart by pushing for the annulment, hoping to keep from manipulating her into doing what I really want, like an arse.

After their brief discussion after church the day before, Liam knew he needed to finish having that serious talk with Rylie. And he'd fully intended to bring it up that morning, so they'd have talked everything out before going to his lawyer's office. But then, once he'd found out they couldn't meet with the attorneys after all, he'd decided it might be in his best interest to put it off for a little while.

It wasn't that he didn't want to have the discussion to determine how she wanted to move forward. But he enjoyed the way they'd slipped back into their easy friendship as they went shopping too much to want to ruin the rest of their time together by talking about ending their marriage. And truth be told, he kind of hoped that spending so much time with him and his family would soften her up to be able to forgive him for his stupidity right after they got married, so she'd want to try to make their marriage work, even if it would only last until he retired from wrestling.

It was probably wrong to hope that she'd fall so in love with him and his family that she'd decide to retire even earlier than she'd claimed she planned to step away from her wrestling career. But Liam couldn't stop himself from secretly hoping that might be the outcome of her spending the holidays in Belle Harbor. He just wasn't going to pressure her to make that decision by blatantly stating that's what he wanted.

He'd always heard that famous quote about letting go of someone you love, and if it's meant to be, they'll come back to you. So instead of staking his claim like a caveman and insisting she stay married to him, Liam was hoping that letting Rylie go, by going through with the annulment, would prove that they were meant to be, when she came back to him after she was finally finished with her wrestling career. But even that would only be possible if she felt welcomed and loved by not only him and his family, but the whole community.

I just hope everyone at this party will be as welcoming to her as everyone was at church yesterday, Liam thought as he rounded the car to open the passenger door for Rylie as they arrived at the O'Donnell house for the party.

While the O'Donnell house was the biggest in the neighborhood, having been built long before Liam was born, when the patriarch of the O'Donnell family first elevated the family's socioeconomic status by making millions on Wall Street, Liam's red Porsche still stood out as the most expensive vehicle there among the staid sedans and mid-grade SUVs in the driveway. Liam didn't care if some of the people in attendance thought he was a tool for driving a flashy car, or believed it was just his way of showing off his wealth. He knew the truth about why they'd switched back to driving his Porsche after Rylie's panic attack in the Navigator. And he was more concerned with making sure she didn't have a repeat, just in case the third row of seats was part of the reason she was triggered after their shopping trip.

But maybe I should see about talking her into helping Ma cook tomorrow, so I have time to drive the Porsche back to the house and use the Navigator to drop off the presents early to both Ma and Da's house and Granda and Granny's, then go back and get the Porsche for us to drive home after dinner, so she won't have to ride in it again.

"Are you sure we didn't need to bring anything for a gift exchange? Or a hostess gift?" Rylie questioned again as she took Liam's hand and got out of the car.

"No, Ma said to just show up and make sure we were in our ugly Christmas sweaters," Liam reassured her, even though he felt ridiculous in a light-up sweater with jingling bells around the collar and tinseled up presents embroidered under the words "BIG GIFT ENERGY" across his chest. But he supposed his sweater wasn't any worse than Rylie's, since hers also lit up and had actual glittery, plastic ornaments attached to it, as well as the ones that were only embroidered on and made of material like the presents on his sweater.

Especially since the placement of the ornaments on hers made a couple of them look like they were hanging from her nipples. He'd wanted to point that out to her while they were shopping for them that morning, but she was so excited about the sweaters she'd picked out for them that he hadn't wanted to ruin the mood by pointing out the sexual connotations. They sure gave him ideas though.

Feck! If only we were at home and she was naked, so I could see if those little wire ornament hangers would work as nipple clamps. Liam had to quickly push his dirty thoughts about his wife from his brain, so he didn't walk into the party tenting his slacks. *But feck, I'd love to decorate her like a sexy Christmas tree.*

When they got to the door, they were greeted by Barry and Ashleen O'Donnell, who were a few years younger than Liam's parents, as well as Barry's mother, Deidra, who'd been friends with his granny since shortly after his grandparents emigrated from Ireland. It seemed strange to see the matriarch of the O'Donnell family in a Charlie Brown Christmas sweater, when he'd only ever seen Deidra dressed to the nines in years past. The trio directed them to drop their coats with an attendant in the foyer before going out to the den, where they'd find the rest of the O'Donnells, along with Liam's parents and grandparents, and several other local families gathering for drinks near the wet bar.

Liam knew Deidra had lived with her husband Fitz, short for Fitzgerald, in the large mansion until Fitz's untimely passing a few years ago. But he wasn't sure if Barry and Ashleen, or one of her other children or grandchildren, had moved in to take care of her in her twilight years, or if she still lived alone in the family home. To be honest, he only knew Deidra and Fitz's names because his grandparents had spoken fondly of the couple for as long as he could remember. But he'd had to be told Barry and Ashleen's names just then because it had been so long since he'd spoken with anyone in the O'Donnell family that he couldn't remember ever hearing them introduced with their first names.

The same could be said for the Murphys, O'Briens, and Walshes of his parents and grandparents' generations, who were all huddled in small groups with Liam's parents, grandparents, aunts, and uncles. So, as he and Rylie made the rounds, he simply introduced them to her by their surnames, so Rylie wouldn't think he was being rude by not introducing her. *Hopefully, she's not too uncomfortable with me introducing her as "my wife, Rylie" all night.*

They made it about halfway around the room before he finally saw someone his own age there, whom he could actually introduce by his first and last name. *And I don't feel so bad about my sweater, since at least mine isn't a parody of a Sir Mix-A-Lot song. Feck, now I'm gonna have "I like big bulbs" running through my head until I can come up with plausible lyrics to finish the song with a holiday theme.*

"Rylie, you've gotta meet this guy, Sean Lynch." Liam punched his old friend in the shoulder, carefully avoiding the large lightbulb dangling from Sean's bicep, as he walked up to where he was standing with a very pregnant woman, who was wearing a sweater that said, "Baking more than cookies this year." Liam thought she was one of the O'Donnells, but she was so much younger than him and Sean that he didn't know her name. "Sean, this is my wife, Rylie."

"Liam Fecking Connery," Sean smiled as he slugged Liam back. "There's no way you conned a woman this far outta your league into marrying you. She's gotta be like a shrink or some other kind of doctor the GWA hired to keep the world from seeing what a nutjob you are."

"Don't listen to him, Rye." Liam shook his head as he hugged Rylie to his side. "He was my best friend all through school and always in trouble with the sisters for making up the wildest stories. So if anyone needs to have a doctor following him around to keep his crazy from showing, it's Sean." They both chuckled before Liam continued. "Man, it's been a long time since I've seen your ugly mug."

"Only because you haven't come home in ages," Sean pointed out. "And changed your number so I couldn't get a hold of you to ask you to be the best man in my wedding."

Liam didn't want to explain that he'd had to change his phone number a few years ago when it got leaked to the dirt sheets and he started getting bombarded with calls and texts from ring rats propositioning him. While that incident had been the wake-up call he needed to slow down his man-whore ways, it hadn't completely stopped him from having the occasional one-night stand with a ring rat. And he didn't want to put that image of him in Rylie's head, even though he'd stopped even looking at other women when he first met her. So, he did the only thing any sensible man in his position would do. He ignored that part of Sean's statement to focus on the fact that his childhood best friend, who'd never been serious about a woman in all the time Liam knew him, apparently got married.

"Seriously, you got married too? When?" Liam assumed the pregnant woman at his side was Sean's wife, so he didn't question who would be brain damaged enough to willingly say, "I do," to Sean.

"Yeah, seriously. Back in February," Sean informed them, squeezing his wife to his side and rubbing his free hand over her rounded belly. "I was blessed enough to be able to change Briana's last name to Lynch and now we're expecting our first baby."

"Congratulations!" Liam smiled at his childhood friend and his friend's wife, even though he was seriously envious of Sean starting his family, when Liam wasn't sure babies were in his future. "For both the wedding and the baby."

"Congratulations," Rylie chimed in shyly, directing her words to Briana. "When are you due?"

"Two days ago," Briana chuckled wryly, cutting her eyes to Sean. "But apparently Sean Junior is just as perpetually late for everything as his daddy."

So, it's Sean's wife they postponed the party for, so she wouldn't have to miss it if she had the baby early. I guess that kinda backfired on them, since she still looks like she swallowed a basketball.

"I'm not perpetually late for everything," Sean protested. "I just sometimes get stuck on a scene and can't leave when my shift is supposed to be over."

"He's got a point," Liam pointed out. "He can't exactly stop in the middle of fighting a fire just because it's supposed to be time for shift change."

"Exactly," Sean agreed, motioning for his wife to listen to Liam. "And even if I did, I'd still be stuck on scene until everyone else was done and ready to head out, since I can't exactly get in an Uber in full turnout gear."

"Oh, no, I completely understand when your job is the issue," Briana defended, holding up her hands in surrender. "It's when you get caught up in watching football or playing video games and don't get ready in time for stuff like tonight, when I was supposed to be here early to help set up, but barely made it five minutes before the guests were due to arrive, that I have a problem with. Especially since you don't like either of the teams that were playing tonight."

"Yeah, I think we're gonna bow outta this discussion," Liam offered playfully, pulling Rylie a step backwards as she giggled at his side. "'Cause we were late to the party because we were both watching the Gators game."

"Seriously?" Briana arched an eyebrow at Rylie. "You're with the guys on this crazy football obsession."

"In our defense, Liam is actually a Gators fan," Rylie defended them, raising her hands in surrender. "And I was enjoying the stories he was telling me about when our friend Dion introduced him to the Gators' tight end and half the team ended up partying with them a couple years ago."

"I suppose you're forgiven," Briana grinned at Rylie. "Since you're still in the honeymoon phase and haven't heard his stories a million times yet."

"Are you saying our honeymoon phase is over already? How can that be, when we haven't even been married a year yet?" Sean shook his head at his wife. "What happened to never letting the honeymoon end?"

"Sorry, Sean, the honeymoon ended when growing your son resulted in not being able to see my own feet."

Liam and Rylie both chuckled at Briana's quip. Before Sean could respond to his wife, several people in the crowd around them jumped back and squealed as three muddy dogs ran in through the open patio doors.

"Oh, goodness, what are Nana's dogs doing outside? They were supposed to be in their room so they wouldn't wreck the party." Briana joined Barry and Ashleen in following the dogs, though Liam wasn't sure how successful she'd be at catching them when she waddled more than walked and had no chance of being as fast as the slippery little mutts.

Luckily, it looked like there were several more of the younger generation of O'Donnells who also joined the chase, so Liam pulled Rylie toward the wall, hoping to stay out of the way until the animals were corralled. He wasn't the only one with that idea, either, since several members of his family and most of the other guests all sort of sidestepped to the edges of the room.

Somehow, in all the commotion caused by the O'Donnell's dogs running in from outside, Granny Breena ended up with what looked like red wine spilled on her sweater, which was mostly white with a picture of Bob Ross painting happy little Christmas trees on the front. Liam assumed the wine or possibly cranberry juice belonged to someone else at the party, knowing neither were the drink of choice for any of the elder generations of his family, who were all now standing fairly close to him, Rylie, and Sean.

Rylie was drinking cranberry juice earlier, but I don't think that was her drink, since we finished off our drinks when we ate those pinwheel things and I can still see the empty glasses on the bar across the room.

"Oh, dear, Breena, I'm so sorry. Let me get the dogs back outside and I'll get you some club soda to get that stain out," the elder Mrs. O'Donnell proclaimed as she walked by them in her attempt to help the younger members of her family, including her pregnant granddaughter, Sean's wife, catch the dogs. "And I'm sure there's a hairdryer in one of the upstairs bathrooms, so you can dry the spot after rinsing it out with the soda."

"Is the club soda in the pantry? If so, then one of us can go get it, so you don't have to worry about it," Liam's ma suggested.

"Yes, a whole case of it," Deidra O'Donnell agreed, pointing toward the kitchen while walking away in the other direction.

"Excellent," Cathleen beamed. "Breena, why don't you and I go upstairs and check all the bathrooms for a hairdryer." She redirected her attention to Rylie before asking her to assist them in the stain clean up. "Rylie, will you please go into the kitchen, get the club soda, and bring it up to us. The pantry is the door right beside the refrigerator."

"Sure," Rylie agreed, only looking slightly apprehensive about searching through the unfamiliar pantry.

"You want me to come help you find it?" Liam offered to be polite, not really thinking she needed his help.

"No, I've got it," Rylie assured him, smiling and waving him off. "You stay and catch up with your friend. I'll be right back."

Liam watched her walk away, appreciating the view of her glorious ass in the black dress pants she wore below her light-up Christmas ornaments sweater.

"Wow! I never thought I'd see the day when Liam Connery would not only settle down and get married, but would also be so smitten that you can't take your eyes off your wife," Sean joked, shaking his head at Liam.

"Oh, like you weren't just as much of a player back in high school and college as I was," Liam scoffed. "Or even just a few years ago, when I last saw you, and you were bragging about being Mr. July in the Hot Firefighters of the FDNY Calendar. And now you're not only married, you're about to be a dad."

"I wasn't near as much of a player the last few years as we were in high school and college," Sean chuckled, turning his head to look around the room, presumably scanning for his wife, who'd somehow cornered one of the dogs, who were so muddy Liam couldn't tell their breed, for one of her relatives to grab it by the collar. "That all stopped three years ago, when Briana came home from college all grown up. Even before I got over my hang up about what everyone else thought about our ten-year age difference to ask her out."

Liam knew the O'Donnells of his generation were all younger than him or Sean, but he'd thought it was only by five or six years, not ten. Hearing that his childhood best friend also married a woman ten years younger than them made him wonder if he was off base in thinking his and Rylie's age difference mattered a whole lot in the grand scheme of things. "How did everyone respond to that age difference when you first started dating Briana?"

"Erin called me a dirty old man and accused me of being as much of a dog as Quinn." Sean shook his head, clearly exasperated by his younger sister. "But she still blames me hanging out with you all the time for why she and Quinn dated in high school. And since she's still pissed about their breakup, and refuses to even speak to him now, she's obviously got a warped perception of relationships. So, I take her opinion with a grain of salt. Nobody else said a word, other than being happy for us when we announced we were getting married and again when we got pregnant almost immediately after the wedding. Even her dad was glad when we started dating, saying she needed someone more mature than the yahoos her age."

I wonder if that's what Rylie's dad would think about me?

"You getting pushback from anyone because Rylie's so much younger than you?" The concerned expression on Sean's face brought

Liam back to the conversation before he could get lost in his head with thoughts of how Rylie's parents would have felt about their daughter marrying him if they were still alive.

"No, Rylie doesn't have any family left to object," Liam confided. "So, I'm the only one who's been thinking of our age difference as an issue. And even then, I'm not really worried about the age difference so much as I'm worried about us being at different points in our careers and not being able to make things work when I retire and she's still touring."

"Yeah, but that's still years down the road, isn't it? By then I'm sure she'll be ready to quit wrestling too, so you guys can have kids. Even if she's one of the modern generation of women who want to wait until their mid-thirties to have children, you're in good enough shape that you shouldn't have a problem with E-D, even in your mid-forties."

"I would hope I don't have any of those issues until I'm in my eighties," Liam scoffed. "But even if it were to strike tomorrow, E-D won't be the reason I retire from wrestling. That'll be my knees and back, which are already starting to ache after my matches, so I'm probably going to have to end my in-ring career in the next couple of years, long before Rylie is ready to have babies."

Liam didn't mention that Rylie had said she wanted to have kids in five or six years, thinking that even if she followed through with that plan, the three or four years between when they each planned to leave the wrestling business would be torturous to endure being apart. And there was no way he could survive ten-plus years without her with his full mental capacity intact.

"Oh, damn, man, I'm sorry to hear that," Sean offered sympathetically. "And she's pretty new to the business, isn't she? Well, at least to the GWA, since I'm assuming she wrestled somewhere else before we started seeing her on TV earlier this year."

"Yeah," Liam agreed with a sigh. He didn't elaborate on what he knew of Rylie's wrestling experience before the GWA. "She's only been with the GWA since March, and with as good as she is in the ring, I know she could have a very successful ten- or fifteen-year career. And I can't ask her to give that up just because I'm ready to settle down and have a family."

"So, what are you gonna do? Live apart while she's finishing her career? Or keep traveling with her until you can talk her into retiring early?"

Liam was surprised his friend didn't ask about the possibility of annulling the marriage. Though considering Sean had also been raised in an Irish Catholic family, he supposed he shouldn't be surprised that he just assumed they'd do whatever it took to make their marriage work. *I'm sure if Sean and Briana were in our shoes, they'd make it work to stay married.*

"We're still trying to work that out," Liam replied vaguely. "But it's hard when I don't want to pressure her to give up the business before she's ready."

"Yeah, I get that," Sean nodded. "But speaking from experience, plans like that change dramatically when it's someone you love asking you to change them."

"Oh? What kind of experience are you speaking from?" Liam eyed his old friend curiously.

"You know I always planned to stick with the FDNY until I actually hit retirement age in my sixties?" Sean questioned, causing Liam to nod in acknowledgment of remembering his friend's plans back when they were in school together. "Well, when Briana and I first got together, she wanted me to change jobs and work with her dad, so I'd be safer. But since I know absolutely nothing about stocks and bonds, and think I'd be miserable in a stuffy office job every day, we compromised. I promoted to captain, so I'm not in as much danger while on the job, and plan to retire as soon as I get my twenty."

Liam felt suspicious of his friend's definition of compromise, unsure how Sean's promotion was a concession since he assumed Sean would have promoted to captain regardless.

"As much as I love being a firefighter, I love Briana more," Sean elaborated. "So it didn't bother me in the slightest to promote from lieutenant a few years earlier than planned and cut my time on the job in half. Now instead of working 'til I'm old and gray, I'll start collecting my pension in seven more years and have plenty of time free to spend with my wife and kids while we're all young enough to actively enjoy it. So, Briana isn't the only one who's happy with the new plan to lessen my risk of injury on the job."

"Yeah, but that's a win-win for both of you," Liam argued. "You still get to work in the job you love until you've been there long enough to collect a pension, and you're both able to live together in the same city between now and when you retire. Rylie and I's situation is different because I'm almost ready to retire and come home, and she's still going to be touring for years after that, so we won't be able to see each other but about fifteen percent of the time until she gets out of the business."

"Only if you insist on staying here instead of traveling with her, or she insists on waiting a few more years to retire and have kids with you." Sean shrugged. "It just seems to me that you could compromise by traveling with her for a couple of years and she could compromise by retiring sooner than you expect. Then you'd have your win-win."

"Yeah, well, we'll see," Liam acquiesced. "But since our wedding was kind of spur of the moment when we were drunk and just following along 'cause some of our friends were getting married, I'm not sure she's going to want to compromise like that."

"If the way she was looking at you like a woman in love is any indication, I think you'll be able to work things out just fine," Sean said encouragingly before changing the subject. "So, what was Rylie talking about when she said you partied with the Gators?"

"My tag-team partner grew up with Jamal Fontenot," Liam explained before telling Sean all about the first time Dion introduced him to the football player and invited Jamal and his teammates to hang out in the VIP section of Xavier's, the club in New Orleans Dion co-owned with his brother, for a GWA after-party.

After talking to Sean for a while, Liam started to wonder what was taking Rylie so long, hoping none of the younger guys there that he didn't know had caught her attention. Or as was more likely to happen, he hoped none of the guys there had hit on her. When he saw his ma and granny rejoin the party, with his granny's sweater now free of the red wine stain, Liam really started to get concerned. So, he excused himself from talking to Sean and made his way over to where his family members were gathered, talking to another set of their peers.

"Did Rylie come back to the party with you?"

"No, she never made it upstairs," his mother informed him. "I thought she might have gotten sidetracked since Nora brought the club soda up to us."

Liam spotted his Uncle Flynn and Aunt Nora across the room, and moved over to check with them to find out where Rylie went after giving Nora the club soda from the pantry. Unfortunately, they weren't much help. All his Aunt Nora could tell him was that she hadn't seen Rylie when she went into the kitchen to get a bottle of club soda from the refrigerator after seeing Granny Breena and Cathleen walking upstairs.

I guess I'll just have to retrace her steps then, Liam decided, heading to the kitchen to start at the pantry and see if he could figure out where else Rylie might have gone from there if she couldn't find any club soda. Other than a couple of members of the catering staff putting the finishing touches on the next round of hors d'oeuvres before serving them, the kitchen was mostly empty. Unfortunately, neither of them had seen Rylie. *Surely, she's not still in the pantry, right?*

Just to be sure, Liam walked over and opened the door beside the refrigerator. *What the feck?* He was surprised to see a staircase down to what he presumed was the basement and not a closet-sized pantry as he'd expected. *Maybe she went down the stairs, thinking the pantry was down there instead of in the kitchen?*

Deciding to check, he stepped through the doorway, letting the door close behind him just as he took the first couple of stairs down.

"No, don't close the door!" Rylie appeared at the base of the stairs just after the door slammed shut behind him. She was backlit by the dim glow of the light behind her, giving her an ethereal incandescence until he flipped the switch to his right and illuminated the stairs.

Feck, she's beautiful, even in that hideous sweater.

Liam hated seeing the dejected look on her face at the sight of him. "Sorry," he apologized, hoping her upset expression was brought on by the door slamming and not because he'd been the one to come looking for her.

"It apparently locks on its own and I can't find a key anywhere in this wine cellar to open it back up," Rylie informed him, just as he turned around to try to reopen the door.

"Seriously, shouldn't this have a way to unlock it from the inside?" Liam fiddled with the door handle, trying to open it as he heard Rylie telling him he was wasting his time.

"You'd think, but apparently not," Rylie scoffed, rubbing her hands together like they were cold and she was trying to warm them up.

Knowing he'd just seen the catering staff in the kitchen, Liam banged on the door, calling out, "Hey, can someone please open this door? We're locked in here."

"And it's apparently a heavy enough door that nobody could hear me banging on it from the other side to let me back out," Rylie added sardonically, as his attempts to get someone's attention in the kitchen failed. "But please keep trying. Maybe they'll hear your deep voice better than they heard mine."

Liam was tempted to ram the door with his shoulder to try to bust it down. But when he banged on it with his fist, he realized that it was a heavy duty metal door that was painted to look like a wooden door, and not an actual wooden door that he might be strong enough to bust through. Luckily, he realized that in time to prevent the unwanted shoulder injury that would likely result from trying to muscle their way out of the wine cellar.

"No, I think the caterers who were just in the kitchen were on their way out to circulate with the trays of hors d'oeuvres they were finishing up when I walked into the kitchen and asked if they'd seen you," Liam advised her, running a hand through his hair as he looked down the stairs at where she was standing. "I'm betting since they hadn't seen you, they were circulating when you first went through there and didn't come back until you were down there looking for a key. And now they're gone again, so it'll be a little while before they might come back for the next round of whatever they're serving."

"Yeah, there wasn't anyone in the kitchen when I walked through there," Rylie agreed, tucking her hands inside the sleeves of her sweater.

"Are you cold?" Liam queried, feeling like an idiot for asking such a stupid question when her shivering was obvious. While he wasn't cold in the slightest, he also hadn't been in the refrigerated room for at least half an hour like she had. Plus, he was always naturally warmer than Rylie, probably because of his size.

"Yeah, we're basically standing in a giant wine cooler, and I left my coat with the attendant at the front door." Rylie rolled her eyes at him.

"Sorry, dumb question. Why don't you come back up here? Since heat rises, maybe it'll be a few degrees warmer." Liam hoped his suggestion would make up for putting his foot in his mouth a few moments earlier.

"Good point," Rylie agreed as she walked back up the stairs.

When she got to the top of the stairs, Liam finally noticed she didn't have the wristlet wallet she usually carried everywhere with her. *Feck, I bet that's why she didn't try calling me to come let her out of here.*

Noticing that it was missing was enough to remind him that he could call for help though, so he pulled his phone from his back pocket to call Da to come let them both out. Unfortunately, when he tried to make the call, he found that he had no service. "Seriously? Does this heavy metal door block cell signals too?"

"Of course it does," Rylie laughed, hugging herself in a feeble attempt to get warm. "But at least now I don't feel so bad about leaving my phone in my coat, since I didn't think I'd actually need it during the party."

Liam attempted to send a text to his da when he moved his phone around and got the very briefest hint of one bar. Even if it wasn't enough of a signal for a call to go through, he hoped maybe a text still might make it out.

Liam: Trapped in the wine cellar with a Rylie popsicle.
Please come let us out.

As soon as he hit send and saw the checkmark that indicated it had been sent, he put his phone back in his pocket and opened his arms to Rylie. "Come here and let me at least share some of my body heat with you."

"Thank you," Rylie gushed as she eagerly pressed her body against his, wrapping her arms around his waist as he encircled her shoulders and mid-back. Neither of them mentioned how the ornaments, bells, and light bulbs on their sweaters poked them uncomfortably as they snuggled together.

Liam only felt slightly guilty for taking advantage of the situation to get Rylie in his arms, knowing it wouldn't be but a few minutes that he'd get to take care of her before they were rescued. Of course, knowing it was just going to be a few minutes that he'd get to hold her to keep her from edging toward hypothermia didn't stop his dick from jumping to attention with ideas of being skin on skin to warm her up even more. Between the alluring light floral scent of Rylie's bodywash and perfume tickling his olfactory system and the feel of her curvaceous body pressed against him, it was pretty much impossible for Liam to control his arousal.

"Ignore him," Liam instructed when Rylie looked up at him nervously and started to pull away. "He's too stupid to understand that this is just for warmth and not because you want to get naked with him again."

"I don't know," Rylie teased, grinning mischievously. "They do say that skin to skin is the best way to share body heat. We could strip down and sit on the landing while using our clothing as blankets to get warmer than we are now."

Is she just wanting to get warm? Or is she suggesting we get naked to create our own heat? And if it's the latter, does that mean she's forgiven me and wants us to add the benefits back into our friendship? Or could she possibly want us to try to make our marriage work?

Not that I can really act on either of those last two options here and now, when I know Da is going to come open the door for us any minute.

"If you're cold enough that you need skin-on-skin contact to get warm, you're gonna hafta settle for just warming up your hands by putting them under my sweater," Liam advised, shaking his head. "'Cause if you take off even a stitch of clothing, we're gonna do a lot more than just get warm. And I don't think either one of us wants Da seeing us naked when he gets my message and comes to open that door."

"True," Rylie agreed, even as she worked her hands under the hem of his sweater. "So, I guess I'll settle for warming up my hands."

"Holy Feck!" Liam was so shocked by how ice cold her hands felt on his low back that he jumped slightly, having to squeeze Rylie tighter to his body to keep her from jumping back and falling down the stairs. "I thought I was just joking with Da about being trapped with a Rylie popsicle, but you really are freezing cold."

"But somehow, you're still a furnace," Rylie teased as she turned her hands to warm the other side against the skin of his low back, making him shiver from the extreme difference in their temperatures.

At least, Liam was blaming their difference in temperatures for why he shivered, trying not to think about how amazing her gentle touch felt. But when he looked down into her topaz eyes, he couldn't resist sliding his hands under the back of her sweater. If asked, he'd say it was to warm her up with his hot hands against her cool back. But in truth, his whole being was overcome with the need to touch her and connect them body and soul. And the temperature in the room had absolutely nothing to do with it.

"Liam," Rylie purred his name as she pushed up on her tiptoes, tilting her head in the perfect angle for him to kiss her.

"Yes, Mo Ghrá?" Liam dipped his head, eagerly awaiting her confirmation that she wanted the kiss her body language was begging for, and totally forgetting that he'd texted his da to come let them out of the wine cellar.

"What are we doing?"

"Whatever you want, Mo Stór."

She didn't reply with words, instead moving her hands from his low back to the back of his head, so she could pull him down a little further and press her lips to his.

Thank feck! Liam quit thinking completely as he took over the kiss, parting her lips with his tongue and tasting her for the first time in way too long. Yeah, technically, it'd only been a little over three weeks since he'd last kissed Rylie, but in Liam's opinion, it felt more like a lifetime.

She tasted like cranberry juice, probably from the cocktail she'd been drinking before she went to find the club soda, and something sweet that Liam couldn't identify as anything but Rylie. *Perfection,* he thought, recognizing the sweetness as something he'd only tasted when kissing her.

His hands dropped to her ass of their own accord, lifting her up so she could wrap her legs around him as she returned the kiss with equal ardor. He ground his hard cock against her core, wishing they'd removed their clothing earlier so there would be no barriers between them. As it was, he feared he was at risk of blowing his load in his pants like a virginal teenager. But if he could get Rylie to come from making out as if they were playing Seven Minutes in Heaven, he wasn't sure he'd mind the embarrassment when they finally got out of the wine cellar.

As Rylie writhed and whimpered in his arms, Liam knew she was close. He pulled back from the kiss just enough to command, "Feck, yes, come, Mo Ghrá."

Rylie bit his lower lip as she kissed him once more, the slight sting quickly morphing to pure pleasure as her whole body stiffened with the convulsion of her release as she obeyed his directive. Making her come with just a little friction on her clit and the sound of his voice gave him almost as much gratification as if he'd orgasmed too. Being in control of her pleasure was a heady rush, making him feel way more powerful than he ever had before, even when he pulled off an amazing move in the wrestling ring.

Feck! I hope she feels this the same way I do, so maybe she'll decide being with me is just as much of an endorphin high as performing in the main event, and we can retire together to start our family.

Deciding that the best way to make that happen was to make her come a few more times before busting his nut, Liam doubled down on the dry-humping as he continued feasting on his wife's luscious lips. He pressed her back against the door, so she couldn't pull back as he thrust his hips to rub his cock over her clit.

With her weight supported by the door, his hands were free to explore her body. He squeezed her bodacious ass in one hand while sliding the other up under her sweater, aching to cup her breasts without accidentally stabbing his palm with the lights weaved through her sweater or the hooks attaching the ornaments. Unfortunately, before he could get his hand up to grab a handful of her tit, the door opened behind her, causing him to have to quickly readjust his grip to support her back and prevent her from falling backwards into the kitchen while he adapted his stance to keep from toppling over with her.

"Oh, shit!" Rylie squealed as their lips parted, digging her nails into his shoulders in an attempt to stay upright.

"I got you, Mo Ghrá." Liam tightened his hold on her, even as he stepped through the door to keep them from being trapped in the wine cellar again.

"Sorry, I thought you said you needed rescued," his da chuckled. "But I guess you found a way to warm up your popsicle."

Feck, I should have waited a little bit to send that text. But I guess it's probably best that they interrupted us now, 'cause if Da had waited a few more minutes, I'd have had a helluva mess to clean up in my pants.

Rylie buried her face against his shoulder, even as she unwound her legs from around his waist. Liam tried to lower her feet to the floor and step back from her, now that his cock was standing down in the presence of his parents and grandparents. But unfortunately, their sweaters didn't seem to want to comply. Her ornament hangers somehow got tangled in the weave of his sweater, holding them together.

"Oh, dear, we should have thought about the hazards of their ugly Christmas sweaters before we sent them into the wine cellar to look for club soda," Liam's ma gasped before covering her mouth, as Liam and Rylie worked together to carefully detangle their clothing so they weren't attached chest to chest.

"I dooehght dey'd be smart enooehgh ta take dem ahff befahre makin' whoopie," Granny Breena added.

"Wait, so the two of you planned for us to get stuck in the wine cellar?" Liam looked back and forth between his ma and granny, wondering how they managed to pull off their elaborate scheme.

"Nora and Deidra 'elped," Granny Breena admitted with a shrug.

"Why?" Liam and Rylie asked in unison, as they finally managed to unhook her ornaments from his lights to step apart.

Feck! We really flattened a couple of those plastic balls, he thought as he noticed Rylie's sweater appeared much more worse for wear than his, even though he did have a couple of places where the weave of the sweater had bigger holes than it had previously.

"Because we felt bad about making you come to the party tonight when you could be at home enjoying an intimate evening alone with one another," Cathleen explained, not appearing the least bit sorry for the shenanigan. "So, we thought you'd appreciate a private place to sneak in a few kisses before coming back to the party. And if things went well enough, then maybe you'd sneak out of the party early to go home and *do what newlyweds do*."

Liam wasn't sure if they'd continue what they started in the wine cellar once they got home or not. But considering the condition of Rylie's sweater, he knew his mom would get her wish for them to sneak out of the party early. "Then I guess you won't mind helping us get out of here now, without anyone else seeing the smashed bulbs on our sweaters."

"Oh, dear," Cathleen covered her mouth as she looked over the damages to their current attire. "Yes, um, wait here while we go get your coats and then you can sneak out the side door."

Liam didn't feel the least bit bad about making his ma and granny explain why he and Rylie left without saying "goodbye" to their hosts. But he did regret taking things too far when Rylie didn't say a word the whole way home and rushed to hide in her room for the rest of the night.

Guess we should talk things out a little more before trying to win her over with our insane attraction to one another.

Chapter Four

Rylie couldn't believe she'd actually volunteered to help Cathleen cook for the Christmas Eve dinner with the maternal half of Liam's family after the way Cathleen and Breena had conspired to trap her and Liam in the wine cellar at the party they'd attended the night before. She still wasn't sure what they'd expected to happen between her and Liam while they were sequestered for half an hour. *Although, I suppose they weren't really wrong about us being in a private space alone leading to a little kissing. And it definitely would have led to more than the make-out session they interrupted if Liam hadn't remembered that he'd texted his dad to come let us out.*

If that was the typical way the Connery women worked for trying to fix up Liam, his siblings, and cousins, she now understood why he'd preferred to deal with the matchmakers in Heart's Destiny and had spent all his breaks there for the last year. *Not that I'm really gonna complain about the Connerys' version of matchmaking, since I thoroughly enjoyed "warming up" with Liam last night. Now if I could just figure out how to convince him that our combustible chemistry is a sign that we're meant for one another, so he'll call off the annulment and actually start trying to work on our marriage to make it real.*

She wasn't sure if she'd done the right thing the night before by going to her room as soon as they got back to Liam's house after sneaking out of the party. She'd thought at the time that it was better to let him chase her a little, instead of coming on too strong and pushing him to finish what they'd started in the wine cellar. But since he hadn't come knocking on her bedroom door, like she'd hoped, when she ran upstairs to change into some sexy lingerie, and had been completely hands-off with her as they'd surfed on their phones and made small talk while eating the muffins Liam had snuck out to pick up that morning, she was starting to think she'd screwed up by playing a little too hard to get.

Since Cathleen is clearly as on board with us staying married as I'm sure my mom would be if she were here, maybe I can ask her advice today while Liam is helping his dad set up and going back to the house for his other vehicle to drop off all the presents.

She still couldn't believe how he'd insisted on driving the Porsche anytime she'd had to be in the vehicle with him since her panic attack the day before. Or that he was so considerate of her feelings that he was willing to make extra trips to drive her in the Porsche and then go back to get the Navigator to deliver the presents while she was otherwise occupied before going back to get the Porsche for their drive to Midnight Mass and back to his house.

Geez, how can he expect me to want to end our marriage when he's doing such a good job of taking care of me when I'm a basket case? And let's face it, he did everything right yesterday to ease my anxiety. The only other thing he could have done that might have helped was scheduling me a therapy appointment. And even I can't do that right now, since I don't currently have a therapist I'm working with and it'd be impossible to get a last minute, new patient appointment on Christmas Eve.

Looking over at Liam as he drove them to his parents' house, she couldn't help but wonder if his thoughtfulness with regard to her recurring anxiety held meaning beyond just being a good friend. *And what about that make-out session last night? Was that just because he's horny and wants to add the benefits back to our friendship while I'm conveniently staying at his house? Or was he just as unable to resist me last night as I was powerless to hold out against him because we both have deeper feelings for one another?*

She didn't have time to contemplate the possibilities as they quickly arrived at his childhood home. He'd shared stories with her before about growing up there with his brothers. She specifically recalled how he'd mentioned that his brothers had all complained that he was the only member of the family who didn't have to share a room when they all lived in the four-bedroom house. Once Liam moved out,

Quinn moved into his old room, so he and Rory finally had their own spaces. Then, when Quinn moved out a couple years later, Aiden took over the room, so he and Finn finally got a turn at having more privacy.

Of course, when Liam told her the story, he'd mentioned how he'd dropped out of college to tour with the GWA at about the same time Quinn moved out to start his time at John Jay College of Criminal Justice. Apparently, Liam threatening to move his stuff back into his parents' house, so Aiden and Finn still had to share a room, caused such an uproar with his youngest brothers that he had to store his stuff at his grandparents' house for a little while, until he was able to rent an apartment with his first GWA paycheck.

I wonder how long he kept the apartment before he bought his house? I'll have to ask him next time we're alone, she thought as Liam walked around to open her car door and escorted her up to the house with his hand on the small of her back, which sent goosebumps tingling along her spine.

Will I ever get used to this tingly feeling every time he touches me? Or will his innocent, gentlemanly gestures always make me want to jump his bones like I did last night? Because if this relentless need in my core to be constantly connected to him in some way doesn't go away, then the only way I'll ever be content is if we work things out to get our happily ever after together.

As they walked into the brick Tudor style home where Liam and his brothers had all grown up, Rylie couldn't help but imagine her dream future with Liam as her loving husband and the father of her children. She could see him teaching their sons and daughters to wrestle and roughhouse, much like she knew Liam had as a little boy.

In her mind's eye, the images of him with their children morphed back and forth with her imaginings of Liam as a child, running through the house and scuffing the hardwood floors with all four of his brothers hot on his heels. Especially when she saw the wall of family photos lining the stairs as they walked through to the kitchen. Those pictures reminded her of the ones she'd seen on Sunday at Neilan and Breena's house, only these appeared to only be of Liam and his brothers, and didn't seem to encompass all his cousins. *Oh, what I would give for our children to have some of those same experiences at their granny and granda's house as Liam did when he was a little boy.*

"Hey, Ma, what smells so good?" Liam asked as soon as they stepped into the kitchen, where Cathleen was already hard at work.

His words brought Rylie back out of her head, just as she realized she was smelling sweets and not the savory dinner she expected to be there to help prepare. *Guess she did the baking this morning, so dinner won't be sitting around getting cold all afternoon?*

She looked over at the table where Cathleen was sitting and noticed the cooling racks covered with cookies shaped like ornaments, packages, and Christmas trees and realized they'd be decorating them first before starting on cooking the dinner they'd share with his Sullivan and McCarthy relatives that evening. *Talk about déjà vu,* Rylie thought, remembering back to all the times she'd decorated cookies and cakes and made candy with her mom when she was a kid.

"I made cookies for the kids, so the toddlers have a dessert they can eat without any risk of choking," Cathleen informed them with a grin.

"And so the older kids don't get drunk on all the whiskey in the other desserts, right?" Liam chuckled as he looked over the racks of cooling cookies on the table in the middle of the room.

"The alcohol all cooks out of the mince pies and plum pudding," Cathleen defended, shaking her head at her son, even as she grinned at him. "But the nuts and chunks of fruit in them are choking hazards for BJ, Declan, and maybe even Taryn."

Rylie had to think a moment to remember which of Liam's cousins' children Cathleen was referring to, since there were eight of them, all ten years old or younger. Thanks to their review of Liam's family tree before going shopping the day before, it only took her a second to realize that Cathleen was referring to the three youngest members of the family. *BJ is Brendon and Sheridan McCarthy's one-year-old son, Brendon Junior. Declan is Murphy and Finola Sullivan's three-year-old son. And Taryn is Kiernan and Cianna Sullivan's four-year-old daughter.*

"But the Christmas cake is soaked in an entire bottle of whiskey after it's baked," Liam pointed out as he stole one of the cooled cookies and popped it in his mouth. "And I doubt covering it in that frosting stuff does much to lessen the alcohol content."

"It's called marzipan," Cathleen corrected her son with a light chuckle. "And no, it doesn't do a thing to lessen the alcohol content. If anything, it helps hold it in."

"And here I thought all that sugary sweetness was supposed to mask how much booze is in the cake," Liam laughed as he swiped his finger through the red goop in the bowl his mother was stirring.

"Hands off," Cathleen smacked the back of his hand with the spoon she was using to mix up the sugar cookie frosting. "If you're just going to get in the way, go downstairs and help your da set up the folding tables for tonight."

"Yes, ma'am." Liam licked the frosting off his finger and the back of his hand before kissing his mom's temple and leaving the room.

For a second, Rylie thought he was going to repeat the gesture with her. But instead, Liam just winked at her as he walked by.

"How can I help?" Rylie finally asked, once it was just her and Cathleen in the room.

"Grab a bowl and spoon from that stack by the mixer," Cathleen instructed, pointing across the room at the KitchenAid stand mixer on the counter between the stove and sink. "Then scoop out a couple cups of frosting from the mixer bowl and pick a color for decorating these cookies."

Rylie went to the sink first and washed her hands before following Cathleen's instructions. Once she had a bowl full of white frosting, she took a seat at the table with Cathleen and put a few drops of the green food coloring in the frosting before mixing it up.

"Have you ever piped on frosting before? Or do you prefer spreading it on with a butter knife?" Cathleen questioned Rylie as she scooped her now red frosting into a piping bag made out of parchment paper.

"It's been a few years, but I actually went to a cake and cookie decorating class with my mom when I was a kid, so I have done this before." Rylie smiled at her mother-in-law, enjoying the memories she hadn't thought about since her parents passed.

"Oh, that sounds like fun," Cathleen gushed as she finished getting set up and started decorating an ornament-shaped cookie with the red frosting. "I did a few of those classes with Breena and my mom back in the day, but the boys were never into anything in the kitchen for us to do them together. Of course, they enjoyed the treats we were able to make and send to school with them, but they didn't want to participate in actually helping prepare them."

"Yeah, if your boys were anything like I was as a kid, that's probably a good thing," Rylie chuckled, finally being able to fondly remember the time she used too much red food coloring in the chocolate candies she and her mom made for one of her class parties, instead of being embarrassed for accidentally causing a school-wide medical scare. "I helped my mom make some chocolate candy shaped like Santa Claus one year and kept adding red food coloring to the white chocolate until it actually looked red instead of pink. And apparently, using too much of that red food coloring paste can be an issue."

"Oh?" Cathleen looked at her curiously. "Did you turn your teeth red?"

"Oh, no," Rylie laughed as she finished mixing the green frosting and put it in one of the piping bags Cathleen already had prepared on the table. "It wasn't just my teeth. Or even just the teeth of everyone in my class at school. Apparently, the human body can't process that much dye during the digestion process, so it had to come back out. And with it being red that I used too much of, my entire class of over thirty fifth-graders all thought they were bleeding when they went to the bathroom for a few days after our class Christmas party. And since my mom and dad were both teachers in the same school, they had the same issue with the students in both their second and third grade classes."

"Oh, dear," Cathleen stifled a chuckle as she moved on to prepare the blue frosting to decorate the next ornament-shaped cookie. "I imagine there were quite a few scared parents rushing their kids to the emergency room."

"Oh, gosh, I didn't even think about that!" Rylie stopped in the middle of decorating a tree-shaped cookie, feeling mortified all over again, now imagining how her error could have really frightened the parents, not to mention causing costly trips to the ER. "I didn't actually look in the toilet to notice the discoloration until after Mom asked me about it when she got a call from the principle, who'd apparently gotten all the calls from the parents and narrowed it down to something we brought to the parties right before Christmas break that year because it was only students in mine and my parents' classes that were affected. Then I was just embarrassed by being responsible for turning everyone's poop red and making it where we couldn't bring anything that was made at home to another school party. But they really could have, like, sued my parents to cover the cost of all those ER visits and their pain and suffering from worrying about their kids."

"Well, thankfully, that didn't happen," Cathleen reassured her, reaching over to pat her hand. "But now I have to ask what kind of paste food coloring you used, so I can freak my boys out with too much green on Saint Patrick's Day next year."

"Oh, now I see where Liam gets his ornery streak to prank everyone in the locker room," Rylie laughed, finishing the green on the first tree before setting it aside to put the base coat of green on the next tree. "And I'll gladly share my secret, if you promise to send Liam some of whatever you make with it."

"Of course!" Cathleen agreed with a conspiratorial smirk.

"I don't know what the minimum amount it takes to make the color obvious when it's expelled, but I used two of the larger containers of the gel food coloring, which you have to go to a craft store to buy, for each bag of white chocolate candy melts to get a really deep red color for Santa's suit. And that was definitely enough to affect pretty much everyone who even ate a single piece of the candy. Not the small tubs that you can get at the grocery store, but the bigger ones that we had to go to Michaels to get. And it was the gel or paste, not the liquid like this." Rylie waved her hand at the little bottles of liquid food coloring they were using for the icing going on the cookies.

"You used two of those one-ounce tubs of food coloring for each bag of white chocolate?" Cathleen's eyes widened with the realization of just how much food coloring Rylie had used.

"Yep," Rylie confirmed, remembering how her mom sent her dad back to the store for four more of the little jars, so they could make more candy for her parents' classes after using up all the red they had at home for the candies for Rylie's class. "And that's the stuff you're supposed to add with a toothpick, because even the smallest measuring spoon is too much for most recipes."

"Oh wow, you really wanted some red Santas," Cathleen laughed.

"Well, technically, just the Santa suits were red," Rylie clarified, continuing to put the green base on all the tree-shaped cookies, thinking it would be best to let the green frosting harden a little before adding the different colored decorations on top. "We used tiny little brushes to paint the inside of the molds with the chocolate, so the facial features, black boots and belt, and white fur trim all stood out from the red suit. Then once we had the outer shells of the molds painted with a fairly thick coat of the colored chocolate, we back filled them with regular milk chocolate."

"Your parents must have had a lot of artistic talent to do all that and teach you how to do it too."

"Mom did," Rylie smiled. "Dad, not so much. That's why he volunteered to go to the store when we ran out of red food coloring and acted as the taste tester whenever we baked anything." *Huh? I wonder why Dad wasn't the first to notice the side effect of my excessive use of food coloring that year?*

"Yes, well, hopefully you won't mind the fact that Liam will most likely be your taste tester and gofer whenever your children are old enough for you to teach them, like your mom taught you." Cathleen pointed to the ornament-shaped cookies she'd been decorating with red and blue squiggles and dots. "'Cause artistic talent doesn't run in our family. That's why I stuck with ornaments, presents, and trees for the cookies I'm decorating. And put the Santas, snowmen, and reindeer aside for the older kids to decorate when they get here this evening. I can haphazardly draw geometric designs on ornament cookies and strings of garland or blobs for ornaments on Christmas tree cookies, but there's no way I can draw faces on cookies with icing and have them turn out to be recognizable."

Rylie got stuck on Cathleen mentioning her and Liam having children in the future and totally let her thoughts about her lack of artistic ability go in one ear and out the other. "I won't mind at all if he just wants to be the taste tester," she choked out, fighting back tears because of her fear that they'd never get to that happily ever after. "If we're able to work things out to stay together and have kids one day."

"Based on what I saw last night, I'm sure you'll be able to work things out just fine," Cathleen gushed with a reassuring smile.

"I don't know," Rylie admitted, setting aside her green icing bag and standing to prepare a bowl of yellow frosting to start adding lights to the Christmas trees once she composed herself. She wasn't comfortable looking Cathleen in the eye as she talked about the more intimate details of her relationship with Liam, so she waited until she had her back to her mother-in-law before continuing. "I'm not sure our chemistry will be enough to sustain our relationship."

"Well, no, chemistry alone isn't enough," Cathleen agreed. "If that was the case, then Liam would have married the girl he had a crush on back in school. To be honest, that's kind of what I expected to happen after seeing the sparks flying anytime Ceara was around. But they didn't have everything else needed to make a relationship work the way I think you have with Liam. And when you combine your obvious chemistry with the love, trust, and respect I also see you share with my son, and lots of honest communication, your physical intimacy can build up your emotional intimacy to strengthen your relationship until it's bulletproof."

"Unfortunately, we're lacking in a few of those areas," Rylie sighed as she returned to the table with another bowl of white frosting, added a few drops of yellow food coloring, and stirred it together before putting the yellow frosting in a piping bag with a smaller round decorating tip attached to start adding lights to the trees. "Especially the honest communication."

"Yes, well, that's the hardest part of marriage for a lot of people." Cathleen smiled sympathetically. "And while I love my boys, I know they all take after their da with not being great at communicating. But from the way you and Liam look at one another, I know you're both overflowing with love, respect, and trust in one another."

"Are we, though?" Rylie wasn't so sure. "I mean, I know I love him. And I respect him, both as a mentor in the wrestling ring and as a generally great human being. But after he told me about kissing Jen Burleson just a couple weeks after we got married, I'm not sure I can trust him not to break my heart."

"He kissed who? When?" Cathleen glared at Rylie, looking absolutely appalled.

"Jen is a mutual friend, the cousin of one of the GWA pilots," Rylie sputtered before waving her piping bag in the air as if waving away Jen's importance in the conversation at hand. "But who she is doesn't really matter. It also doesn't really matter when they kissed, since we didn't know we were married at the time. What matters is that he doesn't really want to be with me and thought the best way to get over his attraction to me was to sleep with someone else. Yeah, he picked poorly the first time because he only thinks of her as a friend. But who knows when he'll meet someone he's actually attracted to and will be able to successfully kill his attraction to me by sleeping with her? And I'm not sure I want to risk getting my heart completely shattered by him ending things later, after I've fallen even more in love with him. It hurts bad enough now, just knowing he doesn't really want to be with me when I'm already more than a few steps past having a schoolgirl crush on him."

"Oh, yes, it does matter," Cathleen contradicted her, standing and dropping the piping bag from her hand onto the table. "All that other stuff matters too, but my son being unfaithful by kissing another woman after marrying you most definitely matters as well."

Rylie felt terrible as Cathleen stomped out of the room, heading in the same direction Liam had gone less than an hour earlier. Especially when she heard Cathleen yell, "Brian Patrick Connery!" just a few seconds later.

Oh, dear, maybe I shouldn't have tried confiding in Cathleen after all. I certainly didn't mean to cause any conflict between him and his mother.

She didn't know what to do to deescalate the situation, though, especially since Cathleen was hollering for her husband and not Liam. *Is that because Liam has already left to go get the presents for tonight, so she can't yell at him right now? But I didn't hear him leave yet. So maybe she just wants to talk things over with Brian first for them to decide as a couple how to approach the situation with Liam?*

Unsure what else she could do that wouldn't make things worse, Rylie sat there quietly, trying to listen without actively getting up to go eavesdrop, and appreciating how decorating the cookies helped to calm her nerves. *Hopefully, she'll just get them to come upstairs for us all to sit down and talk. And then I can possibly come up with a better way to explain the situation, so she's not so upset about what Liam described as "two epically bad, failed kisses" that he shared with Jen, so she can help me figure out how to get past my lack of trust in him to start working on strengthening our marriage.*

~ ~ ~

Just as Liam finished setting up the last folding table in the den in the basement, which was the only room in his parents' house that was big enough for his extended family to sit down to a meal together, his ma hollered down the stairs, "Brian Patrick Connery!"

Feck! Da must really be in trouble if Ma's bringing out the middle name.

Not wanting to get caught in the middle of whatever his da did to upset his ma, Liam stayed downstairs while Brian went up to talk to Cathleen. He knew they still needed to cover all the tables with the red and green tablecloths his ma used every Christmas, push them all together to make one giant table big enough for them to all sit around, and then set up the folding chairs surrounding it. So, he stayed busy finishing up what he could until Brian came back downstairs.

"Everything okay, Da?" Liam questioned when his father finally came back down to the den.

"Yeah," Brian nodded, a somber expression on his face that Liam couldn't read as the two men worked together to finish placing the last of the chairs around their large grouping of tables. "Did you say you still need to go back to your house to get the presents for tonight and tomorrow?"

"Yeah, Rylie had an issue with riding in the Navigator yesterday causing her to have flashbacks to the accident when she lost her parents, so I don't want her to have to ride in it again, but there's not room in the car for all the gifts," Liam explained. "So, while she's busy with Ma, I figured I could run home and bring them all here and to Granda and Granny's before going back to get the car for us to drive to Mass later."

"Well, then, I'll go with you to help carry everything in, so we have some extra time to stop by the pub and have a talk."

Liam wasn't sure what his da wanted to talk to him about, but it couldn't be too bad if he wanted to talk in public at the pub. It didn't take long at all for the two of them working together to get all the Sullivan and McCarthy presents put under the tree at his parents' house and then deliver all the Connery gifts to Granda and Granny's. Once those presents were under the tree, Brian insisted Granda Neilan accompany them to the pub for a drink and "the talk" with Liam.

Maybe this is some kind of Connery tradition I hadn't heard about before, where the older generations of men offer advice to the newly married younger men in the family?

Regardless of what they wanted to talk to him about, Liam had to continue driving the Navigator, since the backseat in his Porsche was too small for either his da or granda to ride comfortably. *Obviously, they're not planning to buy me a drink to celebrate my nuptials since I'm apparently their designated driver.*

As they walked into Connery's Irish Pub, the bar owned by Liam's middle brother, Rory, Liam took a moment to appreciate the aesthetic his brother had achieved, which according to Granda Neilan was a near perfect replica of the pub his da had run back in Ireland over sixty years ago. The dim lighting and dark wood used for almost every surface certainly felt a lot like the pub he'd visited when he was in Dublin earlier that year, even though Rory's version included modern amenities, such as flat screen TVs, which the little pub in Dublin didn't contain.

"Don't you have staff to man the bar?" Liam questioned when he saw Rory wiping down the bar top. "So you can slack off and schmooze the customers?"

"Yeah, but at lunch, they're mostly in the kitchen," Rory explained, pulling out three pint glasses and filling them with Guinness before any of them had the chance to order a drink. "The rest of the bar staff won't be here until three or four, depending on the day, when business picks up."

As his da and granda each took a seat at the bar, Liam looked around and noticed that there were a couple of older gentlemen at a nearby table, but otherwise, the bar was virtually empty. *I guess Rory doesn't get much of a lunch crowd here since he put the pub in a mostly residential area.*

"Since it is lunch time, I'll have a Gaelic Burger," Brian ordered as he picked up the beer in front of him and took a sip.

"Make dat two," Granda Neilan added, also picking up his beer and taking a drink.

"What about you, big brother?" Rory tilted his head at Liam, who hadn't yet picked up what he assumed was his beer.

"Sure, make it three Gaelic Burgers," Liam agreed with a shrug as he took the seat between his da and granda before finally lifting his glass from the bar and taking a sip. "And after this beer, I'll stick to soda, so I can drive Da and Granda home."

Once Rory walked away to go put in their lunch order with his staff in the kitchen, Brian finally decided it was time to reveal what he wanted to talk to Liam about. "So, why does your ma think I need to take a switch to your backside for cheating on Rylie?"

Liam was glad he'd already swallowed his drink of Guinness, or else he'd have spit it all over the bar at his da's blunt question. First of all, because he hadn't been threatened with a switch to his backside in over twenty-five years. And second, because he couldn't believe Rylie had shared the details about his ignorant actions back when he didn't even know he was a married man with his ma.

"Because I probably deserve it," Liam admitted with a sigh.

Granda Neilan reached over and thumped Liam on the back of the head. "We raised ye better den dat."

"Yeah, I know." Liam hung his head, hating that he had to confess his transgressions to both his da and his granda. "But in my defense, I didn't know I was married to Rylie at the time and it was only two really bad attempts at kissing. I haven't actually slept with anyone else since the first day I met Rylie."

"Explain," Da commanded. "And start at the beginning, so we know all the details to decide if you actually cheated or not."

"Okay, I guess the beginning would be when I met Jen, Anthony's cousin, when I went to his wedding over a year ago," Liam started, not realizing several of his da and granda's friends had joined them at the pub.

"Who's Anthony?" Da questioned.

"Anthony is one of the pilots who flies the GWA plane, and the childhood best friend of the Dangerous Twins, who has become a good friend to me and several of the other wrestlers since he started working with us a few years ago."

"And it was 'is weddin' ye went ta when ya first stahpped combing 'ahme fahr yooehr 'ahliday breaks?"

"Yeah," Liam clarified. "Anthony's mom and aunt are the ringleaders of the local matchmakers in Heart's Destiny, and they tried to fix me up with his cousin Jen at all the wedding events that week. They fixed Dion up with her twin sister that same week, but apparently, D and Julie felt a lot more chemistry than me and Jen, even though they didn't let any of us know that at the time. Anyway, at the end of the week, D told me that he worked out a deal with Julie to come back for Christmas, so he could be her buffer from all the matchmaking, and asked me to do the same for Jen. Since they weren't super pushy about fixing us up, and Jen's a nice girl, who ended up being a friend after all the times we had to sit together that week, I agreed."

"Then in March, when Rylie joined the roster, I started hanging out with her while we were touring. Just like going to a club or a midnight meal with a whole group of other wrestlers, not like dates, so it wasn't ever really just the two of us, even if we sat together most of the time. But even though I felt an instant attraction to her that I'd never felt with Jen, I kept us strictly in the friend zone because of our ten-year age difference. I didn't want to cause either one of us to get our hearts broken by trying to be more than friends, when I knew it could only last until I retire because she's just getting started with her career. And I figured if we built a good strong friendship for the next couple of years, then maybe we'd stay in touch after I leave the business and could maybe get together as more than friends after she eventually retires."

"Then when we had two more weddings to go to in Heart's Destiny over the summer, the Matchmaking Mommas kept seating me with Jen and actually tried to fix Rylie up with a few of the local guys. But instead of making love matches, we all just went along with the seating arrangements and hung out as friends. Well, everyone but Dion and Julie, anyway. But I already told you about how we figured out they'd been hooking up in secret when I told you about him finding out he's gonna be a dad and Julie is the woman he's been dreaming about since losing his memory."

"Yeah, yeah, back ta de part abooeht you, Rylie, and Jen," Granda Neilan interjected, just as Rory delivered their burgers.

"So, the *Sin City Showdown* rolls around in mid-August, and one of our coworkers, being from there in Vegas, brought her mom to the after-party. Windy, the mom, and her best friend, Kandi, suggested we go take pics outside one of the wedding chapels to create a buzz on social media." Liam didn't think it was the right time to mention Windy and Kandi's former profession, or explain that they'd since moved to Texas to work with the Hunters to turn the bed and breakfast into a resort and winery.

"There was some debate about whether or not that was a good idea, which is a little fuzzy because the club we were in was in our hotel, so we were all drinking more than normal since we didn't have to drive after. Then later, when the shots of Jameson started adding up and Rick wasn't there to talk some sense into any of us, Windy and Kandi managed to get several of us in a limo when we were too drunk to know half of what we were doing." Liam paused long enough to put some ketchup on his fries and pop one in his mouth, chewing and swallowing before continuing.

"The next day, after waking up with the worst hangover ever and no memory of getting out of the limo, we found out that there were lots of pictures posted online, and we all had to go back through remedial social media training to get out of the dog house with Rick. But since none of us woke up with anyone, and we couldn't find any receipts for marriage licenses or ceremony fees with one of the wedding chapels, we all assumed we'd just taken the pics outside and hadn't actually gone in and got married. So, we all went back to our normal routine, promising to cut back on the alcohol to keep from causing more online trouble for the company."

Liam stopped speaking momentarily to take a bite of his burger, not really tasting the Angus beef, Irish bacon, cheddar cheese, or caramelized onions he normally loved because of the regret that seemed to coat his taste buds at the moment. After washing it down with another large swig of his Guinness, he continued. "Two weeks later, it's time for our Labor Day break, and Dion asked me to go back to Heart's Destiny with him for Anthony's sister's wedding to continue being a buffer for Jen and Julie with the matchmaking efforts of their mom and aunt. I didn't know that I'd gotten married at this point, but I did know that I was frustrated with trying to keep from crossing the line out of the friend zone with Rylie, who by the way did *not* go to Heart's Destiny for that break."

"The first event of the week was the joint bachelor and bachelorette party at the only bar in town, which is kinda like the cowboy version of this place, only they have the stage and dance floor in the main room with the bar and restaurant style tables, and all the TVs and pool tables in the back room." Liam waved his hand around to indicate the space around them, which was all bar height tables and televisions while the back room was set up more like a sports bar with more televisions on one side and with the stage and small dance floor on the other side.

"In my frustrated state, I recruited Dion to be my designated driver, so I could indulge in more than the one beer I usually stop at to be safe to drive after the party. Jen was there, obviously, and she was a lot flirtier than normal. And after I lost count of how much Guinness and Irish whiskey I'd had, I stupidly thought I could get Rylie out of my head by acting on the chemistry that Jen suddenly claimed she felt with me. We snuck off to a storeroom in the back to hook up, but then butted heads hard enough to cause a concussion when we both tilted our heads the same direction on our first attempt at kissing."

When Rory and several others around them chuckled at Liam's confession, he finally realized that apparently his da and granda had called in reinforcements to help them figure out Liam's fidelity status. Or maybe Rory, who looked extremely guilty behind the bar, had called some of them in, since not only were there several friends of both his da and granda there, but the rest of his brothers and a few of his Connery cousins were also at the bar and the tables closest to the bar, listening to every word out of Liam's mouth while having a pint or two with their lunch.

Great! As if this isn't humiliating enough to admit to Da and Granda.

"So, what happened next? Did you call an ambulance for the concussion? Or did you keep trying to make out with the wrong girl?" Rory smirked as he replaced Liam's empty beer glass with a full glass of soda, obviously already realizing that no ambulance had been called.

"I made sure we were both still conscious and hadn't actually busted either of our heads open," Liam chuckled ruefully. "Then I held her head in place and actually managed more than a brief tap of our lips together. But it felt...*wrong*. Even though I had this gorgeous woman grinding on me like she was ready to go, I was not turned on in any way."

He wasn't about to mention how he thought his dick wanted to turn inside out in front of his family the way he'd described it to Dion. "So, I stepped back and shook my head to indicate I couldn't go through with it. Jen said something like, 'yeah, this isn't gonna work 'cause that was like kissing one of my cousins,' and we both agreed to just be friends before going back out to join the rest of the party. For the rest of that week, we still sat together at all the wedding events, but we didn't even dance together after that. We were right back in the friend zone, where we should have stayed all along."

He sighed heavily before spending a few minutes eating more of his burger. "It was a month later before Rylie found the marriage certificate and we realized we'd gotten married. And I was a gobshite who reacted poorly and insisted on getting an annulment 'cause I was still trying to fight my feelings for her in a useless attempt to keep from ending up with a broken heart when I retire in a couple years and she keeps touring."

"Definitely a gahbshite mahve," Granda Neilan agreed, nodding before taking another bite of his lunch.

"So, if Rylie wasn't there when this all happened with Jen, how does she know about it to be able to tell Ma that you cheated on her?" Quinn questioned, reaching over to steal a few of Liam's fries.

"'Cause 'e cahnfessed ta 'is wife instead o' a priest," Granda Neilan answered for him.

"No, I confessed to several priests too," Liam clarified, slapping his brother's hand away from his plate and taking another bite of his burger before continuing. "But when we were back in Heart's Destiny over Thanksgiving for Dean and Allissa's wedding, we tried to keep the local matchmakers from pulling any of their stunts with us by pretending to be happily married and sharing a room at the only hotel in town. And while spending all that time together, we couldn't fight our attraction."

Liam popped a couple of fries in his mouth, letting his audience come to their own conclusions about what happened that week instead of sharing the dirty details.

"Oh, come on, you can't stop just as you're getting to the good part of the story," his cousin Cian complained, throwing up his hands. "We need details."

"No, you don't," Liam barked at his cousin. "Other than the fact that the *benefits* ended a couple nights before our break was over, when Rylie asked me point blank if anything had ever happened between me and Jen, and I had to tell her about me being a gobshite the weekend before Labor Day. So, now we're in this weird form of limbo, where we're trying to maintain our friendship and figure out our options, while also fighting our insane chemistry because she can't forgive me for cheating, even though I didn't know I was married at the time."

"Is kissing really cheating though?" Finn questioned as he motioned for Rory to refill his beer. "I mean, I kiss friends all the time and it doesn't really mean anything. So, since you didn't know you were married at the time and didn't take it past a kiss like you'd give a cousin, then I don't think you really cheated."

"But the intent was there to do more than kiss," his cousin Kegan pointed out, tilting his half empty glass at Liam. "So I can kind of see her point."

"But even if he'd actually had sex with this Jen woman, he thought he was single at the time, so he wasn't intentionally cheating," Aiden chimed in, just as Rory placed a plate of food in front of him. "Right, Da?"

Brian wiped his mouth with his napkin, tossing it on his empty plate before providing his two cents. "If he really didn't know he was married, and only considered Rylie a friend at that point, not even a girlfriend, then no I don't think it was cheating. At least, not intentional cheating."

"Yeah, that's what the priests said every time I've confessed to try to ease the guilt I still feel." Liam sighed, washing down his burger with a drink of his soda before elaborating. "But they also pointed out that it doesn't matter what I think, or even that they absolved me of my sin, if it even was a sin. All that really matters is what Rylie thinks and whether or not she can forgive me, so we can move forward."

"You confessed the same sin to more than one priest?" Finn looked at Liam as if he were studying an alien species.

"Yeah," Liam admitted with a shrug. "When my penance didn't feel like enough to alleviate my guilt the first time, I thought I needed to do more, so I confessed a second time. And a third. But after the third priest told me basically the same thing about being forgiven by God and needing to work things out with Rylie before I'll quit feeling guilty, I stopped including it every time I've gone to confession since then."

"So, it sounds like you need to ask Rylie what you can do as penance to earn her forgiveness," his da suggested, sparking a debate among all the men for the best ways Liam could make up with Rylie.

Since they'd all obviously had more beer than Liam, some of their suggestions became rather graphic, making him uncomfortable. *Seriously, how can they fecking suggest eating her pussy three times a day in front of Da and Granda?* Liam tuned out most of the conversation going on around him, focusing on eating the rest of his burger and hoping they'd all stop eventually, so he could get some useful advice from his da and granda.

"Or we can just show her that a kiss or two isn't cheating," Finn suggested with a smirk, bringing Liam's attention back to the discussion. "By each taking a turn catching her under the mistletoe and kissing her."

"Oh, yeah, that would definitely work," his cousin Devin agreed with Finn. "I'll even volunteer to go buy some mistletoe to put up at Granny and Granda's tomorrow, so we can all take a turn kissing Rylie to show her that a kiss isn't cheating."

"No!" Liam glared at his cousin and brother. He wasn't sure if the raging jealousy boiling up inside him was just from the thought of anyone else kissing Rylie. Or if it stemmed from having his youngest brother and youngest Connery cousin instigating the plan to make a move on his wife, when they were both a lot closer to her age. But either way, he had to fight the urge to grab each of them by their hair and slam their heads together until they were unconscious and incapable of kissing his wife.

"Alright, eejits, quit actin' de maggaht," Granda shouted, pointing at each of his grandsons who'd agreed with the idea of each taking a turn kissing Rylie. "Ye're gahnna get Liam pessed enooehgh to keck yooehr arses."

"Yeah, I think it's time we head out, so we can finish setting up for dinner," Brian interjected, waving Rory over to give them the check.

Liam couldn't agree more, needing to leave before he gave in to his baser instincts. He pulled his wallet out and handed Rory his card before Da could. "I'm covering Da and Granda, but everyone else is on their own."

Once his card had been run and he was alone in his Navigator with Da and Granda, he finally felt like it was safe to ask their advice. "So, what do you think I should do to make up to Rylie?"

"Apologize profusely and tell her how much you love her and want to make your marriage work," Da suggested.

Liam didn't get a chance to point out that his retirement and her continued career would make it impossible for them to stay together for more than a couple of years before his granda advised with a grin, "And fahllow throoehgh wit dat soehggestion ta eat 'er poehssy three times a day."

Liam couldn't help but laugh, even though he knew his face was probably as red as his Porsche from hearing the word "pussy" come from his eighty-six year old granda's mouth. *I guess I was wrong about thinking Dion's joke about the chick coming first is too bawdy to tell Granda.*

When Liam caught his granda's eye in the rearview mirror, Neilan added, "What? It wahrks fahr me wit yooehr granny."

~~~

Rylie wasn't sure what she expected to happen when Liam and Brian returned to the house not long before the maternal side of Liam's family was due to arrive for Christmas Eve dinner. But it wasn't that Cathleen would be satisfied by just silently staring at the two men for a moment, instead of insisting on a conversation between the four of them.

Once Cathleen had come back to the kitchen earlier, Rylie had tried to make it clear that she wasn't upset by Liam kissing Jen. Since none of them knew about their marriage at the time, and they'd only considered one another friends, she didn't feel like she had any right to be upset because he hadn't knowingly and intentionally cheated on her. She explained that it was the fact that he didn't want to be attracted to her and was trying to kill those budding feelings that bothered her, not the method he chose to "get her out of his system" that was upsetting.

Cathleen seemed to understand, and had even offered Rylie some advice for ways she could prove to Liam that he could trust her with
~~~

his heart as a means to keep him from wanting to kill those feelings in the future. But she thought Cathleen meant for her to wait until after they'd all talked to enact those suggestions, so Rylie expected Cathleen to instigate a serious discussion between the four of them, the way Liam initially seemed to think his dad meant for the elders in the family to host an "intervention" for their marriage.

Maybe she decided not to sit us all down together now because there's not enough time before the rest of her family gets here? Or maybe it's because the Connery side of the family is all split up tonight, celebrating with each of Liam's aunts' families, so Breena and Neilan aren't here for the intervention?

When the doorbell rang less than a second later, Rylie presumed her first assumption was correct. Still, she couldn't help but wonder if following Cathleen's advice by being more affectionate with Liam now would subtly signal to him that she wanted more than friendship, so he might be more open to the possibility of working on their marriage when they finally got around to having that talk with his parents. Not that she got the chance to implement that plan right then.

As Brian stepped out of the kitchen to go answer the door, Cathleen turned to Rylie and asked, "Rylie, will you please help me get the kids set up to decorate more of the cookies? Since we're eating downstairs in the family room, I covered the table in the dining room earlier, so the kids will have plenty of room without us having to clean everything up before eating dinner later. But other than the cookies, I haven't had the chance to put the rest of the supplies in there yet."

"Of course," Rylie agreed, stepping away from the oven, where she'd just basted the turkey, which still had an hour of cooking time left. She helped Cathleen carry the piping bags and bowls of frosting, which they'd prepared earlier and stored in the refrigerator, to the dining room. They also gathered several kinds of sprinkles and candies for the younger kids to use, since they'd have a hard time piping on features of any kind.

Soon, she found herself happily assisting Liam's cousins-in-law and their children in swapping out decorating tips on the piping bags to add details to the cookies with faces. Apparently, it was only the younger generation of married women who braved cookie decorating with the kids, since Liam's unmarried female cousins all seemed to disappear downstairs with all the guys, and Cathleen's sister and sisters-in-law all joined her in the kitchen to finish heating up the dishes they'd brought.

"Wow, you're really good at this," ten-year-old Sully McCarthy Junior commented after Rylie showed him how to add the facial features on his Santa-shaped cookie. "Have you been practicing a lot 'cause you and Uncle Liam are gonna give us more cousins and you need to be able to make stuff like this for your kids?"

"Um, nah-no," Rylie stuttered, surprised by the little boy's question. She grabbed another Santa cookie and the piping bag of red icing to keep her hands busy as she tried to redirect the discussion. "I learned how to do this with my mom when I was about your age. So it's kinda like riding a bicycle, not something I do regularly, but a skill that easily comes back to me from my childhood."

"You'll have to excuse him," Kelly, his mom, chuckled, rubbing a hand over her stomach, which was sporting the slightest of baby bumps. "Ever since we told the kids about getting a new baby brother or sister in May, they've both been asking every woman they meet about when they're going to have babies too."

"I haven't, Mommy," eight-year-old Casey chimed in, not looking up from the reindeer cookie she was decorating. "Just Sullivan."

Rylie had to chuckle at the sibling dynamics, assuming Casey used her brother's full first name instead of his nickname as a way to reprimand him without being so obvious she got herself in trouble.

"Our mom's gonna have another baby, too," nine-year-old Brady McCarthy informed everyone in the room, pointing between himself, his sister, Cassidy, and their mom, Aisling, who was married to Liam's cousin Riordan.

Aisling nodded and smiled shyly as all eyes turned to her momentarily. "Due in June."

"So's my mommy," six-year-old Ronan McCarthy interjected, beaming a smile up at his mom, Lynn, who was married to Liam's cousin Kevin. "Ain't that right, Mommy?"

"Isn't that right," Lynn corrected her son. "And yes, we're also expecting a new baby in June."

"Wow, it must be something in the water," Cianna Sullivan, who was married to Liam's cousin Kiernan, chuckled as she and her daughter, four-year-old Taryn, spread brown frosting on reindeer cookies to make them match. "We just found out we're having another in August."

Wow! This must be like that phenomenon Fiona's mom mentioned when she told us how she wanted Fiona to hang out with the Burlesons while she was home, so some of their baby mojo would rub off on her. I guess pregnancy really can be contagious in some families and close knit friend groups.

"Same, same," Sheridan McCarthy beamed, holding up the snowman cookie she'd just finished decorating with her one-year-old, Brendon Junior, to Cianna so they could tap cookies together like a toast, neither seeming to care if their brown and white frostings marked the other's cookie. "We're also due in August."

"Do you think our mothers-in-law have all been saying extra prayers for grandbabies this year?" Finola Sullivan, who was married to Liam's cousin Murphy, questioned as she handed her three-year-old son Declan some candies to put eyes on the snowman cookie they were decorating. "Since we're all having babies between May and August?"

"Probably," the other ladies chuckled in unison before they all turned their gazes to Rylie, as if expecting her to announce that she was also pregnant.

"Oh, no," Rylie held her hands up in surrender. "Maybe all your mothers-in-law have been praying for all of you to be blessed with more babies, but Cathleen hasn't known about me long enough to do the same for me and Liam. And hopefully, she now knows we need to wait a little while before even thinking about having babies. But if their prayers work so well that they helped all of you, then I need to put my boss's wife, Fiona, on their baby blessings prayer list, since she's the only woman I know who is currently trying to get pregnant."

"Maybe now isn't the best time to come swipe a cookie." Shay Sullivan took a step back, bumping into Finn Connery and Keenan Sullivan, who'd both followed him into the dining room where the women and children were decorating cookies. "'Cause I don't need to hear any discussions about pregnancy."

"Uncka Shay," four-year-old Taryn squealed, holding up the reindeer cookie she'd covered in chocolate frosting, "look at my Woodolf."

"How do you know it's Rudolph?" Shay questioned the child, narrowing his eyes suspiciously as he walked closer to Taryn, obviously having changed his mind about retreating from the room. "It's just a brown reindeer. Did you hide his red nose?"

"No," Taryn laughed at her uncle, shaking her head and causing her strawberry blonde curls to bounce around her head adorably. "I haven't put his nose on yet, silly."

"Well, then you need to hurry up and put his nose on, so I can eat him," Shay teased his niece, bopping her nose with his pointer finger.

"No, Uncka Shay!" Taryn hugged her cookie to her chest, smearing brown frosting on the front of her shirt as the cookie crumbled from how tight she squeezed it. "We don't eat Woodolf!"

"If he's a cookie, we do," Shay protested before Cianna cut him off.

"Shay Aden Sullivan, quit riling her up," Cianna chastised her brother-in-law as she pointed at what was left of the cookie. "And since you caused the mess, you can clean her up."

"Sorry," Shay held his hands up in surrender momentarily before picking up his niece. "I didn't realize she'd rather smash Rudolf than eat him."

As Shay carried a now whimpering Taryn out of the room, Cianna called out after him, "Good luck getting the chocolate off her top."

"Sorry, Cianna," Finn apologized, surprising Rylie by how close he was standing to her. "We just wanted to come sweet talk our favorite ladies into letting us have a couple of cookies to tide us over 'til dinner. And didn't mean to upset Taryn."

Rylie had been so focused on the interaction between Taryn and Shay that she hadn't noticed Finn and Keenan slinking around the room. As Keenan threw his arm around his sister-in-law Finola's shoulders and made puppy-dog eyes at her, Finn leaned his head on Rylie's shoulder, folded his hands in a prayer position, and wagged his eyebrows at her.

"You can spare a cookie for your favorite brother-in-law, can't you, Rylie?"

Rylie could only laugh at Finn's over-the-top antics, wondering how anyone could take him seriously as a cop if he always behaved so comically. "No," she choked out between chuckles. "We're just decorating them now, but nobody gets to eat them until after dinner."

"Not true," Finn disagreed, trying to sneak his hand between Rylie and Sully Junior to steal a cookie from the table. "I think Shay and Taryn are eating what's left of Rudolf as we speak. So we should all be allowed a cookie now too."

Rylie reached out with the hand not holding a piping bag of frosting and slapped Finn's hand before he got too close to the cookies. Instead of pulling his hand back or saying "ouch" when she smacked him, Finn took ahold of her hand, obviously thinking he was limiting her ability to keep him from using his other hand to grab a cookie.

He apparently doesn't realize I can get him in a wristlock to push him back from the table without even dropping this frosting bag.

"Thankfully, I knew not to put her in her dress for Mass until after dinner," Cianna chuckled ruefully. "'Cause I'm pretty sure Shay is teaching my daughter to clean the frosting from her shirt by licking it off."

"Most definitely," Keenan laughed as Finola shewed him away from the cookies at her end of the table.

"Finnegan Fearghus Connery, get away from my wife," Liam barked, stomping into the room.

"I just want a bite of her cookie," Finn joked, letting go of Rylie as he raised his hands in surrender and took a step back.

"Go find your own woman to make you cookies," Liam directed his brother, stepping up and taking the piping bag from Rylie's hand and placing it on the plate with the cookie she'd been decorating. He then took her hand and pulled her up from her chair.

"Is Uncle Finn's middle name really Fearghus?" Sully Junior asked before Liam could drag her from the room.

"Yes, it is," Liam confirmed, causing the older children to start teasing Finn.

"I'm gonna call you Uncle Fergie from now on."

"Come with me, Moh Graw," Liam insisted, lacing their fingers together as he pulled her from the room.

"Where are we going?" Rylie wasn't sure what was going on, but something had obviously irritated Liam. And she didn't think he was only aggravated by Finn trying to swipe a cookie before they could get them all decorated.

"The bathroom," Liam insisted, ushering her upstairs and down the hall. "'Cause this'll be the last chance either of us have to go alone until they have to untie us so I can drive to Mass later."

"Untie us? What are you talking about?" Rylie stopped in her tracks, really confused by Liam's strange comments. "And there's no way I'm going in the bathroom with you in your parents' house."

The fiery glow in Liam's hazel eyes made it clear that he easily understood her reference to the last time they were in the same bathroom, when they'd made love in the shower while staying in the same room in Heart's Destiny. Unfortunately, the brightening of the gold flecks in his mostly green eyes seemed to dissipate as quickly as it had flared, alerting her to the fact that he had no intention of repeating that encounter anytime soon.

"Exactly, that's why we each have to go on our own now, so we don't have to go together later." Liam pointed to the bathroom door.

"Liam, you're not making any sense." Rylie pulled her hand from his, placing both of hers on her hips indignantly. "Why would we be tied up and have to go to the bathroom together later?"

"It's an Irish tradition, the Celtic Handfasting Ritual," Liam huffed, shaking his head. "Apparently, since we didn't do it during our wedding, we're supposed to do it at our first Christmas dinner as husband and wife. So, when we go downstairs in a few minutes, Ma and Da are going to tie our wrists together, and we won't be released until it's time to go to Mass after dinner and opening gifts."

"Oh…kay," Rylie drew out the word, finally understanding why he was pointing her toward the restroom, but still feeling unsure about why they were doing this ritual when their future as a couple was yet uncertain. "Shouldn't we wait until after deciding whether or not we're staying married before we do something like this?"

"Yeah, you'd think," Liam sighed, running a hand through his hair. "But when I tried pointing that out, I was told that it was originally done to signify an engagement or trial marriage, and the couple could change their minds and go their separate ways anytime in the first year, so I was outvoted."

"And I don't get a say in this at all? Shouldn't it just be our votes that count? Or is this another of your mom and granny's matchmaking schemes?"

"That's kinda what I think it is." Liam pointed at her and then touched the tip of his nose, indicating he thought her guess was *right on the nose*. "Especially since Granny, Granda, and the whole Connery side of the family aren't here, which I'd think they'd all be here for a real handfasting, so the whole family could celebrate with us. But then again, knowing them, I wouldn't be surprised if Granny insists we do this all again tomorrow, since she wasn't here to see it tonight."

"True," Rylie agreed. "So, we're just gonna go along with it?"

"Yeah, unless you have some kind of fear of being tied up and freak out when the first cord is wrapped around our wrists, I don't see how we can get out of it."

"Sorry, I don't have any past trauma I can call on to freak out at being bound," Rylie scoffed. *And I really didn't think the first time I'd be testing the waters with bondage would be in front of half your family.*

"Then we need to hurry up and do whatever we have to in the bathroom, so we don't have to watch each other urinate, or worse, later. 'Cause I don't know about you, but golden showers and defecation are on my hard limits list."

"Gross." Rylie shuddered at the thought. "No, the only reason I'd ever share a bathroom with someone else would be for what we did in the shower in Heart's Destiny." She paused momentarily, fighting her embarrassment from talking about sex in his parents' house, while also hoping to see another flare of interest in Liam's eyes. "Or to bathe my kids one of these days."

"Agreed," Liam smiled wistfully, making her wonder if he was thinking once again about when they'd made love in the shower last month, or if he was imagining them having kids they'd need to bathe one day.

Not that she could ask him about what he was thinking right then, since it was clearly not the right time or place. Instead, they just stood there staring at each other for several long moments.

"Well, I can't go knowing you're standing right outside the door," Rylie finally huffed, shaking her head at her clueless husband.

"Yeah, I'm going to the other bathroom up here," Liam informed her, pointing with his thumb over his shoulder with one hand while pointing her toward the bathroom once more with the other. "So, I won't hear whatever you do in there. And I'll meet you downstairs after."

"Okay." Rylie waited until Liam turned and walked down the hall before going into the bathroom and emptying her bladder. She still had to turn on the water in the sink for a few minutes to get everything moving, but she eventually got the job done. After washing her hands, she made her way back downstairs, where she found Liam had already rejoined his family.

"Oh, there you are, Rylie," Cathleen gushed, waving her over to stand beside Liam at one end of the large table, which was really several folding tables pushed together to make one big enough they could all sit around it. "I thought for a minute there that Finn and his cousins' antics had scared you off."

Finn's antics? With the cookies?

"Rylie's not gonna run off because of me," Finn chimed in, winking at Rylie flirtatiously. "She might change her mind about lame Liam and run to me when she dumps him, but she's not scared of me."

Is he being flirtatious with me? Why? That makes no sense. I mean, I know siblings often like to mess with each other, but does he really think acting so ridiculous is going to rile up Liam?

"Why would she pick you, when she can have me?" Keenan stepped in front of Finn and blew Rylie a kiss.

And his cousin, too? Is this what Cathleen was talking about?

"Or me?" Shay added, elbowing Finn as he carried a now clean Taryn past both Finn and Keenan. "Since clearly I'm the most capable of helping her with our kids one day."

Our kids? Oh hell no! Rylie shook her head, stepping closer to Liam as if he was going to protect her from his insane family members.

"Oh, please, Aunt Shannon helped you clean the chocolate off of Taryn's shirt," Finn interjected.

"Knock it off, all of you," Liam barked, hugging Rylie to his side.

Rylie wrapped her arm around his waist, grateful for the save since it probably wouldn't be received well by the rest of the family if she reacted violently by trying to slap some sense into Finn, Keenan, and Shay.

"Yes, you boys go sit down and be quiet while we join Rylie with her rightful husband in a traditional Celtic Handfasting," Cathleen reprimanded her youngest son and his two flirtatious cousins.

Once the rest of the family got downstairs and everyone was seated around the large table, which was already filled with the food Rylie had helped Cathleen prepare earlier, as well as several dishes that were brought by the other women in the family, Brian started the handfasting ceremony by directing Liam and Rylie to stand facing each other at the head of the table.

"The tradition of Celtic Handfasting began centuries ago as a way for a couple to declare their engagement. At the end of the ceremony performed by their families, the couple entered into a trial marriage, which lasted for a year and a day, before they had to decide if they wanted to go through with the wedding. As the laws have changed over the years and the Irish people have migrated around the world, the handfasting ceremony has evolved, no longer signifying an engagement but now being incorporated into the wedding ceremony. But since not everyone thinks to include it when they get married, our family has carried on the tradition by including the handfasting in our Christmas celebrations, binding together any newlyweds who didn't include it in their weddings in the last year, as a way for the other married family members to bestow upon the couple the blessings we all wish for in our marriages."

"Traditionally, during a wedding, the couple joins hands, right to right and left to left, forming an infinity symbol with their bodies. But in that setting, they're released from the cords after only a few minutes, so they can finish the wedding. At the holidays, we do things a little differently. Instead of joining all four hands, we harken back to the tradition of centuries past, when only the left hands were joined so the couple could partake of the feast while demonstrating their bond to one another for the remainder of the evening. Liam and Rylie, please join your left hands."

Rylie looked up at Liam nervously as she placed her left hand in his. His encouraging smile as he gently wrapped his fingers around her hand made her heart flutter, giving her a sense that this ceremony held more meaning for both of them than just humoring his family, as she'd thought earlier. She smiled back as she squeezed his hand.

Leah Mae Wright

"The black cord signifies strength, wisdom, vision, and success, all things I hope both Liam and Rylie find in their union." Brian draped a black cord over their joined hands.

Cathleen stepped up then, draping a white cord over their joined hands beside the black cord. "The white cord represents purity, concentration, meditation, and peace, all things I hope both Liam and Rylie share in their marriage."

Next, Liam's Uncle Quinlan and Aunt Shannon stepped up and draped a gray cord over their hands, speaking in unison. "The gray cord signifies balance, which we hope you both find in one another."

Liam's Uncle Brogan and Aunt Tara were next, adding a brown cord as they spoke, "The brown cord symbolizes the earth, providing grounding and a sense of home that we hope will be the foundation of your marriage."

They were followed by Liam's Aunt Chevonne and Uncle Ryan, who laid an orange cord over their hands, adding, "The orange cord represents encouragement, attraction, kindness, and plenty, all blessings we pray you have in your marriage."

Once the older generation took their seats, Liam's married cousins and their wives stood and lined up to continue draping cords over Liam and Rylie's joined hands. Sully and Kelly draped a yellow cord over their hands, telling them it symbolized charm, confidence, joy, and balance.

Kiernan and Cianna added a green cord, with Cianna smiling knowingly at Rylie as Kiernan informed them, "The green cord represents finances, fertility, charity, prosperity, and health, which we wish for the both of you."

Rylie had to stifle a giggle at the reference to fertility considering the ladies' earlier discussion. *I wonder if Cianna intentionally picked that color cord? Or if they all knew about this when they started talking about how they're all expecting and looked at me like I'm going to be next?*

Rylie pushed her thoughts aside as Riordan and Aisling placed a blue cord over the others. "The blue cord signifies tranquility, patience, devotion, and sincerity, all traits we hope you both share in your marriage."

They were followed by Kevin and Lynn, who added a purple cord, describing its meaning as power, piety, sanctity, and sentimentality.

Next, Brendon and Sheridan laid a pink cord beside the purple one, signifying unity, honor, truth, romance, and happiness. The last couple to add a cord was Murphy and Finola, who placed a silver cord, representing treasure, values, creativity, and inspiration.

Once the cousins and cousins-in-law were all seated, Brian added a gold cord. "The gold cord symbolizes energy, wealth, intelligence, and longevity, all of which I pray God bestows on Liam, Rylie, and their marriage."

"And finally, the red cord represents passion, strength, lust, and fertility," Cathleen added as she draped a red cord over the top of all the others. She and Brian then gathered the ends of all thirteen cords, working together to tie them into an infinity knot.

Rylie was surprised that the cords were only slightly snug but not uncomfortably tight. *I guess it kind of defeats the purpose if they cut off circulation and have to remove the cords early.*

"In the name of the Father, and of the Son, and of the Holy Spirit," Brian prayed, making the sign of the cross, "I ask that Liam and Rylie be blessed with all the sentiments symbolized in these cords. And as these cords are joined here today, so shall Liam and Rylie be joined as one. Amen."

The adults in the room all chorused "amen," including Liam and Rylie. She just wasn't sure if Liam joined in because he hoped for the blessings in the prayer Brian had just spoken, or if he'd just repeated the word like she had — because it was an ingrained habit from being raised Catholic. Well, at least, that was part of the reason she'd said "amen" along with everyone else. *Nobody else has to know how much I'm hoping God answers that prayer.*

"Can we eat now?" The solemn silence was broken by six-year-old Ronan, who was clearly tired of having to sit still and be quiet.

"Soon," his grandmother, Chevonne, chuckled. "But first Uncle Liam and Aunt Rylie have to kiss to seal their union and then figure out how to sit side by side to eat with their left hands tied together."

"I got this," Liam grinned, lifting their joined hands to spin Rylie until his arm was around her shoulders with their joined hands resting on the front of her left shoulder. Then he wrapped his right arm around her waist and dipped her back to kiss her soundly.

"Yeah, they're not really supposed to kiss until it's time to remove the knot," Cathleen corrected, not that Liam listened to his mom.

Rylie was so surprised by the flamboyant show of affection that she gasped, involuntarily opening her mouth for Liam to deepen the kiss. Not that her response was involuntary for long. Like the night before, she couldn't resist kissing the man she loved, even if she thought his feelings for her were only attraction and lust. She got so lost in kissing her husband that she didn't register the catcalls of his brothers and cousins, clinging to him with her free right hand.

"Now I understand why kissing is a big deal for them."

Thankfully, unlike the night before, Liam kept them from taking the kiss too far in front of an audience. He pulled her back up and released the kiss only seconds after she started returning it. At least it felt like it was only seconds to Rylie. In actuality, it was probably more like a minute or two. Not that she could figure it out right then in her dazed state, especially since she was too busy trying to contemplate the meaning behind the kiss.

Whoa! I get doing the handfasting to appease his family since it's not just us and his parents here. But wouldn't a chaste peck, like we've done on a couple of the GWA shows, have worked just now? Since he seemed to regret what we did in the wine cellar last night, it doesn't make sense that he'd kiss me for real now. Unless he's just making a show of it because of his brother and cousins' silly flirtation earlier?

With his arm around her shoulders, Liam ushered Rylie over to the table, pulling out two chairs so they could sit at the same time once she finally came back to reality. It was a bit awkward trying to keep from elbowing Liam with him sitting so close while they each only had their right arms free to eat. But they managed to work together, having Liam hold the heavy dishes while Rylie served them both before passing the food on around the table.

Once dinner was over, they had to work together in much the same manner to open their presents. Luckily, they were both right-handed, so they had two dominant hands to open each package, while their left hands were still joined. Unfortunately, Rylie's awkwardness wasn't just limited to not feeling comfortable trying to do things one handed or having Liam help her with things she couldn't do on her own. She also felt discombobulated by the disparity in the gifts they exchanged with each other, since he gave her a pair of eighteen karat gold, diamond stud earrings, while she'd bought him a much cheaper, sterling silver, Irish knot tie clip, so he could show his pride in his heritage while sticking to the GWA's dress code. *If he gives me more jewelry tomorrow, I'm going to feel really bad about only giving him a Gators' jersey. But what else was I supposed to get for a man who already has everything else I could think of to get him?*

Finally, once all the food was consumed and the gifts were opened, with the exception of the stack of envelopes containing the **No Remorse** passes and travel information that Liam left in the car, Brian and Cathleen called Liam and Rylie over to stand in front of the Christmas tree to remove the cords from their hands. Rylie had to spin once more to get out from under Liam's arm, so they were facing each other again instead of standing side by side.

"Rylie, if you'll grab this bundle of cords," Brian instructed, pointing at the end of the cords hanging down to her right of their joined left hands. As she followed his instructions, he continued directing Liam, "And if you'll grab the other side, Liam, then the two of you can kiss to seal your union while gently pulling your left hands out and tightening the knot by pulling the cords with your right hands."

Since they had to kiss over the top of their hands, while releasing their grip on one another and tightening the knot at the same time, this kiss remained much more chaste than the last, which seemed far more appropriate for the current state of their marriage, at least in Rylie's opinion. Once they pulled back, they were left holding the thirteen cords tied in one big knot.

"Oh, now I get it," Rylie squealed in excitement. "This must be why getting married is sometimes called *tying the knot*!"

"Yeah," Liam chuckled, along with most of his family. "You didn't figure that out from everything Da said earlier about the tradition?"

"Well, no," Rylie admitted sheepishly. "Because I thought your parents would untie the knot they made in the ropes to let us release our hands. I didn't realize that we'd actually be able to pull our hands out so easily and finish tying the ropes into a knot."

"Yes, that is where the term came from," Cathleen giggled. "And you have the knot to always remind you of the blessings bestowed on you today."

"Now you need to take it home and hang it over the bed in your master bedroom," Chevonne informed them. "At least, that's what your Granny Saoirse insisted we all do with ours, so we'd return the blessings to her with lots of grandbabies."

"That's why you insisted we all hang ours in the bedroom?" Chevonne's daughter-in-law, Kelly, questioned, motioning between herself, Aisling, Lynn, and Sheridan.

"Well, that explains why there's two cords that symbolize fertility," Cianna chortled. "But is the blessing really more potent if the knot is kept in the bedroom?"

"Guess that means you should put yours in your suitcase, so you can hang it in your hotel rooms while you're on tour," Quinn teased Liam before anyone could reply to Cianna.

"No, we've got too much stuff to keep track of on tour as it is," Liam replied, draping his end of the cords down his back with the knot resting on his shoulder, the same way he often carried the GWA tag-team title belt to and from the ring. "This'll be fine at home."

Rylie released her hold on the other end of the cords to let it hang down over Liam's chest, unsure how to take his plan to leave their knot at home when they rejoined the GWA tour. *Does that mean he's planning to hang it in his master bedroom? Like maybe he's hoping we'll stay together and make that room ours? And if so, does that mean the kiss earlier was real and not just a show to get his brother and cousins to quit being flirtatious? Or is he planning on just stuffing it in a box somewhere? Or throwing it away if we go through with the annulment?*

Since it was time for them to leave for Midnight Mass, Rylie knew she'd have to add those questions to the long list she had for Liam, if and when they finally talked about their marriage.

Chapter Five

Wednesday, December 25, 2019, Christmas Day, New York City, New York

Liam wasn't surprised that, immediately after breakfast at his granny and granda's house, his grandparents insisted on repeating the handfasting ceremony since they'd missed it the night before while celebrating with the Donovans, his Aunt Nora's parents. Luckily for him and Rylie, however, Granda and Granny insisted on the four-handed version, so they were released right after his grandparents, parents, aunts, and uncles each took turns wrapping the cords over their hands, with his grandparents tying the knot for them as they pulled their hands back. Granny said it was because they needed Rylie's help in the kitchen and didn't want him in the way, but he knew it was because she secretly believed it didn't mean as much if only their left hands were bound. Regardless of why, he now had two knots to hang in his bedroom.

Although, I guess Rylie could take one as a memento of this week, if we end up going through with the annulment, Liam thought as he took a seat on the sofa in his grandparents' basement and fiddled with the ends of the cords in his and Rylie's second knot. *If she does, I wonder if she'll hang it over her bed. Or will she stuff it in a box somewhere so she won't have to explain it to the next man in her life?*

Just the thought of her moving on with someone else caused a flare of jealousy inside Liam. He found himself gripping the ends of the cords in his fists, pulling them until the knot was as tight as possible. *I guess that's symbolic of how bad I want to stay tied to her. Too bad it's not just up to me.*

He might not have really felt married to her before, since he didn't remember either of them officially saying "I do" to one another, but he felt married to her now, thanks to those handfastings. While they hadn't technically said vows to one another, either the night before or that morning, the way Granda had specifically asked them if they both willingly consented to the handfasting made Liam feel like their "yeses" were somewhat like declaring that they wanted to stay married. Considering each of the handfastings felt like another wedding with Rylie, Liam was even less inclined to want to end their marriage now than ever before.

I wonder if those feelings will just keep getting stronger if we do the convalidation ceremony my family wants in the Church and the vow renewal that Rick okayed for in the middle of the ring on our anniversary? And if those ceremonies keep making me feel more married to her, will she also feel more married to me afterwards, too? If so, then maybe we should plan more than just a couple of them, so neither one of us will want to go through with the annulment.

The more time he spent watching her interacting with his family, the more he knew she was the only woman he would ever love. He wanted nothing more than to figure out how to work everything out for him and Rylie to make their marriage real in every way, for them to not just stay married, but also to live happily in love for the rest of their lives.

He didn't just want her in his bed every night, though he did want that desperately. He also wanted to spend all his days with her and their family, enjoying their favorite hobbies and sharing jokes and secrets along with their love. He wanted to raise kids with her, filling all four of their current guest rooms with cribs that converted into big kids' beds, along with toys, fairytale books, sporting goods, and most importantly, the laughter of their children. And he didn't care if they were able to have babies naturally, or with medical intervention, or if they had to adopt to expand their family. He wanted as big of a family as she was willing to raise with him, even if that meant buying a bigger house to have enough bedrooms for all of them.

Unfortunately, he still didn't know how to go about making that ideal future happen for them. Yeah, he was financially well off enough that he could easily afford to continue traveling with her after he had to stop wrestling without having to worry about money being an issue. And he was willing to suck up his pride to do so if it was the only way they could be together while she finished out her career. But even if it wouldn't drive him crazy to keep traveling with the GWA after his aches and pains got to be too much for him to give an acceptable performance in the ring and he had to just watch from the sidelines to keep from embarrassing himself, he couldn't be her man if she wasn't able to forgive him for being a scared, stupid idiot when they were first married.

If he could go back and have a do-over, there were so many things he'd do differently now. First of all, he wouldn't have fought his attraction to Rylie from the first moment they met. While he would have still started their relationship by being her friend first, he wouldn't have friend-zoned them from the get-go. He would have made it clear his flirty behavior wasn't just the way he acted with all his female friends, so she would have known he wanted more with her.

Second of all, he would have pulled back from acting as Jen's buffer at all the wedding events in Heart's Destiny over the summer. While he would always consider Jen and the rest of the Burlesons his friends, he would have made it clear to the Burleson matchmakers that his heart was taken by Rylie as soon as they got to town back in May for James and Randi's wedding festivities, even if he hadn't convinced Rylie to be his girlfriend in the first two-and-a-half months she'd worked with the GWA.

And finally, when she first found their certificate of marriage and brought it to the arena to reveal their marital status, he would have claimed her with a not-safe-for-work kiss, instead of spouting off about getting an annulment, like an utter and total moron. Of course, she might have slapped him for being inappropriate in front of their boss and coworkers, instead of just verbally sparring with him, but at least she'd have known his real feelings about being married to her. And if he'd just done the first two things correctly instead of being a gobshite, then they might have already been a couple, so she might not have been too upset about the epic kiss he should have planted on her.

She wasn't exactly pissed about the one last night, he thought, remembering the way he'd given into his baser instincts momentarily after the first handfasting, and especially how she'd passionately returned the kiss. *But she also didn't appear mad about the make-out session in the O'Donnells' wine cellar while we were still at the party with other people around. It wasn't until we got home that she hid in her room to keep from having to talk to me about it.*

Come to think of it, she kinda did the same thing last night. Yeah, it was late when we got home, and she did say a little more on the drive than she did Monday night, even telling me a polite "goodnight" before going up to bed, but she still didn't act like she wanted to repeat the experience anytime soon. Guess that means it's a good thing I kept the kiss at the end of this handfasting chaste instead of kissing her like I really want to.

"Hey, why aren't you singing with the rest of us?" Quinn asked as he took a seat beside Liam on the opposite side of the room from where Granda played his Uilleann pipes, Da played the fiddle, Uncle Callen played a guitar, Uncle Flynn played a flute, and Uncle Owen played a Bodhrán drum, while the youngest generation of Connerys sang Christmas carols. The only instrument not being played was Granny's harp because she was upstairs with Rylie, his ma, and his aunts preparing all the food they'd eat for lunch and dinner later.

"Just taking a moment to let you guys get warmed up before I join in and make it obvious how off key you are," Liam joked, grinning mischievously at his brother.

"Oh, like you aren't the worst singer among us," Quinn scoffed, shaking his head. "What was it Sister Francis said about your singing when we were in school? Something about not being able to carry a tune in a bucket?"

"That I couldn't carry a tune in a bucket because my bucket didn't have a bottom," Liam chuckled, dropping his voice down to the deepest bass tone he could. "But I think she was referring to how I was the only eighth grader she ever taught who could sing like Barry White."

"Yeah, I doubt that." Quinn barked out a laugh. "You're more like White Barry singing nasally parodies of Barry White songs."

"Feck, Quinn, now you've got me picturing Barry and Ashleen O'Donnell providing the entertainment at one of their parties by acting out that Claymation video of Barry White and Tina Turner from when we were kids," Liam chuckled.

"How'd you go from me saying you'd be White Barry to thinking of the O'Donnells acting out a video I barely remember?" Quinn tilted his head and furrowed his brow, obviously confused by how Liam's mind worked.

"You said White Barry, and he's the only white guy named Barry that I know," Liam shrugged. "And that video is the only one I remember from Barry White because Wallace and Gromit were in it. Since you pointed them out after watching them on Nickelodeon, I'm surprised you don't remember it."

"Yeah, that's all I remember of it," Quinn huffed, shaking his head. "That and how their limos seemed like traveling houses on the inside."

"Oh, yeah, and we decided if we ever got rich enough to buy a limo, we'd make sure it didn't have a bathtub in it 'cause we didn't want to risk getting in a wreck while we were naked and taking a bath." Liam had to laugh at his twelve-year-old self thinking so rationally.

"I know you haven't bought a limo, but have you stuck to that plan when you've ridden in them?" Quinn questioned, smirking.

"I can honestly say I haven't ridden in a limo with a bathtub in it." Liam raised his right hand as if he was swearing an oath. "And the one I've ridden in that had a hot tub in it, I stayed fully clothed and seated as far away from it as possible."

"Seriously? You rode in a limo with a hot tub in it?" Quinn sighed and bowed his head. "I'm so disappointed that you didn't boycott it for safety reasons."

"Sorry, Bro, it was the only one available for D and I to use at the fan expo and *No Remorse* show a couple years ago because the others were all booked for proms in between when we needed one to make our entrances." Liam remembered back to when he and Dion first started teaming up. He'd toned down his Liam the Red gimmick years earlier, turning into the more every day Irishman simply known as Red. But when he teamed with Dark Chocolate, he dropped all his green shamrock covered ring gear and started wearing tuxedo style wrestling gear to match Dion's ladies' man gimmick. They rode everywhere in limos for the first six months or so, often hiring models to join them in the limos for pay-per-view entrances to sell the gimmick. "But I did veto having some of the models, who accompanied us to the ring, ride in the hot tub and do vignettes in their bikinis, begging us to join them instead of getting out to wrestle."

"Don't let Finn hear you say that." Quinn waved his hand in the universal signal to "tone it down," shushing Liam. "He'll wanna quit the force and have you train him to wrestle, so he can have a shot at enjoying that perk of your job."

"You say that as if he didn't mention it back then," Liam scoffed. "Besides, hiring models for some of our shows wasn't really a perk. They were only there for the career exposure and didn't really give any of us the time of day. In fact, the cattiness of some of the models was why Rick nixed their participation in our gimmick, and without all those women hanging around, we didn't need the limos anymore."

Considering some of the comments he'd overheard from a few of the stick-thin models about the athletic physiques of the women wrestlers, Liam was glad Rick had pulled the plug on that aspect of his gimmick long before Rylie joined the roster. He understood that the physical requirements of modeling and wrestling were vastly different, and he could appreciate the aesthetics of both body types. But unfortunately, not everyone could comprehend the fact that their ideal wasn't the universal epitome of beautiful. And he never wanted Rylie to think her body was anything but perfect. He loved her curves and knew she couldn't perform in the ring nearly as well if she lost muscle in an attempt to trim down to the size of a runway model, so he didn't care in the slightest that she'd never fit in the size zero clothes those models had to wear.

As she walked into the room along with the rest of the Connery women to join in the caroling before opening presents, Liam's eyes were drawn to her curves. He vaguely registered that Quinn was still talking to him, but with his focus pinpointed on Rylie, his brother suddenly started to sound like the adults on a *Peanuts* cartoon. "Wah, wha-wah, wha, wah, wah, wah…"

When he saw Finn throw his arm around her shoulders and Devin point at the mistletoe they'd hung in several places around the room, Liam stood and practically ran across the room to get to her before either of their lips touched hers. "Get your lips away from my wife," he warned, even though they were standing a good three feet away from the nearest sprig of mistletoe attached to the ceiling.

"Whoa, Li." Rylie stepped away from Finn, whose arm dropped to his side. "They were just asking me if I played any instruments or if

I'd rather just sing to join in the caroling. There's no need for you to brandish that knot like a weapon."

Liam looked down at his hands and realized he was indeed holding the ends of the cords like he was about to wrap it around his brother's neck and choke him out. "No, not as a weapon," Liam chuckled, covering for almost letting out the jealous beast inside him by flipping the knot over Rylie's head to rest at the small of her back, looping the cords around her waist, and loosely tying the ends together to make her a decorative belt at the approximate location her waistband would be if she were wearing pants or a skirt instead of a red sheath dress. "I just thought you might want to accessorize this dress while keeping track of our knot, so it doesn't get left behind when we go home later."

"Apparently, big brother has turned into a fashionista since he was home last," Finn quipped, chuckling as the rest of the family started singing the next song.

Ignoring Finn, Rylie wrapped her arm around Liam's waist, pulling him over to join in as they sang *Away in a Manger*. Liam happily wrapped his arm around her shoulders and sang along, memorizing these moments when they really felt like a couple as they harmonized with each other, even if not everyone in the family was on key. Not that Liam would ever openly admit that he was the one throwing everyone off.

After a couple more songs, Granda waved him over to take the Uilleann pipes, instructing him to, "Show ahff a lettle fahr yooehr gurl."

Feck, I hope I'm not too rusty, Liam thought, taking the seat his granda had vacated, strapping the bellows around his waist, pushing up his Henley sleeves before strapping his right elbow to the bellows, and arranging the bag under his right arm and the cantor and pipes on his lap, as his da and uncles discussed what song to play next. It had been quite a while since he'd last played *The Soldier's Song*, which was the national anthem of Ireland, for his ring entrance as Liam the Red, and much longer since he'd learned to play the pipes from his granda as a kid, but he thought he could still remember how to play a carol or two. Instead of interrupting the discussion about what to play, however, he just started playing what he remembered, trying to see what all came back to him.

Surprisingly, his version of **Silent Night** was recognizable enough that his granny started playing along with him. When Granny started playing her harp, her sons quit debating which of them got to choose the next song and picked up their instruments once more. Soon, the rest of the family joined in singing, with Rylie resting her palms on his shoulders as she stood behind him.

Loving the feel of her hands on him, especially when she started rubbing his shoulders, Liam had to fight his body's natural reaction to her. *Feck, I hope I remember how to play enough songs that I can get my dick to go down before I have to move the pipes currently hiding my inappropriate erection.*

Luckily, all he had to do was look up at his family to gain control of his body once more, since he needed sheet music to be able to play more than a couple of songs. Once they'd played and sang those, Liam turned the pipes back over to Granda, who decided it was time to put the instruments away so they could open gifts.

"I didn't know you could really play the Irish bagpipes," Rylie gushed as they all walked upstairs to the living room, where the Christmas tree was set up and all the presents were waiting to be opened. "I remember when you first started with the GWA and carried them to the ring, and I first thought it was cool that you played your own ring entrance music. But my dad pointed out that they can't be played while walking, so your music came from the speakers in the arena like everyone else's and not the bagpipes you carried. And he convinced me you were just being obnoxious by carrying them because you were a bad guy who probably couldn't even play them."

"Yeah, we actually recorded me playing the Uilleann pipes for my ring entrance before my first GWA TV appearance, instead of using generic ring entrance music like most people who are new to the roster. I actually pitched the idea on the tape I hand delivered to the corporate office while pushing to get a try-out match. But carrying them to the ring was Rick's dad, Richard's idea," Liam chuckled, remembering back to his first year in the GWA fifteen years ago. "He wanted me to use them as a weapon against my opponents when the ref's back was turned, and thought nobody would notice that they can't be played while walking. Of course, he also bought a set of Scottish bagpipes at first because he didn't know there was a difference."

"He's also the one who came up with your wrestling name of Liam the Red, isn't he?" Uncle Owen questioned, walking behind them up the stairs.

"Yes, he was," Liam nodded, turning his head slightly to look over his shoulder at his uncle.

"Okay, you have to explain the Liam the Red gimmick to me," Rylie interjected, looking up at him curiously. "Since I was only ten when I first saw you on TV, I didn't understand why you were named after a Viking instead of an Irishman. And even looking you up online didn't help Dad explain it to me."

Feck, did she seriously just say she was only ten when she first saw me on TV? I mean, technically, I already knew she was only ten when I joined the GWA roster at twenty, but hearing her describe her childhood memory of seeing my GWA debut really makes me feel like a perv for all the dirty things I wanna do with her.

"Because when I did a little research about Erik the Red, I found out the Vikings intermingled with the Irish quite often, even having a Viking settlement in Dublin over a hundred years before Erik the Red was born. So Erik might have been born in Norway, but it's possible his ancestors could have been Irish, which would explain the red hair he was so well known for that his last name was basically replaced by the Red moniker." Liam banished his mental images of her as a ten-year-old girl watching him wrestle, as he explained his original ring name to his wife for the first time. "And even if he wasn't at least part Irish, there are documented accounts of Irish explorers who went on similar voyages both before and after Erik the Red, including mentions of Irish monks already having settlements in some of the places he visited in the sagas written about him and the other Vikings. So, when I agreed to my first gimmick with the GWA, I figured my wrestling character could be a modern version of those Irish explorers, since I had the red hair to pull it off."

That's better, he told himself. *Just think of her as the grown woman she is now. The grown woman I married. I'm not a perv for lusting after my wife.*

"Okay, now that makes sense," Rylie grinned up at him.

"And it was way less offensive than his idea to have me dress like a leprechaun to try and convince a team of little people that I was one of them to steal their pot of gold."

"Is that why you have that green suit you wore on Halloween?" Rylie laughed as they walked into the living room.

"Did he really wear the leprechaun suit on Halloween?" Finn asked, sidling up on the opposite side of Rylie from Liam. "And you weren't too embarrassed to be seen with him?"

"Of course not," Rylie replied, sidestepping closer to Liam in an obvious attempt to keep from ending up under the mistletoe with Finn. "Although I'm sure we confused quite a few people that night, since a giant leprechaun and a Black Princess Leia didn't really go together for a couple's costume."

"Yeah, as soon as I saw you that night, I realized that I should have asked you to wear your gold bodysuit to be the treasure I was trying to hoard." Liam slipped his arm around Rylie's shoulders, deciding to take advantage of the mistletoe Finn and Devin had hung up all around the house to make it clear to his brother and cousins that Rylie was all his, and change the subject before anyone asked why they hadn't planned a real couple's costume like all their friends had for Halloween. "Mo Stór, I believe we're supposed to kiss since we're standing under the mistletoe."

"Oh, yes, I suppose we should follow all kissing traditions," Rylie grinned up at him, sliding her arms around his waist and pushing up on her tiptoes.

"Did he just call her his treasure in Irish?" Uncle Flynn questioned.

"O' cooehrse, we've been tellin' 'im fahr days 'ow moehch de ladies lahve de accent." Granda Neilan repeated the same advice his da had given him over the phone before he and Rylie came home for the holidays, and that had been repeated a couple of times in the pub the day before.

Liam blocked out the rest of his family's conversation as he eagerly dipped his head to meet her lips with his, wrapping her in his arms as he turned up the heat once more. *Maybe if I keep her slightly off kilter with random passionate kisses, she might forget why she ended our friends-with-benefits arrangement, so we can use our attraction to one another to start building our relationship to where we can be much more than just friends.*

Whether it would work or not was still anyone's guess. But if the way she kissed him back was any indication, Liam thought he might have a decent chance of winning Rylie's love in the long run.

"Technically, I'm under the mistletoe too, so shouldn't I get a turn kissing Rylie now?" Finn tried to interrupt their kiss.

Instead of responding to his annoying youngest brother, Liam continued to kiss his wife, lifting his hand to facepalm Finn and push him away. *No way, little brother. Rylie is all mine.*

~~~

As Rylie helped Cathleen, Breena, and Liam's Connery aunts carry all the food they'd prepared that morning to the tables set up in the basement for Christmas dinner that afternoon, she couldn't figure out why his brothers and cousins were all acting so flirtatious with her. Until the night before, they'd all been warm and welcoming, but none of his family members had made her feel like they might have a romantic interest in her. But then at dinner the night before and as soon as they got to Neilan and Breena's house that morning, a couple of his brothers and several of his cousins had started winking and throwing their arms around her shoulders, trying to steer her under the mistletoe as if they meant to kiss her, especially Liam's brother Finn and cousin Devin. The only time they seemed to back off was when she and Liam were actively participating in the handfasting ceremonies his family members insisted they had to do at both Christmas meals and when Liam stepped up to kiss her under the mistletoe before they could. She didn't know what had happened to change their treatment of her, but it was getting to the point that she was starting to feel uncomfortable.

I wonder if this has anything to do with me talking to Cathleen yesterday about Liam kissing Jen? Like maybe after she talked to Brian, he let it slip to the rest of their sons, who now think we have some kind of open marriage where it's okay for us to be with other people?

No, that can't be it. Even if that's what they thought about mine and Liam's marriage, they wouldn't act on it in front of the whole family, especially their devout Catholic grandparents.

But maybe they're all being so flirty with me last night and this morning to give Liam a taste of his own medicine, so he feels as jealous and hurt as I did after hearing about him and Jen? If that's
~~~

the case, then I suppose it's kinda sweet that they're taking my side instead of Liam's. But I really wish I knew how to discreetly tell them that instead of getting revenge and making him question my fidelity, I'd rather focus on convincing him that it's safe to trust me with his heart, so he won't ever want to be with someone else to get over me again. Although, I am really enjoying all the kisses I've gotten from him since they started their crazy flirtatious act.

Showing Liam he could trust her with his heart was the advice Cathleen had given her the day before. Well, after she came back from telling Brian to reprimand their oldest son for being an "eejit," which Rylie understood to be the Irish version of "idiot." While Liam's parents, aunts, and uncles all sounded more American than Irish, they all had a bit of a lilt that slipped out at times. Rylie had especially noticed it when they were excited during the football game on Sunday and whenever they used Irish terms in conversation. But as far as she could tell, Liam was the only younger member of the family who intentionally adopted an Irish accent instead of sounding like an average New Yorker all the time.

I know he intentionally changes his accent for his GWA character, but I wonder if the Irish that comes out during sex is intentional or not? And when he's called me "moh graw" and "moh store" the last couple of days, does he realize that he only changes his accent on those words? And were those accent usages what Neilan was talking about right before we opened gifts earlier?

While Liam usually reserved his Irish brogue for when he was maintaining kayfabe as Red, or now as Liam Red since they announced their marriage as part of their current GWA angle, Rylie was surprised to hear him adopt it as everyone took a seat around the grouping of tables that filled the eldest Connerys' basement. *Or maybe he's using it now because of what Neilan said earlier?*

"Can I 'ave yooehr attention please? I know we've already ahpened presents dis mahrnin', boeht I 'ave one mahre ta give each o' you. Startin' wit Granda and Granny." After grabbing Rylie's hand and pulling her along beside him, Liam walked over to his grandparents and handed them the first of the envelopes she knew contained the **No Remorse** passes, along with the flight and hotel information for the trip to Ireland Liam planned for his family.

As Neilan pulled his reading glasses from his pocket and put them on, Breena opened the envelope. She pulled out the papers first, leaving the laminated passes in the envelope, so none of the family could see them to guess what the present included. Then Neilan and Breena scooted closer together so they could each hold an edge and read the paper together.

"What's dis flight and 'ahtel infahrmation all abooeht?" Neilan looked up at his grandson with a confused expression.

"Dat's de plane I chartered ta take de whahle family to Doehblin in April, and de 'ahtel reservation I've already booked fahr you to be able to visit yooehr brahthers and deir families, and go ta Easter Mass in de choehrch where ye and Granny were married," Liam explained, pulling the rest of the envelopes out from where he'd stashed them in a cupboard on the side of the room and splitting the stack with Rylie so they could pass them out to the rest of the family. Once everyone, or every couple, had an envelope, Liam dropped the accent to finish explaining as he pulled out a chair for Rylie to sit down between his mom and the empty chair she assumed was his. "Since it's a chartered flight, I scheduled it to leave in the wee hours of the morning on Good Friday, so we don't have to miss the evening Mass of the Lord's Supper by taking the GWA plane. There's also passes for the *No Remorse* show and fan expo the GWA is doing the weekend of Easter in Dublin for everyone in the family. I just need you to get me a list of the relatives already in Ireland who want to come to those, so I can get their passes printed for us to deliver when we get there."

"You're taking all of us to Dublin?" Brian looked up at Liam in surprise as Cathleen opened their envelope.

"Everyone who's able to get off work and go," Liam replied to his dad as he took his seat. "That's why I decided to give everyone their passes and stuff now, so everyone who needs to has time to put in for vacation at work."

"Oh, man, Shay and Keenan are gonna be so jealous that we get to check out all the Irish lasses and GWA ladies, and they don't," Finn gloated, elbowing his cousin Kegan.

"Sorry to burst your bubble, little brother," Liam smirked at Finn as he wrapped his arm around Rylie's shoulders possessively. "But all the GWA ladies are happily married, so checking them out is liable to get you in a heap of trouble."

"Well, all the current GWA ladies are happily married," Rylie corrected her husband, eyeing him warily as she tried to decide if he realized she was including herself in that statement. She also wondered if his obvious possessive words and actions meant he was actually staking his claim on her, or just baiting his brother. "But we have Venus and Juno starting with the company in January, and Rick is always having tryouts for more talent he can add to the roster, so we may have a few more women wrestlers by April."

"But are you sure Venus and Juno are single?" Liam arched an eyebrow at Rylie, smirking knowingly. "Or won't be scooped up by a couple of the single guys on the roster by the time *No Remorse* rolls around?"

Is he implying that he knows a couple of the guys are already interested in Venus and Juno? Or is he hinting that he might be interested in one of them and plans to make his move once we annul our marriage?

"Well, no, I didn't ask them about their personal lives when they came for their try-out match," Rylie admitted with a shrug before making sure her next words were pointedly directed at the overly flirtatious younger men in the Connery family. And also hoping her husband got the hint about how she really felt. "So, I can't say for sure that they'll be available for your brothers and cousins to flirt with then. But they're a potential option since the *rest of us* are completely *off the market*."

"Okay, I'll concede that point," Liam smiled before leaning over to brush his lips over her temple, making her wonder if he understood her unspoken message. Then he redirected his next words back at his youngest brother. "But even if there are new additions to the women's division of the GWA for you to flirt with, Shay and Keenan aren't going to be jealous of you, since I gave Aunt Chevonne, Aunt Tara, and Aunt Shannon all the passes for the McCarthy and Sullivan side of the family last night as they were leaving. They're just waiting for me to video call them after we eat, so they can pass out the envelopes 'cause I didn't want to ruin the surprise for Granda and Granny by giving half the family their passes last night."

"Yeah, you probably should have made those calls right before handing these out," Aiden chuckled, waving his envelope at Liam before stuffing it in his front shirt pocket. "'Cause you know Finn's probably already texted the good news to rub it in their faces."

"Well, den he'll look like an eejit when dey get deirs," Granny interjected, looking first at Aiden and Finn on the other side of the table before redirecting her gaze at Liam and Rylie. "Dank ye, Liam and Rylie. I can't wait ta show ye bot where we grew oehp. Now, everybahdy 'oehsh so we can say grace and eat befahre ooehr food gets cahld."

"Yes, ma'am," all the men at the table chorused, tickling Rylie's funny bone with how all those six-foot-plus tall men cowered to their petite grandmother.

Like I'm any better, since I didn't correct her in thanking me for the trip when it was one-hundred percent Liam planning and setting it all up.

While she didn't outwardly laugh, she did smile as Granda Neilan said a prayer to bless their food before they all started digging into the various dishes on the table, passing everything around until all their plates were full.

The conversation soon turned back to the trip, with questions about everything from the size of the plane to the inclusion of rental cars. Liam had to explain that he hadn't included rental cars, since only Granda and Granny were likely to be comfortable driving on the left side of the road. That led to a story about how long it took his grandparents to adapt to driving on the right side of the road when they first moved to the States. One story about their early years in America rolled into another tale of their childhoods in Ireland, which rolled into two, then three, and just kept going until they'd all finished eating.

Rylie loved hearing all about Liam's family history, but it did make her wish she knew more about her own. Oh, she knew about how her parents' families had disowned each of them when they chose an interracial marriage. And thanks to her mom's journals, she'd read a little about her mom's parents, as well as a firsthand account of how her parents met and fell in love, as she was going through their things after they passed away. But other than originally being from Atlanta, and that her paternal grandfather had a penchant for phallic names for his sons, she knew nothing about her dad's family.

Maybe I should ask Aiken and Crockett what service they're using for the DNA tests they mentioned on Thanksgiving? Even if I wait until after I see what kind of results they get with theirs before deciding, that might be a way to get some more family history without having to try to contact anyone that had disowned Mom and Dad.

She quit thinking about that possibility as soon as it was time to clear the table and clean up after the meal. Since the older generations of Connerys had prepared the meal, it was up to the younger generation to clean up. So, even though she'd helped Breena, Cathleen, and Liam's aunts some earlier, Rylie joined Liam, his brothers, and cousins with clearing the table, carrying everything back upstairs, and washing the dishes. After they each carried their own place settings up to the kitchen, the guys all made several more trips while Rylie ran a sink full of water to hand wash the dishes, since Neilan and Breena's house was built before dishwashers were standard.

"Alright, Rylie, since you won't let me kiss you under the mistletoe, tell me what you know about Venus and Juno," Finn demanded as he placed a stack of plates beside the sink before moving over to her other side to rinse what she'd started washing.

"Before I do that, maybe you should tell me why you keep flirting with me," Rylie countered, refusing to tell him anything about her future coworkers until he explained himself. Not that she knew much about them to tell him.

"Well, technically, it started out as an attempt to show you that a kiss isn't cheating, so you'd forgive Liam for letting his lips wander a little too much before he knew you were married," Finn admitted sheepishly as he rinsed the clean plate she handed him before putting it in the dish drainer. He looked to make sure the other guys weren't about to walk into the room with them before leaning close to her ear and whispering, "But then, when he vetoed that idea, I remembered how much fun it is to push his buttons."

"Quit flirting with my wife, baby brother," Liam bellowed as he placed two tall stacks of glasses next to the plates Finn had brought up. He then stepped around Rylie to push Finn over and take over rinsing the dishes she washed. "'Cause I wasn't just implying my fellow wrestlers would kick your arse for putting the moves on their women. I was trying to make it clear that I'd be the first to mop the floor with you without outright threatening you at Granny's table."

"You know I didn't mean anything by it, Bro," Finn held his hands up in surrender, just as Quinn walked in and tossed a hand towel at his chest. Surprisingly, he had excellent reflexes and caught it easily to start drying the dishes in the drainer. "I was just making sure you appreciate how lucky you are to have such a beautiful wife, so you'd actually step up and be a good husband instead of continuing with that nonsense about getting an annulment. 'Cause you know if you don't pull your head outta your ass and actually go through with that, you'll be ready to kick your own ass for being stupid enough to step aside so some other lucky guy can snatch her up."

"I don't even wanna think about how hard it'll be to kick his own ass while his head is stuffed in it," their cousin Grady chuckled as he delivered more dishes.

"Finn does have a point there, Li," Quinn added before anyone could reply to Grady, joining the assembly line by putting away the dish Finn just dried. "I might not agree with his methods to get you to pull your head outta your ass, but I do agree it's a lesson you need to learn ASAP."

"I'm not the only one who has a say in things, ya know," Liam protested, shaking his head at his brothers and looking more than a little irritated. "And what happens between me and Rylie needs to stay between me and Rylie, not be fodder for Finn's antics or up for discussion with the rest of the family."

"Then you shouldn't have told us all about what a dumbass you were at the pub yesterday," Devin interjected as he and the rest of the brothers and cousins unloaded the empty serving dishes and utensils onto the counter beside the sink, and stacked plastic containers of leftovers in the refrigerator.

He did what?! It took all Rylie had in her to remain calm and not glare at Liam for broadcasting their business when she wasn't around to tell her side of the story.

"I was trying to get some advice from Da and Granda," Liam huffed. "And you guys shouldn't have been eavesdropping on our private conversation."

"Then you should have talked to them before coming to the pub," Rory pointed out. "'Cause from what I could tell when you started publicly talking about why Ma thought you were a cheater, you needed all the help you could get to set the record straight, so I sent out the bat signal to get everyone I could think of who didn't have to work to come help you out."

Oh. Em. Gee! My talking to Cathleen yesterday really was what set all this off? Rylie felt extremely guilty for being the one to set in motion all the events of the last couple of days. She especially felt uncomfortable that his whole family now knew about the most embarrassing issue they needed to deal with if they ever had a chance of being a real couple.

But I don't understand why Liam and Brian didn't discuss what I said to Cathleen while they were still downstairs setting up the tables for last night's dinner. Or even while they were driving between houses to drop off all the presents. If Liam had just talked to his dad, like I just talked to his mom, then none of these guys would know anything. And none of them would have thought it was a good idea to flirt with me for the last twenty-four hours.

She stood there quietly, almost in a state of shock, as she continued to wash the dishes while tuning out the guys' conversation going on around her. At least, she did until Liam seemed to realize how uncomfortable she was and insisted the guys all stop talking or change the subject.

"Stop! We don't need your opinions 'cause they aren't even worth two cents," Liam bellowed, wrapping his arm around her shoulders. "Especially when all you're doing by arguing your points is making my wife uncomfortable. So, either shut up or talk about something else."

"Notice he called her *his wife*," Finn pointed out with a smirk.

"That's right, I called her my wife, and I'm her husband," Liam pointed out, glaring at his youngest brother. "That's what we are to one another for as long as it works for us. And our marriage is strictly between us and none of anyone else's business. So, butt out and give us the space and time we need to decide on our future plans together."

"How about you two take off early, so you can go discuss all this privately?" Callen Junior, who they all called CJ, suggested. "And we'll finish up washing and rinsing the dishes."

"We'll gladly step aside and let you finish here," Liam replied for the both of them, taking the current dish she was washing from her hands, placing it back in the sink, and then taking her hands in his to rinse the soap off. He then swiped a towel from Finn to dry both their hands before pulling her aside for two of his cousins to take their places at the sink. "But you know Granda and Granny won't let us leave until after football and another round of food."

"True, but we can change the subject to the new women wrestlers Rylie mentioned earlier while you're waiting to rejoin the 'rents downstairs, so they don't send you back up here to help with the cleanup," Cory suggested in response to Liam's statement.

While Rylie still had no clue how things would go when she and Liam finally sat down to really talk about their marriage and what they each wanted for the future, she was happy to share what little she knew about her future coworkers. "Venus and Juno wrestle as a tag team, using a Roman Goddesses gimmick. They tried out for the GWA roster back in October when we were in Tupelo, Mississippi, but they had to finish out their contract with the smaller organization they worked for before they could officially sign on with the GWA. So that's why they aren't starting until we go back after this break."

"And you really don't know if they're single or not?" Sloan questioned.

"No, I don't," Rylie replied, shaking her head. "But I didn't see either of them wearing rings, so I think they are. Or at least, they don't appear to be married, But then again, none of us who got married in Vegas wore rings for the first three months we were married, and I still keep putting mine on my right hand instead of my left 'cause I'm not used to them signifying that I'm married. So, them not wearing rings doesn't necessarily mean anything."

No, no, no! I didn't mean to draw attention to the fact that I'm wearing Mom's rings while Liam is wearing one he bought over our Thanksgiving break to fool the people of Heart's Destiny into believing we're happily married.

Before any of them could ask about her slip-up with mentioning their rings, Liam stepped in and changed the subject once more. "Actually, Rylie and I should probably go conference with our Sullivan and McCarthy aunts while you guys are finishing the dishes, so they can hand out the rest of our gifts before their celebrations with the McCarthys, O'Shays, and Murphys start to break up."

He ushered her out of the kitchen and into the empty living room, pulling her down beside him on the sofa before placing the video call to conference in his three aunts. She wasn't sure why he felt the need to have her at his side for this reveal the way he had downstairs earlier, since she couldn't actively help pass out the envelopes this time, unless it was just to keep his brothers and cousins from questioning her about their rings. Assuming that was the reason, she plastered on a smile to match the dolls on display on the other side of the room and leaned into his side when Liam put his arm around her shoulders and pulled her into the frame on his phone screen, so his Sullivan and McCarthy family could see both of them as they received their passes and travel itineraries.

I guess I'll just keep up the pretense of the happy wife for now. And hopefully, when we finally get to sit down alone and discuss all this, we'll figure out how to make that pretense into our reality.

<div align="center">~~~</div>

After the events of the last couple of days, and especially the discussion earlier that day with his brothers and cousins in the kitchen, when she found out all about what had been discussed at the pub the day before, Liam knew he couldn't stall any longer and had to have the serious talk with Rylie that they should have finished on Sunday. *Feck Sunday! We shoulda had this talk last month, when I first told her about being stupid that first weekend of our Labor Day break. Or better yet, we shoulda had it at the beginning of October, when we first found out we'd gotten married. But I guess it's better late than never.*

He knew as the older of the two of them, it was his responsibility to be more mature and face their issues head on, instead of continuing to try sticking his head in the sand like an ostrich trying to hide from their problems. But for some reason, he'd been struggling with manning up and doing what they needed. *I guess she was right when she said our age difference shouldn't be an issue since I don't act a day older than her. Hell, with the way I've been delaying this conversation to keep from having to follow through with ending our marriage, I'm acting more like I'm ten years younger than her instead of ten years older.*

I'm like a little kid who's standing in a store holding the prize toy I want and throwing a fit, refusing to let it go or leave the store without it. Only instead of being vocal about wanting to keep Rylie as my wife, I've been lying to myself and everyone else about wanting an

160

annulment while secretly dragging my feet on getting it done. Which I guess is kinda like that kid I was just thinking of, only instead of throwing a fit for the toy, he secretly shoplifts it and lies to his parents about how he got it when they find it later.

Feck, that's exactly what I've done. I've shoplifted Rylie and am lying to myself and everyone I know about doing it. And putting off having a serious conversation with her is just like a little kid who refuses to talk in an attempt to keep from getting in trouble for doing something stupid.

Liam shook off his inane thoughts as he carried in a stack of the presents they'd received that morning, setting them on the coffee table in the living room to sort before carrying them up to their rooms, just as they'd done the night before after the Christmas Eve gift exchange with half his family. While they didn't have nearly as much to bring home as they'd had to take to pass out to everyone, it had been a tight fit in the Porsche after both gift exchanges. *I guess it didn't matter that I stuck to earrings and a bracelet for Rylie, knowing she has limited space in her luggage, when it seemed everyone in my family picked huge spa gift baskets for her.*

"I'm going to have to leave at least half this stuff here when we go back on tour," Rylie commented as she placed the stack of gifts she carried on the coffee table beside the one he'd just put down, obviously being on the same wavelength as his thoughts. "And come pick it up when we're in New York again. And even then I might need to get another suitcase to be able to take the majority of it with us once I can take it straight to the GWA plane instead of having to worry about whether or not it's all allowed with the airline regulations and baggage limits."

I wish you'd leave all your extra stuff here, including whatever you have in Atlantic City, Liam thought as he smiled at her, not bothering to point out that they were taking the GWA plane back to San Antonio after the new pods were installed, so she wouldn't think she needed to take everything with her when it was time to go back on tour. "You're welcome to leave as much of your stuff here as you need to. For as long as you want."

"Thanks," Rylie grinned back as she flopped down on the sofa, presumably to start sorting through the stacks of gifts to take hers up to her room like she had the night before.

The guest room she's staying in, Liam mentally corrected himself as he took a seat beside her. *It's not like she's actually moved in and claimed a room of her own. And feck, if she had, then I'd want her to be in the master bedroom with me.*

"So, um, now that we're alone, I want to apologize to you for how I screwed up by talking to your mom yesterday, and inadvertently caused whatever craziness you had to endure from your family at the pub and the stupid flirtation with me that Finn and the other guys started last night." Rylie surprised him by being the one to instigate the serious conversation they needed to have.

"You have nothing to apologize for, Rye. Regardless of whatever you said to Ma, you are not responsible for Finn, Devin, and the others acting the maggot, as Granda would say." Liam hoped using one of his granda's phrases would lighten the mood, while still making his point clear.

"But it is my fault," Rylie disagreed with a heavy sigh. "If I hadn't told your mom about you kissing Jen to explain why we have trust issues when I asked her advice for how to deal with them, then they wouldn't have thought they could help us by showing me that kissing isn't cheating."

"And they were warned not to act on those thoughts yesterday, so the extra flirtation last night and trying to get you under the mistletoe today was all about getting under my skin, not because they thought it would work to get you to forgive me." Liam ran a hand through his hair in frustration. "And that is completely all on them, not you for talking to Ma, or on Ma for telling Da, or on Da for asking me about it at the pub. If anyone else shares even a sliver of responsibility for their actions, it's me for getting so drunk that night that I actually thought kissing Jen was a good idea. I'm sorry for that, by the way. So beyond sorry, and I promise it won't ever happen again."

"You have nothing to be sorry for, Liam. We didn't know we were married then, and didn't even consider each other anything more than friends," Rylie sighed, seeming to blow off his apology. "But I accept your apology. I should also apologize for overreacting when you told me about it."

"You have nothing to apologize for, Mo Ghrá." Liam shook his head, ready to get back to the other discussion so he could finish taking the blame for anything his family did that made her uncomfortable in the last couple of days. "And if I'm being honest, I'm also sorry because Finn and the others' actions are all on me for not paying attention to who all came into the bar while I was asking Da and Granda for advice."

"So, did they at least give you some good advice?" Rylie questioned, tilting her head curiously and causing her curls to bounce lightly as they fell to the right with the movement of her head.

Yeah, to eat your pussy three times a day until you forgive me, Liam thought while resisting the urge to run his hands through her hair while it wasn't braided. He knew she kept her hair in braids to protect it while wrestling, but he really wished she'd leave it natural more often. Even when she twisted and pinned the front back to keep it out of her eyes, he was still drawn to playing with the shoulder length curls in the back, almost aching to feel how they'd twist around his fingers.

"Some," he finally admitted, knowing it wasn't the right time to share the pussy eating recommendation. "Since none of the penance I was given by the three priests I confessed to has alleviated the guilt I feel for those stupid kisses, Da suggested I ask you what I can do as penance so you can forgive me, 'cause neither one of us will feel better about it until I make it up to you."

"That's funny, 'cause your mom had kinda the opposite advice for me," Rylie chuckled ruefully. "Telling me that I need to prove you can trust me with your heart before I'll be able to trust you not to want to be with someone else again."

"You mean, she thinks you need to make it up to me, instead of the other way around?" That made absolutely no sense to Liam. And apparently, Rylie could tell from the expression on his face how her statement confused him.

"Not exactly." Rylie shook her head, causing her curls to bounce adorably once more. Liam was so lost in a fantasy of weaving his fingers through her ebony tresses to hold her head in place as he kissed her that he almost missed her explanation. "More that neither one of us need to do anything as penance, but that we both need to communicate more in a way that's less confusing for how we each feel about things."

She paused and looked deep into his eyes as if studying his soul. "You know it's not the actual kisses that bother me about that whole situation, right?"

"No?" Liam shook his head, surprised that it wasn't his cheating that upset her.

"At that point in time, we didn't know we were married and just thought of each other as friends, so I have no right to be upset by you kissing or even having sex with someone else back then. So, it wasn't the physical act of you kissing Jen that bugged me, even though I didn't realize that when you first told me about it." Rylie sighed and dropped her gaze down to the sofa between them momentarily before looking back up into his eyes and continuing. "It's the fact that you were so upset by being attracted to me that you wanted to try to kill that attraction by sleeping with someone else that bothers me. It feels like you're rejecting our biological reaction to one another and saying I'm not worthy of your affection. And since I thought we were really good friends before we found out we were married, it really hurt to realize I'm good enough to be your friend, but not someone you can love. I wasn't sure if it was my appearance, or the age difference like you claimed, or if we weren't really friends, but I was more like the annoying coworker you just couldn't avoid, so you pretended to be my friend to keep from making things awkward when we have to be around each other all the time. And since I had a crush on you, almost from my very first day with the GWA, it was heartbreaking to not know what you found lacking in me, so I could fix it."

She had a crush on me? I mean, I knew she found me physically attractive, but I thought it was just a sexual chemistry thing, not a full blown crush. Is that good 'cause a crush can turn into love? Or is it bad because she mentioned it in the past tense, like I've already killed whatever budding feelings she had for me? Or is it a totally moot point because she's really talking about a schoolgirl crush from when she was a kid and watched me on TV? Or could a childhood crush like that turn into an adult lust after meeting me fifteen years later? Liam got so caught up in his thoughts about her having a crush on him that it took a moment before the rest of her words registered in his brain.

"There is nothing lacking in you," Liam growled, angry at himself for unintentionally hurting her that way. "You are absolutely perfect,

Mo Ghrá. You're smart, beautiful, talented, friendly, funny, and just an all-around amazing person. My stupidity in trying to quash my feelings for you had absolutely nothing to do with thinking you weren't good enough for me. Feck, it was the exact opposite. You're so vibrant and special that I know you have a fabulous future ahead of you. And I don't want to be the reason that future is derailed because I'm too old and decrepit to keep up with you. So I was trying to preemptively break my own heart to keep from ever dimming the light in your eyes by saddling you with a broken down geezer who'd just hold you back from soaring the way I know you can."

Liam stopped short of declaring his undying love for Rylie, knowing that, even if she was able to forgive him for his previous stupidity, he needed to take the time to earn her love before overwhelming her with his. Plus, he didn't want to blurt it out in the heat of the moment and put her on the spot to reciprocate saying those three all-important words when he didn't know if she really felt them for him.

"But shouldn't I be the one to decide how I want my future to go?" Rylie asked, wringing her hands in her lap as her nostrils flared and her lips pursed in an ominous scowl. "I may be ten years younger than you, but I'm still a grown woman, who doesn't need you or anyone else deciding whether or not I'll *soar,* assuming you mean that with regard to my career. While, yes, Rick and the other bookers have a little bit of a say in that, they can only book title runs for me for as long as *I* decide to keep working in the GWA."

"Agreed." Liam held his hands up in a placating gesture, trying to be understanding of her obvious anger at his apparently poorly worded clarification of his previous thought process. "But at the time, I didn't know about your plan to only wrestle for another five years. So, I was basing my decisions on how long I assumed your career would last, which again was based on what I've seen of others during my time in the business."

"So, once you found out my plans, you were cool with exploring our attraction to one another?" Rylie arched an eyebrow at him, appearing somewhat guarded, instead of taking his answers to her questions at face value. "That's why you went along with the friends-with-benefits arrangement over Thanksgiving?"

"Yes," Liam agreed, even though he knew that was only half the answer. "That and because sharing a bed made it impossible for me to resist you any longer."

"Then why did you keep insisting on the annulment, even when it seemed like we could easily make our marriage real and lasting?" The dejected look of pain in Rylie's topaz eyes as she muttered the question gutted Liam, making him feel like the most despicable human on the planet.

After taking a moment to close his eyes and compose his thoughts, Liam tried to elaborate in a way she'd understand without being hurt any further by his idiotic actions. "Partially because I still feel so guilty for kissing Jen and didn't think you'd ever forgive me when I eventually came clean about how much of a gobshite I was. And partially because I still didn't see a way for us to be together in the time between when I retire in a couple of years and when you retire in five. And honestly, I'm still not sure how we can work that out, even if you forgive me for being an eejit and decide you want us to try staying together. For a moment there, I thought maybe I could take the booker job Dion turned down, so we could still travel together for the two or three years when you're still wrestling and I'm not able to any longer. But then I found out Cooper is retiring and taking that spot, so now I'm back to thinking I'll have to be here to open a gym and keep working as a trainer for the next generation of wrestlers, and maybe do a few more endorsement deals like I've done in the past, so I don't feel like a lazy oaf for not working. And I think us having a long-distance relationship while you finish out your time in the GWA will be torturous."

As much as he'd almost convinced himself that he'd be able to suck up his pride and travel with her while not actually working, he knew it would drive him crazy to not feel productive in some way. So, he'd already reverted from his thoughts that morning to his previous way of thinking. Unless there was some kind of job he could do while traveling with her as she finished out her career, he didn't think they'd be able to make things work for them both to be happy.

"And what if I told you that I'd be willing to retire in two years and work alongside you as a trainer here in New York?" Rylie implored, her facial expression softening with compassion.

"I'd tell you that I'd welcome you as a trainer at my gym," Liam partially conceded. "But only if you have to step away from performing in our dream job for some reason other than just following me." *Like being pregnant with our baby, not because you got hurt,* he mentally clarified, not wanting to think about the possibility of an injury shortening her career, but also not wanting to scare her with talk of having babies sooner than she planned.

"And if I told you wrestling was never my dream job?" Rylie bit her lip, almost like she was afraid of how he'd respond.

"No? Then what is your dream job?" Liam tried desperately to keep his expression blank, not wanting to get his hopes up that they really could work things out to have a future together that didn't include years of being in a long-distance relationship because of her continuing to wrestle after he had to retire from performing in the ring.

"Being a stay-at-home mom," Rylie stated matter-of-factly. "That's why I planned to wrestle for another five years, so I can save up a few years of my million-dollar-plus salary to afford the medical intervention that might be necessary for me to get pregnant and still have enough to live on without having to leave my babies to go to work. But working long enough to be financially independent first is only necessary if I'm doing it as a *single* stay-at-home mom and not blessed with finding true love with a financially secure man, who shares my dreams for a family and doesn't think it's too old-fashioned for him to be the breadwinner in the family while I'm at home with the kids until they're old enough to go to school."

"That's not too old-fashioned." Liam smiled, thinking her dream sounded perfect to him. "That's a couple treating their relationship like a partnership, the way it should be. It doesn't matter which parent works and which one is home with the kids, they're still each contributing to the family. It doesn't matter if they're financially even, or equals when it comes to the distribution of labor, as long as they're working together to meet the needs of their family. And let's be honest, I'd be more than happy to contribute more financially if it means I'm not the one responsible for cooking, which I'm sure you can appreciate after I burnt breakfast the other day."

"True," Rylie chuckled, smiling beatifically. "So, theoretically, I could quit wrestling as soon as March, when my current contract expires, if…"

"If we fall in love and start trying for those babies, instead of filing for an annulment?" Liam blurted before she could finish her thought, unable to take the chance that she might mention the possibility of meeting and falling in love with another man.

"I was gonna say, 'if I get a miracle and don't end up needing medical intervention to get pregnant,' but your suggestion works too," Rylie smirked. "Especially since it's highly unlikely that I could get pregnant the old-fashioned way if we don't get past our issues and start having sex again."

Liam scooted a little closer to Rylie on the sectional, aching to pull her into his arms and start practicing for baby making, even though he still had another month before he'd feel safe forgoing a condom while making love to his wife to try to make a baby for real. After being exposed to Marcus Gardner's blood when the Avington Security team shot and killed Allissa's stalker back in October, Liam didn't want to take a chance that the tests performed by the coroner's office only showed the stalker was disease free because he was still in the incubation period when he could be a carrier but not yet test positive. So, Liam was now waiting out his own ninety-day incubation period from his exposure before completely believing his own negative tests. But since they still had other things to deal with in their marriage, he knew it wasn't the right moment to tell her he wasn't quite ready to start trying to make those babies. *I just have to remember to bring it up when we get closer to having sex again and actually need to decide when we want to have kids. And since I now know she's Catholic, we also have to decide whether we want to keep using condoms or if she agrees with the Church that using them is a sin. Feck! If that's the case, we're gonna hafta abstain for another month.*

"Since the retirement timeline discrepancy is no longer an issue, what else do we need to work on before I can start trying to make you fall for me?" Liam tried to pull off a flirtatious smile to cover for his fear that they would disagree on condom usage and wouldn't be able to make love for another month, even if they worked everything else out and officially decided to stay together before then. But he wasn't sure he nailed the right expression when she rolled her eyes at him.

"We still need to review, pray, and meditate over the scriptures Father O'Malley gave me the other day, so I can move past my hurt feelings and we can both learn to trust one another to be faithful and not unintentionally hurt each other again before we decide whether to stay married or not."

"Okay," Liam agreed with a thoughtful nod as he pulled his phone out of his pocket. He didn't think she sounded as confident about them as she had a moment earlier. But since they probably had a month before they could make love again, he was okay with taking his time to convince her. "Do I need to go get my Bible and rosary first, or can we just look them up online?"

"I tried looking them up online and didn't feel like I really got much out of them without being able to read the rest of the chapter around them," Rylie confided with a shrug. "So maybe it would work best if you get your Bible and rosary."

"Then hold that thought and I'll be right back." Liam stood and rounded the sectional, pausing only long enough to bend over and brush his lips over the top of her head before running up to his room to get the items they needed.

When he got back downstairs, they sat close on the sofa so they could read the scriptures together, starting with the forgiveness passages. When Rylie told him about needing to forgive herself for her anger and rebellious actions after losing her parents, he realized that he also needed to forgive himself for his poor choices the last few months. While she made it clear that she didn't think he'd done anything wrong when he'd kissed Jen to need her to forgive him for, she also told him she forgave him in case that was what he needed to hear before he could forgive himself.

As they sat there holding hands and praying together for all the forgiveness they both needed, Liam felt closer to Rylie than he'd ever felt to any other person, making it clear that their marriage could be so much more than just acting on their physical attraction to one another. *I guess, considering everything I've realized today, my plan to win her over with passion isn't really the best approach. While a fulfilling sex life can eventually be one of the benefits of our marriage, we really need to build a strong foundation on our friendship and shared beliefs first.*

"So, um, I also asked Father O'Malley about whether or not we should be having sex while we're trying to decide if we're staying married or getting the annulment, and he gave me some other scriptures to review about marriage, so we can make that decision together."

"Okay, then we should probably review those next, then." Liam released her hand, so she could find the first of those scriptures in the Bible.

As she read First Corinthians seven, verses three through five aloud, Liam really let the words sink into his brain. "The husband should fulfill his duty toward his wife, and likewise the wife toward her husband. A wife does not have authority over her own body, but rather her husband, and similarly a husband does not have authority over his own body, but rather his wife. Do not deprive each other, except perhaps by mutual consent for a time, to be free for prayer, but then return to one another, so that Satan may not tempt you through your lack of self-control."

"So, that sounds like we're each giving ourselves exclusively to one another, which I think we've both done pretty well since finding out we got married." He would have made it clear he'd only wanted her since the day they met if it hadn't been for those two stupid kisses with Jen. But since they were forgiving and forgetting those, he didn't want to bring them up again.

"Yes, unless masturbating counts against us, since we've both done that solo instead of giving our bodies to each other." Rylie bit her lip nervously.

"But I've only fantasized about you when I've jerked off, so I don't think it's as bad as cheating," Liam pointed out. "And honestly, that's one of the things I disagree with the Catholic Church about. I can see where it could be sinful if it's replacing sex with a spouse or mentally cheating on your spouse by jerking off while thinking of someone else. But if it's to keep from having sex before marriage, or if it's mutual masturbation with your spouse, or while thinking about your spouse when you can't be together, then I don't think it's a sin."

"True," Rylie giggled, smiling beatifically. "And I only fantasized about you when I touched myself, so I haven't mentally cheated. And since you still have my rabbit, I haven't replaced you with a toy either."

"Yeah, I think I'll wait until we're able to use it together before I give that back, just to help keep both of us from having to confess to using it." Liam smirked, wishing they could play with her toy together a lot sooner than he'd started to realize they were going to have to wait.

"You don't think using a toy is a sin as long as we use it together?" Rylie tilted her head curiously.

"No. I don't think anything we do together is a sin."

Rylie's smile widened, making him wonder what kinds of things she wanted them to explore sexually. But they still had a lot of other things to discuss before they could get to the point that they could add sex back into their relationship without it possibly overshadowing the non-physical aspects of their marriage. So, Liam knew he had to steer them back to a more spiritual discussion and quit bringing up sex to keep them on the right track for strengthening their chances of staying married.

"But I guess if we really want to be as faithful to God's teachings as possible, we should probably stop any solo sessions while we're in this time of prayer, too, since masturbating while thinking of each other isn't really abstaining. That is, assuming you agree that we need to take some time to abstain while we're working on everything else, so we can have a strong marriage going forward?" Liam already dreaded the cold showers he'd have to take to keep from jerking off, but if that was what was necessary for him to get to be Rylie's husband for the rest of his life, then he'd happily endure daily ice baths to keep his cock under control.

"I do want us to have a strong marriage," Rylie smiled.

With that decided, they moved on to the other passages about marriage, talking each of them out before they prayed to ask for God's help in applying them to their daily lives. Unsurprisingly, they both agreed with each passage that mentioned how a husband and wife should treat each other with love, grace, and respect, and that a marriage should be a partnership marked by teamwork.

Liam wasn't sure if it was good or bad that Father O'Malley hadn't given her any more scriptures about what was allowed and not allowed sexually between a married couple. On the one hand, he knew they needed to discuss those things and make sure they agreed on what they both wanted in their sexual relationship. But on the other hand, any further discussion about sex with Rylie might be too much for him to handle without having to jerk off as soon as they went to their separate bedrooms for the night. So, ultimately, he decided it was definitely in the best interest of their future together that they saved any further sexual discussions for after they had a strong foundation of friendship and love for their marriage.

It's probably best if we work on the spiritual aspect of our marriage before we tackle the emotional and physical anyway, he decided, hopeful for their potential future together. *And what better day to do that than Christmas Day?*

By the time they walked upstairs to go to bed for the night, he was much more resigned to proving that he wanted more than sex from her, giving him the ability to answer her honestly when she asked, "Are you sure we shouldn't use our physical attraction to strengthen our connection, now that we've prayed about everything?"

"I want to earn your love before we make love again," Liam replied, fingering one of her curls as they reached the fourth floor landing. "When we share our bodies in our marital bed, I want to know that we're solid. That our marriage is going to last for the rest of our lives. I don't want us to jump too fast into having sex, only to fizzle out like a fling from not doing the work on anything but the physical aspect of our relationship. In order for us to have a bond that can't be broken, we have to connect spiritually and emotionally too. And I think we've made some good progress with the spiritual connection tonight, so I want to make sure we're a hundred percent in sync with our faith before we change our focus to what I think will be the easier aspects of marriage."

Rylie smiled and nodded up at him in agreement.

"Besides, we can still kiss and show each other affection without making it sexual. And when we talk to Father O'Malley on Friday, we'll ask him how long our prayer time needs to last, since it wasn't really clear in any of those passages, before we make love to truly consummate our marriage."

"You're right." Rylie nodded again. "And who knows, once we tell him about tonight, he might think we've done all we need to do before working on the other stuff."

"Maybe?" *Hopefully, she'll agree it's not a sin for us to use condoms, so we won't have to wait much past the weekend. But I still want to make sure everything else is right between us first.* Liam bent down and pressed his lips to hers, hoping to show her how much he loved her without crossing the line by deepening the kiss. "Goodnight, Mo Ghrá."

"Goodnight, Liam."

As Rylie walked to the guest room she was currently using, Liam decided to find out just how cold he could set the water in his shower. While he still didn't think masturbation was a sin, since it kept him from acting on his lustful thoughts and actually having sex, he did want to try to honor his marriage vows by reserving all forms of sexual activity for when he and Rylie could enjoy them together. *Surely, God and the Church can't object to mutual masturbation as foreplay between a husband and wife, right?*

Chapter Six

Rylie felt so much better about her relationship with Liam after their talk the night before. Not only had they cleared up some of the misconceptions between them and finally reviewed the scriptures Father O'Malley had given her to help her be more forgiving, but they'd also looked over the ones the priest had mentioned about marriage when she'd questioned whether or not she and Liam should be having sex while they were trying to decide if they should end their legal union or not. While sitting close to him on the sofa as they shared his Bible to read all the passages together, his enticing bergamot and sandalwood scent caused her libido to adamantly vote yes for sex. But ultimately, after reading, praying, and meditating together, they'd decided to wait until after they met with Father O'Malley again on Friday before deciding if they were ready to take that step or not. Surprisingly, waiting was Liam's idea, telling her that he wanted to prove he wanted more than just sex with her and completely quash all their doubts about them as a couple before they came together in that way. His words from the night before still made her tingle just thinking about them.

"I want to earn your love before we make love again," he'd stated confidently just after they walked upstairs to go to their separate rooms. "When we share our bodies in our marital bed, I want to know that we're solid. That our marriage is going to last for the rest of our lives. I don't want us to jump too fast into having sex, only to fizzle out like a fling from not doing the work on anything

but the physical aspect of our relationship. In order for us to have a bond that can't be broken, we have to connect spiritually and emotionally too. And I think we've made some good progress with the spiritual connection tonight, so I want to make sure we're a hundred percent in sync with our faith before we change our focus to what I think will be the easier aspects of marriage."

Yeah, sex certainly seems to be the easiest part for us, Rylie thought, remembering back to the times they'd made love over their Thanksgiving break, as she dropped balls of biscuit dough into a pot of boiling chicken broth to cook the dumplings, while she cut up the boneless chicken breasts she'd boiled that morning to make a huge pot of chicken & dumplings to take to the community center for the feast of Saint Stephen that afternoon. *If all we had to worry about was nonverbal communication, we'd be golden. Of course, we'd also never leave our bed and would be at risk of starving to death, or losing our jobs at the very least. But Liam is right about the other, nonphysical aspects of our relationship being just as important for building a strong marriage. So, as much as I really want to jump his boner, I have to agree that it's better to build that solid foundation before we make love again. And hopefully, taking his Porsche to the grocery store this morning while he was still asleep won't chip away at that foundation before the concrete is dry.*

Since they'd stayed up well past midnight the night before, she wasn't surprised when Liam slept in that morning, instead of going for his normal run on the beach, which she'd witnessed a couple of times while doing her version of sunrise yoga on the balcony of her bedroom. But after everything that had happened in the past few days, and especially after their talk, Rylie couldn't quiet her mind enough to sleep, even with an extra, middle-of-the-night yoga session. So, after tossing and turning for hours, she'd gotten up and dressed in order to be the first person at the grocery store as soon as it opened, wanting to make a few of her mom and dad's favorite dishes to take with them later.

She'd already finished the smothered fried chicken and macaroni & cheese, keeping them both warm in disposable aluminum pans in the oven while she finished the chicken & dumplings. She would have made collard greens, black-eyed peas, and potatoes, as well, but from eating with Liam's family for the last few days, she knew they'd already have all the vegetables covered.

One of the things she'd done with her parents on Saint Stephen's Day as a teenager was going to serve food to the homeless. When she'd mentioned it to Liam the night before and asked if he'd be willing to go with her to find a place they could carry on the tradition, he'd told her about how the parishioners of Saint Stephen's Cathedral took over for the sisters at the community center who normally cooked and served lunch to the homeless population daily. Only on Saint Stephen's Day, the food was brought in by the parishioners, almost like a potluck, and everyone ate together. Since the homeless population already knew they could go to the community center to eat, shower, and connect with other services, this intermingling often led to networking opportunities to help them find jobs and get off the streets, if they were so inclined.

Rylie loved the idea of how his community combined her family tradition of serving the homeless and the comradery of the potluck dinners she'd seen at the Heart's Destiny Community Church on their visits to the small Texas town. She was eager to do her part to not only honor the lessons of her parents, but also to feel like she was truly joining Liam's community. And if it worked as well as Liam claimed, she knew she had to share the experience with Fiona when they went back on tour with the GWA, since the boss's wife was the daughter of the pastor at the Heart's Destiny Community Church and had told her about the homeless outreach she and the rest of the congregation did with a shelter in San Antonio.

Even if there doesn't seem to be a homeless population in Heart's Destiny that they can welcome to their weekly potlucks, maybe she can plant the seeds for her mom and dad to recruit the parishioners of their church to take their potluck to the shelter in San Antonio on a regular basis, so the Hunters, Burlesons, Walkers, and other prominent families with businesses that need employees can find promising talent that might not have the resources to apply in the traditional manner.

"What is that amazing smell?" Liam questioned, his stomach growling loudly as he walked into the kitchen where Rylie was working.

"Smothered fried chicken, macaroni & cheese, and chicken & dumplings," Rylie answered as Liam hugged her from behind so he could peer over her into the pot, where she was returning the chicken now that it was diced, so all the seasonings could meld as the broth thickened from the flour in the dumplings. She completely lost her train of thought as she practically melted in his arms, reveling in the way he'd started showing his affection recently.

"Not the normal stuff I'd make for breakfast, but I'm cool with that, since they smell way better than the eggs I burnt the other day." Liam chuckled at his own joke as Rylie remembered why they'd ended up eating out or at his grandparents' house for breakfast every day since Liam's failed attempt at cooking on Sunday morning.

"This isn't breakfast. This is for taking to the community center later." Rylie shook her head at Liam as she turned the heat back on under the pan she'd used earlier to make her breakfast before spinning in his arms to return the good morning hug. "But I do have some pancake batter in the fridge, just waiting for you to wake up."

"Aw, you didn't have to do all that." Liam pecked a kiss on her forehead before releasing her to walk over to the Keurig to make himself a cup of coffee. "Though I do have to ask how you got everything to fix all this so early, when it normally takes a couple hours after the store opens to get a delivery?"

"I, um, borrowed your car to go shopping as soon as it opened at seven," Rylie admitted with a half shrug as she stirred the chicken & dumplings.

"You should have woken me up, so I could have gone with and helped you carry everything."

"Are you kidding?" Rylie chuckled, relieved that he didn't seem upset that she'd driven his car without asking first. "With everything I bought to be able to cook the rest of our time here, there wasn't room in the car for you. I was honestly afraid I was going to have to put a couple bags on my lap for the drive back."

When she opened the refrigerator to get out the pancake batter and then the cabinet she'd commandeered as a pantry to get out the syrup, Liam's eyes widened when he saw just how full she'd stuffed them. "Feck! What all are you planning on making?"

"Breakfast, lunch, and dinner for the next week," Rylie shrugged as she splashed a little water on the griddle pan to make sure it was hot enough to start Liam's pancakes. When the water sizzled on the griddle, she opened the plastic container of batter and ladled out enough to make one pancake before asking, "How many pancakes do you want?"

"Depends on how big you make them," Liam stated before stepping back over to the stove and looking at the first one she'd started to see for himself that it was about five inches in diameter. "If they're all about that size, I'll need at least half a dozen."

Rylie ladled out a second as Liam got out a plate for her to stack them on as she finished each one. He got the butter from the fridge, topping each finished pancake as she stacked them up, but didn't add the syrup, presumably because he was going to add it to all of them at once before eating.

The whole scene was so quintessentially domestic that it reminded Rylie of a typical Saturday in her parents' kitchen growing up. She couldn't help but smile at just how right it felt to be following in her mom's footsteps as she made breakfast for her husband for the first time, while the two of them chatted about the plans for the day.

"Well, hopefully, seven will be enough," Rylie advised as she poured the last of the batter she'd mixed up earlier onto the griddle after the first six were done.

"Aren't you going to eat any?" Liam questioned, pointing to the other plate he'd gotten down as he sipped his coffee.

"I already ate three earlier," Rylie admitted, slightly embarrassed that she'd practically gorged on them and one of the pieces of fried chicken while simultaneously boiling the pasta and chicken breasts for the macaroni & cheese and chicken & dumplings. "I also set aside a couple pieces of fried chicken that I didn't smother with gravy, in case you want them to go with your pancakes, even though I couldn't find a waffle iron to make chicken and waffles."

She grabbed a potholder, turned toward the oven in the wall opposite the stovetop, opened it, and pulled out the foil-wrapped fried chicken to give him a little protein with his carb-heavy pancakes, placing the foil packet down on another potholder to protect the countertop. "But if that's too weird for you, then I can still shove them in the pan with the rest of the smothered chicken to take with us later."

"No, chicken and pancakes sounds just as good as chicken and waffles," Liam chuckled, putting the extra plate he'd gotten down for her back in the cabinet.

Once she put the last pancake on the stack, Liam opened the foil and put the two pieces of fried chicken on top of the pancakes, dousing the whole tower of food with what Rylie estimated to be about a cup of maple syrup. "Now I see why your plates have such high sides," she chuckled as she turned off the heat under the griddle pan. "I think I just got diabetes from seeing how much syrup you're about to eat."

"It soaks into the top one and the edges," Liam pointed out as he carried his plate and coffee cup over to the table and took a seat where he'd already laid out silverware. "But the middle bites all end up dry if I don't have a lake of syrup to dip them in while I'm eating."

"How did I not notice your syrup quirk before now?" Rylie wondered, thinking back to the various times they'd eaten breakfast together since she joined the GWA, as Liam ate his breakfast and she started cleaning up from making it.

"Probably because I rarely eat stuff like this in order to maintain my abs for TV," Liam replied, suggestively running a hand over his flat stomach.

She had to turn away from the sink in the island, where she'd rinsed the bowl and utensils she'd used for the pancakes before putting them in the dishwasher, because she didn't trust herself not to forget everything she was doing to go strip Liam's shirt off and lick some of that excess syrup off his abs. *Why did we decide to wait to enjoy the sexual side of our relationship again?*

Luckily, she was able to focus on finishing the chicken & dumplings and placing the finished dish in two more of the disposable aluminum pans she'd bought that morning to transport it to the community center. The pans all came with plastic lids, but she only used them on the two trays of chicken & dumplings, covering the trays of smothered fried chicken and macaroni & cheese with foil instead, since they were still hot from the oven.

Once she had everything ready to go and finished cleaning up the kitchen, she went upstairs to freshen up and change into something a little nicer than the jeans and sweatshirt she'd worn to go to the store and cook. Since Liam wore a pair of black slacks and a red button-down shirt, Rylie changed into a similar look with a long black skirt and red turtleneck. It was probably silly that she liked matching him whenever they went to the various gatherings with his family and friends, but she couldn't help it. Matching him made her feel like they were showing the world they were a couple, so since they seemed to be working through their issues to strengthen their marriage and start to act like the newlyweds they were, she embraced that extra show of coupledom. By the time she'd finished upstairs, Liam had finished his breakfast and put his dishes in the dishwasher, so they could start it before they left for the community center.

"So, am I dropping you off in the car and coming back to get all this, since we can't exactly stack it in the backseat of the Porsche? Or would you rather drive separately and take both vehicles?" Liam questioned when she got back down to the main living area.

"We'll just take the Navigator," Rylie decided, not wanting to let her anxiety get the better of her. "While I appreciate how wonderful you've been with trying to keep me from freaking out again, I need to get over my issues with that third row of seats before we go back on tour, since we can't control what kind of vehicle I might be stuck riding in when it's a different rental every day. So, I need to suck it up and deal with it now, while I know it's only going to be a short ride, so hopefully I'll build up a tolerance to be able to ride in anything again when we can't control it."

"If you're sure." Liam looked a bit skeptical, but he smiled and pulled her into another hug, which she found reassuring as they prepared to leave. "But if it's too much, just say the word and I'll turn around and bring you back to the Porsche. Or come get it to pick you up after, if we're able to make it there but you don't feel up to riding home in the Navigator."

"Deal." Liam referring to his house as home for both of them distracted her enough from her trepidation about riding in his SUV that she was able to easily smile and agree before helping him carry the trays of food down to load them into the back of the larger vehicle, where they could lay them in a single layer instead of having to stack them and risk tearing the foil or ending up with a big mess stuck to the foil from being squished into the food.

Does he really think of his house as my home too? Or did he just say it that way because it's his home and there wasn't any additional meaning behind his use of the word?

"How about I fold down the third row of seats?" Liam's question brought her back out of her thoughts. "If that's the major trigger for you, then maybe not being able to see them will help. And if so, then we'll know to fold them down if we get stuck with a rental that has them, too."

"Yeah, that might work," Rylie agreed, placing the pan of chicken & dumplings she was holding beside the pan of smothered fried chicken Liam had carried down and already placed in the cargo area of the Navigator.

She left him to make the adjustment to the vehicle while she went back upstairs to get the next tray of food. But somehow, speedy Liam managed to only be a few seconds behind her when she reached the kitchen, making it clear that he intended to make equal trips to carry all the food, since she wouldn't just sit down and wait while he loaded it all in the SUV for the trip to the community center.

"You know I'm more than capable of carrying this stuff, right?" Rylie looked at him with a little smile.

"Yes, I know," Liam easily agreed, bending down and pecking a kiss on her temple as he took the tray of macaroni & cheese from her hands. "But you already carried it all in from the store and cooked it, so it's my turn. Actually, scratch that. Since I'm pretty much useless when it comes to cooking, it shoulda been my turn when you were cleaning up while I was eating earlier. So, now you need to take a break and let me do all the carrying, so Ma doesn't have any reason to suggest Da take a switch to my arse for being lazy and making you do all the work."

Rylie had to chuckle at the way Liam always used the Irish form for curse words, thinking they were less offensive if he accidentally said them in front of any of the kids who traveled with the GWA. "Fine, you can carry the rest of the food down and also into the community center when we get there," she conceded with a smile.

She waited until he picked up the last tray of food before grabbing her purse and both their coats from the back of the sofa and following him down to get in the vehicle. As soon as he placed it alongside the other five trays and shut the tailgate, she handed him his coat. Instead of putting it on, however, Liam stepped around her and opened the passenger door for her to get in. She put her purse on the floorboard and put on her coat first, then took Liam's hand for him to assist her into the tall SUV. It wasn't until she was in and buckled up that he put on his own coat as he walked around to the driver's side, and finally got in so they could drive over to the community center.

As soon as he'd closed the garage door behind them and gotten them on their way, Liam reached over and took her hand, driving one handed so he could comfort her on the short trip. If she wasn't already pretty sure she was head over heels in love with him, she was sure she'd have fallen right then from the gentle way he tried to take care of her when he knew her anxiety was elevated. Feeling that connection to Liam as they drove was all Rylie needed to make the short trip with zero thoughts about their risk of an accident from being in a vehicle that reminded her of the one her parents had died in.

Easing anxiety might not be what most people think of as the perks of finding a soulmate, but if you ask me, Liam's innate ability to calm my nerves is certainly one of the sexiest things about him. And I know it's only possible because he's **The One***.*

<center>~~~</center>

For the first time he could remember, Liam actually enjoyed helping serve lunch at the Saint Stephen's Day feast. Since he'd helped serve the dishes his ma, granny, and aunts had prepared every year since he was tall enough to stand and reach across the table, except for the few years he hadn't come home for Christmas while touring with the GWA, he had plenty of experience to know where to have Rylie set up the dishes she'd made that morning, so they'd be among the first to finish serving to be able to sit down and eat. But working with her as they passed out each serving of food was so enticing that he almost didn't want it to end. Of course, part of that could be because he'd just eaten a big breakfast right beforehand. But Liam knew the biggest reason he didn't want to sit down was because of how great it felt to introduce Rylie to each and every person there as his wife and watch her interact with everyone she met as if she'd known them all her life.

Rylie lit up as she found something about every person in line to compliment, eliciting smiles from each and every one of them, even the grumpy homeless man who complained about how he shouldn't have to listen to a sermon before eating. Liam had almost pointed out that Father O'Malley had just delivered a prayer to bless the food and not a full Mass service, but he bit his tongue when his wife took the lead in the interaction.

Rylie had just smiled at the older man, complimented his blue eyes that reminded her of her dad's, and offered him a double serving of her smothered fried chicken, which her dad had claimed was so good it was worth having to wait to eat it while sitting through the three-hour long sermons the preacher where he grew up always gave, at least according to the story she told the older man. She not only got that man to smile back at her before moving on through the line, but a few minutes later, he came back to give her a hug and thank her for making the same kind of chicken his momma used to make, which he hadn't had in over twenty years.

I guess it's a recipe that was passed down in both their families. But from what she said in our earlier conversations about her parents both being disowned by their families for marrying outside their races, I wouldn't think she'd have a recipe from her paternal grandma for her dad to have commented on it being worth waiting to eat back when he was growing up. But maybe I misunderstood the story she just told and it was actually a recipe she learned from her mom? I'll have to ask her later, Liam decided as they finished dishing up their plates to sit down and eat.

As they were looking to see if any of his family had procured a table yet, Sister Mary Katherine, one of the sisters who taught at Saint Stephen's Catholic School when Liam was a student, waved them over to sit with her and several of the people Liam and his brothers had gone to school with, who were apparently catching up on one another's lives since graduation, or maybe they were just still hanging out together since they all still lived in the same area. "Oh, Rylie, I have to know what you did to get Mr. Willie to smile and actually seem to start opening up some?" Sister Mary Katherine gushed as she pointed to two open seats at the table for them to sit.

"I'm sorry, I've met so many people today that you're going to have to refresh my memory," Rylie apologized as she took the seat Liam held out for her. "Who's Mr. Willie?"

While the older, homeless man hadn't introduced himself, Liam assumed he was the Mr. Willie the sister was referring to, but he didn't want to take a chance on embarrassing Rylie by stating as much.

Instead, he just took his seat and immediately dug into the food, appreciating what a wonderful cook he had the good fortune to marry.

"He's the gentleman in the green Army coat." Sister Mary Katherine pointed across the room at the table where the older man was sitting and talking with a couple of the dads of Liam's childhood friends before turning back to speak directly with Rylie. "He's been coming in here for meals once or twice a week for about six months, but other than complaints about not liking to be inside or having to listen to prayers, we haven't gotten him to tell us more than his first name. So, the reaction you got out of him today is a huge breakthrough. And hopefully, it'll lead to us being able to help him with more than just a couple of hot meals a week."

"I didn't really do anything special," Rylie replied humbly. "I just told him how his eyes reminded me of my dad's, and since he looked a little like my dad, maybe he'd like an extra piece of my dad's favorite chicken. And apparently, it was the chicken that broke down his walls, 'cause he came back to tell me it was just like some his mom used to make."

"Well, now you have to tell me where you got your chicken recipe," Sister Mary Katherine insisted with a smile. "And if you don't mind, share it so we can make it here more often to hopefully get Mr. Willie to open up to us even more."

"It's a recipe my mom used to make all the time," Rylie explained, seeming to be happy that the sister's focus was now on the chicken instead of her. "Apparently, my dad told her about his mom's recipe that he loved when they first met, and between his memory and a mix of recipes Mom found online, they worked together to recreate it. Of course, it took them a few years since Dad wasn't very knowledgeable when it came to stuff in the kitchen, especially identifying specific spices, so they didn't perfect it until I was in kindergarten. But once Mom got it right, she wrote it down and made it so often that, by the time I was a teenager, neither one of us had to look at the recipe to make it anymore. But I'll write it down for you before we leave today, so you have it."

Ah, now that makes more sense.

"Thank you," Sister Mary Katherine beamed before turning her gaze at Liam. "I'm so happy to see that you finally settled down with such a kindhearted wife, Liam. After you and most of your brothers and cousins avoided having girlfriends in high school, we were all really worried about all of the Connerys there for a while."

"I didn't avoid having a girlfriend," Liam started before he was rudely interrupted. *I just didn't meet a girl I could see getting serious enough with to go on more than a few dates and actually label her as my girlfriend.*

"But you never took the same girl out twice," Kody Doyle, whom Liam had once considered a friend, chuckled. "And other than Quinn, neither did any of your brothers or cousins. Well, at least in high school. But even Quinn adopted your dating strategy in college."

Yeah, but it was you who encouraged him to break up with Erin to date other girls back then, since you had a crush on her. Feck, maybe you still have a crush on her, since you seem to be following her around like a puppy today.

"That's because Liam was such a *wonderful* influence on Quinn and the rest of his brothers and cousins," Erin Lynch snapped snarkily from her seat beside Kody. "Too bad him settling down with one woman probably won't have near as much impact on the behavior of the rest of the Connery boys now as his always dating a different girl every week did in high school, since he's not home often enough for any of them to see if it's a change he can maintain."

Wow, maybe Quinn dodged a bullet back then, since these two seem to be a perfect pair now.

Before Liam could defend himself against Kody and Erin's implied allegations that his lack of a serious girlfriend influenced Quinn's decision to date other people in college or that he couldn't possibly be serious about just one woman now, Rylie surprised them all by speaking up. "Obviously, I didn't witness Liam's dating habits in high school, since I was in elementary school in New Jersey at the time. But from what I've seen since I joined the GWA and what I've heard from his brothers and cousins this week, I don't think his dating habits had near as much of an influence on them as you seem to think. And even if it did, I know for a fact that he hasn't dated a different woman every week for quite a while, long before we met, became friends, and our friendship turned into more."

Was that elementary school comment a dig at their ages, since Erin and Kody are both behaving like they're still back in high school?

"I don't know if you can really rely on what his brothers and cousins told you this week," Bridget Walsh chimed in, shaking her head.

Feck! Please don't tell me she's still holding a grudge 'cause I wanted to go out with her twin sister and not her back when we were in high school. While they were fraternal twins, it wasn't their different appearances that made Bridget's sister Ceara more appealing to Liam back then, it was her personality and their shared interests. Bridget was all about fashion and being the queen bee of the school, while Ceara was more easy-going and into sports. So of course, Liam was more attracted to the girl who didn't care about messing up her hair and would jump into an impromptu game of whatever sport they could scrounge up the equipment for when everyone was hanging out in the local park.

"They were probably just too embarrassed to admit that they all idolized him for how he strung all us girls along in high school," Bridget sneered.

"I did not string you along in high school," Liam blurted, needing to set the record straight so Rylie wouldn't get a bad impression of his younger self. "In fact, after I turned you down when you asked me out, I didn't even follow through with my plan to ask Ceara to Homecoming because I didn't want to cause trouble between you and your twin, even though I had a huge crush on her at the time."

"What is it with you and twins?" Rylie chuckled, shaking her head before taking a bite of her lunch.

"They're nothing but trouble," Liam chortled, glad to see Rylie was finding humor in the comparison between the Walsh sisters and the Burleson twins that nobody else at the table comprehended.

"Oh, has he come between another set of twins lately?" Bridget chided haughtily.

"No, actually, until we got married, the only woman he even remotely appeared to be recently dating was his best friend's girlfriend's twin sister, who he was only pretending to date to help her keep from being fixed up with anyone and everyone her mom and aunt could think of that came within a twenty-mile radius of their small town," Rylie clarified, sort of. "Wow, that sounded much less convoluted in my head."

She shook her head as if shaking off the confusion before elaborating. "You see, pretty much all of our holiday breaks have been spent in this fabulous little town in Texas, Heart's Destiny, because so many of our coworkers are either from there or were marrying people from there, so they planned their weddings and all the parties surrounding them when we could all attend. Anyway, the first time Liam went to Heart's Destiny, the local matchmakers set him up with Jen and paired his tag-team partner with Jen's twin sister, Julie. Well, Dion and Julie fell in love at first sight, which meant Dion needed to go back to Heart's Destiny for every holiday break, even the ones when there wasn't a wedding planned that we all had to attend. And Liam, being the wonderful friend he is, went along to help provide cover for Dion and Julie, and so Jen would have a friend to sit with at all the gatherings and events and wouldn't be targeted by the matchmakers with a bunch of guys she wasn't interested in, even though they only considered each other friends. Thankfully, after we got married, her family was able to step up for her, so she sat with them at all the parties for our friends' wedding there last month."

Rylie turned to look directly at Liam before asking, "Do you think Dion's brother will take your place sitting with Jen at the parties for her brother's wedding this weekend? I hate to think of her having to go back to having the guys she grew up with, and has absolutely no interest in dating, pushed at her again."

"I don't know, but I'll call D later and suggest it," Liam smiled, trying to cover for his doubts about Rylie's sincerity with regard to her concern for Jen. But being completely ready to be off the topic of his past dating habits, he decided to use her bringing up Dion's brother to transition the conversation to what he hoped would be a less dangerous subject. "But speaking of brothers, where's your brother today, Erin?"

"Sean's over at the hospital with Briana," Callahan O'Brien, another of Liam's old friends, replied when Erin only glared at Liam after his question. "Erin was just telling us all about Sean Junior's birth interrupting Christmas before you sat down."

"Oh, what a wonderful day to be born," Rylie gushed at hearing the news. "I know Briana wasn't too happy about going past her due date when we saw her Monday night, but surely that special birthday makes up for any discomfort she felt."

"Yes, she's thrilled," Erin admitted with a wan smile.

"Show them the pictures, Erin," Sister Mary Katherine commanded.

Reluctantly, Erin pulled her phone out of the bag hanging off the back of her chair and swiped to the photo album before holding it up for Liam and Rylie to see the photos that apparently everyone else at the table had already seen. She rattled off the baby's stats as if anything other than length and weight made sense to Liam or anyone else at the table.

What the feck is an Apgar score? And why is it a big deal that it went from seven to nine?

"Oh, he's so precious," Rylie cooed as Erin swiped through several shots of the infant.

He looked like any other baby to Liam, but he wasn't about to disagree with his wife, especially when that dreamy look on her face seemed to indicate she was even closer to ready to have their babies than she'd previously let on. "Adorable. I'll have to call and congratulate the proud papa later."

After an uncomfortable silence settled around them as Erin put her phone away and they all continued eating, Liam finally decided to see if he could get the rest of the group to speak, instead of just staring at him and Rylie like they were observing the animals at the zoo. "So, you all know what's new with me, now fill me in on what you've all been up to since the last time I saw you."

Before anyone could reply, Rylie's phone blared from Liam's pocket, where he'd held onto it for her while they were serving food, so it wouldn't be in the way hanging from her wrist in the case she kept it in. He pulled it out and handed it to her, looking to see who was calling her as she opened the case. *Who's Bill Dobson?*

"Oh, excuse me," Rylie blurted, as her face contorted with a look of concern. "I should probably take this."

When she stood and walked away from the table, Liam also excused himself from the uncomfortable looks being thrown his way. "Actually, I need to go with her, so please give us a moment before we continue catching up."

He then followed her to the hallway leading to the restrooms, catching up quickly due to his much longer stride length, thanks to being almost a foot taller than her. It wasn't that he was jealous and didn't want to give her some privacy to have her conversation, at least not entirely. But his motivation to follow her was more because he wanted to make sure everything was okay after seeing her worried expression when she read the caller's name.

"Hello, Mr. Dobson," she chirped nervously as she answered the call. "Are you having a happy holiday? Or did we have another pipe burst this year like last Christmas?"

Since she called him Mr. Dobson instead of Bill and specifically asked about a pipe bursting, I'm guessing he's either an older friend of her parents or somehow affiliated with her apartment building, and not an old boyfriend trying to hook up with her while she's supposed to be home for the holidays.

Liam couldn't hear the caller's reply with Rylie holding the phone to her ear, but from the way Rylie's eyes widened to be as round as her mouth when she cried out, "oh no," he was pretty sure this wasn't just a cheerful holiday greeting from an old family friend.

"Was anybody hurt?" Rylie sobbed, her eyes filling with unshed tears. "Oh, um, okay. I'll be praying for him and his family. What about the other apartments? Were they all destroyed, or is there anything left that might be salvageable?"

Unable to withstand seeing her upset, Liam stepped up to her side and pulled her into his arms. He might not be able to do anything about whatever had happened to upset her, but he could be there to comfort her while she cried.

"No, of course you can't know that when they won't let you back in the building." Rylie sighed heavily as she wrapped her free arm around Liam's waist and leaned her face into his chest. "I just hoped maybe they were able to contain things to only part of the building, so maybe some of the residents whose apartments weren't burned could get in and see if they had anything left that wasn't water damaged. I know the lockbox I had in my room is supposed to be fireproof, so if anyone else had something like that maybe they could find it to get their important documents or whatever. But I suppose even a box like that doesn't do much good if the floor around it burned and it fell through to get lost."

Oh feck! Her apartment building caught on fire? Thank you, Lord, for keeping her safe here with me! Liam squeezed her tighter, brushing his lips over the top of her head to reassure himself that she wasn't in any danger since she was nowhere near the fire.

"Yes, I'm actually in New York right now, but I'll see what I can do about getting down there as soon as possible." Rylie paused to let her caller speak. "No, I don't have any way of writing it down right now. Can you text it to me? Yes, thank you. I'll call you as soon as I know when I'll be able to get there, so we can meet then, but that probably won't be until sometime tomorrow."

After a few more "yeses" and "uh-huhs," Rylie ended the call by saying, "See you soon, Mr. Dobson. You stay safe, too."

Liam was at a loss as to what to say to comfort her, so he just held her as she sobbed and clung to him while softly whispering her prayers for healing, shelter, safety, and no major losses of the personal mementoes of the other residents of her building. When she stuffed her phone back in his pocket, so she could wrap both her arms around him, Liam's cock jumped to attention in response to her being so close, even though it was a completely inappropriate reaction to have given the circumstances. Instead of acknowledging his poorly timed biological response to her, however, Liam decided to join her in prayer.

Dear God, please provide Rylie with the same blessings she's asking for you to grant her neighbors, since she's too selfless to include herself in her prayers. I can give her the shelter, but I really need your help with the other things she needs. And please, dear Lord, help me to be the man she can count on to support her, love her, and give her the strength to deal with whatever we find when we get to her hometown. Through Christ our Lord, Amen.

"Oh, Liam, I'm so sorry," Rylie wailed as she pulled out of his embrace. "I got mascara on your shirt."

"I'm not worried about that," Liam assured her, wiping the leftover mascara and tears from under her eyes with his thumbs before wiping it on his black pants where it wouldn't show. "I just need to know that you're okay. And if you have to cry it all out to feel better, then you're welcome to cover all my shirts in mascara, just as long as I'm wearing them and holding you in my arms when you do, 'cause I don't think empty shirts make good handkerchiefs."

"They don't really make good handkerchiefs when you're wearing them either," Rylie chuckled sadly. "But if it doesn't have to be dry cleaned, then I'm sure I can get the stain out tonight before I have to leave to go to Atlantic City in the morning. Well, assuming there's a flight I can get a last-minute ticket for, anyway."

"I'll call the charter service Rick recommended for the Dublin trip," Liam decided, thinking they might need to have the ability to carry more than just a couple of suitcases coming back if she was able to get into her apartment and salvage anything. "That way, we won't have to worry about airline delays or luggage limits if they're able to let you into your apartment to get your things."

Liam pulled his phone from the opposite pocket from the one Rylie's was in, quickly dialing the charter company and booking the flight for first thing the next morning. As part of their services, the charter company had a concierge to book any necessary hotels and ground transportation for when they reached their destination, so Liam gave them the details of what he thought they'd need for however long they ended up needing to stay in Atlantic City. When the company representative asked about when they wanted to book the return flight, Liam posed the question to Rylie.

"I don't know." Rylie looked so despondent as she stood there trying to decide how long she'd need to be in Atlantic City that Liam knew she was too overwhelmed to make a decision. "It depends on how long it takes to do all the paperwork for my insurance and if we're able to get into my apartment or not."

"Sunday," Liam decided, thinking that gave her all day Friday to do the paperwork with her insurance company and all day Saturday to go through her apartment if her side of the building wasn't too damaged for the residents to be able to enter safely to get what was left of their things. "But that could change, depending on what we find when we get there."

After explaining the possible need to carry cargo on the return trip, Liam verified that they still had his information on file to bill him for this charter the same way he was being billed for the ones in April. He then disconnected the call, needing to focus on taking care of Rylie since she appeared to be on the brink of going into shock. As soon as he put his phone back in his pocket, Liam pulled Rylie back into his arms to comfort her.

"Thank you," Rylie sighed, wrapping her arms around him once more, resting her chin on his chest to keep from smearing more mascara on his shirt, and closing her eyes momentarily, as if she needed another moment to regain her composure. "I guess you figured out there was a fire in my apartment building yesterday?"

Liam only nodded in response to her question as he stared down into her alluring topaz eyes, thinking it was best to let her talk it all out. He was there to step in when she needed him because it got to be too much for her, but he wasn't about to make her feel worse by talking over her when she needed to vent as she processed everything.

"It started on the other side of the building, so Mr. Dobson, the manager and maintenance man for the building, isn't sure if there's any damage to my place or not. But apparently, he's got a meeting with someone in the fire department tomorrow to find out if and when any of us will be allowed to enter the building. But even if we're not able to get in there and try to get what's left of our things, I have to do some paperwork with the condo management and my renter's insurance to file a claim."

"Did he say if anyone was hurt? Or if there's anything we can do to help the rest of the residents?" Liam's brain was already spinning with ideas for covering the cost of hotel rooms for everyone affected, as well as enlisting local stores to deliver toiletries and clothing to those who were displaced without the basic necessities.

"Only Mr. Dooley, who after seeing his son deep fry a turkey at Thanksgiving thought he could do the same in a large stockpot on his stove to surprise his family when they came over for Christmas." Rylie sighed heavily, rolling her eyes. "And apparently he didn't think to turn off the stove when the oil splashed out and burned his hands, so by the time he went to the bathroom to wash it off and put on burn cream, his kitchen was too engulfed in flames for him to get to his fire extinguisher. So, he just ran out into the hall, pulled the fire alarm, and started banging on doors to get everyone else out of the building. But everyone made it out safely, and that's the most important thing."

"Yes, it is," Liam agreed. "I'm assuming that everyone in the building was able to find a place to stay last night?"

"Yes, most of them are staying with family, either in town or wherever they'd already gone for the holidays. But there are a few who were able to get into a hotel nearby."

Liam was just about to ask her if there was someone he could call to cover the cost of the hotel when her eyes widened and she derailed his train of thought by blurting, "Oh, Liam, what about our appointments with Father O'Malley for tomorrow and Saturday?"

"I'm sure he'll understand that we need to reschedule them," Liam assured his wife, pecking a kiss to her lips. "But since we aren't leaving until the morning, and he's just down the hall eating, why don't we go ask him about possibly meeting later this evening or whenever we get back in town?"

"Yes, definitely," Rylie squeezed him briefly before stepping back from their embrace and taking his hand to walk back into the banquet hall.

"Is everything okay?" Liam's da asked as soon as they stepped out of the hallway and found themselves surrounded by his immediate family.

"Yeah," Liam replied at the same time Rylie answered, "No, but it will be."

"Well, that sounds complicated," Finn quipped.

"Did Erin say something offensive to you?" Quinn questioned, glaring over at the table where his ex-girlfriend still sat with Sister Mary Katherine and several of Liam and Quinn's high school classmates. "I get that she still can't forgive me fifteen years after we graduated and broke up, but it's not right for her to childishly lash out at my family instead of limiting her grudge to just me."

"Oh, yeah, she still blames me for you wanting to date other people in college," Liam chuckled ruefully. "But that wasn't why we walked away a few minutes ago." Liam looked to Rylie to see if she wanted to be the one to fill in his family or if she wanted him to do it. When she only half-smiled before dipping her chin once, he continued, speaking much more somberly than only a moment earlier. "Rylie actually got a call from the manager of her apartment building to let her know there was a fire yesterday. So, now we need to go to Atlantic City to deal with the fire department and her insurance company to find out if any of her stuff is salvageable and file a claim for whatever needs to be replaced."

"Oh, dear," Liam's ma gasped, throwing her arms around Rylie and inadvertently pulling her hand from his. "No wonder you look so upset. I can't imagine how you must be feeling, especially not knowing if any of your precious mementos of your parents were lost in the fire."

Leah Mae Wright

"Yeah," Rylie sobbed, tearing up once more. "But thankfully, I put digital copies of all the pictures in Mom's photo albums in the cloud the last time I was home. Though now I regret not doing the same with her journals."

"Hopefully, since the fire was on the other side of the building, we'll find them fully intact to be able to digitize them this week," Liam said encouragingly, pulling Rylie from his ma's arms, so he could be the one she leaned on. "But before we can go do all that, we need to find Father O'Malley to reschedule the times we were supposed to meet with him over the next couple of days."

"Yes, of course," Brian nodded at Liam, silently reassuring his son that his priorities were on track. "I believe he's completed his duties for today, so he was sitting with his family the last time I saw him."

"We also need to clean up our dishes from earlier," Rylie pointed out as they scanned the room looking for the priest.

"We'll take care of that," Cathleen assured her just as Liam spotted Father O'Malley sitting with his mother, brothers, sisters-in-law, nieces, and nephews.

"I'll take care of that," Quinn interjected gruffly. "So I have an excuse to approach Erin's table to tell her, *once again*, to leave everyone else out of the issues she has with me."

"You might want to deliver that message to Kody Doyle, too," Liam advised, pointedly looking at the table where Erin and Kody were seated side by side. "Since he seems to have forgotten that it was him who encouraged you to break up with Erin and not me."

Quinn grumbled something unintelligible as he held his hand out to Liam for a fist bump before stomping off in the direction of the table where Erin and Kody had their heads together.

"Don't go starting a fight in the middle of what's supposed to be a celebration," Cathleen advised, following Quinn.

"Do you think we should go back him up?" Aiden asked, looking at their da and the rest of their brothers. "Or maybe just have the cuffs ready to stop a fight?"

"Don't look at me for cuffs," Da laughed. "I'm retired. Remember?"

"Same here," Rory agreed with their da, holding his hands up at their two younger brothers who were still on the force. "So, if I go over there, it'll just be to back him up if anyone else decides to jump in the fray."

"It's a good thing we're off duty then," Finn added with a chuckle. "So we can just help hold everyone else back while Quinn kisses Erin into submission."

As the rest of his family dispersed to go assist Quinn, Rylie giggled, "Maybe Quinn should use his handcuffs on Erin and take her somewhere private, where they can work out their issues by releasing the sexual tension between them."

"Yeah, since she's still just as ticked off at him now as she was when they broke up fifteen years ago, I don't think that'll do anything but risk Quinn's badge," Liam chuckled, shaking his head.

"Oh, Liam," Rylie smirked as they stood there watching the show for a moment. "Now I understand why you didn't get any of my hints that I wanted us to be more than friends. You are absolutely clueless when it comes to women."

"Hey, I'm not totally clueless," Liam protested, turning away from the heated discussion going on over by the table where they'd been sitting earlier to step in front of Rylie so she had to look only at him.

"If you weren't totally clueless, then you'd know that the only reason a woman is still angry about a breakup fifteen years later is because she's still madly in love with the clueless guy who broke up with her. And considering the way Quinn has been looking at Erin all day, I think he still loves her too. And if I'm right, then the best thing they could do is go bang out all their residual anger, so they can calm down enough to talk, forgive one another for their past, and move forward as a couple." With that, she turned and walked over toward the table where Father O'Malley was sitting and chatting with his family.

Feck! Is she basing those assumptions on what she feels for me? Like she's been pissed at me because I immediately insisted on an annulment as soon as we found out we were married and then her anger was only compounded by finding out I'd kissed Jen in that stupid, futile attempt to fight my feelings for Rylie? And now, in addition to the counseling from Father O'Malley and following his advice that we started last night, she thinks we need to bang out our anger before we can really move on as a couple? If so, then why didn't she say something when I stupidly suggested waiting to have sex again?

Realizing he could only get the answers to his questions from Rylie, Liam dutifully followed her to speak with the priest while trying to figure out when it might be the appropriate time to ask her. *Probably not until we get back from finding out how much she lost in the fire.*

Obviously noticing something was wrong as soon as he saw Liam and Rylie walking up to the table where he was sitting with his family, Father O'Malley stood and ushered them out of the main dining hall to one of the rooms used as a classroom or meeting room in the community center. "Let's go talk privately."

"Sorry to interrupt your lunch, Father," Liam apologized as soon as the three of them were alone. "But we just got some bad news that we need to go out of town to deal with in the morning, so we were hoping we can reschedule our counseling sessions with you."

"Of course," Father O'Malley agreed, looking back and forth between Liam and Rylie. "Is this bad news something I can help you with in some way?"

"It's my apartment building in Atlantic City," Rylie informed the priest. "There was a fire yesterday, but thankfully, the only injuries were some minor burns on one of the resident's hands. But apparently the damage is bad enough that none of the residents are allowed to stay there, so if you could pray for everyone to have an easy time finding new homes, I'd really appreciate it."

"Of course," Father O'Malley agreed. "And you're both going down there in the morning?"

"Yes, I have to see if any of my keepsakes from my mom and dad are salvageable and deal with the paperwork to terminate my lease and file an insurance claim while the apartment manager and building owners have a representative from my insurance company in their office tomorrow."

Father O'Malley quickly said a prayer for all those affected by the fire, as well as for Liam and Rylie's safe travels. When he was done, he asked, "Have the two of you talked and prayed about your marriage, so we can do the first session now? Or do we need to schedule it for when you get back?"

"We have talked," Liam assured the priest, smiling down at Rylie as he hugged her to his side. "And after reading the scriptures you mentioned last Sunday, we prayed about them together last night. Now, I'm pretty sure we've nixed any plans for an annulment, but we still need to keep talking and come up with a plan for building a strong spiritual foundation for our marriage going forward."

"I'm thrilled to hear that," Father O'Malley smiled, motioning to the chairs in the room for them to take a seat. "Why don't we have a seat while you fill me in on which scriptures you read and prayed over, so I have a better understanding of where you are to know how I can best guide you forward together?"

Once they were seated, Liam briefly recapped the events of the night before, mentioning the specific scriptures he remembered with Rylie filling in the exact chapters and verses for the ones he only remembered well enough to paraphrase. They talked about how they'd both worked through their issues with needing to forgive themselves before being able to forgive each other. Then they moved on to discuss the scriptures about marriage and how they'd decided they wanted to follow God's teachings in their daily life as a couple.

Rylie seemed a little uncomfortable when Liam mentioned their decision to wait to have sex until they had a stronger foundation for their marriage, so they weren't blinded by the physical and likely to miss a step with the spiritual or emotional aspects of their union. Since Liam felt his own cheeks heat up when he started talking about sex with the priest, he completely understood her stiffening up beside him. He reached out and took her hand, hoping to make her feel more comfortable by making it clear she wasn't alone.

"I think that is definitely the right approach to take," Father O'Malley nodded solemnly. "While intimate relations are a vital component to a strong marriage, there are a lot of things that need to be discussed before a couple can decide when it's right for them to incorporate sex into their relationship. For most couples, it's easy for me to advise them to wait until their wedding night, knowing they'll go through the Pre-Cana and natural family planning classes first. But since the two of you are already married, I can't exactly offer that suggestion. So, I think our best option will be to enroll you in the Pre-Cana classes, which you can do online while you're on tour for work. And the two of you should try to abstain until after you've completed the fifth lesson, which covers the theology behind natural family planning, and ideally, until after you complete the Natural Family Planning Basics class."

"How long do these classes take?" Liam questioned, unsure if they could abstain that long, especially after Rylie's earlier comment about couples needing to "bang it out" to get to where they can communicate most effectively.

"If you were taking the in-person classes, they'd take three months each, which is why we normally only schedule a wedding in the Church for six months after you start the Pre-Cana classes," Father O'Malley informed them. "But with the online version that we'll put you in because of your jobs, you can work at your own pace and will most likely get through them much faster."

So much for my hope that he'd tell us we're good to go since we're already married and have covered the scriptures he wanted us to pray about first. But I guess, since I still need to wait to go condomless until after my blood tests at the end of January, it's probably best for us to keep waiting anyway, so I don't have to ask her to go against the Catholic Church's views on condoms.

"But since you're already married, it's not a sin for you to have intimate relations before you complete the classes, unless you use contraception."

"Yeah, I stopped taking the pill after you mentioned that on Sunday," Rylie informed both him and the priest.

Feck! I probably ought to make it clear that if we slip and have sex, I'm gonna be the one insisting on condoms, so maybe she won't have to feel guilty for sinning.

"So, if we can't wait another month, until I feel safe to say I wasn't exposed to anything in Allissa's stalker's blood, then will we both have to confess each time we use a condom, or just me since I'm the one making the decision to keep wearing them until I know for certain I'm disease free?"

Before Father O'Malley could answer him, Rylie spoke up. "Oh, Liam, his blood tested negative for everything, so you should be fine." Rylie squeezed Liam's hand, trying to be reassuring. While he appreciated her gesture, all she really did was draw his attention straight to her. Their connection felt stronger than it ever had before, causing everything around them to disappear until all he could see was her, effectively making him feel like they were the only two people in the room. As if they were the only ones hearing this conversation. As if Father O'Malley had stepped out of the room to give them privacy.

"Yes, I know that," Liam sighed, locking his gaze on hers. "But when Doc drew the blood for my first test after the *Horror* fan expo, the one before they got the results from the medical examiner's office, he told me that we'd want to watch my tests for the next three months because there was always the possibility that he was in an incubation period when he could be contagious but not have enough of a viral load for it to show up on his tests yet. So, to be on the safe side, I don't want to do anything where you might be exposed, which means wearing a condom."

"Yeah, well, you should have thought of that before we did anything oral, too." Rylie rolled her eyes at him. "While it's highly unlikely that just kissing will spread something, I'm pretty sure I've already been exposed to the same things you were back in October. If not that same night, then definitely our first time in Heart's Destiny."

FECK! Liam groaned, hanging his head as he remembered how she'd licked a drop of precum from his cock right before she sucked him. He'd stopped her before he got too close to coming and put on a condom before taking her in the shower, but he hadn't even thought twice about her potentially already being at risk by then. *Why didn't I think about the possibility of exposure to precum having the same risk of transmission as cum? I guess I was thinking the same thing I thought every time I went down on her, that most things aren't highly transmittable in saliva, so I didn't think it was much of a risk.*

"Not that I think you were actually exposed to anything, even if he'd tested positive for all the diseases," Rylie continued, her voice sounding harsh as she ranted. "Yes, your clothes were covered in blood spatter from him being shot. But you didn't have any open wounds for his blood to mix with yours. And you'd turned your face away from him when you tackled Dean to get him out of the line of fire, so his blood didn't get in your eyes, nose, or mouth to contaminate you through your mucous membranes. Not that it would have reached your face anyway, considering the way you guys landed with your feet closest to the stalker, so most of the spatter was actually on your boots and pants with only a little on the lower part of your shirt. It just looked like more to everyone freaking out when you walked out of the locker room because you were wearing a red shirt, so they couldn't really tell where the spatter ended unless they looked really closely, like I did. And with your hands under Dean when you guys landed, you didn't have any of his blood on them to accidentally wipe it on your face either. So, yeah, you could have been exposed, but since none of those diseases are transmitted via osmosis through clothing and skin, and you removed your contaminated clothing and showered almost immediately after it happened, you've got less than one-one-hundredth of a chance of getting anything. And since I know both the tests you've taken since then have been negative, as have mine, then I think we're okay."

"How do you know *both* my tests have been negative?" Liam had mentioned the first one being negative when they'd talked with Dion and Darius on speaker in catering while Dion was still in the hospital, when Rick announced to everyone that the stalker's blood had tested negative because he wanted to reassure the wrestlers who had to work with those exposed that they weren't at risk of contracting anything while working with them in the ring. But he hadn't mentioned to anyone that he'd also tested negative again at the beginning of December.

"Because you're still allowed to wrestle." Rylie rolled her eyes at him once more, clearly thinking he was an idiot for not realizing that would make it obvious to everyone that he was negative. "It's very clear in our contracts that testing positive on any of our tests will prohibit us from being able to work, effective immediately. So, I might not know what anyone tests positive for, if it's a disease they could pass on by bleeding in the ring, or if it's drugs that they have to go to rehab to kick the habit before they can come back, but we'd all know when someone tests positive because they'd be sent home."

Since it had been a couple of years since Rick had sent anyone home for popping positive on a drug test, Liam hadn't thought about how everyone in the company would know if one of them tested positive for anything. *Feck, she's right. And I'm an idiot for not realizing that. And I suppose, if any of us tested positive for something contagious, then Doc would have to inform the rest of us if we'd potentially been exposed to make sure we continued monitoring things, like he did with me at* **Halloween Horror** *when we weren't sure what we might have been exposed to from the stalker's blood.*

"Still, I want to follow the advice Doc gave me and keep wearing condoms until I get past that ninety-day window at the end of January with only negative tests," Liam decided, lifting their joined hands and pressing his lips to her knuckles. "Even if it's a sin to use a barrier to procreation, I think the greater sin would be not protecting you when there might still be a risk, even if it's only one-one-hundredth of a chance."

"And I will be here to take your confessions, no matter which way you choose," Father O'Malley interjected with a knowing smile.

Liam winced when he remembered the priest was there and realized he'd just overheard all that. Considering how Rylie's cheeks flushed, it was obvious she'd forgotten the priest was there, too. *Yeah, everyone talks about how great it is when you connect with your soulmate to the point that you feel like you're living in a bubble with them. But nobody warned us how embarrassing it can be when we get so lost in our bubble that we don't filter what we say and do in front of an audience.*

"Although, since you only have a month left of that window, I recommend you continue to abstain and use that time, when you're alone and would normally engage in intimate relations, to complete your Pre-Cana and Natural Family Planning Basics lessons and continue praying for your marriage."

It would be tough, but Liam was hopeful that they'd be able to hold out for another month. *Even if I have to schedule three or four ice-cold showers a day.*

Chapter Seven

Since Liam was able to charter them an early morning flight that arrived hours earlier than she expected, Rylie wanted to go by her apartment building to see the destruction for herself before meeting Mr. Dobson and the insurance representative at the main office for the Carson Condominiums to take care of the paperwork to terminate her lease before her rent was automatically drafted on January first, and start the paperwork for whatever claim she might need to file. While none of them thought they'd be able to enter the building until after the meeting with the fire department that Mr. Dobson had scheduled for later that afternoon, she needed to be alone with Liam for her first time seeing the damages. If it was as devastating as she feared, then she didn't want anyone but Liam seeing her break down, knowing he'd be her stoic rock to lean on in her weakest moments.

The way he'd wrapped her in his arms and held her as she cried right after hearing about the fire the day before was so comforting that she didn't know how she could have endured the news without him. *Yeah, I probably would have cried myself to sleep, feeling alone and devastated the same way I did right after I left the hospital when Mom and Dad died, and wouldn't have gotten anything done to even plan for coming here to deal with everything. Maybe I wouldn't have holed up in bed for days before making the arrangements like I did to delay Mom and Dad's funeral, but I'd probably still be in bed now if Liam hadn't taken over to take care of everything for me.*

She didn't have time to examine what it meant for her to lean on him the way she was because the GPS on his phone instructed him to make the last turn onto her block. As the building came into sight, she couldn't help but gasp, "Oh, em, gee!"

The northeast-facing side of the formerly white brick building was now a ghastly gray with darker spots of black soot above several of the windows, which were now missing. She wasn't sure if they'd been intentionally broken out by the fire department as they tried to douse the flames, or if they'd been blown out by the fire building up too much heat and pressure in the stairwell and apartments most affected. But as they passed the northernmost corner of the building to get their first glimpse of the longer, northwest-facing front side of the building, it became glaringly obvious that the flames on this end of the building had escaped the confines of the structure to burn up all the wooden railings on the balconies for Mr. Dooley's second-floor corner unit and all fourteen stories of apartments directly above it.

"Didn't you say the fire was on the opposite side of the building from your apartment?"

Rylie was in such shock at seeing how this part of the building appeared to be reduced to just the outer shell that she could only nod in response to Liam's question, momentarily unable to find her voice. She also couldn't bring herself to look away from the worst of the damage to notice how far along the front of the building the fire had spread, just as she'd been too captivated by the destruction on the end of the sixteen-story building to look down the side street before they passed it to see if the damage was limited to the front of the building or had spread to the apartments in the back.

I bet the firefighters couldn't use the north staircase at all. Which means that unless they were able to get through the doors from the parking garage to use those stairs too, they had to evacuate everyone through the south staircase at the other end of the building.

Having not looked away from the damage on the westernmost corner of the northeast-facing side of the building to notice if the five-story parking garage attached to the back at that end of the building showed signs of fire damage or not, Rylie wasn't sure if the stairways at the corners of the parking structure would have been safe to traverse during the blaze.

And since I doubt the fire department would have pulled a firetruck into the parking garage attached to a burning building, and they would have only had access up to the fifth floor from there anyway, they probably had to drag their hoses through the south staircase, too, in order to keep the fire from spreading to the other end of the building. That had to be a nightmare to try to escape with everyone trying to use the same staircase. Or God forbid, trying to drive out of the parking garage while that end of the building was on fire.

"So, your apartment is at the other end then, where there doesn't appear to be any damage to the balconies or even any soot above the windows?"

Luckily, Liam's hopeful tone of voice helped snap her out of her stunned state, so she could turn her head to see what he was talking about. She was relieved to see that about halfway down, approximately where the lobby was located, the gray sooty appearance of the outside of the building lessened, along with the damage to the wooden portions of the balconies on the upper floors of the building. At about three-quarters of the way across the front of the building, the balcony destruction and soot deposits on the brick seemed to stop completely, causing that end of the building to look totally normal.

"Yeah, but on the seventh floor in the back, so you'll have to drive around to the short street leading to the parking garage in back to see my balcony," Rylie croaked out, hopeful that the lack of damage on the front of the building approximately even with the location of her apartment in the back meant her place was possibly spared.

Liam drove slowly past the building, where she finally noticed that the main entrance to the lobby and the tunnel entrance to the parking garage were both blocked off by metal barricades wrapped in what looked to Rylie like crime scene tape, only this tape said, "Fire Line — Do Not Cross." The tape extended from the metal barricades in both directions and was secured to the street signs on the corners of the side streets on either end of the building.

Huh? How did I not notice that before?

Duh! Because as always, you were looking up and not at ground level. Rylie could hear her dad's voice in her head as if he was sitting right beside her, speaking to her just as he had when she'd fallen from stepping off a curb, or when she'd ran her bike into the neighbor's hedges. *But when I taught you to do that, I meant it metaphorically, not literally. I was trying to teach you to look up to set your goals high, but I didn't mean for you to look up when you're walking or riding your bike or doing anything else when you really need to see where you're going.*

Rylie consciously redirected her gaze to the street in front of the vehicle as Liam sped up slightly to finish traversing the front of her building. When he reached the southwest corner of the building, he flipped on the blinker in the rental sedan and made the left turn for them to drive past the southwest-facing end of the building, which again, appeared to have no damage, even though the entrance doors were also blocked with metal barricades and more fire-line tape.

When they made the second left at the southeast corner of the building, Rylie realized that the entire building, including the attached five-story parking garage the road they were on dead-ended into, was surrounded by the tape, even though the metal barricades were only blocking the actual entrances. She only barely noticed the soot covering the walls of the parking garage, which only stretched along the north half of the back of the apartment building. Instead, her focus moved upward once more, as she leaned across Liam to count up seven floors and over two balconies to find hers. She sighed with relief as she noted that her balcony and windows were still intact with no soot on the brick around them.

Liam pulled over as far as he could to the side of the road and put the car in park before following her gaze. "Which one's yours?"

"Seventh floor, second apartment from the end," Rylie informed him as she pointed at her balcony.

"Is that the first or second balcony?" Liam questioned, obviously confused by the extra windows on the ends of the building without balconies.

"The second balcony," Rylie explained. "The end apartments are bigger, either two or three bedrooms, and they all only have balconies off the living rooms. Then the three in the middle, like mine, are only one bedroom, with the balcony off the living room stretching to just under the bedroom window."

With them temporarily parked on the side of the road while there wasn't any traffic trying to get down the narrow street that only led in and out of the parking garage, Rylie finally took a moment to look away from her apartment to see how close the damage came to her place on the back side of the building. Much like the front of the building, there seemed to be a definite line of demarcation where the soot deposits ended, only at the center of the building, basically running right down the middle of her next door neighbor's apartment, instead of spreading as far as her unit like it's counterpart at the front of the building.

"From here, it looks like they were able to stop the fire at my neighbor's place," Rylie pointed out, leaning her head on Liam's shoulder as she continued looking up at the building. "Do you think that means my stuff is fine and possibly accessible from the south stairwell? Or will they have doused everything with water and ruined Mom's journals and photo albums unnecessarily?"

Rylie had the tiniest sliver of hope that the journals and photo albums were protected from water damage by being in a plastic tote in the top of her closet. But since it was a cheap tote that didn't have a tight seal with the lid, she was pretty sure if the firefighters hit the side of it with their high-powered hoses, then the top would pop off and everything inside would be soaked.

"I'm not sure." Liam put his arm around her shoulders, comforting her as they sat there just staring at the building for several long minutes. "And honestly, even if the stairs at this end of the building are passable, it's possible that the support beams on the other side of your apartment are too damaged to stabilize the floor, making it unsafe to get to your apartment to even check and see what's salvageable."

"The only things I'm really worried about are those journals, photo albums, and the lockbox in the closet with their important papers in it. The furniture is all second-hand stuff I bought at the Salvation Army store when I moved in here from the dorms after college, so it's not worth trying to restore if it's water or smoke damaged."

"You didn't have anything else from your parents?" Liam stroked his hand down from her shoulder to her elbow and back up again, surprisingly calming her even as she gave him more details about her life immediately after losing her mom and dad.

"Just their wedding rings," Rylie replied, holding up her right hand before remembering that her mom's rings were on her left and lifting it too. "I was staying in the dorms at school when they passed, so I didn't have room for everything in the house. That room was so small, I didn't really have room for all *my* stuff, much less theirs. So, when their life insurance wasn't enough to cover their funeral expenses and their medical bills after the accident, I had to use what they had left in their savings to finish the repairs to the house after Hurricane Sandy and sell it to cover everything. Luckily, my college roommate's parents own Mancini Estate Specialists, so Sienna, my roommate, asked them to help me with the estate sale. She also didn't let me wallow in my bed every weekend, actually spending all her free time between classes and studying for the next several months going with me to sort through everything, so I didn't miss anything I wanted to keep, or expose their personal information to everyone coming to the sale."

"You mean like the journals you mentioned?" Liam questioned, still rubbing her arm soothingly.

"Yeah, and making sure I kept the paperwork I needed for dealing with the insurance companies and taxes and stuff, and shredded any paperwork I didn't need, or want to keep for sentimental reasons, so nobody could steal their identities and open up credit cards and stuff with their social security numbers. Sienna was a godsend for helping me deal with all that when we were only eighteen and I was totally clueless."

"Do you still keep in touch with Sienna?"

"Oh, yeah," Rylie nodded, enjoying the feel of his soft cotton shirt rubbing against her cheek, since he'd thrown his coat in the backseat when they got in the car at the airport. "In fact, she's one of the people I mentioned at Thanksgiving, when I told you I'd try to catch up with some of my old friends while we're on break."

"Then you should definitely call her while we're in Atlantic City," Liam suggested with a smile. "Maybe we can meet her for dinner or drinks this evening."

"No can do," Rylie informed him, unsure if she was sad she'd miss seeing her friend, or excited for Sienna because of the reason she wasn't in town. "When I texted her a couple weeks ago to try to set something up before I knew I'd be going to New York with you, she told me all about the two-week long ski trip she's taking with her parents for the holidays. Apparently, her new boyfriend went along to meet the family, so it was kind of a big deal. And if things go well when they meet Ben, I think she's hoping to come back with an engagement ring on her finger."

"Well, you should still try to meet up with some of your other friends while we're here."

Before Rylie could reply to tell him that her other friends were all otherwise occupied for the holidays too, the city fire inspector's truck pulled up and parked right behind them. Liam unwrapped his arm from around her, turned off the car, unbuckled his seat belt, and got out of the vehicle, leaving her sitting there confused.

"Good morning. I hope it's okay that we parked here," Liam greeted the fire inspector as he also exited his vehicle, causing Rylie to scramble to get out of the passenger side, so she didn't miss any of their conversation.

"Yeah, it's fine," the older man replied just as Rylie caught up with Liam at the back of their rental car.

"I'm Liam Connery." Liam extended his hand to shake the fire inspector's. "And this is my wife, Rylie. She got a call yesterday about the fire, since we haven't had the chance to move her stuff since we got married because we travel for work. And we wanted to see how bad it was as soon as we got into town."

"Nice to meet you. I'm Leo Newman," the fire inspector introduced himself as he shook Liam's hand. "I'm sorry. I can't let you into the building. Even the owners of the property or the contractors they hire to rebuild won't be allowed in until after I've finished my inspection and determined it's safe. And even then, I'm afraid most of the building will be completely off limits to anyone not trained to safely remove fire debris and rebuild."

Rylie's heart sank at the realization that she wouldn't even be allowed to go look to see if her mom's journals and photo albums survived. Thankfully, Liam seemed to recognize her nonverbal cues, so he knew to wrap his arm around her shoulders and pull her into his side to console her. She wrapped her arms around his waist, needing to hold onto him as much as she needed him to hold onto her at the moment.

"We completely understand," Liam said stoically, as Leo smiled sympathetically at Rylie, obviously able to read her stricken expression as well. "Like I said, we just wanted to see how bad the damage was before going to meet with the building manager and had no expectation of going inside." Liam smiled down at Rylie before turning back to the inspector and asking a couple of questions. "Do you have any idea when you'll release the building back to the company? Or if it will be possible for them to send any personal items that are undamaged to the tenants whose apartments are still intact, if we're unable to stay in town that long to pick them up?"

"That's all going to depend on what I find when I go in and do my inspection," Leo advised, reaching into the breast pocket on his jacket to pull out a business card holder. He got one of his cards out and handed it to Liam before returning the leather card holder to his pocket. "But give me a call this afternoon and I'll be able to let you know if the shell is stable enough that the guts can be rebuilt or if it needs to be demolished without anyone being able to retrieve anything. And don't hold your breath waiting to see your stuff again, 'cause unless your apartment is in this corner of the building, I doubt there'll be much that wasn't damaged to be retrievable."

"It is in this corner of the building," Rylie informed him, releasing the arm wrapped around Liam's abs and pointing up at her balcony. "Apartment seven-oh-nine, the second one from the end on the seventh floor. And it doesn't look from here like the fire reached my place."

"Well, then you might get lucky," Leo smiled at Rylie, but she could see it clearly didn't reach his eyes, which she assumed meant he wasn't optimistic that they'd be able to access the seventh floor to retrieve her things. "But you have to understand that getting anything out of your apartment will only be possible if there hasn't been any major issues with the floors collapsing. And with the holidays, it'll probably take a couple of weeks before the building owners can get anyone to even come look and give them an estimate, much less start working on clearing it out to possibly find your stuff."

"I guess that means you don't want me to give you the key to my apartment in case you can get to the seventh floor while doing your inspection, then, huh?" *Surely, if he can get up there, he can carry down that one tote, right? I can always reorder copies of mom and dad's birth, marriage, and death certificates if he can't get both the tote and the lockbox. But Mom's journals are irreplaceable as the only first-hand account of my family history.* Rylie just couldn't bring herself to think about the possibility of her mom's journals being destroyed along with what was left standing of the building without someone at least trying to get to them.

"I don't need a key," Leo informed her, shaking his head. "I actually have special tools to open locks if necessary to inspect a space."

As another SUV with the Atlantic City Fire Department insignia on the side pulled up and parked in front of their rental, Liam squeezed her shoulder, silently letting her know it was time for them to go. "Thank you for the information. We'll call you later to find out how your inspection goes. Have a good day and stay safe in there." He tapped the breast pocket on his shirt, where he'd put the fire inspector's card, and lifted his chin at the building before walking in front of Rylie to turn her around and escort her back to the passenger side of their rental car.

"You have a good day as well," Leo called out as they walked away.

Rylie wasn't sure how she felt about Liam maneuvering her the way he did before she could ask the inspector to look for her mom's journals and photo albums if he could get to her apartment. On the one hand, she was hurt that he seemed to block her one chance at possibly being able to save them. But on the other hand, she was grateful that he'd stopped her from embarrassing herself by begging a total stranger to risk his life for her mementoes, especially when there were over a hundred other residents who'd likely lost everything in the fire.

Feeling guilty for being so selfish, she was quiet on the drive to check in at their hotel before calling Mr. Dobson to get the address of the main office where they were supposed to meet. Since she'd done all her paperwork with him at the small office in the building when she'd first signed her lease in 2016, she'd never actually gone to the main office for the Carson Condominiums. While she had their address on her lease paperwork, that paperwork was all still in her apartment, so it was just easier to ask her landlord when and where to meet than to try to hunt down the information online when she knew the complex's website only listed the building address.

She also didn't say much as they carried their bags up to the two-bedroom suite Liam had reserved for them at the Basiation Hotel and Casino, a Burleson Resorts property, where they stopped to freshen up before leaving for the tenant meeting at the Carson Condominiums office. Even though they were both committed to working on their relationship and staying married, they'd agreed it was best to keep staying in separate bedrooms at night, so they wouldn't be tempted to make love while they were still working through everything and Liam was adamant about needing condoms.

While Rylie didn't agree with him about the risk of having sex without a condom since he didn't have any open wounds for the stalker's blood to have infected him, and especially since the coroner had informed the GWA security team that the stalker tested negative for everything, she understood his desire to protect her just in case. If their roles were reversed, she'd want to protect him too, only she knew she'd probably want to wait at least a year to be sure, since the incubation period of some sexually transmitted diseases could be as long as six to eight months, instead of just the ninety days that Doc had told Liam. *Maybe Doc only said ninety days because the lack of contact with open wounds or mucous membranes meant he couldn't have been exposed to the viruses with those longer incubation periods?*

Regardless of why, she understood his hesitation. And since she'd re-embraced her Catholic faith, she was glad to know he was also taking into account their mutual religious beliefs in making the decision. It was those same beliefs that led to her decision to stop taking the pill after her first talk with Father O'Malley. Technically, she knew she could still take it now to control any P.C.O.S. symptoms she might have while she and Liam were abstaining. But even after having that confirmed in their conversation with the priest the day before, she couldn't bring herself to take her pill that morning, not wanting to decrease their chances of conceiving if they weren't able to control their sexual attraction to one another the way they planned.

As she passed the king-sized bed in her room after leaving the bathroom, she felt saddened by the way they had to stay in separate beds to maintain control of their libidos. She wished they could at least share the space to cuddle at night, so maybe she wouldn't have another nightmare like she did the night before, when she'd dreamed about being caught in the fire, as if she'd actually been there when it happened instead of over a hundred miles away. Not wanting to dwell on the negative memories of her nightmare, she attempted to shake off her melancholy mood and at least appear to be optimistic about everything going on as they left the hotel to go to the meeting with her apartment manager and the insurance representative.

"Are you mad at me for not letting you try to sweet talk Inspector Newman into checking your apartment to see if your keepsakes were damaged or not?" Liam broke the silence as they drove to the Carson Condominiums office.

"No," Rylie sighed. "Honestly, I'm mad at myself for being so selfish that I almost asked him to risk his life to try getting up to the seventh floor to even look."

"That's not selfish, Moh Graw." Liam reached over and took her hand, lifting it to his lips for a reassuring kiss. "That's just being human. He just wasn't the right person to ask about retrieving your things. But we'll find out who will be going in there once the fire department releases the building, and have them send anything they're able to get out of your apartment to Belle Harbor, where Da can be there to sign for it and make sure it's safely stored until the next time we're home for you to go through it."

Rylie noted once again how Liam had referred to his place as home for both of them, which made her tingle at the realization that he truly was on board with wanting to give their marriage a go. She was glad the center console in the rental was much lower than the one in his Navigator, so she could easily lean over and peck a kiss on his cheek just as he parked for their meeting. "Thank you. I was afraid I'd have to list the address of the GWA headquarters for anything they might retrieve, since I'm basically homeless now."

"You're not homeless, either, Moh Graw," Liam smirked as he put the car in park. "Technically, as my wife, half my home belongs to you, so you really should consider it your home now, too."

"No, Liam, it doesn't belong to me," Rylie protested, shaking her head. "Yeah, we're working on our marriage and have put all the annulment and divorce talk on hold for now. But until we decide for sure that we're not ending things between us, I don't think it's right for us to combine our assets, so if we do go our separate ways, there's no fighting over who gets what. If we end our marriage, I don't want to leave it with anything more than what I already had before we got married. Well, other than what I've earned with the GWA since then, anyway. We may not have signed a prenup, but I want you to know that I'll gladly sign a postnup now, saying we each walk away with only what we brought into the marriage, so you know your assets are safe."

"So, I guess that means you're planning for us to file our taxes for last year as *'married filing separately,'* instead of filing them together?" Liam questioned, not moving to exit the vehicle for their scheduled meeting. His expression remained stoic, not giving her a clue as to how he felt about their options for filing their taxes.

"Yeah, I guess," Rylie replied, having not really thought that far in advance.

"And how are you going to file yours without an address?" Liam arched an eyebrow as a slow grin spread across his face.

"I, uh, I…" Rylie sputtered before trailing off, unsure how to answer him.

"It just seems to me that, while we're trying to work through everything, we might be more successful if we treat our marriage as if we're certain it's going to last forever," Liam smirked. "Besides, it would just be easier to officially move you to Belle Harbor and let my accountant deal with filing our taxes jointly, so neither one of us has to worry about trying to do them ourselves while on tour."

Does that mean he really thinks our marriage will last forever? He no longer has any doubts? He'll actually let our love for each other grow instead of trying to kill it again?

"You realize that if we do that, then we'll have to put off any of the legal work to end our marriage until after it's all filed and approved by the IRS, right?" Rylie couldn't tell from Liam's suddenly blank expression if he thought that delay was a benefit or a hindrance. "Even if we decide in the next couple of weeks to call it quits."

"We'd already said we can't do any of that until at least April, and most likely would have to wait until our Memorial Day break anyway," Liam shrugged. "So, I guess it works out that the last day to file our taxes is just a few days after we go through New York in April, when we can go to the accountant's office to sign them before leaving for the European tour. And then we have six weeks between then and our Memorial Day break to get our refund before we file anything, *if* we decide not to stay married."

The extra emphasis he put on the word "if" gave her hope that they were both thinking it was unlikely that they'd end their marriage. And it was that extra hope that swayed her into agreeing to officially "move" to his house as her legal residence.

"Okay, I guess I'm officially changing my address to the same as yours," Rylie smiled at Liam. *I wonder if he realizes that I'm also going to have to change my last name on all my government records to make this move and filing joint taxes completely official.* "But since I'm pretty sure it takes more than just putting in a change of address with the post office to make everything legal for filing our taxes together, you have to go with me to the DMV and social security office next week when we're back in the city. Do you think we'll have time to do both on Monday? Or should I plan one of those appointments for Tuesday?"

"We have to go inspect the GWA planes Monday morning, so you should probably schedule one for Monday afternoon and one for Tuesday morning," Liam suggested with a grin. "And if we're going to the social security office to change your name, we should probably do that on Monday, so you have more than just our marriage license to show the DMV to get them to put Rylie Connery on your New York driver's license."

Yeah, I guess he did realize I'll have to change my name. And that grin can only mean that he hopes it's a permanent change to sharing his last name.

"Rylie Ann Long Connery," she corrected with a smirk before opening her car door to get out and go into the meeting with the apartment manager and insurance company representative, loving the sound of her new last name.

Unfortunately, even the joy of thinking they were another step closer to her keeping that new name forever wasn't enough to keep the smile on her face as they walked into the Carson Condominiums office and saw the dejected looks on so many of her neighbors' faces. She just felt too guilty for being happy for her blessings when so many others were suffering through the loss of all their worldly possessions, and especially their irreplaceable photos and mementos.

At least I was able to read Mom's journals and save cloud copies of the pictures in her photo albums before the fire. So, I have to be thankful for having the memories. And maybe I can type up some of the stories I remember from her journals to keep them digitally, too. I just wish I knew how to help everyone else hang on to their memories as well.

~~~

As they sat through the informational meeting with Bill Dobson, Jeff and Jack Carson, the owners of Carson Condominiums, representatives from several different insurance companies, and at least fifty of Rylie's former neighbors, Liam pulled out his phone and texted his business manager, Bradan Murray, giving him the names of the hotels and other organizations the Carsons passed along to their residents in case they still needed assistance in meeting their basic needs since the fire. He usually only dealt with Bradan when he had to coordinate appearances for his endorsement deals and charitable donations with his GWA schedule, so he'd been giving him the same holiday breaks as the GWA for the last year, since he'd done his annual visit to the Children's Hospital in New York over the *Christmas Chaos* weekend and had been scheduling the photo shoots for his endorsements in various cities all over the country instead of just in New York. But even though Liam didn't have any photo shoots for endorsements or charitable hospital visits scheduled for his time off from the GWA, Bradan had to be called in, so he could set up the financial donations needed to help Rylie's former neighbors get back on their feet. Liam had actually called Bradan the night before to give him a heads up, but without knowing any of the details earlier, he hadn't been able to do anything to help yet.

"Who are you texting?" Rylie whispered once the building manager finished telling everyone who to reach out to for assistance and informed them they'd be taking each tenant into a private office to take care of the paperwork to terminate their leases before their next rent payment automatically drafted out of their bank accounts, and then sending them for one-on-one meetings with the insurance representatives for the preliminary claim paperwork.

"My business manager," Liam whispered back, showing her his screen before tucking his phone back in his pocket while they waited for Rylie's turn to be called back to sign her paperwork. "Setting up donations to each of the organizations the Carsons and Mr. Dobson just mentioned."

"Oh, Liam. Thank you."
~~~

While Liam didn't think it was that big a deal, Rylie apparently did. Her expression softened as her shoulders seemed to sag with relief, right before she leaned over and pressed her soft lips to his cheek.

*Huh? I wonder if that's what Kay meant in **Kissing Kat** when she described Katrina as appearing to have "melted" in response to something Anton said? If so, then maybe my plan to read her books to get ideas for how to win Rylie's heart is working?*

*Feck, that was fast, since I haven't even finished reading the first one yet. Of course, I didn't really get the idea to help her neighbors from the book either. But since Rylie doesn't have kids like Kat does in the book, I can't exactly make her swoon by befriending them and helping to rescue her and her kids from an evil ex. So, I guess trying to help her and her neighbors after the fire is as close as I can get to emulating the things Anton did in the book to get Kat to fall in love with him. But maybe I should hurry up and finish reading the first book so I can see if there are any better ideas in **Winning Rhonda**, since I wanna win Rylie.*

After their talk with Father O'Malley the day before and making the decision to wait another month before making love to Rylie again, Liam had gotten the bright idea to read romance novels to get ideas for other ways he could woo his woman that didn't include sex. Unfortunately, he hadn't realized just how graphic romance novels could be before he downloaded all of Kay's books to his tablet. Yeah, he'd definitely been inspired with ways to pamper Rylie that weren't sexual, but he'd also had to go take an ice cold shower after reading each sex scene to keep from jerking off while imagining reenacting them with Rylie.

Although, if I actually do win Rylie over so we can start sharing a bed again, I'm gonna hafta come clean about the real reason for my new nightly reading habit, so she doesn't think I'm just reading those books for the hot sex scenes. But then again, maybe if we compare notes on the books we've both read, we might find a few ideas we'd both like to try once we add sex back into our relationship, like that sexy as feck shower scene.

Feck, I'd love to start the day off eating Rylie's pussy in the shower, even if I'd have to kneel to do it since I don't have a shelf big enough to sit her on in my shower at home. But maybe I can call the contractor to come out and install one? And fecking feck, it'd be amazing to soap her up and fuck her perfect tits while watching her finger herself. Liam couldn't stop himself from picturing Rylie naked in his shower at home, emulating Kat's actions from the book with him in the role of Anton. *And if we can recreate that scene the next time we're home on break, maybe we could actually finish with my cock in her pussy, instead of having to stop before penetration like Anton and Kat did in the book.*

"Um, Liam…" Rylie's soft voice brought him out of the fantasy, as she purposely cut her eyes from his face to his crotch and back again, the slightest hint of a blush brightening her golden brown cheeks. "I don't know where you just went in your head, but you might want to come back to reality so nobody else notices how *happy* you are to be here."

"Sorry," Liam whispered his apology, fighting not to smile as he leaned forward to rest his elbows on his knees and hoping the shift in position would camouflage his erection until he could somehow get it to go down. "I can't seem to get him to understand that just being close to you isn't a signal that he's supposed to come out and play."

When Rylie lightly giggled and her terra-cotta cheeks darkened to a rich russet, Liam quit fighting the upturn of his lips.

"If you have any ideas for getting him to go back to sleep, I'll gladly take them," Liam added when her coquettish expression just made him harder.

"Oh, I have an idea, but I don't think you'll like it," Rylie teased, grinning mischievously.

"If it's your idea, then I'm sure I'll love it, which might be a problem, since everything about you seems to elicit this reaction." Liam dipped his chin to refer to his swelling issue.

"Close your eyes and go back to wherever you went in your head a few minutes ago," Rylie suggested, keeping her voice low, so nobody else in the room could hear her.

Liam did as she recommended, enjoying the image of her naked in his shower once more with his cock nestled between her voluptuous breasts.

"You there?"

"Emmm-hm," Liam nodded, licking his lips as he imagined dropping to his knees to lick her pussy.

"Now, replace me in that picture with Granny Breena."

"Feck no," Liam hissed, barely keeping his voice modulated to keep everyone else in the room from hearing him as he bolted upright in his seat and turned to face her. He popped his eyes open to keep from accidentally following her directions. Luckily, he didn't have to actually picture his granny for his cock to deflate faster than he even thought was possible. "What are you trying to do? Mentally scar me for life, so I'll never be able to…"

Liam let his words trail off, assuming she could fill in the blank when her bark of laughter drew the attention of several other people in the room, none of whom needed to know how his wife just risked his ability to ever get another erection.

"I told you, you wouldn't like it," she sputtered out through her laughter.

"Oh, no, my feelings for that idea are so far beyond not liking it," he susurrated, still trying to keep his voice low so nobody else in the room could hear him. "It's more like I'm disgusted by it. Revolted by it. Nauseated by it. Trying to put that image in my head is the epitome of cruel and unusual punishment."

Liam swallowed down the bile that tried to come up at even thinking about his granny doing any of the things he fantasized about doing with Rylie, even if she was with his granda. Yeah, theoretically, he knew his grandparents had to have had sex or else his da and uncles wouldn't have been born. But he didn't want to picture either of them doing more than the hugging and kissing they still engaged in often enough that they'd been caught by their grandsons at least three times on Christmas Day alone.

"Sorry," Rylie giggled as her laughter died down somewhat, leaning over to rest her head on his shoulder as she clutched his hand. "Would you rather I'd have said to picture your mom instead?"

"No, that's not any better," Liam protested, unable to keep from smiling at how she laughed at him, even though he found nothing funny about picturing any of his family members having sex.

He wasn't smiling for long though, as an older couple, previously seated across the room, stood and walked toward them. *Feck, this really isn't the appropriate time or place to smile or laugh like that.*

"I just want to let you know how refreshing it is to see a young couple in love, finding reasons to laugh and smile even when facing tough situations like this." The older woman reached out and patted their joined hands resting atop Liam's knee. "You remind me so much of when Henry and I were newlyweds. And I really needed that today."

"*We* really needed it today," the man Liam assumed was Henry clarified, smiling at them as he rested his hands on his wife's shoulders.

"Thank you, Mrs. Tomkins." Rylie smiled at the older woman, reaching out with her free hand to cover Mrs. Tomkins' hand on top of their joined hands. "Being compared to you is the highest compliment anyone's ever given me. Though I don't feel like I've really lived up to your graciousness since I've been rude and haven't introduced you to my husband, Liam Connery. Liam, this is Betty and Henry Tomkins."

"It's nice to meet you." Liam extracted his hand from under Rylie's and extended it to Henry to shake. "I just wish it was under better circumstances."

"Likewise," Henry agreed as he shook Liam's hand. "And congratulations on your nuptials, assuming the fact that you're here and wearing wedding rings means you're really married and it's not just a storyline for your GWA characters."

"Yes, we're really married," Liam and Rylie assured them in unison, turning to look at one another and smile at how they'd shared the same thought at the same time.

"Are you staying at the Econo Lodge or with family?" Betty questioned. "If you're at the hotel, we'd love to have you join us for dinner to have a proper toast to your marriage."

"We're actually at a different hotel," Rylie replied with a sad smile, obviously not wanting to rub their noses in the fact that he'd picked a five-star luxury resort for their short stay in town, while the rest of the residents were in an economy hotel. Not that there was anything wrong with the Econo Lodge, it was a fine establishment, but it wasn't part of the top of the line hotel chain the Burlesons had purchased a few months earlier. "We were in New York, spending the holidays with Liam's family and didn't know where everyone else went when we made the arrangements yesterday to fly in this morning."

Before Liam could suggest possibly meeting up with them later, even though they weren't staying in the same hotel, Rylie's name was called for her to go meet with the property manager. So, they politely excused themselves from the conversation with Henry and Betty to go speak with Bill Dobson.

Once they were seated in his office, the man who looked to be in his early fifties informed them that she simply had to give him the address where she would like her deposit and anything of hers they were able to retrieve from her unit sent and sign a form stating they were terminating her lease due to the fire. Liam assumed there was a clause in the document she was signing that stated she wouldn't sue the owners for damages since the fire was not their fault, but he couldn't check by reading over Rylie's shoulder because his phone rang.

Seeing Bradan's name on the screen when he pulled his phone from his pocket, he knew he couldn't send it to voice mail. "Excuse me, I have to take this." Liam held up his phone to show Rylie the screen, so she'd know he was going to make sure there wasn't a problem with the donations he was making to help her neighbors.

"Of course," she smiled up at him as he stood to leave the office. "If I'm not here when you get done, I'll be in the next office giving the Rent Pro Insurance rep our address."

Our address. Yeah, I like the way that sounds. Liam smiled as he swiped to answer the call and stepped out into the hallway. Instead of turning right and going back to the large conference room where everyone who was still waiting for their turn sat, he turned left down the hall, hoping for some privacy to talk to his business manager.

"Hey Bradan," he greeted the other man as he walked. "Please tell me you're not calling because of a problem with the donations."

"No, those are all taken care of with no problems," Bradan assured him. "I don't remember if I told you at the time or not, but a couple of years ago, the building where my cousin and his family lived burned down. When they lost everything, my cousin's son had to sit out a few games after the fire because nobody thought about him needing new football pads and uniforms. So I thought we might prevent that same kind of issue for any of the families you're helping now by setting up some Visa gift cards for each of the families to cover incidentals that nobody else might have thought of, like replacement equipment and uniforms for any athletes or kids whose schools require them, or whatever else the residents might need, even if they don't have kids in their household."

"That's a fabulous idea," Liam agreed. "What do I need to do to set those up?"

"We can go online and order them," Bradan explained. "I just need to know how many and how much to put on each of them. And if you want to take the time for the plastic cards to be sent to you, or to someone there already coordinating donations to the residents. Or if you can get the email addresses of each family, would the emailed version be acceptable, since those will get there faster?"

"Faster would definitely be better," Liam decided, turning around as he got to the end of the hall and noticing that Rylie was being escorted across the hall to another office by one of the Carson brothers who owned the building. "But I'm not sure if all the residents are tech savvy enough to use email like that."

As Jack Carson walked back toward the main room where everyone was waiting, Liam flagged down Jeff Carson, thinking one of the owners might be able to get him a list of email addresses and an exact count of the number of families displaced. "Hang on a second, Bradan. I'm going to ask one of the building owners how many cards and if we'll be able to do the e-versions or not."

"Yes, how can I help you?" Jeff questioned when he and Liam walked within speaking distance to one another.

"I'm Liam Connery," Liam extended his hand to introduce himself to the building owner who'd been introduced at the beginning of the meeting earlier. "My wife was one of your residents and when we found out about the fire, I started setting up some donations to the organizations you mentioned in the meeting to help everyone else get back on their feet."

"That's very kind of you," Jeff smiled as he shook Liam's hand.

"Anyway, I'm on the phone with my business manager and he suggested setting up Visa gift cards for each of the families to help cover the cost of incidentals that aren't already covered, like replacement school uniforms or athletic gear or whatever," Liam continued. "But in order to set those up, I need to know how many families we need to order the gift cards for, and if it's possible to get their email addresses so we can get them the cards faster than actually sending plastic cards. Can you help me with that?"

"Yes, of course," Jeff agreed eagerly. "That building has sixty condos that are individually owned by the residents, and ninety apartments that we lease out, for a total of one-hundred-and-fifty units, but there were ten apartments that were unoccupied while being updated for new renters to be able to move in next year."

"Did you hear that, Bradan?" Liam questioned as he put his phone on speaker. "We need one-hundred-and-forty gift cards."

"And how much do you want to put on each of them?" Bradan asked, his voice now echoing down the hall.

Apparently realizing that this discussion needed to be kept more private, Jeff motioned for Liam to follow him back down to the end of the hall and into his office. Liam didn't say a word as he tried to remember how much his school uniforms and athletic gear had cost, assuming he should probably double that amount to account for inflation in the seventeen years since he'd graduated high school. But as Jeff sat behind his desk and Liam took a seat in the chair in front of it, he realized he had no clue how much his parents had spent on any of that stuff.

"I don't know," Liam finally answered Bradan, looking at Jeff as if he might know how much was needed by each family. When Jeff just stared back at him with a blank expression, Liam guessed he didn't know how much uniforms and stuff that wasn't covered by the various aid organizations cost either. "What's the maximum we can put on a card?"

"According to the website where I've ordered cards like this before, five-hundred dollars," Bradan replied.

"Then go with that," Liam decided, hoping it would be enough to cover the most important items, even if it wasn't enough to replace everything the families needed that wasn't already being provided by the other organizations he'd donated to that morning.

"Okay, the gift card website won't let me do a transaction that big," Bradan sighed. "So, let me call the bank and do another wire transfer. Maybe they'll be able to set it up so you can pick up the plastic cards at one of their branches in Atlantic City to pass them out this afternoon."

"Thanks, Bradan. Be sure and give yourself a bonus for doing all this today when I know you'd rather be spending your time off with your family."

"Oh, please," Bradan laughed. "My three ladies are all off exchanging the gifts that don't fit and taking advantage of the after

Christmas sales to get the stuff they really wanted, so I needed something to do to keep me occupied between trips outside, trying to potty train the new dog, anyway."

"I tried to warn you that you'd get stuck with that job," Liam chuckled, thinking back to the conversation they'd had a week earlier when Bradan had asked if Liam knew anything about Pomeranians, since that was the predominant breed of the mutt Bradan's wife had picked out for their daughters from the local shelter. "Did you at least convince them not to name him Fluffy?"

"No," Bradan sighed. "It's bad enough that the poor guy has so much fur that everyone assumes he's a girl because his junk's well covered. But they wouldn't go for Spike, or Butch, or even Fuzzball to try to make it obvious he's a boy. But when they get home, I'm going to see if I can get them to let me call him Fluffernutter, so they can keep the fluff they want and I can have some reference to him having nuts. Or rather that he had nuts before he was neutered."

"Good luck with that," Liam laughed, noticing Jeff even smiled at the predicament Bradan found himself in with his wife and daughters over their new pet. "And just let me know where I need to pick up the gift cards later."

"Will do, Li. Happy holidays."

"Happy holidays," Liam replied as they disconnected the call. Once he put his phone back in his pocket, Liam enlisted the assistance of the building owner once more. "So, I'm assuming you have a way to contact everyone for me to set up a way to pass out these cards once I get them?"

"Yes, we have two more of these meetings set up for tomorrow morning, one for the resident owners and another for the tenants who weren't able to make it today, so you can pass out a majority of them then," Jeff informed him. "And I believe everyone who was here today is staying at the hotel set up by the Red Cross, so if you get the cards this afternoon, I'll gladly meet you there with a list of the residents to pass them out and keep track to make sure every family gets one."

"Thank you. That would be great," Liam agreed, understanding the need for a checklist to make sure they didn't miss anyone, while also leaving the list in the hands of the building owner to maintain the privacy of the residents. "While I have you here, I wanted to ask what's the protocol for getting Rylie's stuff from her apartment, since it didn't appear to be damaged when we drove by the building this morning?"

"The fire chief is supposed to be coming by here in about an hour to let us know what the inspector found," Jeff explained, shaking his head as if he didn't think it would be good news. "He'll let us know then if we'll be able to hire a clean-up crew to remove items from the intact units, or if the structural damage is so bad that we'll just have to demolish the whole building because it's not safe to try to retrieve anything. If we're able to get a cleaning crew in there, then we'll have them retrieve anything salvageable and sort through it here before returning anything we can to the address on the paperwork your wife signed today."

"Yeah, she's probably done, so I don't think she'll want to wait around another hour to find out." Liam pulled his phone from his pocket along with the business card Leo Newman had given him that morning. "So, why don't we go ahead and call the inspector now instead of waiting for the fire chief."

"You have the inspector's number?" Jeff sat up straighter in his chair, obviously intrigued by Liam having a contact that he didn't.

"Yes, he gave it to us when we drove by the building this morning just as he got there to start his inspection," Liam explained as he dialed, putting the phone on speaker as it started to ring. "And he told me to call him this afternoon to find out when we might be able to get some of Rylie's things."

"Newman," the inspector greeted them when he picked up the call.

"Good afternoon, Mr. Newman. It's Liam Connery, we met this morning at the Carson Condos."

"Ah, yes, Liam, I've been expecting your call. Is your lovely wife with you? I have some news I think she's going to appreciate."

"Actually, she's not in the room at the moment, but I am sitting here with Jeff Carson, one of the owners of the condo building, while she's off dealing with paperwork with the manager and insurance company. So, if you think Rylie's going to be happy with your news, then I bet Jeff will be, too."

"Maybe," Leo chuckled. "But he might not be as happy about having forty-five undamaged units, and another thirty only smoke damaged units, which he now has to pay a clean-up crew to empty out, as Rylie will be to find out her unit is one of the undamaged units."

"And the floors are structurally sound, so it will be safe to go in and clean out those units?" Jeff questioned.

"Yes, there are some places on the north end of the building where the damage is bad enough that you're going to have to go back to the steel framing to rebuild, specifically in the apartment where the fire started. But the majority of the damage in the rest of the building was from smoke, where a lot of furniture, draperies, and wood fixtures burned, and water from where the fire department put it out, but for the most part the fire-resistant building materials used in the original construction are still intact."

"So, Rylie's apartment doesn't even have smoke or water damage? Her mom's journals and photo albums are still just as she left them?" Liam was hopeful that they'd be able to retrieve those precious memories for her.

"I didn't go through anything in the apartments, so I can't say exactly what is in her unit, but from what I could see while doing the inspection, I'd assume she'll only need to air out her possessions for them to be as good as new, and that's only if they picked up any of the fire smell since we opened the door to the unit."

"Thank you, sir. Rylie is going to be thrilled to know she hasn't lost the last link she has to her parents. Is there a fire department fund I can donate to as a way to show my thanks for all the hard work of the men and women in your precinct?"

"The ACFD is actually funded by the city, but we have the Fallen Firefighters Fund you can donate to that benefits the families of firefighters who've been injured or died on the job."

"Excellent," Liam beamed. "Do you have a contact person, whose name I can pass on to my business manager, so he can wire over the donation?"

Leo Newman gave Liam the information, then briefly discussed the details of releasing the building to the Carsons for a clean-up crew to start in the new year before they ended the call. Liam then called Bradan back and gave him the instructions for setting up the donation to the Fallen Firefighters Fund before going to find Rylie and tell her the good news.

Leah Mae Wright

The smile on her face when she found out she would most likely get her mom's journals and photo albums back was so bright it could likely be seen from outer space. But it was the exuberant way she threw herself into his arms that made all of Liam's donations and phone calls that day worth it. *If only I could tell her when she'd see those special keepsakes again, instead of just telling her they'll probably be sent to the house sometime next month.*

Chapter Eight

Rylie luxuriated in the feel of Liam's hands and mouth moving over her skin as he caressed and kissed his way down her torso. The way he alternated featherlight, teasing touches with firmer strokes and squeezes amped up her arousal almost as much as the way he titillated her with light licks and nips interspersed with open-mouthed, sucking kisses. He took his time, focusing on her breasts with his mouth while trailing his hands lower and delving between her legs.

"Oh, yes, Liam," she moaned in pleasure, rocking her hips to meet him as his fingers dipped between her folds.

"You're so wet, Moh Graw," Liam growled as he released her nipple from between his teeth. "So hot. And all mine. Only mine, as I am only yours."

Just as Liam sucked her breast back into his mouth, the room around them seemed to darken as if it was filling with smoke. The bedside lamps cut off at about the same time the acrid smell overrode the scent of Liam's bergamot and sandalwood bodywash, making it clear they now had to escape from a fire in the hotel while unable to see to find their clothes, much less how to navigate out of the room and down the hall to the stairwell.

"Oh, em, gee, Liam, I think the hotel is on fire!" Rylie grabbed Liam's shoulders, digging her nails into his flesh to get his attention as he continued to make love to her, seemingly not noticing the smoke in the room.

"Rylie! No! Not Rylie! My Rylie!"

Rylie bolted up in bed, startled from her sleep by hearing Liam scream her name, and feeling momentarily confused by what was real and what was just part of her dream. As she realized she was alone in her room, and was still wearing the sleep shorts and tank top she'd worn to bed the night before, Rylie felt grateful that she'd woken up before her normal sex dream about Liam turned into another nightmare about the fire in her building, like she'd had the night before after first hearing from Mr. Dobson.

"Rylie!" Liam's anguished howl vanquished her nightmare memories before they fully resurfaced in her mind.

She didn't take the time to think about why, she just jumped up and ran from her bed to the other bedroom in the suite they were sharing at the Basiation Hotel and Casino, needing to go to him if he needed her. Out of habit, she turned on the overhead light as soon as she opened his bedroom door, seeing him thrash around in the bed as if he was fighting some unknown demon in his sleep. *Oh, no, he's having nightmares too.* "Liam, I'm here. Wake up, Li, so you can see it's me, Rylie. I'm right here."

Liam didn't respond as if he heard her, continuing to struggle with the blankets while crying out her name over and over again. "Rylie, Rye-Rylie…"

After reading several romance novels with military heroes who suffered from nightmares as part of their PTSD, she knew better than to move close to him to try to wake him up from his bad dream. Seeing him fight the covers, it was obvious that he'd keep striking out at anyone who got near him until he woke up, and she was smart enough to avoid being accidentally hit. So, she stayed standing by the door as she spoke softly to him, not wanting to frighten him by yelling. "I'm right here, Liam. Whatever you're seeing isn't real. I'm here. I'm okay. Close your eyes in the nightmare and open them here in reality, so you can see for yourself that I'm fine."

When his movements started to slow, she thought she was starting to get through to him, so she took a step closer as she cooed to him. "It's okay, Liam. It's me, Rylie. I'm here with you and we're both safe. So, please, just wake up for me now."

Unfortunately, even when he seemed to quit fighting the villain in his mind, he didn't wake up. Instead, he started sobbing and whimpering her name, tears leaking from his closed eyes as he cried in his sleep. Seeing him in such a vulnerable state was even more heartbreaking for Rylie than it had been to see him distraught with the earlier part of the nightmare.

She was tempted to crawl into the bed with him and try to wake him with affection, but she didn't want to be like the clueless women she'd read about, who almost ended up being choked out by not realizing the fight was still going on in her hero's nightmare, even though he'd quit physically acting it out. Instead, she started brainstorming ideas for how she could wake him up from afar without making the bad dream worse.

"Do I need to shout your full name like your mom said she had to do to wake you up for school when you were a kid? Or will shouting just make the nightmare worse?" She paced back and forth a couple of feet from the foot of the king-sized bed. "Or maybe I could get close enough to tickle the bottoms of your feet without you being able to kick me? No, as fast as you are in the ring, I'm sure you'd either connect with your foot or spin around and grab me before I could back up. And if it's not enough to wake you up, that could really end up going badly for me."

As she passed the bedroom door in her pacing, she caught a glimpse of the kitchenette in the outer room of the suite and got another idea. "Or I could go fill the ice bucket with water and toss it on you. Surely a bucket of cold water would be enough to wake you up."

When she turned to go get the ice bucket, she noticed the television was on and displaying a screensaver, where apparently whatever he'd been watching after they got back from dinner and passing out some of the gift cards he'd bought for the other residents of her building earlier had cut off. "I bet I could play the opening of **Guardians of the Galaxy Vol. 2** and maybe hearing **Mr. Blue Sky** playing while Baby Groot is dancing during the first fight scene will help him realize the fight in his dream isn't real, so he can wake up."

She spun around to look for the remote and hoped she'd be quick enough grabbing it from the bedside table to wake him up before he started fighting the nightmare again and could reach out and grab her while she was that close to the bed. Just to make sure she was safe, she ran to the bedside table, grabbed the remote, and ran back to just inside the door, before backing out to the home screen on the Roku TV. She signed into the Disney+ app as fast as she could, then turned up the volume to its maximum as she started the movie.

When ***Brandy, You're a Fine Girl*** started playing, she mentally kicked herself for not remembering the actual opening scene of the movie. But luckily, the specific song didn't seem to matter, just hearing music blaring from the television was enough to wake Liam.

"What the feck?" Liam sat bolt upright in bed, his eyes wide as he looked at first the TV and then at Rylie, who was standing by the door holding the remote.

Seeing his bare chest momentarily distracted her, especially when she noticed the light smattering of chest hair on his pecs where he'd slacked off on his hair removal routine while they were on break. *Eyes up, Rylie. Right after he's had a nightmare is most definitely Not the appropriate time to drool over how hot he is, especially since we're supposed to be abstaining for the next month.*

She turned away from Liam, looking back at the television as she lowered the volume, leaving the movie playing as she explained. "Sorry, you screamed in your sleep and I couldn't figure out how to wake you up without getting hit because you were thrashing around like you were in a fight for your life. So, it was either this," she motioned with her thumb over her shoulder toward the television as she turned around again and walked over to put the remote back on the bedside table, "or filling the ice bucket with cold water and tossing it on you."

"So, of course, you went with Baby Groot," Liam half-snorted as he smiled slightly, rubbing his eyes with the sides of his fists to clear the crustiness from crying in his sleep.

"Of course," Rylie smiled at him as she sat down on the edge of the bed, fighting to keep her eyes on his face instead of looking down to see what color boxer briefs he was currently wearing now that the covers were pushed down enough that she could see them. "I knew you'd realize the fight in your nightmare wasn't real when it was interrupted by a dancing Baby Groot. But you didn't even have to get that far in the movie before you woke up."

"And hopefully, the hotel guests in the next room won't call the front desk to complain about us blasting music at..." Liam looked over at the alarm clock on the opposite bedside table before finishing his sentence. "...three a.m., so we won't get a visit from hotel security in a few minutes."

"Naw, if they were gonna complain about that, they'd have called to complain about you screaming in your sleep. Besides, I'm sure the hotel staff would much rather come up here for a noise complaint that has already been dealt with than have to replace a waterlogged mattress, so I picked the better option, even if we get someone knocking on our door in a few minutes."

They sat there in silence for a little while, both turning to focus on watching the movie, even though she'd turned the volume down so low that it might as well have been muted. After the silence got to be unbearable, she finally asked, "So, what was your nightmare about?"

"Just the same ones I've been having since October," Liam sighed, scooting back to lean against the headboard and reaching out to invite her to join him, presumably because he needed to be reassured she wasn't in danger by holding her for a few minutes.

"You've been having nightmares since October? About the shooting?" Rylie questioned as she slid her legs under the blankets to warm up, since her sleep shorts and tank top weren't exactly winter sleepwear. She moved the extra pillow to have it as a cushion between her and the headboard before scooting closer to Liam, reveling in the comforting feeling of snuggling with her husband.

"Yeah," Liam confirmed as he put his arm around her shoulders.

"Then why were you calling my name instead of Dion's or Allissa's?" Rylie rested her head on his chest, turning her head to face the TV, hoping he might feel more comfortable confiding in her if he didn't have to look her in the eyes while doing so. *Just don't give into the temptation of licking and kissing his bare chest. That definitely won't get him to open up, no matter how good it might feel for both of us.*

"Because in my nightmares, it's not always Dion and the stalker who get shot. And even that first day, it was you I pictured in Allissa's place." Liam shuddered as if just the thought frightened him.

Rylie pulled the blankets up over both of them, even though she knew he wasn't shivering because he was cold. "You have these nightmares regularly? Why haven't I heard you before now?"

"Because most of the time the screams are just in my head." Liam brushed his lips over the top of her head. "And I had my contractor use soundproofing insulation in all my walls at the house because I didn't want to take a chance on my kids overhearing me in the bedroom the way I overheard my parents when I was a kid."

"But I should have noticed you fighting the stalker when we were in Heart's Destiny, even if you didn't vocalize whatever you were saying in the nightmares." Rylie couldn't believe she'd slept through him having bad dreams while they were sharing a bed for over a week, not with how violently he reacted to the nightmare she'd just woken him up from. *The only night I might have been so out of it that I wouldn't notice was the night of the bachelorette party. But I should have known the rest of the nights. Unless, maybe that's why I woke up when he went to jerk off in the shower, but I didn't completely wake up until after he'd gotten out of bed?*

"They weren't as bad that week as they are now. I only had a couple at the beginning of the week and they completely went away when we started our friends-with-benefits thing."

I wonder if they're worse now because of the fire? I mean, I just woke up from what was about to be a nightmare, too. And since I've even had a couple of bad dreams after finding out about it yesterday — or I guess day before yesterday now — I have to wonder if hearing about the fire has triggered his brain to combine the shooting back in October with the possibility of us being in a fire now to make his dreams twice as scary?

"Are you trying to tell me sex banishes your nightmares?" Rylie chuckled, hoping to lighten the mood in the room as she snuggled into Liam's side. "Is that your way of trying to convince me not to wait another month?"

"No," Liam laughed, squeezing his arm around her a little tighter and resting his cheek on the top of her head. "It's gonna be hard as feck to wait, but I know we need to, so we'll both feel connected spiritually as well as physically."

Rylie felt blessed by Liam sharing her faith and being just as determined as her to try to live according to God's word. When she really thought about it, she realized she had him and his family to thank for her realization that she wanted to reconcile with God and finally start to move into the acceptance phase of her grief over losing her parents. If she hadn't had to attend Mass with them at the beginning of this break, she wasn't sure if she'd have ever gotten there on her own. While attending the non-denominational church in

Heart's Destiny might have started opening her heart to religion again, it took the barrage of memories that were triggered by attending a Catholic Church again to really emphasize the importance of her faith in her life.

"But maybe we could try sleeping in the same bed, even if we have to have the wall of pillows between us like we did before, since being able to look over and see you sleeping peacefully whenever I woke up from the nightmares seemed to help me fall back to sleep and not have another one?"

"Yeah, I suppose that could help with my nightmares too," Rylie admitted, yawning as she turned to drape her arm over Liam's stomach. "But I'm afraid it might be skating on thin ice for our temptation levels."

"You've been having nightmares, too?" Liam questioned, rubbing his hand up and down her back comfortingly and not commenting on how tempting it would be to make love if they slept in the same bed.

"Just the last two nights," she elaborated, fighting to keep her eyes open as she got comfortable. "Since hearing about the fire, I've had a couple, mostly imagining what it was like for my neighbors trying to get out of the building. But the one earlier tonight morphed into having to get out of one of the hotels we stay in on tour."

"Yeah, I imagine that would weigh heavy on your mind," Liam crooned in a soothing tone. "But that possibility makes it even more clear why we should start staying in the same room, so I can make sure you get out safely if it ever happens."

"Emmm-hm," Rylie agreed, no longer able to stay awake now that she was safely ensconced in Liam's arms. *I'll ask him tomorrow, or I guess that'll really be later today, if he means sharing a room like we're sharing this suite with separate bedrooms, or if he wants us to risk giving into temptation by sharing a bed.*

Liam couldn't believe how quickly Rylie had fallen asleep while half sitting up in his bed. From their time together in New Orleans and Heart's Destiny, he knew orgasms knocked her out pretty quickly, but he hadn't realized how easy it was for her to fall asleep without them.

Feeling guilty for having woken her up with his nightmares of being caught in a fire with a stalker trying to take her from him, Liam just sat there holding her as she slept, watching the movie she'd started even though he couldn't hear it. Since they'd watched it together previously, when they were just hanging out as friends with several of the other GWA wrestlers before that night in August when they got married, he knew the story well enough that he didn't need to hear it to know what was going on. Besides, knowing how much she needed her sleep, it wasn't worth waking her up to reach around her to get the remote from the bedside table to turn it up.

Surprisingly, even with her soft curves pressed against him, Liam wasn't tempted to act on their intense sexual attraction. Oh, he was hard as steel, and thoroughly enjoyed the way her soft breath wafted across his nipple as she lightly snored in her sleep, but holding her right then was more about comforting both of them after their nightmares than their explosive chemistry. And after a couple of days of attempting to live a sin-free life to be worthy of being her husband by not even jerking off in the shower the way he used to, he'd started acclimating to his constantly aroused state while the head on his shoulders maintained control, instead of letting the head between his legs lead him astray.

That being said, when he woke up a few hours later while still holding Rylie in his arms, he also knew he had to get up and go take a cold shower to keep from thinking with his dick-brain. Apparently, she realized it wasn't the best idea for her to still be in his bed when he came back from the bathroom to get dressed for the day, since she'd vacated the room by the time he finished taking the world's coldest shower.

They went about their separate routines to get ready for the day, meeting up in the living room area of the suite before going down for breakfast in the hotel restaurant. After being so lost in her thoughts the day before that she was quiet when they first checked in, she finally asked him if he knew the meaning of the name of the hotel, since basiation wasn't a word she'd ever heard before. He'd hated having to tell her about a conversation he'd had with Jen, Julie, and Dion over their Labor Day break. But once he told her that Dion actually came up with the name when Julie asked them to help her brainstorm name ideas for the hotel chain the Burlesons had bought a few weeks earlier, she seemed to relax and not care when the conversation happened or that it was one of the times he was paired with Jen at a wedding shower.

After he explained that basiation is an obsolete Latin word that means kissing, Rylie really thought it was funny that Liam hadn't realized there was more going on with Dion and Julie. *Yeah, I suppose she's right that I should have figured out there was more going on when he suggested she should covertly name their hotels the Kissing Hotels.*

While neither of them said a word about what happened in the middle of the night, or mentioned their nightmares, they'd continued their conversation by planning out their day as they ate. First, they had to go to the Carson Condominiums office to pass out the rest of the gift cards they hadn't been able to give away the night before. Liam wanted to just let the Carsons handle the rest of them, but apparently, Jeff and Jack felt uncomfortable with being responsible for seventy-thousand dollars' worth of someone else's money.

Unfortunately, they didn't seem to understand that Liam had wanted to anonymously donate everything he'd given to help the residents recover after the fire, not wanting anyone but his business manager and accountant to know the final total of his donations. He also didn't want to be recognized and thanked for doing something he knew any of his friends would've done in his position. The reward for him was knowing he was using his wealth to help others, but the way the Carsons talked about what a huge tax write-off he'd have somewhat cheapened that feeling for him. Thankfully, they only knew about the seventy-thousand dollars in gift cards and the hundred-thousand dollar donation to the Fallen Firefighters Fund that he'd done in Jeff's office the day before. So, they didn't bring up the five-hundred-thousand dollars in donations to the various organizations providing shelter, clothing, and medical assistance to the displaced residents that he'd done via text while sitting through their meeting the day before.

Since more than half of that was earmarked to pay for a month at the Econo Lodge, instead of the week or less the aid organizations could normally afford, Liam already had plans to donate more if it took longer than that for the residents to find new permanent housing. Still, even though he knew the Carsons had no idea how much money he'd already contributed to the recovery efforts, he felt uncomfortable every time they mentioned his generosity as each of the rest of the heads of the households signed the resident list to acknowledge they'd received one of the gift cards.

"Did I tell you how cute you are when you blush the way you did every time someone thanked you for the gift cards?" Rylie questioned as they finally left the condo office with only one gift card left in their possession. Hers.

She'd argued about accepting it, saying she didn't need it since her belongings would all be returned to her eventually. But since neither Liam nor Bradan had thought to exclude her when they requested them from the bank, the Carsons had insisted she sign off on their list and accept it, so Liam wouldn't foist it off on them to have to explain to their accountant.

"Cute?" Liam scoffed, shaking his head as he opened the passenger door of their rental car for her to get in. "I'm not cute. Between the two of us, you're definitely the cute one, especially when you pout about not getting your way, like you did about that gift card."

"I don't pout," Rylie protested, putting her hands on her hips indignantly, and apparently, not realizing that she stuck her lower lip out a little farther than her top lip when she scowled.

"You do, and it's cute," Liam chuckled as he dipped his head to peck a kiss on her pouty lips. "Now get in the car, woman, so you can show me where you grew up."

"Fine," Rylie huffed, her smile keeping her from pulling off the irritated act.

As soon as Liam was in the driver's seat, Rylie gave him directions to her old neighborhood. First, she showed him the school where both her parents worked and she went for her elementary years.

"Wow, I bet you couldn't get away with anything with both your parents teaching at your school," Liam observed as they drove around the building after she pointed out the windows to each of her parents' former classrooms.

"No, but I was always the good girl and didn't want to get away with any mischief, so it was cool. Although, having them both there did make it pretty obvious when I was the one who put too much red dye in the chocolate candies we made for the Christmas parties when I was in the fifth grade."

"How do you know you used too much red dye?" Liam questioned.

"Because pretty much everyone in my class, as well as Mom and Dad's second and third grade classes, had red poop after eating the Santa candies we brought for the parties," Rylie confided with a self-deprecating little huff. "And since it was limited to only the three classes with a Long present, it was clear that we provided the contaminated chocolates."

Liam had to stifle a chuckle, assuming Rylie would still be embarrassed by the situation, even though it sounded kind of funny in hindsight, like something one of their coworkers would do as a prank.

"When I shared that story with your mom the other day, she wanted to know how much food coloring I used, so she can make you and your brothers some special treats for Saint Patrick's Day," Rylie giggled, apparently not as embarrassed as he'd assumed. "So, if she sends you some green chocolates in March, I think we should pass them on to prank some of our friends."

"Oh, we will definitely be passing those on to the guys," Liam laughed, trying to decide which of their coworkers deserved to have green shit the most. Blade, Sawyer, Kade, the Benningtons, and Protection Detail were tops on his list, considering they'd all gone along with the Vegas pictures without informing any of the rest of them that they'd gotten married, even though they'd claimed they weren't so drunk they blacked out too. *Definitely Kade and Protection Detail, since they were in the background of the pictures from inside the chapel.*

"So, did your parents meet when they both started working at the same school?" Liam questioned, wanting to know more of Rylie's history as she navigated their drive to the other schools she'd attended.

"No, actually they met at a conference for excellence in education that was held in one of the hotels near the Boardwalk," Rylie informed him. "I didn't know it was at a hotel until I read Mom's journals after they passed and realized that Mom was actually from Newark and not here. Of course, the version they told me growing up was much tamer than what actually happened."

"Oh? How so?" Liam questioned as he drove around her high school.

"Well, in the version they told me, they met at the opening mixer, which was true apparently, but it was in the bar at the hotel and not a

dinner in a conference room at the convention center like they said."
Rylie smiled brightly, moving her hands around animatedly as she
continued with her voice filled with mirth. "Everyone there had name
tags on, but they'd been printed by the conference organizers, so the
names were listed last name first. And after a few drinks, Mom saw
Dad's name tag and asked how much truth there was in advertising
because his name was listed as Long, Peter instead of Peter Long.
And of course, Mom had to write in her journal about how he showed
her there was absolutely no false advertising in his name later that
night in his hotel room."

"Wow," Liam barked out a laugh as he envisioned the scene. "I
wonder if his parents realized what they were doing when they named
him?"

"Apparently, they did it on purpose," Rylie giggled. "Since Mom
wrote in her journal that after he claimed the advertising was one-
hundred percent true, they sat and talked, and he told her all about his
dad Richard, who went by Dick, and his brothers, Willie and Johnson.
After reading that, I finally understood why Dad always went by Pete
instead of Peter."

"Because he was embarrassed about how they were all named after
his dad's favorite body part?" Liam wondered aloud.

"No," Rylie snorted. "Because Mom didn't want other women to
hit on him because his name was such perfect advertising. Talk about
information I didn't want to learn about my dad."

"I bet," Liam laughed along with her. "And thankfully, they didn't
carry on the naming tradition with you."

"Oh, no, that's another thing I learned from Mom's journals," Rylie
confided, her tone turning serious. "She had to veto his suggestion of
naming me Tatianna, and calling me Tata as a nickname. I really hope
he only meant that name idea as a joke, since he was constantly
coming up with cheesy Dad jokes when I was a kid."

Liam didn't know how she managed to say all that without cracking
up, since he couldn't contain his smile at the breast-focused nickname
suggestion. "Yeah, I'm sure he was joking, Tata Long."

Rylie actually chuckled then. "But whether he meant it as a joke or
not, Chastity was also on his list of baby name suggestions, which is
why I chose it as my ring name."

"Do you think he was hoping the name would help you remain *chaste* for a *long* time?"

"Either that, or he pronounced it *Chas-titty* too, and was still joking about droopy boobs," Rylie chortled before pointing out where he needed to turn to show him the house she grew up in. "And since it was spelled C-H-A-S-T-I-T-T-Y in mom's journal, I'm leaning toward them pronouncing it Chas-titty, which was my original ring name. The gimmick was all about emphasizing the size of my chest while being flirtatious, but then turning down all the wrestlers who asked me out. Or at least pretending to turn them down, but then being caught in compromising positions backstage to rile up the other women who thought I was stealing all their men. But then when their babyfaces started getting heat for slut shaming me in their promos, we changed it up to be more of a prudish character and I switched my ring gear to the mock-turtleneck catsuits. But it still wasn't until I started with the GWA that Chas-titty became Chastity."

"I'd love to see video of some of your earlier shows to see how this gimmick compares to what you're doing now," Liam commented, thinking about how her manager outfits had started revealing more cleavage in the past three months, and especially how his dick had responded accordingly when they worked together on the flirtation angle.

"Pull over here." Rylie pointed to a house on the right side of the road. "That's the house I grew up in."

As he parked on the side of the road in front of her modest childhood home, Liam couldn't help but wonder if she would like to maintain a home in Atlantic City, either as a vacation house for their family or as her place should their marriage not work out the way they hoped it would.

"I used to climb up in that tree and sit to read for hours," Rylie informed him as she pointed to a large red maple tree with sturdy leafless branches close to the trunk, where he could easily picture her sitting even now as an adult. "It used to drive Mom crazy 'cause I kept snagging holes in my clothes. Then Dad trimmed off all the smaller branches to make almost like a cubbyhole just big enough for me and a friend to fit among the lowest bigger branches. He even used sandpaper to smooth off any rough spots in the bark."

"Did that help keep you from snagging your clothes?" Liam wondered, grinning as he pictured her dad using a hand sander on the branches of the tree.

"Oh yeah," Rylie laughed gleefully. "But then a couple months later, I had to stop climbing that tree because it started leaking sap from all the places he'd cut off the smaller branches. While Mom had a much easier time washing the sap off my clothes than having to repair or replace them, I couldn't stand getting my hands sticky and ruining the pages of my books. So, Dad ended up hanging a hammock between a couple of the trees in the backyard for me to read in after that. He also tapped that tree for Mom to *try* making syrup."

"I take it the extra emphasis on *try* means she wasn't successful?"

"Oh, she was successful," Rylie cackled. "And the spoonful we each got to eat tasted great. But apparently the tree had already leaked too much sap, so they weren't able to collect enough for her to make a sufficient amount of syrup for even one pancake breakfast for the three of us."

She turned away from staring at the tree to look directly at Liam for the first time since they arrived at her childhood home. "Did you know it takes ten gallons of maple sap to make a quart of syrup?"

"No, I didn't." Liam shook his head, smiling at how happy she was sharing her memories with him.

"Yeah, sap is mostly water and only like two-and-a-half percent sugar, so to get it the right consistency for syrup and kill any bacteria, it has to be boiled down multiple times and then strained through a coffee filter or cheesecloth to get out any sediment before it's edible."

Liam was impressed with her knowledge of things he'd never even considered studying. But he was more interested in learning more about her childhood than how to make maple syrup, so he changed the subject back to her parents and when they'd moved into the house they were parked in front of at the moment. "So, is this the only place you lived as a kid? Or just the place you lived in the longest?"

"It's the only place I remember," Rylie shrugged. "Mom's journal entries mentioned an apartment that they lived in right after they moved to Atlantic City and for the first couple of years they were married, but she didn't mention when they moved into the house. I'm guessing she got too busy after having me to journal much, since her entries slowed down quite a bit after I was born, turning into more like monthly or yearly recaps of the major milestones of my life instead of the in-depth thoughts and feelings they were in the earlier editions."

"I know you said before that your dad moved from Georgia to Jersey to be with your mom, but did they live in Newark for a while, since that's where she was from? Or did they both move here right after they met?" Liam reached over and took her hand, needing to feel connected to her as she told him more about her family history.

"They actually both went home after the conference and finished out the semester teaching in their previous schools, running up monstrous phone bills while staying in touch until they could both get hired at the school here." Rylie squeezed his hand, silently showing her appreciation for him listening to her family stories. "Apparently, while they were just talking on the phone in the months after the conference, it became clear that neither of their families would accept them as a couple. So, they decided to see if there were any openings in the school district here, since it was where they met. They just got lucky that there were multiple openings at the same school the following fall, so they were able to both live and work together. Although, living together before getting married seemed to cause some issues with them finding a church willing to marry them. At least, according to what Mom wrote in her journal. But I'm sure that part of it was because she was Black and he was white. She just didn't want to think the churches were as discriminatory as their families."

"But they were able to get married in the Church? Or did they have to have a civil ceremony?" Liam wondered how her parents' wedding compared to his parents' wedding and also to the Vegas wedding he and Rylie shared.

"Eventually," Rylie nodded. "Why don't we start the mural tour while we talk, so nobody thinks we're casing the house I grew up in?"

"Yeah, that's probably a pretty good idea," Liam chuckled, turning on the car as she pulled up a map on her phone to show him where over seventy murals were located around the city as part of 48 Blocks Atlantic City, a program of the Atlantic City Arts Foundation. It was a program started after the death of her parents, but she told him how much they'd have loved to tour the various works of art. They weren't able to get the GPS to talk them through a route, but it wasn't difficult to follow her directions as she directed him to each point marked on the map to honor her family tradition of finding fun, inexpensive ways to enjoy their adopted hometown.

Once they were on the way to the first mural, Rylie continued telling him the story of how her parents got together. "Anyway, they apparently tried going to a few different churches, since they didn't grow up in the same religion, and eventually decided they felt most welcomed at Our Lady of Hope. They both had to convert to Catholicism first, but they ended up getting married about a year after they met."

"And the priest at Our Lady of Hope was okay with marrying them even though they lived together first?"

"Yes and no," Rylie sighed as she pointed out the first mural, which he slowly drove past since there wasn't any place he could park to look at it for very long. "There were several entries in Mom's journals about how hard it was to live chastely in separate bedrooms while they were converting and going through marriage preparation before the wedding." Rylie paused as they viewed the artwork through the car window. "Wow, I just realized they had to go through the same Pre-Cana classes we're starting next week."

Now that he thought about it, he was pretty sure everyone in his family had taken them, too. Well, at least the married members of the family, since they'd all been married in the Church. "I guess that's one thing we'll both have in common with our parents."

"Yeah, it is," Rylie beamed at him before directing him to the next mural. Once they were on their way, she softly sighed before speaking once more. "I wonder if we should ask your parents what to expect when we meet with Father O'Malley on Monday?"

"We can if you want," Liam agreed, wondering how the courses might have changed in the years since his parents had attended them, besides now having online options that weren't available back then. "Or maybe we could talk to some of my cousins who've gone through them more recently, so we know what to expect from the most updated versions of the courses."

"Yeah, we can do that," she softly sighed once more, making him wonder what was weighing on her mind so heavily. "But I was thinking the classes your parents took would be most like what my parents did, since I won't have Mom's journals back in time to compare notes to her daily journal entries as we go through the lessons."

Realizing she yearned for that connection with her parents more than she really wanted advance information about what they were about to learn as a couple, Liam decided to see what he could do to get access to her mom's journals before they left Atlantic City the next day. He knew it was a long shot, but he hoped to convince Leo Newman to escort them through the building to get a few of her things. *But even if he's not willing to take us up there, maybe he'd be willing to make a quick stop by the building tomorrow to go up and get the journals for her if I double my donation to the Fallen Firefighters Fund? And if he is, then I need to know where those journals are located in her apartment, so I can tell him where they are to surprise her.*

"Where did you keep the journals? Like in a special place on a bookshelf? Or in your bedside table so you could read them at night?"

"They're actually in a plastic tote with the photo albums in the top of my bedroom closet," Rylie confided with a sad smile as she pointed to the next mural they were about to pass.

"Well, maybe if they're already packed up, then they'll be the first of the things they'll send you when the cleaning crew is able to go through the building."

"Maybe." Her smile brightened at the thought.

Definitely, Liam decided, planning to call the fire inspector as soon as they got to the Absecon Lighthouse and had to separate briefly for a bathroom break before climbing all 228 steps to see the original Fresnel lens from 1857. *And if I don't have time to call him then, I'll call him when we get to the Boardwalk. Surely, we'll have enough time apart for multiple bathroom breaks between lunch, the Central Pier Arcade, and the Wheel at Steel Pier, even if I have to just text him the information a little at a time to convince him.*

<div align="center">~~~</div>

After the stress of finding out about the fire, dealing with the paperwork to terminate her lease, passing out all the gift cards Liam generously donated to her neighbors, and sharing her heart-wrenching memories while touring her hometown with her husband, Rylie decided to take advantage of the large soaker tub in the ensuite bathroom attached to her bedroom in their hotel suite to take a nice hot bath and enjoy one of the bath time gift baskets she'd received for Christmas. Liam's family might not know her very well after only a few days, but giving her all the supplies to turn her hotel rooms into mini spa retreats made it clear that they understood how all women need a little pampering to feel their best.

She placed the flameless candles on the vanity counter by the sink and turned them on as she filled the tub. Then she opened her Audible app and started an audiobook before blowing up her tub pillow, placing the pillow, towels, and bath bomb where she could reach them from the tub, stripping down, turning off the overhead light, and stepping into the tub. She was currently about halfway through **Dungeon Royale** by Lexi Blake, trying to get caught up on the books in the **Masters and Mercenaries** series that the other ladies had read the year before. Apparently, there were a couple of new books in the series coming out in 2020 that her friends were anxiously waiting on, so she knew they'd be what everyone was reading in a couple of months. Which meant she needed to get caught up on the series before then, so she wouldn't be lost in their book discussions.

She didn't bother putting a shower cap over her hair, knowing she'd want to rinse off in the shower after the bath and would wash and condition her hair then. Since she'd taken her braids out at the beginning of the holiday break, she didn't need to go sit under a hair dryer for hours to get her hair to dry afterwards. So, she planned to just towel dry it, apply her usual products to lock in the moisture, and wrap it overnight as usual. Then, if it was still a little damp in the morning, it could air dry on their way back to New York.

As soon as the water was as deep as it could get without reaching the overflow drain, Rylie turned off the water and relaxed her head back on the pillow. She let the smooth, sensual tone of Ryan West's voice carry her away to a world of spies and sex in a lavish BDSM club "across the pond" as the British characters in the book would put it. When she put the Earth Bomb in her bath, the sea breeze scent added to the ambiance to help her relax, even though she couldn't see much of the ocean blue color of the bath bomb in her water with the only light coming from the flameless candles.

Now that she was trying to reconnect with her spiritual side, she had to wonder if her choice of leisure reading and listening material would be considered sinful due to the graphic descriptions of the spicy scenes. *No, I don't need to confess to enjoying books and audiobooks with multiple chili pepper ratings. If reading or listening to these kinds of books were a sin, then every priest in America, or possibly the world, would be constantly booked in the confessional booth for all the readers who make romance the most profitable and popular genre of literature of all time. Besides, it's not like I'm actually doing the stuff in the books. And even when I fantasize about some of the things I've only heard about in romance novels, I'm only thinking of doing them with my husband, so it's all fine.*

Once she convinced herself she wasn't doing anything wrong, Rylie closed her eyes and let the bath wash away her stress. She'd been soaking for about half an hour, relaxing with her eyes closed and really getting lost in the audiobook playing on her phone, when she suddenly felt something brush against her inner thigh.

"What the…?" Rylie jumped slightly at the slight tickle, assuming it was the last little bit of the bath bomb that sunk down under the water.

Instinctually, she reached down to move it away from her leg just to keep it from settling on the bottom of the tub close enough to her that the last of the bubbles could tickle her again. What she found when she scooped the approximately two-inch long object into her hands, however, wasn't the blue bubbly bath bomb she expected.

"OH FUCK NO!" Rylie screamed, tossing what looked like a slug or a snail or some other slimy creature she didn't want in her bathtub across the room, just as she also attempted to bound to her feet.

Unfortunately, a slippery, completely full of water bathtub wasn't as easy a surface to kip up from as the wrestling ring where she was accustomed to easily performing the maneuver. She only got about halfway up before her feet slid out from under her instead of sticking as her stable base to stand. She landed with a hard thud, banging her left side against the edge of the tub and her ass against the bottom, splashing water over her head and half the bathroom.

"Fuck, fuck, fuck! I need outta this tub full of slimy slugs!" Before she could get her bearings to more safely push up with her hands on the sides of the tub to get out, the bathroom door crashed open.

"Rylie!" Liam shouted as he flipped on the light, looking around as if trying to see if there was an intruder he needed to defend her from while raising his fists to show he was ready to fight whoever, or in this case whatever, had attacked her. "Who's in here? What happened? Are you okay?"

Neither of them acknowledged the male voice of the audiobook narrator still playing from her phone on the counter, even though it was probably what made Liam think there was an intruder he had to fight to protect her.

"Slimy slug in the tub," Rylie replied, finally being successful in standing up to get out of the bath in case there were more, and not caring that Liam was seeing her buck naked in her attempt to get away from the revolting creatures that had invaded her time of tranquility.

"Where?" Liam stepped closer to the tub, looking down into the water only briefly before examining her body as if looking to make sure none of the monstrous mollusks were still attached to her skin. His eyes flared with desire and the bulge in his workout shorts obviously enlarged when his gaze reached the apex of her thighs and again when he examined her breasts. But after that, he was a perfect gentleman, keeping his eyes locked on her face, seeming more concerned with making sure she was okay than ogling her like a horndog.

While she appreciated his concern, she kind of wished he hadn't controlled his lusty look so quickly, even though they'd both agreed to wait another month for more than kissing. *At least he hasn't completely gotten his cock under control yet,* she thought as she glanced back down over his t-shirt covered torso and landed her gaze on the swelling appendage in his shorts. *Yeah, we can come back to that once the slimy slugs are dealt with.*

"I tossed the one I felt brush my thigh over there." Rylie pointed behind Liam, toward the vanity and door. "But with the lights off to appreciate the candlelight, I couldn't see if there were more or not."

Liam turned around as Rylie finally realized she needed to cover up to keep from pushing them both past the point of temptation, instead of standing there in the nude, discussing whatever had invaded her peaceful bath. *He must really be serious about wanting us to wait since the only indication he's noticed I'm naked is that he's obviously hard. Hopefully, he didn't notice my nipples doing the same when I saw his semi and now thinks I'm turned on by these slimy slugs.* She grabbed the towel she'd put on the bar between the tub and toilet, wrapping it around herself, even though it was just as wet as she was from when she'd splashed down into the tub a moment earlier. Even if it wouldn't do a bit of good to dry her off, it was necessary to help limit their desire.

"You mean this?" Liam bent over and picked up the orange and brown snail-looking thing and laughed. "It's a plastic toy, not a slug. But I can't imagine how it got in your bath."

"Seriously? It's plastic?" Clutching the lump between her breasts where she'd tucked the end of the towel to hold it up, Rylie stepped closer to Liam to look at the approximately two-inch long hunk of plastic resting in his palm. Getting a better look at the ugly thing in his hand, now that the lights were on, effectively killed Rylie's arousal. "Not alive?"

"Yeah, probably a bath toy left behind by the last guest's kid," Liam claimed, shrugging as his eyes momentarily dipped to where she gripped the towel before moving back up to her face. "Though I would have thought you'd have noticed it before you ran your bath."

"No, that can't be it." Rylie disagreed, knowing she would have seen the orange toy against the white tub if it had been in there before she got in. Then she remembered the bath bomb and stepped around Liam to get the package from the otherwise empty wastebasket. "I think it might have been in this." She held up the package to show him where the bath bomb package said it had a "surprise sea creature inside," which she'd assumed would be a charm like for a necklace, similar to the ones she'd gotten in bath bombs before, only in the shape of a whale or dolphin. "They really should make it more clear that the surprise inside is something creepy and not the cute little necklace charm I was expecting."

"Yeah, I'm not really a marketing expert to say for sure," Liam chuckled. "But if this is what they're putting in their bath bombs, I think they missed the mark with inserting a surprise that would be enjoyable to their primary demographic, which I imagine is mostly female. Even if these bath bombs are marketed for kids, I doubt Cassidy or Casey would want a plastic snail when they could have a piece of jewelry, even plastic kids' jewelry."

Leah Mae Wright

"Actually, the ones I've gotten in the past were mostly metal charms shaped to match the scent of the bath bomb, like a surfboard for the ocean surf bomb, flowers for the different flower scented bombs, and even a cute little frozen drink for the daiquiri scented bomb," Rylie clarified. "Only the superhero bath bombs had plastic charms. But those were bigger, more like for attaching to the zipper-pulls on backpacks than to a necklace or charm bracelet."

"You mean like that plastic Groot you have on the handles of all your suitcases to make them more recognizable as yours when you have to pick them up from baggage claim?" Liam arched an eyebrow at her as he referred to her favorite Marvel movie character.

"Yep," Rylie nodded. "They all came from *Guardians of the Galaxy* bath bombs. I just went to Michaels and bought the chains and clips to attach them. I also made several necklaces with the other charms, but they're all hanging on a necklace tree on my dresser at home. Or they were before the fire. Who knows how they'll be boxed up when they finally send me my stuff?"

Her bringing up the fire in her apartment building brought down the mood in the room until Liam tried to cheer her up. "Are you sure this bath bomb didn't come with a charm you could make into another necklace? And this snail thing isn't just a toy left behind by a previous guest?"

When Rylie just shrugged, they both walked back over to the tub to look and see if they saw anything else through the blue water, just to be sure there wasn't a small piece of jewelry that would get caught in the drain when she pulled the plug. She didn't see anything, but that didn't stop Liam from squatting down and running his empty hand through the water to feel all along the bottom of the tub.

"Yeah, I think this one just contained the plastic snail," Rylie sighed, shaking her head when Liam kept feeling around as if he thought he'd just missed the little charm in the light blue, but still see-through water.

When Liam didn't reply for a moment, the story playing on her phone filled the silence between them, embarrassing her when the flogging scene playing out on the stage in the BDSM club was very explicitly described. Not because of the content, since she kind of wanted to find out if a flogger could really feel like a massage, but because it just made her more tempted to ask her husband not to wait like they'd agreed. Rylie quickly turned back to the vanity and fumbled to stop the Audible app as Liam chuckled behind her.

"Please, don't turn that off on my account," he instructed, causing a light splashing sound as he stood and removed his hand from her bath. "I'm not really an exhibitionist, but we can leave it playing to make it seem like we have an audience if you want."

"No, I don't want," Rylie sputtered, interrupting him before he could suggest forgoing their plan to wait. Luckily, she felt too mortified at the thought that Liam believed she was an exhibitionist to turn around and face him, so she was only slightly tempted to give in to their lust for one another and change their plans.

"You don't have to be embarrassed, Moh Graw." Liam obviously tried to coax her into turning around by softening his voice and trying to sound serious instead of joking around like he had a moment earlier. "I know how authors can surprise you with some of the content of their books, and just because you read or listen to all the books in a series to keep up with a mystery or suspense plot, they can add in settings that are places you'd never go in real life. I also know that just because someone likes a certain genre of books, it doesn't mean they want to do the things in those books. For instance, I like reading murder mysteries, but I have no desire to be a murderer or a detective solving those cases. So, I don't think you're into BDSM just because the book you're listening to seems to be set in a BDSM club. But if there are some things you hear in that book that interest you, just know I'm willing to explore our kinks whenever you want. Well, whenever you want after my ninety-day negative test, anyway."

"I'll keep that in mind, *if* anything happens later in the book that's more my speed," Rylie croaked out, clutching the edge of the counter to keep from turning around and telling him all the other book scenes popping into her head that she'd love to one day act out with him, including the one just playing only not with an audience. *No, I can't tell him my fantasies now! Not when we're trying so hard to not have sex until the other aspects of our marriage are solid.* "But right now, I just want to drain the tub, clean up all this water on the floor, and take a shower, *alone*, before going to bed, *also alone*."

"Then I'll leave you to it, Moh Graw." Liam stepped up behind her and bent to kiss her bare shoulder. "Right after I bring you back some dry towels, since yours are obviously too wet to do you much good after your shower."

With that, he left her alone in the bathroom, standing there shivering. She just wasn't sure if it was because she was cold now that she wasn't sitting in the formerly steaming hot water. Or if the tingling was solely her body's response to that brief affectionate contact from Liam. Either way, she waited until he returned with two dry towels and vacated the bathroom once more before she dropped the wet towel covering her to the floor and tried to use it to sop up the rest of the water.

Mom was so right in her journal entry about how hard it is to abstain while staying in such close quarters with the man you love. But if she was able to do it for six months, then surely I can do it for one.

But then again, Mom wasn't already married to Dad, so it would have been a sin for them. Even Father O'Malley said it wouldn't be a sin for me and Liam. If only we could find a way to get around that whole condom issue.

Chapter Nine

Sunday, December 29, 2019, Noon, Atlantic City, New Jersey

Rylie felt a crazy mix of emotions as they left Our Lady of Hope after Mass on Sunday. Being in that Church without her parents still felt wrong, even seven years after the last time they'd attended Mass together. But at the same time, taking Liam there, where she could introduce him as her husband to everyone who recognized her and remembered her parents fondly, made her almost feel like she'd truly taken him home to meet her family. Requesting her baptism, confirmation, and first Communion records be sent to Saint Stephen's Cathedral felt bittersweet, almost like she was officially saying "goodbye" to her first Church, even though she knew she would always be welcome there whenever she was back in town.

It's not a permanent goodbye, though, she mentally told herself as she looked back at the Church one last time, as they drove away to head to the airport for their flight back to New York. *Just a see you later, since I'm sure I'll come back to another Mass here the next time the GWA is in Atlantic City. Hopefully, with Liam by my side.*

While she was a lot more optimistic about being able to make her marriage with Liam work for a long and happy life together since their recent talks, the fact that neither of them had said those three magic words yet still caused her a sliver of doubt. Oh, she knew she was hopelessly in love with him and could easily say "I love you" first. But she didn't want to take the chance that he wouldn't really mean them if he said those three words back only because she'd initially said them. So, she was still holding her tongue, waiting for him to say "I love you" before revealing her feelings, so she could trust that he really meant it.

He has referred to sex as making love, though, she thought as she let her mind wander while Liam drove, not realizing he wasn't going in the direction of the airport, even though the stop at the church was the only surprise delay in their flight that he'd told her about that morning. *And the way he's been there for me to lean on during all this fire stuff, not to mention how generous he's been to help my former neighbors too, definitely shows he cares deeply for me. So, maybe he's not as far away from saying he loves me as I feared.*

She also knew it wasn't just the fact that they hadn't declared their love that worried her. Honestly, she was most afraid that they'd disagree about whether or not to try IVF if she was unable to conceive a baby in the traditional manner, and problems having children would lead him to want to be with someone who didn't face her potential medical issues, leading to the demise of their marriage. But as she assumed those issues would be covered in their natural family planning coursework in the next month, she didn't want to bring it up and risk imploding their marriage when they didn't have Father O'Malley or their mentor couple to help guide them through the tougher topics they still needed to discuss.

But even though she wasn't ready to bring any of that up in conversation with Liam just yet, she still ran through the potential scenarios in her mind on a constant loop. She assumed it was her way of trying to figure out the best approach to take when she finally got brave enough to talk to him, so they'd have the best chance of success as a couple. She might not know everything she needed to know about being married yet, but she did know she didn't want to have a repeat of the rash angry reactions they'd both had when they first found out they'd gotten married while drunk in Vegas. So no matter what the topic, she knew she shouldn't aggressively bring it up with an accusatory tone, the way she had that day back at the beginning of October.

No, I need to approach this topic much more humbly, with a demure tone, almost like I'm his submissive, deferring to his opinion on whether IVF is a sin or not. Huh? Maybe I took too much of that book last night to heart.

She didn't get the chance to finish her thoughts, however, realizing when Liam pulled over that they were at her former apartment building and not the airport, as she'd expected. "Um, Liam, why are we here? Aren't we supposed to be at the airport, so we're not late for our flight?"

"Yeah, I pushed that back to later this afternoon," Liam informed her, picking up her hand and brushing a kiss over her knuckles. "So we have time for another surprise first."

"Another surprise? Here?"

Liam didn't answer, smiling as he got out of the car and walked around to open her door, just as she looked around and saw a couple of other vehicles parked on the little side road with them. *Wait! That's the fire inspector's vehicle. Is Inspector Newman here, too? And if so, why?*

She didn't voice her questions aloud as Liam took her hand and assisted her from the vehicle. Instead, she just kept looking around, hoping to get a clue about what kind of surprise Liam had in store for her. When she saw Leo Newman and two other men carrying a couple of boxes and a tote from the fire damaged building, she gasped, covering her mouth with her free hand when she recognized the tote in Inspector Newman's hands.

He's bringing me Mom's journals and photo albums? How? Why? I thought the clean-up crew the Carsons are hiring wouldn't be able to send them to me until next month at the earliest?

"Good afternoon," Inspector Newman greeted them, passing the tote to Liam, who'd just popped the trunk of their rental car. "I believe this is the box you were most concerned about getting from your apartment."

"Yes, thank you!" Rylie barely waited for Liam to take the tote before she threw her arms around the older man, thanking him with a bearhug as she fought not to cry so she didn't spread her makeup to his coat. "You can't know how much this means to me. And I don't know how I can ever thank you enough for getting Mom's journals and photo albums for me."

Leo awkwardly patted her back to return the embrace. "No need to thank me. Thank your husband for sharing the significance and specific location of your box of mementos. And for his generous donation to the Fallen Firefighters Fund."

"It was the least I could do," Liam stated humbly, as Rylie stepped back from hugging the fire inspector to see her husband rearranging their luggage so the other two men could squeeze in a couple of boxes she didn't recognize in beside the tote. Before she could ask about them, Inspector Newman continued.

"We have three more boxes upstairs, about the same size as those. I wanted to make sure you have room for everything we were able to pack up from the closet and dresser before we brought them all down."

"Yes, they should fit in the back seat, and there's plenty of room on the plane I chartered," Liam informed them.

"Then we'll be right back," Leo smiled before he and the other two men returned to the building.

Once they were alone once more, standing on the sidewalk beside the car, Rylie wrapped her arms around Liam. "Thank you. I don't know how you convinced him to get these things for me, but thank you."

"All I did was ask," Liam claimed as he hugged Rylie against him, brushing his lips over the top of her head. "And I might have mentioned how hard it would be on you to not be able to look at the photos of your parents on the anniversary of their passing next week, so he'd understand why I didn't want to wait on the cleaning crew to retrieve that one tote. Everything else they packed up is thanks to Leo looking at you and seeing what he'd want someone to do for his daughter if she were in your position, since I only asked him to get the journals and photo albums."

"Still, even asking for one of the journals or photo albums is more than what most people would have done," Rylie sniveled, hating that she couldn't control how emotional she got while they were standing on a public street.

"Yeah, well, most people don't care about you the way I do, Moh Graw." Liam pulled a handkerchief from his pocket and dabbed under her eyes, obviously having learned to be prepared for her to be a blubbering mess.

Though he said "care about" and not "love" the way she longed to hear, Rylie could see in his eyes that he meant more than just caring about her as a friend. He might not be as in love as she was, but his open expression made it clear he was starting to fall. The deeper feelings she saw in his eyes, combined with his recent actions, gave her hope that his affection for her would eventually grow into a long and lasting love. A love so strong that she could trust him to never do anything to try to "get over" her in the future.

That realization made it difficult not to blurt out "I love you" right then and there. But somehow, she managed to just smile and say, "thank you," before pushing up on her toes and pressing a chaste kiss to his lips, just as a light drizzle started falling. Liam rushed her back to the car, so they could stay mostly dry while waiting on the men to come back down with the rest of her things they'd packed up.

Once the men returned, Liam got back out and helped load the other three boxes of her things into the back seat. She said her goodbyes to Inspector Newman through the open back door of the car. Then Liam drove them to the airport, where Rylie was able to board the plane back to New York, knowing that she'd finally let go of the hurt from their recent past, fully forgiving him for kissing Jen to try to fight his budding feelings.

While she wasn't sure how to make herself forget the pain she felt, she envisioned herself stuffing those bad memories in a box in her mind. One she hoped to never open again, as she looked forward to a long, happy life with her husband. The man she loved with her whole heart, body, and soul.

<div style="text-align:center">~~~</div>

Sunday, December 29, 2019, 7 p.m., New York City, New York

After some freezing rain in Atlantic City delayed their flight, Liam opted to skip the end of the normal weekly family dinner at his grandparents' house, taking his wife out for dinner instead. After feeling like he only had a few minutes alone with Rylie while they were driving because there were always other people around for the rest of their activities that day, he was really looking forward to some time when they could talk. Unfortunately, since he'd chosen a restaurant with other patrons seated close enough to overhear them, they had to limit their dinner conversation to more small talk, like they did while waiting on the plane with the flight crew hovering nearby.

So, they had to wait until after they ate and drove home before he could bring up the topic of where to put her things as he carried the boxes inside. "So, um, we didn't exactly finish talking about changing our sleeping arrangements the other night, urh, um, early yesterday morning. And then the snail in your bath kinda kept us from discussing it before bed last night. So I don't know if you want me to just put all this in the bedroom you've been using this week, or if you want some of it in the master bedroom, since I'm assuming we'll be sharing it by the time we come back in April."

While Liam hoped them sleeping separately was only a temporary way to help them stick to their plan to wait until he felt safe going without a condom before having sex again, he didn't want to pressure her into sharing his bed on a permanent basis when she still had doubts about them as a couple. Yeah, they'd made progress with working on their marriage, but they'd been sidetracked by the fire and spending time in Atlantic City and hadn't really spent enough time talking about how they each wanted to move forward.

"Yeah, sorry, I kinda fell asleep before we could finish that talk yesterday morning," Rylie apologized unnecessarily with a self-deprecating eye roll as they stopped to put the first two boxes down on the coffee table in the living room. "But I planned to ask you if you meant sharing a two-bedroom suite when you mentioned sharing a room to be able to make sure we both get out of a hotel safely in case of a fire, or if you meant sharing a bed, which could prove to be way too tempting for us to hold out on sex for the next month, even though it seriously worked to banish my nightmares the rest of that night."

"Did they come back last night?" Liam had only been able to sleep peacefully during the few hours he'd held Rylie in his arms in the wee hours of Saturday morning. But if she'd remained nightmare free even when they weren't cuddling, then he wasn't about to tell her that his night terrors had come back full force when they went to their separate beds Saturday night, even though seeing her naked during her bath bomb scare had also caused him to have a pretty erotic dream before the nightmare began. He didn't want to pressure her into sleeping with him if it would increase the temptation for both of them while only he received the horrific dream reduction benefits.

"Yes and no." Rylie bobbed her head from side to side, her expression turning wary, as if she wasn't sure if she could trust him enough to elaborate more.

"Okay, let's sit down for a minute, so we can talk this out some more." Liam took her hand and gently tugged her to the sofa, where they sat side by side. "Tell me about the part of your nightmares that came back."

"It wasn't really the nightmare part that came back," Rylie sighed, her normally golden brown cheeks taking on a coppery undertone that made him wonder what she'd dreamed about that would make her blush so profusely. He didn't have to wait long to find out, as Rylie took in a deep breath and blew it out quickly before elaborating.

"So, I, like, normally have sex dreams. And that part of my dreams hasn't changed at all, whether we're in the same bed or not. But for the last three nights, my dreams of us making love have been interrupted by the nightmares. Thursday night, we had to stop and get dressed to escape from the fire in my apartment building, actually going door to door to help my neighbors and almost getting caught in the fire when we tried to use the north stairwell. When we realized the fire was on the north side of the building, we had to rush everyone to the south stairwell, which was hard to find in all the smoke. And once we found it, we had to squeeze by the firehose and firefighters coming up the stairs to get out, since it was the only stairwell available for any of us to use."

She paused and took a deep breath before continuing. "Friday night's dream was a little different, since we were in a hotel instead of my apartment building, but it still started with us making love. The lights had just gone out and I'd started smelling smoke in the dream when I woke up hearing you scream for me in your nightmare. When we were cuddling to sleep Saturday morning, I actually finished the sex dream without a recurrence of the nightmares."

"But then last night, my dream was really freaking weird. It still started out with us making love, but when I started smelling smoke, the sprinkler system came on, so we had to run through the downpour instead of us having to fight our way past the fire to get out of the building. But it wasn't just water that came out of the spouts, so as we were running naked from the hotel room, we were being pelted by slugs and snails coming out of the sprinkler heads with the water that doused the fire."

It took a moment for Liam to process everything she'd just said. And in that moment, he felt like she'd taken him on an emotional roller coaster. He was elated to know that she'd been dreaming of them making love regularly and wanted to ask her how long she'd been having those fantasies. But then she mentioned the nightmare on Thursday night and his heart plummeted from hearing she had to endure something so scary in her sleep. Then he was back to feeling excited by hearing he'd banished the fire from her dreams when he held her in his arms Saturday morning, only to crash back down to earth upon hearing that her nightmare had partially returned Saturday night. Finally, her mention of the slugs and snails attacking them after her plastic snail bath incident made him almost lose control of his composure to literally laugh out loud.

"So, are you saying that plastic snail in your bath bomb Saturday night was as traumatic for you as the fire in your apartment building?"

"Obviously, since I actually lived through that and only heard about the fire," Rylie nodded profusely, her smile shining through even though she tried to act scared. "But at least in that dream, you kinda wrapped yourself around me from behind as we made our way out of the building, trying to keep any of the slimy slugs from hitting me. But then we had to wait until the paramedics were able to pull them all off before we could even wrap up in an emergency blanket to cover where we were naked, and it wasn't until we went to the hospital to make sure there weren't any stuck in unmentionable areas before we could put on some scrubs to go find a new hotel. And even once we got to the new hotel, we couldn't have sex until after all the wounds healed from where those slimy things had latched on and tried to suck us dry like vampires."

"I think you're confusing slugs and leeches," Liam chuckled, no longer able to hold it in. "And neither one of them are anything like the plastic snail that was in your bath bomb."

"Slugs, snails, leeches, whatever." Rylie rolled her eyes as she laughed along with him. "They're all slimy and that was the only thing that really registered when I first felt that thing in the bath yesterday. So apparently, my subconscious can't differentiate and just doesn't want me anywhere near any of them. And my conscious self totally agrees."

"Noted," Liam grinned, glad to see Rylie smiling brightly again. "And I promise I'll do everything I can to protect you from all things slimy from now on."

"So chivalrous," Rylie cooed, covering her heart with her hands dramatically. "But I want to point out that I actually threw the snail out of my bath myself last night. So you need to step up and be a little more proactive in your slimy creature patrol."

"I'll try," Liam smirked. "But it's hard to be your knight in shining armor when you're so strong and capable that you take care of business before I can step in to ward off the plastic toys in your bathtub. But maybe if we only use those bath bombs when we're both in the tub, then I'll be able to do a better job of defending you from slimy surprises."

"Yeah, I think the two of us in the same tub would end up with you *sliming* me with your *big surprise*," Rylie chortled.

"Yeah, probably," Liam agreed, chuckling and nodding. "But as long as we wait until it's safe for me to slime you, I think we'd both enjoy it."

"True," Rylie concurred. "But what am I supposed to do to keep from being attacked every week when I use a bath bomb between now and then?"

"I guess I'll have to run your bath for you," Liam suggested, reaching over to brush her hair off her shoulder before trailing his finger down her arm until he could take her hand in his. "And sit beside the tub to observe, so I can catch any further sea creatures before they attack you. It'll be *hard* to keep my clothes on and not get in with you, but I think I can endure the torture of seeing you naked without taking my own clothes off, so I can protect you from any slimy surprises."

Kind of like it was last night to keep from doing anything about the erection I got after seeing you naked again.

"But it's the good kind of *hard*, right?" Rylie bit her lip, making it clear she understood his innuendo.

"Absolutely."

"I know we probably can't add stuff to our vows for a Church wedding, but if we get booked into doing that vow renewal in the middle of the ring on our anniversary, I fully expect you to include protecting me from gross, slimy creatures in your new vows," Rylie teased, snorting lightly as she laughed. "And I'll vow to defend you from…I don't know…overzealous ring rats."

"Deal," Liam chortled, nodding in agreement and wishing she'd have made her part of that vow before Halloween. He knew better than to mention anything that might allude to even the flimsiest implication of him noticing other women, though, so he didn't bring up how uncomfortable he'd been that night when he found himself surrounded by fans who shouldn't have been allowed in the VIP section of the club where the GWA was celebrating after their show. "But if we're coming up with things to add to our vows, I think we should both promise to fight off the other's nightmares by cuddling every night."

"That's definitely something we should add to our vows," Rylie nodded, smiling. "But I don't think we should wait until after the vow renewal in August to follow through with these new vows, especially that one."

"No?" Liam was curious about how soon she wanted to implement these new vows to one another. "Should we start cuddling away our nightmares tonight? Or wait until my end-of-January-beginning-of-February test comes back negative, so we're not tempted to take things farther than snuggling?"

"I think that depends on exactly how long we have to wait, since it's less than a month now for that ninety-day incubation period to be up." Rylie bit her lip nervously. "I know Doc did all our November tests a week early because of what happened at *Halloween Horror*. But since he went back to the first week of the month for December and January, do you think he'll make us wait until the first week of February to do yours, even though your ninety days after exposure will be up over a week before then?"

"I assumed he just went back to the normal schedule because of our holiday breaks at the end of November and December," Liam groaned, running a hand through his hair. "But even if he did it because the negative tests at the end of October made him feel like our standard schedule is fine, I can ask him to do my tests the last week of January."

Waiting four more weeks to make love to his wife was going to be hard enough, he didn't want to arbitrarily add another week to that restriction when he could easily take the tests a week earlier than they were normally scheduled with the GWA.

"Then if we only have to wait until the twenty-sixth of January, do you think we can handle four weeks of cuddling like we did yesterday morning? 'Cause it wasn't too difficult for me to resist doing more then, but that's at least partially because I was so exhausted that I couldn't keep my eyes open and then we were able to go to separate bathrooms when we woke up."

"Honestly, I don't know," Liam sighed, tracing circles with his thumb around her mom's engagement ring. "I don't even know if I'll be able to hold out the whole time, even if we aren't sharing a bed. Though I'm pretty sure if we have to extend that time frame to five weeks, then I definitely won't be able to resist making love to you that long. That's why I asked Father O'Malley about needing to confess to using condoms the other day, even though I don't really think using a condom to keep you safe is a sin."

"Even though using a condom isn't remaining open to procreation?" Rylie eyed him skeptically.

"No, because I'm not insisting on continuing to use condoms to keep you from getting pregnant. I'm doing it to keep you from getting HIV or Hepatitis or whatever else I might have been exposed to in that psycho's blood." Liam gently squeezed her hand in his, needing to make sure she understood where he was coming from. "If we believe that it's entirely up to God when we'll have kids, or how many kids we'll have, then we have to believe it doesn't matter if we use condoms or birth control pills or even the things we'll learn in the Natural Family Planning classes we're about to start to try to postpone pregnancy until we're ready. I mean, come on, how long have we heard the only one-hundred percent effective form of birth control is abstinence? Yet abstinence wasn't effective for Mary. If God can impregnate a virgin, he can definitely make a condom break or the pill fail, or even cause a woman who's had a hysterectomy to grow a new womb to have a baby. That being said, I'm really looking forward to making love to you without a condom, just not until I know I'm outside the window of when one of those tests could come up positive, 'cause the only positive test I ever want for either of us is a pregnancy test."

Feck, I hope I didn't just screw up by hinting at how ready I am to start trying for our first baby. But I also don't want her to think I'm still insisting on using condoms because I don't want us to have babies either.

Rylie stared at him for a moment, obviously needing to take her time to comprehend everything he'd just said. Liam sat there letting her think, knowing they'd need to be on the same page before they brought sex back into their marriage. "Okay, then let's go ahead and start sharing a bed to ward off our nightmares. And hopefully, it won't be too much of a temptation for us, but if it is, then we'll just confess to using condoms."

She paused and looked over at the boxes on the coffee table. "And I think we should put these boxes of my stuff in the guest bedroom until I can go through them and decide where everything in them needs to go."

"Done." Liam leaned over and pecked a kiss on her lips before standing and taking the first two boxes up to the guest room she'd been using.

Rylie joined him in carrying in their things, being surprised when he showed her the empty drawers and closet space in the master bedroom for her to use. Once both their suitcases were unpacked and their dirty clothes sorted to be laundered or dry cleaned the next day, she asked him to help her move the rest of her clothing and personal belongings from the guest room, leaving only the five boxes and the tote containing her mom's journals and photo albums from her apartment in Atlantic City in her former room. By then, it was late enough that they decided to call it a night, planning to go through those things and digitize her mom's journals the next night.

After taking turns in the bathroom for their nightly routines, they settled into bed with Liam giving Rylie the side of the bed closest to the balcony so he was on the side slightly closer to the door to the rest of the house.

"Um, is there a reason why we've swapped sides of the bed?" Rylie questioned, rolling on her side to face him.

"Swapped sides? What do you mean? This is always the side of the bed I sleep on when I'm home." It took him a moment to realize that she was referring to when they'd shared a bed in Heart's Destiny a month earlier, since he'd also started out on the right side of the bed in Atlantic City.

"Well, Friday night, or rather early Saturday morning, you were more in the middle of the bed, so I got in on the right, but I guess you did have your stuff on that bedside table like you started out there. But in Heart's Destiny, you slept on the left side of the bed and I was on the right, so it's like we've swapped sides from when we shared a bed before."

"I guess I just always pick the side of the bed closest to the door," Liam half-shrugged since he was laying on his left side to face her in the bed. "So, in hotel rooms, I go back and forth. And since the door was at the foot of the bed in Atlantic City, I picked the side closest to the bathroom. But then the next morning, I had to get out on the other side and walk around since you'd come in and were asleep on that side."

"Is this some alpha, you-have-to-sleep-closest-to-the-door thing to protect the little woman in case of an intruder?" Rylie narrowed her eyes, like she was offended by him thinking she was incapable of defending herself.

"Well, considering the door into the room is at the foot of the bed here, too, and only slightly closer to this side of the bed, while you're actually closer to the sliding-glass doors out to the balcony, I don't think so." Liam pointed out.

"You say that like an intruder might scale the side of the house to come in the balcony door," Rylie scoffed, rolling her eyes at him. "Which is highly unlikely."

"It might be unlikely, but it's not impossible." Liam rubbed his chin as if deep in thought. "But regardless of how an intruder might try breaking into the house, or which one of us will be closer to them if they do, I don't think I picked this side of the bed in some alphahole move to try and act superior to you. And if it was because of some caveman tendency to want to protect my woman, then it was only subconsciously."

"Uh-huh, sure." Rylie shook her head doubtfully. "All your caveman tendencies are only done subconsciously. That's why you always take the lead when we're planning our angles and get all growly and dominant in the bedroom."

Her sarcasm wasn't lost on him. Nor was her introduction of kinky sex to the conversation. But since he was trying not to listen to the head pushing valiantly to escape the confines of his boxer briefs, Liam knew he couldn't let her change the subject.

"Honestly, I think it's just a lazy thing, so I don't have to walk as far to go to the bathroom now that I'm getting so old I have to get up at least once in the middle of the night to go. Well, that and the TV is on this side, so it's easier to see from this side of the bed."

"Alright, old man, you can have that side for now," Rylie smirked mischievously. "But just so you know, you're gonna hafta give it up anytime I'm pregnant and don't want to waddle around the bed to get to the bathroom. And anytime I wanna watch a movie and don't feel like propping up to see it over your clown feet."

"Clown feet? I do not have clown feet. I wear a respectable size thirteen shoe. Thank you very much."

"Respectable size thirteen?" Rylie laughed. "Ha! Your feet are like flippers, they're so big!"

Liam couldn't resist reaching over and tickling her ribs when she laughed at him. "My feet are not flippers. They're proportional to my body, unlike yours, which are tiny."

"I do not have tiny feet," Rylie protested, trying to retaliate with the tickling, turning their playful argument into an impromptu wrestling match in the middle of the bed. "My feet are a size seven, which is pretty average for women. If you want to see small feet you should look at Aiken or Kay with their tiny little size five feet."

Liam didn't care about anyone else's shoe size right then. Honestly, he didn't even care about his or Rylie's once they started rolling around in the bed and she ended up under him. All he cared about right then was kissing her, so that's exactly what he did.

As his mouth crashed down on her plump lips, Liam stopped tickling her, preferring to caress her curvy flesh instead. Rylie responded in kind, wrapping her arms and legs around him as she opened her mouth to his tongue's invasion.

You're supposed to be abstaining, his subconscious tried to warn him.

But Liam quickly shut down his inner voice, mentally declaring, *We're just abstaining from sex, not kissing and touching and showing each other how we feel in other ways. So, it's all good as long as I keep my boxers on.*

As Rylie rocked her hips to grind her sweet pussy on his hard cock, Liam lost the ability to think coherently. All he could do was feel, and taste, the woman he loved. Rylie's kiss tasted sweet and minty, like the toothpaste they'd both just used a short time earlier. Her breasts felt soft and lush under his palms, with diamond hard nipples protruding against the cotton of her tank top. But the most exquisite thing he felt right then was the turgid nub of her clit rubbing against his frenulum. It felt amazing, even through their clothing, which meant he couldn't stand the way they were grinding on one another for long or he'd blow his load in his shorts.

Reluctantly, Liam broke their kiss, trailing his mouth along her jaw to whisper in her ear. "Unwrap your legs, Mo Ghrá."

She released both her arms and legs from around him. But she didn't ask why, so he didn't take the time to explain that he wanted to give her pleasure, even though he still felt like he needed to hold back his own release. Not that he wanted to think about all the reasons for that right then. He preferred just focusing on doing the things he knew she loved, starting with kissing his way down her neck while pushing her tank top up to uncover her bodacious boobs.

Liam slid his body to the side of hers as he continued kissing his way down her torso, hating the loss of pressure against his dick, even though he knew he had to stop dry-humping her. He rested on his left elbow, twisting his forearm around so he could pinch her right nipple between his left thumb and forefinger, while freeing up his right arm to move down far enough he could delve his right hand beneath her sleep shorts and panties.

Not wanting to neglect her left tit, he dipped his head and laved it with his tongue, just as his fingers stroked across her slick cunt. She was so aroused that his first two fingers slipped easily inside her as he circled her clit with the pad of his thumb.

"Feck, you're so wet," Liam groaned against her skin before sucking her taut tip into his mouth and lightly grazing it with his teeth.

"Oh, Liam," Rylie moaned, rocking her hips in time with his thrusting fingers. Once she realized he'd stopped moving down the bed, she ran her hands over his shoulders and arms once more.

Liam loved the way she stroked her hands over him, almost like she needed to touch him. He especially loved the way her gentle caress turned almost feral the closer she got to reaching her peak, knowing he'd have marks from her sex kitten claws after she came.

As she writhed on the bed, Rylie spread her legs, giving him even more access to her sweet sex. In doing so, however, she seemed to be seeking out his cock with her right leg, rubbing her knee against his side in an attempt to get him to roll his lower body off the mattress, so she could stroke his cock with her leg.

"Not this time, Mo Ghrá," Liam growled after popping his mouth off her tit. "This is all for you tonight."

"But I want to make you feel as wonderful as you're making me feel right now," Rylie protested, sliding one hand up to cup his face.

"Trust me, I feel amazing right now," Liam assured her, inching his way back up the bed to look her in the eyes as he elaborated. "And I'm gonna feel even better when you come on my fingers, Mo Ghrá."

He silenced any further pleas with his mouth on hers, kissing her longingly as he continued to finger-fuck her until her inner walls clamped down on his digits like a vise.

"Oh, yes, Liam," Rylie cried out, tearing her mouth from his as her whole body convulsed with her explosive orgasm. "Yes, Li, yes!"

Liam relished being the one to give her such intense pleasure, while he also wished he could go over the edge with her. But no matter how much he wanted her and longed to make love to her, he wouldn't put her at risk by forgoing a condom. And now that he knew she was a Catholic, he also wouldn't make her feel like she was sinning because he felt the need to protect her. He had to banish those thoughts for the time being, needing to focus back on his beautiful bride as he assessed whether she needed another orgasm or if the one was intense enough to put her to sleep.

Since she started wiggling against his hand again as soon as the spasms in her pussy slowed down, Liam teased his thumb over her clit as he bent his fingers to stroke over her G-spot. He slid back down to use his left hand and mouth on her breasts once more, knowing if he hit all her erogenous zones at once, then he could make her come repeatedly with no breaks in between.

It only took three before she went limp, completely spent. She was so satiated that she almost instantly drifted off to sleep with a beatific smile on her lips.

Liam eased his fingers from her body, readjusting her clothes so she could sleep comfortably. He then got up and went to the bathroom to clean up where he hadn't been able to stop the precum flowing from his dick. He was still hard as stone, but thankfully, he was able to get his cock under control with the shower set at the coldest temperature possible.

As he stood in the shower, fighting not to jerk off since Rylie wasn't awake to participate, Liam thought about all the ways he could pleasure her while still keeping her safe. That led to his thoughts about how to reconcile their religious beliefs with the sexual part of their relationship. He didn't want to do anything to make her feel like she was going against her religious upbringing just because he believed the Catholic Church was misinterpreting the Bible to make condom usage a sin. Knowing he wanted to honor her wish to be a better Catholic now that she'd re-embraced religion after lapsing for a few years only strengthened his resolve to wait until he got that ninety-day negative test before making love to her again, so he'd know it was safe for them to lose the latex.

And what happens if one of your January or February tests comes up positive? Liam felt taunted by his inner voice bringing his worst fear to the forefront of his mind.

No, that's not gonna happen! He mentally screamed. *God wouldn't bless me with Rylie as my wife, allowing us to work out every other obstacle that I thought would prevent us from staying together, only to rip her away from me so cruelly.*

But just to shore up his faith, Liam said a silent prayer as he got out of the shower, dried off, and put on a clean pair of boxer briefs, asking God to ensure they only tested positive on pregnancy tests in the future. When he crawled back in bed, he pulled Rylie into his arms, fulfilling his promise to cuddle away their nightmares.

Chapter Ten

As Rylie walked with Liam into the hangar at the airport, where he had to inspect the new pods being installed in the GWA planes, she couldn't help but wonder why he'd been given the task of overseeing this aspect of the business, instead of someone from the GWA's corporate office there in New York. Liam told her when they first went to pick out the new seats that he was the largest person in the company who would be in town, so that was why Rick asked him to pick the seats to make sure the larger guys on the roster would be as comfortable as possible. But if size was the only thing they needed to go by, then whoever they sent could have easily picked the largest seats without having to be the largest person who worked for the company who was also in town. So, it just didn't make sense to her.

When she mentioned as much to Liam on the drive that morning, he seemed to think Rick had too much on his mind because of the IVF cycle he and Fiona were doing this month, so he wasn't exactly at the top of his game with the minutia of running his company. *I suppose that could be the case. But it still feels like there's more to it than just Rick being preoccupied and thinking he needed a wrestler's opinion, instead of going with the opinion of someone who actually knows all about airplane seats.*

Thinking about Fiona trying to get pregnant while dealing with P.C.O.S. brought her own potential issues with getting pregnant to the forefront of her mind. While she and Liam hadn't yet discussed their views on IVF and whether or not they aligned with the Catholic Church, after their talk the day before, she kind of thought that might be another area where he disagreed with the Church. Unfortunately, having lived as a lapsed Catholic for the last several years, she didn't feel like she'd studied the Bible enough to decide for herself about the aspects of the Catholic Church's doctrine, where Liam saw gray areas in what she'd been taught were black-and-white beliefs.

"That's not a racial thing. It's also not a one-is-good-and-the-other-is-evil thing, either. It just means that it's written in black ink on white paper, so you can clearly read what God expects of us as Christians."

She had to smile at how her thoughts brought back another memory of her parents teaching her about life. She'd tried arguing that being able to read the words didn't mean she was able to understand all the nuances of the Bible verses. But her parents had told her that just meant she needed to study more. *I guess Mom and Dad were right about that. And I guess we'll both get to study more when we start our Pre-Cana classes, so maybe we can come to an agreement about what's explicitly clear and what still might be a gray area for me, as well as for Liam.*

She had to put those thoughts on the back burner, however, as they were escorted onto the plane by Gianni Marconi, the avionics technician who was tasked with showing them the progress on the seat installation to see the upgrades to the seats, since the sales manager they met with when they first got to town wasn't available. She'd thought they were just installing the new seats on the upper level of the GWA talent plane and on both levels of the new plane Rick had bought for the ring crew, catering staff, and other roadies. But as they entered the main cabin, it was clear they'd upgraded all the seats to now include entertainment systems and privacy screens, which could be tucked away in cabinets behind each seat, as well as tables in each quad that could be folded up to provide a privacy screen between the pairs of seats facing each other, instead of just having the fabric privacy screens that rolled down from the underside of the overhead compartments to separate a quad of seats from the aisle that they'd had in the past.

They'd also reconfigured the seats to go back to the original two-aisle configuration, with a third set of two seats on each row in the middle of what had previously been an extra wide aisle. The center seats were also arranged in a quad layout, with the seats on the odd rows facing the back of the plane. So, in addition to the eight rows of four-wide seats they'd added to the upper deck, they'd also added an additional two seats to each of the rows on the main deck. Or at least, she assumed they'd added them to all the rows. It also appeared that the rows were farther apart to accommodate the cabinetry, so she couldn't tell if they'd kept the original layout of thirty rows or not, since she couldn't see around the stairs and three sets of bathrooms in the middle of the plane to count the rows, or if there was room for that third set when the plane narrowed just before the back galley.

I guess we have to decide which side of the plane we're planning on sitting in now before we go past the front galley and bathrooms, or else we won't be able to cross over until after we get to the stairs or one of the other three sets of bathrooms.

The new seats were still capable of laying down flat for anyone who wanted to sleep on a flight. But now they could do so in a completely private space, instead of being watched over by the other three people in their quad with only the fabric curtain-like privacy screens along the aisle. While she didn't think they'd use those privacy screens on the majority of their daily flights, since they hadn't really used the curtain-screens previously, Rylie thought they might come in handy on long, overnight, international flights.

She wasn't quite so sure about the entertainment systems, however. Not that they wouldn't be used quite regularly, but that Rick wouldn't be upset by Liam picking out seats that basically included a tablet computer for each person to be able to watch a different movie, or play a different game, without having to get out their own electronics.

"Are you sure Rick's okay with you upgrading all the seats to include these tablets?"

"The tablets aren't really an upgrade," Liam informed her, shaking his head as he pointed to the space where two seat backs met, which was now a cabinet the same height as the back of the seat when it was set upright, where the privacy screens could be hidden away when not in use. "Well, other than adding over fifty more of them, since the old seats also had them. They just weren't accessible because they were mounted on the back of the seats, since those seats were meant to be set up in rows with the in-flight entertainment systems being used by the people in the seats behind them. Though, now I'm curious if he's going to go through the trouble of licensing movies and games and stuff for them now that they're accessible. Or if he'll just have them set up with the Wi-Fi, so we'll have to log into our own streaming services."

"We were actually instructed to set them up with exclusive access to a new streaming service from Burleson Entertainment," Gianni informed them. He sat down in the nearest seat and demonstrated how to pull the tablet up from the cabinet in front of the seat between the rows, as well as how to access the catalog of movies already streaming on the new service. "Currently they only have the back library of movies produced by PEAR Productions before they changed their name, but it's my understanding that they'll be adding more content as the distribution contracts for their newer material expires, and of course, for the movies they're currently producing that won't ever be distributed through other streaming services."

Rylie knew the Burlesons had purchased the production company Aiken's dads co-owned with a lesbian couple they'd been friends with since the 1980s, having heard all about the newer movies they were making when everyone from the GWA was in Heart's Destiny in November. Aiken had mentioned the history of PEAR Productions, specifically how the four friends had started it in the late eighties to provide more opportunities for people of color and those identifying as part of the LGBTQIA2S+ community.

At the time, they knew they couldn't rock the boat too much by making their diversity agenda obvious in their company name and logo. So, Theo Pearson, Shawn Aiken, Abby Easley, and Raven Romero took the first letter of each of their last names and played around with the words they could make from them, finally settling on pear because the fruit was the easiest to make into a logo and seemed somewhat innocuous.

By the time the two couples were able to enter into legal domestic partnerships and eventually marry, the production company was well established, so they kept the name even though Shawn changed his last name to Pearson and Abby and Raven hyphenated their names. But when the founding partners all reached their sixties and were ready to start thinking about retirement, they opted to sell the company to the Burlesons because none of their children were interested in taking over the upper level executive positions of their parents. Apparently, they also liked that Julie Burleson had made it clear that her department of Burleson Incorporated was Diversification and Asset Management, and she felt that meant working with a diverse group of people as well as expanding the company with a diverse group of assets. Since Julie's vision went along with their original agenda for the production company, they were happy to sell to a company owned by a family they considered allies to their community.

But when Aiken mentioned how much her dads were enjoying being able to focus exclusively on producing and designing costumes for the newer movies, instead of having to split their time between the work they loved and the tediousness of running the office, she hadn't mentioned anything about the Burlesons planning to start a streaming service with the movies produced by the studio formerly known as PEAR Productions. *I think she might have been too focused on trying to make our guys jealous by talking about the actors she's planning to pitch to her dads to play each of us in the movies they're making from Kay's books to get into the details of what all the Burlesons plan to do with the production company they bought.*

"Yeah, they'll also have the entire GWA library soon, too," Liam nodded, obviously knowing more about the entertainment division of the Burlesons' business than she'd overheard the last time they were in Heart's Destiny. "They're just waiting until all the shows from the eighties, when Richard first started the company, are digitized to roll it all out at once."

"For real?" Gianni looked excited by that prospect. "I'm guessing you know this because of working for the GWA?"

"Yeah, that and one of the Burlesons is also one of our pilots and a good friend, so I've overheard a few things, both when we're hanging out on tour and when we're in their hometown for weddings and stuff. And when I heard they were talking about putting our shows on their new streaming service, I was excited to get to see the old shows I remember watching as a kid again."

As Liam and Gianni talked about early GWA shows they remembered watching as kids, Rylie walked toward the back of the plane, not waiting for them to go see just how different the upstairs looked now that it was no longer a bedroom. She didn't want to hear anything more about how Liam might have overheard those tidbits while he was hanging out with Jen. It wasn't really that she was still having doubts about his feelings for the other woman, or even that she was jealous of their friendship. It was more that the way he'd insisted on getting her off while not taking any pleasure for himself the night before had stirred up her insecurities about him not wanting to develop feelings for her. And she knew hearing Jen's name would only make those anxieties worse right then.

I know he wouldn't make the same mistake of trying to hook up with Jen again, she mentally told herself as she climbed the stairs. *So, it really shouldn't bother me to hear him talking about his friendship with her. I guess that's something else I need to pray about, so I can stop feeling irrationally jealous for no real reason.*

As she looked around the upper level that had previously been set up as a bedroom, she was surprised by how much smaller the space seemed now that it was filled with the eight rows of seats. Previously, it held what looked like a queen-sized bed, along with two separate seating areas, one set up with a sofa and two recliners and the other set up with a dining table and banquette seating. *I guess it makes sense that it looked bigger when it held less furniture. But I have to wonder just how much Rick is planning to expand the roster that he had to double the seating capacity up here as well as add almost as many seats on the main level as he added up here.*

It felt strange to enter the upper cabin from the back of the space instead of from the front as was always the case when they boarded the plane on the main level. But still Rylie appreciated the private moment to check out the new pods while contemplating what she should do about her relationship with Liam.

I know he thinks we should wait to make love again, but I'm not so sure that's really the best thing for us. Yeah, I know he's going to point out how Father O'Malley recommended we wait until he feels safe going without a condom as his excuse for only pleasuring me last night. But since he doesn't believe using a condom is actually a sin, I'm not buying his claim that he's trying to keep me from sinning against my will.

She decided to check out the new in-flight entertainment system to see if the tablets had an internet browser built in, along with their access to the Burleson Entertainment streaming service. After popping open the cabinet between the seat she sat in and the rear-facing seat in front of it, she pulled up the tablet on the attached arm, so she didn't even have to hold it or lay it on the tray table that folded down from part of the privacy screen between the pods in that quad. She quickly powered it on, noticing immediately that there was an internet browser icon right beside the icons for Burleson Entertainment and the GWA.

Curious about the GWA icon, she clicked it first, finding it went straight to their employee portal on the company website, where they could sign in to see their payroll and benefit records, as well as their upcoming travel schedule. After clicking back out of that, she opened the internet browser to do a search for Bible verses pertaining to contraception, wanting to figure out why the Church considered using it a sin, after Liam had pointed out that it couldn't explicitly be listed in the Bible because condoms and the pill hadn't been invented back when the Bible was first written.

Wow, I guess Liam's not the only one who disagrees with the Catholic Church on this. Her search garnered page after page of links to debates on the topic of contraception being sinful or not. After opening a couple of them to find they were talking about passing out condoms in schools and how that's sinful because it promotes sex before marriage, she realized she needed to narrow her search parameters to find out if a married couple using a condom was a sin.

Once she'd narrowed down the topic, she found it was still debatable. Some of the priests, pastors, and biblical scholars who posted online considered condom usage by married couples sinful because of a passage in Genesis about Onan being put to death for withdrawing and spilling his seed on the ground instead of impregnating his brother's widow. Apparently, a lot of people thought that meant the withdrawal method of avoiding pregnancy was sinful. While quite a few others pointed out that Onan was being punished for not obeying the laws of the Old Testament, and that the sexual act was actually rape because the widow didn't have a say in the matter at all. Still others pointed out that having a man sleep with his dead brother's wife to provide his dead brother an heir was one of the Old Testament laws that Christians no longer obeyed, therefore we couldn't interpret that passage in the Bible as how we're supposed to handle family planning nowadays.

Even looking at the links where the priests, pastors, and biblical scholars didn't list Onan's story as a basis for their belief, there was still a lot of debate about whether sex had to be both procreative and unitive, or if it was okay for it to be unitive without always being procreative. The more she read, the more she realized that, while God did intend his people to "be fruitful and multiply," he also meant for sex to unify a couple as one, even if they didn't conceive every time. And she didn't have to read the arguments about it not being a sin for a woman who'd gone through menopause to have sex with her husband to figure that out. She just had to look back at her parents and how they'd remained openly affectionate, and most likely sexually active right up until the day they died, even after they figured out her mom's P.C.O.S. had progressed so far that they couldn't conceive another child.

Once she read that some priests were even condoning condom usage in marriage to prevent the spread of HIV from one partner to the other, Rylie realized she had to point that out to not only Liam, but also to Father O'Malley when they met with him later that day. *Since it's only going to be for a few more weeks, until Liam feels safe after his next negative test, and we both believe that God could bypass a condom for me to get pregnant regardless, even Father O'Malley should see that it's not sinful for us to make love now instead of waiting. In fact, us making love now will be better for our marriage because of how much closer we'll feel as a couple. You know, since God intended sex to be unitive for married couples and all.*

"Whatcha watching?" Liam startled her from her thoughts when his voice came from the front of the plane, since the stairs were behind her.

"Not watching anything." Rylie clicked the X to close the internet browser, not wanting Gianni to see the screen and figure out what was going on in their marriage. "Just surfing some religious forums online, trying to find some other Bible verses that might come up when we start our Pre-Cana classes this afternoon."

That was not a lie. She fully expected to see some or all of the Bible verses she'd just been reading about in the marriage prep material later. Maybe not in the first session, but definitely when they got to that fifth lesson Father O'Malley had already mentioned.

"How'd you come up here from the front of the plane?" Rylie questioned, needing to change the subject so she didn't have to reveal what she'd learned until after she and Liam were alone.

"There's a second set of stairs for the pilots," Liam replied, pointing over his shoulder with his thumb at a door she hadn't noticed before, "since the cockpit is up here. I don't know if that spiral staircase is normally standard on a seven-forty-seven, but it was cool to see where the extra flight crew rides when we're on a long international flight that requires more than just the normal two pilots, and how they could trade out in the middle of a flight without disturbing the passengers, who might have been using this space as a bedroom before it was switched over."

"Seriously? There's a spiral staircase on the plane?" Based on the smirk on Liam's face, Rylie wasn't sure if she could believe him or if he was just pulling her leg. "Show me."

"Yeah, seriously," Liam confirmed, taking her hand and pulling her up from the seat she was sitting in.

"Spiral staircases were standard on the first seven-forty-sevens," Gianni informed them as he showed them the cockpit. He then took them down the spiral staircase to show them the flight crew luggage closets and small six-pod seating area in the nose of the plane on the main deck before going back through the front galley to expound on the new seat configuration in the main cabin of the plane.

Rylie learned that they'd taken the main cabin from thirty rows of seats down to twenty-four rows to accommodate additional closets for all their hanging garment bags, as well as specialty cabinets for their oversized luggage in the narrower section at the back of the aircraft. But since they'd added two seats to each row, they now had one-hundred-and-forty-four seats in the main cabin instead of the previous one-hundred-and-twenty. With the addition of the thirty-two seats on the upper deck, the GWA plane was now equipped to carry one-hundred-and-seventy-six passengers, not counting the crew.

"Please tell me Janice and Mia, and whatever flight attendants work on the roadies' plane, don't have to sit in those tiny jump seats in the galley the whole time we're on a long international flight," Rylie beseeched Liam as they left after seeing that the roadies' aircraft looked very similar to the talent airplane, only with a full kitchen set up in the back galley and storage for food and kitchen supplies taking up the space where the oversized and hanging luggage cabinets were on the talent aircraft, with those specialty cabinets occupying the space in front of that, where the last four rows of seats in the main cabin were located on the talent plane, so it was only designed to hold one-hundred-and-fifty-two passengers. "Can't they set up the call buttons to notify them on the tablets in their pods in the nose, so they can be comfortable on the flight too?"

"I honestly don't know," Liam admitted, tilting his head thoughtfully as he drove them to the Social Security Administration office for her to change her name on her social security card. "I didn't really pay attention to where they sat on the European tour, even though we had both flight crews with us on all those flights. But even though I've been flying on this plane since Rick bought it, until today, I hadn't ever gone through the doors off the front galley to see that it was flight crew seating and didn't just go straight into the cockpit like I thought."

On their trip to New York, Mia and Noelle York had sat in the main passenger cabin, right across the aisle from Liam and Rylie, since they were the only passengers. But that was only because Liam had basically told Mia to relax and enjoy the flight with her daughter instead of working as if it was a normal GWA tour. Liam also insisted on Mia taking the day of their flight back to San Antonio off, after talking to Mia on the trip to find out that her husband Derek was trading days with Anthony, so he could catch a return flight to New York on the first to meet with the pilots and cabin crews being hired for the roadies' plane on the second and third. Apparently, hiring pilots required a lot more paperwork than hiring wrestlers. So, since Derek was familiar with all the FAA regulations, he was tasked with making sure they were all good to go before they flew the new plane across the country to meet the road crew in Bakersfield, California, before the flight to Hawaii on January eighth.

"So, both flight crews have to go with us on international tours?" Rylie wondered if that was an FAA requirement because of the long flights to and from, or if it was just a precaution in case there were issues on the international flights the crews would have to make every few days to swap out as they did while the GWA was in North America.

"It might have something to do with the long flights to and from and how many hours each pilot is allowed to fly," Liam explained, half-shrugging as if he was unsure. "But I know at least part of the reason Rick insisted on it for the first European tour was because he didn't want anyone to miss out on the sightseeing excursions he had the office set up for us every day, especially the kids."

"You're talking about the excursions they do with all the kids, like the one to Niagara Falls you convinced me to sneak onto back in April?"

"Yeah," Liam chuckled, not looking even slightly embarrassed for tricking her into thinking she'd get in trouble with the boss for not going when it was supposed to just be for the kids to have a history lesson. "But everyone in the company went, not just the families who needed the educational experiences for their kids, even the roadies."

"What all did you see last time? And since everyone did them last time, do you think he'll do the same ones on the European tour this year too?" Rylie hoped they wouldn't skip some of the places she was most excited to see just because most of the company had seen them the year before.

"We went to a lot of castles. Dublin Castle, the Palace of Holyroodhouse, Buckingham Palace for the Changing of the Guard," Liam stated, listing off some of the excursions from the previous European tour. "But we also went to museums, like the Louvre and the Leonardo da Vinci National Museum of Science and Technology, as well as cool tours like the Beatles Magical Mystery Tour and a boat tour of the Grand Canal in Venice. I don't know if we'll do the same things again or not, but even if we do, I'm sure there'll be things we'll notice that we didn't last time. Plus we're going to several cities we haven't been to before, so I'm sure he'll want both flight crews to come along so their kids don't miss something on their normal days off. And that'll probably be the same for this South Pacific and Southeast Asia tour in a couple of weeks."

For the rest of the ride to the Social Security Administration, they talked about all the things they hoped to see on the upcoming international tours. While Rylie was excited about the prospects of all the fabulous sights they would soon see, she felt a little guilty about not talking to Liam about what she'd looked up online on the plane earlier. *I suppose all that can wait until we meet with Father O'Malley, so we have some spiritual guidance to review those scriptures. Though hopefully, he won't tell us we need to go to confession again after what we did last night in bed.*

~~~

Liam couldn't believe how quick and easy it was for Rylie to change her name and address on her Social Security records. Apparently, she'd started the application process online from her phone on Friday afternoon, while he was meeting with Jeff Carson and talking with Bradan about the gift cards for the other residents of her former building. Since the agent for her renter's insurance company was only there to give everyone their contact information for filing a claim later, once each resident knew the extent of the damages to their units, she was finished long before he was done with his calls. So, once they got to the office for the Social Security Administration for her scheduled appointment, it was just a matter of showing the clerk her documentation to get everything changed. They were in and out in fifteen minutes, which boggled Liam's mind, considering he was expecting to wait at least an hour, like he'd had to do with the DMV in the past, so they had plenty of time to stop for a late lunch before their next session with Father O'Malley. Her new social security card would be in the mail to his house within the next two weeks, even though they'd already given her a printout to show the change had been made for her to get her passport and driver's license changed the next day. Oh, yeah, she'd also apparently already made an appointment to change her name on her passport, too, right after she got her braids put back in and had a new passport picture taken.

Tomorrow is going to be crazy with everything she's scheduled. I know she and Teagan always scheduled their hair appointments on days they weren't booked on the card, so they could spend all afternoon and evening getting them done, so I don't know why she thinks she'll have time tomorrow morning for a six- to eight-hour appointment, and still have time to get a manicure and pedicure before getting her passport picture taken, and then trying to squeeze in the passport office and the DMV before we go to the new year's party at the pub.

"Are you sure we'll have time for your hair appointment tomorrow along with everything else?" Liam questioned as they drove back to Belle Harbor.
~~~

"Yes, I'm sure." Rylie reached over and patted his leg reassuringly. "I found a salon in Harlem that's open twenty-four-seven. And when I called to schedule the appointment, I specifically asked them to look at my pic on the GWA website to estimate how long it would take for them to do my braids. And they assured me that if I'm there for a six a.m. appointment, then I'll be done at noon. The girl I talked to also turned out to be a fan, so she hooked me up with the nail salon next door for my noon appointment for a manicure and pedicure, so I'll have plenty of time before my three p.m. appointment at the passport office and my four p.m. appointment at the DMV."

"You realize Harlem is at least an hour away from the house, right?"

"Yes, but according to Maps, it's not too far from the passport office and DMV in Manhattan, which are both kinda on the way back home if we just make a big loop around the city, so I don't think it'll be a problem." Rylie shrugged. "We just have to leave the house at four-thirty in the morning to give us plenty of time for everything. And if you don't want to be bored sitting and watching me get my hair braided, then you'll have plenty of time to come home, catch a nap, and come back to get me at one when my nails are done. Or I can just go on my own, since you don't really have to be there for any of my appointments."

"No, I'll go," Liam decided. *There's no way I'm spending the day at home while you're on your own in Harlem and Manhattan where anything can happen. But I can't exactly tell her that, or she'll get pissed that I'm being overprotective.* "I wanna watch and see how your braids are done, so I can be more helpful when it's time to take them out, instead of fumbling around like I did when you needed help taking the pins out of your updo last month."

"Okay, but once you see the first few, you might wanna go find something else to do or catch a nap in the car, so you don't get bored." Rylie grinned at him mischievously as she reached up and ran her fingers through the longest part of his hair. "'Cause if you fall asleep in the salon, you might just wake up with extensions braided into your hair too."

"Yeah, I'll bring my Kindle and read if I have to." Liam knew taking a nap in the car wasn't an option, so he figured he'd just have to take his chances with being bored if he couldn't hide his reaction to his current choice of reading material. Since he'd finished the first two books in Kay's **Devine** series on Saturday night in Atlantic City, he looked forward to reading the third book in the series, **Ronnie's Runaway**.

They'd already decided to drive the Porsche to her appointments the next day, just in case she had to do an actual driving test and couldn't just transfer her New Jersey license to New York. While she hadn't had another panic attack in the Navigator since he'd folded down the third row of seats, even when they'd had to take it to and from the airport to have room for the stuff they brought back from Atlantic City, it was best not to take any chances when she'd already be nervous for a test in an unfamiliar city.

Liam appreciated getting to drive his sports car as often as possible on this trip home. Especially since he had a feeling he'd be giving it up to Rylie anytime they were home in the future and weren't always going to the same places throughout their days. *Maybe I should go get an extra set of keys made to give her after she gets her driver's license changed tomorrow, so I can make it clear I now consider this her car?*

"So, before we go in for our session with Father O'Malley, I should probably warn you that I plan on asking him to reconsider his stance on condoms being a sin, considering our special circumstances and what I read online earlier about some priests giving couples permission to use them to prevent the spread of diseases."

Rylie's words surprised Liam, just as he turned into the parking lot at the community center adjacent to Saint Stephen's Cathedral, where they were meeting Father O'Malley and the couple he recruited to be their mentors for the Pre-Cana classes they were taking. "That's what you were reading on the plane earlier?"

"Yeah, I wanted to understand why the Church considers condoms a sin, so I could decide for myself if I agree with them, or with you that they aren't." Rylie shrugged as if it was no big deal.

Liam could only smile as he parked, feeling relieved that she'd chosen to do her own research, instead of just arbitrarily going along with the opinions of others. Knowing she'd been raised to follow the Catholic doctrine the same way he had, he'd felt guilty about using condoms every time they'd made love in the past without thinking about how it could have made her feel as if she was sinning against her will. That was the number one reason why he was holding back from making love to her again until after his ninety-day incubation period was over and he tested negative for everything, so his insistence that they continued using condoms wouldn't force her to go against her beliefs.

"And what did you learn in the short time I was talking to Gianni about old school GWA shows and the upgrades to the plane?" *And if you decided to agree with me that using condoms right now isn't a sin, does that mean you don't want to wait until the end of next month for us to make love again?*

Liam thought he'd done the right thing the night before by only focusing on making her come, while showing that he was capable of waiting to achieve his own release. But now he had to wonder if he'd taken things too far and made her feel pressured to find a way they could have sex without feeling guilty.

"I learned that Reddit has forums specifically for Christianity and Catholicism," she started explaining before Liam interrupted her with a chuckle.

"Yeah, I don't think Father O'Malley is going to change his mind based on anything you read on a Reddit forum."

"No, but Reddit isn't the only site I read today," Rylie contended. "Apparently, priests and pastors of all denominations have blogs and forums on their church websites, where they openly express their opinions on a lot of topics I never would have thought would be so vastly different from parish to parish."

Liam immediately thought of the old saying about opinions being like assholes, but he didn't think that was appropriate to mention when they were talking about various church leaders.

"And I know, opinions are like…noses, everyone has one and some of them smell," Rylie grinned, obviously realizing they were both thinking about the same old saying, she just modified it to be more politically correct. "But a lot of the blogs listed biblical references to back up their opinions, including several who pointed out that Onan's story in Genesis can't be the basis for thinking contraception is a sin because it was based on an Old Testament covenant that was abolished when Jesus died for our sins. They also quoted Proverbs to show that sex between a married couple isn't just for procreation, saying love, and meaning sex, should invigorate us always. *Always*, not just until the wife goes through menopause and can't bear children anymore.

So, if it's okay to use birth control pills to regulate my periods and not call it a sin, then it's okay to use condoms until you know for sure you didn't get anything from that stalker's blood, so we can still make love for the unitive aspect of it without considering it a sin."

Before Liam could respond to verify that Rylie wanted them to make love sooner than when he got his next test results, they saw Father O'Malley walking toward the community center. "I guess it's a good thing we got here early then, so we can see if he's available to discuss everything you read this morning before we're supposed to meet our mentors."

They got out of the car and met Father O'Malley at the door of the community center. The priest smiled at them when he saw them walking up holding hands. "Good afternoon. Is it safe to assume that the smiles on your faces mean the fire damage wasn't as bad as you expected when you left here last week?"

"Yes and no," Rylie replied before Liam could. "I'm not sure I really knew what to expect, so when I first saw the end of the building with the most damage, I thought it was much worse than I expected. But then when we saw the other end of the building, where my apartment was located, I had hope that it wasn't as bad as the other end of the building, but I was still expecting possible water or smoke damage to my stuff. But when the fire inspector brought out the tote of my mom's photo albums and journals, with only the faintest scent of smoke from the other boxes they packed up for me, it became very obvious that God truly watched over my apartment. I just wish all my neighbors would have been so blessed."

"But the only injury in the whole ordeal was a very minor burn to one of the resident's hands from the oil spattering out of the pot he was trying to deep fry a turkey in, which should be fully healed in the next few days. So, I think God was watching over all of them, as well as the firefighters who responded to the blaze, since there weren't any casualties." Liam smiled as he added his opinion.

"He was indeed," Father O'Malley agreed as they all walked into the building.

"So, um, I know we're early, but is it possible we can talk to you privately before the others get here for our first lesson?" Liam asked, not sure what they'd do for the next thirty minutes if Father O'Malley was already booked.

"I'm actually supposed to be meeting with Sister Mary Katherine to plan for sorting through everything from our recent clothing drive to restock the closet for our homeless outreach," Father O'Malley informed them. "But that should only take a few minutes and then I'll be able to meet with you in the classroom."

"Oh, that reminds me," Rylie released Liam's hand to open her wristlet and pull out the gift card Liam had bought for all the residents of her building in Atlantic City. "I wanted to ask her about who to talk to here to donate a Visa gift card to help pay for the food and clothes and stuff you all distribute."

"Normally, donations are done online now," Father O'Malley explained, giving Rylie a quizzical look. "Even when we used to pass an offering plate, those donations were always cash or checks, not gift cards."

"I can show you the online portal when we get home, if you want to donate more than what I already have set up to automatically draft from my account each month," Liam assured Rylie.

"So, I can't donate this gift card?" Rylie waved the card around as she refastened her wristlet. "Liam bought all of them for the people who lost stuff in the fire to replace the things that were damaged, but I don't need it. That's why I haven't even activated it to put my name on it, so I can give it to someone who actually needs it or can put it to good use. And what better use for it is there than going to buy food and clothing and whatever other supplies you guys need to help people like Mr. Willie get back on their feet?"

"I suppose we can treat it as an in-kind donation," Father O'Malley offered. "And use it to purchase the items we didn't receive enough of during our recent clothing drive."

"Perfect." Rylie handed the card to Father O'Malley, who insisted on them accompanying him to the office where he was meeting Sister Mary Katherine, so they could write out a receipt for the donation.

After that was done, Liam and Rylie went on to the classroom where they were supposed to meet, while Father O'Malley had his quick discussion with Sister Mary Katherine. "Are you happy, Mo Ghrá, now that you don't have to figure out what to do with that gift card?"

"Yes, very," Rylie beamed as she sat down in the chair Liam pulled out for her. "But I'd have been just as happy if the parish wasn't able to take the card. I just would have asked for a list of what they needed, so we could go shopping tomorrow between our other appointments and then donate the goods purchased with the card instead."

"And what would you have done if they'd told you they didn't need anything because the clothing drive is over?" Liam sat down beside his wife, wondering just how far she'd go to keep from having to spend that gift card on herself.

"Then I'd have found a soup kitchen, or a boys and girls club, or some other nonprofit that could accept it," she said with a shrug. "And if I couldn't find an organization that could accept it, then I'd have just cancelled my nail appointment and come back up here tomorrow at lunch time so I could give it to Mr. Willie directly."

"Meeting him really affected you, huh?" Considering he knew she had a thing for painting her nails every other week, being willing to skip her nail appointment was a big deal for her, even if she planned to paint them herself once they got home from their other appointments.

"Yeah," Rylie nodded, then looked down as if she was slightly embarrassed by what she was about to say. "I know it's ridiculous, since there's probably thousands of men named Willie in the US, but knowing my dad had a brother named Willie and seeing that Mr. Willie has the same color eyes as my dad, I've kinda wondered if he could be my uncle. Not that it's very likely, since Dad's family is from Atlanta and Mr. Willie doesn't have as strong a southern accent as my dad did. But it's kinda cool to think it's possible, you know."

"It's not impossible," Liam offered encouragingly, not mentioning that he'd heard the slightest southern accent in the older man's voice on Saint Stephen's Day to keep from giving her too much false hope. "Especially since he mentioned his mom making the same chicken dish your dad loved so much from his childhood."

"Yeah, that's probably the biggest reason why I've imagined he could be my uncle," Rylie chuckled. "Is it crazy that I kinda want to find him and ask him to do one of those online DNA tests with me to see if we could be related? I mean, I know Dad's family disowned him when he married mom, so Mr. Willie being cool with hugging me the other day would indicate he's not related to the racists my dad came from. But then again, I can't help but wonder if it was just Dad's parents who were racist and his brothers might not be. Like maybe Willie was in the Army when Dad moved up here and had no say in him being shunned back in Atlanta. And then when he got discharged and found out what happened with Dad, he came up here to try to find him?"

"That wouldn't be the craziest story I've heard about people discovering when they did those online DNA tests," Liam chortled, taking her hand and rubbing his thumb over the back reassuringly. "I mean, look at how the Burlesons found their Avington cousins after a hundred years of the family not knowing what happened to their aunt after World War I. Or how Dion found out his white mom was actually at least fifteen percent African, since his test showed he's sixty-five percent African when he only got half his DNA from his dad. So, no, I don't think it's crazy to want to test to find out. Just don't ask me to do one with you."

"You don't want to find out if you have any long lost cousins out in the world somewhere?" Rylie squeezed his hand in excitement. "Like maybe some of your ancestors had siblings who migrated to other parts of the world besides the ones who moved to the States? That's kinda what I'd like to find, distant relatives who didn't have issues with my mom and dad getting married. Or maybe some fourth or fifth cousins I could catch up with while we're on the South Pacific and Southeast Asia tour or on the European tour next year."

"Actually, after studying the history of Ireland, I don't want to take a chance on finding out I'm not one-hundred percent Irish, 'cause I'm pretty sure finding out we're part British, or Scottish, or Norse would cause Granda to have a heart attack." Liam went on to give her a brief history lesson, explaining how his granda was born when Ireland was still known as the Irish Free State, and how Neilan remembered what a big deal it was for Ireland to be declared a republic in 1949, when he was sixteen. He'd just finished telling her about how Granda Neilan and Granny Breena had emigrated from Ireland and immigrated to the US in the 1950s because of how hard it was to find jobs after so many years of conflict, specifically strife in Northern Ireland that often spilled across the border into the Republic of Ireland, which continued for decades after the Connerys moved to America, when Father O'Malley joined them in the classroom.

"Sorry to keep you waiting," the priest apologized as he walked in and took a seat across the table from them. "So, what did you need to discuss with me privately before we start your first Pre-Cana lesson?"

Rylie surprised Liam by jumping in immediately. "We need to reevaluate the whole wait-to-make-love-until-we-can-do-it-without-condoms thing. I was doing some research and found that there are some instances when it's not a sin to use condoms, and I think our situation qualifies."

She went on to lay out her reasoning, including several specific scriptures to show that God meant for sex between a husband and wife to be unitive in their marriage, regardless of whether it was procreative or not. Liam had to smile when she referred to the same "always" quote she'd shared with him in the car, only adding that "always doesn't mean only when the wife is ovulating" to really get her point across. She then quoted more scriptures about Rebekah and Sarah conceiving after previously being barren to show that God has the power to overcome any birth control method, so if He wanted them to conceive, they would, even if they used condoms.

She even found an instance in 2010 of Pope Benedict XVI saying that condom use is acceptable in certain cases, specifically to reduce the risk of infection with HIV. When Father O'Malley pointed out that the Pope was specifically referring to condom use by prostitutes being the first step in taking responsibility for their actions to eventually see that they were engaging in immoral sexual acts, and his statement had no bearing on whether or not it was sinful for a married couple to use condoms, she brought up how Father O'Malley had stated that even using the pill wasn't sinful if it was used for the treatment of a legitimate medical issue and not primarily for the prevention of pregnancy.

"But I believe you said last week that you stopped taking the pill after our initial discussion in the confessional?" Father O'Malley countered.

"Yes, I did, but that's only because I'd started taking it to regulate my periods for the prevention of P.C.O.S. symptoms because I have a high probability of developing it because of my mom's history. I was never officially diagnosed with it, so it's kind of a gray area as to whether or not it counts. And the only way I'll know if taking the pill actually prevented me from getting P.C.O.S. is to go off of the pill for a few months and see if the symptoms develop for a doctor to officially diagnose me with it. But that's irrelevant because I already pointed out that condoms can't prevent pregnancy if God wants me to get pregnant, so using them wouldn't be for contraception. Using them would be for preventing the possible transmission of HIV, which Pope Benedict the sixteenth considered an acceptable reason for using condoms, regardless of the population he was referring to."

Rylie followed that up with giving examples, such as if a nurse in a hospital is exposed to a patient's blood and wants to make sure her husband isn't exposed by using condoms when they make love until they're assured she didn't contract any blood-borne diseases that could be spread via sexual activity. At which point, Father O'Malley had no choice but to agree that it wouldn't be sinful for the nurse and her husband to use condoms for a short time. Seeing she was winning the debate, Rylie then relayed the whole story of what happened at the **Halloween Horror** fan expo to wrap up her argument without even bothering to mention why Onan's story in Genesis was no longer a valid reason to believe God deemed the use of contraception as a sin.

Liam was quite impressed with how she'd done her research and laid out a logical argument to plead their case. *If I wasn't already convinced that using condoms isn't really a sin, she definitely would have just convinced me.*

"And if you remember, you told me that first Sunday in confession that First Corinthians seven means that we can't withhold sex from one another unless we've mutually agreed and only for a brief period in time so we could focus on prayer, otherwise not having sex becomes a sin. So, since we've prayed about it and decided that we're not ending our marriage, and would actually like to do the convalidation ceremony in the Church, I think it would be sinful to stretch out our abstinence period for several more weeks, until Liam is certain that he didn't contract anything when he heroically helped save Allissa from being kidnapped and raped by her stalker and Dean from being shot by him. So we should be preemptively absolved of the not really a sin of using condoms for the next month, so we aren't forced to commit the greater sin of withholding sex in our marriage."

"Should we have met in the reconciliation room, so you could each confess to using condoms since we spoke last week?" Father O'Malley questioned, obviously fighting to keep his expression stern.

"No, Father," Liam replied stoically, also fighting not to grin at how his wife had clearly won that debate. "We haven't used condoms."

"But I'm not sure if we need to confess to only being partially intimate without completing the act last night," Rylie interjected. "Since that wasn't fully giving ourselves to one another the way God intended for married couples."

Feck! Liam mentally groaned, realizing how he'd screwed up and inadvertently made her feel like they were still sinning the night before. "If either of us sinned last night, it was me, Mo Ghrá, not you."

"How can you say that when I came but you didn't?"

"Because you gave yourself over to me completely, while I held back and didn't give you access to my body," Liam countered, lightly squeezing her hand to get his point across. He didn't mention how he'd held back his orgasm from her while she'd given him multiples of hers, thinking that was probably too much information for the priest.

"Yeah, that did kinda make me feel like you were reverting back to before we knew we were married and you wanted to try to stop yourself from developing feelings for me," Rylie admitted, looking down shyly.

"No, that's not what I was doing at all," Liam asserted, reaching over to lift her chin so she had to look him in the eyes as he continued. "I only held back because I don't want to risk your health or make you feel like I'm forcing you to sin by using a condom. I promise, Mo Ghrá, I'm not fighting my feelings for you anymore. And I won't fight against us ever again, even in my head."

When she looked up at him with hope shining in the depths of her topaz eyes, Liam couldn't resist leaning over and pecking a kiss on her plump, cupid's bow lips.

"I think it's safe to say that neither of you sinned, since it seems your actions were intended to bring you closer as a couple while actively trying not to sin." Father O'Malley's words effectively prevented Liam from taking the kiss farther when he'd almost forgotten where they were and that they weren't alone. "And based on everything else we've discussed so far today, I believe the use of condoms until you know you're outside the window of when you might have contracted HIV from your exposure to a stranger's blood while acting in a heroic manner is acceptable. But continuing to use them after you get those negative test results would be sinful."

"Understood," Liam and Rylie agreed in unison, smiling at one another for their unexpected synchronicity.

"Now, since you have decided you want to have a convalidation ceremony in the Church, we need to look at the calendar and pick a date for your wedding Mass."

"I'm thinking toward the end of our Memorial Day break," Liam decided, pulling out his phone to pull up the GWA schedule for 2020 to get a better idea of the dates. "When I talked to Dion this morning, he seemed to think the Independence Day break would be the earliest he could convince Julie to get married, so we'll have to go to Heart's Destiny for that. And I know the other couples who got married in Vegas are planning on doing receptions there over our Labor Day break, or they will be if D's right about his wedding being in July. But even if he's wrong and they end up swapping those two breaks, we won't be able to be here for either of them. So, that leaves us with the only options of Memorial Day, Thanksgiving, or Christmas next year. And I don't wanna wait almost a year for our Church wedding."

"But isn't Julie due to deliver their babies on Memorial Day?" Rylie questioned, arching an eyebrow at him curiously. "Dion won't want to leave her or the babies so soon to be able to come to our wedding, and I know you'll want him to be your best man."

"Yeah, he said their official due date is May twenty-sixth, but since they're having twins it's possible they could be born as early as the end of April," Liam elaborated. "And if they're born three or four weeks early, then they should be able to fly up for our wedding, especially if we schedule it as late as possible that week. And if they're not born until their due date, then I'll ask Josh or Crockett to stand up with us, depending on which of their wives you want as your matron of honor."

"Are any of the people you're considering as witnesses Catholic?" Father O'Malley questioned.

"Dion is, but I'm not sure about any of the others," Liam admitted with a shrug.

"Neither Teagan or Aiken are Catholic," Rylie chimed in, shaking her head. "Honestly, I don't think anyone else in the GWA is, or at least they haven't mentioned it if they are."

"I know there are other Christians in the company, but the only church I've ever seen any of them attend was the non-denominational church in Heart's Destiny, which I think is kind of a mix of several Protestant faiths," Liam agreed. "Do the members of the bridal party have to be Catholic?"

"Only if you just have the two witnesses stand up with you," Father O'Malley clarified. "But if you have a large bridal party, then the best man and maid or matron of honor need to be Catholic, while the rest of the bridesmaids and groomsmen can be Christians of any faith."

"Well, thankfully, we have a little time to decide which of our friends and family we want to stand up with us," Liam pointed out, smiling at Rylie.

"And you have a huge Catholic family, so we have plenty of options," Rylie chuckled, "even though I can only think of one of my friends from school who is Catholic. Though, honestly, we drifted apart after high school, so I wouldn't feel comfortable asking him to be my man of honor."

"Yes, well, that's something you can discuss later," Father O'Malley interjected, getting them back on track to pick a date. "What days will you be on your Memorial Day break from touring, so we can pick a date for your convalidation ceremony?"

"Saturday May twenty-third through Sunday May thirty-first," Liam replied.

"So, we're picking a weekday between Ascension Sunday and Pentecost," Father O'Malley informed them, explaining that because both Sundays were solemnities they couldn't have their wedding as part of the Saturday evening Mass preceding them either.

They had just settled on Friday evening, May 29, 2020, for their wedding Mass when they were joined by the couple acting as their mentors, Bryant and Erin O'Shay, for their Pre-Cana course. After introductions were made and they figured out that Bryant being cousins with Liam's Aunt Tara didn't preclude the O'Shays from being their mentors because Liam and Bryant weren't blood related, the five of them got to work, reviewing how Liam and Rylie would access the materials online while traveling with the GWA before discussing each question on a questionnaire specifically designed for Father O'Malley and the O'Shays to get to know Liam and Rylie better. An hour later, they were on their way to dinner and home, feeling even closer to one another than they had previously and looking forward to finally feeling like they were in the right place in their marriage to officially consummate it.

After dinner, digitizing her mom's journals, and sorting through her other boxes to fully integrate her things with his in their home, Liam finally convinced Rylie to snuggle up on the sofa for a Marvel marathon. He wanted to show her how he envisioned their life together after retirement, while also making it clear that he'd paid attention to the things she said in all their talks. He knew that she loved the superhero movies because she'd originally started watching them with her dad, and he thought watching them with their kids one day could be a great way to share her father's memory with the next generation. She may have only been able to watch the first half dozen movies in the Marvel franchise and only the older versions of the DC movies with her parents, but Liam knew she always went to see each new comic book movie in honor of her dad's love of the genre. And he wanted to show her how they could carry on the tradition with their children in the future.

"You do realize we're not going to be able to marathon watch all the Marvel movies before going back on tour, right?" Rylie pointed out as she carried a bowl of popcorn from the kitchen while he pulled up the first *Iron Man* in the Disney+ app. "Even if we skipped all my appointments and the New Year's party tomorrow to veg out in front of the TV from now until we're supposed to fly out on Wednesday, that only gives us like thirty-six hours to watch over fifty hours of movies."

"Yeah, I know we're only going to get a couple of movies in tonight and maybe one more tomorrow evening before the party," Liam agreed, reaching into the bowl for a handful of buttery goodness while she settled in beside him. "But I figured we can continue watching them on our flights and in our hotel rooms, so we can get completely caught up before the next one comes out. With the long international flights coming up in a couple of weeks, we should be able to get through all twenty-three movies by the end of January."

"Okay, I'll concede that we might get through a few on the plane." Rylie grinned as he munched on the popcorn in his hand and started the movie. "But only on those long flights because we both know that you'll spend at least part of each of our normal short flights talking to Rick about all your ideas for angles, and I'll spend at least part of that time talking to friends, or more likely reading so I'm not totally lost when I'm pulled into an impromptu book club meeting."

"Speaking of the book club you and the other ladies started, I'd like to be included next time you guys discuss Kay's *Devine* series." Liam dropped the remote on the coffee table and picked up his bottle of Guinness to wash down the popcorn.

"You've read Kay's books?" Rylie's jaw dropped as she stared at him incredulously, not paying a lick of attention to Robert Downey Junior on the television.

"Only *Kissing Kat* and *Winning Rhonda* so far," Liam shrugged, enjoying the surprised look on Rylie's face when he filled her in on how much he'd read in bed on Saturday night. "But if you're reading them for your book club, then I'd love for us to read the rest of them together. Maybe compare notes on which scenes we really liked and might wanna try."

"Is that why you started reading them? To get ideas for us in the bedroom?" Rylie asked curiously, glancing sideways at him while dipping her hand into the popcorn bowl. "Or were you just curious after finding out that her characters are loosely based on everyone who works for the GWA or lives in Heart's Destiny?"

"Actually, I started reading them to get ideas for how to romance you," Liam admitted with a half-shrug as he put his bottle back on the coaster on the coffee table after taking a sip. "But none of the stuff those guys did to win the hearts of their ladies really fits for us, so now I'm only thinking they might be fun for us to read together. And if we agree on which scenes might be fun to try, then maybe we could collaborate on how to modify the shower in our bathroom, so I can get a contractor to work on it before our next time in town."

"I take it you liked the shower scenes in both books?" Rylie cooed, putting the popcorn bowl on the coffee table before turning to face him. "Are you thinking of adding a high ledge or a bench for those epic oral scenes? Or maybe a shower massager so I can put on a show for you like Rhonda did when she and Jack were Skyping while he was on the road?"

"Whatever you want, Mo Ghrá," Liam offered, not caring if the contractor had to rip out the entire bathroom and reconfigure it to match whatever ideas she had for her shower fantasies.

"Actually, I think we did just fine without using any of those things in the shower in Heart's Destiny." Rylie ran her hand over his thigh, causing his already half-hard dick to swell to full size instantly. "But I wouldn't mind recreating the New Year's morning scene from *Ronnie's Runaway* when Bethany had to bend over and grip the stair railing for the first time Ronnie ate her out. Or maybe one of the sofa sessions when they were rounding the bases before she eventually gave him her virginity."

"Yeah, I haven't read that book yet, so you'll have to show me what they did," Liam smirked as Rylie crawled into his lap, both of them ignoring the movie playing in the background. *And I definitely need to read the third book in the series tomorrow while she's getting her braids and nails done, so I'll know how to recreate that New Year's morning scene she just mentioned.*

"Like I said, she was a virgin their first time, and hadn't even had a real kiss before meeting Ronnie, so they spent a lot of time watching movies and practicing kissing before she finally made it clear that she was ready for more." Rylie ran her hands over his torso, stopping to tease his nipples as she settled in straddling him. "But the first time they did more than kiss, he was insistent that he would only touch her where she touched him, so it was all over the clothes nipple play while they dry-humped until they both came like teenagers."

"So, you just want foreplay for now?" Liam questioned as Rylie dipped her head and started to kiss his neck. As his cock strained against the zipper of his slacks, he reciprocated her moves, imagining that was what the male main character had done in the book Rylie was describing. "Just to get us warmed up before we go upstairs to bed?"

"Maybe a little bit of foreplay like that," Rylie teased, lightly nibbling his earlobe as she pinched his nipples between her thumbs and forefingers. "But since we're married and now have full permission to do more than make out, I think we can lose our clothes long before we go upstairs to bed."

Liam was really glad he kept a condom in his wallet, so he didn't have to stop what they were doing to go get one out of his bedside table before he made love to his wife. "I like the way you think, Mrs. Connery."

Their lips met in a soul-searing kiss, just as Rylie dropped her hands to tug his shirttails from his slacks. As she pulled it free and then unbuttoned his shirt, he lifted the hem of her blouse, surpassing how far she'd undressed him as he momentarily stilled her actions by insisting she raise her arms for him to sweep it off over her head. As soon as the silky garment was out of their way, Rylie went right back to unbuttoning his shirt, pushing it off his shoulders as soon as the final button slipped from the hole. Once he had use of his arms once more, Liam made quick work of unfastening the front closure on her red lacy bra, whisking the straps off her shoulders and down her arms, so they each had full access to one another's upper bodies.

"Feck, you have the most perfect breasts," Liam groaned, aching to get his hands and mouth on her once more. It took more self-control than he thought he possessed to wait until she'd touched him before he repeated the same moves, especially since she pulled back and focused more on getting them undressed than on the foreplay he craved. "Ugh! Where are you going?" Liam grumbled when Rylie stood and took a few steps back.

"Just giving you room to take off your pants while I take off mine," Rylie cooed, shoving her black stretchy dress pants down along with her red lace panties.

"I thought we were going to focus on foreplay for a little while first?" Liam stood and pulled his wallet from his pocket, dropping it on the sofa before shoving his pants and boxer briefs down to join hers and both their socks in a puddle on the floor.

"We were…" Rylie bit her full bottom lip as she let the word trail off while staring down at his dick, which was standing proudly at attention as he sat back down. "But once we started kissing, I kinda forgot how those scenes went…and decided I didn't want to bother recreating them when I could have all of you instead."

Liam picked up his wallet once more, retrieving the condom inside before tossing the wallet on the coffee table beside their discarded bowl of popcorn. "You definitely have all of me, Mo Ghrá. But we still need to make sure you're completely ready before you try riding every inch."

"So, we keep going with the foreplay now that we're naked," Rylie suggested with a seductive grin.

Liam stroked his cock a couple of times, loving the way her eyes widened as she watched. Unable to wait any longer to get her back in his arms, he opened the foil package and rolled on the condom, not wanting to take any chances with his precum leaking onto her before he knew for sure he was negative. "Most definitely. Now come back over here and rub your wet pussy on my thighs while I take my time enjoying your perfect tits and sweet kisses."

Rylie's boobs bounced beautifully as she practically hopped back over to land on his lap on the sofa. Liam reached out and cupped her face, pulling her lips to his for another kiss as she ran her hands over his torso.

As much as he wanted to lose himself in the kiss, he had to focus to make sure she was completely ready for him. He dropped his hands from her cheeks, taking one to her breasts and massaging, while dropping the other between her legs. *Feck! She's already so wet,* he thought as his tongue delved between her lips and his fingers slipped easily into her slick cunt. But even though his fingers could breach her opening effortlessly, he knew she needed to come at least once before her inner walls would relax enough to take all nine inches of his dick.

If he were on top, he knew he could maintain enough control to only give her half until she was ready for more. But with her on top, he knew she'd try to take all of him on the first stroke, so he targeted her G-spot with his fingers to force her first orgasm, trying to keep his impatient woman from rushing them to the point that she'd be too sore to make love again for a few days.

He knew he'd hit the perfect spot inside her when she stopped lightly pinching his nipples and her nails dug into his pecs, as her whole body convulsed in the first wave of her release. Liam broke the kiss to growl, "Feck, yes, Mo Ghrá, come on my fingers."

Rylie's pussy clamped down so hard that he couldn't move his digits for several long moments, as her whole body writhed and spasmed with pleasure. "Oh, yes, Liam!"

Liam reveled in her enraptured expression as she came, feeling his precum already beginning to fill the reservoir at the tip of the condom. After not even jerking off the past several days, he suddenly started to worry that the condom wouldn't be able to hold the sheer volume of cum he was about to shoot off. *Feck! If I'm already feeling this close to blowing my load when neither one of us are touching my cock, I'm gonna embarrass myself with how fast I come once I'm inside her.*

"I'm sorry, Mo Ghrá," Liam apologized as he was finally able to pull his fingers out of her. He couldn't wait for her to move into position, gripping her hips and lifting her up so he could line up the head of his cock with her opening. "This first time is gonna be quick. But I promise I'll take my time for round two."

"Hmmm, I like hard and fast," Rylie purred, running her hands up over his shoulders as he thrust up inside her while also pulling her hips down to meet him.

"Good, 'cause that's what you're about to get," Liam promised as he filled her completely, hitting her cervix with his tip while grinding his pubic bone on her clit.

With her hands on his deltoids for leverage, Rylie lifted herself up until only his head was still inside her, then quickly plunged back down to take him to the hilt. Liam met her with his thrusts, unsure which of them was really in control of their rhythm. Not that it really mattered since they were so in sync as their mouths crashed together once more. Deciding to let her take the wheel, he lifted his hands and massaged her breasts, loving the feel of their weight in his palms as he tweaked her nipples between his thumbs and forefingers.

Making love with Rylie felt so amazing that Liam completely lost himself in her. He didn't notice how they were bouncing closer and closer to the edge of the sofa, or that his knees were getting precariously closer to the coffee table. He didn't even hear the movie still playing on the big screen television across the room. So, it wasn't until his shins made contact with the edge of the table that he realized he was about to bounce them off the couch and onto the floor. Thankfully, he noticed just in time to push through his heels and scoot them back onto the sofa without any risk of injury. Too bad the items on the coffee table weren't so lucky.

As the rug under his feet slid across the tile floor, it took the coffee table a couple of feet farther from the sofa than its usual position, causing the popcorn bowl and both their drinks to skitter across the table and fall off the edge closest to them. They were showered with beer and popcorn at the exact same moment Rylie convulsed with her second orgasm, her inner walls squeezing his cock perfectly to trigger his uncontrollable release.

"Feck! Mo Anam Cara. Is Tú Mo Ghrá. Rylie!"

"Oh! Oh! Liam!"

Liam wrapped Rylie in his arms, holding her close as he twisted them around and laid back on the sectional, lifting his feet from the floor and wrapping his legs around Rylie's legs to prevent either of them from accidentally stepping on any shards of glass from their broken beer bottles and popcorn bowl.

Once they caught their breath, Rylie started laughing, presumably at how they'd made a mess of the living room, causing Liam to chuckle with her. She pushed up on his shoulders, as if she was doing a modified yoga cobra pose, to look him in the eyes as she joked, "I guess that's one way to find out if all the hype about rinsing your hair in beer is for real or just a waste of time."

Liam reached up and plucked a piece of buttery popcorn from her ebony curls and smiled. "Yeah, I think the added butter and salt from the popcorn might negate any benefits of the beer."

"Probably," Rylie giggled before looking around at the mess on the floor beside the sofa. "Um, how are we gonna get up without risking getting glass in our feet?"

"Very carefully," Liam suggested, tilting his head toward the dining room behind the sofa. "Up and over the back of the couch, where we can check to make sure we're both glass and popcorn free before going up to the shower? Then I'll come back down and clean all this up while you do all your extra hair stuff to be ready for your early morning appointment tomorrow."

"Hmmm, I might have to bring my stuff down here to work on my hair at the dining table while watching you," Rylie cooed before pecking her lips to his. "'Cause I've heard cleaning is one of the sexiest things a man can do, and I'd really like to see it for myself to verify if Holly and Shauna's claims are true."

"Really? Cleaning is one of the sexiest things you want me to do?" Liam arched an eyebrow at his wife. "Surely that's only like maybe number ten on the list. I'm pretty sure making you come by fucking you, fingering you, and eating your pussy are numbers one through three, unless you break those down further by picking specific positions you prefer for each. And based on how you looked at me when I was stroking my cock earlier, I think watching me jerk off might be in your top ten too, bumping cleaning way down the list."

"Oh, no, sexual acts don't count," she playfully argued. "So cleaning is right up there with cooking, playing with kids, and taking care of a baby in the top four spots. Building something that requires wearing a toolbelt would be number five, followed by doing a job that requires a uniform like being a cop, firefighter, or serving in any branch of the military to round out the top ten."

"Well, then you'd better be happy with watching me clean 'til we have kids, since none of those uniform jobs are options for me, and my building skills are right up there with my cooking skills." Liam smirked as he got a few ideas for adding some mild kink to their lives. "Unless you'd enjoy a little fantasy role play with costumes…"

"I don't need role play, Liam," Rylie assured him with a sexy smile. "Your sexy suits work just fine for me."

Chapter Eleven

Since Connery's Irish Pub was only about a mile away from Liam's house, Rylie suggested they walk to the New Year's Eve party, so they could have more than one drink earlier in the night along with a glass of champagne at midnight without having to stay there long enough for a buzz to wear off before going home. But considering the temperature was only in the mid-forties for the high, she seriously questioned what she was thinking when she made the suggestion. Especially since the ruby red Alice + Olivia Elia asymmetric fitted midi-dress she'd bought at Saks when they were Christmas shopping the previous week required wearing heels because it was obviously made to fit a model who stood a good five inches taller than her five-foot-five.

"Maybe we should have gotten an Uber or Lyft," Rylie muttered, clinging to Liam's arm to keep from tripping over the uneven sidewalk where it dipped down for every driveway along their route. *Or I should have carried a bigger bag, so I could have walked to and from in a pair of ballet flats, instead of trekking a mile each way in five-inch stilettos like a ditz.*

"I can still order one if you want," Liam offered. "But after seeing you start getting anxious on our way home earlier, I assumed you wanted to walk because you didn't want to be on the road at all after sunset tonight, and especially after midnight."

"No, I don't really wanna be on the road tonight," Rylie admitted, realizing that he'd figured out before she did that she'd subconsciously picked their mode of transportation for the evening to decrease their risk of being hit by a drunk driver, like her parents had seven years earlier. *And he didn't even see how anxious I was doing my driving test as the sun was setting earlier, since he wasn't allowed to come with me and the examiner then.* "But since I only run on a treadmill, I didn't realize that a mile would be so far to walk in these shoes and with only stockings covering my legs from the cold. So, now I'm wondering if maybe a mild panic attack might be better than getting callouses on my feet from walking too far in these shoes, or freezing my legs off when the temperature drops even lower before we have to walk back home after midnight."

How messed up are we as a society that women are expected to wear dresses with our legs exposed to the cold and men get the extra layer of a jacket with their suits, when most of the time men are naturally warm and women are naturally already cold?

"Well, I can't do anything about the cold until we get to the pub, where I know Rory stocks sweats with the bar logo to sell to anyone who might need a change of clothes for some reason before they can leave the bar. But I can save your feet from any damage due to the walk." Liam surprised Rylie by scooping her up into his arms bridal style before continuing on their way to the party.

"Liam! What are you doing?" Rylie squealed as she flung her arms around Liam's neck, her question about why Rory's patrons would need to buy sweats before leaving the bar flying right out of her head.

"Carrying you, so you don't have to walk," Liam replied matter-of-factly, as if it was no big deal for him to walk the last half-mile while carrying an extra hundred-and-twenty pounds.

"You don't have to do this," Rylie mildly protested, even though her feet were already singing his praises.

"I know I don't have to," Liam grinned, pecking a kiss on her temple. "I want to."

"Well, thank you. My feet definitely appreciate it. Especially since the first half of this walk totally negated all the benefits of the foot massage I got with my pedicure today."

"I guess that means you're gonna want me to give you another foot massage when we get home later?" Liam arched an eyebrow at her.

"I wouldn't turn one down," Rylie teased. "But since I don't think either one of us have a foot fetish, I certainly don't expect one either."

"I don't know," Liam hummed as if deep in thought. "I might develop a foot fetish as part of my Rylie fetish if I start giving you foot massages. But then again, I might just prefer to massage you all over and not just your feet."

"And I definitely won't say no to an all-over massage, either." Rylie enjoyed finally feeling free to flirt with her husband, knowing they were both fully committed to making their marriage work. She certainly loved the way Liam had started flirting more with her. Now she just wished he'd hurry up and say those three special words to her, so she didn't accidently let them slip when she didn't want to be the first to say them. "But I think that's something we should plan to give each other in one of the guest beds, so we don't have to change the bedding before going to sleep if the massage oil ends up everywhere."

"Smart thinking," Liam agreed, grinning wickedly. "In fact, maybe we should rotate through all the guest beds whenever we're home, so neither one of us has to sleep in the wet spot in our bed. 'Cause I imagine it's only gonna get bigger once we ditch the condoms."

"Probably," Rylie cringed at the thought before grinning as she realized how all the best book boyfriends dealt with that issue. "But now I know what you need to learn from Kay's books."

"Oh, what's that?" Liam questioned curiously.

"How it's your gentlemanly duty to clean us both up afterwards," she whispered just as Liam walked up to the door of Connery's Irish Pub.

"Oh, we'll definitely be reading all those books together, so you can point out where that's mentioned, since I don't remember it from the ones I've read," Liam replied as he opened the door and carried her inside before setting her down on her feet.

"Bro! You're supposed to carry her over the threshold at home, not here!" Rory shouted from behind the bar.

"Yeah? Guess that means we can turn around and go home," Liam replied, moving to pick her up once more.

"No, it'll have to wait until after the party," Rylie objected, as she took off her gloves and stuffed them in her coat pockets. She then placed her hand on the center of his chest and blocked him from picking her up a second time. "I need to spend some time indoors to warm up before we make the trek back home."

"Want me to rub your legs to warm them up?" Liam offered, wagging his eyebrows suggestively as he also removed his gloves and put them in his coat pockets.

"Unfortunately, that'll have to wait 'til next year too," Rylie chuckled, shaking her head at her handsome hubby, who helped her remove her coat and scarf before taking off his own, "when we're alone at home."

Rylie couldn't believe how easily she'd transitioned to calling his house their home.

"We don't have to wait 'til next year, or go home to be alone, Moh Graw," Liam smirked. "In fact, I think you should come with me to stash our coats in Rory's office, so we can be alone for me to spend a few minutes warming you up now."

"Oh, no, we're not doing *that* in your brother's office," Rylie chastised, playfully pushing him away from her when he tried to wrap his arms around her to pull her along with him. "The next time you get more than a chaste kiss, it'll be twenty-twenty, and we'll be at home in bed for one more round before we have to go get on the plane to head back on tour."

"Thank feck, next year is only a few hours away," Liam groaned before pecking his lips on hers. He then pulled out a stool at the bar for her, which she promptly sat on to relieve the pressure on her feet from her new shoes.

"Lucky for both of us," she giggled lightly, grinning at the man she loved and whom she could hardly wait those few hours to make love with once again.

"Now be a good wife and order our first round while I go put our coats away." Liam took two steps away from her before turning back to add, "And don't let my brother get you drunk while I'm searching for sweatpants to put with our stuff for the walk home."

"Yeah, I don't think that'll be a problem," Rylie chuckled as she flipped through the menu to get to the alcohol options. "Since I learned my lesson on our wedding night and will avoid the Jameson."

"Oh, no, I won't let big brother get away with being a cheapskate and keeping you from enjoying the best of the best of Irish whiskey," Rory interjected as Liam disappeared through the door behind the bar.

"At almost sixty dollars a shot, I don't think that Jameson Eighteen is the drink of choice for a cheapskate," Rylie scoffed, pointing to the price on the menu while overlooking the other three Jameson options, which were only fourteen dollars per shot.

"Maybe not for most people," Rory conceded, bobbing his head from side to side. "But for someone who can afford the top shelf bottles, it is. So, tonight, we'll make him spend what he can afford and give you your first taste of Teeling Thirty and Bushmills Thirty, so you can learn for yourself how the longer aging time in wine and sherry barrels changes the flavor of Irish whiskey. After seeing how you prefer sweeter stuff this last week, I'm sure you'll like one of them better than the woody spice of Jameson."

After looking through the menu to see the approximately seven-hundred-dollar price tags on each of the liquors Rory mentioned, and thinking those were the prices per shot and not for a full bottle, she decided she'd stick to the wine and beer menu. Yeah, she knew with their GWA salaries, both she and Liam could easily afford the outrageously expensive drinks. But she just couldn't bring herself to spend that much on something she was pretty sure she wouldn't enjoy. And she especially didn't want to spend that much on something that would possibly cause her to end up so drunk she blacked out before she could ring in the new year by making love with her husband. "I think I'd rather just have a glass of rosé and a Guinness for Liam. If he wants anything stronger later, he can order it himself."

"I told you she wasn't gonna fall for your scheme to sell some of those super expensive shots, just so you can open the bottles and have a shot too," Quinn chuckled from behind her.

"Yeah, well, maybe Liam will fall for it later," Rory shrugged as he placed a bottle of Guinness on the bar in front of Rylie before pulling down a glass and pouring her rosé.

"What's he planning to try and con me into later?" Liam asked as he rejoined them.

"Paying for the two most expensive bottles of whiskey in the bar, so he can justify opening them and taking a shot or two of his own," Quinn replied before Rylie could.

"I can't just arbitrarily take shots without accounting for them in my inventory. I may own the bar, but I still have to pay for my food and drinks, just like everyone else," Rory argued.

"Or you can get your big brother to buy them for you?" Liam questioned, eyeing Rory dubiously as he handed over a card to open their tab.

"Only if you want to buy all your brothers a shot to celebrate the new year," Rory offered with a mischievous smirk. "And if so, might I suggest the Bushmills Thirty? It's the best Irish whiskey in the bar."

"Yeah, maybe later," Liam laughed, shaking his head at his brother. "Right now, I'm going to take my wife in the back to listen to the band and dance."

They picked up their drinks and weaved their way through the bar height tables in the front room of the pub to get to the back, which was divided between a music venue with a stage and dance floor, and what reminded Rylie of a sports bar with televisions and dining table seating. There they found more of Liam's family and friends, who were all eating, drinking, dancing, and occasionally glancing at the muted televisions broadcasting the ball drop from Times Square while listening to a rock band, whose name Rylie didn't recognize. "Spanking Maire? What kind of band name is that?"

"They're a Flogging Molly cover band, who picked their name because Maire is the Irish girls name with the same meaning as Molly," Liam explained, shaking his head as he directed her toward the restaurant side of the space. He didn't have to explain why they'd picked spanking for the first word in their band name, though Rylie thought paddling would have been just as apropos. "One I honestly thought would have broken up years ago, once they got too old to be cool with the college crowd where they used to play."

"So, you've seen them before?"

"Yeah, back when I was in college," Liam chuckled. "But thankfully, they've improved dramatically since then, so we don't have to drink our weight in Irish whiskey to enjoy them."

"Yeah, good thing," Rylie laughed along with him.

They quickly found seats at a table with several of Liam's cousins and placed an order for food when the waitress came by, making sure she knew their dinners were to go on Liam's tab. They made small talk most of the night, filling everyone in on the fire to explain why they weren't at Saint Stephen's for Mass on Sunday. Between food and drinks, Liam shucked his suit jacket and pulled her out on the dance floor several times, dancing much more provocatively than they had in the past. It was one of the best nights out Rylie could ever remember, right up until she had to excuse herself to go to the ladies' room and came back to find a beautiful redhead in her seat, obviously flirting with Liam.

Rylie felt the jealous rage inside her growing with each step she took back to the table. Her fury was only amplified when she noticed the other woman reaching over to place her hand on Liam's forearm. She didn't care that his red button-down kept them from having any skin-on-skin contact. She still wanted to rip that woman's hand off her husband and break her fingers for daring to touch him.

She didn't get the chance to voice her protest, however, since Liam pulled his arm out from under the woman's hand and reached out to clasp Rylie's hand so he could pull her onto his lap. "Ceara, I'd like to introduce you to *my wife*, Rylie. Moh Graw, this is Ceara Walsh, an old friend I haven't seen since high school. If she looks familiar, it's because you met her twin sister, Bridget, on Saint Stephen's Day."

While it was obvious they weren't identical twins, she could clearly see the family resemblance between Ceara and the catty sister they'd spoken to the previous week. Bridget might be an inch or two taller than Ceara, who was still obviously several inches taller than Rylie, but they were both model thin with what looked like natural red hair. *Bridget might have gotten her blonde highlights from a salon, though.*

"Nice to meet you, Ceara," Rylie said in as polite a tone as she could muster, wrapping her arms around Liam's neck instead of extending a hand to shake Ceara's. While Liam's extra emphasis on the words "my wife" and blatant public display of affection eased her inner green-eyed monster somewhat, they weren't enough to make her want to be best friends with the woman Liam's mom had called his first love and the woman she'd always expected him to marry one day. Still, she wanted to be polite while also staking her claim on Liam. "Sorry we missed you at the community center last week."

"Oh, you didn't miss me. I wasn't there," Ceara corrected her, shaking her head. "Unlike your jobs, or Bridget's modeling gigs, I can't take off from the hospital just because it's a holiday, even if it's for a good cause like feeding the homeless."

"Oh, no, of course not," Rylie agreed, feeling bad for coming across as if she was trying to shame Ceara for not being at the community center. "Doctors, nurses, and every other kind of first responders like you deserve medals, and awards, and probably at least a hundred times your current rate of pay, for how you selflessly give up your holidays and family time to save lives during emergency situations. So, what do you do at the hospital?"

"I'm a physical therapist, not a first responder," Ceara said flatly. "So, I assign exercises for the patients who are still in the hospital after surgery."

"Oh." Rylie felt terrible for trying to overcompensate for her earlier jealous feelings. But she had no idea what to say to help dislodge her foot from her mouth.

"Physical therapists might not be considered first responders, but you're still a vital part of the treatment team to help patients recover from the heart attacks and accidents that happen on holidays," Liam pointed out, just as the waitstaff rescued them from more awkward conversation by circulating to take everyone's orders for champagne to prepare for the midnight toast. "We'll take two glasses of champagne for the toast, and a bottle of Dom Perignon to take with when we leave."

"Why are you getting a bottle to take home?" Rylie didn't think they needed more than one glass each, considering they'd already had several drinks throughout the rest of the night, even though they'd stuck to wine and beer instead of getting anything harder.

"Because I never made it back up front to order those seven-hundred-dollar shots Rory wanted, so I figured I'd try to partially make it up to him by ordering a five-hundred-dollar bottle of champagne instead," Liam confessed with a shrug before his lips turned up in a smirk and the amber flecks in his hazel eyes seemed to sparkle with desire. "Besides, I'd kinda like to continue ringing in the new year by showering us both in champagne and taking turns licking it off any body parts we don't want to leave sticky before going to bed."

"Oh, I think I'm going to enjoy the way you wanna ring in the new year," Rylie agreed, not thinking about how she'd need to put on a shower cap first to cover the braids she'd just had put back in that morning. She pressed her lips to his and totally forgot that anyone else was in the room.

~~~

He wasn't proud of it, but Liam thoroughly enjoyed seeing how jealous Rylie got from seeing him talking to Ceara. He knew there was absolutely nothing going on for Rylie to be jealous about, since all he and Ceara had talked about prior to Rylie coming back from the restroom was the fantasy football league she tried to recruit him to join. But since Rylie had walked up just after Ceara slapped Liam's arm because she was so surprised by him switching allegiance to the New Orleans Gators, it was clear Rylie hadn't heard a word they'd said and was only responding to the fact that another woman had dared to touch him.

But as much as Liam loved knowing Rylie felt as possessive of him as he felt of her, he also didn't want her to misinterpret the situation to the point that it caused problems for them as a couple. That was why he'd immediately pulled her onto his lap and made a big show of introducing her as his wife. Even though it wasn't enough to completely keep her jealousy from showing, he hoped stepping in and trying to soften the verbal blows Rylie dealt was enough that they could move on with the night without anyone getting their feelings hurt.

Or maybe I'll just kiss Rylie until she realizes I only want her, Liam decided as he passionately kissed his wife, feeling grateful she was on his lap, so nobody else would see how his body responded to her. *Feck, with the way she's wiggling though, it's obvious she feels what only she does to me.*

When they finally came up for air as the waitress delivered their champagne, Ceara had vacated Rylie's seat, hopefully returning to whoever she was there with to finish out the celebration. As Rylie's glazed over eyes seemed to come back into focus, she apparently noticed Ceara's absence as well.

"Oh, dear," Rylie exclaimed, looking around frantically. "I wanted to apologize for being rude to your friend, but totally got sidetracked. I hope she didn't leave altogether before I could tell her how sorry I am for acting like a jealous shrew."

"I'm sure she just went back to the rest of her party," Liam assured his wife, hugging her to his body just as the band stopped playing and
~~~

announced it was one minute 'til midnight. "And if she did leave, I'm sure Ma can track down her email address for us to apologize later."

They joined in with the rest of the crowd as they counted down the last thirty seconds of the year, not bothering to pick up their champagne glasses to toast at midnight. Instead, Rylie wound her arms around Liam's neck as he hugged her closer until their chests met. He was thankful he'd taken off his suit jacket when he got hot dancing earlier, so he could appreciate the feel of her breasts pressed against his pecs, the thin material of his dress shirt, and her sexy red dress and bra, not doing a thing to dull the feel of her hard nipples poking his chest.

"Ten. Nine. Eight. Seven. Six." They counted down in unison with the rest of the room, but Liam only heard their voices as their gazes locked on one another and it seemed as if the world shrunk down to just the two of them. "Five. Four. Three. Two. One. Happy New Year!"

Their lips met once more, quickly parting for their tongues to delve into each other's mouths as their new year's kiss turned far too passionate for their surroundings. Not that either of them cared who might be watching as they shared their love for one another without words. As much as Liam wanted to start the new year off right by saying, "I love you," as soon as their lips parted, the way she wiggled on his lap had too much of his blood flow redirected to his southern head, rendering him incapable of forming words as she pulled back and twisted around to pick up their champagne glasses.

He did his best to shake off the momentary brain fog, taking his glass and clinking it with hers as they toasted to 2020 being their best year ever. They each downed their flutes of Dom Perignon in one swallow, eager to take the party home where they could do more than kiss.

"Ready to go home and ring in the new year right, Mrs. Connery?" Liam smirked at Rylie as they each put their glasses back on the table.

"Absolutely, Mr. Connery." Rylie quickly pecked her lips on his before standing from his lap. She grabbed their bottle of champagne as Liam stood and put his suit jacket back on before escorting her back to the front of the bar. "Though maybe we should have that shot of whiskey to get nice and warm before our walk home."

"We can definitely do that, Mo Ghrá," Liam agreed, catching the eyes of each of his brothers and motioning for them to join them at the bar. Once they were all there, he pointed to Rory behind the bar. "Pour us a round of the Bushmills Thirty while I go get our coats."

It only took him a minute to go back to Rory's office and grab his and Rylie's coats, scarves, and the size-small sweatpants he'd laid with them earlier, but that was long enough for his brothers to round up the rest of the cousins in attendance. While none of his married cousins were there, he knew his tab just jumped up significantly to cover twenty-five shots, instead of the six he'd thought he ordered. Liam just shook his head, laughing and not caring in the slightest that he was about to spend enough on one-and-a-half bottles worth of shots for Rory to buy at least eight more bottles.

"While he's pouring those up, I'm gonna go to the ladies' room to put these on," Rylie informed him, holding up the sweats and handing him back her coat and scarf.

"Good idea," Liam grinned, pecking a kiss on her lips before she walked back toward the restrooms.

"You guys aren't really leaving already, are you?" Quinn questioned. "The party's just getting started."

"Yeah, we're leaving," Liam chuckled at his clueless brother. "We've got much better ways of spending the first few hours of the new year than hanging around here any longer. Besides, we have to get some sleep before we have to fly out tomorrow."

"Like we believe you're gonna go home and *sleep*," Finn scoffed. "More like you're gonna go home and work on making those grandbabies Ma wants so bad."

Liam just grinned, not bothering to tell his family that they were still using condoms for a few more weeks and were only practicing for making babies until he knew it was safe for them to start really trying.

"Look at that fecking smirk." Aiden pointed at Liam's face. "They really are planning to start popping out grandbabies for Ma."

"Don't rush too soon into having kids, Li," Quinn cautioned. "You need to wait until at least after your Church wedding, so Rylie's not walking down the aisle with a baby bump. And honestly, if you want us to consider you the best big brother ever, you'd give us at least a year of Ma focusing on you and Rylie with the hard sell for giving her grandbabies, so maybe we can have a breather from how she's been pushing all of us to settle down."

After they'd called both his ma and granny the day before to get them started with all the planning for the ceremony in May that Liam and Rylie wouldn't be in town to do before that week, word had quickly spread to the rest of the family to save the date. Of course, once they found out about the planned ceremony to validate their marriage in the Catholic Church, Liam's family had quickly figured out that they'd worked through their issues and were planning to stay married. To be honest, it kind of surprised Liam that his brothers and cousins had held off this long before starting to comment on their reproductive plans.

"Don't you think Ma will be too preoccupied with planning for her first grandchild and then busy doting on that child once it's born, so she won't have time to worry about matching us up?" Rory questioned Quinn as he started passing out shots after finishing off the first bottle.

"Oh, no," Quinn disagreed with Rory's assessment of the situation. "Once she gets a taste of being a granny, she'll be ten times worse with trying to get each of us married and giving her more grandbabies."

"If she's anything like our ma, Aunt Cathleen will double up her efforts to marry the rest of you off just because Liam got married," his cousin Kerry pointed out, motioning between herself and her brother, Shay, and sister, Caitlyn. "Ma certainly didn't wait for Taryn to be born to double down on pushing us to get married and have babies."

"I don't think she even waited until Kiernan and Cianna got married," Caitlyn chimed in, chuckling.

"They're right," Aiden agreed, already picking up his shot, even though they weren't all poured yet. "Just since finding out Liam and Rylie got married, she's already doubled her efforts for suggesting potential wives for us. You just haven't heard it, Rory, 'cause you eat here half the time, instead of going to Ma and Da's for dinner all the time like me and Finn."

Liam couldn't believe his two youngest brothers were still eating most of their dinners with their parents, even though the youngest of them had turned thirty on his most recent birthday. "Alright, I understand going to family dinners every Sunday and on holidays, but shouldn't you guys have figured out by now that still eating at Ma's table every night is just setting yourselves up for her to keep fixing you up with whoever she can convince to come to dinner?"

"I've tried pointing that out to them," his cousin CJ pointed out, waving a hand at his younger brothers as well as Liam's. "But I think they secretly want our moms to find them wives, so they don't ever have to learn how to take care of themselves."

"No, I just don't have time to learn to cook," Finn smirked. "And the women I go out with start getting ideas if I let them cook for me. At least if Ma invites a girl to dinner trying to fix us up, I'm able to scare them off of thinking about marriage and babies by showing them what a mama's boy I am. They won't ever want to cook for me when I make it clear I only like Ma and Granny's cooking, so I won't have to worry about them wanting to marry me or have my babies."

"One of these days, Finn, you're gonna meet a woman who's smart enough to know that she can get around that objection by learning to cook your mom and granny's recipes," Rylie pointed out, giggling as she walked up with her new sweatpants on under her dress. "Or more likely, a woman, who for whatever reason needs to be mothered as much as you do, and she'll get that mothering from Cathleen and Breena as they're grooming her to be your perfect match, and you won't be able to keep yourself from falling for her."

"Shuhh, don't say that so loud," Finn objected, darting his eyes around as if looking to see who all heard Rylie. "You'll give too many women ideas about how they can trap me."

"Only the dumb ones who aren't smart enough to figure you out for themselves," Caitlyn teased, causing the large group of cousins to laugh as Rory handed her a shot now that he was finished pouring all of them.

Liam draped their coats and scarves over a barstool and sat the bottle of champagne they were taking home on top of them, as he and Rylie each took one of the shot glasses Rory passed out, while everyone else quickly discussed who should give the toast. "Um, shouldn't I be the one to give the toast, since I'm the one who's paying for all the shots?"

"I can see your point, but since we're toasting to the two of you, I think it would be kind of crass for you to give it, big brother." Quinn slapped a hand on Liam's shoulder.

"Actually, as the owner of the bar, I think I should be the one to give the toast," Rory chimed in. "Since I know more Irish toasts than the rest of you, and I especially need to thank Liam for running up the biggest tab in the history of Connery's Irish Pub."

"You're welcome, Roar," Liam grinned, raising his glass to his brother.

Once everyone else nodded their agreement, Rory began his toast. "To Liam and Rylie, may you be blessed with the luck of the Irish all the days of your lives. May your troubles only be wee ones, and when you're blessed with wee ones, may they be only as mischievous as a leprechaun. I wish you many years of lying…in each other's arms, stealing…kisses and moments alone, and celebrating it all with lots of drinks with friends and family here at my bar."

"Isn't that the same toast you gave at Allissa and Dean's bachelorette and bachelor party?" Rylie queried, arching an eyebrow at Liam, who nodded to indicate it was almost exactly word for word the same toast.

But since everyone was already clinking their glasses, he thought it best to give her some advice before she pointed out to Rory that he didn't know more Irish toasts than Liam. "Be sure to sip this, so you can enjoy the flavor, and still have some to drink with the next toast," Liam advised as he clinked his glass with Rylie's before they each clinked with several of his family members.

As he took his first sip, he watched Rylie do the same. She then made a face that clearly showed she still wasn't a fan of Irish whiskey. She then turned back to Rory and demanded, "Yeah, I've heard that toast before, so you've gotta try again."

"Seriously?" Rory shook his head at Rylie.

"Sorry little brother, but I used that toast at our friends' wedding in November," Liam informed his brother with a shrug.

"Fine, since Liam obviously stole one of my favorite toasts, here's another one for you that I know he hasn't heard before." Rory intentionally turned to look directly at Rylie and Liam and smirked. "If liquor were a pond and I were a duck, I'd swim to the bottom and never come up. But liquor is not a pond and I'm not a duck, so tip your cup and let's get fecked up."

Rylie clinked her glass with his once more before she shot the rest of the amber liquid back and shook her head while cringing from the burn on the way down.

Liam could only chuckle as he took his next mouthful of the smooth, lightly sweet liquor, savoring the flavor and agreeing with his brother that it was the best Irish whiskey in the pub.

"Yeah, I don't think I need to do a DNA test to know that whatever variety of white my dad's ancestors were, they weren't Irish."

"That's alright, Sis," Aiden assured her with a huge smile as he also sipped his shot. "We'll count the Irish DNA Liam leaves in you as making you part Irish, especially if you're really going home early to make a grandbaby for Ma."

"Thanks, I think." Rylie's brow furrowed as if she was confused by Aiden's words.

"And on that note, I need to close out my tab, so we can go," Liam decided, finishing off his shot with a third sip.

Rory tapped the screen of the point-of-sale system several times before swiping the card Liam had left with him earlier and printing out a receipt for Liam to sign.

When the total was about ten grand lower than he expected, Liam questioned his brother instead of looking at each individual item. "Do we suddenly have a fifty-percent family discount or something? 'Cause this seems too low."

"No, there's not a family discount," Rory scoffed, shaking his head and placing the half-empty bottle of Bushmills Thirty on the bar in front of Liam. "I just charged you for two bottles instead of twenty-five shots. So, you still have six or seven shots left for later."

"Hey, when are we going to Liam's for another round?" Finn questioned, smirking roguishly.

"You're not," Liam disagreed, fighting not to roll his eyes at his youngest brother before turning back to his middle brother. "Ring me up for a third bottle, so you guys can have another round tonight while Rylie and I head home to enjoy this bottle of Dom."

"Done," Rory grinned as he followed Liam's directive.

Liam signed both receipts and put his card back in his wallet before helping Rylie put on her coat, scarf, and gloves, and donning his own. Once they were bundled up for the walk, he handed her the bottle of champagne and then scooped her up in his arms for the trek home.

"Liam, you really don't have to carry me the whole way," Rylie protested, even as she looped her arm around his neck to hold onto him while clasping the neck of the bottle in her other hand. "I can walk until my feet start to hurt again."

"Why do that when I can just carry you the whole way, so your feet don't hurt at all?" Liam arched an eyebrow at her as one of his cousins opened the door for them to exit the bar.

"So you don't end up with a sore back that might limit what we can do when we get home," Rylie replied with a sexy waggle of her eyebrows at him. "I know you're trying to be a good husband and take care of my feet since I didn't bring better shoes for walking in tonight, but I also want to be a good wife and not overtax your aging back. So, I'd rather you save your strength and stamina for when we get home."

"My back may be aging, but I've still got plenty of strength and stamina to carry you home and sex you up 'til sunrise," Liam asserted confidently.

"Yeah, I don't think *I* have the stamina to make it 'til sunrise," Rylie laughed, rolling her eyes. "Besides, we have to get some sleep before we go to breakfast with your parents and grandparents and fly to San Antonio. Unless you're planning on sleeping on the plane?"

"No, I have other ideas for on the plane." It was Liam's turn to wiggle his eyebrows suggestively. "Since it'll just be us and the pilots on the flight, this'll be our only chance to join the mile-high club, so I don't think we should miss it."

"Did you tell your brothers about that? Is that why they were going on about us having babies soon?"

"No," Liam chuckled. "They just assumed that since we're staying together, then we must already be trying to make a baby. And I didn't want to get into the whole discussion about needing condoms for another month, or try to give them an idea of when we'll actually start trying, since we haven't really discussed it yet."

"I just assumed we'd start trying once your ninety-day test comes back negative," Rylie admitted, looking sheepishly down at the bottle resting on her midsection.

"If that's what you want, we can," Liam smiled, hoping to reduce her obvious nervousness about this discussion. "But since we'll probably learn more about natural family planning by then, I figured we'd talk it all over during those lessons and come up with a plan that works for both of us."

"Yeah, I'm a little worried that going off the pill will cause my periods to not be as regular and make it hard for us to time things with my cycle the way they teach in those classes." Rylie rested her head on his shoulder, no longer looking him in the face as she spoke. "I mean, we can try counting the days and stuff while we're doing the classwork, but if my cycles don't stay regular now that I'm off the pill, then it may not work for us."

Since he kinda had to watch where he was going as he walked them home, he couldn't really look her in the eye anyway, so he let her get by with hiding for now. "Yeah, that's what you were reading about in your mom's journals yesterday, right?"

Liam hadn't actually read the entries, focusing more on making sure the pages were legible in each of the photos he took. But when they got to the journal when her mom started writing about the Pre-Cana and natural family planning classes she and Peter took before they were married, Rylie took a moment to read a few of the entries to decide which ones she wanted to bring with them on tour. As she was reading, he noticed a few keywords on the pages to know she'd specifically read about her mom's period problems.

"Yeah," she nodded, rubbing her cheek against his shoulder. "From what she wrote, it seems like she struggled with figuring out when she was ovulating because her periods were so all over the place. Like one month it would be super light and easy, or she'd skip it, and then the next month, it would be super heavy and last for two weeks instead of one. So she was really worried that they wouldn't know when she was actually ovulating to try to get pregnant. Was it two weeks after her period started? Or one week after her period ended? Or maybe not at all in the months it was light or nonexistent."

"Yeah, I guess that would be hard to figure out." Liam could only partially sympathize, considering he was a man, but he hoped his agreement would help her feel more comfortable talking to him about this stuff. "But I think it's less important for people who are trying to get pregnant to know than for people who want to time their pregnancies with their careers. I mean, if you're trying to get pregnant, you just make love every day, so you'll eventually hit the target on the right day."

"Yeah, that only works if there aren't issues like P.C.O.S. or fibroids or whatever that make it difficult to conceive, even if you do hit the target on the same day I ovulate," she scoffed, sounding dejected.

"Well, if it's a problem when we decide we're ready to start trying for kids, then we'll look into adoption or fertility treatments or whatever to have a family." Liam didn't care how they built their family as long as she was willing to have one with him.

"Are you thinking we need to plan for having our babies to sync up with when you want to retire?" Rylie questioned, finally lifting her head to look at him once more.

"Not necessarily." Liam turned his head to look her in the eyes, surprised she hadn't commented on his plan to look into their other options. "But I won't have to stop wrestling during the pregnancy like you will, so I thought you might want to hold off on getting pregnant until we're both ready to leave the business."

"How does that work with the GWA? I mean, I know they have some kind of maternity and paternity leave, 'cause Kay and Anthony just took time off this year. But they aren't wrestlers. How did it work with Holly and Shauna when they had their kids?"

"Shauna was pregnant with their daughter when Vaughn first signed with the GWA," Liam explained, remembering back to when the other guys had joined the roster. "That was right before Rick took over for his dad and bought the company plane, so she didn't travel with him until we all started flying together in January of twenty-twelve. By then, his paternity leave was over. And she didn't actually wrestle for the GWA until after their son was born a couple years later. And just like with Anthony and Kay, he went on paternity leave when she was far enough along that she couldn't fly."

He thought for a few moments to remember if it was the same with the Everetts or not. "Now that I think about it, it was a couple months after we started flying together that Everest and Olympus joined the roster, when Olympus's daughter was a couple months old. And Holly didn't start wrestling until after their son was born in twenty-thirteen, so again he just took paternity leave when she couldn't fly anymore."

"Were there any female performers before them who got pregnant while they were actively on the roster?"

"For the first ten years of my career, it seemed like there was a revolving door of women wrestlers," Liam chuckled. "I suppose some of them could have left because they got pregnant, but if that was the reason they chose not to renew their contracts, they didn't share that info with the rest of us. I just assumed it was because of age or injuries, or Richard got tired of the complaints from the rest of us when couples broke up and caused drama in the locker room, so he didn't renew their contracts."

"He didn't renew the women's contracts because they had nasty breakups with the guys on the roster?"

"Not just the women," Liam defended the former boss. "Both Richard and Rick have refused to renew the contracts of the men in those feuding couples too. Honestly, I was a little worried that Rick would terminate my contract after how I acted like a gobshite when we first found out we got married. But thankfully, I was able to apologize to him for my outburst that day, and he assured me then that as long as we managed to act professionally from then on that our jobs were safe."

"Yeah, I was terrified he was going to fire me when I first found the certificate, which is why I was shaking like a leaf and babbling like an idiot when I first got to his office. And I don't even remember the cab ride to the arena."

"Thankfully, we no longer have to worry about any of that." Liam smiled at her once more.

"No, but now I have to read my contract to find out what happens if I get pregnant and can't fulfill the terms. Not that I'm really worried about that being a problem with my possible P.C.O.S. issues." Rylie sighed and rested her head on his shoulder once more. "Were you serious when you said we could adopt or do fertility treatments if I can't get pregnant?"

"Absolutely," Liam declared whole-heartedly.

"Even though the Church considers IVF and other medical interventions to get pregnant as sins?"

"I think you've already learned that I don't always agree with everything the Church considers sins," Liam pointed out as he finally turned down their block. "While they claim IVF and artificial insemination take away from the unitive aspect of sex for couples, I don't think that's the case at all. I mean, I'm sure you've seen how

Rick and Fiona are just as close now as they were before starting preparing for IVF. But I don't know if you realize that Rick actually had to give her daily shots for like two weeks to prepare for the egg retrieval, so they're still working together to create their baby."

"How do you know that?" Rylie eyed him curiously, appearing confused by his knowledge of what went on in their boss's marriage.

"Because he told me when he asked me to pick out the new pods for the planes, 'cause he had to explain why he didn't want me to call him that first Saturday," Liam explained. "Apparently, while we were looking at pods, Fiona was having her eggs retrieved. And Rick had to give his sample at the same time, so the doctors could do their thing to make the embryos to be implanted a few days later."

"And that's why you couldn't call him about the pods?"

"Yeah, we both agreed it was best if I didn't video call him to show him the pods I liked, so I didn't see more of the boss than I ever wanna see by interrupting him mid-jerk."

"T-M-I!" Rylie giggled, shaking her head.

"Exactly," Liam laughed along with her. "But my point is that they're doing it all together, so I don't think it's taking away from their marriage in any way. It's more like they're using the God-given talents of those doctors to bring them closer together and follow God's directive to 'be fruitful and multiply' when the old-fashioned way isn't working for them."

"So, if it comes down to it, you'd want us to try IVF to have babies?"

"I want us to do whatever you feel comfortable with," Liam clarified, not wanting her to feel pressured into going along with IVF just because he didn't think it was a sin. "I fully expect you to do all the research like you did with the use of condoms, and decide what you feel is the right path for you, probably having another debate or two with Father O'Malley, before we decide together how to build our family. I'm not going to push you to do IVF just because I don't think it's a sin."

"And if I decide I agree with the Church and don't want to do IVF?" Rylie's topaz eyes looked pensive as she stared into his, as if she needed to see his truth in his eyes.

"Then we'll adopt, if that's what you want. Or we'll be the cool aunt and uncle who spoils all my brothers' kids when they come along, if you decide you don't want kids at all."

"No, I definitely want kids," Rylie quickly blurted. "And I'm cool with adopting if that's what we have to do. But you're right about me needing to do more research before deciding on IVF or fertility drugs or whatever other medical intervention we might wanna try."

"Then we're in perfect agreement," Liam smiled, leaning his head down to peck her lips with his. "Now, how do you feel about trying to plan for when we have our first one?"

"Like I said, I don't think I'll be able to tell when I'm ovulating to know when we need to skip a day to keep from getting pregnant for the next couple of years until we both quit wrestling," Rylie confided. "At least, not if my periods start getting wonky like Mom's did. And I'll try to count the days and stuff the way they'll teach us in the natural family planning classes for as long as my cycle stays normal, so we can maybe hold off on getting pregnant until after you're ready to retire, so we won't have to worry about maternity and paternity leave. But if my cycle gets off to where that system isn't accurate, I won't be upset if we end up pregnant sooner. I'd just consider us lucky to be blessed with a baby and would be perfectly happy with leaving the business sooner than I planned."

"Then I think we should just enjoy being married and not worry too much about trying to track your cycles or whatever once we've done the convalidation ceremony in the Church," Liam suggested with a grin as he dipped down to open the gate to their house without having to put Rylie down. "And just leave it in God's hands as to whether or not we have a baby before we retire. And if we don't have a miracle before then, we'll look into our other options when we come home after our time with the GWA is over."

"Agreed," Rylie grinned up at him as he dipped his knees once more to activate the biometric scanner on the front door.

Once it was open, Liam paused momentarily before entering the house. "Now I think I'm supposed to kiss my bride as I carry you over the threshold."

He didn't give Rylie the chance to reply, claiming her mouth with his as he stepped into their home.

Chapter Twelve

Rylie felt as giddy as a schoolgirl as Liam carried her over the threshold of their home. If anyone had told her two weeks earlier that she'd start the new year happily married and planning for the future with her husband, she wouldn't have believed them. Honestly, if anyone had told her back on Wednesday, December eighteenth that Liam would ask her to come home with him for Christmas two days later, she wouldn't have believed it either, much less that this break from touring would lead to them moving past all their issues to cancel his plans for an annulment. Oh, when he'd first invited her to New York, she'd been hopeful, but she hadn't dared to fully believe it was possible for them to work things out. Now she was kissing the man she loved, planning to make love with him to finish ringing in the new year with a bang, and fully believing that all her dreams were coming true.

While she still thought it would require a miracle for her to get pregnant without medical intervention, she knew they'd eventually have a family together. Yeah, it might require adoption or going against the teachings of their religion, but after their talk on the way home, she knew they would one day have a family. *And if I have any say in it, then we'll be the first Connerys in almost a century to bring a little girl into the family, even if we have to adopt her to make it happen.*

Her bark of laughter at the thought caused Liam to break the kiss. "I'm glad you're happy, Moh Graw, but I'm not sure how I feel about you laughing at me kissing you during such a solemn moment."

"Carrying me over the threshold is a solemn moment?" Rylie chuckled even more. "Maybe if you'd have done it on our wedding night, but I don't think it counts four-and-a-half months later."

"Nope, the timing doesn't matter," Liam disagreed, shaking his head as he set the alarm and carried her up the stairs. "It counts as solemn because it's the first time I carried you into our home. It's also a very momentous occasion when I carry you into our bedroom for the first time, so I think I'll wait until after you finish your giggle fit before I go any farther than the living room."

Rylie wanted to protest that she wasn't having a "giggle fit," but she was laughing too hard to say the words, making it clear he'd accurately identified her current condition.

"What's so funny?" Liam chuckled along with her as he sat down on the chaise lounge portion of the sectional since it was closest to the stairs, holding her on his lap.

"I…ha…he…ha…thought…ha-ha…about…huh-ha…us being…ha-ha…the first to…ha-he-ha…have a daugh-daughter…" Rylie gave up trying to speak, unable to control her laughter.

"You think we're gonna break the Connerys' century-long streak of only having sons?" Liam chortled, shaking his head.

"Yes," Rylie asserted once her laughter died down enough that she could speak once more. "Even if we get a miracle or two and only conceive boys, I'm determined to break that Connery curse by adopting a daughter. Maybe two, so they have each other to team up with against their brothers and boy cousins."

"If you're planning on adopting even if we're able to get pregnant, does that mean you might want to start our family now?" Liam looked at her with such an open loving expression that she instantly knew he'd go along with whatever she wanted for planning their family.

"I'd love to, but I don't think it will be as easy for us to adopt as it was for Kay and Anthony," Rylie admitted, thinking back to the conversations she'd had with Kay and the other ladies over the last few months, specifically when Kay had given Fiona the info for who they went through back in May. "From what I understand, they were only able to adopt Antonio because they were home on maternity and paternity leave for all the home visits they had to have with social workers to get it approved through the court. That's why Fiona decided to go with IVF to try to have a baby, since she and Rick can't be home long enough for those social worker visits to get approved to adopt."

"Yeah, I guess that means we can't adopt now either," Liam nodded, his lips turning slightly up in a sad smile. "But I suppose that's okay, 'cause we still need to decide how many kids we want before we can start that process anyway. Not to mention how we should probably focus on each other and our marriage for the next couple of years and enjoy practicing for baby making, even if God doesn't bless us with a child before we come home and can adopt."

"Yeah, have you thought about how many kids you want? Or are you just thinking about practicing now?"

"Oh, I'm definitely thinking about practicing now," Liam crooned, wagging his eyebrows suggestively. "But I've always thought four sounds like a good number for kids. That's why I picked this floor plan for the house, so they'd each have their own bedroom and bathroom."

"So, you were planning for your future family when you had this house built?" Rylie wondered how many women had shared his bed, trying out for the role of the mother of his children.

"Yeah, I was," Liam agreed, nodding once more. "And just so you know, you are the only woman who's ever been here who isn't a blood relative or paid to be here as part of the cleaning service I hired. I knew before I even signed the paperwork with the building contractor that this would be the home where my wife and I would raise our children, so I didn't want any other woman to ever taint the space."

Rylie could only smile at the way he seemed to be able to read her mind at times, especially since he always used that ability to ease her worries. "Good," Rylie grinned, pecking a kiss on his lips. "And I agree that four kids sounds like the perfect amount for us. Though I'll be happy with however many we're blessed with as long as it's at least two. Now, how about you carry me up to our room, so we can get started practicing for making some of them."

"As you wish, Moh Graw." Liam easily lifted her as he stood, not bothering to stop and remove their winter outerwear before practically sprinting up the two flights of stairs to their bedroom on the fourth floor.

Rylie wasn't sure how he saw where they were going as he kissed her passionately the whole way up to their bedroom. She also wasn't sure how she maintained the wherewithal to not drop the expensive bottle of champagne she still clutched to her stomach with one hand while running her gloved fingers through the short hair on the back of Liam's head with her other hand.

Nothing registered in her mind but the taste of Liam's lips and tongue, which still held traces of that last shot of Irish whiskey they'd had at the bar. While it would never be her favorite drink, Rylie had to admit that the sweeter flavor of this particular brand didn't taste so bad when mixed with Liam's kiss. It wasn't until Liam broke their lip lock to gently place her down on their bed that she opened her eyes and realized they'd made it up to their bedroom.

As he stood after stooping to lay her down, Liam took the bottle from her hand, placing it on the bedside table. "We need to lose some clothes before we get into that," he grumbled, quickly removing his gloves and scarf before helping her do the same, as she first sat up and then stood beside the bed. It didn't take long before their coats and her sweatpants joined their discarded scarves and gloves on the floor. "Feck, Moh Graw, as much as I love seeing you in this sexy red dress, I need you naked now."

"I'm not the only one who needs to get naked," Rylie pointed out, reaching up to grab Liam's tie and pull him down for another kiss as she worked to undo the knot at his throat.

Liam wrapped his arms around her, unzipping the back of her dress, just as she pulled the tie from his collar and dropped it on the bed behind her. Rylie focused on the buttons of his shirt, planning to push his suit jacket and shirt from his shoulders at the same time. She didn't get the chance however, when Liam stepped back, pulling her dress down the front of her body to pool at their feet.

"Feck! You're gorgeous, Moh Graw." Liam dipped his head to trail his mouth from her collarbone to her cleavage, while tracing the edges of her red lace panties and garter belt with his fingers.

"Then enjoy the view while I finish undressing you," Rylie commanded, gripping his lapels to push him back so she could see what she was doing.

"Yes, ma'am," Liam smirked, straightening his posture as he dropped his hands to his sides, allowing her access to finish removing his black suit jacket and red satin shirt that perfectly matched his tie and her dress. Since he rarely relinquished sexual control to her, she didn't waste a moment of the short stint in charge that he gave her.

Rylie knew they should probably be hanging all this formalwear up, but as she removed his belt, she couldn't care less about preparing the designer garments to go to the dry cleaners right then. So, when she finished unfastening his pants, they quickly joined everything else in a pile on the floor. As did his red boxer briefs.

Rylie reached for his cock, longing to stroke him, even though she knew he wouldn't let her suck him again yet. Liam gripped her wrists and pulled her hands away before she got ahold of him, stepping back slightly as he toed out of his shoes and socks and took control of their lovemaking once more.

"No, not yet," Liam groaned, shaking his head and looking pained at having to tell her no. "I need to finish getting you naked first."

Liam started to slowly and reverently remove her undergarments, beginning with her bra. But once her breasts were free, he fumbled with her panties and garter belt, not watching what he was doing because his face was buried in her chest.

Rylie reveled in the exquisite feel of his mouth suckling her nipples, probably making things harder for him as she writhed in pleasure. Not caring if it took him an hour to remove her lingerie as long as he kept up with the teasing licks and nips, she ran her fingers through his hair, appreciating the softness of his strands now that her gloves no longer impeded her sense of touch. When he sucked harder on her right breast as if he wanted to mark her, she tried holding his head in place as she felt her arousal building in her core.

"Feck this! I'll buy you new ones later," Liam roared as his mouth popped off her breast. He then surprised her as he ripped through the soaking wet lace covering her sex.

Rylie kicked off her Louboutin pumps, hoping landing in the pile of clothing would keep them from being damaged as Liam lifted her from the floor and tossed her on the bed. He tugged the lace panties and garter belt from her body along with her stockings, not caring about tearing them. The rough, animalistic side of Liam coming out turned her on more than ever before, making her pussy gush with anticipation.

Just as he appeared to be about to pounce on her, he paused and pulled out the drawer of his bedside table, grabbing both a box of condoms and the box containing her rabbit vibrator. Although she was curious, she didn't say a word as he placed both on the table, before getting out a condom and rolling it on. Then he pulled out the toy and held it up between them. "I think instead of risking pouring half that bottle of champagne down the bathroom drain, I'd rather play with this tonight."

Since she was feeling the effects of that shot of Irish whiskey on top of a glass of champagne and three glasses of rosé, she agreed that it was probably best if they waited to open that bottle, so she'd just feel a little buzzed while they made love and wouldn't end up getting so drunk that she passed out first.

"I was wondering what you'd done with that," Rylie cooed, eager to find out how he intended to torture her with the toy before finally making love to her.

Liam apparently intended to keep her guessing, crawling on the bed beside her and laying the toy on her stomach without switching it on. He kissed her passionately once more, surprising her by covering her eyes with his tie just as he pulled back.

"What are you doing?" Rylie questioned, her voice coming out an octave higher than normal due to her excitement.

"I'm blindfolding you, so you won't know where I'm going to touch you next, or what I'm going to use to tease you, and I'm not gonna stop until you're so worked up you beg for my cock," Liam informed her as he lifted the red satin away from her face and looked her eye to eye. "That is, if you're willing to trust me to surprise you with something a little kinkier than what we've done in the past. I promise I don't want to do anything as hardcore as the flogger scene in the book you were listening to in Atlantic City. Just tease you a little by touching you with more than just my hands…" Liam ran his hand down her side. "…or my mouth…" Liam trailed light kisses along her jaw, down her throat, and over the top of her cleavage before flicking her nipples with his tongue. "…or my cock." Liam emphasized his plan by thrusting his dick against her thigh. "But only if you agree that I can blindfold you, so you won't know what I'm going to touch you with next."

"Yes, Liam, I trust you," Rylie panted out breathlessly, only slightly anxious about what he might use, since he specifically mentioned the flogger scene she'd had to go back and relisten to later, which was essentially Simon giving Chelsea a massage to ease her pain from injuries as a child, so not as hardcore as she was interested in trying with him someday.

Liam's smile was the last thing she saw before he covered her eyes once more and tied the strip of red satin around her head, carefully securing it at the side so he didn't mess up her braids. "When you first tossed my tie on the bed, I thought about tying you up with it, so I'd have you completely at my mercy. But since this bed isn't really designed for bondage, I figured I'd just have to trust you to lay perfectly still while I play."

"Yeah, I don't think I'll be able to lay perfectly still," Rylie chuckled, already feeling the urge to wiggle and squirm until he touched her pussy to relieve her need.

"Oh, I think you will," Liam assured her as she felt the bed dip when he got up. "'Cause if you don't, then I'll have to stop so I don't accidentally hurt you with the other toys I'm planning to play with."

"What other toys?" Rylie barely squeaked the words out, as she heard Liam rustling around, opening doors and drawers both in the master bedroom and the attached bathroom. She was really confused when she heard him turn on the water in the bathroom, but assumed he was washing his hands before doing whatever it was he had planned to tease her.

"Just a few things I think we'll both enjoy," Liam claimed, as she heard more sounds of him continuing to move about the room as the water still ran in the bathroom. "Nothing that will really hurt. Well, unless you move at the wrong time."

When she heard the flick of the candle lighter and smelled the strawberry pound cake scented candle she'd placed on her bedside table after unpacking it Monday night, she wondered if he was filling a bowl in the bathroom sink so he'd have cold water on hand to soothe her skin after wax play. *No, he specifically said he's not into any hardcore kinks like that.*

"Do we need a safe word for this?" Rylie wondered aloud, thinking it sounded like they might have different definitions of "hardcore" kinks. Considering the books she read often mentioned how a flogger could feel like a massage, including the one he'd partially overheard a few days earlier, she thought hot wax might be more painful than a flogging. *But I've also been turned on by those wax play scenes, so if that's what he's planning on doing, then I don't think we're too far off in what we think is too hardcore for us. Especially since I've pushed the unmelted wax on the sides of this candle down into the pool of melted wax to know that, even when the candle is lit, the melted wax isn't too hot to handle on my fingers.* "Or go over a list of hard limits first?"

"We can use a safe word if you want," Liam assured her as she felt the bed dip once again, presumably because he was crawling back onto it with her. "But if you don't like the feel of something, you can just tell me and I'll quit using that toy. And since I'm only planning on using things that enhance your pleasure, I don't think there's any chance I'll come close to doing something that would be on your hard limits list."

"Promise?" While Rylie was so excited that her nipples felt as hard as diamonds and she was pretty sure she'd already created a wet spot on the comforter, she was also a little nervous about what he might use that could be painful if she moved at the wrong time. But that was only because she knew she couldn't always control the movement of her body in the throes of an orgasm.

"I promise, Moh Graw." Liam peppered light kisses across her face and down her neck. "I only want to make you feel good, so I will absolutely stop if you don't like something I'm doing. Just as you have to trust me not to do anything that could harm you, I have to trust you to tell me when anything I do feels like too much. That's why I think this is a great way for us to build our trust in one another. But if you're not into it, I can remove the blindfold and skip all the toys if you want."

"No, I'm into it," Rylie quickly responded, not wanting him to stop. "I'm just nervous because I've never done anything like this before."

"Neither have I," Liam admitted with a chuckle as he finally moved her rabbit vibrator off of her stomach, his warm breath wafting across her skin as he moved down to lavish her breasts with his oral affection once more. "But after reading about something similar in **Winning Rhonda**, I thought this would be something we'd both like to try. Now, lift your hands over your head and then be very still so I can get started playing with you."

"Yes, Sir." As Liam licked and sucked and teased her to the point that she was about to come from breast play alone, Rylie scanned her memory of the book, finally remembering how Rhonda had gushed about how their sensation play was the most erotic experience of her life, and how Jack keeping her on edge led to the most explosive climax she'd ever had. When Liam lifted his mouth from her breasts just as she started to feel her arousal building in her core, Rylie knew he planned to recreate that scene, keeping her on edge without letting her go over too soon.

I know this is supposed to result in an epic orgasm, but I really hope he doesn't make me wait too long. Dang, now I wish Kay had been more specific in her writing to give me an idea of how long this teasing is supposed to last. I'd also love to know what Liam remembers from that book to know what he's about to use to torture me.

"Feck, I just wanna touch you everywhere, so I can memorize every single inch of you," Liam moaned as he proceeded to do just that. First, he trailed his hands up her arms, following them with his mouth, kissing up her left arm and back down her right.

When he reached her shoulder, Liam teased her by trailing his fingertip over her collarbones, also following that soft touch with his lips. Then he skimmed his palms down her sides, peppering kisses across her chest and abdomen before skipping over her sex to repeat his earlier movements on her legs the same way he had on her arms.

Just as she started to think about what Jack had told Rhonda he'd used while they were shopping at an adult store, Liam got up from the bed, leaving her bereft of his touch. She couldn't tell where he was going from the sound of his footsteps alone, but when she heard the water turn off, she assumed he went to the ensuite bathroom.

"Tell me if this is too hot, Moh Graw," Liam instructed as she felt the bed dip once more, letting her know he'd returned to continue their play.

The next thing she felt was a warm liquid dripping onto her breasts, making her think he'd gone to get the bowl of water to soothe her skin after dripping the hot wax on her. As Liam ran his fingers through the liquid and massaged it into her skin, however, she realized it wasn't candle wax like she'd briefly thought he might use, even though it also smelled like strawberries.

But it's too thin to be lotion, and too warm to be one of the oils I use in my hair. Not that any of those smell like strawberries.

What did Jack say he used in the book? Chocolate sauce? No, it can't be that. If it was, it would smell like chocolate and not strawberries. Unless he has some kind of strawberry syrup. No, Liam would have had to go downstairs to the kitchen to get anything edible like chocolate sauce or strawberry syrup.

As he massaged and blew on the areas where the liquid soaked into her skin, it warmed even more, making her wonder if he had some kind of warming massage oil or lube that smelled like strawberries and was designed to make her skin tingle. *I suppose he could have something like that without me knowing about it since I didn't look in his bedside table when we put away my stuff the other night after deciding it was time for us to share this room.*

No, he said he's never done anything like this before, and he hasn't ever brought a woman here to share his bed, so I doubt it's something he had laying around in his drawer.

Unless maybe it was a gag gift from one of the guys from before we met? Or a lube he likes to use while jerking off?

No, when he did that in Heart's Destiny, he used my bodywash, not lube. Of course, he could have just used my bodywash then because it was already in the shower, so he didn't have to dig through his luggage in the dark to find his special lube. Or risk having to explain why he had lube in the shower the next day if he forgot to put it away after.

She didn't get the chance to ask him before he stopped kneading her breasts and switched out his implement of titillating torture. She wasn't quite sure what soft item he trailed down from her wrist to her shoulder, but she liked it. Well, she liked it until he ran it down her side, tickling as it crossed her ribs.

"Oh, oh, oh!" Rylie giggled and squirmed, knowing whatever he was using right then wouldn't hurt her, even if she moved to where it was touching her more sensitive areas like her nipples or clit.

"Is it too much, Moh Graw? Do I need to stop?"

"No, you don't have to stop altogether," Rylie assured him, shaking her head. "Just maybe avoid the really ticklish spots, like my ribs, inner thighs, and the bottoms of my feet with whatever that is."

"I can do that," Liam chuckled, moving whatever he was using to trail over her already warm flesh where he'd rubbed in the liquid earlier.

She didn't think it tickled there, but whatever he was using did make the tingles come back stronger than before. *Is that a feather? No, it's not flat and wide like a single feather. And I don't know of anything that has several feathers together that would feel round and about an inch in diameter. The only thing I can even think of that might be similar to what he's using is a microfiber duster like the one I saw his cleaning lady use the other day. But that thing was like six inches in diameter, so the only way it could be that would be if he has a mini version of it. And I can't think of a single reason why he'd have a mini version of it since he's not exactly having to clean out test tubes or dust the small spaces inside a computer on a regular basis.*

Oh well, whatever he's using for the tickler, I hope it's something he can bring with us on tour, so we can play like this all year.

Just as she was starting to get used to the feel of what she was calling "the tickler" in her head, she heard a click that sounded an awful lot like Liam had just opened a pocketknife. She instantly froze, no longer sure it was safe for her to squirm, even though the only thing she felt was him running the tickler over her belly and down to the top of her mound.

When she felt the sharp point of what she assumed was the knife he'd just opened tracing circles around her areolas, she did everything she could not to even let her chest rise and fall with her breath. The contrast of the cold metal against her warm flesh made it clear that he wasn't improvising with a plastic pen cap like Jack had in the book from which he got this idea. While her body certainly responded with tension from the slightest bit of fear, Rylie knew Liam had no intention of cutting her, so she trusted him to pay close attention to her reaction and lift the blade to a safe distance when necessary.

Thankfully, he seemed to recognize when her heart rate sped up and she couldn't keep up the exceptionally shallow breathing much longer, so he replaced the knifepoint with the tickler once more. As soon as she realized it was safe, she took a few deep breaths, needing to fill her lungs completely for the first time in minutes. But just as she started to relax, she felt the edge of the knife, and his knuckle where he held the handle, scraping down her abdomen. Once again, the feel of the cold metal caused her to try to keep from breathing too deeply so as not to get cut.

No, that doesn't feel sharp like a knife. But maybe he's using the backside of it, so it's scary because it's a knife, but he's only touching me with the blunt edge that can't cut me.

"You like that, Moh Graw?"

Still unsure if she was correct about which side of the blade he was running over her skin kept her slightly afraid of taking too big a breath in order to speak, so she only nodded her agreement.

"Or is the metal too cold? Maybe I should warm your pussy up a little before I test how close you shaved earlier?"

"Umpm," Rylie squeaked when he lifted the tickler from her breast. Then she felt the warm liquid drizzling over her pubic bone.

Leaving his hand holding the knife resting on her lower abdomen, Liam used his other hand to massage in the warming oil, spreading it down over her folds and putting extra emphasis on rubbing it into her clit. She just thought it was warm on her breasts earlier. Her clitoris felt like it was on fire, and she couldn't decide if she loved it or hated it.

"Oh, I think you really like that," Liam chuckled as Rylie whimpered and moaned.

She was shocked at how the sensations made her pussy gush with arousal, pushing her right to the brink of orgasming. She felt desperate to move, needing more pressure on her clit to push her over the edge from pain to pleasure. As much as she wanted to grab his hand and use the digit he'd had circling her clit to finger herself to her first orgasm of the new year, she knew it wouldn't be safe for her to reach down, not knowing where that knife was now that Liam had lifted his hands from her body.

Did he just lift his hands a few inches straight up, waiting to surprise me by lowering them back down to touch me somewhere else? Or did he move them away from me completely, and possibly put the knife down on the comforter beside us, so he can pick up something else to tease me with? Since she couldn't see to know the answers to those questions, she just gripped the comforter above her head, knowing he hadn't laid anything right there at the edge of the bed.

"But I bet you'll like this even more." Rylie recognized the buzz of her vibrator as Liam turned it on.

Oh, yes, yes, yes! She was eager for him to insert the toy, hoping the pressure of the rabbit ears on her clit would be enough to ease her need, even if it was only a small orgasm compared to the ones she got when Liam was inside her.

Instead of doing as she expected, however, he ran the vibrator over her nipples, while scraping her mound with the edge of the knife. "Spread your legs a little more, Moh Graw, so I have better access."

Rylie carefully did as she was told, not wanting to move too far too fast and accidentally hit anything else he might have laid on the bed beside them, or raise her hips any to press the top of her pussy into the edge of the knife. However, as she spread her legs, the only thing she touched was Liam's cock.

She tried to rub him with her thigh, wanting to tease him a little too. But Liam pulled back, lifting the knife from her mound and the toy from her breast as he rolled away from her.

"Uh, uh, uh. You don't get to play with my cock until you beg me to fuck you with it. And I think it's gonna take a lot more teasing before you do that."

She was tempted to start begging right then, but she also wanted to know what else he had planned to work her up even more. So, Rylie clamped her mouth shut, eagerly anticipating what he would use and where he'd touch her next. He didn't make her wait long, going back to using the tip of the knife to trace along the edges of her slit while softly blowing on her clit.

Rylie lost all track of time as Liam titillated her, alternating between his hands, mouth, her toy, and several other items she couldn't be sure she accurately identified to work her up to the edge repeatedly without inserting anything or allowing her to reach her peak. Though she came exceptionally close when he wound what felt like a necklace chain around her nipples to tie her breasts close enough together that he could fuck her tits while propping her toy on her ribs so the rabbit ears brushed along his balls with each thrust.

"You need to start begging, Moh Graw," Liam warned, his voice sounding strained as he kept thrusting between her breasts. "Or else I'm gonna come from fucking your tits and not make it into your pussy before we have to stop and nap."

"Please, Liam, fuck my pussy with your big cock," Rylie eagerly pleaded, wishing she could see his face. "Please. I need you inside me. My pussy is so empty without your long, thick dick."

"Since you begged so beautifully." Liam pulled back, walking backwards on his knees down her body. He picked up the toy and flipped it off, just before she heard the click of him closing what she assumed was the pocketknife he'd been using. She felt him get off the edge of the bed before gathering most of the things he'd used and clunking them down on the nightstand. "But I'd better change condoms first, 'cause this one is already pretty full of precum."

She heard him walk to the bathroom to dispose of the first condom before coming back and crinkling the foil packet to open a new one. Then he grabbed her feet and pulled her across the bed until her butt was barely on the edge. Propping her feet on his shoulders, he shockingly entered her in one thrust.

"Oh, yes! Liam!" Rylie cried out, gripping the comforter to ground herself since she didn't think she could reach him in this position. She was so aroused from all their earlier play that he didn't need any kind of lube to repeatedly fill her with his full length, not stopping until his balls slapped against her ass on every powerful thrust.

"Oh, I suppose I should remove this, too," Liam chuckled, pulling the chain from the middle so the loops tugged on her nipples. "But it looks so pretty on you that I wish you could wear it all the time for me."

"Yes, oh, Liam, yes," Rylie panted, too lost in the beginning waves of her orgasm to really register what he was doing to her breasts as he continued to pound into her.

Just as her whole body spasmed with the most explosive release she'd ever felt, Liam pulled the chain off her tits, causing a sharp sting as the blood flow resumed to her previously numb nipples. "Oh, fuck, Liam!"

Rylie lost all control of her body, squirting on his cock as he moved her legs down, wrapped them around his waist, and leaned forward to soothe her aching nipples with his mouth. Surprisingly, Liam didn't come with her that time. He just kept thrusting relentlessly, fucking her through the orgasm, until one rolled into two, then three, four, who knows how many more.

"Feck, I need to see your eyes," Liam roared, undoing the tie around her head as she floated in an unprecedented state of nirvana. "Open your eyes, Moh Graw."

It took a moment for her to come back into her body to be able to follow his command. When she did, she found he'd braced his upper body with his hands placed on either side of her shoulders, so he could look directly into her eyes while thrusting deep inside her. She couldn't resist moving her arms a moment longer, reaching up to grip his head and pull him down for a kiss.

Even as their tongues tangled in passion, Liam didn't stop pistoning in and out of her, quickly working her back up to another orgasm. Rylie tightened her grip with her arms around his shoulders and her legs around his hips, intentionally squeezing her pelvic floor muscles in an attempt to hold him inside her as she started to go over the edge once more.

"Feck, Rylie," Liam groaned, breaking their kiss and staring into her eyes once again. "Come with me now, Moh Graw!"

"Yes, Liam, yes!" Rylie reveled in the love she saw in the depths of his hazel irises. But even though she suspected they both felt it, she still didn't want to be the first to say those three little words. So, as her body convulsed in the ultimate pleasure, she clamped her mouth shut, hoping he could see her love for him in her eyes as they came together.

Liam plunged inside her one last time, holding still as deep as he could go as his body shuddered with his release. As soon as the trembles subsided, he collapsed on top of her, resting his head on the mattress beside hers with his arms extended out to their sides.

Rylie wished they could forgo the condoms sooner than the end of the month, curious to know what it felt like to have him come inside her with no barriers between them. Not that she could complain about how wonderful it felt with the condom, especially considering she came so hard that she felt like she was floating once more.

As she came down from her orgasm high, Rylie couldn't help but laugh from how hopeful she was that the superstition about New Year's Day she'd been taught when she was young would be true for her and Liam.

"Now what are you laughing about?" Liam pushed up on his elbows, looking down into her eyes as he smiled at her. "'Cause I know you don't think orgasms are funny. Feck, normally you're passed out by the time you have as many as you have so far tonight."

"You mean so far this morning," Rylie corrected him with a grin. "But no, I'm not laughing at the amazing O's you've given me so far today. I'm laughing because I'm hoping the superstition my parents taught me about as a kid is true."

"And what superstition is that?" Liam arched an eyebrow as she felt him start to harden inside her once more.

"That whatever you do on New Year's Day is what you'll be stuck doing all year. That's why we never cleaned the house on January first." Rylie shrugged before letting her excitement show through in her expression. "So, if it's true, then you need to pack extra ties and all your special toys, so we can play like this regularly to make up for having to sleep in the wet spot all year, since we didn't think about breaking in the other beds like we said earlier."

"Then we'd better make love multiple times today, Moh Graw," Liam suggested with a wide grin. "That way we know we'll have multiples every day for the rest of the year and I have another chance at figuring out how to tie you up."

"Hmmm, I like the way you think, Hubby. But you'd better pull out and change that condom before we start on round two."

"Of course," Liam agreed, pecking her lips before pulling out and getting up to go dispose of the condom. When he came back from the bathroom, he grabbed another from the box on his bedside table, donning it before crawling back over her on the bed. "Now, where were we?"

"I think it's my turn to blindfold you and tease you like you teased me," Rylie suggested with a grin.

"Yeah, no," Liam disagreed, shaking his head as he rolled off of her and pointed to the other items on his bedside table that she hadn't had the energy to look over while he was in the bathroom. "I don't think it'll have the same effect, since I know what everything is that I used earlier, and won't be able to suspend disbelief enough to be turned on or frightened by any of it, and I'm not ticklish enough for one of those tassels to do anything for me either."

Rylie pushed up on her elbows to half sit up and looked over at his bedside table to see her vibrator, a bottle of strawberry flavored warming lube, a large silver set of toenail clippers, one of the necklaces she'd made from a surfboard charm she'd gotten in a bath bomb and a chain from the craft store, and the knot from their handfasting on Christmas Eve, which made her wonder which of the tassels he'd used as the "tickler." She also quickly figured out she'd been right about the chain he'd used on her nipples, that the pointy end of the surfboard charm was what he used when she thought it was the tip of a knife, and that the toenail clippers had to be what he used to mimic the blade since they were the only other metal item on the table. But she was still confused about a couple of things.

"Okay, I think I know what you used for everything you touched me with, and even how you made me think that lube was candle wax since it's a similar scent to my candle, but I'm confused about how you made the sound of opening and closing a pocketknife and why you ran the water in the bathroom sink for so long."

"Yeah, I got lucky that the lube Dion gave me as a gag gift for my birthday is the same flavor as your candle," Liam chuckled, sitting up on the side of the bed and reaching over to pick up the toenail clippers. He flipped the lever on the clippers up and down a few times, making it clear those were the sounds she mistook for opening and closing a pocketknife. "And I held them like this to cover the blades with my finger and just ran the side of the lever over your skin, so you were never in any danger of being cut."

"Yeah, well, that worked to convince me it was a pocketknife," Rylie snorted, unsure how to feel about falling for his trick, as he laid back down beside her and demonstrated by running the lever over her thigh now that she could see what he was doing. "Which I'd like to point out shows just how much I trust you, since I thought it really was a pocketknife the whole time, even though I wondered if you were only touching me with the dull side of the blade."

"Yeah, if I ever had to actually use a knife, I'd skip it and wouldn't risk dropping it and hurting you, especially if my hands were slippery from the lube." Liam explained as he closed the clippers once more and tossed them back on the bedside table. "And the running water was to heat up the lube so it would be warmer than room temperature when I first dripped it on you, 'cause I wanted you to think it was candle wax until I rubbed it in. But it wasn't thick enough to stay in one spot, so I had to massage it in sooner than I planned and didn't get to leave drops of it all up and down your body to really sell it as wax."

Rylie couldn't help but chuckle at the faux irritation on Liam's face from how his plan had gone awry. "I kinda thought it was strawberry syrup at first. But then I realized you hadn't gone down to the kitchen for anything, so that couldn't be it. Though now that I think about it, I wonder if we could use that Magic Shell ice cream topping that hardens in seconds to mimic wax?"

"Yeah, I think that stuff has to freeze to get hard, so it'd only work if we ran an ice cube over it." Liam pointed out the fallacy of her plan as he trailed his finger over the upper curve of her breast where he'd first dripped the lube earlier. "But even then your body heat would probably melt it as soon as the ice cube was removed."

"True," Rylie agreed, wrapping her arms around his neck and running her fingers through his hair. "So, I guess I'll have to take some time coming up with other ideas of things to use to tease you before I blindfold you."

"Yeah, we're not gonna wait for that now," Liam informed her before dipping his head and bringing their lips together to start round two. While she had her eyes closed for the kiss, Liam somehow managed to lift her hands over her head once more, twisting his tie around her wrists to bind her arms together.

Happy New Year, indeed!

~~~

Wednesday, January 1, 2020, New Year's Day, Flying from New York City, New York to San Antonio, Texas

After being up most of the night making love to his wife, and then getting up earlier than he wanted to so they could go to breakfast with his parents and grandparents, Liam was more than ready to convert the new seats on the plane to lay flat, so he could catch a nap for at least half of the four-hour flight. But before that, he wanted to take advantage of him and Rylie being the only two people in the main cabin of the plane to join the mile-high club. *Too bad that's one thing we'll do today that we won't be able to repeat daily to fulfill Rylie's superstition,* Liam thought as they walked to the back of the plane to stow their luggage, knowing they'd never trust the privacy screens on the new pods to keep the rest of the GWA from knowing what they were doing to try making love on one of their normal flights.
~~~

As soon as their coats, garment bags, and oversized luggage were all safely stored away in the new closets in the tail of the plane, Liam took Rylie's hand, pulled her to the center pods on the back row, and quickly stowed their carry-ons in the overhead bin. Not only were these the least likely seats anyone else would use the next day, so they wouldn't have to worry about their coworkers noticing if they still smelled like sex, but they were also the seats farthest from the cockpit, so they'd have plenty of time after landing to make sure their clothing was all back in place before seeing the pilots as they exited the plane.

"Why are we sitting way back here?" Rylie questioned as Liam stepped between the pods, taking the right seat and buckling up for takeoff.

"Because it's the farthest from the cockpit," Liam pointed out, wagging his eyebrows suggestively as she took the left seat and buckled up. "And I was thinking that as soon as they turn off the seat-belt lights, we can lay these two seats down to make a double bed for joining the mile-high club. And if we don't manage to get all our clothes on again before napping for the second half of the flight, then we'll have plenty of time to finish getting dressed when they announce that we're landing before they come back down to this level and see us."

"You were serious about wanting to make love on this flight?" Rylie's eyes widened as she stared at him, clearly thinking he'd been joking when he suggested it before.

"Yeah, I was serious," Liam chuckled, reaching over and taking her hand once more now that they were both buckled into their seats. "Why do you think I insisted on Mia and Noelle not coming on this flight, only to fly right back to New York like Derek and Nick?"

Liam wasn't entirely certain where Nick Ledger, the second pilot on the flight crew with Derek and Mia York, would actually go on his time off. He just assumed the more reserved pilot also lived in New York like the Yorks. But since he knew Nate Rogers, the pilot who worked with Anthony Burleson on the other flight crew, lived in Atlanta and not in the San Antonio area, and he had no idea where Janice Smith, the flight attendant on the crew with the Burlesons and Nate Rogers, lived at all, he was probably wrong about where Nick was actually from. *Though, I guess Nick isn't gonna fly out with Derek today, since I think it was just Anthony and Kay switching days*

Leah Mae Wright

with Derek and Mia tomorrow, instead of riding with us as passengers on their normal travel day between flight rotations since we're flying out of San Antonio.

"I thought it was just to save them from having to deal with flying commercial when Mia wouldn't have anything to do on this flight."

"Yeah, but it was also so it would just be us and the pilots on the plane today," Liam smirked, not pointing out that he'd made that suggestion on the flight to New York, when he didn't think he and Rylie would ever have sex again, much less want to join the mile-high club together.

"But that was when you thought we'd be annulling our marriage while we were on break," Rylie argued, shaking her head at him when she obviously realized what he wasn't saying. "Did you think we'd do all the legal paperwork and then reinstate our friends-with-benefits arrangement?"

"No," Liam chuckled, just as Nick made the announcement to prepare for takeoff. "I was honestly thinking you'd want fewer people around so you wouldn't have to pretend we were still friends on this flight, not having much hope that Da's idea to talk things out with the family and Father O'Malley would work. But I also secretly wished for us to work things out to stay married, so we could break in these seats on what will most likely be our only opportunity to be alone on the plane."

"Emmm-hm, sure you did." Rylie rolled her eyes at him as the plane taxied out to the runway.

"Just because I was still afraid to even admit my feelings for you to myself, doesn't mean I wasn't feeling them, Mo Ghrá." Liam lifted their joined hands to his lips to reinforce the statement with a kiss to the back of hers, since he didn't think it was the right time to say those three little words yet.

Yes, he knew he was madly in love with her and longed to share the sentiment, but he wanted it to be special the first time he said it. With the way they'd ended up married without ever going on a date, couldn't remember their first kiss because it was presumably when they were standing at the altar after saying "I do" on their wedding night, and how their first time making love had been hurried when they were half asleep and emotionally distraught after Dion got shot, Liam wanted to make their first time saying "I love you" to one

340

another meaningful for both of them. That's why when he looked at their upcoming schedule after they decided to stay married and saw that Las Vegas was one of the first tour stops in January, he called the hotel and changed their room reservations to a honeymoon suite. He wanted to give them a do-over of what their wedding night should've been and thought a champagne toast after their show in Vegas was the perfect way to say those three little words the first time.

Feck! It's hard to keep from telling her I love her until I can make that first time special. But since I screwed up and haven't made any of our other firsts meaningful, I really don't wanna mess this one up, too.

"I know," Rylie smiled at him. "I felt the same. Too bad neither one of us was brave enough to tell each other we hoped your family's intervention would work. But I am willing to admit now that you telling me they planned to try to talk us out of the annulment was what made me decide to go to New York for the holidays. Before that, I was planning on pretending to look for a hotel and then telling you I couldn't find a room available because the city was booked up for the ball drop, so I couldn't go."

"Why were you gonna do that?" Liam couldn't believe how close they'd come to not spending that time together to work things out.

"Because I didn't want to make it easy for you to get the annulment by going to the lawyer's office with you," Rylie admitted with a shrug. "I know it was ridiculously petty and vindictive, but I was still hurting from you rejecting me and trying to kill any attraction to me by sleeping with someone else, so I wanted to make the divorce process difficult to get back at you."

"Well, while we're making confessions to one another, I suppose I should tell you that your plan to get back at me wouldn't have worked," Liam smirked, hoping to steer clear of rehashing his idiocy at the beginning of their marriage. "'Cause even if you hadn't come home with me and the lawyers' office was open for the meeting I thought Boyle had set up, I wasn't really planning to file anything that day. I wanted to get the information in case it was ever needed, but I secretly hoped to delay it long enough for you to forgive me for being an eejit and help me figure out how we could make things work long term."

When Rylie eyed him skeptically, Liam reached over and cupped her face in his free hand, silencing anything she might have said to contradict him with a claiming kiss. As always seemed to be the case when he kissed Rylie, he felt an intense vibration throughout his body and the distinct feeling of all the blood in his system shooting straight to his cock. And those sensations only seemed to be amplified by the aircraft lifting off the ground.

Rylie pulled her hand from his as she opened her mouth to return the ardent kiss. He only vaguely registered her moving the armrests down to be flush with their seats before she ran her hands up his torso to wind her arms around his neck. With his hand now free, Liam stroked along her hip to wrap his arm around her, pulling her as close as they could get while they were still buckled into their seats.

Liam lost himself in the sweet taste of his wife, tangling their tongues and not paying attention to whatever announcements Nick and Derek made over the intercom from the cockpit. He already knew approximately how long the flight would last. And since they didn't have anything planned but grabbing some food and going to their hotel room once they landed, he didn't care what time the pilots estimated they'd arrive in San Antonio. Even if he missed the announcement that it was safe to move about the cabin to go get a drink from the galley or hit the head, he knew he could figure it out by simply looking at the seat-belt lights above their heads to find out if they were on or off. So, he let everything else around them recede into nothingness as he focused exclusively on showing Rylie how much he loved her.

At least if our mouths are otherwise occupied, I can't accidentally blurt out "I love you" in the middle of making love, instead of waiting until I can make the moment special for her.

Liam relished the feel of her delicate touch as she raked her nails through the short strands on the back of his head, imagining the pointed tips of her manicure felt a lot like the way he'd ran that surfboard charm across her flesh early that morning, only multiplied by ten. *Feck! I'd love to feel her running those nails over my chest and abs before gripping my dick and stroking me until I come all over her tits. I'll have to add that to our list of things we want to do once we know I'm safe.*

Liam let his hands wander, cupping her breasts since they couldn't turn enough in their seat belts to press their bodies together the way he wanted. He circled the pads of his thumbs over the hard nubs that were in no way hidden by her top and bra, making her shudder even as her nipples poked out a little more. He loved being able to easily arouse her, the heady sensation making him feel a little lightheaded. Though part of that could be from a lack of oxygen since he was only shallowly breathing through his nose while they continued to meld their mouths as if they were going for the world record for the longest lasting single kiss. Or the lack of blood flow to his brain, since it seemed every ounce of blood in his body had rushed to his dick.

When she pulled back to take a breath, Liam trailed his lips down her neck until he was blocked by the high collar of her mock turtleneck shirt. "Feck, you taste so good, Mo Ghrá."

"So do you, Hubby." Rylie trailed her mouth down his jaw as she pushed his suitcoat off his shoulders. "But I bet you're gonna feel even better when you get inside me."

Wanting to make sure it was safe before they started losing clothing, Liam glanced up to see the seat-belt lights were off. *Thank feck!* He didn't have to wait any longer, quickly stripping off his suitcoat before reaching for the bottom of Rylie's stretchy top to lift it up off her body.

As their clothes practically flew off, they landed on the seats in the row in front of them that made up the quad seating area. Somehow they didn't stop kissing and touching each other even as they stripped off his shirt, tie, and pants, her skirt, bra, and panties, and both their shoes and socks. Liam then pulled back to step around the cabinets between the rows of seats to grab a condom from his wallet before shucking off his boxer briefs and rolling it down his hard length, while Rylie hurriedly reclined both their seats to make them into beds.

As he walked back around the cabinets to get back to his seat, he saw Rylie pulling a pillow, sheet, and blanket from the cabinet behind her seat. He followed her lead by opening the cabinet on his side and pulling out the sheet to cover the leather seat before crawling into the bed. "I know the sheets are probably necessary to keep from sticking to the leather seats when we get sweaty, but do we really need the pillows and blankets now?"

"I thought whichever one of us is on bottom might like the neck support," Rylie replied as she put the pillow at the head of the bed on her side while tossing the blanket at the foot now that the sheet was fully in place. "And even if we don't need the blankets now, it's better to have them more easily accessible than in the cabinets, just in case

Nick or Derek come down here for a snack or bathroom break before we get dressed. Though now I wish I had an empty bag to put them in when we get to San Antonio, so we can take them to be laundered before our flight out tomorrow."

"They have lavatories and a galley on the upper deck for the pilots if necessary," Liam pointed out, shaking his head, even as he put his pillow and blanket in the same positions as hers. "And if what Gianni told me when I asked about these things when he first showed them to me is true, then we just need to leave them on our seats when we exit the plane for the cleaning service the GWA contracted with at each airport to launder and return them."

"Oh, good. I was afraid we were each going to have to keep track of any of this stuff we used each day, like we do with our clothes and ring gear we have laundered through the hotels." Rylie gracefully lowered herself down on the bed.

"That's because our clothes and ring gear all belong to each of us, even if it was purchased by the GWA wardrobe department," Liam explained as he walked on his knees onto the bed beside his wife. "But this stuff all stays with the plane, so it's taken care of by the same people responsible for cleaning the cabins and restrooms and restocking the galley after every flight."

Liam crowded in close to Rylie, cupping her face in his hands. "Now, where were we?"

Rylie wrapped her arms around his neck. "I believe we were right about here."

Liam claimed her lips once more, reveling in her sweet taste as he gently laid her down on her back, rested her head on her pillow, and covered her body with his. Again, he let his hands wander, tenderly kneading her breasts before trailing his mouth down her body to suckle the turgid tips.

He wanted nothing more at that moment than to memorize every inch of her beautiful bronze body, inspecting her skin everywhere he'd touched her with the metal implements that morning to make sure he hadn't left any marks. As he kissed and stroked her flesh, he knew he'd always remember her just like this. Even when they were old and out of shape, he'd still see her as the perfect goddess of a woman that he somehow got lucky enough to marry.

When he got down to her mound, the heady scent of her arousal mixed with the residual aroma of her lightly floral bodywash overwhelmed him to the point that he couldn't resist eating her pussy a moment longer. While he knew he couldn't let her give him a blow job until after his tests at the end of the month, he didn't think him going down on her presented any greater risk of transmitting something than they were already taking every time he kissed her mouth.

He loved the moans he elicited from her as he swiped his tongue through her folds, ending with just the tip twirling around her clit before he sucked that sweet little nub between his lips. He couldn't stop his hips from moving, humping the sheet-covered seat as he spread her lower lips open and inserted two fingers.

She was so wet, he didn't have to do much to open her up enough to take his cock. But he still wanted to make her come at least once before he filled her up and took his pleasure while giving her another orgasm. Not that he had to wait long. Between crooking his fingers to hone in on her G-spot and sucking on her clit, Liam soon had Rylie writhing in the throes of her release.

"Oh, yes, Liam," she cried out as she gripped the back of his head and pressed his face down harder against her pussy, her inner walls gripping his fingers like a vise. She barely took the time to come down from her high before she pulled on his ears to get him to move back up her body. "Inside me. Now. Don't make me wait any longer for your cock."

"Yes, Mistress," he teased as he crawled up to cover her once more. He lined up the head of his cock with her slit, sliding home in one smooth thrust, just as he crashed his mouth down on hers once more, plunging his tongue between her lips.

He held most of his weight off of her by resting one elbow and forearm beside her head, freeing up the other arm to go back to playing with her bountiful breasts. She wrapped her legs around his thighs, rocking her hips in perfect time with his long, slow thrusts.

Unlike that morning when he'd teased them both with toys until they were so far gone they couldn't hold back their mutual need for a fast and furious fuck, Liam was able to savor every moment of their coupling this time. Since it was likely the only chance they'd ever get to join the mile-high club, he wanted to take their time and really appreciate every moment, every kiss, every touch.

There was no more need for words as they let the joining of their bodies speak for them. Every swivel of his hips or rake of her nails down his back spoke volumes about how they felt for one another. But still, he felt the need to keep his mouth occupied so he didn't accidentally blurt out those three little words. Even when he had to stop kissing her to let her breathe, he kept trailing his lips and tongue over her flesh. And when they reached the precipice and he absolutely couldn't hold his tongue any longer, he switched to Irish.

"Is tú mo ghrá." *You are my love.* "Mo anam cara." *My soulmate.* "Táim i ngrá leat." *I am in love with you.* Liam punctuated each phrase with a deep thrust, finally holding still inside her as his balls drew up and his cum exploded into the condom.

"Oh, oh, oh, yes, Liam," Rylie exclaimed as her pulsing climax milked his cock of every last drop.

He rolled them so she was on top, not wanting to crush her as his muscles gave out from the intensity of their simultaneous orgasms.

"Feck," he groaned as soon as he caught his breath, realizing that he'd have to walk on spaghetti legs to get to the lavatory to dispose of the condom and get some paper towels to clean them up. "That was amazing. But we really should have pre-gamed a little better to be able to clean up and dispose of the condom without having to walk to the bathroom."

"Guess it's a good thing we were smart enough to only try this while it's just us in this part of the plane," Rylie giggled, rolling off of him and disconnecting their bodies long before he was ready. "'Cause we'd have just ended up with a mess in our pants if we'd trusted the privacy screens to keep the rest of the GWA from knowing what we did on one of our normal flights."

"True," Liam chuckled as he rolled to sit up on the side of the seat, gripping his dick to hold the condom in place so he didn't drip as he stumbled on shaky legs down the aisle. He also grabbed the empty condom wrapper before he started down the aisle toward the back of the plane, wanting to throw it away where it wouldn't be super obvious to the cleaning crew what they'd done on the flight. "And another good reason I picked these seats, so it's not far to walk."

As soon as he got to the closest lavatory, Liam removed the condom and tied it off, wrapping it and the empty wrapper in a paper towel before disposing of the whole bundle in the wastebasket. He then wet a couple of paper towels to clean off his now flaccid dick, also disposing of them in the wastebasket along with the towel he used to dry off. Finally, he wet a couple more paper towels, ringing them out well before taking them and a couple of dry towels back to their seats to clean Rylie up before their nap.

After he cleaned between her legs, Liam returned to the lavatory to dispose of the paper towels, glad that the cleaning service would be emptying the waste bin before the rest of the GWA boarded the plane the next day. When he returned to their seats, he found Rylie putting on her underwear and hated that she was covering those perfect tits.

"Do you really think we'll have time to get dressed later?" Rylie looked up at him imploringly. "'Cause I really wasn't thinking about laying down for a nap when I got dressed this morning or I would have picked my pants that wouldn't totally wrinkle in my sleep."

"Yeah, I'm sure we'll have plenty of time to get dressed," Liam assured her as he put on his boxer briefs. They weren't as much of a barrier from his precum as a condom, but hopefully, he wouldn't leak much while they napped. "We might not have enough time between the prepare-for-landing announcement and when we have to be buckled in to put everything back on and get our bed converted back into seats, but it won't be a big deal if the pilots see you putting your boots back on or notice I'm not wearing the tie I had on earlier."

"Then I'm not putting on anything else now," Rylie declared as she crawled back into the bed.

"Me either," Liam agreed, joining her and opening his arms for her to cuddle into his side. "No point in risking getting my suit wrinkled if my nightmares come back from me not being used to sleeping on the plane."

"Hopefully, still being able to snuggle will keep them away for both of us." Rylie laid her head on his shoulder and adjusted her braids so they weren't trapped under his arm as he wrapped it around her torso.

"Do I need to get one of your scarves out of your bag before this nap?" He knew she normally wrapped her hair up to keep from messing up her braids at night, so he assumed she'd want to do the same for their nap.

"No, I think it'll be fine for a short nap," Rylie yawned. "And if not, then I know exactly who to call in Heart's Destiny to fix my braids before our flight out tomorrow."

Considering the only hairstylist he'd met in Heart's Destiny was white, Liam wasn't sure how much experience she had with fixing braids. But he wasn't about to argue with his wife about something he really knew next to nothing about. Instead, he changed the subject. "So, how surprised do you think everyone is gonna be tomorrow when we tell them we're officially together and not getting an annulment?"

"I'm sure some of them might be shocked, but they'll all be happy for us."

Liam closed his eyes as Rylie's breathing evened out as she fell asleep. *They'll be happy for us, but they won't be nearly as happy as I am right now.*

Chapter Thirteen

Thursday, January 2, 2020, Flying from San Antonio, Texas to Tucson, Arizona

As they met up with the rest of the GWA that morning, Liam couldn't keep the smile off his face as he and Rylie walked through the airport hand in hand. They didn't have to make an announcement that they were staying together because it was obvious to everyone around them as they lined up to board the plane. Especially when his grin only got bigger when Rylie started to blush from him leaning down to whisper in her ear to recap what they'd done on the flight between New York and San Antonio the day before. Unfortunately, before Liam could talk her into joining him in the back row again, so they could silently relive the memories in their minds without anyone around them being the wiser, her friends all called out to her, insisting she had to ride in the upper cabin with them, so they could share their honeymoon stories without being overheard by any of the kids who traveled with their family members who worked for the company.

It was a little slower to get everyone on the plane now that they had to maneuver their luggage down the two narrow walkways instead of the wide open single aisle they had previously. But since they tended to fly into private airports with stairs that rolled out to the plane for the passengers to board, instead of having to line the door of the plane up with one of the gates, Liam didn't see why they couldn't use more than one of the doors on the plane to help them all board quicker.

"Yeah, I see your point," Rick agreed when Liam pointed out that possibility to the boss as he and Rylie walked into the galley behind the Robertsons. "I always just asked for one entry point, so I could catch whoever I need to talk with on each flight easier than having to watch both a front door and a back door. But maybe since we've added those new luggage compartments at the back of the plane, it might be best to have us enter back there, so we don't all have to try to squeeze by each other multiple times, first going back to put up our luggage and then again to get past everyone else to get back to our seats."

"Or maybe you could have the airports set up for those of us with oversized luggage to go in the back and those with just carry on sized stuff to come in the front, so we can meet in the middle at our seats? And text whoever you need to talk with on a flight so they know to sit up front with you?" Liam suggested, hoping to speed up the boarding process for all the international flights they had coming up when they might already have delays because of going through Customs.

"Yeah, that will work better than this," Rick agreed, lifting his hands, which were full with his carry-on and the handle of his rolling suitcase as he turned to go down the first aisle in the main cabin, while Liam and Rylie passed through the galley to walk down the second aisle. "But since I have my hands full and can't text, I'm just going to have to ask you to sit up front on this flight, so we can go over a few things."

Rick nodded his head toward the first front-facing aisle seat to indicate where he wanted Liam to sit, which was directly across from the first rear-facing aisle seat on what Liam considered the left side of the plane, but Anthony had explained was the port side, where the company owner always sat. Well, the general position on the plane where Rick always sat anyway, since this flight would be the first time anyone but Liam or Rylie used any of the new seats.

"Will do, Boss," Liam agreed, stepping between the center pods from the right aisle to the left and putting his carryon-sized bags in the overhead bin. He then followed their boss and his family the rest of the way down the left aisle to meet his wife at the back of the plane to hang up their garment bags and strap their oversized suitcases into the specialized luggage compartments that had been added to the plane. They each showed a couple of their coworkers and their family members how to do the same, so none of their oversized luggage had to take up an empty seat for their future flights. When they started back to the front of the plane with her still carrying her smaller bags, he asked, "Do you need me to come help you put those in the overhead bin upstairs, Mo Ghrá?"

"No, I think I can get it," Rylie replied, smiling as they stopped in the open space beside the stairs out of the way of the two aisles before pushing up on her tiptoes to peck her lips on his for a quick kiss.

A quick peck wasn't enough for Liam, though, so he wrapped Rylie in his arms, dipped her back, and kissed her heartily. While he'd intended the kiss to show her how much he was going to miss her while on the flight, it also did a pretty good job of making it clear to any of their coworkers, who hadn't already figured it out, that they were most definitely staying together, especially when Rylie made that swoony face as he lifted her back into an upright position and stepped back to give her room to go up the stairs.

Ignoring more than a few catcalls from their coworkers, Liam just smiled as he walked back to the front of the plane and took his seat across from Rick. He assumed the boss wanted a report on why these pods had been chosen over the other options of similar sizes. *I wonder if he's gonna care that I picked these because the armrests between the seats can be pushed down to allow cuddling when they're converted into beds, or to give a couple extra inches of padding on each side of the beds even if the privacy divider is up between the two side-by-side seats?* While he hadn't thought he'd get to use the cuddling benefit when he first picked out the pods, Liam appreciated how he'd gotten to use it the day before. And he thought for sure Rick would appreciate being able to cuddle his wife on the long international flights they had coming up in a couple of weeks, as would several of the other couples who worked for the GWA, even if they didn't always sit with their spouses on the shorter daily flights.

"I'm guessing you need a demonstration of where everything is and how to use these pods?" Liam questioned as he buckled in.

"Yeah, it's probably a good idea if you show all of us," Rick chuckled, shaking his head. "So we don't break anything by trying to adjust the seats the same way we did the old ones, when these aren't designed the same way. But that's not really why I wanted you to sit here."

Before Liam could ask why Rick wanted him to sit there, the boss called over both of the flight attendants to have Liam show them how to adjust the seats, access the in-flight entertainment system, and put each of the privacy screens in place as well as back into the cabinets attached to each individual pod. *I guess it was the whole flight crew that swapped days, since Janice and Nate are here. I wonder if that's because Mia had to be in New York to assist the other new flight attendants with everything they need to know before our South Pacific and Southeast Asia tour and they didn't want Kay to try to do both her and Janice's job on this flight? And honestly, I'm kinda surprised that Rick hasn't filled that mother's helper position on the other flight crew, since Kay is constantly bouncing around between the kids on the days she works.*

Once Liam demonstrated everything he knew about the new pods, Rick then instructed Janice and Kay to demonstrate the same to the rest of the crew in small groups once the flight took off and it was safe for everyone to move about the cabin. After converting his pod back to a seat so he could sit and talk to Rick, Liam sat back down and buckled in once more, just as Anthony came over the intercom to tell them to prepare for takeoff.

Rick didn't wait for them to actually get into the air before he started explaining to Liam, the bookers, and the production crew, who were all in the first two rows of seats on the plane, how he wanted to make some changes to the company over the next few months. "So, I'm sure you're all wondering why I insisted you sit up here."

"Yeah, I think I'm the only one who doesn't normally sit up front to discuss your show plans for the day, Boss," Liam chuckled.

"That's because I don't just want to discuss the show plans for today," Rick smiled and shook his head. "I want to explain how I want to restructure the company over the next year or two. As you all know, I've had to delegate some things recently because of needing some time off to start growing my family. And as we add new members to the Robertson household, I'm going to have to keep delegating more and more. That's why I gave Liam a little test over the break to see how well he deals with some of the businesses we work with that aren't in his comfort zone." Rick turned away from where he'd been directing his comments to all of them to look directly at Liam. "A test that you passed with flying colors, by the way."

Liam only smiled, unsure where Rick was going with this conversation.

"Gianni Marconi is my cousin," Rick elaborated with a smirk.

Why didn't Gianni mention that on Monday? Liam briefly wondered.

Because it was part o' de test, eejit, Liam's inner voice replied in his granda's distinct Irish brogue.

"Marconi, as in the Marconi crime family?" Ethan Abrams interjected before Rick could finish explaining why Gianni being his cousin mattered. Ethan looked confused as his eyes darted back and forth between Rick and Liam.

"Gianni isn't involved in our grandfather's business." Rick held up his hands in a surrender position. "Or I guess I should say his father's and our uncles' business, since our grandfather passed on. And it was purely a coincidence that we reconnected after I hired the aviation company he works for to get and set up our second plane and redo the interior of this one. But since we did reconnect once he found out he was working on my planes, I asked his opinion on the way Liam went about completing the task of picking our new pods and inspecting the work after it was done."

"And I'm assuming Liam was smart enough not to ask your cousin if he was part of the Marconi crime family," Cooper Stafford joked, pointedly looking at his fellow booker, Ethan.

"Sorry, it just shocked me that Rick *Robertson* is related to a mob family," Ethan defended his earlier question, emphasizing how Rick's surname was distinctly not Italian to explain why he hadn't figured out the connection.

Rick and Cooper looked each other in the eyes. Then in unison they both reworded a famous line from the movie **Fight Club**. "The first rule of being related to the mafia is *don't talk about the mafia.*"

When Liam joined the GWA roster in 2004, Rick had already been wrestling for his dad's company for eight years, and Cooper had been with the company for three. Being the same age and two of the youngest guys on the roster, Rick and Cooper had quickly become friends, even though they often quipped that with Cooper being from Chicago, they came from rival mafia families. Liam always thought they were only joking about being connected to the mob in some way, like maybe they were just throwing out a gimmick idea for changing up their characters. But just like when he'd recognized the Marconi name on Monday, Liam didn't ask if either of them really had a mafia connection because he had no desire to end up in a pair of cement shoes. Since they quit joking around about it when Rick quit wrestling to take over running the company from his dad, Liam had completely forgotten about the mob references without ever finding out if either of them were made men or not.

Yeah, now he knew both Rick and Cooper well enough to know he was safe to ask, even if the connections were legit. But there was no reason for him to put his foot in his mouth when Ethan was more than willing to do it for all of them.

"Wait," Ethan's eyes widened as he turned to stare at Cooper. "You're related to the mob too?"

"Are you saying you can't see the resemblance to my great-uncle Al?" Cooper sat up straighter in his seat, flattening his smile to imitate the deadpan expression seen most often on Al Capone's face in pictures, the same way he had back when they'd joked about the gimmick years ago.

"Al as in Al Capone?" Ethan's jaw dropped. "He's really your great-uncle?"

"No," Cooper laughed. "Surprisingly, most people from Chicago aren't related to mobsters."

"Neither are most people from New York," Liam pointed out, hoping to make Ethan feel a little vindicated in his original assessment of Rick's likelihood of being connected to a major mafia family.

"True," Cooper agreed. "But when I first started with the company, I thought it would make a good gimmick. Until Richard pointed out that his in-laws would find it offensive at best, and might order a hit on me at worst. So, from then on, Rick and I just joked about doing a rival mob family gimmick whenever Richard suggested something we thought was ridiculous. It was our way to make it clear that we'd rather face off with his in-laws than dress up like a turkey, or Baby New Year, or whatever other off the wall idea he had for a pay-per-view."

"Yeah, I remember how some of the gimmicks from back then seemed kinda preposterous," Liam chuckled, shaking his head. "Seeing that turkey costume, or that crazy fat suit that he claimed was for a sumo wrestler but actually looked more like a giant volleyball, made me really glad I only got stuck being a confused Irish Viking, who didn't know the Uilleann pipes can't be played while walking to the ring."

"Alright, before I start having nightmares about all the bad masked gimmicks Dad stuck me with as a teenager, let's get back to the changes I want to make to the company," Rick interjected, getting them back on topic as he turned to point at Liam. "The number one being that I want you to step into a new position I'm creating. It'll primarily be acting as a liaison between the talent and staff on tour and the corporate office in New York. Mostly, I want you to focus on getting everyone to set up more endorsement deals and charity outreach appearances, like what you're already doing for yourself. But it'll also include doing anything I can't on our breaks because I'm in Texas with the family, like what you just did with the planes, and catching anything I might have missed with adding in-house catering crews, as well as handling any issues the ground crews might have come up that I don't have time to deal with. For now, it'll be a part-time traveling position, so it won't interfere with your wrestling. Once you're ready to step away from the ring, we can make it a full-time traveling position, until Rylie's ready to quit wrestling. At that point, you'd transition to working in the corporate office as the company president, where you can physically oversee the support staff at corporate, which I'm sure you'll have to hire to help you out with everything now, and you'd have to designate someone else to be your eyes and ears on tour. You might still have to fly out to meet up with me on occasion, but eventually you'll be able to spend ninety-nine percent of your time in New York. So, what do you think? Is that a job you'd be interested in?"

"Well, yeah, but aren't you the president of the company?" Liam was flattered to think Rick trusted him to step up and partially fill his shoes, but he was also more than a little wary of his ability to fulfill all the duties Rick was laying out for him in this potential position.

"Technically, I'm the C.E.O. and C.O.O., and we don't have a company president," Rick clarified before nodding his head in the direction of the bookers. "But if the time comes that we need to settle down in one place to be able to adopt, then I'll be promoting one of these guys to the C.O.O. position to deal with everything I currently handle on tour."

Liam had to wonder if it would be Cooper or Stone, knowing they were the two bookers with the most wrestling experience. Stone had actually started wrestling for the GWA the same year Liam did. But unfortunately, a back injury ended his in-ring career after only ten years with the company. So, in 2014, after several months off for physical therapy, the Fields family rejoined the tour with Stone in his current role as a booker. Ethan, on the other hand, didn't start wrestling for the GWA until 2012, eight years after Liam and Stone, and only wrestled for five years before he had to retire from the ring because of a neck injury. After surgery to relieve the pressure on his spinal cord from herniated disks in his neck, he came back to the GWA as a booker at the end of 2017.

Probably Stone since he's been a booker the longest, even though he doesn't have as many years in the ring as Cooper. But I'm sure either one of them would do a good job.

"How are you planning to handle the tour stuff when you go on paternity leave?" Stone questioned, glancing back and forth between Rick and Liam. "Will Liam as company president act in the C.O.O. position? Or will you task one of us with stepping up to temporarily fill that role until the baby's born and you can rejoin us?"

"I'm actually hoping you'll all step up to help out with those tasks, if we're lucky enough to be successful with IVF to get to where I can take paternity leave," Rick clarified. "I would expect Caleb to handle anything to do with the networks for our weekly TV shows and the pay-per-views." Rick nodded to the head of production, who was sitting in the same seat as Liam but on the opposite side of the plane.

Then he redirected his focus to the three bookers in the center seats. "And the three of you to deal with anything to do with the arenas, wardrobe, and props for whatever gimmicks you write while I'm out."

Rick then redirected his gaze to Liam. "If he accepts the job, then Liam will handle anything the corporate office would normally report to me that doesn't fall into one of the categories I've already laid out for the rest of you, like hotel issues, problems with our catering staff and ground crews, and rerouting everyone if a show has to be cancelled or rescheduled, like we've had to do a couple of times over the years for weather issues."

Liam remembered back to when they'd had to scramble to reschedule an entire week's worth of shows, and all the talent travel arrangements for all of them, because of Hurricane Katrina. That was during Liam's second year with the company, back when they were all responsible for their own travel arrangements, and several years before the August pay-per-view became the **Sin City Showdown**, when it was permanently set in Las Vegas. So it not only affected two weeks' worth of live television shows and several house shows, it also caused one of the six highest grossing shows of the year to be completely cancelled that year. *Feck, this job sounds like it's a lot more work than just getting the rest of the guys to do more endorsement deals and charity outreach appearances, which is really just gonna be hooking them up with business managers and publicists, like the ones who work for Bradan at Murray Business Management. I hope I'm capable of handling all this extra responsibility.*

"You have the whole scheduling department at corporate to work their magic with the arenas and hotels for stuff like that, though, right?"

"Yes, but once they work their magic, then as the liaison between talent and corporate, it'll fall on you to make sure everyone else knows about the changes," Rick explained. "Plus you'll have to monitor the roadies and decide if it's necessary to call in a backup ground crew if the first one can't break everything down and get to the new city in time, like we had to do back in October. But that won't be nearly as challenging now that we have a plane for the support staff, so they won't have to try to drive across the country in less than a day."

So, it's just a matter of making the decisions, delegating the legwork, and passing along the information from corporate to the talent and staff on tour. Yeah, I can handle all that, Liam decided, smiling at Rick. "Then yeah, I'll definitely take the job. But we might need to be flexible with the timeline to transition from traveling all the time to working in the office."

"Oh?" Rick arched an eyebrow curiously. "How so?"

"I'm a newlywed, Boss. A *Catholic newlywed*," Liam stated pointedly, grinning from ear to ear at what he was implying. "I might need to work exclusively from the office a lot sooner than the two or three years I was planning to keep wrestling if we get pregnant."

"You know the Church has natural family planning classes you can take to learn how to plan when you have kids," Cooper pointed out. "Tiffany and I had to take them, so we could get married in the Church her parents attend."

"Yeah, I know," Liam nodded, hoping Rylie wouldn't be upset by him oversharing with their boss and coworkers. "We're actually already enrolled in that and the Pre-Cana classes to prepare for our Church wedding. But Rylie has a family history of P.C.O.S. and doesn't think her periods are regular enough to accurately predict when she's ovulating. So, as soon as I get my end-of-January-beginning-of-February negative test to know I've made it past the incubation period without contracting anything from my blood exposure in October, we'll have to ditch the condoms."

"Technically, as a Catholic, you're not supposed to be using condoms now," Connor pointed out.

"Yeah, you'd think," Liam chuckled, shaking his head. "But in trying to decide for herself if she agrees with me that using condoms isn't really a sin, or if she concurs with what she was taught growing up Catholic, my beautiful, brilliant bride did enough research to debate the topic with Father O'Malley and got special permission for us to keep using condoms to keep me from spreading anything I might have contracted and don't know about to her, without having to go to confession every time, at least until after that incubation period is over."

"And if you pop positive on this next test?" Rick arched an eyebrow at Liam.

"Then I'm pretty sure Rylie will go back to Father O'Malley and convince him that we have to keep using condoms and just adopt to build our family without passing anything along to her or the next generation of Connerys," Liam shrugged. "Which will mean I can transition straight to that full-time traveling position, since I won't be able to wrestle anymore, but she won't have to leave the ring behind to have our babies."

They all stared at him for several long moments before Rick finally broke the silence. "Of course, we'll work with your family situation to determine how this job needs to evolve and at what pace. But I hope you won't be too disappointed if Rylie's issues with P.C.O.S. are anything like Fiona's, and we have to go with my original timeline."

"Yeah, I'm sure I'll be a little disappointed if that's how things turn out." Liam shrugged once more. "But with both Ma and Granny praying for grandbabies, I'm hopeful we'll get a miracle and be able to conceive the old-fashioned way."

"Then I'm sure I speak for everyone in the company when I say that we hope you get your miracle," Rick smiled sadly, which Liam assumed was because he and Fiona hadn't got their miracle yet. "And I will gladly speed up that timeline if you're blessed with a baby sooner than expected."

"Thanks. And just so you know, you and Fiona have been added to Ma and Granny's baby prayer list, too."

"I'm sure Fiona will appreciate that," Rick chuckled.

Liam knew Rick wasn't really a religious man, even though he never specifically stated what he did or didn't believe. Needless to say, they all thought it was ironic that his new father-in-law was a preacher. While none of the GWA crew felt it was appropriate to officially place bets on it, they'd all stated unofficial guesses for how long it would take before Fiona and her family convinced him to go through the process of being saved and baptized in the Heart's Destiny Community Church. Unfortunately, Liam had been completely wrong in his guess that Pastor Harrison would have made it a requirement before he performed the ceremony uniting Rick with his daughter as husband and wife back in July.

"So, when are you planning this Church wedding?" Rick asked, pulling Liam from his thoughts. "And will we need to write you off TV for a week afterwards so you can go on your honeymoon?"

"Friday, May twenty-ninth," Liam replied, suddenly realizing he and Rylie hadn't discussed anything about a honeymoon. "We planned it for our Memorial Day break so we'd all have the time off, hoping you might spend the break in New York and attend. But we haven't talked about a honeymoon. Though now that I think about it, since it's on a Friday, we could take a couple of days then for our honeymoon. Maybe at a B and B in the Hamptons or the Catskills, so we can be back in the city in time for our flight out on the following Monday?"

"I guess I need to make sure our travel department knows we'll be in New York for that break instead of Texas," Rick agreed with a smile. "But you don't have to stay at a B and B. You can have our house in the Hamptons for the weekend."

"Thanks, Boss," Liam grinned. "That sounds like the perfect honeymoon plan."

Now I just have to figure out the best time to give Rylie the Claddagh wedding band I bought her back in November, so I don't have to try to keep hiding it from her until I can officially put it on her finger in May.

~~~

Rylie wasn't all that surprised when the whole GWA women's division took over the upper cabin on the plane. At first it was just the seven of them without kids, so they almost completely filled up two rows of seats in the upper cabin. They didn't want to sit too far forward, where they might be overheard by the pilots. But they also didn't want to sit too far back, where they could possibly be overheard by the kids sitting closest to the stairs in the main cabin. So, they picked rows five and six to be in the center of the upper level, thinking the flight of stairs and a door provided more soundproofing from the main cabin than just a couple of doors between them and the cockpit. As the plane taxied to the runway, they started their conversation by getting to know the two newest members to the roster, Amoura Valentine and Juno Johnson, who used the ring names Venus and Juno for their gimmick as the Goddesses. Then once they were airborne, the seat-belt lights turned off, and the announcement was made that it was safe to move about the plane, Holly and Shauna joined them, squeezing into the one empty rear-facing seat directly in front of Rylie, where they could see everyone else without having to stand up to look over the back of a seat, so they didn't miss out on any of the gossip.

"You know you can drop the armrests down to make that seat a little wider, right?" Rylie pointed out as the two women wedged into one seat. "And if Aiken feels exceptionally nice today, she can lower hers too, so you can get comfortable instead of imitating a can of sardines."

"No, how do we do that?" Holly started fiddling with the armrest that was digging into her ribs.

Rylie demonstrated by lowering the armrest between her and Teagan, answering their questions about which button was which as Aiken, Holly, and Shauna each lowered their armrests to effectively turn their two seats into a bench seat with enough space for them to sit three-wide without even having to touch one another.
~~~

"Alright, what did we miss?" Holly asked as soon as they'd adjusted the armrests so she could scoot to the middle. Instead of looking at everyone else the way Rylie expected, though, both Holly and Shauna focused in exclusively on Rylie, making it clear they wanted the juicy gossip about her and Liam.

"Just us getting to know Amoura and Juno a little better," Rylie replied, nodding to the two new female additions to the roster, where they sat across the aisle with Randi and Allissa.

"Yeah, we already got to know them when they had their try-out match last year," Shauna grinned at the two newcomers before redirecting her gaze at Rylie. "So we can skip more of that for now to get to the deets on you and Liam."

"Yeah, no offense, ladies, but you're old news already," Holly joked and winked at the tag team known as the Goddesses, who just grinned and chuckled at Holly's antics. Holly then turned back to Rylie. "Chastity, on the other hand, has some serious splainin' to do. Tell us everything about how you and Liam went from barely speaking before the break to kissing like newlyweds when you had to separate on the plane."

"I thought ya'll had to sit downstairs with your kids?" Randi Hunter arched an eyebrow at the two women wrestlers, whose children were still downstairs in the main cabin.

"Cheyenne, Sarina, and Jana are watching them for us," Shauna informed them, waving off Randi's concern. "So we can come get the deets to share later, when our kids are all occupied with the tutors."

"But I'm sure Fiona and Jax will probably take turns either asking us what we learned while they aren't busy with the kids' lessons later, or they'll corner you themselves at dinner to get more specifics," Holly added with a chuckle.

"There's not really much to tell," Rylie shrugged and quirked her lips up in a half smile. "He originally asked me to go with him to New York for the holidays, so we could meet with his attorneys on the Monday before Christmas to do the annulment. But instead, I met his entire family. Like seriously, he has such a huge family that I'm still not sure if I can remember all their names. In addition to his parents and four brothers, I met his granny and granda, six sets of aunts and uncles, like two dozen cousins, another half-dozen cousins-in-law, and eight of his cousins' kids. Oh, and all six of his cousins-in-law are pregnant, so there'll be another six kids in the family by the end of August."

"I knew he had a big family 'cause it seemed like he introduced us to a different brother or cousin every time we've had a show in New York," Holly chuckled. "But I didn't realize it was that big."

"Oh, yeah, his parents and all of their siblings each had four or five kids, and now his married cousins are well on their way to following in their parents' procreating footsteps."

"Please tell me you at least got to meet them in small groups, instead of being overrun by all of them at once like when we first met the Burlesons and half of Heart's Destiny." Shauna looked at her hopefully.

"Oh, no," Rylie laughed, shaking her head. "They were all in his house when we first got there, with Granny Breena just finishing up cooking what one of his brothers called our *wedding feast.*' And of course, at that point, his dad was the only one who knew we were planning for the annulment, so when he went outside with the guys, I had no idea how to respond to the warm, welcome-to-the-family sentiments of all the women. It actually took his cousin, Caitlyn, pointing out that I was wearing my rings on the wrong hand for me to look out the floor-to-ceiling windows separating the dining room from the pool area to see Liam had put on his wedding band. Since he'd introduced me as his wife and was wearing the ring, I assumed he wanted everyone to think we were happily married. So, I quickly moved my rings over, morphed into Chastity, and acted the part until they all finally left, like, eight hours later."

"Wait, so the guys all went outside to use the pool in December in New York?" Teagan asked incredulously, reaching over to slap Rylie's arm since they were sitting side by side. "I mean, yeah, I went swimming with Josh on our honeymoon, but we were in Bali, not freezing cold New York."

"No, they didn't go swimming, even though Liam did say his pool is heated." Rylie shook her head as she turned in her seat to face Teagan beside her.

"Yeah, I don't think I'd even want to swim in a heated pool in New York in December," Allissa shivered.

"I don't know," Aiken disagreed, wrinkling her nose in thought for a moment before smiling. "I think it'd depend on how warm the pool is kept. If it's just like the eighty-something degree water for the aqua aerobics class I took in college, then no, I'd only swim in that if it was an indoor pool. But I really enjoyed sitting in the hot tub with Brent on our deck in Lake Tahoe while it was snowing."

"Oh, yeah, hot tubs in the snow are awesome," Holly agreed, fist bumping Aiken since they were sitting side by side.

"Yes, well, Liam doesn't have a hot tub, and his pool is outside, so we didn't go swimming," Rylie interjected, getting back to the explanation about her first day in New York. "But there was barely room in his dining room for all fifteen of us women to sit for lunch, so the guys and the older kids all went out to sit at the tables set up by the pool to eat. They also had several patio heaters set up, so it was warm enough they could eat without freezing."

"And while you were sitting with all the women in his family, you had to act like ya'll are happily married?" Randi questioned from her seat across the aisle from Rylie.

"Yeah," Rylie nodded. "But then once everyone left, we talked about how we each responded to his family's questions about us earlier before going to our separate rooms for the night."

"And how did he respond?" Allissa inquired from her seat on the other side of Randi. "Did he also act like the happy hubby? Or did he start telling his family about his plan for the annulment?"

"Oh, yeah, he happy-hubbied it that whole weekend, including when we went to church the next day and his mom and granny started trying to plan our convalidation ceremony. But then once I was in the confessional, his family left, so when we came out, he spoke to the priest about doing marriage counseling to help us decide if we should stay married or get the annulment."

"So, he wasn't as adamant about the annulment as he led all of us to believe?" Teagan questioned.

"No, he wasn't," Rylie smiled sadly, remembering how stupid her husband had been in dealing with his feelings for her. "He tried to frame it as us just getting the information from Father O'Malley to annul the marriage in the Church as well as legally. But once we found out the lawyers' office was closed the whole time we were on break, so we couldn't do anything about legally ending the marriage, and we ended up making out in the wine cellar at an ugly Christmas sweater party, we actually started talking, and followed the advice

Father O'Malley gave me in the confessional, and realized that neither one of us wanted the annulment."

"Oh, you have to tell us how you ended up making out in a wine cellar before you talked it all out," Teagan insisted, slapping Rylie's leg.

"Yeah, that's because Liam's mom and granny are much more mischievous matchmakers than the ladies in Heart's Destiny. And I think his dad and granda are just as bad, but they're a little more subtle with it." Rylie chuckled before telling them all about how she and Liam got locked in the O'Donnell's wine cellar, and were subsequently caught kissing with their sweaters snagging on one another so they couldn't separate for several minutes. She also told them about the handfasting ceremonies, the talk at the pub that led to some of Liam's brothers and cousins flirting with her, and the first Pre-Cana class they attended after getting back from Atlantic City. Of course, that led to her having to tell them all about the fire in her building, meeting with the priest before they left to deal with the fallout of the fire, and the details of their trip, including the snail in the bath bomb story.

"Hold up! Wait," Amoura held up a hand in the universal symbol for stop as she tried to get her laughter under control after hearing how Rylie had freaked out so bad about what she thought was a slimy slug in her bath that she only half realized she was naked when Liam first came into the bathroom. "He comes into your bathroom while you're naked, with an erotic audiobook playing, and you didn't end up sleeping together right then and there?"

"No, we were still trying to follow Father O'Malley's advice to abstain while we were praying for our marriage," Rylie explained. "But wanting to was what led to me doing all the research to convince the priest that we didn't have to keep waiting."

"I'm still confused about how his family was so welcoming at first but then gave you bath bombs for kids as a Christmas present," Juno added, shaking her head.

"You think it was a dig because she's ten years younger than Liam?" Randi asked Juno, who only shrugged in response.

"I don't think it was intentional, even though I'm a couple years younger than even his youngest cousins." Rylie disagreed, thinking about how Caitlyn and Kelsea, who were each two years older than

Rylie, also got gift baskets with bath bombs in them on Christmas Eve, as did Kerry and all their McCarthy and Sullivan cousins-in-law. "I've bought that same brand before and always got charms for like necklaces and bracelets as the surprise inside. Even the superhero ones had charms in them. Although, they were big and plastic, instead of metal like for jewelry, more like for kids to attach to the zippers on bookbags, so I ended up clipping them on my luggage to make it easier to identify as mine in baggage claim. So, I'm sure they saw a sea breeze scented Earth bath bomb and assumed the *sea creature* inside was a dolphin shaped charm, the same way I did. Though now that I think about it, I should probably text Caitlyn and Kelsea to warn them, so they don't freak out the way I did when they use theirs and can warn Kerry and the cousins-in-law, whose numbers I don't have."

"So, it wasn't just you they gave these bath bombs to for Christmas?" Aiken surmised, arching an eyebrow at Rylie.

"No, I think one of Liam's brothers gave them to all the female cousins and cousins-in-law on their mom's side of the family, then suggested the bath gift baskets to the Connery cousins when they didn't know what to get for me. Since all the Connerys apparently only have boys and Liam is the first of them to get married, his cousins on his dad's side were all pretty clueless about shopping for women."

"Actually, his single male cousins were all pretty clueless about women in general, not just shopping for them," Rylie snorted, turning to look at Amoura and Juno. "You guys should probably be prepared for a bunch of horny Irishmen to flirt with you mercilessly the weekend of **No Remorse**, 'cause Liam's Christmas gift to his whole family is a trip to Dublin and passes to the GWA events that weekend."

"And you think they're gonna flirt with us?" Amoura asked as Juno gave Rylie an incredulous look.

"Oh, yeah, Liam's brother Finn especially," Rylie nodded and chuckled. "One of the first things he mentioned when we passed out the passes and flight information was how he couldn't wait to flirt with the GWA ladies. And when Liam warned him that all of us were married, I may have mentioned that you two were joining the roster and I thought you were single. But I also mentioned that Rick could hire several more single women between now and then, or I could be wrong about you two being single, so it wasn't like I was intentionally trying to set either of you up with Finn or any of the other Connerys."

"Uh-huh, sure," Aiken laughed, shaking her head. "You started getting some from Liam and now you're as bad as the rest of us with wanting to fix up everyone else in the company."

"Speaking of getting some," Teagan interjected, wagging her eyebrows. "When exactly did you and Liam start banging again?"

"I'm not giving you any of those details," Rylie scoffed, turning to look at her most outrageous friend.

"Oh, please, we're not asking for who was on top or how big his dick is," Holly quipped, grinning impishly. "We just need to know a date, so we know who won our betting pool."

"You guys were betting on when Liam and I would have sex?" Rylie hoped her embarrassment wasn't blatantly written all over her face.

"Of course," Shauna shrugged. "We knew you two couldn't spend almost two weeks alone at his house without getting it on, even if you still stubbornly went through with the annulment. So, what date was that ugly Christmas sweater party, since it sounds like what you did in that wine cellar counts."

"That was the first Monday we were there, the twenty-third," Rylie automatically replied, but she shook her head to make it clear it didn't really count since they didn't have sex that night, even if she did have an orgasm. "But we just kissed and, um, *rubbed on each other* to get warm and didn't even remove our clothes. So that doesn't count."

"Did you *O* from the *rubbing*? 'Cause if you did, then I think it counts." Randi pointed to Rylie's very warm face, obviously trying to indicate that her blush gave away her secrets.

"You're only saying that because you have the twenty-third in the pool," Allissa snorted. "But the bet is for when there'd be actual penetration."

"Yeah, I don't think my desperate-after-he-stole-my-rabbit O counts, since I could have come from any extra friction at that point, with or without Liam's participation, and we still weren't sure we weren't ending our marriage."

"He stole your vibrator?" Teagan screeched, way louder than the rest of them were talking. "When the hell did that happen?"

"After Allissa and Dean's bachelorette and bachelor party," Rylie confessed, pointing with her thumb at Allissa while looking the opposite direction at Teagan. "He told me he had it later that week when we started our friends-with-benefits thing, but we never got around to using it together. Then when that ended, I couldn't bring myself to ask him to return it."

"Does he still have it? Or did he finally give it back now that you're officially together?" Aiken inquired.

"Oh, yeah, he gave it back," Rylie smirked, not wanting to share the details of all the delicious things he'd done while he had her blindfolded to ring in the new year, or that he'd insisted she pack it and a few other things they could use for sensation play before rejoining the GWA. "But I'm not sharing *those* details."

"Yeah, I think we can all guess those based on the satisfied look on your face." Shauna pointed her finger at Rylie's face before moving it around in a circle.

"And our own experiences with our men and toys," Teagan added with a huge grin.

"But we still need a date when there was actual penetration, so we can settle the bet," Holly pointed out, trying to get them back to their earlier topic.

"Well, that depends," Rylie shrugged, masking her expression to appear innocent, the way she often did for her Chastity character. "Are you only counting dick-in-vajayjay as penetration? Or do fingers count?"

"They weren't on the same day?" Amoura appeared surprised as Rylie shook her head.

"Nope." Rylie popped her lips together momentarily before smiling and explaining. "Remember we were supposed to be abstaining per Father O'Malley's recommendation when we met with him before the trip to Atlantic City?"

When everyone around her nodded, she continued with a nonchalant shrug. "Well, Sunday when we got back, we decided to see if sleeping in the same bed would help banish our nightmares after the fire and snail incident. And we kinda agreed that abstaining just meant from sex, not kissing and cuddling and other stuff."

"Sunday the twenty-ninth?" Holly's expression appeared hopeful, leading Rylie to believe that was the day she'd guessed in their betting pool.

Rylie only nodded.

"I guess if you finished each other off then it still counts, even if there was no actual intercourse," Aiken offered with a sigh. "Though I still can't believe I was wrong for picking Christmas day. I thought for sure you two would give each other orgasms for your first Christmas together."

"And I told you she'd make him grovel longer than that," Teagan taunted at the same time Rylie opened her mouth to let them know that Sunday didn't count either. She quickly closed her mouth without saying a word as Teagan continued. "And she wouldn't be so cliché as to pick a specific holiday like Christmas or New Year's Day for their first time back together."

"You're right, I didn't pick a specific holiday," Rylie agreed with Teagan. "But Sunday doesn't count either, since Liam wouldn't let me reciprocate the handy and took a cold shower instead."

"Seriously?" Holly's mouth dropped open for a second. "I didn't win with the twenty-ninth?"

"Sorry, it wasn't until the next day after our first Pre-Cana meeting with our mentors and Father O'Malley," Rylie shrugged, not thinking her friends needed the details of how she'd debated with the priest to get permission to use condoms for the next few weeks before she and Liam made love again. She also didn't think they needed the details of how they'd gotten a beer and popcorn shower in the middle of their mutual climax.

"Monday the thirtieth?" Teagan asked for clarification, her expression deadpan. "That's when you finally had sex?"

"Yes," Rylie confirmed.

"Who had Monday the thirtieth?" Shauna asked, looking around at the other ladies. "Was it one of the guys? 'Cause I know they were all picking later than us or not at all."

"Nope, it was me," Teagan announced with a broad smile. "Pay up bitches! And be sure to let all your guys know they lost, too."

"I suppose you want us to let the tutors know who won the bet?" Holly arched an eyebrow at Teagan as she pulled a hundred dollar bill from the pocket in her skirt and passed it to Teagan.

Rylie only shook her head as she watched Aiken, Holly, Shauna, Randi, and Allissa each hand over Teagan's winnings.

"If you wouldn't mind," Teagan agreed, straightening the stack of bills in her hand before folding it and tucking it in her bra, instead of getting up and grabbing her purse from the overhead compartment.

"Liam and I really should get a cut of that," Rylie teased her friend.

"You can keep whatever you collect from the single guys if you're daring enough to tell them they lost," Teagan offered with a smirk.

"Oh, no, I'll leave that to you," Rylie declined, knowing the only two single guys she'd feel comfortable enough to discuss the bet with were Cameron and Harrison, since she'd become friends with them while working so closely with Protection Detail for the majority of her time in the GWA. "But I suppose it would be nice of you to extend that same offer to Amoura and Juno, since they weren't able to put in their guesses before the break."

"I think Rylie really is trying to fix us up." Juno nudged Amoura with her shoulder. "If not with one of her in-laws, then with one of the guys we've gotta work with daily."

"No, I really was just trying to make sure you feel included from day one," Rylie protested. "If I was trying to fix you up, I'd tell you to avoid the man-whores we work with and hold out for one of the Heart's Destiny hotties you'll meet whenever we go back there for another wedding."

"That could be as early as our Memorial Day break if Dion is able to convince Julie to marry him that soon," Allissa inserted with a smile. "And while we've already claimed the Hunters, and most of the Burlesons are spoken for, the Walkers and Deeres are all easy on the eyes and available."

"And most of them aren't man-whores like the rest of our single coworkers," Randi added. "Well, the single guys who've worked with us for a while anyway. I don't know if the new guys are man-whores or not."

Rylie knew she was referring to the new three-man team that had signed on with the GWA right before the holiday break, but since she didn't even remember all three of their ring names, much less know their real names, she didn't want to discuss them right then. She'd wait to form an opinion about them once they were formally introduced to everyone again and she had a chance to observe them interacting with the fans and ring rats who might catch up with them after a show in the next few weeks.

"Actually, Liam talked to Dion, and he's not planning to marry Julie until at least our Independence Day break," Rylie interjected, thinking this was as good a time as any to ask her friends to come to her and Liam's convalidation ceremony. "So, we're doing the whole Church wedding thing on May twenty-ninth, and I'd love for all of you to come to New York during our Memorial Day break to attend or possibly be in the bridal party."

"Of course, we'll be there," Teagan agreed as the other ladies chorused their yeses. "How many bridesmaids are you planning on? Or are you gonna try to stand all of us up there with you as co-matrons-of-honor?"

"Actually, Liam's best man and my matron-of-honor both have to be Catholic since it's in the Church. So, we decided to wait until we could talk to all of you to see who might meet that stipulation, and also to make sure whoever we pick for bridesmaids and groomsmen will be comfortable standing up with us, since a wedding Mass is a little different than the weddings we've attended in Heart's Destiny."

After finding out the Staffords were the only other Catholics in the company, at least according to Holly and Shauna, Rylie spent the next few minutes trying to explain to the other ladies how a Catholic Church wedding differed from the other Christian weddings they'd all had or attended in the past. *I wonder if Liam will want to ask the Staffords to stand up with us if Dion can't make it? Or would he rather just stick to asking a couple of his cousins?*

When most of the women looked uncomfortable about standing up with them when they couldn't take Communion, Rylie dropped the subject and asked Aiken and Teagan about their honeymoon trips. Thankfully, her girlfriends were able to entertain them for the rest of the flight with talk about skiing, surfing, and spa days between rounds of newlywed sex.

I just thought Liam and I were adventurous with our sensation play. But we're tame compared to Teagan and Josh on a surfboard or Aiken and Crockett in a hot tub. But maybe I can talk him into doing that hot tub thing next time we're someplace cold enough for snow. Or maybe just at a hotel with jacuzzi suites, so we don't have to worry about someone seeing us having sex outside. We can always fill our ice bucket first and use the cubes instead of snow to tease each other with the hot and cold sensations.

~~~

As Rylie and the other ladies spread out in the locker room to change into their workout clothes before their daily ringside meeting to get their match assignments for the night, Allissa surprised her, Teagan, and Aiken by handing them each a manila envelope filled with their Vegas wedding pictures. She then dug into a side pocket of her computer bag and pulled out three USB flash drives, holding them up for the ladies to see that the pivot points, where the black flash drives normally appeared as a black circle surrounded by the silver USB protector, had each been painted a different color.

"We wanted to make it easier for me to make sure you each got the right wedding video, so Mom marked these with nail polish based on your gimmick colors." Allissa handed Teagan the one marked with glittery green polish, Aiken the one marked with a pretty purple polish, and Rylie the one marked with fire engine red polish. "I'm sure you'll all want to watch them later with your hubbies, but I also brought my laptop, so maybe we could all watch them together at some point tonight, like maybe at ringside before the meeting or in catering over dinner."

"I didn't know there was video of the ceremonies," Rylie commented as she took the flash drive from Allissa. "Why didn't the chapel tell us about these or send them when they emailed the digital copies of the photos?"

"I guess the files were too big to send in an email," Allissa suggested with a shrug. "Either that, or they didn't want to take the chance that they'd end up on TV, like when they sent the pics, just in case they'd get in trouble for marrying you when you were all obviously drunk."

"Oh, God," Teagan groaned, holding up her flash drive and looking at it as if she could see the video on it without plugging it into a computer. "Is it that obvious how drunk we were?"
~~~

"Oh, no, I don't know." Allissa held her hands up as if she was being robbed. "I haven't watched the videos. I didn't feel right about seeing the weddings before any of you, so I trusted Mom and Kandi to check the files to figure out how to mark the drives, since they were there to see your ceremonies in person."

"Well, now I feel like we should go ahead and watch them now," Aiken huffed. "'Cause I don't think I'll be able to wait until dinner time to find out how much of a train wreck our wedding ceremonies were. And as soon as Brent knows we have video of them, he's gonna wanna see it, too."

"Then I'll bring my computer to ringside now," Allissa offered with a wry smile. "Mom said you and Crockett got married first, so we should start with your video, even if we don't have time to get to the other two before dinner time."

"How about you just hold onto the flash drives until after we watch them?" Rylie suggested, extending the hand still holding hers out to Allissa. "That way we're not trying to each keep track of them during our match run-throughs."

"Yeah, I can do that," Allissa agreed, taking back all three flash drives and putting them in the side pocket of her computer bag.

Rylie put the manila envelope of her and Liam's pictures in her locker and finished changing into her workout clothes before joining the rest of the roster at ringside. Before Allissa could pull out her computer and start the videos, Rick started the meeting by reintroducing the newest members of the roster.

"For anyone who didn't meet them when they did their try-out matches last year, I want to start by reintroducing the performers joining us today. Juno Johnson and Amoura Valentine, also known as the tag team 'The Goddesses' and individually as Juno and Venus, had their try-out match back in October. And the three-man faction known as 'The Celestial Bodies,' Kaleb 'Quasar' Miller, Ryker 'Pulsar' Wilson, and Zane 'Blazar' Brown, signed on last month just before our break. They'll all be working as heels, eventually, but the Goddesses will start out more as tweeners until we start their feud with the Precious Stones, or the Stone Family as the four of them will be referred to when they reunite as faces starting in March."

"I also want to let you ladies know that if the women we have scheduled for tryouts in January work out to join the roster, then I'm planning to unveil women's division tag-team titles at the ***Saint Valentine's Day Massacre*** show and announce a tournament to crown the inaugural champions at ***No Remorse***." Rick went on to let them know that in addition to the five women he had scheduled to tryout in January, he was still looking for another babyface men's tag team and a few more men under two-hundred-and-twenty-five pounds, so he could bring back the lightweight title that had been quite prominent when the GWA was first started.

I guess that explains why he added so many seats on the plane. He's planning to accommodate all these new additions to the roster and their families. If the ten people he's planning to hire are all married with kids, he could theoretically add forty or more people who have to ride in the plane with us.

Rick also gave them a general overview of the booking plans leading into the ***Saint Valentine's Day Massacre*** show on February ninth. In addition to the current plan for Liam to keep teaming with Blade as the tag-team champions until Blade jobbed to Protection Detail at ***Massacre*** to lose the titles, so Liam could claim that he had to be the one pinned to lose Chastity's managerial services since they were married, Rylie also paid special attention to the plans for the GWA heavyweight championship and women's division championship, since those matches at ***Massacre*** would be pivotal for her and Liam's future angles.

With Crusher Cooper still holding the heavyweight title, the plan was to have him job to Vaughn Valor at ***Massacre*** in a loser-must-retire match to set him up to transition to booking full time. And the current women's division champion, Victoria Vicious, would also job to Shauna Valor at ***Massacre***, so it would appear that the babyfaces all went over at the Valentine's-themed show. But then in a twist to swerve the fans, the previously babyface Valors would set up their heel turn by declaring themselves the king and queen of the GWA, who were suddenly too haughty to associate with the commoners who previously cheered for them. As Chastity was supposed to insist her husband cut back on his underhanded tactics if he wanted her to keep managing his career, it would set them up for Liam Red to turn face to appease his wife and challenge the now heel Vaughn Valor for the heavyweight title with Chastity challenging Shauna for the women's division title.

Finally, just before giving them each their match assignments for that night, Rick announced to the rest of the company that Liam would be taking on the role as the company president. While he would still wrestle at first, he'd also be the official liaison between the GWA talent and corporate office to help all of them capitalize on their fame with endorsement deals and give back to their fans with charitable appearances. Liam had told her about the job on their drive from the airport to the hotel, apologizing for not talking to her about it before accepting the position. At first, she'd kind of been surprised that he hadn't at least mentioned it to her before making the decision. But when he told her about how flexible Rick was with the location of the job so they weren't locked into traveling for so many years before settling in New York to build their family, it seemed like a no brainer to her. If their roles were reversed, she would have taken Rick up on the offer immediately too.

"Any questions before I turn over the ring so you can start running through your matches for tonight?" Rick looked around at the performers sitting at ringside and staring at him where he was seated on the ring apron.

"Not really a question about the company or tonight's show," Allissa replied, holding up her hand where she grasped the three flash drives. "But I have the Vegas wedding videos that my mom picked up back in August, since she finally got all her stuff moved and unpacked now that she's living in Heart's Destiny. And I'm sure I'm not the only one who wants to see them before I pass them along to the couples they rightfully belong to, so I wondered if you might wanna play them on the jumbotron instead of us all crowding around my computer."

"Oh, absolutely," Rick agreed with the biggest grin Rylie had ever seen on their boss's face. "Caleb, if you'll take care of cuing those up for us, while I text my wife to let everyone else know to come to ringside for the show."

It took a few minutes for Caleb Quinn, the head of production, to take the flash drives from Allissa to the AV booth and for Fiona to bring Jax, all the moms, and the older kids down to the ring, so they could all watch the videos.

"Why do I have a feeling this is going to be extremely embarrassing?" Liam wrapped his arm around Rylie's shoulders as they settled into a couple of ringside seats facing the jumbotron, instead of staying where they'd been sitting facing the side of the ring, getting comfortable to watch their wedding for the first time.

"Oh, it's definitely going to be embarrassing," Josh chuckled self-deprecatingly as he took Teagan's hand.

"Before we start playing the videos, I say we need to place bets on who looks the drunkest and which couple's first kiss is the most inappropriate for a wedding," Dane Bennington suggested with a smirk.

"Josh and Emerald," several of their coworkers chorused in unison, obviously thinking the most openly affectionate couple would be the ones to make out like teenagers while standing at the altar.

"Oh, yeah, we'll definitely take first place in that competition," Teagan chortled. "But I'm betting Chastity looks the drunkest, since she's a total lightweight when it comes to taking shots."

"Wait, are you saying the Vegas weddings aren't just a work for TV?" Kaleb Miller, one of the new additions to the roster, looked around at the group and seemed to finally notice that the Connerys, Crocketts, and Parkers had paired off to watch their weddings with their spouses, instead of moving to sit with their opponents for the night to start planning their matches.

"Oh, no, we all got married that night," Crockett clarified for the group while squeezing Aiken to his side. "We just didn't know it for a couple of months because Victoria's mom challenged us to a drinking contest and we got so drunk we still don't remember the actual ceremonies."

Before anyone else could put in their two cents to make either of the bets official, the first video appeared on the jumbotron, causing everyone to stop talking and pay attention as Elvis Presley's **Can't Help Falling In Love** started playing while Crockett and Amethyst walked down the aisle together. Aiken wobbled a little in her heels, but Brent steadied her as soon as they reached the Elvis impersonator acting as their officiant. As they said their vows, it wasn't obvious either of them were blackout drunk as they clearly took it seriously enough to focus so they didn't even slur a single word. Even the extra "I love you, Princess," Brent added to the vows was loud and clear, making him appear perfectly sober. But then again, the camera angle was far enough back that it wasn't clear how glossy their eyes were from their earlier imbibing.

When they went to exchange rings, they had to pause for a moment so Aiken could take the plastic spacer Rylie wore on her dad's ring off before putting it on Brent's hand. She then handed him the spacer to put on Rylie's mom's rings before he slid them on Aiken's hand. They finished the ceremony with a perfectly polite, chaste kiss as they were declared husband and wife. Then they posed for several pictures at the altar before walking back up the aisle to the same Elvis song that had played for their processional.

When they got to the end of the aisle, where Rylie, Liam, Teagan, and Josh were waiting their turns, Aiken and Brent took off the rings and passed them to Teagan and Josh. The video cut off just as Josh pulled the plastic spacer off Rylie's mom's rings. But they didn't miss what happened next, as the next video started with Josh handing the spacer over to Rylie, so it wouldn't be lost before she could put it back on her dad's ring when all their ceremonies were over.

The music changed to *All Shook Up* for Josh and Teagan to take their turn walking down the aisle hand in hand. After the Elvis impersonator gave his opening remarks, Josh interrupted to ask if they could say some of their own vows in addition to the standard ones the officiant would have them recite.

"Uh huh huh," fake Elvis replied in character, causing a few of their coworkers to chuckle around them.

The Josh on the screen turned to Teagan, holding both her hands in his as he started them off with alternating statements of their personal vows. "Emerald, Teagan, my love, I vow to spend at least an hour every day watching crime shows with you."

"Oh, I'm gonna hafta start holding you to that," Teagan snorted from a few seats over, just as the drunk version of her on the screen slightly slurred, "Josh, my Joshy-Josh, I vow to go watch you every time you get the chance to surf, even though I have no desire to get in the ocean and ruin my hair."

"Aren't you glad I found a way you can surf without ruining your hair?" Josh leaned over and pecked a kiss on Teagan beside him, just as on-screen Josh continued their vows. "I promise to sex you up so good that you won't ever have to complain about there not being any hot male ring rats ever again."

"And I promise to go full Emerald Stone on any of the ring rats who think it's okay to hit on you, making it clear that you're mine and I don't share," on-screen Teagan added.

"And I promise to never even look at another ring rat, so you won't have to use any of the stuff you learned about how to dispose of a body where it can't be found," on-screen Josh vowed with a smirk.

"And I promise to fuck you so often and so good that you won't ever be at risk of breaking that vow."

"Maybe we should have screened this before allowing the kids to come watch it," Rick quipped from where he sat on the ring apron with his wife and daughter.

"Hey Boss, maybe you should have included a swear jar in the upgrades to the plane," Taylor Olson, who used the ring name Tank, suggested with a grin.

Rylie missed the other personal vows Josh and Teagan made because several of their coworkers debated on where Tank could stuff his swear jar. Rick shushed them just as the officiant began the standard vows (well, the standard vows for an Elvis-inspired wedding), which Teagan and Josh completed with only minor slurring to show they might be a little drunk.

Once they exchanged rings, Josh dipped Teagan back, kissing her to seal their union much more passionately than Aiken and Crockett had at the end of their ceremony. Then they posed for a few pictures at the altar before finally walking back down the aisle to the same song they'd used a few minutes earlier, passing the rings back over to Rylie and Liam just as their video cut off.

The final video started with a shot of Liam and Rylie clutched in a kiss so passionate that it put Teagan and Josh's kiss to shame. Rylie had her arms around Liam's neck and her legs around his waist, while he held her up with both hands squeezing her butt. The way they were gyrating made it clear they weren't just kissing.

Holy…wow! I can't believe we were dry-humping in the chapel before we even got to the altar to get married. Rylie was mortified that everyone in the GWA was witnessing their outrageous public display. *That's PDA that neither one of us would've done with an audience if we weren't drunk.*

Leah Mae Wright

"I can't believe we were all wrong about who would have the most inappropriate kiss," Dean Hunter joked as several of the parents covered their kids' eyes.

Love Me Tender started playing, but it still took Crockett slapping Liam on the back and saying, "That's your cue to walk down the aisle," for them to break the kiss and start to actually walk toward the imposter Elvis officiant.

Instead of holding hands like the other couples had, Liam and Rylie each kept an arm wrapped around the other, with Liam's around Rylie's shoulders and Rylie's around Liam's waist. As they swayed their way down the aisle, they took turns slurring out "I love you" to one another, almost tripping more than once from looking at each other instead of where they were going as they repeated the words over and over.

"I can't believe Liam looks as drunk as Rylie," Dean's wife, Allissa, chuckled.

"Feck, Moh Graw, I'm sorry," Liam leaned over and whispered in her ear to apologize, as the others debated which of them appeared to be the drunkest and the officiant started their ceremony on the screen. "I've been trying to think of some way to make it special the first time I told you I love you. And now I feel bad that I thought I should wait until we get to Vegas tomorrow to say it the first time in the honeymoon suite, since it won't actually be the first time."

"Oh, Liam." Rylie turned in her seat to look into her husband's green and gold eyes, thinking this was the perfect time and place for them to each hear those three little words from one another for the first time, especially since as recently as the previous week, she'd doubted he'd ever allow himself to feel more than friendship for her. "Finding out we both shared those special words on our wedding night is perfect. And considering our careers, sitting ringside seems pretty special for us to say it again for the first time that we remember it. I love you, Liam."

"I love you, too, Rylie." Liam bent down and kissed her, not quite as passionately as their drunk counterparts kissed on the jumbotron to seal their union after saying their vows, but still more ardently than was truly appropriate for their current audience.

We'll have to watch this again in our room later, Rylie decided when she realized that they'd talked and kissed over their ceremony and didn't really see it.

After catcalls from their coworkers broke their kiss, Liam made a perfect suggestion, grinning at her while speaking loud enough everyone else could hear him. "Hey, guys, since we're in Vegas tomorrow, whaddya say we have a do-over of our weddings? Complete with tuxes, bridal gowns, all our own rings, and actually standing up with each other in a triple ceremony the way it shoulda been, instead of loitering at the back of the room while waiting for our turn to say 'I do,' like it's three separate weddings."

Rylie loved that idea, looking over to the other two couples to confirm they were on board before nodding her head in agreement.

"I'll just have to call Papa to bring my dress," Aiken agreed, as Caleb brought the flash drives back to Allissa, who passed them out to the three couples.

"I know it's way too short of notice for him to design dresses for us and get them made," Teagan pointed out, looking hopefully over at Aiken. "But do you think he might use his contacts to help us find our wedding dresses in time for a ceremony after the show tomorrow night?"

"Absolutely!" Aiken squealed, nodding so fast she looked a little like a bobblehead. "Papa will love helping make our wedding re-do perfect. In fact, he'll probably want to pick the guys' tuxes too. Though don't be surprised if he and Daddio insist on walking us all down the aisle at the same time."

Rylie wasn't sure they'd fit walking down the aisle five-wide, but she was happy to be included in letting the Hollywood fashion designer dress them for their first vow renewal. *And if the dress is too risqué for our Church wedding, then maybe I'll just wear it again for the TV vow renewal Rick approved for the three of us in August and let Cathleen and Breena pick my dress for the convalidation ceremony in May.*

Chapter Fourteen

As he put on the black shirt to match the tuxedo Shawn Pearson had declared "perfection" that afternoon, Liam second guessed his decision to surprise Rylie with the Claddagh wedding band when he put it on her finger during their Vegas vow renewal. While he firmly believed they needed to exchange their own rings and save her parents' rings to pass down to their children, he worried that he should have talked to her about the rings beforehand, instead of surprising her in the middle of the ceremony in front of everyone in the GWA.

I probably should have mentioned this when she gave me her mom's rings on the way to the chapel, when I could have just suggested she move them to her right hand right before walking down the aisle. But no, I had to keep the fact that we have matching bands a surprise right up to the point I'm putting it on her finger.

Feck, I probably should have double-checked that I bought the correct size before now too. 'Cause if I try putting a different ring on her hand that's too small, she's probably going to be upset and think I lost her mom's rings. No, I can fix that by putting her mom's rings on her right hand first, so she knows I've kept them safe and sound.

When she'd put his ring on her left thumb in the car as they swapped rings, he'd put her mom's rings on his pinky, even though they were only able to slide a little past the most distal joint on his much larger finger and looked quite ridiculous on him. As soon as he'd stepped into the changing room, he'd removed the rings and put them in the box with her Claddagh band.

Feck! What was I thinking? I have her rings that fit, so I can check to see if they're the same size as the band now. And if so, then I'll put her mom's rings on her right hand and the new band on her left during the ceremony. But if the band isn't the right size, then I can just use her mom's rings again until I can get the band resized.

Liam quickly pulled the box from the pocket of his tuxedo jacket, where he'd put it as soon as he'd put her rings in it, and was thrilled to verify that he'd bought the correct size ring back in November. Back when he bought the ring, he'd had a vague flash of memory of the ladies talking about ring sizes before their first wedding, and picked the size he thought he remembered her saying her mom's rings were back then. But until he saw that he had the correct size ring, he still wasn't sure those flashes of memory were anywhere near accurate and was afraid he might have fallen prey to his faulty memory and bought a ring that would fit one of the other girls who'd been talking about their ring sizes at the time. He quickly put the box back in his jacket pocket before picking up his black tie and slipping it around his neck to finish dressing for the ceremony.

"How'd you manage to get to wear a regular tie and not a bow tie like us?" Crockett questioned as he struggled to tie his purple bow tie.

"And why don't you have a red tie and vest to go with your gimmick colors?" Josh added as he tied on his green bow tie.

"Because I told Shawn that I'm planning on wearing this same tux for our Church wedding in May," Liam explained as he finished tying his black tie much faster than either of the other guys. "And I may have mentioned that Ma and Granny explicitly vetoed red as one of our wedding colors, since it apparently clashes with Rylie's favorite color, so black everything ensures I won't clash with whatever they choose for the bridesmaids' dresses and groomsmen's ties. And by not choosing to wear a vest now, I'm leaving them the option of picking a different colored vest and bow tie if they decide they want me to match the rest of the bridal party."

He still wasn't exactly sure if mauve was more pink or more purple, since Rylie picked out several options in the dress catalogues his ma had brought to breakfast on New Year's Day for them to narrow down the options for the bridesmaids' dresses. All he knew was that it was Rylie's favorite color, so he'd happily wear a mauve vest and tie if that's what his wife wanted for their wedding, even if she decided the groomsmen should wear the sage green accessories that she thought went best with mauve to make up their wedding color scheme.

"Speaking of your bridal party, Teagan said something about your best man and matron of honor needing to be Catholic," Josh pointed out as he put on his emerald green vest. "And that the rest of the bridal party won't be able to take Communion if they aren't Catholic. So, I guess that means you won't be asking any of us to stand up with you in May?"

"Yeah, that's one of the reasons I suggested this re-do of our Vegas weddings," Liam admitted with a sigh, as he put on his tuxedo jacket. "'Cause I really want us to all stand up for each other, even if Rick changes the booking plans and we don't have a triple ceremony in the ring on our one-year anniversary."

"So, who are you going to have stand up with you for your Church wedding?" Crockett asked as he too put on his tuxedo jacket.

"We're going to have my married cousins for our bridal party then," Liam informed them of the current plan he and Rylie discussed the night before. "Well, maybe, some of them anyway. Since they're the cousins I was closest to growing up, I'd probably pick Sully and Riordan and their wives to keep the bridal party small, instead of having all six of my married cousins and their wives taking up all the space at the front of the church. But with them expecting babies in May and June, I doubt they'll be able to stand up with us through the whole Mass to be in the bridal party."

"But you still have four other cousins whose wives aren't pregnant, though, right?" Josh eyed him curiously. "So you still have options for picking two couples to keep the bridal party smaller?"

"Oh, no," Liam laughed, shaking his head. "They're all expecting between May and August. So, Ma's planning to talk to all of them and see who'll be the farthest from their due date. Rylie thinks that'll be Kiernan and Cianna, which serves them right for picking the cord that represents fertility during the handfasting we did on Christmas Eve. But if it's not possible for any of them to do it, then we'll probably go with my brother Quinn and cousin Caitlyn as the best man and maid of honor and leave it at that."

When both men looked at him like he'd grown a second head, Liam explained the Celtic Handfasting ritual and told them about the two handfastings his family insisted they had to do while they were home for Christmas. He also explained how those handfastings felt like weddings and made his union with Rylie seem more tangible, since their official wedding back in August didn't seem real until they saw the video the day before.

"And I thought Teagan was a little over the top with wanting to renew our vows now, in the middle of the ring in August, and whenever we do our reception and stuff in Heart's Destiny, so we'd basically have four weddings. But you've already done two extra renewals, so tonight will be like your fourth wedding. And you're still planning to do a fifth, for sure, and possibly a sixth and seventh?"

Liam shrugged and smiled. "I'd happily marry Rylie every day for the rest of my life if that's what it takes to show her how much I love her. So why not have as many ceremonies as she wants?"

"Great, now we have to come up with times to do three more ceremonies, too," Crockett groused, throwing up his hands in frustration. "'Cause after doing our ancestry stuff over the break, Aiken has started studying more of her Vietnamese culture and now considers the number four unlucky."

"So, we'll skip the renewal in Heart's Destiny and just do a reception there," Josh suggested. "That way you won't have to worry about her feeling unlucky between the fourth renewal and whenever you can schedule a fifth."

"Yeah, you'd think that'd work," Crockett huffed, pacing around the room. "But I know my wife better than that. Three isn't a significant number, but seven is like sacred or something, so having seven weddings would be like finding the Holy Grail."

Crockett continued stalking around the room while running his hands through his long hair anxiously. "Okay, I can add another wedding in L.A., which will thrill her dads, so they can invite all their Hollywood friends. And maybe I can get Dad to plan something in Portland next time we go through there. Now I just need one more."

"Um, since she's been studying her Vietnamese culture, maybe you can talk Rick into giving you a couple of days off while we're in Southeast Asia, so you can go find someplace special in the city where she was born to recite your vows to one another, even if you can't throw together a full wedding on short notice," Liam suggested, hoping to ease his friend's anxiety before they had to walk down the aisle in a few minutes.

"Yeah, that could work," Crockett agreed, seeming to relax somewhat. "And even if we can't get to Vietnam on this South Pacific and Southeast Asia tour, maybe we can convince Rick to add a show there for the next one."

With that issue somewhat settled, they all made sure they had everything they needed to go out and meet with the officiant, who only went by Elvis to stay in character, and get into their positions to begin the ceremony. Since they weren't walking down the aisle with their spouses this time, they couldn't use the same three songs for the same couples that they'd used back in August. So, they opted to rearrange the songs, playing **All Shook Up** as the men walked into the chapel, **Can't Help Falling In Love** as the women were escorted down the aisle by Aiken's dads, and **Love Me Tender** as they walked back down the aisle in pairs after the triple ceremony.

Liam couldn't believe they'd seriously picked the Elvis theme for their first wedding, knowing none of them were true fans of the iconic rocker who'd died before any of them were even born. But as he followed the other two Vegas grooms down the aisle, he supposed the re-do with the same gimmick seemed apropos.

I guess it would be kinda weird to have a more traditional wedding in Vegas, since this is where people come to specifically have an Elvis impersonator do the honors instead of a priest.

When the music changed for the ladies to walk in on Aiken's dads' arms, he barely noticed how Aiken was flanked by her dads with Teagan on Shawn's other arm to her right and Rylie on Theo's other arm on her left. He only had eyes for his beautiful bride, and honestly couldn't see what any of the other four people walking down the aisle with her were wearing. Rylie took his breath away in what almost looked like a traditional wedding gown with a long train and veil.

Holy feck! She totally Vegased-up the top half of that dress.

While there were layers upon layers of lace making up the skirt of the dress, the veil, and even lace half-sleeves that covered from her wrists to her biceps, the corset-style top of the dress looked like something he'd expect to see on one of the showgirls Vegas was known for. Her copper complexion popped against all that white lace, drawing his eyes directly to her bountiful breasts, especially since they weren't completely covered.

Now I understand why she said she won't be able to wear this dress for our Church wedding.

Feck! With at least a third of her tits showing over the top and between the laces of that corset, Rick might not even let her wear that for our in-ring vow renewal because it's too risqué for GWA TV.

Not that he minded her showing off just a little, since she had the most perfect round breasts he'd ever seen. And honestly, the dress covered more than the bikini she'd worn over the summer, so he didn't think it was too revealing for anywhere other than inside the Catholic Church.

"You're a true vision, Mo Ghrá." Liam couldn't stop himself from enjoying the up close view of his wife as the officiant started the ceremony by welcoming everyone.

"We are gathered here today to renew the vows of Brent and Aiken, Josh and Teagan, and Liam and Rylie. If there are any ***Suspicious Minds*** here today, ***It's Now or Never*** to speak up. Their love won't wait."

While Elvis's words elicited a few chuckles from the audience, obviously nobody objected, so Elvis quickly transitioned into the ceremony. "Brent, Josh, and Liam, are you ready to take Aiken, Teagan, and Rylie as your brides? Do you promise to love her tender, love her sweet, and always be her loving ***Teddy Bear***?"

"Yes. I do," the three men chorused in unison.

"Then repeat after me," Elvis crooned. "I promise to never step on your ***Blue Suede Shoes***, or treat you like a ***Fool***."

Liam, Josh, and Crockett all repeated the first vow before the officiant continued. "I promise to never leave you in ***Heartbreak Hotel***, or treat you like ***You're the Devil in Disguise***."

Again, they repeated the Elvis impersonator's words before he gave them the next line.

"I promise to always be your ***Puppet on a String*** and give you everything I've got to make our lives together ***Viva Las Vegas***."

Since the chapel was full to capacity with all the GWA talent and their families attending, the three couples opted not to say their own vows. They didn't want to take a chance on Josh and Teagan repeating the same ones from their first wedding with the younger kids present, so once the officiant finished having the men say their "I do's" and repeat their Elvis-song-themed vows, Liam leaned down and whispered in Rylie's ear, "And I promise to protect you from all things slimy, including but not limited to snails, slugs, leeches, and snakes, both human and reptile.”

Rylie's grin widened in response, making him curious about what she planned to add to her Elvis-song-themed vows, since he didn't think her previous vow to protect him from overzealous ring rats was appropriate in case any of the kids could hear them. Thankfully, he didn't have to wait long for the women to take their turn saying “I do” when asked if they took the men as their husbands and repeating the Elvis imposter's words. Rylie finished her vows by pushing up on her toes to whisper in his ear, “And since you just vowed to be my 'loving teddy bear,' I promise to have your grandparents teach me how to say 'teddy bear' in Irish, so I have an Irish endearment to call you whenever you call me Mo Ghrá.”

Liam thought for a minute, trying to remember what his granda had taught him as a child. If he remembered correctly, there were multiple Irish Gaelic words for bear, depending on the type of bear being discussed, so he tried to remember which one his granny used when talking about a small stuffed toy and not the actual animal. “Teidí béirín,” he blurted when the memory came back to him, smiling at his wife. “I think. It's been a while since I've had to use either of those words, so you might wanna double check with Granda and Granny.”

“Is he translating their vows to Irish?” Liam wasn't sure which of the new guys commented, but he was pretty sure he must have supersonic hearing to have overheard him from the middle of the chapel. “That's some serious commitment to living the gimmick.”

Thankfully, fake Elvis talked over the chuckles of their coworkers as he talked about how the rings they were about to exchange were symbols of belonging to each other's hearts. Not waiting to be told when to put the rings on each other's hands, Liam pulled out the box from his pocket and took out her mom's rings without letting her see the Claddagh ring before closing the box and putting it back in his pocket. He then placed Rylie's mother's rings on her right ring finger.

“Um, Liam, aren't you supposed to wait and put these on the other hand when Elvis tells you to?” Rylie barely hissed the words, looking up at him with wide eyes.

“No, Mo Ghrá,” Liam whispered back, smiling as he released her right hand, took the box back out of his pocket, and finally pulled the Claddagh ring from the box, holding it up for her to see while putting the box back in his pocket. "I want you to be able to pass your parents' rings down to one of our children in about thirty years, which means you need a different ring to show we're married, so you don't have to remove the symbol of our love whenever our son or daughter wants to use your parents' rings for their wedding. And since it's a symbol of our love, I figured you need a ring that matches mine."

"Gentlemen, place the rings on your brides' left hands and repeat after me," the Elvis impersonator directed. "I give you this ring as a symbol of my hunk, a hunk of *Burning Love* for you."

"I give you this ring as a symbol of my hunk, a hunk of *Burning Love* for you," Liam repeated with a chuckle as he spun the ring around so he could place it on her finger with the tip of the heart facing her hand and the crown facing her finger. Even though it was a band with the Claddagh design carved into the gold instead of a more traditional Claddagh ring, he still wanted to make sure it was worn in the proper direction to show she was married and not just engaged.

Since he'd told her about the significance of how a Claddagh ring was worn when he handed her his in the car, Rylie also made sure to spin his ring around when she removed it from her thumb and placed it on his finger, reciting the same words as directed by Elvis.

Once they'd exchanged rings, the officiant continued speaking. "Now by the powers vested in me by the state of Nevada, I now re-pronounce you husbands and wives. You may each kiss your spouse."

Liam pulled Rylie into his arms, dipping his head down to kiss his bride. It took all his willpower to keep it mostly chaste, even though he really wanted to recreate the first kiss he wished he'd remembered from their first wedding night after seeing it on video the day before.

"Remember, you can't *Return to Sender*. And sometimes, *A Little Less Conversation*, a little more action can help solve all your marital conflicts." Elvis's words caused both of them to chuckle, effectively breaking the kiss before it got out of hand.

"It is my honor to present to you, Mr. and Mrs. Crockett, Mr. and Mrs. Parker, and Mr. and Mrs. Connery. Thank you. Thank you very much."

The photographer asked them to each pose for their first official couples' photos before *Love Me Tender* started playing for them to walk back down the aisle, which they did in the same order they'd gotten married back in August.

Now we get to enjoy that honeymoon suite, Liam thought, glad he'd made that change to their reservation, even though he no longer needed it for his original plan to make their first time saying "I love you" to one another special. *And our "I love you's" tonight will be just as special as they were yesterday, both at ringside and once we got to the hotel after the show.*

~~~

While Rylie had fun at the small reception after their ceremony at the chapel, and appreciated Aiken's dads surprising them all with three cakes and a champagne toast for each of the Vegas couples, she was really glad to finally get in the limo to head back to the hotel with her husband. She couldn't wait to have a re-do of their wedding night once they got to the honeymoon suite Liam had reserved for them. *At least, now I know better than to start the sexual part of our celebration in the stairwell, so we won't take any chances on making another risqué video when Windy and Kandi aren't here to make sure it gets erased, like they did last time. But then again, if our stairwell escapades were half as hot as I dreamed they were, maybe I should ask Liam if he might want to recreate them against the wall in our room?*

"What are you thinking about, Mrs. Connery?" Liam eyed her curiously as he opened the bottle of champagne waiting for them in the limo.

"Just remembering the dream I had right before I woke up the day after our first wedding," Rylie admitted, hoping it was dark enough that he couldn't see how hot her cheeks felt. "Which I think might not have all been a dream."

"Oh? You think you remember something we did that night?"

"I don't think I really remember what we actually did. It's more like I was just dreaming about how far I wished we'd have gone in the stairwell while on our way up to our rooms." Rylie half shrugged as she held up the two empty champagne flutes.

"So, this was after the chapel?" Liam questioned as he poured them each a glass from the bottle of Dom Perignon.
~~~

"Yeah, right before I woke up the next morning, so part of it could have been what actually happened when we got back to the hotel after getting married, but I'm sure we didn't actually go as far in real life as we did in my sleep-fogged fantasy. In my dream, we couldn't wait to go back to our separate rooms and pack up to move to the honeymoon suite, so we consummated the marriage in the stairwell. Then we fixed our clothes and went up to the floor where our rooms were, kissing once more before going to pack our things. But I woke up before I dreamed, or remembered, actually going into my room."

Rylie clinked her glass with Liam's and took a big gulp for the liquid courage to continue telling him what she thought actually happened. "But since I wasn't sore…" She trailed off as she looked down at her lap. "…you know, down there, when I woke up the next morning, I think I only dreamed that we had sex in the stairwell. Especially since Windy and Kandi said they only saw us kissing and dry-humping, and only my boobs were exposed when they were in the security room with their friend Chuck."

"Windy, Kandi, and their friend Chuck all saw your boobs that night?" Liam's eyes widened right before he downed his entire flute of champagne.

"Yeah, on the security cameras, where they were watching to make sure we all got to our rooms okay." Rylie had heard of seeing red when getting angry, but apparently Liam also turned beet red as he squeezed the glass in his hand until the stem broke off the bottom of the vessel. Hoping to alleviate his anger, Rylie quickly added, "But Windy told me she made Chuck delete the video as soon as we were back in our rooms. So we don't have to worry about it ever leaking to CNZ."

"When did you talk to Windy about that night?" Liam placed the two large pieces of his now broken glass in the small wastebasket in the cabinet beneath the built-in bar. Then he grabbed a napkin, dipping it in the ice bucket to get it wet before brushing it over his tux to pick up any slivers of glass that might have fallen when he broke the champagne flute. Once he was satisfied that there were no stray pieces of glass that might cut one of them, he discarded the wet napkin in the same wastebasket.

"The morning of Allissa and Dean's wedding," Rylie replied, taking another gulp from her glass before telling him the whole story.

"While we were getting our nails done, we were talking about how it was Crockett who first suggested actually getting married, and how Teagan and Josh were groping each other in the limo, when Kandi said something about how you might have been the last one to say you wanted to really get married so we could use the angle between Red Velvet and Protection Detail to keep everyone from getting in trouble for the pictures, but the way we were making out the rest of the night made it clear that wasn't the only reason you wanted to marry me. Only she worded it to make it sound like we were on the verge of earning a public indecency charge, which freaked me out a little, until Windy backtracked for her to say we were just leaning on each other getting in and out of the limo and didn't kiss until it was time for the ceremony in the chapel."

"Then someone changed the subject to what Kay needs to know about each of us for writing her books, so she can be accurate when describing the sex scenes, like with the piercings in *Claiming Carlita*," Rylie continued until Liam interrupted her.

"I haven't read that book yet, so I don't know what piercings you're talking about," Liam pointed out.

"Yeah, Micah, the male main character in *Claiming Carlita* has his dick pierced," Rylie elaborated, wondering if she needed to explain that the fifth book in Kay's *Devine* series was loosely based on Charlotte Burleson and Ian Campbell. "And apparently, Kay got that idea based on a suggestion Charlotte made for piercing one of Ashlyn's products before anyone knew she was seeing Ian."

"Yeah, maybe I shouldn't read any more of Kay's books," Liam shuddered. "I really don't need to know if any of my friends have pierced dicks."

"Technically, we don't know if Ian's dick is pierced or not, since Charlotte hasn't confirmed it. We just know that Kay based the description for that book dick on the pierced dildo Ashlyn now sells for her It's My Pleasure business. And when we were asked if there were any special characteristics we wanted mentioned in our books, other than her standard description of long and thick, Teagan and I both said that her typical depiction worked fine for you and Josh." Rylie paused and took a deep breath before continuing. "But that's when Kandi pointed out that she and Windy couldn't vouch for you on that, but they could say that my boobs are the most perfect natural tits they've ever seen because they saw them on the security video in the stairwell on our wedding night."

"They're not wrong about that," Liam snorted, pointedly looking down at her chest. "I just hate that their friend and who knows how many other security guards saw them, too."

"Yeah, me too," Rylie sighed. "But when I asked exactly what they saw, since at the time I thought it was only a dream and couldn't possibly be memories trying to come back, they told me that you were fully dressed the whole time and had only pulled down the front of my dress and bra to fondle them while we were dry-humping against the wall in the stairwell. Then Teagan pulled me aside, while Aiken started talking to Kay about Crockett being uncircumcised, to make sure I was okay."

Rylie had to stifle a chuckle at the way Liam cringed when she shared a little too much information about their friends. Since Liam wasn't circumcised either, she didn't see what the big deal was about mentioning he wasn't the only one of their friends who still had a foreskin. But since she'd never seen Liam's dick when it wasn't so hard that his foreskin didn't have to be pushed back to put on a condom, she also hadn't understood what Kay and Aiken had to talk about back in November, either. Regardless, she dropped that subject to keep from making him more uncomfortable, going right back to recapping her conversation with Windy Walters instead. "And when I told her that I was worried about the possibility of that security video leaking to CNZ, Windy came over to make sure I knew it was just her, Kandi, and their friend who were in the security office to see the video, and that they made him delete it while they watched, so we don't have to worry about anyone else ever seeing it."

Rylie didn't mention that she'd intentionally looked away whenever she saw any of the security officers at the hotel on this trip, since she didn't know which one was Windy and Kandi's friend Chuck. She hoped that he'd seen enough in the last four-and-a-half months that he wouldn't remember her if she ran into him while they were in town, but just in case, she didn't want to do anything to draw attention to herself at the hotel. *Surely, with all the debauchery in Vegas, he'll have seen several other women's boobs by the time we come back to town in August, so I won't have to be embarrassed if I see him then.*

"She also swore up and down that they only intended for us to take some fun pictures and maybe start to take a chance on falling in love, not do anything that would actually cause a scandal for the GWA. She even said something about trying to sober us up with iced coffee before we went to the license bureau and chapel, but it apparently only worked long enough to make us appear sober to the officials issuing the licenses. Then we negated the effects of the coffee with champagne in the limo on the way back to the hotel, which explains why we passed out in our rooms before packing up to meet back up in the honeymoon suite."

"So, she didn't intend for us to actually get married that night?"

"No, I don't think so." Rylie shook her head and downed the last of the champagne in her flute glass, just as the limo pulled over in front of their hotel. "But I did thank her for everything she did that night because if she hadn't pushed us to do those pictures, I wouldn't have ever tried the friends-with-benefits thing with you."

"Feck, I should probably thank her too," Liam sighed as he took her glass and put it in the small sink that was part of the built-in bar. "'Cause if she hadn't drunk me under the table that night, then we'd still be stuck in the friend zone and I'd probably end up with carpal tunnel from jerking off to thoughts of you twice a day."

Rylie had to laugh when the driver picked the exact right moment to open Liam's door, so he basically made an announcement to everyone in the general vicinity about his previous masturbation habit. Luckily, Liam just chuckled along with her, taking her hand and helping her from the limo.

"As you can all see, I'm no longer at risk of carpal tunnel 'cause we're married," he boasted, only waiting long enough for Rylie to bend down and pick up the end of her train before rushing them into the hotel.

Thankfully, they didn't have to deal with their garment bags for the clothing they'd worn to the chapel earlier, since Aiken's dads had insisted on collecting their things from the changing rooms for all three couples and would be taking them back to the arena, where Rick had someone from the wardrobe department meeting them to put them in their individual wardrobe trunks before the ground crew left for Reno. And since the only other personal item she'd taken to the chapel earlier was her wristlet, which was a combination of a phone case and wallet that fit in Liam's pocket along with his phone, they didn't have to wait for the chauffeur to get anything from the trunk.

Rylie tugged on his hand to get him to change direction as he aimed for the elevators. "Obviously, I don't want a re-do of our wedding night in the stairwell, but I thought it might be fun to have a quick kiss there to commemorate it and then maybe recreate the events of that dream once we get to our room?"

"Can we recreate that dream while you're still in this dress?" Liam's eyes flared with excitement as they changed direction and walked swiftly toward the stairwell.

"Yeah, you'll have to help me unlace it in the back and I'll have to remove the wardrobe tape holding it up in the front, but it should be doable," Rylie grinned at her husband.

"Then by all means, Mrs. Connery, lead the way to the spot you remember from your dreams, so we can quickly commemorate our wedding night before retiring to the honeymoon suite."

They walked hand in hand through the stairwell door.

"Yeah, I think I know why we couldn't wait to get to one of our rooms that night," Liam chuckled, shaking his head as they started up the steps. "As drunk as we were then, it's a miracle we made it up the first flight without tumbling down the stairs."

Rylie only chuckled in response as they passed the second floor and continued up.

"Obviously, we needed a break before going up twenty flights to where our rooms were. And what better way to take a break than to make out for a few minutes."

Rylie looked at the paint on the walls as it changed with each landing they passed, trying to remember what color the wall behind her was in her dream.

"Seriously, what were we thinking with taking the stairs and not the elevator? And were we really planning to carry all our luggage up another five flights of stairs to the honeymoon suite?" Liam chuckled incredulously.

She stopped them when they got to the landing between the fourth and fifth floors, where she believed she remembered their wedding night festivities happened based on the pale blue wall.

"No, I don't think we'd decided exactly how we were getting up to the honeymoon suite, especially since we'd have had to go back down to the desk to get the staff to give us a key to it first. As for our thoughts before taking the stairs to our rooms, we were probably thinking that we wanted some privacy, instead of riding up in the same elevator as Teagan, Josh, Aiken, and Crockett," Rylie chuckled along with her husband, as she turned so her back was facing the wall. "But even though I'm not nearly as drunk tonight since we've only had a couple glasses of champagne, I'll happily agree to go grab the elevator on the next floor, instead of walking up the rest of the stairs to the twenty-fifth floor in these shoes."

"Oh, but we have to make sure we're in the right spot in the stairwell before I kiss you, Moh Graw," Liam declared as he stepped up close and loomed over her.

"This is the right spot," Rylie assured him breathlessly as she pointed to the wall behind her with her head. "I remember the pale blue wall from my dream."

"Guess it's a good thing they change colors every floor," Liam chuckled, releasing the hand holding hers to cup her face in his palms. "So we know we're on the right landing."

He held her where he wanted her as he dipped his head and brushed his lips over hers. Rylie released her train and ran her hands up his lapels until she was able to loop her arms around his neck, moving her lips against his even though neither of them opened their mouths to deepen the kiss.

Unlike what they'd done in this spot on their first wedding night, this kiss was sensual and sweet, and perfectly chaste, so neither one of them would be embarrassed if the security video leaked to CNZ or the dirt sheets. It was the ideal way to commemorate their drunken beginnings and start their marriage anew.

But even though the kiss was tame in comparison to their norm, Rylie still felt swoony when Liam lifted his lips from hers. She had to hold onto him for a moment, though she only released her clasped hands to place her palms firmly on his shoulders, looking deep into his gold-flecked green eyes as he smiled down at her.

"I love you, Mrs. Connery."

"I love you, too, Mr. Connery."

She recognized the twinkle of mischief in his gaze less than a second before he bent his knees and scooped her up in his arms, somehow catching her train so it wasn't dragging the floor as he carried her the rest of the way up the stairs to the fifth floor, where he exited the stairwell.

"What are you doing, Liam?" Rylie instinctually wrapped her arms around his neck once more, needing to hold on to feel secure, even though she knew Liam would never drop her.

"Carrying my bride to our honeymoon suite," he replied as he practically ran down the hall to catch the elevator while the doors were open after another couple exited.

"I think you only have to carry me over the threshold to the room, not up twenty floors in the elevator beforehand," Rylie laughed as they passed the other couple and barely slid into the elevator just as the doors started moving. Thankfully, the sensors recognized they'd blocked the doors, so they opened back up immediately, giving them time for him to make sure no part of her dress might get caught in the doors when they closed.

"But carrying you makes it much faster for us to navigate the halls," Liam teased with a grin as he leaned over to push the button for the twenty-fifth floor. "And I thought you'd appreciate giving your feet a rest without having to take off your shoes and traipse through the hotel barefoot."

"I do appreciate that," Rylie agreed, pecking a kiss on his cheek. "Thank you, Teddy Barren."

"We've really gotta work on your Irish accent," Liam chuckled, just as she realized they weren't alone in the elevator. Before he could correct her very poor imitation of the way she imagined Granny Breena would enunciate the Irish terms, the older woman standing beside her husband's electric wheelchair on the other side of the car finally spoke up.

"Oh, Dave, I miss the days when you were able to carry me around like that." The dark-haired woman with streaks of silver that almost looked like intentional highlights in her shoulder length tresses placed one hand over her heart while clasping her husband's shoulder with the other.

"What are you talking about, Kim?" Dave looked up at his wife with an impish expression while patting his lap with the hand not resting on the joystick that obviously controlled his chair. His previously dark hair sported a few more gray strands than his wife's, giving away his late fifties or possibly early sixties age much more than the smile lines on his face. "I might not be able to walk while carrying you like when we were newlyweds, since I'm not always steady on my prosthetic, but you can still sit on my lap for me to wheel you around anytime you want. Just because it won't help me walk again, doesn't mean we can't still enjoy the way having you on my lap causes me to grow an extra leg."

Rylie couldn't help but giggle at the way the older man flirted with his wife, not seeming to care that they weren't alone. She turned away from the other couple, missing Kim's reply, to look directly into Liam's eyes. "Promise me we'll always be just as in love and..." Rylie trailed off while she thought of the right word to imply being sexually active without being graphic about it, "...*playful* as they are, even when we're old and unable to be as physically active as we are now."

"Hey, who're you calling old? I'm not even sixty yet," Dave grumbled, knocking on his shin, which she wouldn't have recognized as a prosthetic if he hadn't mentioned it earlier, even with the strange sound it made when he hit his fist against it. "And I'm still plenty capable of being physically active. I just have to limit how much time I spend standing on my bionic leg to keep from getting blisters on my stump."

Oh, no! Why can't I take a moment to think before I speak, so I can quit being rude and insulting when I don't mean to be?

"I'm sorry," Rylie apologized emphatically, feeling terrible for unconsciously insulting someone she actually found inspirational. "I didn't mean to imply that you're old or physically incapable in any way. I just found your obvious love inspiring and want us to emulate it for the rest of our lives."

"You'll have to excuse my husband," Kim interjected, shaking her head and waving off Rylie's apology. "The closer he gets to sixty, the more sensitive he gets about hearing the O-word. It was very clear you weren't talking about us in an insulting manner."

"And you'll have to excuse my wife," Liam piped up, appearing disappointed momentarily before giving her a half smile. "She's still got a few years before she hits thirty, which is when I'm assuming she'll start to object to age references. And we haven't been married long enough for her to learn that there's only one O-word a man wants to hear cross a woman's lips."

"Sorry, but our vows didn't include me promising to *obey* you," Rylie snarked, rolling her eyes at her caveman husband.

"Alright, maybe there's two," Liam laughed.

"What's the other one?" Kim questioned, looking back and forth between Liam and her husband, who was also chuckling.

"He was talking about *orgasms*," Dave grinned up at his wife just as the elevator stopped and the doors opened on the twenty-second floor. "Now hop on my lap, woman, so I can carry you over the threshold and give you as many tonight as I did on our wedding night."

Kim quickly stepped in front of her husband's wheelchair and plopped down on his lap. Dave then wheeled them out of the elevator before turning around and adding, "Congratulations. And I hope you're both as happy and in love as we are for many years to come."

Rylie and Liam barely managed to get out their thanks and reciprocal wishes for the other couple before the doors closed between them.

"Do you really think he believes me that I wasn't commenting on his age or physical abilities?" Rylie still felt guilty for coming across even the slightest bit rude to the other couple.

"I'm sure he does," Liam assured her with a peck on her temple. "With the way he was fighting to hide a smile, I think he's one of those guys who thinks playful arguments are flirtatious. And I'd be willing to bet that he's in his wheelchair instead of walking on his prosthetic because he had a couple of drinks tonight and that's why he didn't limit his flirting to just his wife."

"Oh, please, he wasn't flirting with me." Rylie rolled her eyes, just as the elevator door opened once more, this time on their floor. "It was clear as day that he only had eyes for his wife."

"Oh, I didn't say he meant anything by it," Liam defended as he stepped out of the elevator and strode confidently down the hall to their room. "Just that he's an outgoing guy, who doesn't always realize he's flirting. We have several coworkers who are the same way. Hell, some of our coworkers would say I used to be the same. It doesn't mean anything 'cause there's no intent behind it other than being friendly."

Rylie thought back to when she first met Liam and realized that she could definitely see what he was talking about. "Yeah, I get it," she sighed as he stopped in front of their door. "When we first met, I was actually jealous every time you complimented or playfully teased one of the other women. But then after a couple of weeks, I realized you ribbed the guys just as much as the girls, so I knew it was just your nature and not actually flirting. Of course, then it crushed me to realize you weren't flirting with me either."

"Oh, I was definitely flirting with you, Moh Graw," Liam practically growled. "I just had to cover it up by spreading the compliments around, so you didn't realize how bad I wanted to step outta the friend zone with you. Now can you please reach into my back pocket and get my keycard outta my wallet so we can go in our room and get started on our honeymoon?"

"If I *have to*," Rylie joked, releasing her hold around his neck to snake her arm under his to try to get to his pocket. When she finally managed to move his jacket enough to reach the correct pocket in his pants, she pulled his wallet out and brought it around to rest on her midsection before opening it to look for the keycard. She was surprised to see the clear pocket, where she assumed most people would put their driver's license, held one of the pictures they'd gotten from the chapel of their first wedding. In the photo, they were looking at one another instead of at the camera, but it was clear that their eyes held nothing but love for one another, even back then. *How did I not notice that when we first saw these photos back in October?* "Oh, Li, when did you put this in here?"

"Back when we first got the pics emailed from the chapel," Liam admitted with a sad smile. "I'll be glad to tell you all about how hard it was to find someplace that would print them off for me once you grab that keycard from the opposite side of my wallet and open the door to our room."

"Sorry," Rylie cringed, quickly pulling out the keycard and sliding it into the slot on the door until the light turned green to allow them entry. "I'm probably getting pretty heavy, huh?"

"No, you are not getting heavy at all, Moh Graw," Liam disagreed as he strode through the now open door, kicking it shut behind them before he finally put her on her feet. "But I believe we have some work to do on your dress before I pick you back up in the right position for officially consummating our marriage up against the nearest wall."

"That we do," Rylie agreed as she handed his wallet back to him. Then she turned around and pulled her braids and veil over her shoulder, so he could get to the laces on the back of the corset portion of her wedding gown.

"Feck," he groaned as he started trying to undo the knot at the top of her dress. "Who tied you in this thing? And why didn't they just tie it in a bow like we tie our shoes?"

"Teagan," Rylie replied with a chuckle. "She tied it in a bow at first, but as soon as I started moving around, it loosened enough that the front slipped down, even with the wardrobe tape. So in order to keep me from having a nip slip in the middle of the ceremony, she tightened the laces and tied it in a way that it wouldn't loosen up no matter how I moved."

"Yeah, I'm not sure even Houdini could untie this knot," he grumbled, tickling her as he continued to struggle with it. "Feck, I may have to call Blade and see if I can borrow one of his daggers to cut you outta this dress."

"You are not cutting the laces on this dress," Rylie protested, turning around to glare at her husband.

"Then I hope you're happy wearing it for the rest of your life." Liam threw up his hands in frustration. "'Cause my fingers are too big to work between the layers of the cord to pull the knot apart. And I don't have fingernails long enough to pinch it and pull it out either."

"Could you maybe get it with tweezers? I have some in my toiletry bag."

"Maybe?" Liam shrugged.

Rylie picked up her train and quickly ran across the suite to the bathroom. When she opened her bag to get out the tweezers, she also noticed the bundle of bobby pins she'd stuck in there after Allissa and Dean's wedding, so she grabbed one of those as well.

"Okay, here's the tweezers." She handed them over as soon as she walked back into what she considered the living room portion of the suite before explaining why she'd also grabbed the bobby pin. "But if that silk cord is too slippery to pull out with the tweezers, maybe you can work one side of the bobby pin under it to be able to hook it in the end and pull it out that way."

"Yeah, that'll probably work better than the tweezers," Liam agreed, handing them back to her before having her spin around once more so he could work on the knot with the bobby pin.

She dropped the tweezers on the table by the door while she waited until he quit pulling the binding tighter in the back, so she could try to work the front of her gown down to remove the double-sided tape adhering the corset-style bodice to her breasts. To be honest, she was a little nervous about removing the tape, since she'd always had a mild allergic reaction to the adhesive in bandages, and couldn't imagine the red rash would be all that attractive to her husband when he went to play with her boobs. But Aiken's papa had promised her that if she used the skin barrier spray he passed into her dressing room before applying the wardrobe tape, then she wouldn't have her typical allergic reaction to the adhesive.

But maybe I should completely take the dress off and go wash off the barrier film, so Liam won't lick off something he probably shouldn't ingest.

"Um, Li, maybe we should wait to try to recreate that dream when I'm wearing a different dress," Rylie suggested, suddenly fearing she could accidentally poison her husband if she didn't warn him about the skin protectant covering her breasts. "'Cause I just realized that I need to go wash my chest before you use your mouth on me there."

"Got it," Liam exclaimed, just as she felt the gown open in the middle of her back. "Wait. Why do you have to wash your chest?"

Rylie explained how she'd followed Shawn Pearson's instructions to spray the skin barrier on her breasts before applying the wardrobe tape to keep from having an allergic reaction to the adhesive, as she pulled the front of the dress down and peeled the tape off her skin, tossing it in the nearby wastebasket. The film left behind from the spray did an excellent job of making it easier to remove the tape, and it was clear that Aiken's costume designer papa was correct in recommending it to prevent the rash she normally got whenever she was exposed to adhesives for any length of time. But it was also obvious where she'd over sprayed her breasts and part of that protective film remained since it wasn't actually in contact with the tape.

"Then I guess you'll just have to be happy with me only using my hands on your tits this first time," Liam chuckled after she elaborated on how she wasn't sure the chemicals were safe for oral play. "And round two will have to be in the shower, so I can suck your pretty nipples as soon as we get you clean."

"Yes, Sir," Rylie agreed as she wrapped her arms around his neck and Liam bent slightly to kiss her.

She got so completely lost in the kiss that she didn't realize at first that she was the only one actually using her hands to touch him. It wasn't until she heard the crinkle of a foil packet being opened that she realized he'd adjusted his clothing to free his cock and was rolling on a condom before touching her. *I wonder where he put the bobby pin?*

Once the latex was in place, he carefully started lifting the layers of lace and satin making up the skirt of her wedding gown. Apparently, unlike putting on a condom, finding her under the voluminous lower half of her dress wasn't a task he could do without looking, causing him to break off the kiss to squat down so he could gather all the layers of material at once. "Feck, Moh Graw, there's enough lace here to cover all the tables we used for Christmas dinner."

Rylie only giggled as she released her hold on his shoulders to help him pull the bottom of her dress up to her waist, revealing the baby blue satin and lace thong she was wearing that said "I do" right over her mound.

"Yeah, I'm gonna wanna see these on you again later, but without the dress," Liam declared as he released his hold on her skirt now that she was holding it up, so he could slide the panties down her legs. His hot breath wafting over her sex made her pussy gush, soaking her thighs when the barrier of her panties was removed. "Hmmm, maybe I need just a little taste first."

Liam swiped his tongue through her folds, lapping up her cream as he caressed down her legs to push her panties down to her ankles and causing her to moan in pleasure. Once she stepped out of them, he stuffed them in the pocket of his tuxedo jacket as he stood back up, licking his lips in appreciation of her taste. He then gripped her thighs to lift her up, so she could wrap her legs around him while his cock poked her entrance.

As soon as they were close enough that the press of their bodies held up the bunched up lace and satin, she wrapped her arms around him once more, hanging on tight as he pushed her back against the door and covered her mouth with his. Keeping one hand on her ass to hold her where he wanted her, he fondled her breasts with the other while spearing both his cock and his tongue inside her.

Tasting herself on his tongue was almost as intoxicating as the way his cock filled her up. She reveled in the slightly taboo aspect of the act, only wishing it could be made better by tasting the two of them mixed together, his salty with her tangy sweet. She mentally added kissing him after an orgasmic sixty-nine to their list of things they wanted to try once his ninety-day test came back negative, hoping she'd remember to run it by him later.

After holding still a moment to allow her to adjust to his invasion, Liam pulled halfway out then thrust deep inside her once more. He didn't stop kissing her, even as he pinched her nipple between his thumb and forefinger while setting the perfect rhythm of stroking his cock in and out of her pussy.

It wasn't as hard and fast as she'd dreamed on their first wedding night, but his gentle insistence was exactly what she needed to fly off to the heights of nirvana as the waves of her first orgasm of the night crashed over her. She tore her mouth from his as she cried out, "Oh, Liam, I love you!"

"I love you, too, Moh Graw," Liam replied as he plunged inside her once more, holding still as he reached his own release. "Feck, moh anam cara."

He continued speaking in Irish, but she had no idea what any of it meant, as his climax extended hers. Or possibly triggered her second. Either way, it was a great way to kick off their all night honeymoon lovemaking. They could sleep on their morning flight to Reno. And if that wasn't enough, maybe they could skip lunch and their workout time to take a midday nap.

Chapter Fifteen

Friday, January 10, 2020, Flying from Hilo, Hawaii to Suva, Fiji, Crossing the International Date Line

Liam was excited about his first flight over the International Date Line for the South Pacific and Southeast Asia tour. While technically, they'd started the Pacific portion of the tour when they flew from Bakersfield, California to Honolulu, Hawaii on Wednesday, he didn't feel like it since the two-hour time difference meant they landed at 12:30 p.m. in Honolulu, after their 9 a.m. flight from Bakersfield was in the air for five-and-a-half hours. But this seven-hour flight was going to feel like time travel, since they were jumping ahead by almost a full day. They still took off at their normal 9 a.m. local time from Hilo, but instead of landing at 4 p.m. on the same day as they would if they stayed in the same time zone, they would land at 2 p.m. on Saturday, the eleventh, in Fiji. It was the first time in all his years with the company that Liam saw two dates listed on their schedule for their appearances, one for the local date and time of each show until they headed back to Hawaii in two weeks, and one for the date and time at the corporate office in New York during those shows.

And they wouldn't all get a night off from wrestling until they went back to Hawaii in two weeks, because the eight-hour flight and twenty-hour time difference between Guam and Hawaii meant they'd land at 9 p.m. local time in Lahaina, Hawaii on Friday, January 24, 2020, after flying out of Andersen Air Force Base at 9 a.m. local time on Saturday, January 25, 2020 in Guam. They'd put on a show in Lahaina the next night, on the twenty-fifth, but they wouldn't get their normal amount of sleep afterwards because they had to fly out of Hawaii at 6 a.m. on Sunday to account for the two-hour time difference and five-and-a-half-hour flight, so they could get to the arena by 3 p.m. local time in Tijuana, Mexico for the next show.

On top of all the craziness of time zone differences and flight times between cities, they also had to account for how long it would take them to get through Customs each time they entered or exited a country, which would affect the time they needed to arrive at the airport each morning, so they wouldn't be on their normal schedule at all for the entire South Pacific and Southeast Asia tour. And all this logistical craziness was just for the people traveling on the talent plane. The roadies had to be on their plane at least six hours earlier than the talent, so they had time to set everything up in the next arena before the wrestlers arrived.

Thankfully, Rick realized the ring crew couldn't possibly break down everything after the show in Lahaina and make it to Tijuana on time. So, he already had it arranged for the ground crew that worked the GWA show in Bakersfield to meet them in Tijuana and give the crew who worked the South Pacific and Southeast Asia tour a couple weeks off. And Liam knew this because Rick had started teaching him everything about scheduling their shows, including all the talent and support staff needed for everything to run smoothly, so he'd be prepared to oversee the corporate departments, who normally handled all that, once his new job landed him in New York full time.

While they were in Bakersfield on Tuesday, Rick had also introduced Liam to the people responsible for supervising the roadies on both crews, as well as the new head chefs on both catering crews, so they knew he was another resource they had on tour to act as their liaison with the corporate office if they had any issues. Apparently, the transition to having their own catering staff and traveling kitchen, both on the roadies' plane and in one of the big rigs the second support crew drove around the continental US and to neighboring cities in Mexico and Canada, hadn't gone as smoothly as Rick had hoped.

While Cole Zaring, the head chef on the ground crew, was experienced in running the catering operation for a music tour and already had the pantry stocked on the big rig, there was some confusion about who was responsible for stocking the pantry on the roadies' plane. That head chef, Tristan Nelson, had apparently only worked in restaurants, where he submitted the list of ingredients he needed each week to the owner, instead of shopping himself. Needless to say, Tristan thought the service that stocked the planes' galleys with drinks and snacks for the GWA's daily flights would also stock the pantry. And of course, everyone at GWA corporate knew that service only stocked prepackaged drinks and snacks, which didn't include pantry staples for cooking all the meals for the talent and support staff to be served at the arenas daily. The purchasing department at the corporate office also assumed the head chefs, or possibly their assistant chefs, would shop for their favorite ingredients themselves to have everything on hand before they left the US, just in case some things weren't available in some of the cities they visited on the international tours, which was exactly what Cole had already done to feed everyone their first week back on tour.

So, Liam's first real assignment in his new liaison position was to make sure they had food on the plane for the international tour before they departed Bakersfield. He had to get both head chefs together to come up with a list of staple ingredients they both wanted available. Then he got someone in the purchasing department at corporate to schedule regular grocery deliveries to the chefs before they swapped rotations on tour, including having them contact Josh Burleson to find out how to get their beef direct from the ranch as if they were a local restaurant. He then had to break the news to Tristan that he would now have to find time in his and his assistant chefs' schedules to supplement the staples they could keep on the plane with fresh produce from local stores and farmers' markets in the various cities they visited.

They'd cut it close and had to go with a local Bakersfield supermarket delivery for everything for the first couple of weeks. But thankfully, Tristan and his staff were able to come up with a game plan on the flight to Honolulu, so they were able to start their meal prep while still in the air and finish everything after a trip to a farmers' market. To be honest, Liam had been a little surprised that dinner Wednesday night in catering had gone off without a hitch. But apparently, the only reason most of the GWA talent knew they'd switched from having the arenas cater their meals to having their own GWA catering crews was because they'd heard Liam on his many phone calls Tuesday.

Now he couldn't wait to find out how Tristan and his staff handled meshing local fresh foods with the nonperishable staples they brought with them to feed everyone for their first international stop on this tour. Not that he could call or even text the chef to find out the plan right then, since the other plane had left Hilo six hours earlier and the crew might not have phone service once they disembarked in Suva and didn't have access to the plane's Wi-Fi while shopping or at the hotel or arena.

Thinking about trying to contact the chef reminded Liam to switch to Wi-Fi on his phone as he settled into a seat next to Rylie for the seven-hour flight. He didn't expect to hear from his family unless there was an emergency, but just in case, he always linked his phone to the network on the plane for flights more than a couple hours long and maintained an international calling plan for anytime they weren't in the States. He was just leaning over to remind Rylie to do the same when Rick and Fiona boarded the plane, and Rick whistled to get everyone's attention.

Unlike normally, the boss and his wife didn't board the plane at the same time as the rest of the crew for this flight. From what Cage said when he escorted Britney on the plane and secured all of the Robertsons' luggage, they had to finish a phone call in the back of their limo before joining the rest of them.

"I know several of you have been almost as anxious as Fifi and I," Rick announced as soon as everyone quieted down and turned to face the front of the plane, where he was standing with his arm around Fiona. "So, we wanted to share our test results with all of you first thing after calling our parents this morning."

"Quit stalling, Boss, and tell us already!" Jax Nolan, the history tutor who was best friends with Fiona and dating the GWA head of security Cage Dalton, shouted and bounced in his seat.

"We're pregnant!" Fiona proclaimed with a huge grin, just as Rick rested his hand on her still flat belly.

Amongst the chorus of "congratulations" that echoed throughout the plane, Jax squealed the loudest as he fumbled to unbuckle his seat belt so he could run up the aisle and hug his bestie.

Liam and Rylie joined the others in celebrating the news, but he could tell the announcement brought up more than a few uneasy feelings for his wife. He knew she was over-the-moon happy for Rick and Fiona, but she was also anxious about the possibility of having the same condition Fiona had that forced them to have to go with IVF.

And since she was Catholic, he knew she was already struggling with making the decision about whether or not they should attempt IVF if they weren't blessed to conceive without medical intervention.

Wanting to put her mind at ease about whatever her decision was if it became necessary, Liam decided that it was probably best to discuss things with her while they were as secluded as they could get on the plane with it only being the two of them in this "pod quad," as everyone had started calling the groupings of four seats on the plane. "You okay, Mo Ghrá?"

"Yeah, I'm fine," Rylie replied, seeming to be off in her own thoughts, instead of really paying attention to anything other than her seat belt.

"Are you sure?" Liam had to pause and not fully express his concern for her because the speakers above them drowned out his words as Derek made his preflight announcements. But as soon as the pilot was finished speaking, he elaborated, leaning down to whisper close to Rylie's ear to make sure he wouldn't be overheard. "Because I'm pretty sure Rick and Fiona's situation has you thinking about the possibility that we'll have to go with IVF as much as I am right now."

"Them successfully getting pregnant is good news," Rylie hissed in response, also keeping her voice low. "I'm thrilled for them."

"Yes, I know, and so am I," Liam agreed, smiling to make sure she knew he wasn't accusing her of being resentful of their friends. "But we can be excited and happy for them, and still feel anxious about going through the same fertility issues they have, and struggle with whether or not we can handle the spiritual ramifications of making a similar choice in how to grow our family. So, I just want to make sure you know I'm here for you if you need to talk it all out."

"I know you are, Teidí Béirín." Rylie leaned her head over on his shoulder, physically leaning on him the way he wanted her to emotionally lean on him, as her version of the Irish terms came out sounding more like "Teddy Barren."

Since it wasn't the right time to try again to teach her how to do an Irish accent, Liam just wrapped his arm around her shoulders and hugged her into his side, effectively moving her cheek from his shoulder to his chest.

"A month ago, I would have said I was a hundred percent sure I'd go with IVF if that's what's necessary to have a baby." Rylie sighed as she slipped her arms around him. "But I also wasn't going to Mass or trying to live like the Christian I was raised to be. Now IVF is another of those gray areas where I'm not sure I agree with the Church that it goes against canon law. But I'm also not sure I could go through with it without feeling guilty and going to confession daily."

"I understand, Mo Ghrá." Liam brushed his lips over the braids on the top of her head. "And like I said before, if you decide it's not something you're willing to try, then I'll be happy to adopt all our kids."

"And if I do want to try IVF?" Rylie tilted her head to look up at him without pulling away. "Will you be okay with that? Or will you schedule us both standing appointments with Father O'Malley for daily confessions?"

"Well, since I agree with more of the Jewish philosophy about IVF, I'd be more than okay with trying it to have a baby," Liam informed her with a smile. "And I don't think I'd feel a need for daily confessions. Honestly, I'm pretty sure I wouldn't even mention it in my regular monthly confession until after the baby was born, 'cause it's not exactly repentant to confess to things I'm planning to continue doing."

"True," Rylie smiled in agreement. "But I'd still feel so guilty that I'd probably at least say a prayer after every appointment, test, or injection, if only for my own peace of mind."

"And if the time comes when we decide to try IVF, I'll gladly pray with you." Liam squeezed her shoulder as he leaned down and pecked his lips on hers. "Though if I have to give you some of those shots, like Rick had to do with Fiona, then I might want to pray for God to guide my hands before each injection too."

"Yeah, after you mentioned that the other day, I asked Fiona about the process and she told me a little about all those shots." Rylie shuddered in his arms as if just the thought of the two weeks of daily injections required before the egg retrieval disturbed her. "If we ever have to do that, you'll definitely have to be the one to poke me, 'cause I'd pass out before even being able to give myself the first one. And honestly, even if you're the one to give them, I'd still want to lay down beforehand, just like I do when Doc does a blood draw, so it won't be a big deal if I do go out."

Liam felt his stomach flip at just the thought of having to stick Rylie with a needle. Yeah, it would be for the very best reason, for them to have a baby, but he still didn't think he was capable of intentionally doing something that would cause her pain or so much distress that she passed out.

"So, what's the Jewish philosophy about IVF? And how did you decide you'd rather follow it than the Catholic philosophy?"

"The way it was explained to me by a Jewish college friend is that God's first commandment to 'be fruitful and multiply' takes precedence over all the other commandments, as does the second commandment that human life should be preserved above all. So, even though he wasn't supposed to eat pork because of one of the other rules of Judaism, if he was ever in a situation where the only thing available to eat was pork and if he didn't eat it he'd starve to death, then he had to follow the commandment to preserve human life and eat the pork. And since having children was the first commandment, even before preserving human life, they have to do so by any means necessary, including IVF."

"So, Jewish people who are really strict with following their faith wouldn't have the choice to just adopt if they can't get pregnant? They'd have to try every medical intervention available first?"

"Oh, I'm sure they can adopt too," Liam assumed, rubbing his hand down her arm and back up reassuringly. "But if they're super diligent with living according to their beliefs, then they'd also have to try every medical intervention they could afford."

"And you agree with that instead of the Catholic belief that IVF is immoral because it replaces the marital act with conception in a lab?" Rylie pulled back to look into his eyes as she asked the question.

Liam could see she was confused by his earlier statement. "I don't agree with taking the choice away from the couple, no matter whether that's the Catholic Church saying we can't use IVF or the Jewish Synagogue saying Jewish couples have to try IVF. But I also believe that God wouldn't have given medical doctors the knowledge of all these different methods to overcome infertility if He didn't want us to have the option of using that knowledge to have babies. So, I don't think it's sinful to try IVF, especially since most of the steps in the process can be done with the couple working together and leaning on each other, so it's still a unitive process."

"I get that the two weeks of shots can be unitive, since you'd have to give them to me the same way Rick had to give them to Fiona last month. But how is it unitive when the woman goes off to surgery to retrieve the eggs and the man goes off to a room alone to jerk off to give his sperm sample? Or when neither parent is actually present in the lab when the egg and sperm are combined to make the baby?"

"I said most of the steps can be done together, not all," Liam clarified. "But if it's something we end up having to do, I'd specifically ask the doctor to have you in the room with me for my part, so you can do the honors, instead of it just being me masturbating to thoughts of you. For that matter, I don't see why I couldn't scrub up to observe, the same way a medical student would if the procedure was being done in a teaching hospital, and sit beside your head, holding your hand, while they do the egg retrieval and embryo implantation. And even if we couldn't be in the lab together when our samples are combined, we would be together at the time of conception, praying for a successful outcome."

"Okay, yeah, I can see how you can make it a more unitive process than what Fiona described," Rylie conceded, resting her head back on his chest. "But I'm still not sure if I want to go through all that, especially since she also mentioned how it limited when they could have sex."

Liam didn't remember Rick mentioning that drawback to IVF, just that he had to give his wife daily injections for two weeks, then they had to go to a clinic for a final injection to trigger ovulation a couple of days before the egg retrieval. He also remembered it took six days before the embryos could be implanted and they had to wait two weeks after that to take the first test to see if it was successful. "Rick didn't say anything about that when he told me the general timeline of everything they had to do."

"Oh, yeah, apparently, they couldn't have sex for like five days before he had to give his sample, both at the beginning to be tested to make sure he didn't contribute to their fertility issues, and then again for the sample they actually used for the IVF. And then she had to be on pelvic rest after the egg retrieval and implantation to give them the best chance of it working." Rylie lifted her head once more to look up at him. "Did you know that a female orgasm can cause a woman to eject the embryo because of the strong uterine contractions?"

"No, I didn't know that." Liam started to understand a little more of the Church's view on IVF not being unitive for a couple if they had to abstain from making love for several weeks at a time. "How long do they have to wait after the implantation before making love to make sure the baby sticks?"

"A week or two," Rylie shrugged before relaxing back into him.

So, with having to stop having sex five days before the sperm and egg retrievals on the twenty-first, and not being able to make love again for two weeks after the implantation on the twenty-seventh, they've had to go almost a month without? Yeah, that's gonna totally suck if Rylie wants to try IVF.

"Well, thankfully, we've got a couple of years before we'll have to make that decision," Liam offered, lightly running his hand over her braids. "And even when we finish the Pre-Cana classes, we'll have our mentors to talk to about all our options."

"True, and by then, it'll be much easier for us to schedule times to talk to them," Rylie sighed. "'Cause we'll be just a couple miles away, instead of having to wait a couple of weeks to be back on the same calendar day."

Liam had to chuckle at the reminder of how they'd confused the O'Shays the last time they'd video conferenced them from Honolulu because the five-hour time difference meant Liam and Rylie had the call interrupted by room service delivering their lunch while the O'Shays were planning to go out to dinner right after their call. When they'd tried to schedule another video call for a week later, the fact that the Connerys would be fifteen hours ahead of New York time while in Brisbane, Australia, made it impossible to coordinate a time to connect around all their schedules. So, they'd decided to postpone their next video call until they were back in the US.

"But even though we can't meet with them until we get back to Hawaii and have a night off, we can probably get through several of our assignments on this flight," Liam suggested, popping open the cubby to pull out the tablet for the in-flight entertainment system, so they could go to the website.

"In seven hours, we can probably finish all our assignments for the next couple of weeks and still have time to watch a movie or two," Rylie agreed, pulling from his arms and, now that the seat-belt lights had been turned off, getting up to grab the bag with their Bibles and personal electronics, so they had all the supplies they needed.

It wasn't quite as much fun as some of the other things they'd done on the plane recently, but this flight was still excellent for strengthening their marriage.

~~~

Saturday, January 11, 2020, 2 p.m., Suva, Fiji
(Friday, January 10, 2020, 7 p.m. in Heart's Destiny, Texas)

As soon as they landed in Suva, Fiji, Kay informed the ladies that she'd be Skyping with her sisters-in-law, cousins-in-law, and the rest of the Heart's Destiny book club as soon as they got to the arena, in case any of them wanted to join her to hear the latest gossip. While Rylie wasn't normally interested in gossip, she did want to check out the book club to see what all was involved, wanting to find out if they had some kind of system to their meetings, so she could get the GWA women more organized, instead of just having impromptu book discussions backstage or on long flights. So, once they made it through Customs, checked into their hotel, and rode a tour bus around the city on their way to the arena, she left her husband at the locker rooms to go find the rest of the GWA women. *Hopefully, I've read the book they're discussing in the Heart's Destiny book club today. Or is it tonight, since it's still Friday night in Texas, but it's Saturday afternoon here?*

Rylie had a hard enough time keeping up with what time it was while traveling between time zones in the United States, so she felt really off now that crossing the International Date Line meant they'd jumped ahead a day, especially since traveling west usually meant going back an hour for each time zone they crossed. *Yeah, now I understand why Liam suggested waiting until we get back in the US before scheduling our next video call with Erin and Bryant O'Shay. Hopefully, his experience with traveling so many years with the GWA will come in handy for keeping us on schedule for the next couple of weeks, until we get back into our normal hemisphere.*
~~~

When she found the other GWA women, they were crowded around Kay's laptop, which she'd apparently connected to a mobile hotspot on her international phone plan to be able to Skype with everyone in Heart's Destiny. Fiona had apparently already informed her friends back home about being pregnant, as they were all offering her their congratulations, just as everyone in the GWA had before they left Hawaii that morning. *Yesterday morning? This time change is confusing. But now I understand why we were all instructed to try to nap for at least half of our flight to keep from getting too sleepy to wrestle tonight.*

In addition to the Heart's Destiny women cheering for the Robertsons' baby news, the GWA ladies all congratulated Amy for her wedding to Justin over the holidays. Amy then promptly turned the attention to Cait, so the GWA ladies not in attendance could extend their praise to her for the "surprise" marriage ceremony Cait and Josh Burleson had the day after Amy and Justin's wedding. Apparently, that wedding was just a surprise for their friends, since Josh had told Cait he would propose and plan the wedding all in the same day before the end of the year, so she knew he'd pick the anniversary of the day they met to make it all happen.

With all the wedding updates being talked about so excitedly, Rylie was almost tempted to mention that she and Liam had decided not to end their union. But then she remembered how they'd intentionally kept their plan for an annulment a secret from the younger generation of Heart's Destiny residents, so she just smiled politely and let the subject drop.

Luckily, the book club finally got around to mentioning the book they were discussing, *Rocked* by Cari Quinn and Taryn Elliott. Since she'd been a longtime fan of the writing duo, who sometimes used the pen name of Taryn Quinn, she'd read the *Lost in Oblivion* series a couple of years ago. So she was familiar with the characters and the basic premise of the story, even though she hadn't read it again recently to remember all the details.

"Oh, oh, Amethyst, while we've got you here, I have to ask, has Crockett ever done any modeling for book covers?" Lexi Wilder blurted from where she was crowded onto a sofa with the rest of the glam squad, who'd done all their hair, makeup, and nails for Allissa and Dean's wedding. "'Cause if the guy on the cover of **Rocked** isn't Crockett, they are definitely doppelgangers."

"Not that I know of," Aiken replied, shaking her head. "But I do see the resemblance, so maybe we'll meet that model when Brent gets his DNA match list in a few weeks."

Hearing once again about the tests Aiken and Crockett had done over the holidays caused Rylie a pang of regret that she hadn't followed through with her own plan to do one while she was in New York. She knew it was crazy to think she'd felt a familial connection with Mr. Willie at the feast of Saint Stephen, but it still weighed on her heart that she had to do something to reach out to him and make sure he was okay, even if it was extremely unlikely that he was her uncle. So, she decided that the next time they video called Father O'Malley for their Pre-Cana counseling, she'd ask him to pass her phone number along to Sister Mary Katherine. Hopefully, the sister would be willing to give her an update on Mr. Willie and give her some guidance on what she could do to help the man who reminded her so much of her dad. Even if it was just sending extra money to help with finding him shelter from the cold winter, or making sure the community center staff had everything they needed to insure he ate smothered fried chicken at least once a week, if he refused to let them help him get off the street, she had to do something the way she'd want someone to help her dad if he were in the same position. She knew in her heart that helping him would be what her parents would do if they were still alive and able to, so she wanted to honor their memory by doing something to make Mr. Willie's life better.

As the women around her started discussing the scenes they liked best in **Rocked**, Rylie pushed away her thoughts about doing more for the homeless outreach at the community center once she and Liam quit wrestling, trying to be more present in the moment.

"Yeah, the golf course scene was hot, but the one I could relate to most was the one after Oblivion performed at Red Rocks," Randi sighed.

"Because the adrenaline rush of performing makes you horny?" Teagan asked with a smirk.

"Maybe a little," Randi shrugged and smiled. "But mostly because up against the rock wall reminded me of the night I met James."

"It didn't remind you of all the times you and James have snuck off to the rock quarry on the Hunters' land since then?" Kay questioned her sister.

"Well, yeah, but those times were all to recreate our first time together," Randi admitted with a huge grin. "But we don't actually go to the quarry, since we couldn't ever be sure there wasn't someone around to see us while they were digging up and cutting the stones for the elevator shaft on the Heritage House. So, we found a secluded rocky outcropping halfway between the quarry and where they're putting in the vineyard."

Rylie wasn't sure how that would be any more private, but since she hadn't ventured out to see the fields they were preparing for the vineyard when she was in Heart's Destiny, she had no idea if the land between the two areas of the Hunters' estate was an open grassy field or covered with dense forest. *Hopefully, it's got a lot of tree cover like the area between their houses and the bed and breakfast, so once they finally get it up and running, we can go on a winery tour without catching James and Randi in the middle of their sexcapades.*

It was hard to keep track of the conversations going on with so many women talking, both at the arena and on the computer in Heart's Destiny, but eventually they seemed to coalesce into a conversation where the women on the computer asked the GWA women about how realistic the rock band's tour seemed compared to the GWA's wrestling tour.

"It's sort of similar, I think," Holly offered, looking around at the other GWA women for confirmation. "But with us traveling by plane instead of on a tour bus, we don't get several days between shows like they do in the book."

"And we only stay in the same city for a couple of days on pay-per-view weekends," Shauna added. "But on long flights like the one we did today, it's nice to have these new pods that kinda feel like bunks on a tour bus."

"But now that we've brought the catering staff in house, instead of relying on each arena to provide catering, I suppose it could be possible for a wrestler to fall for a chef, like Deacon and Harper." Teagan pointedly looked over at the Goddesses as they walked up to get their first introduction to the Heart's Destiny gals.

"I wouldn't hold your breath on that one," Amoura offered, shaking her head. "Cole is hot, but I can't see starting anything with him when the catering crew swaps out every couple of weeks, and even when he's on tour with us, our schedules only line up for us to barely say more than 'hello' and 'goodbye' at dinner each day."

Rylie knew Amoura was talking about the head chef who'd been responsible for feeding all of them their first week back on tour, and who'd been left behind in Bakersfield when the support staff swapped out between the ground crew and the air crew for the South Pacific and Southeast Asia tour. Unlike the flight crews, who swapped out every five days like clockwork, the support staff schedule was extremely flexible. While Rick said he hoped to have the support staff swap out every two weeks for the most part, they had to modify that anytime the GWA tour took them outside the continental United States and the cities in Canada and Mexico where the ground crew could drive to the arenas. So, for the first month of 2020, the ground crew worked from the second to the seventh, with the air crew taking over for the entirety of the South Pacific and Southeast Asia loop between the eighth and the twenty-fifth, before the ground crew finished out the month. They'd then be able to stick to a two-week rotation through February and March. But when they left for the European tour in April, the air crew would have to work for a full month before the ground crew could take over again when the GWA was back in the US. The air crew would then get a month off before they got back to a two-week rotation for the summer.

Yeah, I hope she doesn't really have it bad for Cole. As cool as it would be to have a romance similar to the plot of a book, it would suck to not get to see her man for weeks at a time like that.

When Rylie tuned back into the conversation, she realized they'd moved on once again, this time to discussing the importance of reading the prequel to the **Lost In Oblivion** series, **Seduced**, before reading **Rocked**. As she tried to remember when in the series the conflict over the band's recording contract and previous band member came in, Julie Burleson chimed in, reminding her that it was toward the end of **Rocked** and not in the next book, **Rattled**, as she'd momentarily thought.

"While ***Seduced*** wasn't what I'd classify as a romance, I think the information about the band dynamics in the prequel was vital for the contract and Snake drama to make sense."

"Yeah, but they could have done the same thing with just a few references in ***Rocked*** without us having to read a whole other book that didn't have the romantic happy ending we all want when we pick up a book," her twin sister, Jen, added.

"But then we wouldn't have had that hot threesome scene," Ashlyn Lawton pointed out as she fanned herself with the hand not holding her e-reader.

Rylie cringed, not thinking the scene they were talking about was all that hot. While there were some ménage books she'd enjoyed, knowing the trio in question didn't end up together after that one threesome, she couldn't enjoy a scene where the woman called out one guy's name while having sex with the other guy. *And even ignoring how ménage doesn't align with my religious beliefs, I really don't see how a woman can handle having sex with more than one man. Liam wears me out as it is. I'd end up in a coma if I had to try to keep up with two of him.*

"I'm with Ashlyn," Kori Ingleman, who was in a permanent threesome with Reid and Tait, even though Rylie didn't think their marriage was technically legal, interjected. "I just hope that scene is a prelude to a why-choose book for Jazz, Gray, and Nick later in the series."

"Sorry, Kori, you'll have to wait 'til the ***Found in Oblivion*** series for the why-choose books," Fiona informed the only woman among them who'd lived out that book plot.

I really don't see how Kori does it, especially while also raising two kids. But I guess at least she doesn't have to try to keep up with all their laundry while we're on tour, since she can send it all to be laundered through our hotels.

"Kori, I really need to get your number, so we can text for you to help me figure out how to get Dare and Cade to make my why-choose fantasies come true," Ashlyn declared, moving closer to the computer on their end, so she dominated the screen on Kay's laptop. "Well, the permanent part like you have with your guys anyway, since they did a pretty good job with the bedroom activities the last couple of weeks."

"Dare, as in Dion's brother, Darius?" Teagan questioned, crowding in between Kay and Kori to talk to Ashlyn.

"Yep, that's the one." Ashlyn beamed.

"But who's Cade?" Kori asked.

"He's the director working on the **Devine** and **Heart's Desire** movies," Ashlyn replied.

"Caden Starling?" Aiken queried as Ashlyn nodded in agreement. "I know Caden from when they've worked with Daddio in the past. They're hot. And you hooked up with both Caden and Dare Davis the last couple of weeks?"

"Oh, yeah, I did," Ashlyn grinned, looking exceptionally pleased with herself. "They even let me try out the cock cages we just added to the It's My Pleasure catalogue. Let me tell you, those are fun! But now that Cade's gone back to L.A., and Dare's talking about going back to New Orleans before Cade comes back to town to film, I'm afraid these two weeks will be the only taste of my why-choose fantasies I'll ever get, if I don't come up with some way of convincing them that we can be more than a fling."

As the ladies all inundated Ashlyn with questions about the new additions to the sex toy catalogue and started brainstorming for ideas for her to try to make her ménage permanent, Rylie decided it was time for her to bow out of the book club meeting. While she didn't begrudge her friends for wanting to live an alternative lifestyle, and would in no way judge them for their choices, talk of cock cages and Ashlyn wanting to be the Domme that both Dare and Cade submitted to in the bedroom was too far outside Rylie's comfort zone.

I need to go find Liam, she decided as she walked back toward the locker rooms to change for their match run-throughs. *And discuss more of our limits, so he knows I'm not interested in trying anything Kay writes about when she gets to Ashlyn's book.*

~~~

Friday, January 31, 2020, Jackson, Wyoming

Liam was thrilled to get the official lab report from Doc that his blood work came back negative as soon as they got to the arena. But still
~~~

having to get through the afternoon and evening before he could get his wife alone in their hotel room to finally make love without a condom for the first time was excruciating. Especially when he and Rylie both had the night off from actually wrestling and could have gone straight back to their hotel after the pre-show meeting if not for his additional duties as the new company president.

Just like he had in Hawaii when they hired the Hula 'Ōlapa women's tag team of Kai Iona and Lani Kahananui, Liam had to stay and watch the local talent trying out that night to give his opinion on their performance as well as sit in on the interviews and contract signings, so he knew what to do if they were able to hire anyone else while Rick was off on paternity leave later in the year. In addition to learning what Rick normally did when signing new talent to the roster, Liam also had to spend time with the newcomers to make sure they had everything they needed to start working with the GWA, like passports (or all the paperwork for the legal department to get their passports expedited if they didn't already have them), new ring entrance music that was either written by the musicians at corporate or was properly licensed for them to be able to use an outside musician's songs, and everything else they needed for wardrobe and new GWA-specific social media accounts.

Liam had actually gotten out of those tasks in Bakersfield, when Rick signed Laci Lopez to the roster, due to spending all his time dealing with the catering issues, and her already having a valid passport. But back when Kai and Lani had their try-out match in Honolulu, Liam really had to push the legal department at corporate to expedite their passports, so the ladies could join them when they came back through Hawaii after the South Pacific and Southeast Asia tour and participate on the show in Tijuana.

At least if Cady Clark and Alexa Peterson, the two women trying out that night with the tag-team gimmick of the Park Rangers, didn't have passports, he wouldn't have to pressure the legal department at corporate quite as much, since the GWA wasn't scheduled to leave the contiguous states until March when they went back to Puerto Rico and the Bahamas for a couple of days. And if their passports didn't come through in time for their show in the Bahamas, then they could fly commercial from Puerto Rico to Miami to meet back up with the rest of the crew after a day off. The legal department would then have another month to expedite their passports before the European tour.

As he sat and watched the Park Rangers challenge Holly the Hottie and Shauna Valor in their try-out match, Liam pulled his wife onto his lap, wanting to get her opinion of the women after she'd spent some time with them in the locker room earlier. While they seemed to have a fairly high workrate in the ring, he was worried they wouldn't be able to pull off the heel gimmick on a worldwide level. Yeah, in the wilds of Wyoming, they could probably piss off a few hunters with their khaki uniforms and rules about how to behave in the wilderness. But with having grown up in New York City, he couldn't see Park Rangers as a group of people who could be universally considered the bad guys. Or bad gals in this case.

"What's your opinion on Alexa and Cady?" Liam whispered in Rylie's ear, not wanting to take anyone else's attention off the monitors.

"They seem nice," Rylie shrugged, obviously not getting what he was asking. "But I only talked to them for a few minutes earlier."

"Yeah, but do you think they can pull off working heel?"

"Maybe?" Again, Rylie shrugged as she continued watching the monitor in front of them. "I'm waiting to see how they do with the spot they were talking about earlier to see if it draws heat from the fans before I decide."

Since Liam hadn't overheard anything they were planning as they were choreographing their match earlier, he had to sit and wait with his wife and the rest of the GWA crew to see what Rylie was talking about. Luckily, he didn't have to wait long, as it soon became apparent when Alexa distracted the ref with accusations that the babyface team was cheating while Cady snuck in a right hook on Holly, which was supposedly an infraction that would lead to a disqualification in professional wrestling.

As the crowd roared, trying to get the ref to reprimand the Park Rangers for breaking the rules they claimed to be sticklers about upholding, Liam decided they could definitely pull off working heel, even if their gimmick wasn't universally hated.

"Yeah, I think they'll be good as heels," Rylie giggled, watching the monitor to see where Cady claimed to have hit Holly with a forearm instead of a closed fist to knock her out. "Especially since they just pulled off a Red Velvet signature spot and were almost as good at it as you and Dion were."

"Like anyone could ever pull off being sneaky heels as well as me and D," Liam playfully scoffed, earning a smile from his wife for his feigned cockiness.

As the referee counted Holly out to give the Park Rangers the victory, Liam kissed Rylie's temple, picking her up off his lap as he stood, so he could go meet with Rick and the bookers to give his opinions on the match. She took over his chair, staying with their friends and coworkers to continue watching the next match on the card, as he went to perform the duties of his new job.

A couple of hours later, he finally had everything done to successfully incorporate the newest members of the roster into the GWA family. He'd also sent off an email to the human resources department about hiring some public relations staff to specifically focus on scheduling endorsement deals and charitable appearances for all the talent, now that he'd clarified with Rick that he wanted that done in-house, instead of hiring an outside firm like Liam had with his business manager.

Since Bradan had declined Liam's offer to work for the GWA, claiming his company didn't normally handle scheduling endorsement deals and charitable appearances for their clients and that he'd had to contract it out to a PR firm for Liam, he'd had to have some video conferences with the PR firm Bradan had hired to set up his endorsement deals and charitable appearances, so he could learn the process they went through to complete those tasks. He'd made it clear that he was primarily asking to be better prepared to interview potential candidates when the GWA was ready to hire more people, so he half expected the publicist he'd spoken with to apply when the jobs became available on the GWA website. Not that he wanted to hire Dan Elsner after his long talk with the publicist, as he wasn't really impressed with the man he later found out was his cousin Caitlyn's boss. *I'd much rather hire Caitlyn to be one of the new GWA publicists, but I don't know how well that'll go over with the human resources department.* But in the meantime, he needed to know what to do, so he could represent his fellow wrestlers in reaching out to the various companies and nonprofit organizations that matched up best with their gimmicks and hometowns.

He'd also had to do a little research on what positions needed to be created in the corporate office, and what positions already existed in the public relations department that might be able to take on those tasks without him having to hire more people. As the GWA's current PR department consisted of only one publicist, whose primary responsibility was to promote their shows in every city they visited around the world; the social media manager, who planned the social media strategies for the whole company; and several social media specialists, who actually posted the content for all their individual talent accounts, as well as the GWA corporate accounts, there wasn't anyone available to take on the extra duty of scheduling endorsement deals and charitable appearances for the talent roster, making it entirely up to Liam to do the job for now. Which was why he was currently working with the human resources manager to establish at least two new publicist positions, one to reach out to businesses who pay for celebrity endorsements of their products and one to reach out to children's hospitals and other nonprofit organizations where the wrestlers could make unpaid appearances to help raise funds and patient morale, and planning to go through the interview process to fill those positions. At this point in time, he was thinking these two jobs could be done primarily over the phone and internet, like the PR firm Bradan had hired for him, only at the GWA corporate office in New York.

If only I could do their interviews the same way we do talent interviews, in person while on tour, instead of having to schedule video conferences with the applicants that work with the HR hours in New York, he thought as he finally parked their rental car at the hotel for the night. That thought made him question if the positions might be better as traveling jobs, so the publicists could reach out in person to more than just the businesses and nonprofits in New York. *Maybe I should call the PR Pro Shop back and ask a few more questions. Or maybe I'll just call my cousin Caitlyn since she works there. She might not be a publicist yet, but I bet she'd know how often the publicists she works with have to travel as part of their jobs. I'll just have to make sure to have the human resources people handle all the interviews and make the final hiring decision if she wants to apply for one of these jobs, so there's no question about me having biased hiring practices.*

"Are you okay, Teidí Béirín?" Rylie questioned, as they got out of the car, leaving their gear bags in the trunk so they didn't have to carry them back down with the rest of their luggage in the morning. "You've been awfully quiet since we left the arena and that's not like you, so now you've got me worried that something went wrong earlier and you haven't told me about it."

"Nothing's wrong, Mo Ghrá," Liam assured his wife as he grabbed his laptop bag and locked up the car before putting his arm around her shoulders to walk into the hotel. "Just thinking about how I'm going to have to find time to schedule online interviews for the PR jobs we're adding at corporate in the next couple of months."

"I know Rick said this new job wouldn't interfere with your wrestling, but I'm starting to wonder if he realizes just how much time you're already putting into it." Rylie sighed as she put her arm around his waist. "Or if he's so distracted with everything baby that he doesn't realize just how much he's put on your shoulders while still expecting you to wrestle five days a week."

"Yeah, he knows," Liam assured her as they walked through the lobby and caught the elevator. "That's one of the things we discussed tonight after signing the Park Rangers. And we decided to cut my wrestling schedule back to just TV nights. Well, as much as we can until we hire the other five guys he wants to add to the roster. So I'll have more time the rest of the week to deal with everything myself, until I can get a couple of people hired at corporate to take some of the outside scheduling off my hands."

"Is it cutting back on your time in the ring that's got you all broody then?" Rylie questioned as Liam pushed the button for their floor.

Liam thought for a moment, trying to figure out why he was in a bit of a dour mood. "Surprisingly, no," he finally replied, shaking his head just as the elevator doors opened on their floor. "I actually think cutting back my ring time will help save my knees and back, so I'll be able to keep wrestling as long as you want to, even if it's longer than the two more years I had in mind. Who knows, if I can stay injury free, I might even make it to twenty years with the GWA and not just twenty years since I first started training as a wrestler."

Rylie waited until he'd opened the door to their hotel room and they were alone on the other side of it before asking her next question. "So, if it's not cutting your ring time that has you scowling, then what is it? 'Cause I'm not buying that it's just because you're stressed about doing online interviews for the jobs you've got to hire for at corporate. Did you get bad news when you talked to Doc earlier and just didn't know how to break it to me?"

"No, that's definitely not it," Liam assured his wife with a huge sigh of relief. "My lab reports are negative for everything. And I'll gladly show them to you if you need the reassurance of seeing them to believe me."

"No, you don't have to do that. I believe you." Rylie put her purse down on the dresser before stepping close and hugging him. "I just want to know what's wrong so I can help you fix the problem and get you to smile again."

"There's not a problem you can fix, Mo Ghrá." Liam placed his laptop bag beside her purse before wrapping her in his arms and lightly kissing the top of her head. "Unless you can convince Rick that it's okay for me to bypass all the hoops human resources are gonna put me through to create these two new publicist jobs and just hire my cousin Caitlyn to take one of them and do all the HR stuff to hire the second one."

"Actually, I think you'd have to set her up as the PR manager and have her hire however many publicists she needs to make that department run smoothly." Rylie ran her hands up under his jacket, kneading the muscles of his back as if she was trying to get him to release the tension he was carrying around.

"Unfortunately, she's only worked as a PR assistant since college, so it would be an obvious case of nepotism if I did that," Liam admitted, relaxing under Rylie's touch, even though he was irritated by thinking about how the publicist Caitlyn worked with had boasted about his qualifications while belittling the women who worked under him for not having the same contacts he did. *Like Caitlyn could possibly have as many business contacts as someone who's been in the business ten or fifteen years longer than she has. But I guess at least having talked to Dan Elsner on the phone last week, I now know his name, so I can veto his application from the get-go. And I can't get in trouble for discrimination for not even considering him for one of these jobs, since misogynistic arseholes aren't a protected class of people.* "Since she hasn't worked her way up from an entry-level position in the company she's worked at for the last few years, I'm sure HR would have problems with it if I just hired her as a PR manager without even looking for a more qualified candidate. To be honest, I'm not sure I'd even be able to interview her for one of the new publicist positions we're currently discussing, since she doesn't have any experience in that position. And that's not even taking into account the fact that we're related."

"So, tell her to apply, but don't say anything about her to the HR department, and let them do all the interviews without you, so there's no hint of favoritism if she gets the job," Rylie suggested.

As much as Liam wanted to agree with his wife that he'd tell Caitlyn to apply for one of the new positions, he didn't think that would do anything but cause a rift between him and his cousin, since he didn't believe Caitlyn would make the cut to even get an interview if he left the screening up to the HR department due to her lack of experience. *But Dan Elsner might.* "But if I do that, I might get stuck with the misogynistic arsehole she works with now, who I talked to last week while trying to figure out what titles to assign to these two jobs and the qualifications to look for when hiring them."

"Okay," Rylie sighed, rubbing against him in a way that made him start to forget what they were talking about.

The pressure of her abs rubbing over his cock felt even better than her pillow-soft tits pushing into his ribcage. Liam instantly hardened, deciding it was time to change the subject to getting naked, so he could finally make love to his wife without a condom for the first time. *Why the feck did I waste all this time talking about work, when I could have been making love to her already?*

"How about you have HR do all the preliminary interviews and send you the résumés of their top five picks, so you can avoid interviewing the misogynist. And if Caitlyn makes the cut to interview with you, you can recuse yourself from all the second round interviews and have Rick sit in on them instead."

"Yeah, I'll do that," Liam agreed, even though he only half understood what she'd said. He pulled back from their embrace just enough that they could look into each other's eyes. "But enough talk about work. I'm ready to celebrate my ninety-day tests being negative by making love to my wife."

Rylie didn't have time to do more than smile in response as he dipped his head and kissed her. She returned his passion by spearing her tongue into his mouth as soon as he parted his lips, not giving him the chance to be the one in control of deepening the kiss.

Liam could only smile in his mind as he let her take charge, wondering just how far she'd take things before she relinquished control to him once more. As she explored the recesses of his mouth with her tongue, he slid his hands down to grip the globes of her ass, pulling her tighter against him as he rocked his hips to grind his hard-as-a-rock cock on her pubic bone.

Rylie glided her hands around his torso, unbuttoning his suit jacket before pushing it off his shoulders. Liam had to release his hold on her long enough to let the jacket fall to the floor, but wanted to get her back in his arms quickly so he could lift her red sweater dress up over her head and off her body. He didn't get the chance however, when she broke their kiss, dropped to her knees, and reached for his belt.

"Feck, Mo Ghrá, what are you doing?" Liam groaned, torn between stopping her so he could get her naked and letting her have her way, since it appeared that she wanted to give him a blow job now that they knew it was safe. On the one hand, he desperately wanted to know what it would feel like to be inside her bare and didn't want to risk coming before he got in her pussy. But on the other hand, he worried that his first time ever without a condom would feel so fecking incredible that he'd end up being a two-pump chump if he didn't prime the pump first.

"Something I've been dying to do for the last couple of months," Rylie grinned up at him as she unfastened his belt and slacks, pushing them and his boxer briefs halfway down his thighs and getting them out of her way to free his cock. "Sucking your dick."

She gripped his shaft in both hands, lapping up the drop of precum oozing from the tip before closing her lips over his crown. He loved the way she squeezed his base tight, holding him exactly where she wanted him as her hot, wet mouth engulfed him.

"Oh, feck," Liam moaned, feeling a tingle in his balls from the pure pleasure of her tongue stroking over his frenulum as she bobbed up and down on about a third of his length. Not wanting to miss any part of the show she was putting on for him, he quickly removed his tie and shirt, so the fabric wouldn't block his view when he instinctually started bucking his hips to gently fuck her mouth. "Yeah, suck my cock. Oh, feck, yeah, that feels so good, Mo Ghrá."

Once her saliva dripped down his dick, she used it as lube and finally started stroking the bottom part of his cock that wouldn't fit in her mouth. As much as Liam loved just watching her as she had her way with him, he couldn't resist reaching down and pulling her braids into a makeshift ponytail, knowing she wouldn't want to risk any bodily fluids getting on them and causing her to have to wash them more than once this week.

Apparently, him holding her hair back as if it was a handle he could use to control her movement was a turn-on for her, causing her to take more of his cock in her mouth. He loved the feel of her uvula stroking over the head of his dick as his tip reached the back of her throat when she swallowed about half of his nine-inch length.

"Use one hand to play with my balls while you suck me," he commanded, unable to stop himself from talking her through it, when her oral inexperience showed as she pulled her head back, even as she tried to suck him back in. "Feck, yeah, just like that."

Rylie's head bobbed up and down, as Liam enjoyed the feel of her testing the limits of what she could handle. He knew from the one other blow job she'd given him in the past that she had limited experience at giving head. In fact, since she'd told him that BJ in November was her first time sucking a dick, he was positive his was the only cock that had ever been in her mouth, so he held out as long as he could to let her find her groove. But even though she was no deep-throat pro, her mouth felt too amazing for him to hold back very long before he had to take over control.

"Keep your mouth open and relax your throat, so I can fuck your face."

Rylie hummed around his dick, obviously smiling as she obeyed his instructions. Liam used both hands to hold her head still as he fucked his cock through her lips and over her tongue. It might look like he was brutally fucking her mouth, but he maintained control of his thrusts, stopping each stroke just as he felt her uvula on his crown, so he didn't take even the slightest chance on hurting her.

When he felt the distinctive tingle in his spine that signaled his balls were about to draw up and shoot off, he pulled from the heaven of her mouth. As much as he knew he'd enjoy coming down her throat, he wanted to come in her pussy more. He just hoped he'd somehow manage to maintain control, so he didn't embarrass himself by coming too soon, like a sixteen-year-old virgin.

"No, don't stop," Rylie begged as he reached for her underarms to lift her back to her feet. "I want you to come in my mouth and then eat my pussy, so when we kiss afterwards, we'll taste the two of us mixed together."

"Feck," Liam groaned, torn between stripping her down to get inside her bare and fulfilling one of the items she'd recently added to their fucket list.

He'd been confused when she first used the term, thinking she meant the fuck-it list he'd heard of, which was a list of things an individual wanted to stop doing. But thankfully, she'd explained that she meant it like a traditional bucket list, only with all the sexual things they wanted to try before they died. Now that they'd checked off the mile-high club, their fucket list mostly contained different positions and exotic places where they wanted to make love, most of which they'd probably never be brave enough to try for fear of getting caught. So, he couldn't bring himself to make her wait to do the first thing she specifically requested they try in the heat of the moment. *At least I know that coming now will help me last longer once I get in her pussy.*

"Okay, but you have to lose some clothing first," Liam acquiesced, releasing his grip on her hair to stroke his cock, spreading his precum down his shaft while she stripped off her long-sleeved sweater dress. "You can leave the boots and panties on for now, but lose the bra. That way, if it's too much for you to swallow, I can shoot the rest on your tits."

"Are you planning to check off multiple items on our fucket list with one orgasm, Teidí Béirín?" Rylie grinned at him as she dropped her dress on the floor after she pulled it over her head. She then unfastened the front clasp on her bra and added it to the growing pile of their clothes.

Liam toed off his shoes and socks, shoving his pants and boxer briefs down and off as he replied. "Of course not, Mo Ghrá," Liam grinned as he stepped back up to her and aimed his cock toward her lips once more. "I want you to finger yourself while you're sucking my cock, so technically it'll be two orgasms, one for me and one for you."

Rylie giggled as she reached out to grip his dick with one hand while pushing the other under her panties. Once she had ahold of his cock, Liam released it, moving his hands back to her hair and loosely holding her braids together at the back of her head. Instead of replying with words, Rylie stuck her tongue out and licked his dick from base to tip, like it was her favorite flavor of ice cream swirling up from a cone.

"Feck, Mo Ghrá," Liam moaned when she tickled the tip of her tongue over his frenulum.

Rylie just smiled in response, obviously recognizing that she'd found his most sensitive spot.

"Quit teasing me, Mo Ghrá, and suck my cock," Liam ordered, his voice coming out gravelly with need. "And don't just rub your little clit. I want you to fuck yourself with your fingers, so they're covered with your cum when you pull them out for me to lick off before I eat your pussy."

"Yes, Sir," Rylie grinned before closing her lips over his cock once more and sucking him to the back of her throat.

Liam tilted his head to see around her glorious tits and enjoy the view of her hand moving under her red lace thong. With the way she'd pushed the panties down in front, he could easily see how she used her thumb on her clit while she had two fingers knuckle-deep in her pussy. The sight was so hot, it didn't take him long before he was right on the brink once more, barely able to hold back his orgasm until he saw her whole body tense up as she reached her first climax of the night.

"Feck, yeah, Mo Ghrá," Liam praised her. "Come from sucking my cock. Such a good girl."

Thankfully, she didn't bite down as she shuddered with each wave of her orgasm, even though she did stop bobbing her head up and down on his dick. Liam took over once more, holding her head still as he pumped his hips to fuck her mouth.

He barely gave her time to finish coming down from her high before he shot his load down her throat, praying she was coherent enough to control her swallow reflex so she didn't choke, as rope after rope of cum exploded from his cock. Since he'd been the one to add coming on her tits to their fucket list, he pulled back about halfway through his orgasm, just in case she couldn't swallow all his jizz, and enjoyed the gorgeous sight of his white sticky cum covering her terra-cotta tipped, tawny brown tatas. As always, he seamlessly slipped into Irish as he cried out his pleasure, her name being the only English word he uttered as he repeatedly declared his love for her while he spurted three more times on her boobs. It might make him a caveman, but he loved marking her as his with his cum.

As soon as the aftershocks seemed to pass, he helped her stand before sucking her sweet cream from her fingers, dropping to his knees, and shoving her panties down her legs. He didn't bother removing her boots before he propped her left thigh on his shoulder and dove into her pussy like a starving man. He squeezed her ass in his hands as he licked and sucked her tender flesh, holding her in place for him to fuck her with his tongue until she exploded in another orgasm.

"Oh, oh, yes, Liam," Rylie cried out, weaving her fingers through his hair to hold his head in place between her legs, as she pumped her hips to push his nose into her clit, while his tongue was buried inside her wet cunt.

He relished the way her inner walls clamped down on his tongue as he swallowed down the gush of girl-cum she released with her second climax. *Feck, she tastes so sweet.*

He waited until she seemed to stop shuddering with the waves of her release before pulling his tongue from her pussy and pecking a kiss on the top of her mound. He then lowered her foot to the floor, unzipped her boots, and helped her remove them and her socks.

Deciding that sex without condoms was messy enough that they should probably do it in the shower to keep from leaving stains on the comforter and sheets before trying to sleep in the bed without rolling in the wet spot, he then stood, picking her up and kissing her as he carried her to the bathroom. *Feck, she was right about her sweet and my salty mixing well to be a tasty treat.*

Even though he'd just come, his dick was already hard again, eagerly seeking out her pussy, as she wrapped her arms and legs around him and returned the kiss with equal ardor. He barely managed to step into the shower before he impaled her on his cock, not even bothering to turn on the water.

"FECK, Rylie!" Liam broke off the kiss, as his eyes rolled back in his head from the exquisite feel of being inside her without any barriers between them. The difference compared to wearing a condom was surreal, probably because of his love for Rylie as much as it was because of it being his first time to ever go condomless.

Even in all his fantasies, he hadn't imagined the wet heat of her pussy would intensify to this extreme. He'd just thought being bare inside her would feel like having sex after putting a lubricated condom on inside out, or lubing up his cock before putting on a condom. But he was way off in his expectations. Yeah, her arousal definitely made condomless sex a wetter experience, but it also allowed for him to feel her inner temperature, literally making the whole encounter hotter. Not to mention how the rough texture of her G-spot felt as he dragged his cock over it with each stroke in and out of her pussy.

Liam buried his face in the hollow where her neck met her torso as he pressed her back against the wall, licking and kissing her between murmuring Irish terms of endearment. He lost all sense of time and space, no longer consciously in control of the thrusting of his hips as he fucked her like a primal animal claiming his mate. They were so connected that it was as if they were one being, making Liam finally understand the Bible passages that talked about two becoming one. As he thrust inside her until his balls slapped into her ass, he couldn't tell where he ended and she began.

Rylie seemed to be just as enthralled in their carnal coupling as he was, writhing and moaning as she nipped and sucked the skin between his pecs and shoulders between soft susurrations of sweet nothings combined with his name. They fucked like beasts for what could have been hours or only minutes without either of them registering the passing of time, until finally her inner walls squeezed his cock in waves, as she reached yet another orgastic apex, milking a simultaneous climax out of him.

Once again, he felt the tell-tale tingle in his spine just as his balls drew up and his orgasm blasted through him, filling her with jet after jet of his cum. It didn't matter that he'd already had one explosive orgasm that night. This release was stronger, more powerfully profound than any he'd ever experienced in his life, leaving him feeling like he'd been drained of his life force and his soul was floating off to Heaven. Only he wasn't alone on this celestial plane. Rylie was right there with him, still wrapped in his arms as he was wrapped in hers.

"I love you so much, Mo Ghrá," Liam whisper-shouted as he stumbled while carrying her over to the bench in the shower, barely able to sit down before his legs gave out.

"I love you, too, Teidí Béirín," Rylie panted out breathlessly, still clinging to him, even though her hold seemed to have loosened.

He wasn't sure how long they sat there catching their breath and embracing in the afterglow of their lovemaking. But once he finally felt like he had control of his body again, he started to wonder what their chances were of conceiving the first time he filled her womb with his sperm.

"After we clean up, I wanna look at the NFP chart to see if we were in the zone or not." He knew from going over the chart with her as part of their natural family planning class that she'd most likely ovulated a few days earlier, but he thought they might still be in the window around the actual day of ovulation when they might be able to conceive.

"We're not," Rylie sighed, her warm breath wafting over his neck as she rested her head on his shoulder. "At least, I don't think we are. It depends on whether we go with the fifteenth for the first day of my period, since that's what day it was while we were in Australia when it happened, or the fourteenth, since that's what day it was in the States at the time. Since we're back in the U.S. now, I think we have to go with the fourteenth, which means today's the eighteenth day of my cycle and one day past that fertile window."

Even though Liam was a little disappointed that they'd missed the optimal days for making a baby, he knew it wasn't the right time career-wise for them. As much as he wanted kids with her, he also wanted to spend the next couple of years watching her reach the pinnacle of her time as a wrestler. Knowing she was about to get her first title run as the women's division champion, he resolved then and there to keep better track of her fertile time each month and try to keep from coming inside her when she was ovulating. At least, he would until she told him she was ready to actively start trying to get pregnant.

"I know you think it's gonna be difficult for us to get pregnant, but I still think we need to be careful around that week each month," Liam informed her before brushing his lips over her forehead. "Coming on your tits and in your mouth was hot as feck. So if you liked that as much as I did, then we have a couple of options to make sure we wait until at least after your first title run before trying for our first baby."

"I did like that," Rylie grinned as she lifted her head from his shoulder. "Even though I now have to wash my braids again to get your cum off them."

"Sorry, Mo Ghrá, I did try to hold them back out of the way when I came. But I totally forgot about needing to keep them behind your back when I lost control from how fecking fabulous it felt to be inside you with no barriers."

"It's fine," Rylie giggled, her smile only widening. "I coulda tied them back too, but I also wasn't thinking about the possibility of them flopping forward and ending up between us then. I'll just have to make sure I schedule washing my hair on the same day I ovulate for the next few months, since I suppose we should at least wait until after our convalidation ceremony in the Church before getting pregnant. But I'll be happy with only a couple of months as the women's champion, so we can tell the bookers I wanna drop the belt at *Gateway to the Gold*, so we can start trying to have a baby this summer."

"As you wish, Mo Ghrá." Liam dipped his head and kissed his wife as he stood to go turn on the shower, looking forward to helping her wash his cum from her braids for many years to come. He still thought she needed more time in the ring to reach her full potential, but he was done being an eejit and arguing against his own interests. So, while he might take control of their sexual encounters most of the time, he'd leave the decisions about when she'd quit wrestling and they'd have kids up to her and God.

Chapter Sixteen

As they were finishing up the final planning meeting that morning before the show that afternoon, Liam was surprised when Rick looked pointedly at him and Rylie and asked, "Are you dead set on doing the TV vow renewal in August as another triple ceremony? Or would you consider leaving that to just the Stones and doing the Reds' vow renewal in Dublin at *No Remorse*?"

"That wasn't something I even knew was a possible option," Liam shrugged as he turned to look at Rylie to see what she thought of the idea. "But I'm always up for another wedding with my beautiful bride. How 'bout you, Mo Ghrá?"

"Sure," Rylie nodded, smiling. "I'm good with whatever works best for all our angles. But will it be okay if I wear my Vegas wedding gown then, so I can keep the dress I'm wearing for our Church wedding in May off the dirt sheets?"

"Oh, yeah, I wouldn't ask you to make any part of your spiritual ceremony available for public consumption," Rick assured her before elaborating on his reasoning for the change to their show plans. "And I think being able to announce a vow renewal in Liam's gimmick hometown right before you two challenge the new heavyweight and women's division champions will reinforce his face turn and the Valors' heel turn tonight. Plus it'll send the fans home happy after they realize the faces they were cheering for earlier just turned on them."

They worked out a basic script for the finish of that night's card, which would be a discussion between Protection Detail and the Reds in the middle of the ring after their match with the new tag-team champions walking away without their manager. Once it was just the two of them in the ring, Chastity would tell Liam that he needed to quit using so many underhanded tactics to get his way in the ring and he would agree to help her get justice for the fans after the way the Valors spurned them earlier in the evening.

The current plan was for Liam to negotiate with Chastity to get him to turn face only if she agreed to renew their vows in his "hometown" at *No Remorse*. But as soon as the meeting broke up and Rylie went to the back to meet with the stylists, who'd been hired by the GWA to do all the ladies hair and makeup that day, to get new braids put in before the show, Liam suggested a change to Rick and the bookers, one that he wanted to surprise his wife with in the middle of the squared circle.

"Hey, Boss, I think I have a better idea for the promo to finish the show tonight."

"Um, shouldn't you have brought this up before we turned everyone loose?" Cooper eyed him dubiously.

"Do I need to call everyone else back out here to rework it again?" Rick only looked slightly irritated, but he also appeared curious.

"No, it's not that much of a change that it'll affect everyone else's parts tonight," Liam informed him and the others still standing around. "Just instead of negotiating with Chastity about cutting out my bad guy behavior and challenging the Valors, I think I should immediately agree when she asks me to quit cheating to win and drop to one knee to *propose* the vow renewal and challenging the Valors at *No Remorse*. That way I won't come off as reluctant about the turn, and it'll give me a chance to surprise her with an engagement ring since I didn't get her one before."

"He does have a point about the current plan making him appear to be reluctant to work face," Stone pointed out, nodding his head.

"Do you have an engagement ring to give her?" Rick asked, obviously seeing the only flaw in Liam's plan.

"No, not yet," Liam shrugged. "But I know what she likes and have some time to go buy one now while she's busy with the hair stylist for the next few hours."

Since she'd taken her braids out a few days earlier to give her hair a rest before putting in more, he knew he had at least six hours before she'd be done in the stylist's chair. She'd be cutting it close for the show's four p.m. start time since they were in the Pacific time zone and had to start the pay-per-view at seven p.m. in the Eastern time zone. But it wasn't a big deal because they were in the main event and not jerking the curtain.

"Then you'd better get out of here now, so you can find one," Rick chuckled, implying he agreed without explicitly approving Liam's script change.

"Thanks Boss," Liam grinned as he ran up the ramp from ringside to find Crockett backstage. While his fellow Vegas groom probably didn't know where to find the best jewelry store in Los Angeles any more than Liam did, he had two fathers-in-law who most definitely would know where to send him. Now Liam just had to hope Crockett hadn't snuck off for a quickie with his wife, since Aiken didn't have to spend hours in the stylists' chairs for braids like Rylie and Teagan.

Luckily, he found Crockett and Surfer Josh in catering, having a mid-morning snack and choreographing their match without either of their wives. Liam momentarily felt guilty for not doing the same when he saw Blade sitting with Protection Detail at the next table. But after almost sixteen years in the GWA and eighteen years in the wrestling business, he felt more than capable of calling it in the ring, even when working with younger guys like Blade and Protection Detail, who were only a couple of years into their careers and weren't as familiar with the old-school style of wrestling he'd been taught.

Liam looked around to make sure none of the other women were within hearing distance as he sat down with Crockett and Josh. "Hey, Crockett, can you call Shawn or Theo and find out where I should go to get Rylie an engagement ring without telling Amethyst, so I can surprise her with it at the end of the card tonight?"

"Yeah," Crockett chuckled as he pulled out his phone to make the call.

"It's about time you got her more than just the gold band you gave her last month," Josh commented, shaking his head.

"Hey, shouldn't you be over here helping us plan our match for tonight?" Blade questioned, turning around to slap a hand on Liam's shoulder.

Liam turned away from Crockett to look at the man he'd been teaming with for the last couple of months. "Naw, since you're doing the job, I just need you to fill me in on the high spots and the finish, and maybe how many times you want us to tag in and out, and I'll call my part in the ring."

"I'll never understand how you can wrestle that way." Blade shook his head.

Blade had only been with the GWA for a couple of years, joining the roster in January of 2018 after spending the last six months of his eight years in the Navy doing physical therapy for a leg injury that cut short his career as a SEAL. He only had one year under his belt of training and working in the indies before his try-out match that earned his spot with the GWA, so Liam wasn't surprised that he didn't have the vast knowledge of wrestling moves that was required to be able to start a match without a plan. But he still thought Blade's Navy training should have prepared him to understand how to change the plan in the middle of a fight.

"It's no different than when you were a SEAL and had to improvise when a mission didn't go as planned," Liam offered, trying to explain to the younger man. "Well, other than the fact that we're not using weapons and actually have to tell our opponents what we're doing so nobody gets hurt."

"Yeah, but back then we at least had a couple of contingency plans in case plan A went FUBAR," Blade grumbled. "And even though I'd prefer having a backup plan, I get that's not always possible when we've gotta cover a botch or if the bookers call an audible and we have to go home early without doing everything we planned. But I can't come up with every move on the fly for a whole match. I need a battle plan to work with so I don't end up with go-away heat from using too many rest holds to think about what to do next."

"That's just because you haven't been in the business long enough for sequences of moves to start to feel ingrained yet. Once you've got a few more years in the ring, you'll get a feel for which moves flow together best for you, so you'll know the next four or five moves that come right after the one you call. And if you work with the same opponent long enough, you'll be able to read each other's body language so well that you won't even have to call them to put on a clinic without a run-through first."

"He's right," Crockett backed up Liam's claim. "If you wanna see it done in person, just ask Rick and Cooper to get in the ring to spar."

Leah Mae Wright

"Or just watch some of their matches from back in the day on our flight tomorrow," Josh added. "I don't know how long they'd been wrestling without even having to call it in the ring when I joined the roster in twenty-ten. But by then, the only time they even decided on the finish was when the bookers wanted their matches to end a certain way, like in a double DQ or a screw job."

"They were already just calling it in the ring when I joined the roster in oh-four," Liam added, nodding along to show his agreement with Crockett and Josh. "In fact, working with Rick and Cooper is how I learned to call it in the ring in the first place. And I'm pretty sure it was the same for Stone."

"Since they're all bookers now, you think they might have time to teach those of us who are newer to the roster how to call it in the ring without looking bad?" Trojan asked, pointing to the tablet where he was taking notes while planning that nights' match. "I have all my match choreography going back to when I first started training, but maybe they know a better way to figure out those sequences than trying to read through all my old matches and look for a pattern."

Liam had wondered why Trojan took notes every time they did a match run-through, but always assumed it had something to do with memory issues or maybe OCD tendencies, which was why he'd always pre-planned his matches with the Canadian tag team in the past, not wanting to throw either of them off their game. He never thought it might be a way for Cameron to review his previous matches to help him plan better for his future performances.

"Yeah, maybe," Liam shrugged. "But even if they don't have time, I'll be glad to help you, starting with just having you follow my lead while we're in the ring today."

"But unless you wanna go jewelry shopping with us now, you're gonna hafta wait 'til we get back to the arena later to start that first lesson," Crockett interjected, cutting off Liam before he suggested some extra sparring workouts over the next few weeks to give the younger guys some practice with calling moves without an audience to make them nervous. "'Cause my fathers-in-law are leaving now to meet us on Rodeo Drive, where there are apparently several jewelry stores to choose from with lots of necklaces, bracelets, and earrings Shawn swears Aiken will love as a Valentine's present."

"Yeah, I'll pass on that," Blade chuckled. "No way I wanna take a chance on running into a ring rat who might get ideas about me putting a rock on her finger."

"Rodeo Drive is a bit too pricey an area for ring rats to troll for hookups, isn't it?" Magnum questioned, looking around at the other guys for confirmation.

"Not if she's also into Hollywood A-listers, like the rat I banged at the club last night," Blade offered with a shrug.

"Yeah, I don't want to hear about your hookups." Liam shook his head at Blade as he stood to go with Crockett. He then directed his parting words to Protection Detail, even though he would also extend the offer to Blade or any of the other younger guys who wanted to learn. "I probably won't have time today because of the early start time of the show, so just follow my lead in our match later to get a feel for how it works. And let's plan to spend some extra time in the ring later this week, so we can go over how to hide your calls during our sparring workouts, since that's really the hardest thing to learn."

"Will do," Harrison and Cameron agreed in unison.

Liam left them to plan the match with Blade, while he went to endure the craziness of shopping on Rodeo Drive for what he hoped would be the only time in his life.

Why do I have a feeling I'm about to spend more on this ring than I did on both our wedding bands in San Antonio? He smiled as he followed Crockett out to the parking lot where their rental cars were parked. *And I don't think it'll even count as a Valentine's present. Good thing I love her enough to not care how much the gifts cost as long as they make her happy.*

~~~

Rylie wasn't sure what to think when Harrison, Cameron, and Blade tracked her down in the stylist's chair while she was getting her braids put in, asking her opinion on their planned finish for their match without Liam with them. Since their plan was for her to be distracted by checking on Liam after he was tossed out of the ring so she couldn't stop Protection Detail from double-teaming Blade to get the pin, she understood their reasoning for filling her in on the details of
~~~

the finish. What she didn't get was why her husband had apparently left the arena when she'd assumed they'd both be there all day. Her confusion was only confounded when the three men only shrugged in response to her question about why Liam wasn't with them.

"I don't know if that finish is really the best idea," she objected, trying not to shake her head at them while the stylist was working on her hair. After working with Protection Detail for almost eleven months, she knew she had to keep the conversation focused on the match if she wanted any answers from them, since they weren't interested in anything to do with committing to a relationship or discussing the dynamics of making a marriage work, even if the marriage in question didn't include them. Since Blade was known to be just as much of a man-whore as the two Canadians, she assumed she had to keep the discussion on the match for him, too. "Maybe you should check with Rick or the bookers to make sure it's okay for Protection Detail to start using heel tactics now, when you're not supposed to turn until after your condom deal expires next month."

"So, maybe not a double team to take me down," Blade suggested, nodding in agreement. "But what about if I'm also distracted by Liam rolling out of the ring after Magnum hits the sperminator splash and don't realize I've been tagged in when Li barely makes contact with my pants? With our size difference, it'll be totally believable if I'm looking down at where you're checking on him at ringside and Magnum grabs me in a belly-to-back suplex to bring me into the ring. And being caught off guard like that, it won't take much for him to knock the wind out of me and roll me up for the pin without any heel tactics."

At six-foot-three and two-hundred-and-thirty-five pounds, Rylie wouldn't normally consider Blade small by any means. But compared to six-foot-seven, three-hundred pound Harrison, he definitely looked smaller than when he was standing by himself. But even with the four-inch height and sixty-five-pound weight differences, she wasn't sure it was enough for it to appear believable that Magnum could seriously hurt Blade so severely that it would be easy for him to get the pin after only one move.

"I think he needs to hit more than just a single belly-to-back suplex before the pin," Rylie stalled, her eyes darting around looking for her husband. "But run it by Liam and see what he thinks will be enough to be believable. Where did you say he went again? To help Cole find something he needs for dinner tonight?"

They hadn't said where Liam was or what he was doing, so she threw out one of the tasks he'd had to do the month before as part of his new role with the company to hopefully lead them to give something away.

"He didn't say where he was going," Blade started as Cameron talked over him.

"But that would explain why he asked Crockett to go with him, since he knows L.A. better than the rest of us after marrying Amethyst."

"Brent doesn't know where to find a grocery store in L.A.," Aiken scoffed, rolling her eyes, pulling out her phone, and quickly swiping her thumbs over the screen, presumably to send her husband a text. While Rylie was tempted to get her own phone out to text Liam, she decided to wait and see what Aiken found out first, knowing her friend would get their husbands' whereabouts now that the guys had finally given her some new information. "Much less a farmers' market, which is where I know Cole goes to find whatever produce he needs each day."

When everyone turned to look at Aiken where she was sitting on the floor near Teagan, so they could choreograph their portion of the mixed-tag match they were working that night with their husbands while Teagan got her braids put in with the second stylist there for the show, she clarified with a shrug, "Cole worked on a movie with Daddio a few years ago. So I'm assuming he still follows the same habits now that he's one of our head chefs, as he did when he was just an assistant chef in craft services back then."

"I swear you know like everyone who's ever worked on a movie set in Hollywood," Teagan chuckled, pointing at Aiken.

"No, not everyone, just the people who've worked with my dads," Aiken refuted with a grin as she put her phone back in her purse.

"Okay, well, we'll go run this finish by Stone, Cooper, and Ethan, and see if they have any better ideas," Blade interjected, obviously wanting to avoid getting pulled into a gossipy conversation.

Once the guys walked away, Rylie arched an eyebrow at Aiken, not having to say a word before her friend filled her in on their husbands' afternoon excursion.

"Don't worry, Chas. They aren't on a grocery run. They're with my dads on Rodeo Drive, shopping for Valentine's Day."

"Damn, now I wish Josh and I hadn't gone to the adult store together last night to pick our Valentine's gifts out early," Teagan pouted. "I wouldn't have worried at all about him thinking more surfing gear is romantic if he'd gone with your dads to shop for me."

"Seriously? You couldn't wait to be surprised because you thought he'd buy you surfing gear for Valentine's Day?" Rylie questioned her friend, while trying to think of something to get for Liam before the actual holiday.

"We're gonna be in South Dakota on Valentine's Day," Teagan pointed out. "So, no, I couldn't wait to go lingerie shopping when the store options are so much better here. And when I told him where I wanted to go and why, Josh agreed that we'd probably have better luck finding a good toy store here than in Sioux Falls, too. So, we went shopping together, which kinda works out since everything we bought is for both of us."

After thinking about how the selection of lingerie and adult toys would probably be better in Los Angeles than in any of the cities they'd visit in Utah, Colorado, North Dakota, or South Dakota before Valentine's day, Rylie agreed that Teagan and Josh had probably been wise to shop early. But since she wanted to do something more romantic and sweet for Liam, she hoped she hadn't waited too late to do her Valentine's shopping. Still, she needed some ideas besides a card and heart-shaped box of candy, which was all she'd thought of so far for her husband.

"I guess that makes sense," she agreed with Teagan before redirecting her gaze at Aiken. "What are you getting Crockett for Valentine's Day?"

"I ordered some stuff from La Perla and had it sent to the house so I could pick it up this weekend. And I plan to surprise him with it, along with a bottle of champagne and a tray of chocolate-covered strawberries in our room that night."

"Yeah, too bad I didn't think about ordering something early enough to have it delivered before Friday," Rylie sighed, knowing there was no way she'd have time to sneak out of the arena to go shopping the way Liam was because of the early start time of the pay-per-view and having to spend almost every minute between now and then in the stylist's chair.

"Do you trust Papa to shop for you?" Aiken asked, referring to her costume designer dad.

"Of course." Rylie rolled her eyes, thinking that was a stupid question after the amazing job Shawn Pearson had done the month before with picking out Rylie and Teagan's wedding dresses as well as all the guys' tuxedos. "But I can't ask him to pick out something for me to wear for Liam on Valentine's Day while he's out shopping *with Liam*."

"Oh, no, he wouldn't pick it out while Liam's with him." Aiken waved off Rylie's concern as she pulled her phone back out and started texting once more. "But once he and Daddio finish showing the guys where all their favorite jewelry stores are, he can stop at Fredrick's after Brent and Liam head back here. He even still has your sizes from dress shopping last month, so he can easily pick something up before the show this afternoon, and then give it to me at the house tonight for me to pass it on to you on the plane in the morning, or the locker room tomorrow afternoon if Liam doesn't have to sit with Rick and the bookers on the plane."

"You don't think he'll mind?"

"Of course not." Aiken shook her head. "He just needs to know if you have a preference for a specific color or style."

"Liam's favorite color is red, obviously," Rylie chortled. "And as hot as that corset style dress was last month, I'd prefer something that doesn't require as much work to get out of it, so no corsets this time around."

"Even if it's more of a waist cincher, pushing up the girls but leaving them and the hoo-hah exposed for easy access?" Aiken questioned as she texted Shawn with what Rylie had already stipulated.

"I suppose that would be okay. But I'd rather have something lacy and see-through, like a loose, flowy nightie with matching crotchless panties," Rylie decided. "And I'll need his info to Venmo him the money to cover it."

"Yeah, no problem. I'll text it to you," Aiken agreed as she continued texting with her papa.

Leah Mae Wright

It only took an hour of going back and forth with texts for Rylie to pick out a crimson red lace and mesh babydoll nightie with a pair of matching crotchless, lace-up back, cheeky panties. Once Shawn texted her the total, she sent him the money, looking forward to sneakily picking up her purchases the next day.

As soon as she was done in the stylist's chair, she ran to the women's locker room, so she could call the hotel in Sioux Falls to set up some in room surprises for her husband while she knew he couldn't walk up behind her and overhear her plans. *Now I just have to hope my period will come early, like tonight or tomorrow instead of the eleventh, or be extra light, or both, so I can actually wear this new lingerie on V-Day.*

When she finally saw Liam again after he returned to the arena, she didn't let on that she'd been the slightest bit worried about why he left the building or that she had any knowledge of his Valentine's Day shopping excursion. He played it off as having errands to run and she just smiled, kissed his cheek, and told him to let her know if she could do anything to help him with his new duties to the company, since they were keeping him so busy.

They then spent the rest of the day going through their normal routine, minus their in-ring match run-through due to the early start of the show to air live at seven p.m. on the East Coast. While they ate an early dinner in catering, the guys filled both her and Liam in on the new plans for the finish of the match. They were still going with Liam rolling out of the ring after taking the splash, which the wrestlers all called the sperminator splash whenever Magnum delivered it from the top rope because of how rare it was for someone of his size to fly, joking that he was sterilizing his opponents instead of pushing for them to use condoms to go along with their gimmick. They were also still going with both Chastity and Blade being distracted checking on Liam, but now instead of Magnum grabbing Blade from behind for the belly-to-back suplex, he'd wait for Blade to turn back to the ring, calling out to distract the ref from counting Liam out, only to be surprised by Magnum standing right there and grabbing him for a vertical suplex. Once Magnum suplexed him into the ring, he would maintain the hold on Blade's upper body while twisting his hips to roll them both over and pull Blade up into a standing position to hit another vertical suplex. He'd then repeat the move one more time to complete the Three Amigos, as made famous by the late, great Eddie Guerrero, before covering Blade for the pin. Which of course, would lead to the discussion in the middle of the ring, where the referee would decide that Protection Detail were officially the new tag-team champions, but they hadn't won their manager back since Liam had snuck in a clause in the contract that stated he had to be pinned to lose his wife's managerial services. Stone Fields had even agreed to make an appearance as the GWA commissioner, carrying a copy of the contract to ringside to clarify it for the in-ring official.

Over dinner was also when she learned that Liam would be calling his parts of the match in the ring, which was a skill she asked her husband to teach her since she hadn't mastered it yet. With Holly and Shauna being the only female performers with enough experience to completely choreograph a match on the fly after only deciding on the finish beforehand, Rylie hadn't had the opportunity to practice the skill since starting with the GWA because they'd all three been babyfaces the whole time she'd been with the company. Now that Shauna would be turning heel and starting a feud with Rylie, though, she hoped to expand her wrestling repertoire over the summer.

Watching Shauna Valor defeat Victoria Vicious for the women's division title after basically putting on a wrestling clinic to kick off the show only solidified Rylie's thoughts about how much she could learn from working with the older woman. It also made her think Liam was right in wanting to wait a little longer before intentionally trying to make a baby. While she'd told him she'd be happy with only holding the title a couple of months before they stopped tracking her cycle to avoid having him come inside her on the day she ovulated each month, she started to think she wanted to wait at least a couple of years before intentionally trying to have a baby. The extra time would not only give her the opportunity to learn a lot and achieve a few career goals, it would also give Liam the chance to achieve that twenty-year career he'd planned for from the first time he stepped foot in the squared circle, without having to take time off for paternity leave.

After a six-man tag match between Heavy Artillery and the Celestial Bodies, the card went on with a couple of singles matches from the mid-carders on the roster. Then the women's division tag-team titles were unveiled with the tournament to decide the first champions announced for *No Remorse* before the Goddesses and Hula 'Ōlapa faced off for their first GWA pay-per-view appearances. They threw in another tag-team match between the Dangerous Twins and the Bama Boys after the ladies-tag match and before the mixed-tag match pitting the Precious Stones and their husbands against each other.

Since the new women's tag-team titles were still on display at ringside, Emerald and Amethyst spent most of their time on the ring apron sneaking longing looks at the belts as a way to make the fans wonder if they would work things out to reunite or find new partners to form new teams before the tournament in April. As Crockett had gone over in the men's match at *Christmas Chaos*, he jobbed to Surfer Josh this time around, setting up the fans to expect a rubber match at *No Remorse*.

Rick planned to swerve the fans, though, booking that match on the GWA's weekly TV show in mid-March, so Protection Detail could come to ringside and try to persuade one of the Precious Stones to take over as their manager because they were frustrated by losing all their non-title matches since winning the titles and thought they needed a manager to help them implement some underhanded tactics to keep from losing their belts at the next pay-per-view. Of course, Crockett and Surfer Josh would take exception to Protection Detail flirting with their wives, abandoning their match to team up and defend their women. After a brawl that would lead to a double disqualification between Crockett and Surfer Josh, the Family Stone would come together, turning Crockett and Amethyst face while also turning Protection Detail heel.

After the mixed-tag match, there were only two matches left on the card, the ones the GWA billed as a double main event. First up, was the loser-must-retire match between Crusher Cooper and Vaughn Valor for the GWA heavyweight title. While closely watching their match and comparing it to the women's title match earlier, Rylie thought Rick and the bookers had screwed up by having the women jerk the curtain instead of the men. It wasn't that it was a bad match, per se, but it clearly wasn't as sharp as the match between Allissa and Shauna. Cooper took a couple of breathers that didn't make sense, selling a knee injury, even though Vaughn hadn't worked his knees at all, and making it obvious to the rest of the roster, and probably a few smart fans, why he was retiring after this match.

Once Vaughn won the title, Cooper took the mic and thanked the fans for their love and support over his twenty-year career, only slightly breaking kayfabe for his heel persona. The fans responding to his retirement speech by chanting, "thank you, Crusher," was the perfect way to set the stage for the Valors' heel turn.

As Shauna ran down to ringside to congratulate her husband, Vaughn took the mic from Cooper and threw a fit that would put most toddlers to shame. He stomped his feet and screamed at the fans. "Shut up! Stop thanking him! I'm the one you should be cheering right now! I'm the GWA heavyweight champion!"

Rolling into the ring as soon as she got to the end of the ramp, Shauna tried to console her husband, patting her hand first on his title, which Vaughn had resting on his shoulder, then on her own, which she wore around her waist. With her standing so close to her husband, she didn't have to take the mic for her words to be heard throughout the arena. "Ignore them, Vaughn. Their cheers mean nothing. We're the king and queen of the GWA now, so we no longer have to pander to these peasants."

"You're right, my sexy queen," Vaughn sneered out at the fans before turning to smile at his wife. "Now that we have our titles, we can quit pretending to care what these low-life losers want."

He dropped the mic and kissed his wife before assisting her out of the ring and walking up the ramp to a chorus of "boos" from the fans. Since they were no longer mic'd, Rylie could no longer hear what the Valors were saying to the fans taunting them on their way backstage. She couldn't even attempt to read their lips on the monitors because it was time for her to go with the guys to the gorilla position for their ring entrances.

Once the Valors cleared the curtain, Chad Westbrook announced the final match of the night, the match pitting Protection Detail against Liam Red & Blade for the GWA tag-team titles and Chastity's managerial services. In order to sell the lack of cohesion between the champs, they did three separate ring entrances instead of two. Protection Detail went to the ring first, as was traditional for the challengers in any title match. But then, instead of Liam, Chastity, and Blade going to the ring together, Blade's music hit next for him to walk down the ramp on his own. He stopped at the bottom of the ramp, not actually getting in the ring where Protection Detail was waiting, and turned to look up the ramp just as his music cut off and the Red Velvet theme song started. As Liam and Chastity walked down the ramp together, Blade kept his head on a swivel, looking back and forth between his tag-team partner and their opponents for the night, as if he wasn't sure which of them might attack him before the match even started.

After taking Liam's ring jacket and making a show of passing it off to the production assistant, who would carry it to the back along with the dagger and dog tags Blade used as props for his gimmick, Chastity smiled across the ring at her former teammates, wishing them good luck before getting out of the ring to stand in Liam's corner. As Blade and Trojan started off the match, she cheered for both of them whenever they successfully completed a move.

Once the ringside cameraman got close enough that their voices could be picked up on the microphone attached to the camera for the television audience, Rylie and Liam started a little banter to sell the angle.

"Hey, ye're not deir manager anymore, so ye should only be encouragin' me and me partner," Liam grumbled, looking down at her from the ring apron instead of paying attention as Blade attempted to reach him for a tag.

"But they're still my friends," Chastity pouted up at her husband. "So, I'm still going to encourage them when they're doing a good job."

Before Liam could argue her point, Blade managed to break away from Trojan to slap him on the shoulder for the tag.

"Go, Red, go!" Chastity clapped, bouncing on her toes with excitement and grinning up at her husband as he entered the ring to take on the smaller of the two Canadian wrestlers. Not that Cameron's six-foot-two and two-hundred-and-twenty pounds was really all that small, but Liam being two inches taller and twenty pounds heavier made Trojan appear to have a slight disadvantage.

Rylie paid close attention as the two men locked up in a collar-and-elbow tie-up, trying to see if she could see Liam's lips moving to guess what move he'd call next. But even walking along the side of the ring away from the corner post, she couldn't find the right angle to see his mouth before he had Trojan in a headlock and flipped him down to the mat. They then quickly transitioned from one amateur wrestling move to another so fast that she couldn't identify all of them, much less fathom how Liam was calling them in time for him and Trojan to trade the advantage back and forth in such a rapid-fire style. The sequence was so impressive that she was legitimately applauding for both men, and not just because she was supposed to continue selling her split loyalty.

This went on for several minutes before Liam used the classic heel tactic of an eye gouge to escape Trojan's half nelson while Blade had the referee distracted by acting like he was about to enter the ring without a tag. That time, Rylie did manage to see Liam use a hand signal to alert Blade to play his part, but she only recognized it because it was slightly different than the signal he'd used in previous matches to let her know it was time for Chastity to distract the ref. In those earlier instances, the distraction was pre-planned so she knew what to do. But with the distraction not being pre-planned this time, she hesitated long enough to try to make eye contact with Liam to figure out what he wanted her to do. That's when she noticed he was looking up at Blade, who was standing on the ring apron on the other side of the corner from where she was standing on the floor, so thankfully, she didn't blow the spot before Blade could duck his upper body under the top rope and start yelling at the ref.

I wonder when they worked that out, since they didn't mention it at dinner earlier. Maybe Liam went over his hand signals with the guys before he went Valentine's shopping earlier?

She momentarily got so lost in thought that she missed how Liam managed to get off the mat and tag Blade while keeping Trojan from making it across the ring to tag Magnum. They then spent a large chunk of the match having Trojan play Ricky Morton while Liam and Blade tagged in and out several times. Then finally, Liam made the "mistake" of whipping Trojan into the ropes on the same side of the ring where Magnum was standing, allowing the babyfaces to get the hot tag due to Magnum's impressive wingspan stretching from the tag rope to the center of that side of the ring.

With Magnum fresh from not having wrestled at any point earlier in the match, and Liam being slightly fatigued from having worked half the match, the hot tag started the sequence where Magnum would dominate Liam. Rylie found it quite amusing that other than the sperminator splash at the end of the segment, Liam was technically the one directing which moves Magnum would use to rough him up.

At this point, her job was to focus on encouraging only her husband, getting mad at her former teammate for intentionally trying to hurt the man she loved. It was her yelling at Magnum for being a "big ol' meanie" after he hit the splash that gave Liam the opportunity to roll out of the ring on the same side where Blade was standing holding the tag rope in their corner. She was impressed with the way Liam was able to barely brush his fingertips over the ankle of Blade's fatigues with one outstretched hand while holding his lower abdomen as if in severe pain with the other hand, just before he went under the bottom rope.

"Oh, Red! Are you okay?" Chastity ran around the corner post to kneel down on the floor beside Liam, catching the referee signaling the tag out of the corner of her eye at the same time Blade turned his back and no-sold the fact that he was now the legal man in the match.

She focused only on looking at Liam, not watching the planned finish to keep selling how concerned she was about her husband. But even without seeing it, she knew Magnum and Blade had pulled off the Three Amigos leading into the pin based on the huge pop they got from the crowd.

Blade was fuming as he got out of the ring, glaring as the title belt he'd worn to the ring was handed over to Trojan while Liam's was handed to Magnum. He turned toward the Reds, narrowing his eyes in disgust before spitting out, "Eff you, Red. If you hadn't insisted on tagging in that last time, I'd have pinned Trojan for us to keep the belts. So, I'm done tagging with you."

While he didn't have a mic in hand, he made sure to yell loud enough that he could be picked up on the mic in the hands of the ring announcer, who climbed into the ring to award the tag-team titles to Protection Detail and now stood halfway between the new tag-team champions and their defeated foes on the floor. Before Liam could reply to his now former tag-team partner, Blade turned and stomped around the ring and up the ramp to the backstage area.

"It's okay, Red, you don't need him," Chastity assured her husband, also speaking loud enough to be picked up on Chad's mic, as she stood from her kneeling position. "We'll find you a better partner. One who doesn't need to cheat to win, so you can be the sweet man I married instead of going along with your partner's bad habits."

As Protection Detail celebrated their first title run in the middle of the ring, Liam slowly got to his feet with Chastity's assistance. "No, Moh Graw, ye're de only partner I need. I'll go back ta singles matches wit ye as me manager from now on."

"Sorry, keener, but you seem to have forgotten who won this match," Trojan boasted, holding up his title belt as if waving it in Liam's face. "Which means Chastity is our manager again."

"No, it doesn't," Liam disagreed, a sneaky smile spreading on his face as he looped his arm around Chastity's shoulders. "I 'ad ta 'ave a partner ta defend de tag titles, so ye could win dem by pinnin' Blade. But ye had ta pin me ta win me wife as ye're manager."

"Yeah, no." Magnum stomped over to the side of the ring to loom down over them. "Chastity's our manager. Your marriage has nothing to do with it."

"Check de contract, boyos," Liam smirked. "Commissioner Stone, please bring de contract we signed last Tuesday down ta the ring ta show these eejits me wife is still me manager."

Liam walked her over to the ringside stairs so they could meet in the center of the ring with Protection Detail, the ring announcer, and the former wrestler, who was acting in the role of company official with the final say on what was legal in each of their matches. Once Stone walked down the ramp to join them in the ring, he pulled a folded packet of papers from the inside pocket of his suit jacket. He then flipped through them to show Magnum, Trojan, Chad, and the cameraman whose video was displayed on the jumbotron for everyone in the audience and watching on television to see the clause stating the only way Chastity's managerial services could change hands was if Liam Red was pinned by one of the members of Protection Detail to end the match.

"As you can see, the fine print clearly states that you could win the titles by defeating either Liam Red or Blade via pinfall or submission. But the only way to win Chastity's managerial services was to defeat Liam Red via pinfall. So, even if you'd have won the titles by getting Liam to submit in the middle of the ring, you still wouldn't have won Chastity's managerial services."

Leah Mae Wright

As Protection Detail stormed off, swearing to get their lawyers to look over their copy of the contract first thing Monday morning, Chastity stood there looking shellshocked.

"Thank ye, Commissioner," Liam smiled as he shook hands with Stone. "Now if ye don't mind, I have somethin' ta run by me wife before we discuss de contracts for our future matches."

Stone held up his hands in a placating gesture as he stepped back, moving over to lean back against one of the turnbuckles. Chad also backed up a step from where Rylie and Liam were standing, but he stayed close enough that everything they said would be picked up on the mic he still held.

"I hope this discussion includes you planning to follow the GWA rules from now on, instead of sneaking in illegal moves and contract clauses to make things go your way," Rylie grumbled, putting her hands on her hips as she set up for the debate with her husband that they'd worked out that morning to finish the card.

"Absolutely, Moh Graw," Liam agreed immediately, cutting her off before she could finish her lines.

She was just about to no-sell his last sentence and launch back into the script they'd settled on for her to suggest challenging the Valors for the heavyweight and women's division titles to avenge the fans for the new champions earlier mistreatment when Liam dropped to one knee in the center of the ring, completely catching her off guard with the last minute swerve on her. *What on earth is he doing?*

"I know ye don't like it when I cut corners ta get me way," Liam smiled, the mischievous twinkle in his hazel eyes coming from more than just the stage lights shining down on them right then. "And I promise ta be a better man wit ye by me side. From now on, me surprises will only be ta make ye smile and show de world how much I love ye."

Liam took her left hand in his before holding up a gorgeous diamond solitaire on a gold band as thick as the Claddagh band she already wore on her left ring finger. "And I dink we should start by renewin' our vows in de middle o' de ring when we're in me 'ometown fer *No Remorse*. Will ye marry me again in Dublin?"

Is that what he went shopping for today? Is that why he didn't tell me about the change of plans for this promo? 'Cause he had to make sure he could find a ring before he suggested it to the bookers?

I bet he decided not to tell me about changing the script because he wanted to see how well I can improvise after I asked him to help me learn how to call a match in the ring. Not that this is what I had in mind.

Looking down into her husband's expressive face, she could clearly see his love for her shining through. So, regardless of why he'd decided to change things up, she knew she had to show him she was up for whatever challenges life threw at them, starting with the challenge her husband just threw down for her to expand her acting and wrestling chops.

"Oh, Liam, yes!" Rylie let him put that gorgeous ring on her finger as he stood back up before she stopped him from sealing their agreement with a kiss. "But only if you're serious about being a good guy from now on."

"O' course, Moh Graw," Liam agreed, dipping his head to try to kiss her once more.

Again Rylie stopped him by putting her hand on his chest and pushing him back slightly. "I'm gonna need you to prove it. And I think the best way to prove it is to help me avenge the fans for how the Valors mistreated them tonight."

"Anythin' ye want, Moh Anam Cara," Liam nodded. "'Ow bout we teach dem a lesson by takin' deir titles at *No Remorse*?" Liam turned to look at Stone then. "Ye can make dat 'appen, right, Commissioner?"

"You want to challenge the Valors at *No Remorse* for both the GWA heavyweight title and the GWA women's division title?" Stone questioned as he stood straighter and took a step toward them, so he could be heard through the microphone Chad still held near the couple in the middle of the ring.

"Yes, we do," Chastity spoke for them as Liam nodded along.

"Then I'll have the contracts drawn up and presented to them on *Tuesday Night Takedown* in Boulder," Stone promised.

"Make sure those contracts are just for standard title matches, with no crazy clauses to put any of us at a disadvantage," Chastity insisted before finally allowing her husband to pull her into his arms and kiss her soundly to end the televised portion of the *Saint Valentine's Day Massacre* show.

Liam kept the kiss mostly chaste, which she appreciated since the fans in attendance in Los Angeles were still watching even after the cameras were turned off. But it didn't matter that only their lips were involved, Rylie felt their soul-deep connection nonetheless. She relished the way he made her feel challenged to improve her workrate while also claiming her in front of the fans to show he was already proud of her.

When they finally broke the kiss, they were alone in the ring, so nobody else heard Liam's outrageous suggestion. "Are you sure we don't want to pay homage to the tuxedo matches of the eighties? Or have you and Shauna wrestling in wedding gowns? With the tape you have to use for the one you wore in Vegas, you won't be able to lose the match by being stripped down to your skivvies."

"No, I absolutely won't ruin one of my wedding gowns by wrestling in it." Rylie rolled her eyes at her husband's reference to the way the winners were determined in the tuxedo matches that had aired on the GWA's weekly television show back before she was born, which they'd recently watched on the GWA streaming channel provided through Burleson Entertainment. "Besides, you're the only one I want wrestling me out of my clothes."

"And I'll gladly wrestle you out of your clothes every night for the rest of our lives, Moh Graw," Liam vowed as he helped her out of the ring before scooping her up in his arms and carrying her off to start their happily ever after.

Epilogue

After the whirlwind of the last few days, Rylie enjoyed spending the late afternoon doing a wedding photo shoot with her husband. Somehow, between supporting her as she served the homeless and did the DNA test to prove Mr. Willie was indeed her uncle, and going to the Mass of the Lord's Supper on Thursday, flying overnight with his family to Dublin in time to attend Mass on Good Friday in the church where his grandparents were married, introducing her to even more distant relatives who still lived in Ireland, and attending to his new duties for the GWA, Liam had scheduled this photo shoot at a gazebo in a park overlooking the Dublin Bay portion of the Irish Sea for the late afternoon between the *No Remorse* fan expo and the joint dinner he had planned with both his large biological family and their GWA family. The only way this trip could have been better would have been if she'd been able to convince her Uncle Willie to come along.

While technically they didn't have the results of their DNA tests back yet, Rylie knew her hunch was right after getting Willie to confess that his last name was Long while they were at the community center on Thursday. She'd felt goosebumps covering her arms as soon as he officially introduced himself as Staff Sergeant Willie Long. But instead of immediately telling him she thought he was her uncle, she followed Liam's advice to ask more about his family first. Apparently, Liam was worried that she'd give him enough information about her family that he could take advantage of her by just agreeing with the names she mentioned, even if he wasn't actually related to any of them. So, she'd waited until she could sit with Mr. Willie before asking him about his family and where he was originally from to get his unusual accent.

When he started talking about growing up in a suburb of Atlanta with his parents and two younger brothers, Rylie's goosebumps got goosebumps. But when he specifically mentioned his brothers' names while relaying the story about his mom's smothered fried chicken being the favorite food of all three of them as children, and then replied to her question about whether or not he was still in contact with any of his family with the story about being upset with his parents when they cut off contact with his brother Peter while he was overseas with the Army, effectively keeping him from knowing where his middle brother was to get back in touch when he came home on leave, Rylie's excitement couldn't be contained. She'd blurted out her hunch about being his niece before he could finish telling her whether or not he still knew how to contact his parents or Johnson.

Willie actually seemed skeptical of her story until she pulled out her phone and showed him a picture of her parents. Then she thought she saw a tear in his eye as he stared at her dad's image for several long minutes. That's when Willie revealed that he was likely her only living relative on her father's side, explaining that Johnson was killed in action in 2007 while serving in Operation Iraqi Freedom, and that his parents had both died in the late 1990s, his dad from lung cancer and his mom from a heart attack.

They'd then spent the rest of the afternoon talking, sharing stories about her dad's life to give her more information about her family history and him some closure from knowing his brother had a happy life after leaving Atlanta. Liam had been the one to insist on the DNA test, going so far as to run to the nearest pharmacy to buy the kits for them to send off when he heard her suggest that Willie take a job as their house sitter to have a place to stay and an income. Willie had turned down her offer of a job and place to stay, claiming he was too prideful to want a handout like that, even from a relative. But he did agree to the cheek swabs to verify their familial relation and agreed to talk more next time she was in town, so she was hopeful that she'd eventually wear him down.

Maybe I can talk to Rory while we're at dinner tonight, and see if he can use some extra help at the pub? If he goes by the community center and posts a job opening, maybe Uncle Willie won't think of it as a handout and might actually apply.

"What are you thinking about, Moh Graw?" Liam questioned as he slid his hands around her waist and up her back under her veil to move into the next pose the photographer suggested. "You've got a bit of a conniving expression going on that has me worried about who you might try to match up with my brothers and cousins tonight and tomorrow."

"I was actually wondering if Rory might need some help at the pub and would be willing to hire Uncle Willie," Rylie confessed as she reached up, cupped her husband's jaw in her hands, and pushed up on her toes to peck a kiss on his lips, not caring in the slightest that the photographer was still clicking away. "But now that you mention it, there did seem to be quite a few sparks flying between Caitlyn and Blade this morning."

"You might think you saw sparks, but knowing Blade, I guarantee they'll fizzle out faster than a sparkler on the Fourth of July." Liam slid his hands down her back, gripping them together under her ass before lifting her off the ground to bring their lips together once more. After another gentle peck, he spun her around in the center of the gazebo before lowering her back to her feet. "And since I know Caitlyn's not the type of girl to end up as one of Blade's one-night stands, I doubt anything will happen between them while we're here in Dublin. Besides, even if they did have some chemistry, it would take him walking the straight and narrow for several weeks before she'd fall prey to him, and with the GWA's tour schedule, they won't ever be in the same city long enough for him to fool her into believing he's not picking up a different ring rat every other day."

"You don't think Blade would try to fool her into sleeping with him, do you?" Rylie didn't know Blade all that well, but he didn't strike her as the type who would try to con a woman like that just to get in her panties. Whenever she'd seen him picking up women while they were all out at a club after a GWA show, he always seemed pretty honest and up front with them about what he had to offer, even going so far as to blatantly state it was a one-time hookup where everyone around them could clearly hear their exchange of consent. She liked to think he was just sowing his wild oats, the same way she thought of her former partners in Protection Detail and the rest of the single guys who worked with the GWA, and that eventually they'd each meet their one true love and settle down.

"No, I don't," Liam smiled and moved to the side of the structure as the photographer directed them to sit on the railing of the gazebo. "He might flirt with her some more this weekend, but once he makes it clear he's only interested in one night, she'll shoot him down and that'll be the end of whatever sparks you thought you saw this morning. He'll move on to flirt with someone else a few minutes later. I just hope he's smart enough not to move on from Caitlyn straight to Kerry or Kelsea."

"And what do you think will happen if Caitlyn applies for one of the publicist jobs you have posting online next week? Since you decided they need to travel with us to book stuff all over and not just in New York, they could be together constantly for those little sparks to turn into a blazing inferno." That was kind of what Rylie was hoping for, thinking Caitlyn and Blade made a cute couple and her sunshiny personality would soften his grumpy broodiness.

"Then she'll see firsthand how he picks up a different woman in every city, so she'll dump a bucket of water on those sparks before they can ignite into anything more," Liam sighed, shaking his head. "Besides, I doubt she'll apply for one of those jobs since I haven't mentioned them to her."

"Why haven't you told her about them?" Rylie questioned, ignoring the photographer's direction to smile as she glared at her husband while climbing up to stand on the top rail around the side of the gazebo. "She'd be perfect for one of them."

"Because she's my cousin," Liam huffed, following her to stand instead of sit and anchoring both of them to the nearest post. "Like I told you before, when I was first talking to HR about setting up the positions, I can't even interview her without raising questions of nepotism, so since I have to be the one to make the final decision about who we hire, I can't tell her to apply."

Maybe you can't, but I can, Rylie thought. "But if she hears about it from somewhere else, or maybe goes looking on a job board and comes across the listing, you can't stop her from applying either, though, right?"

"No, but if she does and makes it past the first round of interviews with HR, then I'd have to recuse myself from conducting her second interview. And if I did that, Ms. Hawkins would have to know why, so she wouldn't likely get the job because we're related, even if I was able to convince everyone to have the HR manager make the final decision."

Liam's words made her realize that he'd actually thought about the suggestion she'd made back in January to get around being the one to interview Caitlyn and found a flaw she hadn't thought of before.

Then I guess I'll just have to come up with another way to get you out of the second round of interviews without letting on that you're related to Caitlyn. Well, if I can convince her to apply for the job in the first place.

"If something comes up to keep you from making some of the second interviews, Ms. Hawkins would have to step up and make the final decision about who to hire, right?" Liam nodded in response to her question while posing as directed for a few final shots before he jumped down from the railing and gripped her hips to lower her down as well. "Then we can just have connection issues for any of the Skype sessions you schedule for those interviews."

"Yeah, Ms. Hawkins is planning to schedule the second round of interviews for the week of our Memorial Day break, so I can be there in person for them." Liam shook his head, thwarting her latest idea.

"But I thought the corporate office was closed during our holiday breaks, too?" Rylie questioned, remembering how they'd had to deal with the security guard to pick up the passes Liam needed for his family to attend *No Remorse* and deliver the gift she'd gotten for Rick's assistant, since he was the only one working in the corporate office at the time.

"Normally, it is," Liam confirmed with a nod. "But Rick also set a precedent when he interviewed for the tutor positions over the Thanksgiving and Christmas breaks in twenty-eighteen, so Ms. Hawkins is planning to take her break the week after to be there when I'm in New York and expects me to come in for the interviews that week."

The week of our wedding? She can't be serious! Especially since he can't move his week off because of his other duties with the company. Nope, I'll go to Rick if I have to, so I can make sure my husband gets all his time off, especially since we'll have so much to

*finalize with the florist and bakery and whatnot, since we can't exactly
be there for all that beforehand.*

"Well, then there's your out," Rylie squealed with excitement,
grinning from ear to ear. "We've got a whole lot of stuff to do to
prepare for the wedding that week. So if you see Caitlyn's name on
the list of interviewees, you have the perfect excuse to recuse yourself
from all the interviews without saying a word about you guys being
cousins. Then if Ms. Hawkins picks her for one of the jobs, you can
let her know the truth, so they'll know you wanted Caitlyn to have a
fair shot of getting the job on her own merit. Problem solved."

"I like the way you think, Mrs. Connery," Liam grinned before
kissing her once more.

Liam's tongue invaded her mouth, practically melting the panties
right off of her. Rylie swirled her tongue with his, wanting to be an
active participant in the action while still letting her husband have
complete control. She only wished they didn't have the photographer
with them, so they could go farther than just kissing before they were
scheduled to meet up with everyone for an early dinner before the
Easter Vigil that night.

As if reading her mind, Liam broke off the kiss and declared, "This
photo shoot is over." He then squatted down and hoisted her up over
his shoulder, securing the train of her wedding gown around her legs
before carrying her back to the park building where they'd changed
clothes earlier.

"Thank you!" Rylie called back to the photographer over Liam's
shoulder.

"Be sure to email those pictures to Caleb Quinn this evening, so he
has time to put together the montage that will play on the jumbotron at
the show tomorrow," Liam added without turning back to wait for the
photographer to acknowledge him.

"Feck, Moh Graw, I can't wait until we get back to our room
tonight to make love to you," Liam growled, turning and locking the
door behind them as soon as they reached the lounge area where their
other clothes and the garment bags for their wedding attire were still
right where they left them earlier. He placed her down on her feet
before gently removing her veil and carefully placing it back on the
hanger in her garment bag. Then he moved her braids out of his way

and made quick work of using the bobby pin they'd stashed in the garment bag to untie the laces of the corset style bodice of the gown.

As soon as Liam finished making it possible for her to remove her wedding gown, Rylie went to work slipping off the lace sleeves and peeling off the tape holding the corset to her breasts. As she was removing the gown, Liam quickly removed his tuxedo. Then, both of them cautiously put the garments they had to wear the next day for the ceremony in the middle of the ring back in their individual garment bags, along with the wardrobe tape and skin barrier spray she needed to hold the dress up in front without having an allergic reaction and the bobby pin they needed to get her out of the gown, so there was no chance of messing them up when they likely wouldn't have time to clean or repair them before the *No Remorse* show.

Once that was done and they were basically standing there in only their undergarments, they quickly stripped them off too. They were much less meticulous when dropping her panties and his boxer briefs on the floor, since they wouldn't have to put them back on again until after they'd had the chance to have them laundered.

They quickly came back together, with Liam lifting Rylie in his arms, claiming her mouth in a drugging kiss, and pressing her back against the wall at the same time he impaled her on his cock. With no time for foreplay, she was surprised with how easily he slid home, not realizing just how wet she'd gotten with every longing look and brush of their lips during the photo shoot.

Rylie clung to his shoulders as she wrapped her legs around his waist, rocking her hips in time with every thrust of Liam's cock. She had to focus to keep breathing through her nose, as she felt her first orgasm building in her core with every stroke of his crown across her G-spot.

Knowing they couldn't be sure the photographer would email the photos as Liam had instructed, instead of waiting right outside for them as soon as they came out after changing to give them a flash drive to take to Caleb, they continued kissing, limiting the dirty talk and trying to keep the noise down. After the way they abruptly ended the photo shoot, it would probably still be obvious to the photographer that they'd had a quickie in the changing room, but at least if they were quiet enough, maybe none of the other park patrons would figure it out.

But even knowing she couldn't cry out his name the way she wanted as she came, Rylie couldn't stop the moans escaping from her throat, as she writhed in his arms with each wave of her release that washed over her. Liam swallowed her sounds as best he could, but nothing could be done to completely silence them when his guttural grunts accompanied her whimpers at the same time he joined her in orgasmic bliss.

Rylie loved the feel of his dick seeming to swell inside her as he thrust in as far as he could go before painting her womb with his seed. Since her period had just ended the day before, she knew they weren't likely to conceive. But not making a baby right then didn't in any way lessen the euphoric experience of having her husband come inside her without any barriers between them.

"Feck, Rylie, I love you so much," Liam whisper-shouted as he broke their kiss to try to catch his breath.

"I love you, too, Liam," Rylie replied, resting her head on his shoulder as she slowly came down from her high. "But we need to start planning these quickies a little better, so we have a sink or at least some wet wipes nearby, so I don't have to worry about anyone seeing your cum running down my legs after. Either that or I'm going to have to start wearing pants instead of skirts, and maybe some more absorbent panties."

"Naw, you won't have to do that, Moh Graw," Liam grinned as he gently pulled out and slowly lowered her feet to the floor. "You can just use a tampon like the cork in a wine bottle, so my swimmers will stay inside you until we can get someplace to clean up later. And feeling it inside you will remind you of how it felt when my cock was there, so you'll be wet and ready as soon as I can get you naked again."

Rylie could only laugh at his ridiculousness. She didn't have the heart to tell him that a tampon was too small to remind her of him in any way. Not because she didn't want him to know it wouldn't make her think of having sex with him, but because she knew he'd just take it as a compliment on the size of his dick.

Life with Liam will certainly be happy. Even if we aren't blessed with babies and have to get creative to grow our family, I know he'll always have me laughing.

~~~

As Liam changed out of his black wedding tux and into his red tuxedo-style ring gear to prepare for winning the GWA heavyweight title in the main event of the show that night, he reflected back over the last few days. While quite a lot had happened, for both him and Rylie, he felt most affected by attending the early morning Easter Mass in the same church where his grandparents were married over sixty years earlier and the big family breakfast afterwards, where several of his distant cousins put on an Irish step dancing performance while decked out in their Irish Saffron Kilts. That morning's festivities really made him want to incorporate even more of his Irish heritage into his daily life, making him think he might want to go back to wearing a kilt in the ring, like he had when he first started with the GWA sixteen years earlier.

On Friday, as the men of his family had toured a local kilt maker's shop, his granda pointed out that it was tradition for Irish grooms to wear kilts for their weddings instead of tuxedos, gifting him a complete Irish National Kilt outfit with all the accessories he'd need for the formal occasion of his wedding. And after seeing his Irish American relatives embracing the tradition by purchasing kilts in the tartan patterns of the counties in Ireland where their ancestors purportedly originated, he was starting to think he'd like to follow that Irish tradition during one of the vow renewal ceremonies he and Rylie had planned, too. Unfortunately, since they'd done all the promotional pictures for their GWA wedding the day before with him in his solid black tux, that's what he'd had to wear for the wedding in the middle of the ring to kick off the *No Remorse* pay-per-view, instead of the new kilt outfit his granda had given him.

But since I know Rylie went shopping on Friday with the women of the family while I was with the men at the tailor's shop, and she picked out her dress for our Church wedding to include my Irish heritage in the convalidation ceremony by wearing a gown made from Irish lace actually produced in Ireland, maybe I can convince her that I should wear a kilt made from the Irish National Tartan. I know she wants our
~~~

*wedding colors to be mauve and sage green, but maybe I can convince
her to change from sage to the brighter green that's the primary color
of my new kilt.*

Previously, Liam had only worn the standard saffron kilt that
matched the one his granda wore while playing the Uilleann pipes.
But that had been back when he first started working with the GWA,
when he'd actually wrestled in the kilt with a pair of matching short
trunks underneath, because it was the only kilt he knew represented his
Irish heritage. He'd also worn his wrestling boots instead of the
special socks and shoes that normally went with a kilt outfit and a
gimmick t-shirt instead of the full formal attire that would be expected
for a wedding, so he knew he'd have to have his granda explain the
significance of each piece of the formal kilt outfit, especially the
dagger he was supposed to wear sheathed in the top of his sock.

As they'd toured the local tailor's workshop on Friday, they'd
learned that in addition to the saffron kilt that had represented Ireland
for over a hundred years, there were now tartans registered for each of
the thirty-two Irish counties, all four of the provinces of Ireland, and
the Irish National Tartan, which represented the country as a whole.
Most of these tartans were designed in the 1990s, but the Ulster Tartan
was based on the archeological findings of fabric, which dated back to
the 1600s, dug up on a farm in the 1950s.

In planning the outing to the tailor's shop with his brothers still
living in Ireland, Granda had gathered the measurements for every
man in Liam's extended family going on this trip, along with the
surnames of his daughters-in-law and everyone who'd married into the
Sullivan side of Liam's family. He used that information to find out
what counties each surname was originally linked to in Irish history, so
the tailor could make sure he ordered enough of each tartan fabric to
make them all kilts to fit that represented their ancestral origins. Only
instead of speaking to Liam about ordering bespoke kilts before the
trip, the way he did with all the other men traveling with them so they
could each choose which tartan they wanted for themselves and cover
their individual costs, Granda had Rylie get his measurements and
didn't give him a choice of which county tartan he wanted, calling the
whole formal outfit and accessories Liam's wedding present.

Rylie had apparently gotten in touch with Shawn Pearson, who
passed along Liam's measurements from the tux shopping they'd done

in January. So, Granda was able to have the Irish National Tartan made into a custom kilt for him, while all his uncles, brothers, and cousins had several choices based on where their parents and grandparents were originally from in Ireland. Since he found out he had four choices based on each of his grandparents alone, and possibly quite a few more if he traced his family tree, Liam was glad his granda had decided for him, even if he still felt a little guilty for the high cost of the gift.

Maybe since Rylie was in on the planning for having my kilt custom made, it won't be too hard to convince her that I should wear it for our Church wedding in May. Feck, I bet Granda already planted that seed of an idea in her head when he asked her to get my measurements, only he didn't tell her exactly what shade of green my kilt would be, so that's probably why she picked the sage green she'd decorated with in her apartment because she already knew it went with her favorite color of mauve.

With that thought in mind, Liam left the locker room to go find his wife, thinking he'd talk to her about going with the more emerald shade instead of sage, so he could wear his new kilt for their Church wedding. *And I bet I won't be the only man in our family wearing a kilt at that ceremony, since Granda probably planned that outing on Friday just to make sure they all have the option, even though none of them will exactly match mine.*

When he thought about it, he realized that the County Wexford Tartan that his granda, da, and brothers all chose came the closest to matching the Irish National Tartan, having the same color scheme but a slightly different pattern. *I bet Granda really pushed for them to all pick his county of origin instead of going with Granny's County Waterford Tartan, so he knew we'd all match. I wonder if he did that before or after we decided for sure to have Quinn stand up with us as my best man and have him and Granny fill in for Rylie's parents to walk her into the ceremony?*

Thinking about asking his brother to be his best man, while taking a seat with some of his friends and coworkers, made him think about how he'd first asked Dion to do the honors. Liam still couldn't believe Dion's response when he first asked him about being his best man. Well, maybe not that he'd turned him down, since their Church wedding was scheduled just a few days after Julie's due date with their twins. But what he'd said when Liam suggested he act as his best man at the vow renewal they had planned for their Labor Day break in Heart's Destiny still made him wonder about his best friend's recovery. *Is he still having issues that he's not telling me about? Is that why he doesn't want to stand at the front of the church throughout the whole ceremony?*

"Naw, the front of the church will be too crowded for a full bridal party with you, Crockett, and Surfer Josh doing a triple ceremony with your women. But if Rylie needs someone to walk her down the aisle, I'll gladly do that job."

If I didn't know how deliriously happy he is now that he and Julie are living together, I might have to wonder why my best friend would rather ditch me to hang out with my wife. Liam found himself smiling as Rylie finally walked out of the women's locker room and over to where he was sitting with some of the other guys to watch the show on the backstage monitors. In honor of their earlier in-ring wedding, she was wearing a white iridescent catsuit for her match with Shauna in the first part of their double main event, but she currently had it mostly covered with a black and mauve warm-up jacket and sweatpants, so she could nosh on an after-dinner snack or protein shake in catering without risking spilling anything on her ring gear. *Feck, she's hot, no matter if she's wearing that sexy as fuck wedding gown that barely covered her tits earlier, or this sporty cute outfit that makes her look even younger than her twenty-five years.*

"What's that look for, Teidí Béirín?" Rylie questioned as soon as she reached him.

"Just thinking about how hot my wife is, Mo Ghrá," Liam replied, taking her hand and pulling her onto his lap. He then pecked a kiss on her lips as she leaned her side into his chest, draped her arm over his shoulder, and lightly ran her fingernails through the short hair at his nape. "I was also thinking about possibly going with Granda's idea to wear my new Irish kilt for our Church wedding in May. But if I do that, we'll have to adjust our wedding colors from sage green to emerald green, so I want to make sure you still think it will go with the mauve maid of honor dress you picked out for Caitlyn and the greenery in your bouquet."

"Yeah, the greenery in my bouquet is already darker than sage, or even emerald," Rylie nodded her agreement. "So, basically, the only real changes are that you'd be in your kilt and Quinn would just need an emerald green tie and vest, instead of the sage green ones we picked the other day?"

"Yeah, I think Quinn, Da, and Granda would all be in their kilts, too," Liam pointed out with a half shrug of the shoulder she wasn't resting her arm on. "So, no need to order Quinn a tux or the tux accessories, since he's already got the full formal kilt outfit."

"Then I definitely think you should wear your kilt," Rylie agreed with a grin before biting her lip. "But, um, maybe don't go as traditional as I've heard some guys do with the undergarments. 'Cause as hot as I think it would be to know you're going commando under your kilt, I think that might be a bit disrespectful during the ceremony. And considering I had to pick a different wedding gown to meet the modesty guidelines while in the Church, I'm pretty sure Father O'Malley won't want to accidentally get a glimpse of your dick while we're sitting right up front during our wedding Mass. In fact, maybe you should double check with him that the kilt is considered acceptable attire."

Liam could only chuckle at the serious expression on Rylie's face, knowing his granda had already confirmed that it was okay for men to wear kilts in church before even making the suggestion. "Yeah, how 'bout I do like I did when I wrestled in a kilt? And wear a pair of Speedo-style briefs under a pair of short wrestling trunks to make sure I'm properly covered in case anyone can see up my kilt?"

"Oh, yeah, those green ones with the shamrocks all over them that you wore before you started teaming with D?" Rylie's eyes lit up with excitement. "'Cause I remember how little they left to the imagination when Sienna and I watched *Tuesday Night Takedown* with the rest of the girls in our dorm in college."

"Did she just call you out on being old? Or out herself for having a crush on you before she started with the GWA?" Cruz Bennington questioned, stopping in his tracks instead of continuing to walk past them to catering.

"I think she outed herself for having a crush on me," Liam smirked, teasing his bride. "'Cause if she was trying to make me feel old, she'd point out that she was only ten when I first started wrestling for the GWA, like she did at Christmas."

"Oh, yeah," Cruz cringed. "That's way worse. I'm surprised you guys stayed married after that. 'Cause I'd think it would make you feel like a dirty old man for marrying a kid who wasn't even outta elementary school when you were probably plowing through some ring rats."

It was Liam's turn to cringe at Cruz's inappropriate, but probably fairly accurate, words.

"I wasn't trying to do either," Rylie protested, shaking her head at Liam, and thankfully, not acknowledging Cruz's last statement. "I was just pointing out that those trunks would match your kilt."

"Uh-huh, sure you were," Liam chuckled, pecking a kiss on Rylie's pouty lips. "That's why you commented on how they look on me. But it's okay, Mo Ghrá, I'm cool with being your teenage heartthrob, since I didn't actually meet you until after you were old enough that it wasn't creepy for me to return the crush."

"Yeah, now that Dane and Blade's match is over, I'm gonna go see if the cuties in catering saved me some leftover roast," Cruz scoffed, rolling his eyes as he started walking once more. "Since seeing all the sappy sweetness between you two tonight is already gonna give me cavities, I need more meat and potatoes instead of my normal extra dessert."

"If he keeps flirting mercilessly with the catering staff, one of these days they're gonna lace his extra desserts with Ex-lax," Rylie giggled once Cruz was no longer close enough to hear them.

"Oh, I wonder if it's possible to melt those chocolate laxatives and mix them with that food coloring you told me about?" Liam grinned at his wife, noticing her eyes lighting with excitement at the prank ideas running through both their heads. "Since Ma didn't send us any green treats for Saint Patrick's Day, we still owe several of the guys a little revenge for not letting us know we got married immediately after it happened and feigning total ignorance when we finally found out, especially the guys who were clearly not drunk on our wedding video."

"Maybe?" Rylie shrugged. "But I don't know how effective it would be for turning the laxatives, or um…anything else, different colors if the food coloring paste isn't mixed with white chocolate or white frosting."

"We'll have to ask Ma to test it on my brothers, so we're prepared for passing out some special wedding favors to a few of the guys."

"Oh, no, I want no part in this prank," Rylie objected, shaking her head. "'Cause you know half the guys you wanna give the green drizzling shits would share any candy they get as wedding favors with the kids. And then you'll have all the moms pissed off and seeking revenge. Nope, not happening. You'll have to think of a better way to rib the guys."

"Yes, Dear," Liam repeated the two words Dion had told him his future father-in-law said were the most important words a man needed to learn before marriage. "I'll think of some other way of getting even with Kade and Protection Detail. Like maybe hiring an actress to show up at one of our shows wearing a costume that makes her look nine-months pregnant…"

His words trailed off as Rylie covered his mouth with her hand, at the same time her eyes practically bugged out of her head.

"Don't even joke about making them think they knocked up a ring rat. There's too much of a chance of that actually happening. And we both know you'd feel terrible if your prank caused one of them to not believe his baby mama when they inevitably find out about a kid with one of their random hookups. Or worse, if karma decided to bite you on the ass by having one of your former ring rats show up with a baby in tow."

"No, don't even go there in your head, Mo Ghrá," Liam commanded, cupping her face in his hands. "I haven't touched a ring rat in well over a year, so there's no way a pregnant woman could show up and claim I'm the daddy. You are the only woman I've had sex with since the day we met, and I'd significantly cut back on the one-nighters long before then, so I highly doubt I had any condom fails to have a long lost kid show up one day. Especially since I haven't exactly been hiding away to make it hard to find me for child support. So, you are the only woman who will ever make me a daddy. Got it?"

Rylie gripped his wrists with her hands, running her thumbs over the backs of his hands as if trying to soothe him as she nodded. "I know I'm the only woman you could possibly impregnate now, Liam.

But I also know you weren't a virgin when we first made love, so I wouldn't be upset if you had a child show up one day, claiming you're his or her dad. I'd welcome them to our family with open arms, while also feeling heartsick over whatever milestones you've missed in their life. But I definitely wouldn't hold their birth against you."

"Then why did you say it'd be worse for me to have a kid show up than for one of the other guys to not believe it if they did?" Liam was confused about what she'd meant earlier.

"I meant that your anguish over the situation would be worse," Rylie elaborated, smiling sympathetically. "'Cause you'd feel bad if you did something that made one of the other guys reject his kid, but you'd feel even worse if you weren't able to be there from day one for your child."

Liam could only nod in agreement before kissing his wife. He was more than ready to change the subject, thinking there was no reason to upset either of them over something that wasn't likely to happen. He was just about to ask her what she thought was a good prank for the guys when she broke their kiss and surprised him with more of an explanation of her earlier words.

"Or maybe I was thinking it would be worse because I pictured your karmic revenge coming in the form of a rebellious teenage daughter, whose mom brought her to you when she couldn't handle her behavior problems any longer, so you'd have to deal with her inappropriately flirting with all the guys, or raiding the hotel mini-bars and getting drunk, or sneaking off to get a tattoo or body piercings."

Rylie might have been grinning as if she meant that scenario as a joke, but Liam could easily imagine it as his worst nightmare. Only with the daughters she'd previously mentioned adopting, instead of the children he could have fathered with the ring rats he was with in his younger years.

"Feck, I really hope my Connery genes run true, so we only have boys," he groaned, resting his forehead on hers. "'Cause if we ever have girls who start to rebel like that, they'll be transferring from Saint Stephen's Catholic School straight to the convent."

"I don't think you can make our daughters become nuns," Rylie laughed.

"Maybe not, but I can send them on a prison tour with their uncles the same way Da took all of us when we got old enough to start acting out," Liam declared, wondering if one of his brothers could take the girls through a women's prison, or if they'd have to get a female officer to lead that tour. *Hopefully, by the time that becomes necessary, one of my brothers will have fallen in love and married one of the women who work with the NYPD, so we know our daughters will be safe with a family member on their scared-straight tour.*

Liam could only smile as he envisioned his future family. Regardless of how many children they had or how they built their family, he knew it would be an adventure with Rylie by his side. And he looked forward to enjoying every minute of their long happily ever after.

~~~

Friday, May 29, 2020, New York City, New York

Brandon "Blade" Braddock felt extremely out of place as he sat in a pew at Saint Stephen's Cathedral, watching Liam and Rylie renew their wedding vows. Again. While he hadn't actually gone into the chapel to see their first wedding in person, this was their fourth ceremony he knew about and the third he'd personally witnessed, if he didn't count watching the video of the first ceremony on the jumbotron with the rest of the GWA, so he knew part of his unease was not understanding why they needed to say "I do" more than once. But he was also uncomfortable because this was his first time visiting a Catholic Church, and their wedding Mass was quite a bit different than the other weddings he'd attended in the last year, and nothing like the Baptist Church services his last set of foster parents made him attend in his hometown of Branson, Missouri, as a teenager. But if he was really being honest with himself, the main reason his tie felt like a noose around his neck was because of the woman standing up with his friends at the front of the church as Rylie's maid of honor. Caitlyn Sullivan.

Blade first met Caitlyn at the fan expo for the *No Remorse* show in Dublin almost seven weeks ago, when the strawberry blonde beauty had taken over all his thoughts by immediately critiquing his gimmick the first time they spoke to one another. If he'd have had his way,
~~~

he'd have hooked up with her at least one of the two nights they had left in Ireland, so he could have walked away without thinking of her again, just like he did with all the ring rats he'd banged since joining the GWA roster a little over two years earlier, and the frog hogs he'd hooked up with during his time as a SEAL before then. But Liam had cock-blocked him by telling her Blade was a player of epic proportion as he ushered his family out of the booth Blade was signing autographs in at the time.

Later that day, when the GWA crew and Liam's family all got together for dinner, Blade tried to move on, just as he would if any other woman had shot him down. But his eyes kept being drawn to Caitlyn, almost like she had a spotlight on her making it impossible for him to see anything but her. The next day at the *No Remorse* show, he tried taking another shot with her, flirting some more when he caught her away from her family backstage. But even though she bantered back beautifully and it seemed to him that their chemistry was off the charts, she refused to give him her number or agree to hang out with him after the show. He'd ended up giving her his number instead, hoping to hear from her so they could hook up the next time they were in the same city.

Since she hasn't even texted, and totally avoided me at the pub last weekend, I really should get over this obsession with her and go back to banging ring rats.

Unfortunately, that was easier said than done, especially since his cock had lost all interest in anyone but her immediately after the first time he saw her back in April. Blade had never thought of himself as having a type before he met Caitlyn, finding all women beautiful and never having a problem performing sexually, no matter who he was with at the time. But since meeting Caitlyn in Dublin, his dick went into hiding every time a ring rat approached him, only standing at attention again whenever Blade saw or thought about Caitlyn. It was like his favorite appendage suddenly had a mind of his own, deciding to act like a divining rod that considered Caitlyn the only source of water on the planet.

Sitting in the church was no different than any other time he saw Caitlyn, which was probably the biggest reason he was uncomfortable. Even someone like him, who believed there was a higher power watching over them but didn't follow a specific religion, knew it was completely inappropriate to have an erection while sitting in church. But seeing Caitlyn in her pale pinkish-purple dress as she stood up with Liam and Rylie still caused Blade's dick to stand up and take notice.

Not being able to control his hard-on in her presence wasn't the only unusual issue he was having at the moment, either. For the first time in his life, Blade found himself feeling irrationally jealous as she placed her hand on the arm of the best man to walk back down the aisle at the end of the service. Considering he knew the best man was Liam's brother and also Caitlyn's cousin, he consciously knew it was stupid of him to be jealous of Quinn. It wasn't like there was anything sexual about the way he escorted Caitlyn into and out of the church. But Blade still wished he could be the one to feel her delicate palm gripping his arm.

"Well, that was different," Sawyer Owens, who used the ring name Owen Sawyer and whom Blade thought of as his best friend in the company and the only wrestler he felt as close to as one of his SEAL brothers, commented as they finally exited the church and followed Liam's family and the rest of the GWA to the building next door where they were having the reception. "I wonder if the reception is gonna be just as solemn since it's in the community center on the church grounds and not at a hotel ballroom like the weddings in Texas?"

"The solemnity of the ceremony is what you thought was different?" Blade eyed Sawyer curiously. "Not that Liam and all his male relatives were wearing kilts? Or that their kilts were several different patterns?"

"No," Sawyer chuckled as they walked. "He's Irish, so the kilts were kinda expected. Some of my Welsh family members have done the same. And the different tartans represent their ancestral family, clan, or location of origin. If I'd have thought about it sooner, I'd have asked Liam about wearing my Owens family tartan kilt today."

Blade only shrugged and shook his head, unsure what to make of Sawyer's unexpected revelation that he too owned a kilt.

"Do you think they were all going commando under their skirts?" Dane Bennington asked, only half turning to look back at Blade and Sawyer as he and his brother walked in front of them into the community center. "Like that guy in Edinburgh said is the traditional way to wear a kilt?"

"I don't know about everyone else, but when I heard Liam and Rylie talking about him wearing a kilt for the wedding at *No Remorse*, he promised to wear underwear and a pair of short wrestling trunks under his," Dane's brother Cruz replied, shaking his head.

"Yeah, I'm not taking a chance that one of his brothers or cousins would flash everyone to show us, so I'm gonna hafta leave that a mystery and not ask." *Though I wouldn't mind if Caitlyn wanted to show me what she's wearing under her skirt.*

When they walked inside and found that, in addition to the family and friends who'd attended the ceremony in the church, there was also a small group of nuns and homeless people sitting down for the reception, Blade knew the kilts and formality of the ceremony weren't the only things that would definitely be dramatically dissimilar from the weddings they'd attended for their other coworkers in the last year. Clearly, the reception was going to be just as unusual.

Oh, they still had a corner set up with musical instruments indicating a band would be playing at some point later, just like the other wedding receptions he'd recently attended. But unlike the country-rock bands that played at the weddings in Texas, the musical instruments waiting to be played here were all acoustic and included a harp and what looked like some type of bagpipes, making it clear that if there was any dancing at all, it would only be slow dancing. *And that's probably only gonna be for Liam and Rylie, so I really shouldn't get my hopes up to dance with Caitlyn tonight.*

They also had a table set up with what looked like a standard wedding cake. But he'd already been warned that the bridal-white fondant covering the multi-tiered cake was the only thing resembling the previous wedding cakes he'd eaten. Under the decorations that made it look like the light, fluffy vanilla or other lightly flavored cake varieties, which most people associated with weddings, lurked a dense fruitcake that had been soaked in Irish whiskey for a couple of weeks to make sure the flavor permeated every nook and cranny.

"Maybe the reception won't be as stuffy as the ceremony," Blade offered as he took a seat beside Sawyer. "Since from what I've heard, the wedding cake is soaked in so much Irish whiskey that anyone who eats a slice will likely get a buzz."

"Really? And they're serving it in a church?" Sawyer looked confused.

"We're not really in the church now," Kade Carrington, who used the ring name Killer Kade, pointed out as he sat down at their table along with the Bennington brothers and Protection Detail. "This is a community center, which in addition to being used for the church's homeless outreach is also available for the public to rent out for different functions."

"Besides, even the priest took a shot of whiskey with us at the stag party," Magnum, the larger member of the Protection Detail tag team, added. "So I don't think Catholics consider alcohol as sinful as some other religions."

As the rest of the guys discussed the wedding for a few minutes, Blade scanned the room to find Caitlyn, unable to contain his desire to at least keep her in his sights, even if he wasn't sure he should bother talking to her. He continued following her with his eyes after one of Liam's cousins came by their table to tell them to go mingle and grab a drink at the bar for the cocktail hour part of the reception. His obsession with her was getting out of hand, making him momentarily wonder if he'd actually fallen in love at first sight with her, the way several of his coworkers claimed they had with their spouses.

No, that can't be it. I've just been around too many happy couples recently and have started confusing my attraction to her for more because she's the only woman who's ever shot me down. If we'd have hooked up back in Dublin, I'd have been over her as soon as we got to Edinburgh the next day, just like all the other women I've ever hooked up with in the past. But since she blew me off from the first time we met, and keeps ignoring me every time we run into each other, I'm suffering from some kind of FOMO, and only want her because I can't just snap my fingers and have her.

Still, it would be nice to figure out how to convince my dick that she's not the woman for me. If only she'd agreed to give me her number. I bet having her turn me down daily over text would eventually make it clear that I need to move on. Not that I'd actually move on to settle down with just one woman.

Regardless of the fact that he'd completely given up his regular ring rat habit since the first time he saw Caitlyn, Blade was still afraid that he wasn't the type of man who could be happy with only one sexual partner for the rest of his life. Having only seen one example of a man capable of fidelity from the time he was born until twenty-seven years later when he joined the GWA roster, Blade was afraid the three years he spent being fostered by the Carpenters and the almost two-and-a-half years he'd seen the happy GWA marriages weren't enough to override the other twenty-four years of his life, when all his male role models had problems keeping it in their pants.

Since the man who provided half his DNA was the first of a long line of cheaters he'd lived and worked with over the years, Blade was afraid that it wouldn't matter that he was now surrounded by several examples of faithfulness in relationships because he'd already inherited the cheater gene. And after seeing how being cheated on affected his mom almost as much as his sperm donor's physical abuse, he didn't want to take a chance on getting serious with a woman, only to find out he was just as much of a monster, who would hurt her the same way his mom had been.

But even though he didn't think he could follow through with anything more than a one-night stand or possibly a weekend fling, Blade was still drawn to Caitlyn like he'd never been attracted to anyone before. It was almost like there was something in their physical makeup that pulled them together like magnets. It was that magnetic pull that caused him to excuse himself from the group he was standing with, claiming he needed to hit the head, when he saw Caitlyn walking out of the room with Fiona Robertson.

He didn't bother asking where the restrooms were located since he didn't actually need one. He didn't know exactly why she went down the hall with the boss's wife, but assumed she was showing Fiona where the restrooms were located and would then be alone for her walk back into the reception.

His mission in following them was actually to catch Caitlyn off by herself, so he could have a few minutes to talk to her alone and hopefully convince her to give him another chance at getting to know her. He knew better than to come on too strong with the flirtation, since she obviously wasn't the type to be into casual hookups. But he hoped to persuade her to give him a chance to at least be her friend.

Even if he never managed to fuck her to get her out of his system, he thought repeatedly being reminded that they were stuck in the friend zone would eventually convince his dick to move on, so he could finally go back to the smorgasbord of ring rats he'd enjoyed prior to meeting Caitlyn. Seven weeks of celibacy was wearing on him to the point that he'd started to wonder if his right arm was bigger than his left from jerking off to fantasies about her so damn often, so he had to find a way to get her out of his head and move on.

When he entered the hallway after the ladies, however, he quickly figured out Caitlyn wasn't showing Fiona to the restrooms. Instead, Fiona directed Caitlyn to a small conference room where Rick and Liam were apparently already meeting. At least, that's what Blade thought, based on the voices he heard as the ladies walked into the room.

"Alright, I'm outta here, so it's clear this isn't nepotism of any kind," Liam chuckled.

Not wanting to get caught eavesdropping, Blade ducked into an alcove and behind a bookcase so Liam wouldn't see him as he walked by on the way back to the reception hall.

Nepotism? What the hell does that have to do with a wedding reception?

"Nepotism?" Caitlyn croaked out, partially repeating his thought, the clicking of her heels as she walked ending suddenly, like she'd been stopped in her tracks by her cousin's words. "Does this mean I got the job, even though you recused yourself from my interview the other day?"

Caitlyn interviewed for a job with the GWA the other day? One of the ones Liam's mentioned, so he can quit trying to schedule us for endorsement deals and children's hospital visits?

"I'll let the boss answer that question," Liam replied, just before he walked out of the room and down the hall, not noticing Blade, who pretended to peruse a shelf of books without noting a single book title.

"I'm afraid Liam's way more concerned about doing everything exactly right to keep from appearing biased than I've ever been when it comes to hiring," Rick scoffed. "If he'd have done this my way, he'd have hired you back in January when I first told him to add a couple of publicist positions to work with the talent roster. But instead of hiring for the jobs first and getting HR to handle all the paperwork later, like I do all the time, he insisted on being meticulous about researching everything about the job requirements and what PR companies look for when hiring people for the same titles, then going back and forth with HR until they got the job posting exactly right before he even listed it to start taking résumés.”

“Oh, please, I remember finding my job listed on the GWA website and submitting my application online a month before I got an interview, so I know you don’t just hire someone and deal with the paperwork later,” Fiona, who worked as the English tutor for all the kids who traveled with the GWA, argued with her husband.

“Maybe not for your job,” Rick disagreed. “But there’ve been a few times I’ve made up jobs on the spot when one of my employees asked me about openings for their significant others. And I certainly didn’t forewarn HR when I made Liam the company president. So, if he’d have told me that his cousin already worked in PR back in January when we first started talking about these publicist jobs, I’d have had him call and hire her right then.”

“Is that why there’s only one flight attendant on the second flight crew?” Fiona questioned. Blade couldn’t hear Rick’s response, so he assumed the boss either nodded or just smiled to keep from confirming his wife’s suspicion. “Well, you’d better never let Kay know that.”

“Yeah, I keep hoping Nick or Nate will fall in love, so I can fill that other job,” Rick chuckled. “Now, back to the task at hand. Since Liam wanted to make sure you knew that you got the job on your own merit and not because you’re his cousin, he didn’t disclose your familial relationship to the HR manager until after she finished all the interviews and told him who she thought he should hire. And after their conversation this afternoon, he asked me to be the one to officially offer you the job as our charitable outreach publicist, instead of making you wait until Monday for Ms. Hawkins to call you.”

Well, damn, maybe I won’t have to push so hard or do anything to try to befriend her to help me get her outta my system. No point looking like a lovesick puppy chasing after her to get her number so I can experience her rejection regularly. I can play this cool and not let on to anyone how she affects me. And working with her regularly will reinforce her lack of attraction enough that I’ll easily be able to get over her now.

Blade didn’t wait around to hear more than her acceptance of the job before he made his way back to the reception. Too bad he didn’t feel relieved that he now had a plan for how to move on from Caitlyn and end his recent dry spell.

Coming Next in the GWA

Blade's Botched Bump

Blade: Ring name of professional wrestler Brandon Braddock.
Derived from the call sign he earned in BUD/S for always
carrying a pocketknife.
Botched: When a wrestler makes a mistake and the move they're
attempting doesn't go as planned. Often leading to injuries to
either themselves or their opponents.
Bump: When a wrestler falls, or is thrown by their opponent, and
lands on the mat, ground, or any object in or around the arena
while performing. Used in this case to simply mean "falling,"
as in falling in love.

Brandon "Blade" Braddock loved his job as a wrestler for the GWA,
living the gimmick as a former special warfare operator who now wore
civilian camo and reproduction dog tags while carrying a decorative
dagger or ceremonial sword to the ring to keep from showing the
terrorists of the world what his brothers in the SEALs actually wore
for their missions. While he worked as a heel and was a little gruffer
than most of the guys on the roster, he didn't think of himself as a bad
guy most of the time. Since the ring rats seemed to be drawn to his
broody attitude, he was perfectly happy not really fitting in with all his
married coworkers. Considering the trauma he'd endured as a child at
the hands of the man who supposedly provided half his DNA, he was
fine with remaining single and fulfilling his sexual needs with one-
night stands, so he never risked hurting a woman the way he'd seen his
mom suffer because he believed evil was an inherited trait. At least,

he was until he met Caitlyn Sullivan at the beginning of the GWA's 2020 European tour, when he metaphorically bumped hard for the petite strawberry blonde.

Caitlyn Sullivan couldn't believe her cousin had gifted the entire family with a trip to Dublin, Ireland to attend the GWA's *No Remorse* show and reconnect with their distant relatives, whom most of the family hadn't ever spoken to in person since their grandparents emigrated from Ireland to the United States. Having spent her entire life in New York City, she thoroughly enjoyed getting to see the country where her ancestors lived. Even though she also wished she could travel to all the exciting places her cousin and the rest of the GWA visited regularly while on tour, she knew that wasn't in the cards for her. At least, not while she still worked in her entry-level public relations assistant job. She would be stuck in New York, writing press releases for her boss, who actually traveled the world to meet with their celebrity clients, probably for several years until her boss finally retired for her to be able to promote to a full publicist position.

Caitlyn's prospects for romance weren't much better than her potential to move up in her current company. Yeah, there were millions of men in the city she could theoretically date, as her mother was fond of pointing out. But still, it seemed like trying to find the one man she was meant to spend the rest of her life with was like trying to find a real, live unicorn. She was starting to wonder if her soulmate was just as mythical as the horse with the spiraling horn. No matter how often she went out with her friends looking for *The One*, she kept meeting guys who were only after one thing. And that one thing wasn't a long-term relationship. The single men her cousin worked with were no exception, no matter how much just looking at Blade made her insides tingle. Even if she wanted to believe he wasn't just like all the other guys, they couldn't actually pursue a relationship when he was traveling all the time and she was stuck in New York.

Or could they? Was she willing to get to know him via texts and calls to let him prove he wasn't the player she thought he was? What if she took the job with the GWA that her cousin mentioned to help set up endorsement deals and appearances to help raise funds at non-profits for all the wrestlers? Could that lead to actually traveling the way she wanted and also getting to know Blade well enough to decide if he was safe to fall for?

Blade certainly hoped so. Being around Caitlyn made him want to be a better man, one who could actually see himself committed to only her for the rest of his life. But that would only happen if he could convince her that he'd changed dramatically on the day they met. Otherwise, falling for Caitlyn could be the worst botched bump of his wrestling career, causing him to end up with a severely broken heart.

And even if fate stepped in, allowing these two the time to explore what could happen between them, would they be able to withstand having Blade's past endanger both their lives to find out if they could have a happily ever after together?

DISCLAIMER: This opposites attract, grumpy sunshine, unconventional workplace, he falls first, sports romance contains references to past abuse, childhood loss of a parent, a former abuser seeking revenge for serving prison time, a hostage situation, DNA test revelations, profanity, and graphic sex scenes. It is intended for adult readers (18+) who are not easily offended.

Also in the GWA

Claiming Cage

Cage Dalton could best be described as broody and reserved. After an IED explosion left him scarred, both physically and emotionally, his career as a Navy SEAL was over. But even though he was free to come out of the closet when he left the military to work in private security with the GWA, Cage kept his sexuality, along with his former outgoing personality, mostly to himself. While his boss, and mostly his boss's kid, became close enough for him to consider them family and let them see the fun-loving uncle he'd once been, rejection from his biological family and the callous words of strangers at seeing his scars, made him close himself off to ever finding love for himself. So, he didn't see the point in risking possible rejection by letting anyone know he was gay. Then one day, Jax Nolen started traveling with the GWA as the history tutor.

Jax Nolen was his exact opposite, proud to be out as a gay man. But after discrimination for his sexuality cost him his last teaching job, he didn't want to make it an issue when he interviewed for the history tutor position with the GWA, especially after learning they'd recently fired a teacher for flirting with the married parents of their students. Wanting to enjoy the perks of a generous salary and constant travel around the world, Jax vowed to be celibate, not wanting to do anything to risk losing the job of his dreams. Little did he know that when he got to Minneapolis for his first day on the job, the man of his dreams would be the one to pick him up at the airport.

But with Jax being wary of blatantly flirting so he didn't lose his new job, and Cage being determined to not torture a lover by letting him see his scars, it seemed they might be forever doomed to longing for one another in secret. But then fate, and their matchmaking coworkers, stepped in, pushing them together, whether they were ready or not.

DISCLAIMER: This MM, wounded warrior, grumpy-sunshine romance contains brusque talk about the casualties of war, grotesque descriptions of scars often left after combat, profanity, and graphic sex scenes between two men. It is intended for adult readers (18+) who are not easily offended.

Coming Next in Heart's Destiny

<u>Destined for Deanna</u>

JJ Burleson met the woman he knew he was destined to marry a few years ago. They spent a wonderful week together at a conference, with JJ planning to propose before it ended and bring her back to his hometown. But for some unknown reason, Deanna Wolfe ended their fling before he could get the words out, leaving him heartbroken.

Deanna had fallen head over heels for JJ when she first met him. But after a whirlwind week with him, she had to end things because she knew she could never give him the family he wanted in the future. She went home and tried to make herself forget the younger man who'd stolen her heart, but it was difficult when her boss at OK Oil kept going head to head with JJ for deals they both wanted for their companies. While she never had to see him, it was still difficult for her to hear his name whenever Burleson Incorporated won a contract her boss wanted.

When JJ's cousin married Deanna's best friend, their longing for one another only got worse because she could no longer avoid seeing him whenever her friend invited her to family events. Especially when she learned that their breakup led him to study the kinks they'd both been curious about years ago.

Somehow she managed to keep her secrets, if not her distance, from JJ for over a year after they ran into one another again. But when Burleson Incorporated bought out OK Oil, JJ moved out of his small hometown to take over as her boss in Tulsa. Fighting their destiny was a lot harder when she had to report to him daily as his executive assistant.

DISCLAIMER: This second chance, older woman, younger man, he falls first, office romance contains profanity, graphic sex scenes including BDSM, and flashbacks to an abusive past, pregnancy loss, and forced infertility, as well as a hostage situation when her former abuser breaks out of prison and comes for revenge. It is intended for adult readers (18+) who are not easily offended.

Books by Leah Mae Wright

Heart's Destiny Series

Galactic Wrestling Association Series

About The Author

Leah Mae Wright lives in Florida with her husband and fur babies.
Her head has been filled with romantic stories for as long as she can
remember, beginning with fairy tales as a small child growing up in
Oklahoma, and carrying through to countless ideas of her own
throughout the years as she has moved around to live in several
different states. Now that her children are grown and life has slowed
down, she's letting them out of her head, so they can join the libraries
of her fellow fans of romance. Leah's literary world is a wonderful
place that has no Covid, no real politicians, and a few unreal towns.
Her favorite part about her characters living in her literary world is
knowing that they are guaranteed a happily ever after.

You can keep up to date with Leah's future book plans at:
www.leahmaewright.com – Be sure to sign up for the Newsletter to
receive emails about new releases, sales, and freebies.
www.facebook.com/LeahWrightAuthor
www.amazon.com/author/leah_wright
https://www.instagram.com/leahmaewrightauthor/

https://www.pinterest.com/LeahMaeWrightAuthor/

Provide your feedback to the author at:
Leah's Literary World Facebook Group
LeahWrightAuthor@gmail.com
Leah@LeahMaeWright.com

You can also review Leah's books on Amazon, Goodreads, Bookbub, and Fictiondb.